TALES OF BRIGANDS
AND BANDITTI.

I Warn & Strike

[I WARN AND STRIKE.—RED GAUNTLET PUNISHES TREACHERY.]

RED GAUNTLET, THE BANDIT; OR, THE BLACK MOUNTAINEERS.

BOOK I.—THE ARTIST.

CHAPTER 1.

THE MOUNTAIN INN.

THE day was waning, but the approach of night was slow, and the sun lay, like a river of fire, deep in the Neapolitan sky.

Vast masses, grand and dusky with a slumbrous purple, loomed heavily over the mountain heights.

Far beneath, and seeming in the distance to share the deep solitude of heaven, lay the city of Naples, with the flashing waters of its Bay lit by the sunlight; and between the

No. 1.

mountain's base and a sequestered valley stood a quaint and Gothic structure with a signboard at the door.

This structure was the inn, and, if rumour did not speak falsely, no place of good repute. Whatever its repute, however, its picturesque appearance had attraction for a young English traveller, who, with his portfolio slung by a belt from his shoulder, paused before the house.

"'The Mountain Guide,'" he said to himself, reading the inscription underneath the figure on the signboard. "The artist evidently had a very savage brigand in his eye when he drew that for a peaceful pioneer. What a name, too, for the innkeeper—Scampia Zatani! Let us see what sort of cheer old Scamp and Satan has for a tired tourist."

Looking up again before he entered, his glance fell upon a latticed casement above. He paused with a sudden hush of admiration, for at the casement was as sweet a face as he had ever seen.

"Not old Scamp and Satan's daughter, surely !" he thought. "Yet one never knows. She is a divinity, and her father may be some shocking old Goth, whose countenance would lend ugliness to a picture. By Jove ! so it would !"

The innkeeper appeared just then.

Our tourist thought of the wolf who invited a lamb in to dinner, and ate the poor thing for accepting the invitation. Scampia Zatani's aspect was the very reverse of hospitable.

Titanic in build, with a face so covered with black hair that a vulture-like nose and a pair of dark, glittering eyes were the only features visible.

He did not seem the sort of man to follow the quiet avocation by which he seemed to live.

"If that fellow's looks do not wrong him," thought our tourist, "Nature ought to be ashamed of herself. His face would convict him before any jury in the world. Now, mine host," he added, aloud, "don't fill up the doorway."

"Will the Senor Englisse enter ?"

"The Senor Englisse will. Can I have some dinner ?"

"Senor, yes."

"'Senor, yes.' I have heard nothing but that ever since I came here. These fellows always put the cart before the horse, as the people say. The people say lots of curious things. What sort of wine have you ?"

"The best, senor."

"If it is as good as your English it will do. Bring a flask."

"Of my Englisse, senor ?"

The tourist looked into Scampia's stolid face—its perfect gravity made him smile.

"No—your wine. Now, I wonder if he meant that as a joke ? What right has he to joke with his customers ? I will have revenge by sketching him in caricature ; but then it would be so ugly I should be afraid to look at it."

Scampia went to fetch the wine, and as he went, called out :

"Nicola !"

The tourist's heart beat as the girl came down the ricketty stairs.

She was very pretty.

Her dress—that of a peasant girl—added no inconsiderable charm to a full, fine form, lithe, round and supple in every limb. A countess would have envied her thin little foot in her tiny sandalled shoes. Her ankles were exquisite—so, at least, our tourist thought, and only, of course, admired them as an artist and a student of the beautiful.

Nicola was not darker in complexion than an English brunette. Her face, throat and neck had the pure olive tint—a soft, warm glow, peculiar to the children of that passionate clime. What her eyes were, our tourist only knew indistinctly. Their first glance thrilled him to his fingers' ends.

"The sort of girl a fellow would like to run away with !" thought the tourist. "But only fancy being chased by old Scamp and Satan ! Ugh !"

Nicola was to wait on him evidently.

He followed her into a room, the door of which she opened.

This room was not badly furnished. It had a comfortable couch, and several cushioned seats, a large centre table, and several smaller ones placed conveniently near the seats.

The couch was occupied. A young Italian student lay upon it, fast asleep.

"I wonder if he would wake were I to lift him off," said the tourist. "I should like that couch !"

He approached the sleeper, intending to lift him off, when Nicola touched his arm.

"Let him sleep, senor. He is tired."

"So am I, and I am going to sketch sunset from the mountains. An awful thing to travel up, that mountain is. Give me a glass of wine, Nicola. Is Scampia Zatani your father ?"

Nicola's answer was an inclination of the head—almost a nod.

"Wonderful are the ways of nature," said the traveller to himself. "This pretty little maid is piquant to sublimity. I ask her a question and she nods. I will talk Italian to her."

"And so Zatani is your father, is he ?"

Nicola laughed outright. The listless concern with which he repeated his question amused her. When she laughed he caressed his whisker in astonishment, and asked her to laugh again.

"That sort of music does a fellow good to hear," he said. "The girls at home never laugh like that If a fellow says anything funny they giggle at him—not that I ever say anything funny."

"Can you give a message for me ?" he asked, tasting the wine, which was excellent. "A friend of mine is coming to the mountain for me in about two hours."

"What will be his name ?"

"Marriott—Viscount Marriott. The same as it is now, you know."

"Is senor a viscount too ?"

"No, he isn't. My name is Oliver St. George. I suppose you are curious, and like to know all about it. All women are curious. Don't forget the message, Nicola."

"Message, senor ?"

Nicola lifted her pretty eyebrows in surprise.

"Ah, ah !—I haven't given it yet. Tell him I shall not be at the place I intended, but at the other place. He will know."

Nicola repeated the message on her fingers.

"Not at the place I intended, but at the other place. He will know."

"That's it, Nicola. Pretty name, Nicola is. Who is cooking my dinner, Nicola ?"

"My father."

"The deuce ! Run and tell him get to, Nicola. I prefer anything you have cold. Why," he added, to himself, as Nicola went away, "the shocking old Goth had his hand full of damp tobacco !"

He lit a cigar and waited for Nicola to return. But she did not ; so, taking a pencil and paper from his portfolio, he commenced a sketch of the sleeping student.

The face was one worth studying as it looked now—with every feature set in repose, its chiselled beauty was perfect. Rich masses of raven hair clustered on a forehead white as marble—a student's forehead perhaps—thoughtful in expression even while he slept, wide and deep of brow, and classic in its entire contour.

The beauty of the face was wild and dreamy. His form, as it lay, was an undulation of graceful strength.

The tourist's sketch was half completed, when Nicola returned with a tray. The sight of a cold fowl and a handsome cut of very choice ham, with new white bread and another bottle of wine, reminded St. George of his appetite.

"Just wake that fellow up and ask him to have some with me," he said to Nicola. "You don't keep Bass, I suppose ?"

"Bass ?"

"Ale—pale—bottled ! Don't you know ?"

Nicola did not.

"Allsopp, then? Bitter, you know—beer!"

Nicola shook her head again. She knew what he meant when he asked for beer. All the English travellers she had seen asked for beer.

"No beer. Never mind, Nicola, but you ought to keep Bass —Allsopp would do. I hate having to drink wine whether I want it or not. Can you carve me a leg out of that fowl? I never could carve a fowl—always shot of the dish when I touch them! Thank you! Just wake that fellow up. Perhaps if I give him some dinner he will let me have the couch."

Nicola crossed the room and touched the slumbering student on the cheek.

"Nice way that of waking a fellow," said the tourist, ruminating while he ate. "If I were him I would pretend to be asleep and let her keep at it. What a lovely Hebe she would make for my picture—'The Feast of the Gods.' I wonder if she would sit to me?—classic drapery, and so on. Perhaps she would not."

Here the stranger woke. His large black eyes scanned Nicola's features inquiringly. Then, more fully awake, he recognised her.

"Well, Nicola?" he said, with a singularly winning smile.

Nicola repeated St. George's request.

"How do?" said Oliver, nodding to him pleasantly. "I detest eating by myself. Will you ——"

He indicated the fowl, minus a leg, the ham as yet untouched, and the bottle as yet unfinished.

The stranger gazed upon him with a glance of unmistakeable hauteur.

"An Englishman," he muttered—"an eccentric people."

St. George repeated his question. He had his mouth full of fowl.

"Thank you," said the Italian, "it is not my hour for a repast."

"Drink, then?"

"Not to-day—I rarely touch wine."

"Do something—have a cigar?"

"With pleasure!"

St. George offered him his cigar-case; the stranger declined it by taking one from his own pocket.

"Funny!" thought St. George. "I wonder what he is?— smokes his own cigars when he might get somebody else's. Pleasant weather, isn't it?"

"It is Italy," smiled the stranger.

"That's very good. We never have pleasant weather in England; if we do, it don't last—all fogs, no sunshine. Sangster is a great institution—he's the umbrella-man, you know."

"That sketch," said the stranger, smiling again at the indolent, shallow style of converse which formed a thin surface to as fine a nature as ever graced a man,—"you are an artist?"

"A little—just for fun, you know. It's your head. Think it good?"

"Equal to the subject, at least. You are sketching in the vicinity?"

"I am going up the mountain to do the sunset if I can— the sunset is glorious here. You love your country, senor?"

"To adoration!"

"I don't mine,—I travel out of it as much as I can."

"I know the clime. It is dull—sombre; there is no life, no light, or gladness there. The people are sordid. Pardon me—I have heard this."

"Quite true, I assure you—the most dismal place in the world! People all keep shops till they get rich, then give parties and spend all the money. Sordid, as you say—awfully so! Can't get a bill done under twenty-five per cent.—extortion, you know. Have you any usurers in Naples?"

"Too many!" said the stranger, bitterly. "There are aliens and robbers from every shore, who come to glut their funds by devising the wreck of our ancient glory. Italy is now a huckster's mart for foreign venturers—a playground for strangers—idlers; its people are hirelings and slaves!"

The room creaked beneath his heavy tread as he strode across the floor.

"True!" said St. George, reflectively. "You want a William Tell sort of fellow—somebody to shoot apples, and that kind of thing. I saw it at the play. One fellow scattered a herd of bulls—at least, he said so; I didn't see any bulls, only a lot of soldiers run away. Funny, wasn't it?"

The stranger broke into a half-fierce, half-ironic laugh.

"We want the generous sympathy of kindred nations," he said—"the help of men who, having liberty themselves, have enough of chivalry to assist us in the fight for ours."

"They mustn't do it, you know. Non-intervention is the idea—political wisdom—that kind of thing."

"I know. They would see a wounded lion torn by wolves, and none would raise a hand to keep the murderous fangs out."

"Think not, do you?"

"Think of Aspremonte—Garibaldi!"

"Brave fellow that! Saw him in London. Lots of cheering he had. General holiday—nobody did any work. Such a crush to see him that everybody came out unwashed—lots of unwashed!"

"Why was he hunted back? Why was it England did not keep him?"

"Political wisdom; gave him a yacht, and that kind of thing."

"Curse their wisdom—it enslaves all that is chivalric and good! Oh for a twelvemonth of the olden time, when a cry like Italy's would have found echo in a million hearts!"

"Lots of fighting there must have been. I say, it's a good thing you would not eat with me—or, rather, it's not a good thing you would not eat with me—shocking fowl! Must be the one that made Peter weep—awfully tough bird!"

"This is an Englishman," thought the fiery student, "and he can mock me with his folly; I have heard that they are as insensible to fear as to feeling. We shall see anon!"

"You are going up the mountain?" he said, after a pause.

"Over the Pontine Marshes. Are you an artist?"

"Only an amateur. I could not sketch a sunset from the mountain, although it is my birthplace. Are you going alone?"

"Yes; I can sketch better when alone. No fellow to bore me with stupid questions and borrow all my pencils. The viscount is coming for me in an hour or so."

"You have no fear in going alone?"

"Fear? Of what?"

"Banditti?"

"Bosh! See this!"

He produced an elegant revolver capped and loaded.

"I could pepper any six vagabonds to their hearts' content, and punch a few if I hadn't enough bullets. I know a little of the science. Do you box at all?"

The Italian shrugged his shoulders in the negative.

"Strange! Very few foreigners do. I could smash any fellow in ten minutes, and I can snuff a candle at ten paces. Just stand quiet a minute, and I'll take the feather out of your hat."

Curious to see such a proof of skill, the Italian stood motionless. St. George did not even rise, but, elevating his weapon slantingly to the level, pulled the trigger.

The feather fluttered to the ground cut clean through the stem—the hat was not grazed.

"An excellent aim!" said the student. "You have great nerve, senor!"

"So have you. Like to try a shot at me?"

He tendered his revolver, which was accepted.

"Pick this off!" he said, putting a cork on his cap, and the cap on his head. "In this kind of target it is better to be a little too high than ever such a small amount too low."

The Italian fired before the tourist had finished speaking. St. George felt the cork go flying from his hat—it rolled to the floor perforated.

"Bravo!" he said,—"shoot as well as I do. Adieu, senor! I must not lose my sunset!"

He took his revolver from the stranger, not noticing that the caps had fallen from the two nipples next in rotation to those which were exploded.

"Good-bye, Nicola!" he said, tendering a piece of gold for the slight repast he had made. "Give me a kiss for the change, and don't forget my message."

And, just touching with his lips the warm cheek offered to him in coquettish frankness, he left the inn and made for the mountain.

Nicola followed him with a glance of admiration. It was well deserved. He was a stalwart fellow, quite six feet in height, and blending in his form the power of a Hercules with the grace of an Apollo. His face was purely Saxon—open, frank, and irresistibly prepossessing.

The stranger watched him too, and with a smile.

"Brave!" he said,—"our Saxon—genial and rich! Such a man should be highly valued by his friends."

Still watching the tourist up the heights, the student took a bugle from his sash, and blew a prolonged, plaintive note. It seemed to find five distinct echoes, one following the other.

St. George looked back. The student replaced the bugle in his sash and waved his hand.

CHAPTER II.

LEON, THE STUDENT.

THE student went back into the inn. There was a strange smile upon his lip as he beckoned Nicola to him, and said:

"There would have been bad work, Nicola, had Cospoletto seen the stranger kiss you."

"Cospoletto!" pouted the girl. "I do not like him."

"Why?"

"He is uncouth—he terrifies me. He cannot speak gently, as you do."

"Perhaps you are not so kind to him, Nicola?"

"I do not like him. He does no work of late, and people whisper that he is a brigand."

"Were it true, would you love him less?"

"Neither less nor more, Senor Leon. I never loved him at all, but were he kinder I could like him a little."

"Suppose you had loved him very much, and he joined the banditti, would you love him still?"

Nicola hesitated. The student awaited her reply with much interest.

"I do not know," she said at last. "Brigands are terrible people, Senor Leon!"

"Not to those they love!" said Leon, with his soft smile. "We hear of them now and then—these bandits."

"And their chief—Red Gauntlet. How I dread to think of him!"

"Poor little Nicola! He would not hurt you. What have you heard of him?"

"That he takes travellers captive, and kills them if they cannot get a ransom."

"As a bandit, even Red Gauntlet may not be so bad as people say. I have seen him."

"Seen Red Gauntlet?" cried Nicola, starting back. "Oh! what is he like?"

"Not half so hideous as people say."

"Not dreadfully ugly?"

"I assure you, no. Am I ugly?"

"Senor Leon!"

"Well, Nicola," he said, smiling at the flattering exclamation, "he is very much like me—in fact, if I wore his dress I might be taken for him."

Nicola opened her lustrous eyes in wonderment.

"Where did you see him?"

"On the mountain."

"Did he not molest you?"

"No—he was attacked by the soldiery."

"And you?"

"I fought for him. I did not like to see so many against one, and he escaped."

"That was brave!" said Nicola, clapping her hands. "I should so much like to see him!"

The student laughed.

"Perhaps you will some day; but you would scarcely believe your own eyes if you were to."

"He would not hurt me, you say?"

"I am sure he would not. He had a mother, Nicola—he had a sister. I have heard him say that, in reverence to their memory, he holds all women sacred. Not the most daring of his band would dare lay a finger on one of your sex!"

"Why, senor?"

"Red Gauntlet would kill him."

His voice made Nicola shudder.

"If he is so noble, why is he a bandit?"

"The story is a sad one, Nicola. He was oppressed—wronged in fortune and in love!"

The student's sympathy for his bandit friend must have been strong, for his chest heaved and his eyes grew fiery.

"There is Cospoletto coming," he said, turning from her questioning gaze. "Be gentle to him, Nicola—then he will be kind to you."

"Do not leave me with him, Senor Leon!"

"Only while I speak to your father. I shall be at hand."

He went into the house seeking Scampia Zatani. Nicola would have followed, but she had not time.

A huge, swarthy ruffian, gaunt and fierce in aspect as a wolf, crossed her path.

"Would pretty Nicola shun me?" he asked.

Certainly, a more ill-favoured lover did never persecute a pretty maiden with an unprosperous love. It might have been him whom the artist had in his eye when he drew the questionable-looking ruffian on the signboard.

Nicola had no answer to give. Cospoletto's very presence filled her with a terror that kept her dumb.

"We used to be good friends, Nicola. You were not so shy in former days."

"You seem so fierce, Cospoletto."

"Seem demons! That guest of yours, the Englishman—maledictions on him!—he did not seem too fierce, did he?"

She shrank from his savage voice and more savage glance.

"Come, pretty Nicola—a kiss, to make us friends again! No shrinking, for I will have one! You were not so coy with the traveller!"

His heavy grip fell and tightened on her dimpled shoulder. She gave a terrified cry, and tried to break away.

The ruffian laughed at her struggles. It gratified his natural liking for brutal mischief to kiss a helpless girl against her will—it gratified his passion to kiss Nicola.

When his lips were so near that another inch would have brought their hot, sullying pressure to hers, she gave a second cry.

"Help, father! Senor Leon!"

The student came out at a single bound, and Cospoletto reeled till he rolled over in a heap. He had received a blow which would have felled anything of the brute creation.

Getting up, blinded by the sudden contact of his head with the dust, he rushed savagely at his assailant.

"Cospoletto!"

The word was not spoken above the student's breath, but the ruffian stopped.

"Kneel in the dust there! Ask Nicola's pardon!"

Cowering like a beaten hound, crouching as though from a merited lash, the ruffian knelt and bowed his shaggy head in low humility. Great drops of perspiration broke out upon his brow.

"Would you raise your hand against me, Cospoletto?"

Cospoletto's teeth chattered audibly, yet the student was smiling, and his voice was sweet and musical, only a peculiar inflection—a thin under-current, ran through it like a vein of ice.

"Pardon, senor—pardon!"

"Rise, Cospoletto—forgiven this time! Never speak to Nicola again, Cospoletto."

"Never, senor—I swear!"

"Your word is enough to me—for those who lie to me I have a way of punishment peculiar to myself! Go, good Cospoletto! You are sorry for having frightened Nicola?"

"Very sorry, senor!"

The student pointed to the mountains. Cospoletto turned his footsteps thither; but his limbs so trembled that he went totteringly and slowly.

He could not have sunk more suddenly into a state of abject, prostrate terror had he seen a phantom, or Red Gauntlet.

"You see, my pretty Nicola, we can tame a brute by kindness," said the student, with a laugh. "Cospoletto went away quite calm!"

"You frightened him, Senor Leon—you frightened me!"

"Did I? Yet I was not angry."

"But your voice!"

"Nay, my voice was low enough."

"But so strange, Senor Leon!"

"Never mind its strangeness, Nicola!—it quieted Cospoletto and saved you. He will not trouble you again."

A sudden thought made her tremble. Cospoletto had gone up the mountain. He might meet the tourist there.

"Senor," she said, clutching Leon's arm, "should he see the Englishman——"

"Never fear! Cospoletto would not trouble him more than would a rat a terrier."

"Senor Leon, is the Englishman in danger?"

"What danger?"

"The banditti."

The student started slightly.

"Why ask me that, Nicola?"

"Only this: should he fall into their hands, you will intercede for him? Do promise me, Senor Leon!"

"Why should you fear for him?"

"I have a presentiment—I know not why! Do promise me!"

"Very well, Nicola. Should there be occasion for my intercession, shall I tell Red Gauntlet at whose request I intrude?"

"No, for then he would know."

"And suppose he did?"

Her beautiful eyes filled with tears.

"He would think lightly of poor Nicola!"

"Pretty child—and so proud, pure, too, in spite of teaching not too good! The Englishman shall be safe for your sake, Nicola! And remember this: Leon, the student, is your friend!"

"I am so grateful! You will save Senor St. George should the bandits capture him?"

"I have promised."

"Nicola—Nicola!" called Zatani, from the interior.

"Scampia's voice! Go, Nicola! Senor St. George shall be safe, even should he fall into the hands of the banditti—quite safe, Nicola—Leon has said so!"

CHAPTER III.

THE BANDITTI.

THE nature of St. George's adventure at the mountain inn was strange enough to set him thinking of the student. About the latter there was enough of singularity to create strong interest in any thoughtful mind, and Oliver St. George was of a deeper mood than he seemed by his usual manner.

He was a great, simple-hearted fellow, frank and brave as a school-boy, and generous to a fault. He detested anything like a sensation, or outward display of emotion. His light, half-jesting style of speech could give him a semblance of carelessness, even when his heart ached with sympathy.

He had conceived a liking for the student at first sight, and every fiery word Leon uttered had fallen on a kindred chord in St. George's soul. Our Englishman had the chivalry of a knight errant, but he was indolent, and did not see the force of getting in a passion when he could do no good.

Just at this moment, he was very earnestly at work upon the sketch. Never had the sun set in more solemnity of majesty—never had he felt greater power to grasp so grand a subject.

The scene above and all around—in the far distance, and striking from the mountain's base, in wild, unbroken solitude

for many a mile—was such as could not but call forth in all its force the poetry of his soul. There was the city, dim and picturesque, viewed from where he sat—the waters of the Bay rocking softly, as though sleeping, hushed to quietude by the slowly-spreading wing of night; the wide, long range of crag and peak sifting through the silvery clouds; and sinking behind crag and peak, the purple sun rolling downward, till it formed a pyre.

He kept his pencil busily at work, save when, ever and anon, he had to pause to take in some new beauty as it came. The time sped on, and he felt no sense of weariness, but almost regretted Marriott had appointed to meet him so soon.

A slight sound diverted his attention from the task before him, and he looked around, expecting to see the viscount. No human figure was in sight, however, and he drew a sigh of real relief.

"I thought it was Cecil," he said, pausing now to study the outline and partial filling of his sketch; "and if it had been, good-bye to work. A deuce of a fellow Cecil is! He chaffs me awfully about wanting to be an artist! I wonder if Nicola gave him my message? Pretty little girl that Nicola—would make a lovely Hebe—classic drapery, and so on. I think I said that before. Very different to the girls in London. I remember the Hon. Selina Mowldy, an ancient party—artistic—used to paint her own face. Funny that! Wanted me to make a match. Didn't see the force of it—would rather have Nicola. How the fellows would stare to see me take Nicola home as Mrs. St. George! Wonder if she would have me? Couldn't have her, if she would. That's funny, too."

He went on sketching again.

"Queer fellow, that artist—capital shot—not sociable, though. Hallo!"

A second time he heard a slight noise behind him, but, turning round, could see nothing. Yet there was a sinister face peering from behind a crag within ten yards of where he sat.

He set to work again at his sketch, fully intending to astonish Cecil by the amount of artistic labour he was capable of getting through, till a new vein of thought occupied his attention, and, becoming absorbed in meditation, he lost the particular period of sunset he had been most anxiously waiting for.

Then, like a philosopher, he put pencil and paper away. His portfolio was open, and he was rather startled by seeing the shadow of a human figure thrown right across it.

"Cecil this time!" he said.

But on looking up he saw he was mistaken. The man who stood before him was Cospoletto.

St. George felt instinctively for his revolver. The fellow's face was in itself a caution.

"A second edition of the Scamp and Satan species!" said Oliver. "What do you want, my good fellow?"

The ruffian laughed, and pointed over St. George's shoulder. St. George turned his head, and in an instant Cospoletto was upon him.

"Clever!" said St. George. "Taken in by such an old trick as that! This, I suppose, is one of the banditti my friend, the artist, spoke about."

And with inimitable unconcern, he, by the mere force of superior strength, forced back the ruffian's brawny hands, shook him off, and, getting him at arms' length, knocked him down.

"If you want to fight," he said, "get up and come on!"

Cospoletto did not want to fight—he did not want to get up; but he put a whistle to his lips, and blew a signal.

The mountain seemed alive with Cospolettoes then,—every crag and crevice had served as a hiding-place for a wretch like St. George's first antagonist.

"I am in for it!" muttered the Englishman, between his teeth. "But if they take me, it will not be yet!"

He drew his revolver. A dozen of the banditti hemmed him in by forming a wide circle.

St. George regretted now that he had not replaced the two shots spent in the trial of skill at the inn.

He did not waste words. He had heard of the recent doings of brigands in the locality, and knew that they wanted him to keep in captivity till a ransom could be obtained.

St. George did not want to put his friends to any expense, and had no money to spare of his own.

So, keeping his revolver hidden till he had mentally taken aim at the desperado who was chiefly in his way, he fired from the hip.

The hammer descended on the nipple harmlessly.

He muttered an oath, half in anger, half despair. The ruffians, whom his resolute aspect had cowered back, now gave a yell of triumph as they saw the failure of his weapon. They advanced and paused. It was a revolver glittering before their eyes now, and only one chamber had missed as yet.

He tried a second at the same man, and again the hammer fell without report. They advanced nearer, and he pulled the trigger once more.

This time the brigand leaped into the air with a jet of blood spurting out between the fingers of the hand he put to his breast. He fell, bounding from crag to crag like a ball, till his mangled form found a resting-place half-way down the mountain's side.

"One shot more I have!" he said, his eyes flashing fire now. "Back! you grimy crew of confounded ruffians! By jove! I wish Cecil would come!"

Cospoletto made a sudden dash at him, and they closed. St. George got the muzzle of his pistol against the brigand's temple, but Cospoletto wrenched his head aside just as St. George pulled the trigger.

The ball went through the brain of a tall bandit, who happened to be in the way.

Though comparatively defenceless then, St. George gave them some trouble. He stood up and fought with his revolver grasped by the muzzle in his left hand, while he guarded with his right.

Nothing but his agility and skill saved him from the long knives with which they now assailed him. Cospoletto, who tried to make an insertion, got the butt of the revolver on his nose, and went back howling.

St. George battled like a lion. His blood was up—his physical power strong to its topmost pitch, and had his foes been not so many, he would have conquered.

In spite of their number, it went against his pride to retreat. Though there were ten against him, he satisfied his conscience by doubling his fifth antagonist as though from the kick of a horse, and, seeing an opening then, he ran for liberty.

They uttered a barbaric yell, and gave chase; but St. George could run well—he was used to mountain travelling.

Still, his recent active conflict had not left him so sound in wind and limb as he could have wished to run with. He stumbled once or twice, and as he recovered his footing, heard the hot breath of his foremost pursuers close behind.

He was about to turn and fight again, when, for the third time, he stumbled.

That stumble saved his life. He was lying full length along the edge of a deep precipice.

Another step, and he must have gone down. Clinging to the strong, rank weeds, he shuddered to think of the hideous fall—the dull crash of bone and flesh on the steep rock.

His pursuers came on. They had not seen him fall, but thought he had gone on ahead.

The foremost struck his foot against St. George's body, and went headlong down the abyss. His death-cry warned the rest, but not in time to save a second from the awful doom.

"Capital!" thought St. George. "I lie here, and they roll over me! Funny, rather!"

A third, in going over, struck his foot heavily against St. George's head. The man went down to death, and St. George lay senseless.

When he recovered, he was lying in a corner of a cavern bound hand and foot, and with Cospoletto as sentry at the cavern entrance.

The savage brigand had a rifle levelled at St. George's head, ready to shoot him if he stirred. Oliver was a captive in the hands of the Black Mountaineers.

(*To be continued in our next.*)

BRIGAND LIFE IN TUSCANY.

THE PRISON OF VOLTERRA AND ITS INMATES.

THE COUNT FELICINI.

The most ancient place in Tuscany is Volterra, situated on the borders of Siena.

Its antique gateway, built of uncemented stone, its ruins of a Roman amphitheatre, its museum of old coins—the whole place being, in fact, a museum of antiquities—give it an attraction to all travellers in Tuscany.

But the great object of interest is its fortress, perched on the highest rock in that rocky region.

The wondrous strength of this old castle has resisted the decay that has overtaken the other remnants of Roman architecture that lie around it.

It is in such a state of excellent preservation that it continues the strongest prison in Tuscany, and is devoted chiefly to the punishment of offenders whose crimes have been most flagrant, and whose punishment extends to long periods of solitary confinement.

As illustrative of the semi-barbarism from which modern Italy is but just emerging, let us take the cases of three of the principal criminals of modern times whose names are associated with this prison.

One is dead and two are living and still pointed out to the visitor.

Deep below the foundations of the fortress is shown a circular cell in which, for twenty years, was confined the Count Felicini, the memory of whose crimes excites to this day a shudder amongst the people of the country.

This man was one of the wealthiest landed proprietors in Tuscany, but of so strangely constituted a mind that, from his earliest youth, his chief happiness lay in the excitement produced by inflicting and contemplating the agonies of human beings.

This modern Caligula amused his leisure by inveigling to his castle chance wayfarers under a pretence of hospitality, and afterwards subjecting them to all the tortures which his diseased imagination could devise.

His favourite victims were monks and friars, and it was proved on his trial, by the evidence of his servants, that he resorted to a system of torture and mutilation to account for which it would be an effort of charity to consider him to have been a merely dangerous maniac.

Even in Italy, in the days of the old *regime*, a barbarian like the Count, compared with whom his Majesty of Dahomey is a refined and humane gentleman, fell into the hands of justice, and he was sentenced to twenty years' solitary confinement.

For this period he inhabited an underground cell five feet in diameter; light and air were admitted by a circular hole bored through the wall, only two inches in diameter at the inside, but gradually increasing in width as it approached the exterior.

A large millstone occupied the middle of this cell, and it is said that he had misgivings that this was a masked trap-door, through which, if touched, he would be precipitated to unknown depths.

To avoid this, he kept himself in one spot, beneath the air-hole, which was, however, too high for him to reach, and visitors are shown marks on the floor and wall which are asserted to have been worn by his feet and elbow.

How flesh and blood could have held out for twenty years pent up in this narrow cistern is marvellous enough, but this stringent imprisonment proved less fatal to him than his liberty.

When his term had elapsed, and he was again free, he was advised to return to air and light by slow degrees.

Disregarding this counsel, in the wild joy of recovered liberty, he rushed into the courtyard of the prison, and instantly fell dead as if he had been shot.

The world was thus relieved from the presence of one of the greatest monsters of modern times.

But this is a tale of the past.

Looking through a loophole through which visitors are allowed to inspect the inmates of the cells, we see a living specimen of another man of blood.

CIOTTI, THE SHOEMAKER.

Munching a piece of black bread, we see a thick-set man of horrible aspect, and the action of whose jaws makes the spectator, acquainted with his history, shudder.

This is Ciotti, once the terror of the Livornians.

This man, a shoemaker by trade, had several associates in crime, of whom he was the leader.

These wretches bound themselves by an oath never to let a single day pass without committing a murder. To these crimes they were impelled solely by a lust of blood.

Every morning corpses were found in the streets of Leghorn of men murdered, but not robbed, as the watches and purses of the victims were left untouched.

A panic seized the inhabitants, and no one dared to stir abroad after nightfall.

This nightly butchery continued for more than three months, and its perpetrators remained undiscovered.

In process of time victims began to grow scarce, and the murderers had to resort to extraordinary arts to fulfil their vow.

Early one morning, Ciotti, having prowled about all night in vain search for food for his knife, rather than forego the nightly sacrifice, turned it against his own wife; fortunately he did not succeed in despatching her, though she was desperately wounded.

Her shrieks brought the assistance of the neighbours and the police.

The wounded woman revealed her husband's long career of crime, which he had hitherto contrived to cloak under the semblance of regular and industrious habits.

Ciotti was seized, tried, and condemned.

We had a piquancy imparted to the awful history of this wretch from the circumstance that one of our party, an Italian officer, had been himself in near danger from the knives of these Tuscan Thugs.

He told us that he was residing at Leghorn during this reign of terror, and growing tired of being kept at home night after night, which to an Italian is a mild kind of imprisonment, he one evening sallied out in spite of the remonstrances of friends.

It was a rainy night, and after spending some hours at a *cafe*, he set out on his return home, carefully keeping the middle of the road, and with his attention on the alert to prevent a surprise.

The streets were silent and deserted; and the splash of his own footsteps through the mud, and the dripping of the rain, were the only sounds audible.

He had proceeded half-way up one of the narrow and tortuous streets that led out of the principal square, when, from beneath an archway, two men rushed out upon him; by the glimmer of the street-lamp he saw the flash of their knives; taking to his heels, he ran with all his might, closely pursued by the homicides.

The chase was fast and furious for some time, but our friend, the narrator, who is blessed with a pair of legs of unusual length, made such excellent use of them as eventually to distance his pursuers.

The last he heard of them was a complimentary speech sent after him—"*Figlio d'un cane, s'hai scapata bella!*" (Son of a dog, a narrow escape you've had.)

After listening to this anecdote, we took another look at the human tiger, who, sensible of this intrusion on his privacy, gnashed his teeth at us in a way that produced a disagreeable sensation; but our tall friend who had once been so nearly in his clutches gazed with marked satisfaction upon the wild beast secured in his cage.

The next amongst the notables of the place was a man who, compared with the two wretches already described, may lay claim to the title of a hero.

This was the once celebrated bandit chief Norcino.

NORCINO, THE BANDIT OF TUSCANY.

Let not, however, any romantic reader imagine that this poor prisoner had the noble bearing, dignified mien, or the picturesque dress often associated with the idea of a leader of banditti.

Whatever he might have been in his palmy days—and we were told that he then had some pretension to gentlemanlike bearing—yet as we saw him, after ten years of solitary confinement, his appearance excited no more elevated feeling than that of compassion.

Years back he had been the Turpin of that part of Tuscany surrounding Pisa.

He and his band had been the terror of the wealthy farmer and trader, but the secret pride of the peasantry, to whom he had the reputation of being a liberal benefactor.

So well concerted were his plans, so secret his spies, so daring and adventurous his character, that it was a rare occurrence for any moneyed traveller to escape him, unless he journeyed by daylight, or was accompanied by a formidable escort.

Norcino was a native of a beautiful little village called Altopascio.

His band consisted of from twelve to twenty men.

Few acts of personal violence are laid to their charge, as it was their practice to treat those they pillaged civilly so long as they offered no resistance.

The motive which led Norcino to resort to a bandit life was not the love of adventure only, but a passionate fondness for play.

When he had succeeded in making a handsome booty, he would cease his depredations until his store was quite exhausted.

Large rewards were offered for his apprehension, and parties of soldiers were often in pursuit of him, but the peasants were his friends, and he succeeded for a long time in eluding capture.

At last he was taken and imprisoned at Volterra, but, strong as the fortress is, he contrived to make his escape from it more than once.

At last, being recaptured, he was consigned to an underground cell.

Even from this dark dungeon he has made several attempts to escape, but hitherto ineffectually.

His spirit seems now completely broken, and in this gloomy cell he will probably end his restless career.

An English lady, the wife of an Italian gentleman resident at Pisa, gave me an anecdote of this bandit chief which exhibits his character in a favourable light, and is illustrative of the state of society in this part of Italy.

The truth of the incident may be fully relied upon, and I shall relate it as nearly as possible in her own words:—

"The Val di Niesole, which lies between Pontedera (a small railway station between Pisa and Leghorn) and Altopascio, is one of the most populous and fertile valleys in Tuscany.

"Altopascio is a large village, about four hours' drive from Pontedera, and is situated in the midst of a district famous for its abundance of game, and consequently much frequented in the shooting season by sportsmen of all classes.

"In the neighbourhood of this village a few farm-houses are scattered, and in one of these my husband, Mr. S., engaged rooms for the shooting season.

"At that time he was living with his family at Leghorn, and his practice was to visit the shooting ground at the end of every week.

"He travelled by railway from Leghorn to Pontedera, and thence in his own conveyance to his farm-house lodgings.

"The drive led through the beautiful valley of Niesole, the road traversing well-kept vineyards, which are here of singular beauty.

"The vivid green of the vine leaves just turning under the touch of autumn into a deep red are a bright contrast to the dull, blue-green monotony of the olive trees, that dot a landscape having for its appropriate setting the blue hills in the distance.

"Leaving the valley, with its oliveyards and vineyards, the road winds over a mountain ridge, where a fresh picture greets the eye.

"On one side the Arno winds in and out like a huge serpent gradually dwelling to a silver thread, till at last it is lost in the distance.

"On the other side is spread out the Lago di Bientina, the largest lake in Tuscany; it is sixty miles in circumference, and its banks are dear to sportsmen from the quantity of snakes and wild ducks that make them a favourite haunt.

"But it is not without danger that the sportsman seeks his game.

"The marshy ground is covered with a treacherous, green, velvet-like carpet, which trembles beneath the tread, so that one unwary footstep may cost a life.

"The peasants say, and firmly believe, that the waters of the lake flow over a buried city.

"The late Duke of Tuscany, with a view to reclaim the land, caused, at great cost, a canal to be dug to carry off the waters of the lake.

"Through this channel the water has been flowing for ten years; still St. Lago di Bientina shows no sign of diminution.

"It was one Saturday evening, now fifteen years ago, that Mr. S. was pursuing the road I have attempted to describe, on his way to his shooting-quarters.

"It was at a later hour than he had intended, for he was quite aware of the dangers of the road, but his ardour as a sportsman induced him to run the risk.

"Provided with a good horse, a favourite pair of loaded pistols, in the use of which he was expert, and with only a small sum of money in his pocket, he determined to brave the danger, despite the remonstrances of friends and the unhappy experience of other travellers.

"He had been driving for about two hours, and had reached that part of the road which wound up the hill before described.

"It was some hours after sunset, but the valley he had quitted was lighted up in the full glory of Italian moonlight, but as he ascended the hill, at a slow walking pace, a wood, on either side, intercepted the moon, that only penetrated the trees in quivering patches.

"He had advanced about half-way up the ascent, when, at a moment when he least expected a surprise, a man suddenly stepped from among the bushes into the road, and laid his hand upon the horse's rein.

"My husband instantly seized the pistol that he had laid in readiness at his side, but a deprecatory movement of the hand made by the man at his horse's head restrained him.

"'It is useless using firearms,' said the figure, with quiet dignity, 'I am Norcino.'

"Mr. S. stared at the intruder in mute surprise and curiosity. He saw a short, stout, dark-looking man, with a good-natured expression of face, and dressed like a farmer.

"It was difficult to realise that this could be the terrible brigand, the terror and scourge of the district.

"After a moment's pause, Mr. S. replied:

"'Well, sir, and what do you want of me?'

"'You are Mr. S., of —— Street, Leghorn,' Norcino said, 'and you are going to —— farm-house for a few days' shooting.'

"'All this is quite true,' said Mr. S., 'and what then?'

"'I want 50 scudi,' replied the brigand, 'and must have them to-night.'

"'You, that seem to know all about me,' replied Mr. S., 'must know that I don't fill my pockets with money to come on a shooting excursion.'

"'Certainly,' said the robber, 'especially when you thought it possible you might have the honour of an interview with me on your road. Come, Mr. S., I am serious; this money I must and will have. I will allow you now to go to your lodgings and borrow the sum amongst your sportsmen friends whom you will meet there, and in two hours bring it to me at the bridge below the farm, where I will meet you. Do not fail me at you peril; and remember this—come alone. Any attempt at deception shall be visited upon you with a terrible vengeance ; on the contrary, do me this favour, and you are free from me and my band this night—and for ever.'

"With this Norcino stepped aside, and with a courteous salute disappeared amongst the bushes, leaving my husband to pursue his way.

"To reach his destination, Mr. S. had to turn from the main road down a by-path that led over a bridge crossing a brook not far from the farm-house where his quarters were. This bridge was the meeting-place appointed by the brigand.

"Mr. S. found two of his friends at his lodgings; to them he communicated his adventure. They, naturally enough, advised him to disregard the robber's demand, but my husband considered that he had, tacitly at least, been a party to a bargain, which, as a man of honour, he was bound to keep. As his friends saw that he was bent upon meeting Norcino, they supplied him with the funds he wanted, but earnestly begged to be allowed to accompany him to the trysting-place. Mr. S. showed his good sense in declining all attendance, feeling persuaded that, with a character such as that he had to deal with, a show of confidence was the wisest and safest course.

"At the specified hour, Mr. S. stood upon the bridge, but not a creature was visible. After a few moments' delay, in a low voice he called 'Norcino,' and immediately issued from beneath the bridge the redoubtable brigand. Without a word Mr. S. handed him the scudi.

"'Mr. S., you are a gentleman,' was the reply, and they parted.

"Several weeks passed, Mr. S. continued his visits to the shooting-ground, but without adventure; when, one evening, at precisely the same spot where he had first encountered Norcino, that notorious bandit again appeared.

"Mr. S. now felt the matter to be serious, and determined at all hazards to resist a fresh demand.

"Norcino, without professing to notice my husband's attitude of resistance, quietly advanced to the carriage, and laid upon the cushion a parcel of money.

"'Here, Mr. S.' he said, 'I return you, with thanks, the sum you so kindly lent me.'

"Mr. S., no little astonished, replied that he never expected to see the money again, nor did he wish to take it.

"'Perhaps not,' said the brigand, 'but your whole conduct proved you to be a gentleman. I wish to be no less honourable. Addio!'"

ITALIAN BRIGANDAGE.—CONFLICT WITH GIARDULLO'S BAND.

THE *Italia* states that Giardullo's band has sustained a defeat.

The brigands, thirty in number, were so energetically attacked by a few carabineers that they hardly had time to take refuge in flight, leaving behind them two of their number—one killed, the other wounded.

The brigands have still in their hands the prisoners in whose fate the whole country is justly so deeply interested.

Had the carabineers been less limited in point of numbers, it is more than probable that the band would have been surrounded.

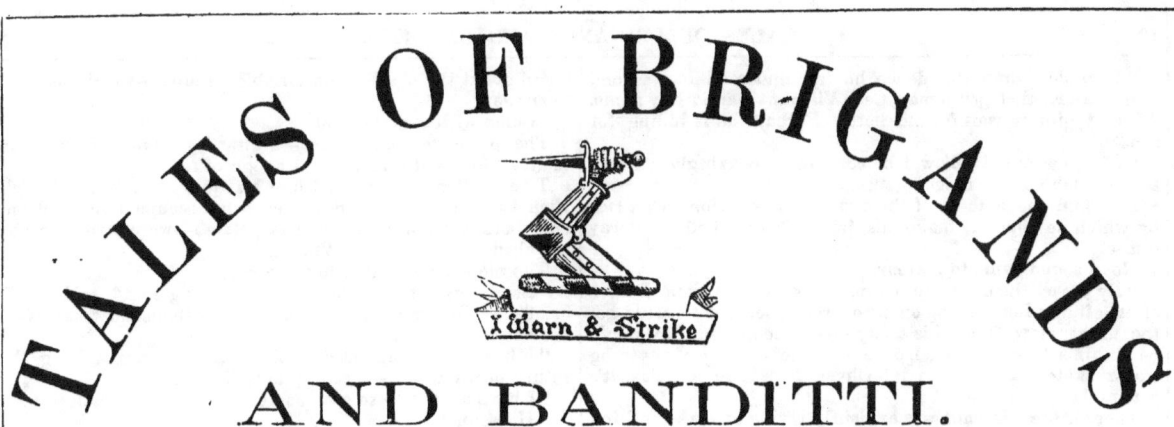

TALES OF BRIGANDS
AND BANDITTI.

I Warn & Strike

[PERILOUS POSITION OF ST. GEORGE.]

RED GAUNTLET, THE BANDIT; OR, THE BLACK MOUNTAINEERS.

BOOK I.—THE ARTIST.

CHAPTER IV.

THE BANDIT'S MESSENGER.

THE sun was setting, like a fire dying out, behind the rugged line of mountain and the sapphire sea of sky, when a second tourist turned his reluctant footsteps homeward, but not before he made Pontine marsh and mountain echo with his voice, as he shouted:

"St. George—Oliver!"

The echo was his only answer.

"I wonder where the deuce he is," muttered our second tourist, an English gentleman, Cecil Viscount Marriott by name. "I told him to wait for me here. Perhaps he is hiding for fun."

"It's no use, old fellow," he continued, coaxingly, "I can see you behind that crag!"

He could see nothing of the sort. His assertion was a *ruse* by which he hoped to make his friend laugh, and so betray himself.

Not a sound came to his ear.

"By Jove!" he muttered again, "this is very odd. I have often left him here sitting on my overcoat, because he could get the finest view from this spiky bit of mountain. He would perch himself on a spire, I believe, if he could see anything worth sketching. I hate it! Oliver, look here, old boy, it's getting late, you know!"

Though the Viscount was evidently trying to see something funny in St. George's absence, his voice was not altogether free from concern. These two were friends, St. George and Marriott.

"I said two hours," he went on, looking at his watch, "and the time isn't up yet. Perhaps he got tired and went home."

Again marsh and mountain rang with the name of his friend.

Silence succeeded the reverberation, and then the Viscount returned to the city.

He had his abode in a handsome palazzo, whose windows overlooked the bay.

Entering his chamber, he rang for his native servant.

Toncilo appeared.

"Has Mr. St. George returned, Toncilo?"

"No, senor."

"Anyone called?"

"Yes, senor—waiting."

"Waiting, is he? Show him in."

Much to the Viscount's surprise, Toncilo ushered in a lazzaroni—a Neapolitan mendicant.

This was something curious. Hitherto Cecil had wondered at the tribe at a distance, and now in the Viscount's own apartment was a perfect specimen—dirty, truculent, and picturesque.

"Who are you?" Cecil asked—"what do you want?"

The man drew a little note from his sash, and presented it.

The Viscount rang the bell.

"Toncilo," he said, pointing to the note, as his servant entered.

Toncilo understood. He set the small epistle on a silver tray, placed it within his master's reach, and, sidling round the mendicant, escaped by the door.

Cecil opened the note and read:—

"Dear Cecil,

"I am in the hands of the Philistines. My life at the present moment is worth five thousand piastres. Send the amount by the bearer. To delay, molest, or follow him is to kill me.

"Yours in faith,
"OLIVER ST. GEORGE."

There was a postscript in Italian.

It ran thus:—

"By dawn in the morning my messenger must return with five thousand piastres, or by eight Oliver St. George will be dead.

"RED GAUNTLET.
"CHIEF OF THE BLACK MOUNTAINEERS."

At the bottom of this postscript was a crest—a strange device—being a shield, on which were a red gauntlet grasping a dagger, a black mask, and a bugle.

The motto was:

"*I warn and strike!*"

This letter—so laconic, so conclusive, confirming all he had heard about the chief of the terrible banditti—Cecil hastened to answer.

"Come with me," he said.

The pretended mendicant—a swarthy, savage brigand, in reality—followed him without a sign of fear.

Two gentlemen—Stuart Linn, Marquis of Leith, and Dick Nicholson, his particular friend, who occupied magnificent chambers in a lower part of the palazzo—were astonished by the abrupt advent of the Viscount.

The messenger waited in the street.

"St. George is in the hands of brigands," said Cecil, briefly. "His ransom is fixed at five thousand piastres—I have two thousand."

"I have not a hundred," said Linn. "I am waiting the return of my fellow—I sent him to Torlonia's."

"I have a little loose cash somewhere," said Nicholson.

"How much?"

"About fifty piastres. But look here. Let us take our revolvers and fight the bandits, then we shall get St. George back for nothing."

"We should kill him," said Cecil, gravely. "Read his note."

They read it. Stuart Linn took out his watch, drew a magnificent diamond ring from his finger, picked the miniature of a beautiful lady from his jewelled case, and put case, watch, and ring into Cecil's hand.

"What are they worth?" he asked.

"Two thousand piastres."

"With the two you have there are four. Now, Dick—what have you?"

"These," said Nicholson, taking from his breast a locket set with pure opals, and from his finger a costly ring. He put them into Marriott's hand. A tear fell as he did so, and glistened like a diamond in the opal gleam of fire. "A relic of the dead," he said—"my dying mother's gift. It may save the living, Marriott, and I may get it back."

"Tell the rascal we shall redeem them," said Stuart Linn—"fifty per cent, interest. By Jove, we will too! We will all go out together in a day or two after we have got Oliver back, and perhaps the brigands will attack us."

Nicholson said he hoped they would.

Marriott went to the messenger, who was waiting for him in the street.

"Will these be sufficient?" he asked, displaying the glistening heap.

"Senor, yes."

The messenger's eyes—keen, dark, Italian orbs—flashed as brightly as the jewels.

"My friend the artist will be liberated immediately on your return?"

"Senor, yes."

"Which way may we expect him? We should like to meet him."

"By the ravine leading from the Pontine Marshes."

"Very well; and now, my good fellow, understand this: If you play us false,—if any of your comrades harm our friend, your band shall be tracked out and hunted down, though you were hidden where a mouse could not hide! Remember!"

The man changed colour. The Englishman had spoken with that cool determination peculiar to his race—the bandit knew the threat to be no idle one.

But, though the ransom was sent, Oliver St. George did not return. His friends waited for him at the ravine by the Pontine Marshes—waited till the close of day, and then returned alone.

They neared the outskirts of the city,—Marriott thinking sadly of his friend, and the Marquis discoursing with Dick Nicholson.

Suddenly a strange, prolonged bugle cry was heard. The horse attached to the *calessini* in which they had set forth came to a dead stand, then started wildly forward.

The plunge broke the rein; the driver had no control over the animal then, and the *calessini* must have been overturned, had not a stranger come upon the scene.

Quick to see and prompt to act, he saw the danger, and

measuring time and distance well, caught the curb and stayed the horse's mad career.

They were safe then.

"That was bravely done!" said the Marquis, as he alighted and shook the stranger warmly by the hand. "We owe you our lives, senor!"

"If you do," said the stranger, in excellent English, "you also owe to me the danger."

He pointed to a golden bugle in his silken sash.

"Is it the fashion," Marriott asked, half smiling, "to startle people's horses with those bugles?"

"Not the fashion, but we students have a fashion of our own. My bugle cry was a warning."

"To whom?"

"A fellow-student."

The reply, at once laconic and unsatisfactory, occasioned a pause.

"Confound his fellow-student!" said Dick Nicholson. "We shall have to walk, and there is a storm coming on."

"You may obtain a coach at the inn," said the stranger, as though answering Nicholson's thoughts. "Accept my earnest apologies for the misadventure of which I am the cause."

"Where is the inn?" asked Marriott, while the Marquis disputed the stranger's self-accusation. "The harness is not fit for use again."

Answering the Viscount's question, the stranger pointed to a building by the road near the mountain's foot. It was an antique structure, quaint with curious gables, and with a signboard on which was a painting intended to represent a mountain guide.

Seen in the dusk, this figure looked more like a swarthy bandit with his rifle than like a peaceful safeguard with his pointed staff.

The inn itself had an inviting aspect. The whole scene, with its rugged background and darkening sky shadowing the little hostel, was just such a one as a painter might have chosen.

The landlord, hearing travellers approaching, came to the door. The picture was perfect then.

For the benefit of travellers, there was an inscription over the door, signifying the nature of the house and the name of its host.

"We want a coach, if you have one—horses, if you have not," Marriott said.

"Alas, senor!" exclaimed Scampia Zatani; "the only coach I ever had rolled over a precipice!"

"Horses, then."

"They rolled over with it."

"That was a loss indeed!"

"The passengers had not paid me," said Scampia.

"The passengers—were they killed?"

"Every one, senor!"

"The deuce! And so you have no horses. Well, gentlemen, one of us must walk to the city. Since the bandit has broken faith with us, we must see what the authorities can do."

The stranger listened with singular attention.

"Pardon, senor," he said—"you spoke of banditti?"

"The rascals!—yes."

"An adventure?"

"A sad one, I fear. The story is contained in this letter."

He handed to the stranger the epistle before mentioned. It was read and returned.

"And you did not send the ransom?" the stranger said.

"We did."

The stranger's handsome, dreamy face underwent a swift and fierce change.

"Did?" he repeated.

"Twice its value—lest their ruffian chief should haggle while our friend was in captivity."

"In money?"

"Two thousand piastres, a locket set with opals, two diamond rings, a watch, and a jewelled miniature case."

The stranger repeated the words one by one.

"Senor," he said, after a brief pause, "I can serve you in this First, let me assure you I believe the brigand chief to be a man of honour. You smile at the conjunction of terms."

"We sent the ransom,—our friend has not returned."

"The fault does not lie with him. I can serve you, because Red Gauntlet would serve me. I have a talisman."

"A talisman?"

"His friendship. How I gained it does not matter; it is enough to know that for me he will do much, and I promise to liberate Oliver St. George."

"We shall be grateful to eternity! And, in return——"

"When I have kept my promise I shall ask a favour. Come with me now. I will take you to the haunt of the Black Mountaineers. That you have been there will for ever remain a secret."

"For ever?"

"This Red Gauntlet, then, is generous," said Stuart Linn.

"To his friends."

"Is there any truth in those stories we hear of him—that he is never seen without a mask—that his face is not known even by his men?"

"Truth—every word! He is a mystery—a terror! No one can guess his identity. Some say he is a prince, others say he is a peasant. He is only known as Red Gauntlet!"

One hour later the stranger had led the three Englishmen into a deep ravine—an irregular passage without an outlet.

"You can climb?" he asked.

All three answered in the affirmative.

"Then follow me."

With extraordinary agility he ascended the steep side of the ravine.

It had seemed inaccessible.

When the others followed, they found footholds and clinging places planned like a stairway.

Behind a huge jutting fragment was a small crevice, imperceptible until within reach of the hand.

The stranger passed through, the others went after him; then through a narrow passage, where men could only go singly, and with care. This led to a scene, the aspect of which struck the beholder with wonder.

Some mighty earthshock had shifted an enormous hollow rock, which, falling in its present place, rested now immoveable, and formed a spacious vaulted chamber. Looking at the exterior of the mountain, its existence would never have been imagined.

"The Bandits' Home," said the stranger. "Now for the banditti."

A faint sound from his bugle brought a wild crew from a hundred hiding-places.

The stranger stood bugle in hand; he raised it, and every head was bowed.

"Wait," he said to the Englishmen—"you shall see Red Gauntlet."

He disappeared. No word was spoken by the banditti, and while the marquis and his friends were wondering at the strange adventure, the chief himself entered.

He was masked from brow to chin.

Just as they had imagined—just as a hundred wild stories had represented him, so he appeared now—a stately figure, graceful, statuesque, and with an air of strange command in his simplest attitude.

His dress, elegant and costly, set well on a noble form. A silken sash round his waist held a jewelled dagger and a golden bugle.

His left hand—slim, white, and delicate—was ungloved, and on the fourth finger flashed a splendid ruby.

On his right arm was that which most of all attracted attention.

It was a gauntlet of chain mail—each separate link formed of a brilliant red metal. It was impenetrable—steel and bullet proof—but so curiously worked as to be of silken flexibility.

Before this gallant presence our three Englishmen bowed with unconscious respect.

The brigand chief's innate nobility showed even through his mask.

They felt he was what the artist had said—a man of honour in spite of his lawless life—in spite of his lawless horde.

"Welcome," he said, approaching Stuart Linn, "if you come with truth. My artist friend has told me what you want—a captive."

"St. George. We sent his ransom—twice its value!"

"I wanted the ransom only—not a piastre more. Look around and see if you recognise my messenger!"

Each of the three took a survey of the swarthy crew. The messenger was not with them.

"He is not here," said Marriott.

"Cospoletto!" said Red Gauntlet. "Where is he?"

A man, who had hitherto remained in the shadow, now came forward.

No sooner did Marriott see him than he said:

"The messenger!"

"Come hither, Cospoletto," said Red Gauntlet, in a tone whose deadly quietude chilled the listeners' veins. "Let us see the man who stole the captive's ransom, and left the captive to die!"

CHAPTER V.
COSPOLETTO.

NOT the quiver of a breath broke the dense silence that fell when the bandit chieftain finished speaking. The guilty, shivering wretch whom he had summoned was the sole object of attention.

"Nearer yet, Cospoletto!" said the chief, as the brigand paused. "Stand face to face with the Viscount. Look into his eye if you can! Deny, if you can, that you are a traitor!"

"When my chief is angry, I dare not speak," said the ruffian, humbly.

"Man to man, then—accuser and accused! Your comrades shall judge between you. Viscount Marriott, this is the man who brought to you my message?"

"It is."

"And you gave him the ransom I desired?"

"Two thousand piastres in money, a watch, and—what most of all was prized—a locket set with opals."

"Why was this prized?"

"As a dying gift—the last token of a mother's love!"

Through the brigand's suit of mail, it could be seen his whole form vibrated with emotion.

"There were other jewels," Marriott continued, "of great value—large intrinsic worth—but of higher value by association."

"And you gave these things to Cospoletto?"

"With my own hand."

"He did not deliver one," cried Cospoletto, "but answered as I have said, chieftain."

"Repeat what you said!"

"Senor, the viscount threatened me—that he would have us hunted out from places where a mouse could not hide."

"In the event of treachery, rascal," said Marriott, raising his hand as though to strike the lying traitor on the cheek. "You had the ransom, and told me we were to wait for our friend by the ravine near the Pontine Marshes."

Cospoletto denied it by all the saints in the Italian calendar.

"Cospoletto," asked Red Gauntlet "what were you hiding in the eagle's nest?"

The brigand gave a shriek of terror, and sank to his knees.

His treachery was discovered. He had hidden the ransom in the eagle's nest, thinking, by doing so, to have St. George killed, and to gratify his own avarice.

"Was it this, Cospoletto," Red Gauntlet went on, holding up, first the bag containing the money, "or this—the watch, or this—the locket—or these two rings? Perhaps all, good Cospoletto! Look at them!"

Then the ransom glittered in his blood-red hand,—then

above the traitor's head. That hand gleamed symbolic of his doom.

Cospoletto grovelled at his chieftain's feet.

"For Nicola!" he groaned—"I kept the jewels for Nicola!"

The bandit chieftain put the ransom back into a pocket in his sash, and dropped his gauntletted hand on Cospoletto's head.

"Rise!" he said.

The touch seemed to draw the ruffian erect as by magnetic power.

"Mercy!" he shrieked. "I have not prayed!"

"There is time yet. Come!"

Dragging Cospoletto with him, he went to the other end of the cavern, where there was a way of exit and entrance, concealed by a massive piece of rock, which acted as a sort of drawbridge.

This was lowered by strong chains.

The chief passed through with Cospoletto.

The band followed one by one.

The three Englishmen last.

They would have interceded for the guilty wretch, but knew it would be useless.

Red Gauntlet led the way till he reached a level lodge of mountain.

He stood there with Cospoletto within two yards of an awful precipice.

"Kneel, Cospoletto!" he said.

The bandit chief dragged the traitor to the very verge of the abyss, and, with a dagger glittering high in his red hand, said:

"Pray."

Forced by that resistless hand to his knees, Cospoletto appealed despairingly for mercy.

Red Gauntlet heard, but did not heed.

He stood like a statue waiting for the doomed man to pray.

"One minute more," he said.

There was something almost sublime in the wondrous fearlessness with which he stood on the edge of the cavern—so near, that had Cospoletto touched him in resistance or struggling, he must have gone over.

But, by the power of his will—the devilry of a nature, that, once roused, had no limit to its destructive wrath—he held that legion of desperate men so completely in his grasp that not even to save his own life would one of them have dared to raise a finger against Red Gauntlet.

"It is time," he said. "Have you courage to take the leap, Cospoletto, or must your comrades hurl you down?"

"Mercy!"

The stern red hand pointed to the precipice.

Seeing no hope of mercy in his chieftain's eye—knowing that the doom once spoken was incommutable,—Cospoletto shut his eyes, and, drawing himself erect, walked towards the brink.

Then he paused again to ask once more for mercy.

"Benito," said Red Gauntlet, with a gesture of disgust, "the coward fears to die! Kill him!"

Benito hesitated. He had been Cospoletto's chosen comrade.

"Did Benito hear me?"

The brigand drew a pistol with reluctant hand, and fired at Cospoletto, who was kneeling now in prayer. The bullet dashed him over.

The dull crushing of his body down the crags ended in a duller splash. He had only uttered one cry.

"Come, gentlemen," said Red Gauntlet. "Now that we have punished the traitor, let me conduct you to your friend."

"St. George! He is safe?" said Marriott.

He was pale, as were his companions. The recent scene had slightly shaken their nerves.

"Quite safe," said the bandit chief. "Suffer me, gentlemen, to give back the ransom."

All started. The brigand's generosity took them by surprise.

"He is ransomed by two promises I made, so to these jewels and this money I have no right. Suffer me also to compliment you on the courage that brought you without fear to the haunt of desperate men."

"Ransomed by two promises?" said Dick Nicholson. "To whom?"

"One to senor, the student—the other to Nicola."

"Nicola?"

"The daughter of Scampia Zatani. Come, gentlemen, you seem reluctant to take the ransom back."

"Hang the ransom! We want St. George!"

"Red Gauntlet can hold a dying gift sacred," the bandit said. "This locket!"

It was taken gratefully by the owner.

"These jewels and this money. Believe me, gentlemen, I can take nothing from the brave; and it needed some devotion to bring you to such a dangerous place!"

"We had the student's word," said Marriott.

"And trusted him. He is my friend, and I thank you."

He led them back to the cavern; then to an inner cave.

"Senor St. George is there," he said.

Marriott entered.

The cave was empty. A stalwart bandit lay stretched at the opening. There were tokens of a desperate struggle, but St. George was gone.

"Escaped!" exclaimed Marriott.

"Impossible!" said the bandit. "Seek for him in the mountains. If he has attempted to escape he is dead!"

He blew a note on his bugle.

"That will insure your safety while you seek," he said. "Farewell!"

He disappeared. The three friends rushed through the opening of the cave.

The bugle note was singularly like what they had heard the student give.

CHAPTER VI.

THE RESCUE.

THAT St. George should have attempted to escape was a matter of no surprise to his friends. They knew his indomitable spirit—the reckless gallantry that would prompt him to dare all for liberty.

The first evidences of his escape existed in the cords which had bound his feet and hands; they were broken into fibre. The second token was his guardian for the time, who lay stunned and very badly bruised indeed.

While Marriott, Stuart Linn, and Dick Nicholson were in fear for his safety, they felt proud of their countryman. He had shown how an Englishman could fight.

When St. George began to look upon his captivity as a fact, he reflected that the sooner he made it a matter of doubt, the better it would be for him, so he began by trying bribery.

They had bound him securely enough—the cords cut into his flesh. Cospoletto was his sentinel then, and, not being aware that the brute had any personal animosity against him, St. George wondered at the vicious nervousness with which his fingers played with the trigger of his gun.

St. George offered him a handsome sum to go to sleep and give him time to get away. Cospoletto answered by setting his rifle on full-cock.

"That fellow is naturally sinful," thought the tourist, on seeing the act. "Nothing less than a pair of thick boots and a horsewhip would soften his heart!"

He waited, thinking of another expedient; and in the meantime grinding the cord on his wrists each piece against the other. Every fibre less in strength increased his chance of liberty.

Cospoletto sat scowling at him. He sat smiling at Cospoletto, till a bugle-note made the brigand leap to his feet. St. George wondered why he started so.

A second brigand, less sinister in appearance, came to relieve guard. Cospoletto gave St. George a final scowl, and departed. St. George did not see him again.

The new sentinel seemed so fully sensible of the dignity attached to his duty, that St. George concluded not to try bribery with him just yet.

The fellow stood like a grenadier, with his gun on his shoulder and his back to the object of his care.

St. George began to whistle an air from Fra Diavolo. The music, being appropriate, soothed the savage's breast. He listened, and, when St. George concluded, muttered a "Bravissimo!"

"Like it, do you?" said the tourist,—"fine ear for melody! The largest ear I ever saw. I wonder if a fellow with a large ear hears more than any other fellow? Perhaps he does,—funny things large ears are!"

The extensive size of the brigand's auricular tickled the tourist's fancy—he laughed.

The brigand turned and stared at him.

"Just untie my hands?" said St. George. "I would not trouble you if I had one loose. Will you?"

He received an oath in reply.

"Hush, my friend—don't swear! I have a purse in my pocket."

The bandit's eyes glistened.

"Pockets?" he said—"money?"

"That's it,—money in my pockets. Just untie my hands, and you shall have it!"

When he said "You shall have it," he meant something besides the money in his pockets.

But the brigand was a very intelligent gentleman;—he tapped his own side-pocket, by way of asking St. George to indicate where the purse was.

The tourist showed him.

"What is your name?" he asked.

"Chneili, senor captive."

"Well, don't grin—I hate to be grinned at! Why don't you wash your face and shave? Are you going to untie my hands?"

Chneili shook his head.

"Then you don't have the money."

Chneili nodded. Laying down his rifle, he crossed leisurely over to St. George, knelt upon his chest, and, putting his dirty hand in his pocket, took the money out.

St. George did not say a word, though he longed to get his hands free, so that he might astonish Messire Chneili by a hit.

His longing to do this was so intense that he tried by a mighty wrench to break his cords. They creaked—a few strands parted; but his wrists were so severely hurt by the effort, that he could not try again just then.

"If I do get a chance," the tourist mentally determined, "he shall have something to Chneili over!"

The brigand had resumed his post at the opening, and now stood grinning to himself like a monkey.

"Chneili," said St. George, coaxingly, "make me a cigarette. Come now—a cigarette isn't much to ask for!"

So Chneili thought. He made two—put one between his own lips, and was kind enough to insert the other between St. George's.

"Thank you. A little more cigarette, and a little less finger, Chneili! Now, a light, please? There's a fusee-box in this pocket of mine. Did you ever see a fusee-box, Chneili?"

"Yes, senor."

"Really! Where?"

"An Inglisse."

"Ah!—somebody you plundered. Well, strike a light!"

The brigand did. The tiny ball of fire adhered to St. George's cigarette, and Chneili walked away to gaze over the mountain and smoke.

St. George quietly applied the tiny ball of fire to the frayed rope on his wrists. The smell made by the burning cord was not noticed, as it blended with the aroma of the cigarette.

St. George smoked leisurely. The cigarette went out, and the rope burned through at the same instant.

The tourist's hands were free.

Chneili's back was turned to the captive. It was not a

handsome back, but St. George admired it under the circumstances.

To draw a keen pen-knife and sever the cord from his ankle was the work of an instant.

He replaced his pen-knife, put his feet together, and kept his wrists close, as though they were still tied, then said:

"Chneili!"

"Senor!"

"Another cigarette, please! I enjoyed the last one very much!"

Chneili appreciated the compliment; he rolled another smoke, put it between St. George's lips, and lit it.

Then he went back to the opening of the cave.

"Have you a good view from there, Chneili?"

"Excellent, senor!"

"Then we will look at it together, Chneili."

He rose. Hearing his footstep in the cave, the brigand turned. St. George stood face to face and within a foot of him.

In an instant the bandit was paralysed.

The magnificent coolness of the act—the wondrous characteristic quietude of nerve—were more than he was prepared to meet or comprehend so suddenly.

Chneili gasped out an oath.

The Englishman's iron hand was on the barrel of the bandit's rifle—the Englishman's iron grip was on the bandit's throat—a struggle and a heavy blow, and Chneili lay insensible at the Englishman's feet.

St. George had a rifle and his liberty.

"Chneili's cigarettes were a bad investment," he said, throwing the burning end of the second one over a crag. "What capital rifles these fellows use! Hallo!"

The end of his cigarette had unfortunately fallen on the beard of a brigand who was lurking behind the crag. It set his beard on fire, and he came up anathematising Chneili in the most choice Italian extant.

The sight of the Englishman with Chneili's rifle told him what had happened at once. He raised a shout:

"The Englisse escape!"

A dozen wild, hoarse cries answered him. St. George's first impulse was to silence the rascal for giving the alarm. A reflection, however, that he might invest the bullet to better advantage, altered his intention.

There were more than a dozen banditti armed with rifles on the scene with magical quickness.

Now, St. George knew that to attempt escape by flight after having once been a captive, would be to seal his own fate—they would shoot him down without mercy.

So he stood his ground.

"Liberty or death!" he said, setting his back against a rock. "Come on—'come one, come all!' as the fellow says in the book! I wish Cecil could see me do the fighting!"

The brave fellow was desperate though calm. It was not in his nature to yield himself captive again while he had a weapon in his hand. He had, too, that strong contempt for brute force which is so characteristic of the patrician. He would have faced a rabble, though its numbers counted thousands, and never thought of giving in while his heart had a pulsation left.

Now, with his single weapon, he stood menacing thirteen foes, his watchful eye on the alert, and his finger on the trigger for the first he should see take aim.

He had not long to wait.

One man, skulking back behind another, levelled his piece by resting the muzzle on his comrade's shoulder.

Only his right eye and part of his face were visible as he sighted, but for St. George there was enough to aim at. The sinister glitter of the brigand's eye quenched suddenly as the bullet from St. George's rifle took it into his brain.

Oliver stood intrepid and at bay with his rifle clubbed, as, with a ferocious yell, the whole savage crew rushed upon him. They fired at him as they came. He felt the shots ping past his head, but not one struck him.

With his athletic form reared up, he swung his weapon round above his head. It went through the air with a dull whizz, and not one of the brigands dared venture within range of its powerful sweep.

He held them at bay. By fair fighting he would have escaped, had not a sneaking wretch—who must have inherited the soul of Judas—slunk round and crept up the crag which hung over St. George's head.

The brave fellow was on the look-out for his enemies in front. He had no sound or warning of the scoundrel above—no token till he was stricken down.

He staggered, then dropped to his knee.

They were upon him like a pack of wolves. Knives were gleaming, and firm hands ready to strike, when a thrilling cry startled all.

Nicola—lithe, agile, and fearless as a panthress in defence of her cubs, leaped right in amid the banditti. She snatched a rifle as she leaped, and its barrel described a circle from which all shrank.

The inspiration of her beautiful devotion gave to her aspect a dignity from which they crouched as from the anger of a queen. Her white breast heaved and fell, her dark eyes glowed, her attitude was statuesque.

"Back!" she said, resting the butt of her rifle on the mountain, and extending her right arm like a prophetess. "Lay not a finger on him—touch not a hair of his head!"

They wavered for an instant, then advanced. Him they meant to kill—for Nicola they had a worse fate—for they did not think the chieftain was near.

Her thrilling cry for help sent the mountain echoes pealing to the sky.

"Leon—Leon!"

That cry was like a talisman—a bugle-note rang out in answer.

The brigands cowered back in terror. Nicola looked up. On a lofty crag, and looking in the night like a black statue on a pedestal, stood—Leon, the student.

(*To be continued in our next.*)

AN ADVENTURE AMONG SPANISH BRIGANDS.

A TRAVELLER'S STORY.

DOUBTLESS most of our readers have heard of the city of Trucillo, in Estremadura, Spain, situated almost at the base of the mountains of Toledo. I spent several months at this city some years since; and between the pleasant society in town and frequent excursions to the neighbouring mountains, the time passed quite happily.

One afternoon, as I sat in my room, reading and smoking my cigarro, a genuine Colaso de Santiago, Senor Pepita, my landlord, came up to inform me that he and several of his friends, male and female, intended riding into the mountains, and to invite me to accompany the party. As there was nothing to detain me at the hotel, I accepted the invitation.

A few moments were quite sufficient to enable me to make all necessary preparations, then I hastened down where the party was waiting for me in the court-yard of the inn.

I instantly vaulted into the saddle, and away we started at an easy trot down the street, in high spirits, towards the mountains, looming up sombre-like and majestic below us.

Wreaths of light, gauzy, purple clouds hung over their towering summits like a bridal veil.

Our road to the mountains lay through a beautiful tract of country. Rich fields of grain and orchards of bright fruit—groves of orange, lemon, citron, fig, and pomegranate trees grew in rich profusion along the way.

The redolent aromas of blushing grapes, the quaint and graceful dresses of the "pastors," and the merry songs of the herdsmen on the distant plains singing in the rich sonorous language of Castille, all tended to form a scene of more than ordinary beauty and interest.

As the day was sultry and the distance not great, we proceeded slowly, not wishing to fatigue our horses, as we all knew from experience that their mettle could be put to the test when we came to ascend the mountain.

In due time we commenced the ascent, and as we followed the narrow and sinuous path upwards, the plain we had left lay unrolled behind us like an immense panorama.

Trucillo lay almost at our feet, and far above us, on the verge of the horizon, the River Tagus lay basking like a huge silver serpent in the sun.

We at last halted upon a broad table-like precipice, which rose may hundred feet above the level of the surrounding country. An ample collation was soon spread, and I partook of one of the most delightful repasts I ever remember enjoying.

Rising and hanging almost over our heads was a peak, the crest of which was partially obscured by a thick mist which was gradually obscuring the higher portions of the mountains.

I imagined if I could gain its apex I could obtain a clear and unobstructed view of the ambient country, and perhaps get a glimpse of Marida, immediately south of us.

As none of the indolent Spaniards would consent to accompany me, I resolved to make the ascent alone; so leaving them to chat and strum their guitars, and dance their catalonas and fandangos, I left them.

At first the ascent was easy enough, but the higher I climbed the more difficult I found it to proceed.

Frequently I would scramble up a few rods, and find my progress suddenly checked by a wall of rock that no human being could scale.

Then I would retrace my steps and follow a new path. At last, panting and breathless, and reeking with perspiration, I arrived at the peak.

Never before had I beheld a scene of such gorgeous beauty as now lay before me.

The whole mountain range, as far as the eye could reach, was flashing and glowing in the setting sun.

Marida could be faintly seen in the south, dark and gloomy in the shadow of the mountain.

As I looked towards Trucillo, I perceived my friends were all mounted, and preparing to descend; several of whom had caught sight of me, and were waving pantomimic adieus—others were making signs for me to join them, and pointing towards the north-west, where masses of dark, ominous clouds were rapidly rising.

After casting a parting glance at the scene, I commenced descending as rapidly as the nature of the ground would admit; and in a short time I had the satisfaction of reaching the rocky table where I left my horse.

The sky was now completely overcast with clouds, and I could already hear the wind shrieking around the rough crags and howling in the deep gorges.

The bright scene of a few hours before was now enveloped in Cimmerian darkness.

I found my horse at last, which stood trembling and neighing with fear.

I dared not mount him, for I could have ridden scarcely one hundred feet ere both "horse et eques" had been precipitated into some one of the many dark and fearful chasms which beset the way. So I saw that he was securely fastened, for I did not wish the frightened animal to dash itself to pieces; and then I commenced the descent as best I could, crawling along cautiously, and feeling the way before me with a stout stick I had secured.

Ere long I came to a wall or ledge of a rock, which barred all further progress in the direction I was pursuing.

I stood irresolute, not knowing which way to turn, when by the glare of a vivid flash of lightning I perceived a rough path apparently made by the chamois and izard, running obliquely to the left of the place where I stood.

I resolved to follow it at once, and I did so for a considerable distance, waiting at times in difficult places for the lightning flashes to illuminate the way.

At last I perceived a light gleaming, like a star, in a glen far below me; I concluded it came from a habitation of some kind, but how to reach it was a perplexing question.

However, no time was to be lost; so I scrambled down towards the light as fast as possible, clinging to the tangled vines and shrubs for support.

At last, just as the storm broke forth in all its fury, when the thunder commenced its most discordant bellowings, and the rain came pouring down in torrents, I struck a mule-path which led me directly to the "poerta trasera" or back-door of a small mountain inn.

The vigorous blows I gave the door with my staff brought the landlord, who looked me over as surlily as a chained bull-dog. Finally he growled, in a tone far from amiable:

"Quiera vuestro?—what do you want?"

"Some supper and a bed for the night," I answered in English.

"No entiendo—I don't understand you," he replied, shaking his head. However, he motioned me to enter, with seeming reluctance, and pointed to a low stool near the wall, in a manner which plainly said, "You can sit if you please, or remain standing."

Then turning to a swarthy, malignant-looking Spaniard, who was busy emptying a bottle of vino tinto, he growled:

"A glorious night for us, Silvano—por Dios! I wish this Englishman had broken his neck among the passes! In an hour Don Raymundo will be here with the silks and the plates from the Franciscan Cathedral—Satanas! What are we to do?"

"Why, give him some supper and put him upstairs, and let Senorita Margarita amuse him with her guitar and her English, for she speaks the language like a native, you know, Senor Benito."

"Por Dios! I will do so, Silvano, and if he give me further trouble——"

Here the courteous landlord dropped his voice so low that I could not hear the remainder of what I had no doubt was a threat.

Presently he motioned me to follow, and leading me into an adjoining apartment, kicked a seat up to a table, upon which were the remains of a supper.

Resolving not to be outdone by mine host in point of ceremony, I sat down at the table, and helped myself to bread and cold fowl with all the sangfroid I could muster, whilst Senor Benito withdrew and left me to my supper and my reflections.

Presently the door opened and a young girl entered, quite pretty, methought, for a barmaid.

Her dark, mournful eyes seemed full of tenderness and fire; skin of that pure transparent brown seldom seen except in Castilians of rank; her eyebrows arched beautifully across a full, fair forehead.

Her nose was not your Castilian half-pug, neither the aquiline of the Moor, but purely Grecian in its contour.

Her hair, soft, glowing, and jetty, hung in luxuriant masses over her shoulders of exquisite loveliness.

"My father," said she, speaking in very good English, and in a voice soft and musical, "tells me that you are an Englishman, and do not speak Espanola."

"No, my pretty Margarita," I replied, taking it for granted that she was the girl to whom Silvano had alluded. "I am not an Englishman—I am an American."

"Santisima, senor! how did you know my name was Margarita?" she exclaimed, in astonishment.

"When you entered I knew your name; also that you spoke English, and played the guitar and bandoline. Moreover, I knew you were pretty, and——"

"Ah, senor," she answered, interrupting me, and simpering at the compliment, "you Americans are all great flatterers."

I confess, the beauty, graceful costume, and coquettish manner of the girl made me feel a little sentimental, and I was about to make a gallant speech to vindicate the character of Americans, when the nymph, with a merry laugh, ran across the room, picked up her guitar, and took a seat near me.

I begged her to favour me with an aria or song.

After complaining of the damp weather impairing the tone of her instrument, and apologising for a slight cold, her delicate fingers commenced dancing and skipping among the chords of her guitar, as she played the prelude.

She sang a letrillas—a kind of wild lyric, so popular among the Spanish.

She touched her instrument with wonderful skill, and the melody was at times so wild, and then again so soft and plaintive, sinking almost to a whisper, and her voice blending so with the accompaniment, as to produce almost one volume of exquisite sound.

I was amazed, spellbound at the wonderful harmony she produced.

I was soon recalled to my senses, however, for a great noise of loud talking, laughing, and shouting was heard outside. Margarita informed me that it was a band of volunteers, preparing to spend the night at the inn—very rough fellows, too, and ones I had better avoid.

Ere long, Senor Benito entered and said something to his daughter, in a kind of patois I could not comprehend. She left the room instantly, and Senor Benito informed me with a pleasant snarl, if I wished to retire, my room was prepared.

So I followed him up a creaking old stairway into a dreary and comfortless room.

Several panes of glass were gone from the windows, and the cold night air blew in with chilling force.

As I entered, he shut the door, and left me to find the bed as best I could in the dark, as he had taken the lamp with him.

However, I found the bed, and sat down upon it.

I wanted a light very much, for I wished to know in what kind of a place I was to sleep.

I soon bethought me of an expedient. I had a small metallic flask of hair oil in my pocket, and by tearing my handkerchief into strips, I soon made a wick, which on lighting with a friction match gave me all the light I required.

I first examined the bed, which was clean and well made, but as I looked under it, what was my astonishment to see the feet and legs of a man lying motionless and quiescent.

Drawing my poniard, I commanded him to come forth, but he did not stir.

I ordered him again, in a louder tone, but with the same effect.

Exasperated at the rascal's obstinacy, I seized him by the leg and drew him out in no gentle manner.

Horror.

Lying supine before me, with sodden eyes glaring in the rays of my lamp, was a corpse!

A faintness came over me.

I reeled—I should have fallen, but I clung to the rafters for support.

Yes, purple and swollen, showing every mark of death by strangulation, lay a murdered man.

I went to the window and looked out.

The storm continued to rage with unabated fury, and the heavens were dark and ominous as the brow of Cerberus.

It was but a short distance to the ground, certainly not more than ten feet.

"Surely," thought I, "this is the easiest and safest way to escape the bloodthirsty band."

So, extinguishing my light, I opened the window with the utmost caution.

I forced myself through it, making as little noise as possible, then hanging down as far as the length of my arms would permit, I let go my hold of the window-sill, and landed uninjured on the soft, yielding earth beneath.

In passing round the house, towards the road, I could not resist the temptation of peering into an open window, through which a flood of light was streaming, and the sound of mirth and laughter was heard within.

I saw about twenty brigands seated about the apartment, smoking and drinking.

The fair Margarita, who had inspired me with so much sentiment scarcely an hour before, was now perched upon the knee of a handsome young ruffian, recounting to the hideous crew her interview with the verdant stranger, while they were constantly interrupting her with loud peals of laughter.

"Come, Benito," said a huge robber, staggering to his feet, "let's—hic—examine your cove up—hic—stairs."

"Wait till he's asleep, Gaspard," said Benito.

"I'll not wait, by San Jago!" roared the drunken Gaspard. "If he's awake I'll administer a sleeping potion," he continued, with a brutal laugh, tapping a huge sheath-knife in his belt.

Seizing a light, he left the room, followed by several of his comrades, whilst I, incited by all the terror the fear of a violent death could give me, fled away into the storm and darkness, and escaped.

FUOCO, THE BOURBONS' BANDIT.

THE Italian clergy, in their desperation, are making a new movement. They are exerting themselves to form a consequential party in the Parliament, and at the elections the loud war cry of the church militant is to be raised. In the last Parliament there were only two clerical partisans, one of whom has recently been to Rome, where he had repeated conferences with the Pope and the leading political personages of the Pontifical Court. He reckons upon having a numerous following in the new Parliament.

The operations of this political force will be damaging, it is expected, to the Government, whom the brigand soldiers in Southern Italy will further harass and weaken, if the King's troops should not be able to catch and subdue them. At present these ferocious legionaries appear to have it pretty much their own way. Incendiarism, murder, and robbery mark where they have been; and in the territory adjacent to the Roman frontier, Abruzzi, Molise, and Terra di Lavoro, they proceed with unexampled daring. Fuoco, the most terrible of living ruffians, who is ravaging the territory of Sessa, is described as having in a few days committed an amount of destruction which is incalculable. To put a stop to his atrocities most pressing orders have been given and most energetic measures adopted, but the troops exhausted themselves in difficult and fatiguing marches under a burning sun, and the chase scarcely affords results proportionate to the labour.

Papal partisans conniving at these atrocities, present a distressing spectacle to the world. They may be desirous of suppressing the new kingdom of Italy, and may also entertain the belief of its instability, and look forward to the restoration of Bourbon rule; these are legitimate ideas and aspirations, however unpopular and unsubstantial, but let them pursue their object by fair and legitimate means. If the Bourbons think they have a chance of regaining power which they lost by misgovernment, let them come out fairly into the open field and there try conclusions with their conqueror. It is dastardly work to employ ferocious mountain ruffians to ruin and devastate the country, plunder the peasantry, besides terrifying travellers in search of the picturesque from pursuing the bent of their inclinations. It is a remarkable circumstance, too, that whilst the brigands flourish on the Roman frontier, political offenders are pounced upon and punished with terrible severity. The *Siecle* states that "there are at present fourteen political prisoners confined in the convict prison at Civita Vecchia, expiating imaginary crimes. Being suspected of patriotism, they were dragged before the tribunal of the Sancta-Consulta, and, without being permitted to defend themselves, were sentenced to confinement in the convict prison, some for a limited period, and others for life, as conspirators against the Papal Government. No intelligence could be obtained of them for a long time, all access to them being refused to their friends and relatives. One of the prisoners, by means of a stratagem, succeeded in forwarding a letter to his wife in which the tortures suffered by him and his companions are described. These political prisoners are, he states, more severely treated than any malefactor or criminal. They are crowded into two damp, filthy, narrow dungeons, scarcely twenty paces long, with seats placed against the walls. The ceiling of the dungeon is so low that the prisoners cannot stand erect. They declare that they are buried alive in a tomb in which their flesh is worn to the bones under a chain weighing 24 lb." This may last for a time, but the days of persecution are numbered.

TALES OF BRIGANDS AND BANDITTI," is Presented Gratis a Picture, beautifully printed in Colours, entitled,

TALES OF BRIGANDS
AND BANDITTI.

THE FOUR-SHEET FEAST IN THE OLDEN TIME,
with an early number will be given the companion Picture, printed in Colours, entitled, THE FORESTERS' FETE OF THE PRESENT DAY.
London : E. HARRISON, Salisbury Court, and all Newsagents everywhere.

I Warn & Strike

[THE DUEL AT THE ALTAR.]

RED GAUNTLET, THE BANDIT; OR, THE BLACK MOUNTAINEERS.

BOOK I.—THE ARTIST.

CHAPTER VII.
ST. GEORGE AND NICOLA.

THE scene was strange—the tableau perfect. There were the banditti cowering back in startled terror, while Nicola, with her white hand still grasping her rifle, stood by the gallant Englishman, and the student looked on from the crag above.

St. George, too weak to fight, and though very faint, too brave to surrender, caught, with an artist's eye, the set and beauty of the striking picture.

[THE RIGHT OF DRAMATISING IS RESERVED..]

He uttered an involuntary " Bravo !"

"Lots of brigands," he muttered, in the succeeding instant, "so an extra bravo or so don't matter ! Funny, isn't it ?"

None other than a man with such cool courage could have seen anything funny so soon after his peril.

He watched curiously to see what would come next, and while he watched, wondered what there was in that quiet student to make the wild horde crouch so low in fear.

No word—no gesture of command did Leon use. He only stood with one hand raised, and in that hand a bugle—such a bugle as Marriott and the rest had seen in the belt of Red Gauntlet.

Leon descended with the steady ease of a mountaineer. He waved his bugle, and the bandits crept back to their covert.

"Hallo !" said St. George—"that's the thing ! Mysterious student waves bugle ! Funny, eh ?"

Leon smiled.

"And enter Viscount Marriott with his friends !" he said. "See, senor—they come !"

Cecil, with Dick Nicholson and Stuart Linn, appeared upon the scene just then. They ran eagerly towards St. George.

"Safe !" said Linn. "Thank heaven, we are in time ! You are hurt, Oliver ?"

" By jove ! you should have come a minute or two ago !— quite a little regiment of brigands—Nicola fighting the lot ! She saved me—and our friend here saved me,—both saved me, you know !"

They shook hands cordially with the student. St. George kept Nicola by his side.

"We owe you many thanks, Senor Leon," said Marriott, "and you too, Nicola !"

The girl drew closer to St. George,—she was shy and tearful now the danger was past. Her whole care was for Oliver,—she wanted no thanks from the others.

"We were wondering where you were," said Marriott, speaking to the student, and noticing with a quiet smile how the pretty peasant girl kept to St. George. "You disappeared."

"To see that your friend was safe. I thought he would try to escape, and knew the attempt would be dangerous."

"How came it that the bandit spared St. George, although the ransom was late ?" asked Nicholson.

"He doubted Cospoletto," replied Leon, "and did not believe that you would let your friend die."

"Not a bad fellow, that bandit," said Dick. "You missed a scene, Senor Leon."

"What was it ?"

"The death of Cospoletto. There was a fine, rude sort of grandeur about his trial, judgment, and doom."

St. George saw a peculiar smile play for an instant on the student's lip.

"My brigand friend is strange in some things," he said, "and such acts as that you saw are necessary. There can be no compromise between him and the savage tribe he rules."

"I should like to know something more about him," said Stuart Linn. "There are many rumours, each differing from the other."

"He is a mystery," observed Nicholson. "I did not believe in his existence till I saw him."

"A prince in disguise, some people say," said Marriot.

"A peasant, others," said Linn.

"A patriot, I have heard," said Dick.

"Everybody says a lot about a fellow nobody knows," said St. George, "and it don't matter—he's a great scamp !—don't you think so, Senor Leon ?"

"He is my friend," replied the student, gravely. "The worst I know of him is, that he is Red Gauntlet."

"That's a good thing," said St. George, drily ; "but I don't see the force of being pitched into by a lot of rascals, captured, and given the choice of sending for a ransom, or having a long knife-kind-of-thing poked into me ! Funny, perhaps— but I object to it !"

"So it would appear," the student said. "You thinned his band a little, Senor St. George."

"I should like to have another go in at them along with Dick, and Cecil, and Linn ! I'll wager we should hurt a few !"

"Doubtless," said Linn. "They found it hard to capture you, and harder still to keep you."

"And then they tried to kill me ! By jove ! my ' Sunset from the Mountain' was likely to have been my last artistic effort ! Some fellow hit me in the head. It aches."

There was a streak of blood down his face, and he looked pale, now that the excitement of meeting his friends was past.

Nicola was pale too. She shuddered when she heard of Cospoletto's fate.

Seeing her anxious glance at Oliver, Marriott proposed they should seek some place of rest.

"Scamp and Satan's," suggested St. George. "Nicola lives there."

That was quite sufficient reason why the party should proceed to the Mountain Guide. The student offered St. George his arm. St. George preferred being helped along by Nicola.

He contrived to drop a little way behind the others—just out of earshot. Then he slid his arm round her waist, saying he could walk better so.

Her beautiful dark eyes were lifted to his with an expression that went thrilling to his heart. Her look—reproachful yet trusting—seemed to ask him a question that set him thinking.

She had saved his life—incurred a danger greater far than death, and for his sake alone. He could not deny himself a pleasant puzzled consciousness that such devotion only grew from one cause.

They had never met before, yet her soul had awakened to its first sense of love. She was nurtured in a clime where passion is the growth of impulse—a love fire never dying, though lit in an instant.

Nicola loved him. This child of Nature, with her quick, passionate senses, had made a rich and handsome gentleman the idol of her dream. He could not doubt it, for she trembled at his touch, and the rich blood dyed her glowing cheek when he spoke.

Her choice was a dangerous one. St. George was not a bad man, neither was he a saint.

He was simply a good, generous fellow, careless by disposition, and slow in temperament. He hated trouble or sensation of any sort, and thought love-making a bore which no sane person could endure.

So far, Nicola was safe. Oliver St. George would rather have cut off his right hand than done her a deliberate wrong. He had no thought beyond the present—only that pleasant puzzled consciousness of being an object of especial interest to the prettiest creature he had ever seen.

But this interest kindled its response. The gentle pressure of her little hand upon his own, her downcast eye and glowing cheek, were the mute eloquence of a language he was not unlearned in.

Yet his pleasure blended with regret. He would have to see her on many occasions before he left the vicinity, for he had his sketch to finish, and in going to the mountain he must pass her father's house.

Each time he saw her thus would strengthen a feeling that would make his ultimate departure painful. Every throb of honour and of gratitude would have risen against an impulse of wrong.

Her beauty was a great temptation. His pulse quickened as, while thinking, he gazed at her again and again.

She was superb, lithe, full and pliant, and graceful as a woman only is in the springtime and strength of her girlhood —from brow to foot every line and curve was a beautiful undulation. St. George gazed upon her till his head swam.

"Were you aware of my danger ?" he asked, at length.

"I only feared because of Cospoletto—poor Cospoletto ! I am sorry for him !"

"Bother Cospoletto ! What did you fear ?"

"That he would kill you."

"Why?"

"He loved me."

"The deuce he did!"

"He saw you kiss me."

"Confound his impudence! He had no business to look! So you were afraid he would kill me, Nicola?"

"I feared so, senor."

"Call me St. George. And so you did not love him."

"No, senor."

"St. George."

"St. George."

"That's it. I never liked my own name so well before. Say it again!"

She said it again.

"That's the thing! Feared he would kill me! Funny that! By jove! I would settle two such fellows in no time!"

"But he was cruel—treacherous—he would have crept upon you from behind."

"So he did. And you came all the way to see if I was safe?"

"I knew you would be safe."

"How?"

"Senor Leon promised me."

"Wonderful fellow, that Senor Leon—does everything he promises! You are a dear, little, good girl, Nicola! I don't know how to thank you! If there's anything I could offer you—diamond kind of thing, you know....eh! what's the matter?"

Nicola had stopped and burst into tears.

St. George did not understand that.

"Of course I don't mean as reward, you know, Nicola. Saving a fellow's life is a kind of thing diamonds don't pay for. But a—eh?—keepsake affair, you know! Don't cry—there's a dear!"

He took her to his breast and patted her glossy head caressingly while kissing away her tears.

"There, there, there!" he said, in very much such a tone and such tenderness as he would have spoken to a child. "Is this my brave, pretty Nicola who fought for me? Come! I only meant something as a keepsake! You would like a keepsake, wouldn't you?"

"I thought so," he went on, responding to an affirmative sob. "All feminines like keepsakes." This was to himself. "You shall have one, Nicola; but I am not going away yet."

His last words seemed to give her greater pleasure than did the perspective keepsake. She smiled through her tears.

"The excitement it was," she said, recovering her delicate pride, now that the first gush of emotion was over—"my fear of Cospolette and the bandits—then your danger, and the conflict!"

"Dear Nicola, I shall never forget you! I shall come and paint your picture—may I?"

"If it would please you, senor."

"St. George."

"St. George."

"That's right! And it would please me, and I should like to keep one for myself—may I?"

"If it would please you."

"It would, and you shall have one of mine. Would you like to?"

"Very much, Senor St. George."

"Say St. George without the sinner, Nicola," he said. "I hate misters, and messieurs, and sinners and all that kind of thing! What's the use of a fellow having a name if everybody calls him something else?"

His question needed no reply. Nicola only heeded his promise—he was to have her miniature to keep, perhaps to wear in his breast; and he had said he would never forget her.

She was to have his miniature to keep. There was not a doubt as to where it would be worn—not a doubt but that it would be enshrined upon as pure a heart as ever beat beneath a love token.

CHAPTER VIII.

THE STUDENT'S STORY.

SCAMPIA ZATANI opened his eyes very wide when his guest of the previous day entered in company with Leon, the student, and Nicola.

The old rascal was himself a sanguinary brigand—one of the worst in Red Gauntlet's band—worse than the chieftain knew as yet.

"Have the senors been in danger?" he asked, with much concern.

"Danger, old Scamp and Satan? I should say so! Settled lots of brigands! Didn't we, Nicola!"

The innkeeper scowled at the speaker and at his daughter. A look from Leon made him smile again.

"Bring wine!" the student said, quietly.

"The best!" added Nicholson.

"When I ask him to bring wine," said Leon, "he would not think of bringing other than the best."

Nicola retired to her chamber. The four Englishmen and the student seated themselves round the table. Scampia brought wine and withdrew.

"When you were so prompt to take us to the rescue of our friend," said the viscount, "and we offered in return, to do anything that friends could do for him who saved our comrade, you said our favour should be asked when you had fulfilled your promise."

"And I have fulfilled that promise?"

"Nobly."

"Like a true and gallant gentleman!" said Stuart Linn.

"You overwhelm me, marquis!" said the student, with his singularly winning smile. "The favour I would ask is slight."

"Be it what it may——"

"I know. The sons of England are generous. Theirs is no niggard gratitude. There is to be a masquerade a week hence, at the palace of the Prince Luali."

"We are invited."

"That I know. You are visitors—intimates—admitted to the family circle. That, I think, is the case—is it not?"

"The correct thing. Go ahead."

"Lulalu—the daughter of Luali," said Leon, his black eyes beaming, and his voice vibrating low—"you know her?"

"A lady of more than earthly loveliness!" said Stuart Linn.

"Ethereal!" said Dick Nicholson.

"A face to make an artist dream—a form to haunt a sculptor!" added Marriott. "You know her too, Senor Leon?"

The student sighed.

"I have a friend who loves her," he said.

"The Duke de Mareosi?"

"He?" said Leon scornfully. "No. The Duke de Mareosi could only win regard from one man in the world."

"And who is he?"

"The Duke de Mareosi himself. A patrician—a noble—claiming some degree of relationship with the royal blood. My friend is Adrian Duscanelli."

"Count Adrian, the young poet," said St. George. "I have heard something of the story. It is romantic, and that kind of funny thing. Tell us all about it."

The student said:

"I will," and he then sat musing awhile.

Shadow after shadow deepened the sombre beauty of his face, as he thought of the recital he was to give. Leon sympathised very deeply with his friend Count Adrian Duscanelli.

"It is an old story," he said; "such as we have often listened to—such as we may have heard at our fathers' knees—such as minstrels have sung and poets have written many a time. We will begin when my hero was a boy—young imaginative, proud, and daring.

"I have heard that his face and form were such as charm

the eye. I know him well, and must not praise him. If I speak in admiration of his nature, it is because I know his nature's truth.

"At this time the boy was one of Fortune's favoured. His father, the Marquis Duseanelli, held high place at court. The boy was proud of his father as a statesman, but his love for his sire was stronger than his pride.

"At this time, too, the Prince Luali was high in place, and he was Duseanelli's bitterest foe. But the marquis feared him not, for he had a home in the people's hearts when Luali was as nothing. The life homage, the flattery of tongue he received, were given not so much for him as for the sake of his daughter Lulalu."

"Betrothed to the Duke de Mareosi," interrupted Stuart Linn.

"By her father," said Leon, with a passionate glow in eye and cheek. "But every love-thought—every hallowed link was given to Adrian.

"This is the old story again, but not a whit less sweet because antique. You have a Shakspere in your land, and you remember that wild and thrilling romance of his—that touching story of old Italy—'Romeo and Juliet?'"

St. George nodded reflectively. The others listened with much interest.

"Adrian and Lulalu loved like these. He would steal at night to her window, though at the peril of his life, and she would speak to him, or if she could not, it was enough to gaze upon the casement and know that Lulalu was there. This was the ecstasy of love say you. But we children of the southern sun live but in passion's dream. She was the sainted idol of his soul—his worship—his idolatry.

"Sometimes she would steal away at night to wander with him by the moonlit shore, and dream beneath the stars. But their dream was broken, their gladness stricken to earth.

"They were watched by a spy, whom de Mareosi sent; and one evening, when Adrian went to his place of tryst, he was set upon by ruffians. He had a friend at hand—a brave old Corsican, a very gladiator when at battle. So Adrian escaped —his Corsican scattered the hirelings.

"From that time Lulalu was closely guarded—from that time the malice of Luali awoke in tireless and deadly enmity. The Marquis Duseanelli was driven from his place— a false charge of treason raised against him.

"He was convicted, though innocent, his title taken from him, his estates confiscated, and himself condemned to exile.

"The rest he could have borne, but not the last. He loved his native clime—as only an Italian can. He could not go forth an exile. Sorrow, humiliation, and undeserved shame broke his failing strength. He did not die—but he went blind.

"In pity, then, he was allowed to stay—to inhabit a little dwelling on his own estate, which had been given to the Duke de Mareosi.

"Before this, Adrian had won renown. He was a poet, people said, but this was when he had a title, and could set his verse in gold. Now that he was poor—the son of a man proscribed—his verse could scarce obtain bread for his sightless sire.

"Soon, then, came the gallant fight for liberty, and Adrian, burning with a sense of oppression, joined the glorious Garibaldi, leaving his father to the care of Labian, the Corsican.

"The result of that struggle we know. It is branded black—a mark of shame on every hand that saw the fetters riveted on liberty, and would not strike to free Italia. The daring band broke up. Adrian returned.

"He was proclaimed an outlaw—a price set upon his head —and he had to seek safety by escaping to the mountains. Once there he was safe. The brigands would die for him to a man.

"I hold my friend in much regard," the student said. "He has dared much—suffered much, and at the worst is noble yet. This masquerade at the Palazzo Luali is the marriage festival of De Mareosi and Lulalu!"

"It is," said Nicholson.

"Adrian would see her once more before fate sunders them for ever. The favour I would ask is a card of admission for the masquerade."

"For him?"

"For myself—for Leon. I will give my card to Adrian, and should discovery take place, the risk is mine and his."

"His life would be in peril," said Marriott.

"No matter," said the student, with his inexplicable smile. "He will have friends near at hand. Will you do this for me?"

"Most certainly—it is so slight, so simple a thing to ask."

"Enough—quite enough for me. His appearance at the masquerade will cause a sensation, for he will assume a strange character."

"What is it?"

"Red Gauntlet. Thanks, gentlemen—and adieu! Leave the card for me here, with Nicola."

And in an instant he was gone.

The four Englishmen looked at one another.

"There will be a row at this masquerade," said St. George. "I have an idea."

"So have I," said Stuart Linn.

"I, too," said Marriott.

"And I," said Nicholson. "Mine is good."

"What is yours?" asked St. George.

"That Leon, the student, is Count Adrian Duseanelli."

"That is mine also," said Marriott.

"And mine," said Stuart Linn.

"Mine is the best idea," said St. George.

"Let us hear it."

"Leon, the student, is the Count Adrian Duseanelli, and Count Adrian Duseanelli is Red Gauntlet!"

CHAPTER IX.

THE DUEL AT THE ALTAR.

BEYOND the mountains, and in a valley far below, though almost within sight of the brigands' haunt, there stood a little cottage, inhabited by an old man whose name was almost forgotten in the city and at court, though the time had been when the proudest of the land were glad to do him homage.

Not so now.

The fallen minister—the father of the outlaw, Adrian Duseanelli—was forsaken by all, save one faithful heart, who clung to his master with true Corsican fidelity.

Change of fortune wrought no change in Labian's affection. He was the last and only one of Duseanelli's servants, as this lowly dwelling was the last and sole remnant of Duseanelli's princely estate. The staunch *retaine* lived but to show his loyalty unto the man whom he had known and loved in boyhood.

But for Labian, Duseanelli must have been alone for many days—forsaken in his affliction, blind and helpless.

The old man and his Corsican were at the cottage door when the student appeared on the heights, and, folding his arms upon his breast, gazed moodily upon the scene.

"The home of a Duseanelli," he soliloquised, bitterly, "and there the outlaw's father. If this be borne, and retribution not sought, let Adrian crouch with timid birds, and hide when men tread by."

He stood there with burning eye and swelling breast, thinking over all the wrongs Duseanelli had endured—thinking over the story he himself had told the Englishmen, and thinking of the outlaw.

The old man, sitting by the door, as was his wont at sunset every eve, looked, with his sightless brow, towards the mountain.

"Is it not time?" he asked of Labian.

"Not yet, my lord—but near!"

As though Leon had heard the question and its answer, his moody expression passed, giving place to a gentle smile.

Taking the bugle from his belt, he sounded a soft, plaintive note, then sprang lightly over chasm and abyss towards the valley.

The old man heard the bugle-cry.

"Labian," he said, leaving his seat, and clinging to the Corsican's arm. "Adrian—my son!"

"Is here."

And the student, Leon, was by the old man's side, looking with deep love into his sire's face.

St. George and his friends were correct in one conjecture at least—Leon, the student, was Count Adrian Duseanelli.

"My father has been well?" he said, as gently as a girl could have spoken to her mother.

"Quite well, Adrian."

"And happy, father?"

"Happy since I knew you were coming. Tell me, Adrian, is it true what Labian says?"

"What says he?"

"That you are not in danger."

"True—all truth! There is not one in Naples—not the boldest soldier, nor our haughtiest foe dare seek me in my mountain home, or molest me here!"

"Yet you are still proscribed."

"Only by the Government."

"A power too strong to be defied."

"A power at which I laugh," said Leon, "for I am free as air in spite of it! I am well protected, father—I am safer than is the King in his palace!"

"How?"

"By the force of faithful hearts and ready hands. Were I molested, a single bugle-note would bring a hundred men to my rescue."

He said this with quiet, defiant pride, as though he knew his own strength and the strength of those on whom he trusted.

The old man's face turned towards his son in that inquiring way peculiar to the blind.

"These men?" he asked.

"Are the Black Mountaineers—Red Gauntlet's band."

"Red Gauntlet, the bandit! He bears a terrible name, Adrian!"

"Ay! for he is daring, and defies the power that wronged my father and made me an outlaw. Let them say their worst of him, and the worst they can say with truth is, that he is a brigand!"

"He has protected you—been your friend?"

"The only one I ever knew with power and will!" said the student, with a strange and bitter smile. "But for him I might long ere this have been a captive, lingering out a living death in the dungeons of the State!"

The elder Duseanelli trembled at the thought.

"My poor boy," he said, with deep emotion, "but for my sudden fall, yours would have been a brilliant destiny! Young as you are—richly gifted by Nature, and with genius rare—this change in fortune must be hard to bear!"

"Not hard for me. It is for you alone I think," said the student. "Could I but see you as you once were—the favourite of a King—the idol of a people!"

"Nay, my son. I have no ambition now. When Heaven struck my sight away it taught me patience and humility! I cannot see the world; but the greater beauty of the realm above is ever before my soul! Had those I loved so well spared me one pang, I should be happier in this little cottage than in our princely home!"

"This one pang, father?"

"Your outlawry."

"Do not let that trouble you. The ban shall be removed."

"How?"

"I have Red Gauntlet's promise."

"That strange, mysterious man! Were he to do so much for you, my prayers should be for his sake—my blessing on his head!"

The student listened eagerly.

"Give them to him, father, always, for he has seen and loves you!"

"Seen me?"

"Very often—has stolen to this little home at night and crept into your chamber, that he might gaze upon the face of one he holds in dear remembrance! Believe me—he would die for you!"

"Singular!" said Duseanelli, wonderingly. "Who is he?"

"That must not be told."

"Have I seen him? Do I know him?"

"He says you have."

"Some one, perhaps, whom I did some service. I tried to have some thought for my fellow-creatures when I was high in place."

"You were kind to all—most kind to him. Do not, for my sake, believe the evil that you hear!"

"He has done many crimes."

"None, save those to which he has been impelled by hard necessity. He has been wronged, as we have been."

"But these wild stories told of him?"

"Are rumours only; in fact, he has done much to take from brigandage its savage aspect. He rules—a monarch under whose sway a lawless horde have learned how to be merciful, and be content with plunder without blood. Had our foes possessed an atom of his gentleness, they would have been more merciful to us!"

"Forgive them, Adrian. The Prince Luali has much to answer for, but let a Higher Tribunal judge and deal with him. We should forgive our enemies."

"I cannot hate them," the student said, "for when my hate would rise in bitterness it is subdued by my love."

"The trial was hard, Adrian. I hoped you had forgotten her."

"Forgotten Lulalu? I could as soon forget my father's love!"

"Poor Adrian—poor boy!"

"I could as soon forget her as I could forget my foe—my rival!"

"The duke?"

"De Mareosi!" the student said between his teeth. "I have a debt to settle with him yet."

"Do not go near the city, Adrian."

"There is no fear."

"You are the last link left to me—my only child—the gift of a sweet saint in heaven!"

"My mother!" said Leon, reverentially. "Fear not, my father, I shall do that which would place in jeopardy a life whose loss would leave you desolate! And now I must go—to be seen here would but endanger you."

"When will you come again?"

"Every evening, while the sun is setting. Should anything occur, danger loom near, or a necessity for caution come, I will send a messenger; so that, when you cannot hear my voice, you shall know I am not in peril."

"Always do this, Adrian."

"I will. Adieu!"

The affection between the outlaw and his sire was the stronger, because of their isolation, their misfortune, and their peril. They parted always as kindred part when they may never meet again.

"Adieu!" the student said, and then he turned to Labian.

"Faithful old friend!" he said,—"staunch and true from the time of my childhood, and through every change!"

"A servant's duty," said the Corsican, while his eye was dim with gratified emotion—"nothing more, Master Adrian."

"In such a case a servant's duty is a friend's devotion, Labian; and, should adversity ever give place to a better time, your service shall be well remembered."

He said "Adieu!" again, and went away, turning, as he left the valley, to look once more upon his sire.

The mute, wistful countenance bent towards him to the last—not even the fair face of the student's love-dream ever made it seem less kind and dear.

The vesper chimes were ringing as Leon entered the city. He had come so far, impelled by a hope that he should see Lulalu where he had seen her many times before, kneeling at the virgin's shrine in the cathedral.

He went slowly and with uncovered head through the kneeling crowd.

The priests were chanting their holy hymn of prayer, while the grand organ made thrilling music. There was a lady kneeling at the altar, and Leon knelt by her side.

"Lulalu!"

Her name—breathed low, and in a voice she knew so well—was only heard by her; those who knelt around only heard the solemn organ and the solemn hymn.

The lady started. Leon's head was bowed, and his long hair hid his brow. She must not seem to recognise him, for her kinsmen were at hand; and even in that sacred place they would have slain her lover had they seen him.

"Adrian!" she said, in the same low tone,—"and here?"

"Here, dearest, with my best hope and worst despair, for you are both to me!"

"Hush! By your love for me, no word, no whisper more! Heaven have grace to save you from this peril! My father and his friend are near—the Duke De Marcosi."

"He——"

"Has sworn to have you hunted down to death. Oh, Adrian, escape!"

"Fear not, dearest! Say, while there is yet time—is it by your consent you wed De Marcosi?"

"Saint Maria, no! I have wept and pleaded till my soul is weary; but my father's will is stern—inexorable!"

"And so is mine. I will not let the sin be consummated, and you shall be my bride, as we have sworn. To-morrow, at midnight——"

"Tell me! Well?"

"I will be in the garden of your father's palace, and toll you a plan I have to save us both from misery!"

"My father's palace? It would be death were you seen!"

"It would be worse than death were I not to come. Say you will be at the casement?"

"Adrian—the peril!"

"Is nothing."

"Hush! The hymn is ended. De Marcosi comes."

The music ceased, the hymn died away, and the kneeling throng arose.

A gentleman, richly dressed, went to Lulalu just as Leon upturned his face.

They recognised each other, for the eye of hate is quick—and De Marcosi knew his rival.

"Adrian Duscanelli!" he exclaimed, with his hand upon his weapon's hilt—"the outlaw!"

Lulalu gave a cry, and threw herself between them. De Marcosi's words were echoed throughout the cathedral, and then Luali pressed forward angrily.

Leon stood erect and calm. He had no weapon, but he placed his hand upon the bugle hidden in his sash.

"The Duke De Marcosi!" he said,—"felon-hearted craven! —we stand in heaven's sanctuary, and you dare not touch me!"

"What ho, there!" thundered Marcosi, in reply. "The Luali here to take this daring outlaw—this rebel excommunicated by the Church!"

His sword flashed out. The Prince Luali snatched Lulalu from Leon, and motioned his companions forward. The student could not seek protection of the priest—the reverend man would not protect an excommunicant.

Yet Leon was unmoved.

He kept his glittering eye set steadily on Marcosi, and as Luali's friends advanced, he leaped forward like a tiger and wrenched a sword from one of them.

In an instant, they were driven back by him alone; an instant more, and Leon's bugle-cry rang out like a battle-note.

"Back, everyone!" he said. "See—I am not alone!"

A crowd of lazzaroni—the mendicants of Naples—now turned silently upon the Luali, and many a long stiletto gleamed in dangerous hands.

Their aspect, strange and unexpected as it was, caused the Luali to shrink. The prince strode with his fainting daughter to the entrance.

"The outlaw and mendicants in league!" he said. "Are they banditti?"

"Shut the cathedral door!" thundered Leon. "Let no man pass or enter!"

The lazzaroni shut the door at his command.

"No, Duke De Marcosi," he said, facing his rival, sword in hand,—"when the outlaw's life is sought, he must defend it! Come!"

He stepped towards his foe, but the duke went back in dread. He knew the student's skill, and dared not oppose him single handed.

The priest saw the young patrician's jeopardy, and, standing on the altar, cried out:

"Here, Duke de Marcosi!—here, with me, before St. Mary's shrine! Back, sacrilegious outlaw, lest outraged Heaven sends its vengeance down!"

"Let Heaven judge me!" exclaimed Leon, his gleaming blade flashing in the light as he leaped forward, even while De Marcosi clung to the altar rails. "Here stands my rival—my bitterest foe—my father's chief oppressor, and my own! He hath sought my life—I did not seek his! Now, and here, before we part, it shall be death to one of us, though I sacrifice him on the shrine!"

Marcosi called aloud for aid, but none could help him, for the passage now kept his friends away. He had to rise and face his gallant foe alone, and foot to foot.

A shriek pealed from the lips of Lulalu as she heard the deadly clash of steel. She clasped her white hands in supplication and exclaimed:

"Adrian—Adrian—do not kill him!"

The student heard her, though he did not seem to heed her. His sword was playing like a snake of steel round the weapon of his foe, and de Marcosi was beaten to his knee.

He was powerless before the student's matchless strength and skill. His blade was as a reed might be unto a scimitar, and so he let him go, trusting that his rival's chivalry would not let him strike an unarmed man.

"Mercy!" he said.

"How? Pick up your sword, and fight again, or like a coward die the death you have sought! Pick up your sword!"

He kicked his kneeling foe in scorn, and De Marcosi, desperate then, took his weapon and resumed the fight.

It did not last a minute. The rapid clash and glitter ceased suddenly, and an awful scream of pain went to the cathedral roof as Leon's blade swept into Marcosi's body.

Resistless and with meteoric swiftness, it made its own red passage, and the hot blood gushing out, descended, splashing on the marble pave.

De Marcosi fell back, bleeding like a sacrifice upon the velvet steps before the shrine.

(*To be continued in our next.*)

THE BLACK DEVIL OF SICILY.

A LITTLE town in Sicily was, some twenty years back, horribly infested with brigands.

Indeed, some bold people declared that a part of the said band of brigands lived in the town itself, and one bold man, two hours before leaving the town for ever as he thought, declared the mayor, whom everyone believed to be a respectable young blacksmith, was the leader of the band.

And to prove his innocence, the mayor punished the slanderer, upon his return to the town two hours after he had left it, to complain of a visit from the brigands to his personal pockets—punished the slanderer, I say, by laughing at his loss, and refusing to exert his authority where it had been so brutally attacked.

It has been said the mayor was a blacksmith, and though the two trades in one person appear unusual to us who look upon a mayor as a kind of bank, it is different in little foreign villages, where the mayor is generally chosen for his respectability and industry, and being chosen he generally drives a good trade, and resigns his apron or his hammer to perform the duties of his mayorship with considerable satisfaction.

It has also been said the mayor and blacksmith was a bachelor; but he sighed at the feet of Marietta, who served wine at her father's little inn, and who utterly disliked the Fortemano, as he was called from the grip of his hand. Somehow, the signoretta, as he flatteringly called her, could not believe in that respectability people declared him to have; and as she was a clever young woman, perhaps she could see as far as most men, and so, perhaps, she was right when she declared that Fortemano's eyes were not the thing, and that his mouth looked cruel.

Old Paulo, the girl's father, vowed flatly she was a fool to be cool to the mayor, and loudly condemned her each evening as the mayor sat smoking and drinking black wine in moderation; whereon Marietta would laugh, say signor the mayor could live without her help, and turn coquettishly to a new customer, for being a clever girl she knew that if she took things seriously, she should have no peace in her life.

So she pretended to listen "half and half" to the mayor, and thoroughly made up her mind she would see the mayor very handsomely hanged before she would marry him.

Fortemano vowed she had no heart—she laughed, and said, perhaps she had not.

Then, with something like a frown, he said perhaps he had a rival; she admitted, glancing at a little glass, which reflected back a very pretty face, that, perhaps, he had—more unlikely things might happen.

Then the mayor said, perhaps, whoever he was, he would not come to find her if she were locked up in the mountains.

She returned, she did not mean to be locked up in the mountains.

"Suppose," said he, "she were carried there?"

"And who," she answered, "was to carry her there?"

"The Black Devil, Marietta."

"La—one once said you were the Black Devil!"

"The Black Devil has a black beard."

"And you a yellow one, yet, truly, have you black eyes, and just now not very pleasant ones, mayor!"

"No man has a kind eye when a woman jilts him, Marietta."

"Ah, mayor! and what woman has jilted you?"

"Thou dost know, Marietta!"

"Truly! Giulia at the mill? No? Well—Anna at the bakery? No—who can it be?"

"It is thou, Marietta!"

"Signor Mayor, one who has never encouraged cannot jilt. I have said no word to you."

"But you have said enough with your eyes."

"La—look at them now!"

"They are as cold as the snow on the mountain up there."

"And they will keep as the snow. 'Tis a shame, Signor Mayor, to weary a girl with your sighings when she has no sighs to return. Is there no other in the whole town who will suit you for a wife? There is Giulia at the mill; and Anna at the bakery. Truly, Anna hath bright hair, and Giulia's hair is not sleek, yet they both look kindly on the mayor."

"Those who do not look kindly on the mayor, the mayor unkindly looks upon."

"La, there is the Black Devil in thy eyes now!"

"Yes, and the Black Devil in my heart."

"Ah, talking of the Black Devil, he will be caught, mayor! Yes, the soldiery are to catch him."

"Truly, the mayor has heard nothing of it."

"Ah, but Marietta has."

"And how did she learn what she has learnt?"

"By listening, mayor."

"Nay, she is not so clever as to tell people's names by serving them a bottle of red wine!"

"I listened to them, mayor."

"What, the horsemen who were here yesterday?"

"The very same—the handsome horsemen."

"They were poor devils."

"Better poor than black—the mayor takes it they were poor. Did they pay him badly?"

"Yes."

"La, was that because the mayor was asleep, and had to be waked that the horse might be shoed. People wonder that the mayor sleeps so much in the day. Giulia at the mill wonders, and also Anna of the bakery!"

"Good—now you—Marietta—will you have me?"

"Good! no, not if you were the Mayor of Palermo. I would as soon marry the Black Devil. See you, mayor, we all have our likes and dislikes, and I do not love you—nay I——"

"You hate me?"

"No—no—we may not hate—the priest says so—but see, you, we may try to love some people hard, and yet we cannot, but—but—but not like them, mayor."

"Good night!"

"Good night! but why break the wine-jug, for thou hast broken the wine-jug? And where are you going?"

"Where I choose."

"To Giulia, at the mill?"

"Where I choose."

"Or to Anna, at the bakery?"

"Where I choose."

It was after this rejection of the mayor that these things occurred.

First:—Old Paulo led his daughter such a life, for depriving him of the mayor as a mayor, of the mayor as a customer, and of the mayor as a son-in-law, that the brisk little body half determined to run away, only she did not know where to run to.

Second:—The Black Devil—which was the common name of the brigand captain, whose band of perhaps ten rendered gloomy ten thousand people,—the Black Devil grew worse and worse, for formerly he would spare priests, women, and peasants, now he levied taxes upon all; on all handsome young girls he was especially hard, vowing he would put out their eyes, and nearly frightening them to death; once he robbed in a gentlemanly way, now he robbed with awful accompaniment of threats; and some people in the village vowed he would soon take to murdering, which as yet he had not done.

Certainly he might be quite willing to murder, but the Government were in the habit of interfering when the brigands went so far.

Third occurrence:—Travellers began to avoid the road; the consequence was that old Paulo's wine remained corked up, and old Paulo complained more than ever that Marietta had deprived herself of an establishment and him of a home, by her refusal of the mayor, and he recommended her to call the mayor back.

Fourth occurrence:—This the young lady refused to do, and the consequence was that old Paulo locked her up in her room, and indeed she was hardly wanted at the inn, for barely any customers came at all.

Fifth occurrence:—One evening the whole town was horrified by hearing that the blessed bishop himself had been robbed, while coming on a pastoral visit.

It was too true.

Five carbines and five brigands had brought the bishop's carriage to a dead stop; the brigands insulted the holy father; they ransacked his box and pockets; they took his watch from his fob, they tore his papal ring from his stout finger; they implored his absolution; and then permitted him to drive on; and, it is a fact, the unlucky priest arrived in the village without a single coin of that realm in his immediate possession.

This was a little too good, so the sixth and last of the chain of occurrences took place.

For one evening, precisely one score of soldiers and one officer marched into the quiet little village, and set the whole place in a ferment.

The officer took up his residence at old Paulo's, and when that gay youth entered the little inn, the old fellow looked at Marietta as though *she* was the cause of this too.

The next day there was a little parading of the soldiers.

They were introduced to the mayor, who hoped they would soon render the roads clear of the vermin who infested it, and who offered all the help in his power.

By that evening the soldiers had grown vastly popular in the town, for somehow—and who shall say how?—French, German, and Italian soldiers are liked by French, German, and Italian civilians far more than English soldiers are liked by English civilians.

Now the young officer had left Palermo, which he loved, for it has cheap operas, cheap concerts, cheap dancing, and 'tis merry always; and he could not love this quiet little village.

So as he was sitting under the vines outside the inn, his elbow on the little table, his head on his hand, and his wine-glass unemptied before him, he thought that just at that moment the curtain was rising, and the magnificent prima donna preparing to "go on."

Thus he sat, and slowly stroking his military moustache, when Marietta stepped gently up; she was more cheerful than she had been for some time past.

"Signor does not like the wine?"

"The signor does—my beautiful!"

"But the signor does not drink it."

"He was thinking—fair one!"

"Of the lady wife at home, perhaps?"

"There is no wife, and no home, fair one."

"Ah, but there is to be?"

"I wonder!"

"Oh, signor, is it possible that you have no dearest one?"

"We soldiers are poor, signora,"

"Truly, you are like us poor villagers, then."

"Truly for you, I have only my pay."

"Ah; he is poor—the poor youth!"

"What are you saying there low—under the vine?"

"I said—doubtless the king will reward you when the Black Devil is in prison!"

"Ah, but first get him there!"

"Truly, there are you and your gallant men!"

"We will do our best. You are very pretty!"

"Signor remarks that!"

"Why, has he not remarked it before?"

"The signor is too great to look at me—and—and he keeps his eyes on the ground—doubtless he thinks."

"And now he will keep his eyes straight before him and still think. And see, they call you, Marietta."

"By that very name!"

"And a pretty one too—and who calls you by that very name besides your father?"

"Oh, signor, the whole village!"

"Ah—but who especially."

"Alas—no one! I am like you, signor!"

"What, not one sweetheart?"

"No—yes."

"Ah, ah!"

"The mayor whom I—but here comes the mayor. Good evening signor—we have not seen you for a long, long time!"

"Oh, I've not been wanted here, signora. Where are you going?"

"To see to the grapes. Soon again to see you, signor."

And she was gone.

The next moment the mayor sat down on the other side of the little table at which sat the young officer, who really *was* as poor as you or I; and his jug of black wine being brought him, he fell to talking with the officer.

"The Black Devil should shake in his shoes, lieutenant."

"If the vagabond wears any, mayor."

Here the mayor started.

"Do you know the number of his band, lieutenant?"

"To a single one."

"Why they say he don't know his band so well."

"Nonsense; he's too clever a fellow for that, and I assure you he is clever."

"You honour him, lieutenant."

"No; but I give everybody his due."

"Ah! And you hope to take him?"

"Surely—I am sure to."

"Ah! then I take it, lieutenant, you are cleverer than he."

The lieutenant blushed.

"Surely, mayor, I do not boast of cleverness, but numbers. We are a score—he and his men but ten. We fight rightly—each man is two, so there are four against one, and he must fall!"

"Ah! lieutenant; but they say a desperate man fights like four—so you and the brigands are equal; and who shall win we shall see!"

"Why, mayor, you seem to befriend the rogues!"

"*I*, lieutenant!—*I*, the mayor!"

"Pardon; I spoke in jest."

"Harsh jests are bad words, lieutenant!"

"True; for you—pardon."

The mayor waved his hand.

"And you know their retreat, lieutenant?"

"No—and yet, yes."

"I should call that bad evidence."

"No, in fact. But to-night I shall know. For, mayor, I need not tell you that amongst ten rogues there must be one coward, and we've found the Black Devil's coward."

"And where, lieutenant?"

"Where? Well, you being mayor, I may tell the chapter through. We met him on the march; it seems the Devil had slit one of his ears for talking of some handsome peasant girl or another, whom he called his sweet mistress, and so he vowed vengeance. My sergeant meets him to-night."

"Indeed, lieutenant, you are a godsend to us, veritably. And pray, may I ask where?"

"Surely, mayor; the first cross on the road from the village."

Here the party was increased by old Paulo himself, who, hearing the mayor had honoured him once more, came forward with all the conciliation he was master of.

But the mayor took little notice of him, and he became taciturn at last, and rose uneasily from his stool to make for home.

The next morning the whole town trembled.

Outside the village the first holy cross on the road had been desecrated—a man was tied to it by the throat, dead.

The parish priest had the cross taken down and burnt.

The body was brought into the town in a hay cart, and the whole place was in commotion.

The mayor and the greybeards had a meeting in the town hall—a barn, in fact, over a market-place,—and passed a good many resolutions; but the mayor said nothing about what the young officer had told him on the previous night.

The meeting over, the mayor paid the lieutenant an official visit.

The latter was being served his breakfast by Marietta; and it is supposed to be a fact that, as the mayor arrived at the open door, the lieutenant was kissing the hand of the pretty little innkeeper's daughter.

"Good morning, lieutenant. This is a bad business!"

"Oh, mayor, terrible."

"If the good signora would permit me to privately speak with the brave lieutenant, how honoured I should be, and the signora will not listen."

"Sir-r-r-r," said the signora, and flung out of the room.

"It is a bad business, mayor. I am ashamed of it."

"You, lieutenant, ashamed! Why?"

"Why, mayor, the whole band of the blackguards came to meet us last night, and we were not there."

"I do not comprehend you, lieutenant."

"Mayor, my sergeant went. Our man was at the cross: he went to open his mouth—crack; in a moment he was gagged; half a score of men were there, too. My man was positively handcuffed; he had the pleasure of seeing the poor devil hanged, of drinking a glass of wine with the scamps, and of being escorted to within twenty yards of your own forge, mayor, when he came on to me, tapped as well as he could at my window, and I cut the rope that tied him with that sword there; and I wish it was among the ribs of the Black Devil himself——"

"As I, of course, do too, Signor Lieutenant. Addio! Perchance horsemen are waiting at the forge. I will, with the lieutenant's permission, see him again to-night."

"Surely, mayor. By-the-bye, mayor, they tell me you think not badly of Marietta: you must have me for a rival, I think. What, you start! oh, then, it is true. Nay, never fear, man, I'll not step in; though if I did, 'tis a fair field, I'm told."

"Yes, lieutenant, and frequently a red one. You soldiers carry all before you, always."

"Except with Black Devils, mayor."

(To be concluded in our next.)

THE FOR=STERS' FEAST IN THE OLDEN TIME.
With an early number will be Given the companion Picture, printed in Colours, entitled, THE FORESTERS' FETE OF THE PRESENT DAY.
London : E. Harrison, Salisbury Court, and all Newsagents every where.

TALES OF BRIGANDS

I Warn & Strike

AND BANDITTI.

[RED GAUNTLET IS RECOGNISED.]

RED GAUNTLET, THE BANDIT; OR, THE BLACK MOUNTAINEERS.

BOOK I.—THE ARTIST.

CHAPTER X.
THE VISCOUNT'S STORY.

"I NEVER told you why I came to Naples, did I?" said Dick Nicholson, when, with his friends, he was seated in Stuart Linn's chamber, at the magnificent palazzo by the Bay. "Perhaps you wouldn't care to know?" He had started a new idea. St. George, who had his back on an elegant lounge, and his feet on the back of an easy chair, opened one sleepy eye a little wider.

"Why did you come?" he asked.

"Don't believe Dick knows!" hazarded the marquis.

"Neither do I. He is trying to invent an excuse," added Cecil Marriott.

"Now I do know why I came."

"Why, then?"

"Because St. George did. I think St. George was always a little out of his senses!"

St. George opened the other sleepy eye and listened. He had been indulging in a fit of indolence since his fight with the banditti, and when he once got indolent, he said it took a lot to set him right again.

"A little out of his senses?" he repeated, in a tone simply of inquiry. "Think away old fellow—you were always good at thinking—some people are. Funny—isn't it?"

"It was a deuced hot morning," continued the Viscount, "and I had been to the 'At Home,' at the Dowager Duchess of Winchester's, you know—an awful thing in receptions—all the staircase full and the servants sliding up and down the bannisters with ices!"

"Go ahead!"

"I liked it rather. You know Sybil Moffatt — pretty, plump, delicious little Sybil? By Jove!—such shoulders—such a lovely neck, and the sweetest ankle you ever saw!"

"Except Nicola's!" put in St. George. "But I don't see what you know about Sybil's ankles!"

"Well, you see, it was a staircase party, on a hot night, with lots of crinoline and tulle. I didn't want to look, you know, but there they were. Pearl silk embroidered, and shoes tiny enough for Cinderella!"

"Nicola has little feet," mused St. George, amid a cloud of fragrant smoke; "but she don't wear pearl silk embroidered. There's an awful lot of sham about ladies!"

This startling statement was received with cries of:

"Question!"

"Well, so there is. See how delightfully shocked they would be if they thought you caught a glimpse of their toes. But if they don't mean to show them, why do they wear pearl silk embroidered? That's the thing!"

"But it was an accident with Sybil," Marriott went on. "However, it got me into a scrape. The pretty ankles haunted me somehow, because, you see, I got a glimpse of just a bit more; and when I reached her stair, I felt like giving her a terrific hug, and telling her how beautiful she was.

"I didn't; but I tell you what—getting upstairs was the most dreadful thing in the world! I tried to do the flunkey's dodge, by sliding up the bannisters, but I slipped over and caught at the first thing to save myself.

"It happened to be the head of a lady—I won't give her name, because her hair came off—and I was so confused that I begged her pardon and offered it back to her. Everybody tittered of course, but a great many wigs were tightened on the sly. I believe that lady is my mortal enemy for life. But I couldn't help it—could I?"

"Certainly not," said St. George. "I remember getting into just such a mess over my uncle—a conceited old donkey! Nearly sixty he was then, and making love to a girl not twenty. I didn't know he wore a wig, and just for fun fastened a bit of curly hair to the back of his chair. He had a shocking habit of being polite with his head, so it didn't take him long to nod himself out of his wig. Funny—wasn't it? But he served me out."

"How?"

"Why, of course, I thought to come in for all the property, and he left it all to be spent in building almshouses for hairdressers! His mouldy old wig was all he did give and bequeath to me."

"How much would you have had?" asked Stuart Linn, laughing with the others.

"Nearly a million," said St. George, quietly—"but I didn't care. It would have been an awful lot of trouble to spend!"

Marriott proceeded.

"I got Sybil out of the staircase, carried her part of the way—I liked carrying her—and managed to find a quiet corner in the drawing-room—at least, on the balcony outside the drawing-room. I was thinking about her ankles, and she had a new pair of ear-drops—a present from me."

"'Do you not think they look very pretty?' said she.

"'I never saw anything so beautiful,' said I—'so round, and not too thin. Such darling little feet too!'

"'Viscount!' said she.

"'Hallo!' thought I—'here's a fix!' However, I said:

"'Do forgive me! I was thinking of my part in the private theatrical.'

"'I see,' said she—'that is one of your speeches.'

"'Yes,' said I.

"'You play Rolando—do you not?' she said.

"'I do,' said I.

"'Ah!' said she. 'How nice! I play Zomora.'

"'Delicious—by Jove!' said I, for how could a fellow help it. Fancy playing Rolando to her Zomora; she dressed as a page—a short tunic and little boots, you know—and I having to pat her on the head, or on the cheek if I like—or kiss her. I have seen a fellow play Rolando in the 'Honeymoon,' and kiss the Zomora. 'You will look lovely—a velvet tunic, with white fur, kid boots with blue heels, and pearl silk, like that you have on.'

"There was no help for it. I had put my foot in it!

"By Jove, it was worth a trifle to see the colour leap to her face, and the fire to her eyes! I forgot what she said, but it was something hot and angry, and then her hand came smack against my face."

"Jolly!" said St. George. "Funny—wasn't it?"

"I would rather have had that blow than a kiss," Marriott went on. "Of course I apologised. I don't know what I did say; but I asked her to hit me again, and so on.

"I did not think the passionate little puss ever cared for me. I knew she was engaged to marry somebody, but somehow in her pet it all came out, and I said a lot, and we both said a lot, and I had my arm round her waist, and she had her arms round my neck, and I was kissing her, and she was hitting me, when all of a sudden the shocking old fright whose wig I had jerked off on the landing pulled aside the curtains and everybody saw us!"

Marriott's friends laughed, although they sympathised.

"I didn't care a hang except for Sybil. I was as cool as a cucumber. But up came old Moffatt—a major-general, you know, come over from India—terrific moustache, and voice like a lion.

"'My daughter, sir-r-r-r!' said he, with lots of r's.

"'I have had the honour of a previous introduction,' said I, politely.

"'Damme, sir!' said he, with a lot more r's. 'How dare you make love to her, knowing that she is engaged to the Duke Tikeypoodle!'

"'Hang the Duke Tikeypoodle!' said I. 'Damme! he's a puppy; and before he should have Sybil, I would run away with her!'

"'Sir!' said he, with such a lot of r's that I thought he was going into extensive Irish.

"'By the lord Harry!' said I, hugging Sybil closer, "if that little monkey presumed to marry her, I would break his neck and elope with Sybil—damme!'

"By Jupiter! I thought the major-general would roar his moustache off! He wanted to eat me on the spot—challenged me to fight next morning—threw his white kids in my face, after the good old style—kicked his footman over the bannisters because he could not get downstairs for the carriage—carried Sybil out like a baby, and made somebody else's coachman drive him home!"

"Bravo, the major-general!" said Stuart Linn. "That was energetic!"

"So I thought. Well, in the morning there came a long fellow, all spurs and whiskers, and lots of orders over his breast.

"'I am the Duke Tikeypoodle!' said he.

"I rang for my valet—a capital fellow! I had him at Oxford. Strong as a bull he is, and no respecter of persons.

"'Jack,' said I 'here is something escaped from a menagerie! Turn it out!'

"Jack tucked up his sleeves.

"'It won't break if I touch it, will it?' said he.

"'Not if you are careful, Jack.'

"His grace of Tikeypoodle tried to stand upon his dignity, but Jack went straight at him, picked him up, and carried him to the street door.

"Of course I couldn't fight the major-general, and I didn't want to hurt the Tikey, so after Jack had turned him out, I said :

"'Jack.'

"'Viscount.'

"'Pack up a few things. We will travel.'

"'Breakfast first,' said Jack.

"'Breakfast,' said I.

"Jack ordered breakfast, and went on packing. Somebody knocked at the door.

"'The major-general come to eat me!' thought I, so I called Jack.

"'If that is a sanguinary old gentleman,' I said, 'with big moustaches and a wonderful voice, tell him to come after breakfast—I never fight before breakfast.'

"Jack went down. It was not the major-general, but St. George.

"He had a travelling bag in his hand, and a cab at the door.

"'I am going to Italy,' said he. 'Will you come? Cab's waiting.'

"'The very thing!' said I. And I was dressed in no time. So we came to Italy."

"What became of the major-general?" asked Nicholson.

"He came with a carriage full of swords and pistols about an hour after we had started. Jack offered to fight him for me; but the old fellow did not see that. He started off in pursuit, and, for all I know, is in pursuit still."

"And Sybil?"

"The old gentleman put her in a nunnery, or a monkery, or some such thing. I shall find out where she is, and get her out some day."

"Rather a vague date," said Stuart Linn.

"Well, what is the use of being in a hurry? She's not of age yet, and if I got her out and married her, it would be invalid on something. I intend to have her, you know, if I have to pull the monkery down! You would help me, would you not?"

"I would," said St. George. "By jove! I should think so!"

"So would I," said the others. "And now, suppose we hear why Dick Nicholson came to Naples."

CHAPTER XI.

DICK NICHOLSON'S ADVENTURE.

"FIRST," said Dick, "you remember the mysterious doctor, who came to London five years ago?"

"And lived near Piccadilly," said Stuart Linn. "I know."

"He was a mesmerist and an opthalmist, and a lot of other ists—a very quaint old card altogether, and knew enough for several people. He had all the ologies at his fingers' ends, understood the science of alchymy, and, I have heard, used to deal with Old Nick."

"Perhaps he did deal in necromancy?" suggested Oliver, lazily. "But go ahead!"

"He did indeed; for he had drained every fount of human knowledge with such purpose, and so studied every phase of nature, that his science partook largely of necromancy in character; but he would explain how it was all done—expound the science of will—the theory of magnetism, and a lot of other incomprehensibilities."

"Awful long word—incomprehensibilities," said St. George, seeming to see its length as he uttered it. "Don't say it again."

"Well, I was curious to see this man. I doubted the stories I heard—that the past and the future were to him but as books, which he could read, so I went to him.

"I had expected to see a strange, weird figure, with a long white beard, velvet skull-cap, loose robe, &c., dark, of course,

and a foreigner. It is a peculiar and universal supposition that all mysterious people must be foreigners or Jews."

"As a rule, they are," said Linn.

"This man was not. I saw an attendant—a very ordinary-looking attendant, in plain livery. I gave him my card.

"'Is Doctor Montena engaged?' I asked.

"'No, sir.'

"'I would see him.'

"The man disappeared with my card, came back in an instant, and led me to a chamber where sat Doctor Montena.

"He was a handsome man, but it would be quite impossible to tell his age. His face had an expression that troubled you—a calm inscrutability which baffled penetration, while his own burning eye searched the depths of your soul.

"'Doctor Montena,' I said.

"He rose. He had been sitting poring over a book that to me was Sanscrit. He seemed to read it with facility.

"When he rose, I looked at him attentively, feeling that I stood before a remarkable man, and wanting to see what outward trace he bore of an intellect almost supernatural.

"Not one. He was simply an elegant, slender gentleman, of middle height, with a splendid figure, and perfectly dressed. My first thought was to envy him his tailor, my next to admire the man.

"His hair was a bright, soft brown, his forehead white as marble, and his face without a line. He was fair, but not pallid. He wore whiskers and moustache, both matchless—soft and brown as his hair, and parted in wavy ripples from his chin. The chin itself was perfect, fine in outline, and just touched by a dimple. His eyes were of no definite colour, but seemed dark, and burned with an inward fire. His brows were slightly—only very slightly arched."

"You must have studied him intently," said Marriott.

"I did. The man was perfect, as though Nature had loved her task, and formed a creature without the imperfections which make most men alike and ordinary. His hands were white and slim, his face entirely passionless.

"'I have come, doctor,' I said, 'prompted by no idle curiosity, but to see if there is truth in what is said of you.'

"He bowed.

"'I am,' I said, 'a sceptic in such matters, because I have seen most of those who profess what you profess, and they have been charlatans.'

"He bowed again.

"'It is said that you can read the past—unfold the scroll on which is written the story of the future. Is this true?'

"'It is.'

"I had been curious to hear his voice, and was glad when he spoke. His voice was calm, low, and had a strange, subduing power. His manner was so free from all charlatanism, so quiet and assured, that I began to have faith.

"We said very much together—spoke of the mysterious sciences, the wonders of the universe, and such things as men speak when their souls are aroused to earnest purpose. I think my discourse pleased him.

"I had not the idiotic bad taste to ask him absurd questions about what would become of me, how long I should live, and whether I should be rich, &c. I chiefly wished to enlarge what he called the inner life—the separate existence of the mind.

"I had dreamed. The science of dreams is not new nor improbable in any way. Most of us have dreamed things that have been realised. I had dreamed of a face which had been with me in my dreams from boyhood.

"Some such face it was as we see pictured for a saint—too sweet almost in beauty to be earthly—weird, spiritual, haunting. My heart ached with longing to see that face in life.

"I am no enthusiast. You, who know me, know me as a man of little ideality or romance to subdue the outward portion of my realistic self; but this face became a part of my existence."

Marriott and Stuart Linn gave him their serious attention now. St. George listened with his eyes shut—a sign that he was very deeply interested.

"Some few nights before I went to Doctor Montena, my

dream had changed. The vision came, but not as before—not with the intense, mute gladness I did so love to see, but with a look of deep reproach and pain.

"She came in a dark shadow. I saw her only dimly, and then she faded back into the gloom, and another head loomed out.

"It was the head of a man—a monk.

"I saw the features distinctly; they were fine and clear, but mocking—sardonic—demoniac. Even in my dream he despised and mocked me,—even in my dream I hated him!

"I told my dream to Dr. Montena.

"What he said I could not now repeat, but he succeeded in fixing an impression that my visions were not dreaming only. He explained to me how my mental organisation had properties which rendered me susceptible to magnetism—that my soul had recognised its earthly idol before I saw her by material agency—he told me, in fact, that she *lived!*

"He was a powerful mesmerist; and, by what he taught me, I was as fully prepared to receive as he to practise the influence of Odic force,—he sent me into a trance.

"At first, all was darkness; but, with what would have seemed a necromancer's power, he secured mastery of my thoughts and set me dreaming again. He established a magnetic link between my mind and his, and so he saw what I saw.

"I dreamed again. There were the faces—my spirit-love and the monk—just as I had seen them last. They came as in a cloud, and went away. Then came another cloud, and when it broke I saw a black chateau.

"It was built of marble, that looked like polished ebony, and I entered. I went direct without a guide to a chamber hung with sable drapery, and on a bier raised in the centre of the floor lay my spirit-love—dead, or seeming dead.

"The monk came in. I saw him force her lips apart, and drop some few drops of a pungent essence into her throat. She awoke—living.

"Then what he said to her I do not know, but she wept, and clasped her hands in supplication. She seemed in bitter dread, as though beneath the influence of monkish craft. I heard him tell her much that seemed most strange, and I knew that she had learned to die—that there had been a funeral masquerade.

"The rest was indistinct; but I remember that I interposed in time to save her from falling a victim to a monkish miscreant. I remember seeing a red pool on the floor, and in its midst the monk lying dead. I remember that he wore rich attire under his gown and cowl. And while I stood wondering in this indistinct tragedy, darkness came again.

"When next the darkness broke, my spirit-love was with me, and I was with a horde of wild banditti,—their chief, and she their queen.

"'Awake now!' said Doctor Montena,—'you have seen enough!'

"Then the trance ended, and I awoke.

"Doctor Montena was sitting near me. I saw by his look that he had seen all I had seen—his words proved it.

"'So it will come to pass,' he said,—'five years hence you will see the lady at the black chateau!'

"'When?' I asked.

"'This is the twenty-ninth of August, in the year eighteen hundred and fifty-five—on the twenty-ninth of August, in the year eighteen hundred and sixty, you will see Dorolie in the black chateau,—the chateau in the mountain-forest near the City of Naples.'"

"Did you believe him?" asked St. George.

"I did—I do."

"And that you will be a bandit?"

"I do not see how that is to happen, yet I do not doubt."

"Well," said Marriott, "we shall soon see,—this is the twentieth of August, eighteen sixty."

"Nine days hence will see me at the black chateau."

At this moment an uproar in the street arrested the attention of all. They went to the window, and saw that the palazzo was surrounded by a host of armed men.

"What the deuce do they want, I wonder?" said St. George.

"Me," said a quiet voice at the door. "I left the Duke de Mareosi dead, or dying, on the altar in the cathedral."

"The deuce! Where can we hide you?"

"Here," the student said. "In Naples, the dwelling of an English gentleman is safer than the sanctuary of the church! The King himself does not pass your threshold without permission!"

"All right!" said St. George. "If they come to the door we will kick them downstairs! What is that they are shouting?"

"Their kindly purpose!" smiled the student. "Listen!" The shout rang out again.

"The outlaw! Death to the outlaw!"

CHAPTER XII.
THE BANDIT AND HIS HUNTERS.

"THAT is me," Leon said. "The rabble are like wolves, who howl in chorus and never change their song, but will as soon howl at the hunter as the hunted. Now, would it not be sport to set them yelling at the priests and soldiery?"

"Do!" said St. George. "It would be funny!"

"They are coming upstairs!" said Marriott. "Senor Leon, you will be captured!"

"No," exclaimed the student, with a quick flash of the eye. "Give me a hiding-place for five minutes, and I will face them singly, yet none shall dare lay a finger on me!"

"How?"

"You shall see. Hark!—how the brutes keep howling!—and mark how soon their song shall change!"

The cry rang out again :

"Death—death to the outlaw!"

"The hiding-place!" said Leon.

Marriott called:

"Jack!"

Jack entered. He was a tall fellow, somewhat bigger than St. George, and he had the muscle of a full-grown gladiator. His chief characteristic was stolidity—his one religion, fidelity to the graceful young aristocrat, the viscount.

"Viscount!"

"Take this gentleman to my dressing-room."

Without a word, Jack led the way into an ante-chamber. Just then the door of the palazzo yielded with a crash, and the infuriated rabble swarmed up the stairs.

The Neapolitans are a superstitious race—worse than heathenish in their indolence, their bigotry, and slavish obedience to the priest. The monk who had been doing service in the cathedral only had to say "Sacrilege" and point out Leon, to set the populace on his track like wolves, as he said.

And had he so pleased, he could with that magic bugle of his have called a hundred men, who would have turned upon the wolves like hunters; but he wished to cause no bloodshed, so fought his way through the crowd backed by the lazzaroni, and escaped as far as the palazzo where the Englishmen resided.

"Death for the sacrilege!" the rabble shouted—"death to the outlaw!"

And they swarmed up to the very door of the apartment where St. George and his companions sat.

"Jack!" called Marriott.

Jack came out.

"Well, viscount?"

"Open the door, and see what the gentlemen want. Don't let them in!"

Jack strode towards the door, when it was sent flying from its hinges and, following its advent, came a big Neapolitan with a long knife and a long nose.

"Mustn't come in!" said Jack; and, with a terrific hit, he caught the big one in the wind, doubled him up, and sent him flying over the balustrade.

The fellow had a long way to fall—down two flights of a well-staircase, through a chandelier, and on to a mat in the hall, where he lay groaning and feeling as though somebody had hit him.

"Bravo, Jack!" said Dick Nicholson. "There's another coming!"

The next comer was an officer of the guard, with his sword drawn.

Jack floored him like a shot, sword and all.

"Messire Englisse," said the officer, rising, very much astonished, and dodging out of Jack's way, "we want the outlaw!"

"Shall I hit him again?" asked Jack.

"Not just now," said the viscount.

Jack drew back, but stood with his fist ready, and mentally singled out a bigger Neapolitan than the first. This one had a longer nose and a longer knife, and on the nose Jack longed to hit him.

"What outlaw?" asked Marriott.

"Count Adrian Duseanelli."

"Are you aware that you stand on neutral ground—the home of an English gentleman?"

"Senor, we traced the outlaw hither."

"Did that give you a right," Marriott asked, sternly, "to break my door and enter my chamber with a crew of ruffians at your back?"

The officer seemed disconcerted.

"Order them down!" said the viscount, more sternly than before—"and sheathe your sword, Senor Neapolitan! How dare you stand with it drawn before me?"

The officer recoiled from the fiery young patrician, and, sheathing his sword, bowed very humbly.

"My duty, senor," he said, respectfully—"I do but do my duty!"

"I think you exceed it! Is it your duty to bring this brutal rabble with you?"

He pointed to the crowd of dark faces reaching from the doorway to the staircase. Several, who heard and understood his words, murmured angrily, and their ominous knives glittered in the light.

St. George, Dick Nicholson, and Stuart Linn rose with one accord. Marriott was already erect.

Jack placed himself behind his master, and picked out another Neapolitan bigger than the second. These two were conspicuous by their extra size. Jack could take the rest as they came.

"Guard the dressing-room, Jack!" said Marriott. "There will be an onslaught presently!"

Jack placed himself before the door. That movement betrayed the student's hiding-place to the mob.

"The sacrilege!" they shouted—"death to him!"

"Death to him who says so!" cried the impetuous Marriott. "Back!—or, by the saints, some of you shall go out less quick than you came in! Back!"

The four formed a living barrier, and a dangerous one.

But the rabble were excited. Their superstition and their cupidity made them bold.

The outlaw had committed sacrilege, and there was a price set on the outlaw's head, so they shouted again:

"Death to him!"

And moved towards the door—moved towards the four Englishmen, who did not flinch from the fierce throng.

The walls of the chamber in which this scene was taking place were hung with curiosities of various kinds. Among these were two Moorish scimitars, a Turkish yataghan, and a crease—a keen, double-edged dagger, long, heavy, and deadly.

Marriott went aside and took them down, keeping the crease himself, giving the yataghan to Stuart Linn, and the scimitars to the others.

"There is no outlaw here," he said. "We are not to know but that what you say is a pretext by which these ruffians come seeking pillage. Now, hearken!—I count ten! If, by the time I have done, one of these wretches darkens my threshold, these weapons will be at work! One!"

The officer half unsheathed his sword. He felt convinced the outlaw was near, and did not wish to go without his prey.

"Two!" said Marriott, steadily—"three!"

Not one moved.

"Four—five!"

Still no sign.

"Six—seven!"

Not a movement yet. The Englishmen gripped their weapons firmly. Those of the rabble who had kept their knives sheathed drew them now.

"Eight—nine!"

The officer bared his blade.

"Stand by me!" he said. "The outlaw is in that chamber! Think of the reward! We will have him!"

"Ten!"

The four strode one step forward. The rabble murmured, and the murmur deepened, but they gave way.

"What," said a voice within the chamber, "going without me?"

The words—the defiant, mocking voice—brought back all the pursuers' ferocity.

"The outlaw!—death to him!—the sacrilege!"

"Let them come, gentlemen," said Leon's voice, and the door opened.

Wondering at his temerity in coming forth—wondering, too, why the crowd shrunk back—the Englishmen turned.

"Come," said Leon's voice, "there is a large reward for the outlaw—there is a large reward for me! Who will take me captive?"

Leon's voice it was. But the figure had not Leon's face or form.

He wore a black mask, covering his features from forehead to chin, an elegant and costly dress, a silken sash, and in this sash a jewelled dagger—a slim, white hand, ungloved, and on the fourth finger a red ruby, flashing fire. On his right arm a gauntlet—a red gauntlet—and in the blood-red hand a golden bugle.

"Red Gauntlet, the bandit!" went from tongue to tongue, and the brigand chief stood like a statue, as he said:

"I warn and strike! Now listen, hell-hounds who have followed!—listen currish rabble!—minions of oppression!—sateless wolves! A word of menace—a finger raised to molest me, or these my friends,—and with a single note to warn, I bring a wild horde to strike and slay!"

The rabble cowered back.

The eyes of death glittering through the mask—the still, calm voice of deadly promise—the red gauntlet on the hand made them cringe in terror, for they knew the terrible bandit, and they feared him.

There was a pause—a silence in which the quiver of a breath would have been heard.

"We shall meet again," the bandit said, speaking to the Englishmen.

Then to his foes he said:

"Give me passage, and still no word, no look, no finger raised! I warn and strike! Remember!"

And not one of the many stood in his path, as, with stately grace, he strode through the passage made in their very midst.

He looked neither to the right nor left, but passed the stricken throng in silent scorn, went out into the street, and through the city.

CHAPTER XIII.

THE MASQUERADE.—AN UNINVITED GUEST.

THE night following this adventure was to have been the night of the masquerade. The Duke de Mareosi was to be formally betrothed to Lulalu.

But his grace of Mareosi had a hole in his body, and his physician advised him to keep his bed till the perforation healed.

The wonder is that he did not die, for the student's sword went well aimed for his heart. Certainly de Mareosi's heart was a difficult thing to find, or Leon's weapon would have found it.

But the result of the duel at the altar was simply an ugly wound, not half so dangerous as ill-looking, costing his grace de Mareosi several pints of the red puddle that filled his ducal veins, and causing masses to be said with much solemnity and a large display of wax candles—to say nothing of the family relics dedicated to the Virgin Mary and appropriated by the priests.

When his grace was carried from the cathedral and the physician summoned, the physician shook his head and said that nothing less than a miracle could save the duke's life.

That physician was a clever old hypocrite.

He saw at a glance that the case was an easy one—he knew that Naples was rather in want of a miracle. There had been a winking saint, which, like the people that believed in and went to see it, had a hollow head. When the votaries of the marvellous dropped gold or silver coins into its mouth, it would open and shut its eyes. It was a very sensible saint —it would not wink for coppers.

But one evening, when her saintship had been winking unusually hard, some thief knocked off its head to look for the money it had swallowed. This was an impious thief, for, finding that the left leg was the receptacle, he unscrewed the saintly limb, emptied it, and screwed it on where the head should have been, and screwed the head in the cavity left by the left leg.

That was making a miracle with a vengeance. The saint was so shocked by the outrage that she never winked again.

That miracle being over and another being in request, the physician made one by curing De Mareosi—a feat of surgery which an ordinary quack could have performed with ease.

Every night the wounded man was carried to the cathedral shrine, and a long mass, with lots of incense, said for his body.

At the expiration of a week he was able to walk out of the church without assistance.

Then the people shouted :

"A miracle !"

And on the next night Prince Luali gave his masquerade.

The assemblage was brilliant in the extreme. There was a mist of light, a scent of perfume, and a glorious thrill of music, a crowd of lovely faces, and a throng of lovely forms, grotesque figures, and the manners and costumes of the world comprised in a living panorama passing continually before the eye in the garden of the Palazzo Luali.

Four gentlemen, who entered early, excited general attention.

One, a graceful, slightly-built gentleman, was habited as an English cavalier of Charles the Second's time. This was Cecil Viscount Marriott. His companion, whose figure was something of the same build, was dressed as a Hugenot. This was the marquis. The two behind, St. George and Dick Nicholson. St. George had his tall form arrayed in the splendid garb of a Greek pirate. Dick Nicholson had the disguise of a man of Grenada.

These four stood for an instant near the door, all gazing in one direction.

The figure of a lady in black stood by a silver fountain in the centre of the hall.

She was strangely beautiful.

Her dress, a simple black robe, soft in texture, clung like statue drapery round her form. The large and supple limbs shadowed through, and set the thoughts of masquers wondering.

Dick Nicholson gazed at her with a thrill at his heart.

"Have I seen her before," he thought, "or have I dreamed of such a form ?"

He was about to take the privilege of a masquer and cross the saloon to speak to her, when a commotion in the corridor stayed him.

A fierce murmur, followed by the flash of swords and a cry of "The outlaw !" drew all observation to a marble pillar, by which there stood a lady attired like the Goddess Diana. By her side was one whom they recognised with a start. Confronting these were the Prince Luali and the Duke de Mareosi, both with weapons drawn. Behind were a crowd of retainers coming at Luali's bidding to arrest the daring outlaw who stood by Lulalu.

"Leon, the student !" said St. George. "The outlaw and the bandit ! There will be hot work, my friends ! We must not see him crushed or slain !"

The bandit was quite calm.

His red gauntlet grasped his sword, the point of which rested on the ground.

"Red Gauntlet !" said the guests. "Down with him !"

The brigand's eye glittered. He watched De Mareosi, who was nearest.

"Once have I warned," he said—"once have I struck ! When I strike twice I never fail !"

(*To be continued in our next.*)

THE BLACK DEVIL OF SICILY.

(*Concluded.*)

On the evening of the day on which the mayor had paid the lieutenant an official visit, he (the mayor) went to the inn, dressed dashingly, and before the visitors—before the lieutenant, before Marietta herself, he produced a bag of gold, such as very few present had ever seen; and as old Paulo gloated at it, the mayor proposed out loud for Marietta.

Whereon Marietta overthrew the table, dashed the mayor's wine over the mayor's beard, and crashed her little foot upon the floor.

"Bravo, signora, you are brave enough to be a soldier's wife," said the lieutenant.

"And I should like to be a soldier's wife."

Which sentence a good many took to be the second offer of marriage made that minute.

"Signor," said the mayor—"signor lieutenant, look, the wine has fallen over the gold, and made it red !"

"Wipe it, Signor Mayor, and the gold will be again yellow."

"I wish I could wipe away the signora's insult as easily as I can dry these coins."

"Nay, then, mayor," said Marietta, "you should not make honest girls blush for you and themselves too."

The mayor put his gold in his pocket, and away he went.

The town was all asleep, and even the Black Devil was forgotten, except in dreams, when there was a cry of fire. Soon, all the eyes in the place were wide open, and all the female tongues were entreating all the men to help in putting the mayor's house out, for it was all in flames.

The score of soldiers were soon on the spot, strangely different as they looked from the trim coquets they were by day—here dashing water, there hewing down an outhouse, now calling, now pushing.

In the middle of the noise, there was heard the report of a gun. All started, but the next moment the bustle was hard on again.

Suddenly, one of the soldiers cried out, "The capitano—the capitano—see to the capitano !"

And, indeed, the lieutenant was leaning against a shed with his right hand pressed on his left arm.

"I am wounded," said he, "'twas a bullet, sure enough."

The lieutenant was carried to the inn; the parish priest, being parish doctor, was sent for; the wound was declared to be very slightly dangerous, or not at all, and a young female of the name of Marietta was very, very, glad to hear that joyful news.

Well, love affairs are managed rather more rapidly in warm climates than in ours; and the honest truth, which may not be blamed or shamed is, that on the fifth night after the fire, the young officer made that proposal to Marietta which she had made to him, and which the mayor had made to her. And it is set down in the chronicles from which I take these presents, that she accepted him at once, and without considering.

And let no one wonder that the lieutenant proposed to sell out, or rather buy out, and go into the inn-keeping business, for a French or Italian officer is but a very small man compared with his English brother.

Well, these young people were prattling away the hours as

minutes, when the sergeant, who had witnessed the execution at the holy cross, came into the room in so uncivil a manner that he had an opportunity of marring the composition of the picture.

He was too elated to "pardon."

"Capitano—capitano (which was a brevet rank bestowed upon the lieutenant), this time we have the Black Devil!"

Whereat Marietta thought, "Then Andrea will have the reward; but he won't run danger in the mountains."

It was perhaps a whole second after this reasoning on the girl's part, that the capitano said, "Have him!—where?"

"In his very hold, capitano. We shall catch him, signora (in whom the man was taking interest, as a probable part of the brigade); we shall catch him like a black rat, as he is in his trap——"

"Well, sergeant, and how did the news come?"

"With a frightened peasant, so it may please the capitano, whose teeth are yet chattering."

The next minute the room, which had been so quiet, was full of clattering soldiers, in the midst of whom was a queer-looking peasant, such as we sometimes see here in London—long-hanging black hair, long black whiskers, searching eyes, brown skin, brown lithe hands, a sheepskin jerkin, and astounding twisted bands about his legs. He looked terribly frightened.

"Speak, comrade," said the lieutenant, giving him a great glass of red wine.

"Signor, I can hardly speak!"

"Let me. You have seen the Black Devil?"

"Oh, yes, I have seen him! I have seen him, signor, with these eyes."

"And where?"

"He is terrible!"

"How came you to see him?"

"He is a giant!"

"Did you speak to him?"

"And there is fire in his eyes!"

"Psha!"

"Come, come, comrade," said the sergeant, "speak out like a man—if he was a score of Black Devils!"

"Yes—yes; but he hath the fire in his eyes!"

"But where—the capitano asks where?"

"Not one-third of a league from the town!"

They all started, for every day had parties of the soldiers been about the country, and no trace of the robbers could be found.

"But who are you?" asked the lieutenant.

"A poor peasant, who watches the sheep cropping the grass of the good God."

"Oh, surely," said Marietta, "hast thou not passed here before, and were there not two or three with thee?"

"Truly, signora, I have passed through this town, and was not I now coming to it?"

"Yes—and the Black Devil?——"

"I saw him, the fire streaming from his eyes, sitting on a ledge of rock, with three others of them; and he smoked, and he drank wine!"

"Well, well?"

"So, please you, as you pass the forge—which I see, signor, is burnt to the ground—behold there is a turning to the rocks above: go creeping along that turning; go on, and on, and then turn, and you shall come to a break in the rock, and through it and far down below there sat the Black Devil and the others—and—and they sit now, doubtless."

"You will lead us to the place, signor peasant?"

"Surely, signor."

"Sergeant, call the men together; they shall smell gunpowder this very night."

The mayor soon heard of the new discovery, and came to make inquiries.

There was a tacit enmity between the two men now, for was not one man master of what the other had striven hard for? Hence the interview was rather cold.

Its aim was that the lieutenant would allow the mayor to accompany the little expedition. "Surely," said the lieutenant, and the mayor declared himself infinitely obliged.

But when the expedition was ready to start in the moonlight,

the mayor was nowhere to be found; and, after waiting a little while, and after a little conversation between the lieutenant and the young Marietta, it set off without him.

"You," she said, "are not going; your wound ——," for woman's love prompts her oft to cowardice.

"I am going!" he returned; "for as the mountains won't come to us, why we must go to the mountains."

"And the capitano will kill the Black Devil," said the peasant, looking up from his jug of wine.

"Yes; and you will have the reward, signor," said the girl, gaily trying to be brave. "And, as you are wounded, lieutenant, you are not strong enough to go first."

"First, capitano, or last," said the peasant, "what matters?"

Ten minutes after, the little troop had marched quietly out of the town, round behind the ruins of the forge, and on towards the rock which towered on one side of the Italian town.

Inasmuch as the soldiery had been in the town a whole week, a good many young females, besides Marietta, did not go to bed that night. Indeed, several little sets of them passed the night together, and dreaded the noise of firearms in proportion as nature had given them hearts and nerves.

Marietta watched by herself.

Up the next day's sun came, and still the expedition had not returned.

The people went about their work, the inn was opened for the day, and as the soldiery had not returned, one of the most inquisitive went to the house of the town barber, whither the mayor's blacksmith had taken refuge when his forge went down.

Some one opened the door of the shop when the inquisitive one knocked at it.

"Good day, father! Is signor, the mayor, in?"

"Why, Pietro, do you not know me?"

"Know you! Holy saints! it is signor, the mayor; and his hair is grey."

"Bah! hair often turns grey in a few hours. What do you want? Some of you been disputing?"

"No, signor; but the soldiers, they have not yet returned."

"Bah! doubtless they have followed the scamps up; traced them to some distance."

"Good, mayor!" said the man; and as he spoke he was looking upwards. "Signor," said he, "behold the fifth black vulture which has flown past, in the last hour, and towards the rock; and see, what a flight of crows are there!—two, four, eight; they are beyond counting!"

"And what, neighbour, do you make of that?"

"Good faith, neighbour mayor, I cannot tell; can you?"

"Not at all. Go, now, to thy work."

But when the frightened townspeople were thinking of sleep, when all kinds of fears had been suggested, behold the inquisitive man of the morning, known to all the town, came amongst them with such terrible news, that it was hard to believe, and the mayor would not believe it at all, until, indeed, the whole town believed it.

The whole expedition had been murdered, without the least resistance on their part, as it was clearly seen.

The apparent peasant was really one of the band, and had led the soldiery to their destruction.

They had evidently arrived at the opening in the rocks mentioned by the brigand; they had then formed single file; each had passed through that terrible narrow opening, and each, when he arrived on the other side, had been quite silently and savagely murdered.

The poor lieutenant was found with a score of wounds about him; his lips cruelly cut, and the very bandage which the girl had put about his arm, torn from it.

But it is a fact, that from that day forward, no trace of the robbers was ever found, nor were they ever heard of again as committing fresh outrages. That night's work was their finishing stroke.

Marietta did not die, lady readers, for 'tis astonishing how much we can live through; she lived through hearing of the murders; she lived through seeing his body, and she lived through going to his burial, for 'tis only diseased hearts that break with grief, as the doctors will tell you: a good, stout, healthy heart can bear the assaults of misery, and very fairly. So Marietta did not break her heart, however much she may have suffered. But, as a compensating, sentimental atonement, I may tell you she never married, and lives single to this day; though I am afraid I shall injure the effect of that information by the admission that she has had to work for her living, and she will deftly flatter you, or me, if either of us go to the old inn, which she keeps now, for her father sleeps in the same cemetery as her young lover.

By-the-bye, the other girls, whose soldier lovers were slain, married again, most of them; and perhaps the two or three who have not, can't honestly say that they are willingly spinsters. You do not often come across a love that lives through twenty long years of assault by lovers good and bad, young and old. Indeed, I am told that the very constancy with which the woman clings to the old love has induced many a man, more vain than merciful, to win her.

Marietta is very good natured and good tempered over this persecution; and, perhaps, if you only stayed one day at the inn, you would not take her for a very sentimental personage. But every All Saint's Day she trims another grave beside her father's.

And, as the innkeeper has quite enough custom to keep her, and as she don't care much about money, I will not tell you of her whereabouts, but I may tell you that 'tis not more than twenty miles from Palermo.

By-the-bye, the mayor became a brother of a very strict order, is very fanatic, and lives in the odour of sanctity.

JAYME; OR, THE GENEROUS ROBBER.

"By San Pablo!" said a tall, handsome man habited in the costume usually worn by the smugglers of Andalusia, and mounted upon one of those magnificent chargers so much prized in that province of Spain; "but that's a sorry ass of thine, friend."

"Sorry indeed, sir!" said the *arriero*, to whom he addressed himself, and who was at the time caressing his favourite and regaling him with the kindest expressions of endearment ever lavished on that species of animal since the days of Balaam.*

"*Pero, tado le que brilla, no es oro*, and although you see my beast so lank, he is nevertheless the most sensuous ass in all Andalusia, let the next best be where he may."

"That may be true enough," said the inquirer, "and notwithstanding you are an old acquaintance, I see no earthly reason why you should not be separated."

"Ah! Senor Jayme, for the love of God, and your mother, don't deprive me of my poor *jamento*—my old friend—my constant companion—my——"

"Tush, fool! do you think I could descend to manners! Hear me! I have seen you often, and know that you are an honest and industrious fellow (of whom, by the way, there is but a sprinkling in the world), that you have really a chatty wife, a numerous family, and gain your livelihood by charcoal, and that you never indulge in more *aquardiente* than you can comfortably carry. Well now, Mr. Fernandez, for such I believe is your name, suppose you were to receive a couple of mules in exchange for that miserable beast, how long would it take you to make your fortune, eh?"

"The Lord only knows, sir; but when shall I have the mules to try?"

"To-morrow," replied Jayme, "or to-night if you like."

"Heaven be praised!" ejaculated the astonished charcoal dealer, while tears of joy copiously bedewed his sunburnt face. "Do I dream, or am I awake?"

"Come, come, none of this foolishness! You know Padre Antonio, the curate of the village, whither you are going, and if you don't you ought, for he is a greater rogue than any within fifty leagues of it. Well, this said padre has a lovely pair of mules; 2,000 reals will buy them; here is the money—give yonder donkey a holiday, and away with you to the curate; I shall see you again soon."

Saying which, the robber spurred his steed and was out of sight ere the astonished Fernandez had well recovered from the fit of surprise into which this unexpected freak of fortune had thrown him. Then turning to his old acquaintance, he

* All is not gold that glitters.

threw his arms around his neck, and gave him a solitary kiss above the left eye, which the creature received with that not-to-be-mistaken humility for which this species of the brute creation is so notoriously conspicuous. . . . . In a few hours he reached the village, bargained for the mules, and joyously trotted homeward to astound his family with so extraordinary an acquisition.

The same evening, as the curate was sipping his chocolate and inhaling the fragrant perfume of a cigarro, while "fanned with cool winds," a majestic figure, completely enveloped in a *Capa*, after respectfully saluting the padre, very politely asked the favour of permission to ignite his *puro*, and after the usual compliments, he threw a searching glance at the father, and inquired if he had ever seen his visitor before. The priest replied in the negative.

"Well, then, Senor Curate, you have now the happiness to see before you Jayme, the robber!"

Had a thunderbolt from heaven descended to within an inch of his toes he could not have been more thunderstruck than he was at this appalling notification, and it required all the energy he was master of to assume that complacency of look which distinguishes the godly from the ungodly—but the perturbation occasioned to the poor priest by this unpleasant announcement did not escape the keen eye of the wily Jayme, who shrewdly observed that he hoped his company was not in the least disagreeable.

"Bless me, senor," faltered the trembling priest. "I assure you I feel the greatest happiness in the honour you have been pleased to do me."

"Well said, father; I don't come to confess, and have little time to lose—therefore, to business! you must be aware that I am, sometimes, short a few reals—it unfortunately happens that my exchequer is as empty as your pate, and I must have 2000 reals this night—you can oblige me I know!"

"Holy virgin!" exclaimed the astonished curate, "2,000 reals! why I have not half the number of maravedis in the world!"

"Pho! pho! that won't do, Senor Cura, I want the money, and *must* have it!"

"Heaven bless *Vouestra Senoria*, how should a poor pastor as I am be possessed of 2,000 reals—*Valgame Dios!* 2,000 reals! would to God I had but a simple 200!"

The robber grew impatient—his eyes flashed, and his brows became contracted. These forebodings of an approaching storm did not escape the watery eye of our poor curate, and without waiting for any additional demonstration of Don Jayme's implacability, hurried out of the apartment, and returned with the identical bag which the robber had that morning given to Fernandez. With a trembling hand the padre poured its contents upon the table, which, when told, fell short of 150 reals, protesting, at the same time, that it was all the cash he had in the world.

"Come, Senor Curate, it's growing late, and I am in haste. Return to your closet, and see if you can't make up the difference. If I were not actually in want of this trifle, I pledge my faith that I would not have troubled you for it. *Vaya, Senor Cura*, see what you can do for me!"

"But, my good——"

"No buts or barrels, curate—the reals, and quickly!" and producing a tolerably lengthy knife, he continued—"You have got the sum I want, I know, and if you do not instantly produce it, this little companion of mine will soon discover your hidden treasure."

It was enough—his argument was irresistible, and the 2,000 reals delivered to the ingenious robber.

"So! so! senor padre, you see what a little exertion will bring about. I dare say your coffers contain more than you imagine, and if you were to dip again you might hook another bag or two; but I'll not give you the trouble now."

Then, presenting the curate with one of his choicest cigaras, and cordially pressing his hand, he bade his victim *buenas noches*, with all the air and satisfaction of a man who had achieved a victory over the wealthy to benefit the poor.

What became of Fernandez and the curate's mules we never heard; but Jayme may be seen to this day in the vicinity of Ronda.

TALES OF BRIGANDS

AND BANDITTI.

I Warn & Strike

[NICOLA RESCUES ST. GEORGE FROM THE BANDITTI.]

RED GAUNTLET, THE BANDIT; OR, THE BLACK MOUNTAINEERS.

BOOK I.—THE ARTIST.

CHAPTER XIV.

THE MASQUERADE.—A FIGHT FOR A BRIDE.

An incident beginning so abruptly, and being of such a startling nature, was sufficient to bring a throng of revellers to the spot.

Lulalu trembled on her lover's arm. He stood self-possessed and quiet, as was his wont.

"There is sure to be a fight," said St. George, seeming as if he rather liked the idea. "I wonder why he was rash enough to take his mask off?"

It was a dangerous thing to do, but to the bandit daring deeds were ordinary. He knew no fear.

But for Lulalu he would at once have made an onset on his foe—for her sake he was calm.

A sudden thought came to him, prompting him to set aside by subterfuge the peril he had incurred by recklessness.

"Come," he said, changing his defiant attitude for one of careless grace, "these hostile intents are not suited to a revel. Do I masquerade so well that I am taken for the veritable brigand, or does his highness jest, as I do?"

"This is no masquerade," exclaimed De Marcosi, hastily. "You are the outlaw!"

"Your pardon, duke! When I assumed this character I did not apprehend so grave an error. My friend, the viscount, will tell who I am."

"What is it, Senor Leon?" asked Marriott, approaching. "No quarrel, surely?"

"You call him Senor Leon," said Luali, "and seem to know him. Is he not the outlaw?"

"I call him Senor Leon because that is his name. I know him, as do my friends."

"He has deceived you, then. His face is known to many here."

"I pray you, gentlemen, forgive my jest," said the bandit—"it has been too successful. I might be angry at this reception, but more than once my close resemblance has got me into trouble."

"A resemblance only!" echoed Luali.

"A trick to juggle us," said De Marcosi. "Do not believe him, prince. Do I not know the man who nearly slew me?"

"It seems not, if you mistake me for the Count Adrian. I am simply Leon, a student of the monastery, and pupil of Fra Paulo, a very renowned man."

"Do not listen to him," interposed De Marcosi. "Was he not followed from the cathedral to the Englishman's residence, where he appeared in his true character as the terrible bandit?"

"A fact which simply bears out the serious assertion," said Marriott, coming to the rescue. "It would seem that when the rabble followed the outlaw, they chanced to see Senor Leon returning from his studies. His likeness to the outlaw, who had fled, prompted the mob to pursue him. He took refuge in my house."

"That does not explain his transformation," said De Marcosi.

"That does," said Marriott, pointing to the bandit's costume. "What he did then was done as this is—rather in jest than earnest. The masquerade dress lay in my room, whither Senor Leon had gone, and in a spirit of mischief not uncommon among the students, he put it on to see what the effect would be."

"But when pursued," said the duke, doubtfully, "he had the sword with which I was so nearly slain."

"He picked it up on the way, and was wondering who could have dropped it."

De Marcosi, dubious still, shrugged his shoulders and stepped back.

"When Senor the Viscount Marriott speaks," he said, "there is nothing further to be said."

"Nothing," said Marriott, with dignity. "My explanation is conclusive."

"Quite," said St. George. "Outlaw fellow goes to the cathedral—nearly kills his grace of Marcosi—runs for it—crowd follow—drops his sword and bolts out of sight. Student—strange coincidence—very much like him—sees the sword—picks it up—crowd see him—pursuit—student comes to us, puts masquerade dress on, and scares the rabble—bravo!"

His bravo was an exclamation of admiration for the clever story Marriott had invented to save the outlaw.

Certainly for nothing else than that there was a life at stake would Marriott have told a falsehood; but he and his friends were strongly interested on the bandit's behalf.

Confidence creates confidence, and by a series of singular adventures, the brigand and the English gentlemen had been strangely thrown in each other's way. The chivalry of his act in releasing St. George without the ransom—the romance attached to his name—the story of his outlawry, and the story of his love for Lulalu, combined to win such regard as would not let them see him outnumbered or oppressed.

"I shall watch our masquerader closely," said De Marcosi to himself; and, as though answering his thought, the bandit said:

"The surest proof I can offer is this—were I the outlaw, his grace of Marcosi would be in peril."

He tapped his sword significantly. The duke bowed haughtily, and turned away.

During all this, Lulalu had remained with her lover.

She felt to the full the nature of his peril, and knew that nothing would so soon endanger him as any act of hers that would reveal his identity.

So she was calm, though very pale, and when the peril passed, she said, loud enough for her father and the duke to hear:

"Surely this seeming quarrel was but a masquers' pastime?"

"That is all, sweet lady," and the bandit, replacing his mask, smiled; only, as he smiled he glanced at the duke, and if a smile would have killed, the duke would have fallen dead.

A dance commenced—a beautiful waltz. St. George looked round for a partner.

The figure of the lady in black, who had stood by the silver fountain quite motionless throughout the scene of excitement, caught his eye.

He was about to go towards her, when Dick Nicholson, the man of Grenada, forestalled him.

St. George watched him with a slight feeling of envy. The lady was superb, and St. George liked superb ladies.

St. George, looking round again, felt a light fan touch his elbow. He turned. An Italian peasant girl stood near.

Her form seemed familiar. He had a pleasant, vague sense of having seen her before.

Even the rich swell of her breast and the full contour of her supple limbs were not altogether unrecognised.

"Senora," he said, placing her little olive hand upon his arm, "I am honoured by this choice. We dance?"

The girl shook her head.

Now, as this refusal took from St. George the privilege of putting his arm round her waist, St. George felt sorry.

"The gardens are pleasant," he suggested.

There was a possibility of opening a little flirtation there.

"We have met before," he said.

"Have we?" asked the girl, with a low, merry laugh.

"I could swear it."

"Why?"

"By the beating of my heart," said St. George, fired from his lassitude by the thrill of the glowing hand upon his arm, "for it has never quickened so except at your voice."

"The senor forgets. He does not know me."

"I do," he said, rashly.

"My name, then?"

"It should be Diana. Surely the queen of beauty was not more peerless."

"I cannot call you my Endymion."

"Why?"

"You are more like a pirate than a shepherd."

"Were I a monarch, I would gladly exchange my crown for the crook and pipe of the Latmos shepherd."

"I do not understand."

"The deuce! and I was trying to be classical and complimentary."

Never an ardent votary of the gentle sex, and by no means the man who could enter into the spirit of a revel except in his own lymphatic way, St. George felt rather embarrassed by his companion's simplicity.

"Don't try," he said, leading her into the garden. "I wish you would dance."

"I never dance, senor."

"A wonder—a woman who never dances! This is not your first masquerade?"

"It is indeed, and will be my last."

Such an irrepressible little sigh set her breast quivering that St. George put his arm round her.

"Why your last? You are not going to a nunnery, are you?"

"No, senor."

Another little sigh. It might have been larger but for the pressure of St. George's arm.

"What then?"

"I stole away by stealth to come here."

"Alone?"

"Alone, senor."

"And have no escort to return with?"

"No, senor."

"And have you far to go?"

"To the mountain, senor."

"Nay, you jest."

"Surely, no."

"Then you must permit me to see you out of danger," St. George said, gravely. "You would run some risk in going home alone on the night of a masquerade."

Her last words had rather troubled him. It struck him that she was perhaps some pretty girl who had chosen to fall in love with his handsome self.

St. George hated to be fallen in love with.

So he began to talk quite gravely about the danger she had incurred—the risk to her fair fame, and other things extremely good and moral.

"I knew I should be safe with you," she said in reply—"Senor St. George is a man of honour."

"You know my name!"

"You know mine!"

"If I hear it, and see your face!"

They stopped.

The full moonlight played upon the peasant girl as she raised her mask.

"Nicola!" said St. George.

Happily they were in a secluded place, or the masquers would have seen a very lovely peasant girl clasped close to the breast of a Greek pirate, who was caressing her with more than the licence granted at a masquerade.

They were startled by an exclamation.

St. George, putting Nicola behind him, saw Dick Nicholson and the lady in black.

The lady was unmasked, so was Dick.

"It would be death to follow," St. George heard her say. "Beware the monk!"

And Dick Nicholson, reeling, said:

"Dorolie, the spirit of my dream!"

The lady in black disappeared.

Dick returned to the revel, closely followed by St. George.

Before they reached the banquet-hall the revel was changed to a scene of strife.

During the dance which St. George had left, the bandit had contrived to get near the door with Lulalu, and then, as the music died away, he stopped.

Keeping his arm round her waist, he drew his bugle, and its powerful notes rang through the hall.

Something in his attitude and manner warned the Luali what was coming.

The bugle was replaced, and the bandit, lifting Lulalu to his shoulder, drew his sword.

"Death to those who stay me!" he thundered. "Red Gauntlet will have his bride in spite of all!"

So sudden was this act, that ere anyone could stay him he was outside with Lulalu upon his breast.

It seemed that he must escape, when he found himself confronted by De Mareosi and a party of the guard.

The duke had expected this, and prepared for it.

"Ha!" exclaimed the bandit. "Then I must fight for my bride! What ho! Labian and the Black Mountaineers!"

The cry was answered.

A party of the masqueraders rallied round him, and in an instant a fierce conflict commenced.

"Here!" echoed the voice of Labian in response. "Fight, comrades!—fight for Red Gauntlet and his bride!"

And the brigand horde, who had mingled with the masquers, fought gallantly for their chieftain, who cut his way through the crowd to De Mareosi.

The duke waited for him.

St. George and his companions, pressing forward to watch how the bandit would succeed, saw him strike his foe down, but in the same moment they saw the captain of the guard strike the bandit in the back.

At the same moment, too, and while the bandit staggered, the Prince Luali, dashing to the spot, struck the fallen brigand with his sword, and snatching his daughter up, bore her shrieking to the palace.

Labian saw his chieftain fall. Like a lion the old Corsican battled to his side and cleared the foe away. But he was driven back; and the captain of the guard, setting his sword to the bandit chieftain's heart, said:

"Attempt to rescue, and I kill him! Back!"

A line of glittering pikes, levelled steadily, kept the banditti at bay, and the captain of the guard stood over the brigand.

More soldiers came, and then they took Red Gauntlet captive.

BOOK II.—THE BLACK CHATEAU.

CHAPTER XIII.

THE BLACK CHATEAU.

THOSE two days which were to elapse before Dick Nicholson was to see the spiritual face of his dream, and to mark in reality the black chateau, had passed, or nearly passed, for it was evening when, as Nicholson was seated by himself on the ground floor of the palazzo to which reference has already been made, he was surprised by the sound of broken glass.

He looked up—there could be no doubt about it. One of the stained-glass panes in the window near him was broken into a hole. Naturally looking towards the ground to see what had caused this disaster, and wondering as he did so whether the glass had been fractured by accident or by design, he saw upon the polished marble floor what appeared to be a little lump of crushed paper, but which, upon nearer inspection, turned out to be a stone wrapped about with a piece of thin writing paper—that thin paper which we associate with foreign letters.

"Strange!" said Nicholson.

And as he spoke, he perceived that the paper bore writing.

To read this was the work of a moment, for the communication was far from lengthy. It said:

"If you are brave, and would aid the unfortunate, come to the corner of the square. There you will see a monk. Say 'Bianca,' and if answered 'Nero,' follow him. To ask an Englishman to help one in distress, is to put a question to one who will be sure to answer yes."

Now, was this missive intended for him? There could not be much question about it. He was seated near the window, could be seen from the street, and the paper and stone were obviously thrown with intention.

And the words made his heart beat rapidly, for all that day he had been wondering eagerly—very eagerly for a sensible Englishman—whether the dream, or rather the trance, would be fulfilled.

He did not hesitate.

He got up at once, flung on a slouch hat, and set out without leaving any message or letter—a most reprehensible action, beyond all question.

No one saw him leave the house—no one was near at hand outside the house to mark his departure.

Reaching the corner of the square, he saw a monk, sure enough, standing at the corner, and apparently praying with great earnestness to a little figure of the Virgin Mary, such as the tourist finds at many a continental street corner during his travels.

For a moment he felt disappointment. The man had nothing of the appearance of the monk he had seen in the trance.

The next moment he determined to carry on the adventure.

Approaching the monk, he said:

"Bianca!"

The monk took no notice.

"Bianca!" repeated Dick Nicholson.

Then the monk trembled, and turned towards his questioner.

"My prayers have been heard."

"What prayers?"

"Nero."

Nicholson felt an odd creeping sensation pass over him, for it was indeed strange, just as the time expired when the fulfilment of his trance was to be accomplished, that this extraordinary adventure with a monk should take place.

"Fra," said Nicholson—the word means brother, and is applied to all monks, the term father only being given to priests in orders—"brother, do you want me?"

"By the blessing of heaven—yes!"

"For what?"

"For Christian charity."

"Where?"

"Outside the city walls."

"Far away?"

"Not far."

"Why am I applied to, fra?"

"Because you are an Englishman."

"And why apply to an Englishman?"

"Because those we know here in Italy are always good men."

"Nay—you flatter!"

"Thank heaven—no! Will you, senor, follow me?"

"Do you give me your word that I can be of service?"

"Holy Madonna, I do indeed!"

"Then I will follow you."

"Good—yet first let me put up another prayer to the blessed Madonna for having softened your heart."

"Nay, fra, 'tis not softened."

"Yes, brother, it is, without your knowing it."

The Englishman laughed, and the fra turned away, raised up his eyes, and commenced a very ardent but indistinct prayer, shutting his eyes and shaking his raised hand at intervals.

This edifying business over, the monk opened his eyes, bowed, smiled, and led the way.

"Fra, will you converse?"

No answer.

"Are you forbidden to converse?"

"Senor—yes. I may only lead you."

And thereupon, crossing his arms upon his breast, he half closed his eyes, and appeared again to be praying.

"A queer monk," thought Dick, "and not over good-looking; but there, as so far it has never yet been my luck to see a good-looking monk, why, I suppose the breed is ugly!"

The monk was certainly not handsome—in fact, he looked little better than a scamp; but, as Dick had said to himself, one rarely sees a good-looking monk; it would seem as though the ugly men only took to the sackcloth and ashes.

On the monk went, never saying a word, and continually praying, as it appeared to Dick Nicholson.

"Well," thought the Englishman, as they left the town behind them, "it appears I am to go a long way to help somebody of some kind, who wants something done by somebody! However, here I am, and on I go with the adventure!"

The neighbourhood of Naples is fearfully hilly, and its hills and rocks are of that jagged character, that a few moments' walk will totally change the scene about one.

So therefore the good reader can readily comprehend that in a very short time the Englishman had lost his bearings, and, the sunlight apart, was quite ignorant of the direction in which the city lay.

This went on for about half an hour, under rock and over rock, at the bottom of ravines and at the top of precipices — the monk meanwhile praying with great fervour.

Suddenly he stopped.

They were under a sapling tree, and on the edge of a precipice extremely deep, and only clothed with trees—pines at a depth of about forty feet.

"Well, fra?"

"Signor Englisse, we are here."

"And where is here?"

"Where you are wanted."

"To do what?"

"To help those who want help."

Now, when an English gentleman is brought to an outlandish spot, in the middle of a rocky forest, under the pretence of helping somebody about some matter of which he knows nothing, and finds himself by himself, but for his guide, why, naturally he becomes suspicious.

Nicholson's eyes were also good, and suddenly he saw the "fra" with a whistle in his hand.

To make sure of this, he quickly jerked the holy man's arm, and away flew a whistle some yards away.

"A thousand maledictions!" cries the fra.

"No monk, but a decoy!" yells Nicholson.

And with a bound he was upon his prayerful brother, kicking, as he did so, the betraying whistle over the edge of the precipice.

The monk was ready for his opponent, as far as two muscular arms went, but he found in a moment that the Englishman had a grip of iron.

"This is a new style of prayer, fra!"

"Cursed Englishman!"

"You shall have cause to curse me before I have done with you!"

"Infamous heretic!"

"Ha, I've no doubt you're a good catholic!"

"I will cast you over the precipice!"

"If you can."

"Pig!" screams the false monk.

Now, these words had passed rapidly, and while they were grasping each other's arms and clothes and attempting to seize each the throat of the other.

"Oh, if I had but my good dagger!" screams the monk.

"A fra with a dagger?" cried Nicholson. "Why, one might as soon expect to meet a little nun carrying home a cradle!"

"Cursed Englishman—let me go!"

"What—over the precipice?"

"No—unhand me!"

"Well, I don't think it an honour to hold a man of your kidney—but I sha'n't unhand you."

"At your peril, let me go!"

"Steady—what, beginning to jerk, are you? Steady!"

Here the monk became very violent in the efforts to loose himself, and failing, tried to whistle.

"Ha, my friend, you can't whistle without help!"

"I will have you cut in strips!"

"Thanks—should object to that sort of thing more than a little. Now kindly let me know why you enticed me out here."

"I will not tell you."

"I shall ask that question three times."

"And what if I don't answer?"

"Why, I shall send you quick to the devil, to see what he has got to say to you—I should say a very great deal!"

"I'll bite on to you—but you shall fall with me!"

"Quite welcome—but hope you use a tooth-brush. Second time—why am I brought here?"

"I would have you torn limb from limb!"

"If you could get your own limbs free. There's such a difference between what we want and what we get—as the lady said who tried to get a husband, and got run over instead."

"Northern pig!" screamed the Neapolitan—for whenever

a South Italian wants to insult you very much indeed, he always calls you a pig, instanter.

"Third time—why here?"

"No."

"Give you one in fourth time—why here?"

"No."

"Then over you go!"

"I'll bite on!"

"Do—and scratch in too, if you can! No, you can't, for I see you've been angry, and bit all your nails down, you beauty!"

The answer was a scream.

Now, during this conversation between the antagonists, each had cleverly been striving, by sheer dint of contraction of the muscles, to overpower the other; but this is a faculty, being one of endurance, in which the Englishman is more at home than any other man.

"One!" says the Englishman.

And nearer the precipice they went.

"Two!" says the Englishman.

And then both could see the tips of the pines waving in the breeze of the coming evening.

"Three!" says the Englishman.

And, according to a proper calculation, over the false monk would have gone—down to the bottom certainly. Whether he would have continued the journey further downward, according to the Englishman's recommendation, we cannot say.

But even Englishmen are not prepared for all chances, and the mishap of stumbling over a bit of rock, and pitching forward the way Nicholson was about to send his enemy, was a mishap for which Dick was not prepared.

A moment, and the opponents would have taken their chances of death—nay, their almost certainties of death,—together.

But Nicholson, in a moment, released his left hand, flung it back and above him, and caught a branch of the half-rotted pine tree leaning partially over the precipice.

"Great Jove!" muttered the Englishman, as he heard a cracking.

He dared not look back, but by the feeling, and judging by the horror-stricken Italian's eyes, he saw what was happening.

The catch at the branch had been quite successful, but the forward force of the two men had been so great that the branch had rent partially away from the trunk, and now it was gradually peeling away under the great weight, and must in a few moments part from the tree.

This peeling, snapping, broken branch stood between these two men and a terrific fall.

What could be done?

The Italian had now the advantage of two hands as compared with the Englishman's one, but he dared not follow up that advantage, for only one foot was on the rock, and the other swinging in mid-air. Any movement on his part would cause the branch at once to part. To struggle, therefore, would be to commit suicide.

And as the Italian saw the parting of the branch, a seen danger being so much more terrible than when it is only known to be present and not seen, his face began to blanch, and he began to tremble.

"My great heaven!" thought Nicholson—"am I safe?—will he tremble until he falls, and so leave me alone, and hanging to this branch?"

Strange! Neither man a moment before feared the chance for one or the other of instant death; but the moment imminent death overtook them both in a fearful form, both men were horror-stricken.

All this occurred in a few moments.

What was to be done?

Questionable, Nicholson felt it would be, whether he could raise the man by the most careful management; but he had no idea of attempting such a manoeuvre. He knew the bad side of the Italian character sufficiently to be aware that it never pardons. He felt that if he gave the man his life he would only attempt his again, or his liberty. A bad Italian cannot be noble—he has no chivalry in his composition.

Either the false monk must tremble till he fell from very weakness into the yawning gulf, or they must both go over together.

This was Nicholson's first determination.

But he felt that perhaps he ought to give this rascal a chance.

Mark, all this was the work of a few moments.

"Scamp," said he, "here is a chance for your life: Why did you decoy me to this place? Tell me, and I will save you if I can."

"I must die whether or no; and this at least gives me vengeance upon you! I will not tell you—never!"

Then, with a scream from the Italian, they were swiftly cutting through the air, for as the Italian uttered the word "Never!" he jerked the tree, the branch parted, and the enemies were swiftly ploughing the blue southern atmosphere.

And during that swift journey, of what did our countryman think?

Some may say that he could not think at such a moment, and that if we said that he did, it would appear as great a parody as that of the Scotchman who, falling from the garret of a six-storeyed house in Edinburgh town, said, as he passed a fellow-occupant sitting at the window of the third floor: "Hey, Sandy—sic a fall as I shall hae!"

But it is a fact that in moments of great danger we are able in a few moments to concentrate the thoughts of hours. No man or woman can be devoid of this experience.

So it was with Nicholson.

As he felt himself falling, his thought was, "I'll try the trapeze dodge."

Fortunately for him, he had at home, in London, belonged to one of those gymnastic societies where is taught, amongst other matters, the power to catch at a bar with the hand while falling.

This ability now saved Nicholson's life.

He remembered the pines, and was prepared to catch at some one of their branches.

A jerk, a wrench, and he was safe, landed in the midst of the upper branches of a huge pine.

He smarted and ached, for the jar to the system was horrible, but he felt no pain for the first few moments, his whole comprehension being engrossed in hearing the sickly crashing of the falling body of the false monk wrenching its way downward, and then thud, thudding from rock to rock on its way to the valley below.

"Saved!" said Nicholson.

He had fallen about forty feet. He looked up.

No chance of reaching the brow of the ravine.

Forty feet of sheer rock. Then he looked below him.

The very tree upon which he was half hanging and half seated was thirty feet from the ground, while below it there appeared to stretch away, in a fierce downward expanse, fields of pines, the sharp peaks of which appeared to be pointing at and mocking him.

All he said was:

"Here goes!"

And "here" he went.

To a man unaccustomed to gymnastic exercises, the descent could never have been made.

Happily for him, this descent was not a work of insurmountable danger.

At last he stood upon level ground—or comparatively level ground.

Then he looked about him.

Suddenly he started.

There—far away as his eye could reach—there was the Black Chateau of his dreams—the building wherein he felt sure he was to meet Dorolie.

Then he felt himself reel.

The shock of the fall, the terrible labour of his descent, and now this wonderful discovery, were all too much for him, and, exhausted nature announcing her sway over his weakened frame and mind, he fell prone to the earth, and there lay senseless, while nature recovered his strength and will to carry on this adventure.

(*To be continued in our next.*)

MARCO SCIARRA, THE ROBBER OF THE ABRUZZI.

"Of no avail," says the excellent Neapolitan historian Giannone, "was the horrid spectacle of the tortures and death of the chief Mangone; for very shortly after the kingdom was disturbed by the incursions of the famous Marco Sciarra, who, imitating Marcone of Calabria, called himself "*Re della Campagna*," or "King of the Open Country," and asserted his Royal prerogative at the head of six hundred robbers."

Favoured by his position in the mountains of the Abruzzi, and on the confines of another government—the Papal States, which for many years have been the promised land of brigandism—this extraordinary robber obtained the highest eminence in his profession. His band, so formidable in itself, always acted in concert with other bands of banditti in the Roman States; they aided each other by arms and counsel; and in case of the Romans being pressed on their side, they could always retreat across the frontier line to their allies in the Abruzzo, while, in the same predicament, the Abruzzese could claim the hospitality of the worthy subjects of the Pope.

The same circumstances have strengthened the banditti in our own days, and rendered the country between Terracina and Fondi, or the frontiers of the Papal States and the Kingdom of Naples, the most notorious district of all Italy for robbers.

But Marco Sciarra was moreover favoured by other circumstances, and he had the grasp of mind to comprehend their importance, to avail himself of them, and to raise himself to the grade of a political partisan—perhaps he aimed at that of a patriot.

His native country was in the hands of foreigners and despotically governed by Viceroys from Spain, who were generally detested by the people, and frequently plotted against by some of the nobility, who, instead of assisting to put down the *fuorusciti*, would afford them countenance and protection, when required, in their vast and remote estates.

A great part of the rest of Italy was almost as badly governed as the kingdom, and consequently full of malcontents, of men of desperate fortunes, who, in many instances, forwarded the operations of the robbers, and not unfrequently joined their bands.

An accession like theirs added intelligence, military skill, and political knowledge, to the cause of the rude mountaineers of the Abruzzi.

In the course of a few months after the death of Benedetto Mangone, Marco Sciarra had committed some ravages, and made himself so formidable, that the whole care of the Government was absorbed by him, and every means in its power employed for his destruction.

In the spring of 1588, he had retreated with his band, before a force of Government troops, into the States of the Church, which the Vice-Royalists could not invade without the permission of the Pope.

In the month of April, the Viceroy, Don Giovan di Zunica Conte di Miranda, applied to the Holy See for an immediate renewal of an old *concordate*, by which the commissaries and the troops of either government were authorised to have free ingress and egress in the Neapolitan Kingdom and the Papal States, to pursue robbers, crossing the respective frontiers as often as might be necessary, and by which the two States were pledged reciprocally to aid each other in the laudable duty of suppressing all bandits and bad livers (*mal viventi*).

The Pope, Sixtus VI., complied with this reasonable request by granting a Breve for three months.

Immediately the troops of the Viceroy Miranda crossed the frontiers in pursuit of Sciarra, who, being properly informed by numerous friends and spies of all that passed, turned back into the kingdom about the same time that his enemies quitted it; and avoiding the pass of Antrodoro, where the Spaniards were in force, he went through the defile of Tagliacozzi, and was soon safe in the mountain solitudes that surround the beautiful lake of Celano.

The robber had the sympathies of all the peasantry on his side, and found friends and guides everywhere.

Not so the Spanish commander in pursuit of him, who did not learn whereabout he was until several days after, when some fugitive soldiers brought him word that Marco Sciarra was in the kingdom, and had just sacked the town of Celano, cutting to pieces a detachment of troops that had arrived there.

The Spaniard then recrossed the frontier of the kingdom, but nearly a whole day before he reached the country about Celano, Sciarra was again beyond the borders.

He had now, however, considerable difficulties to encounter.

The officer had left a body of bold men behind him in the Papal States, and these had been joined by several commissaries of the Pope, who each led a number soldiers, and carried with him his Holiness's command to the faithful, not to harbour, but to assist to take the Neapolitan banditti wherever they might be.

Sciarra had not expected so formidable an array on the side of Rome against him; he was several times hard pressed by the troops, but the peasantry, spite of the injunctions of the successor of Saint Peter, still continued his faithful friends.

The historians who relate these events especially record that wherever he went the robber was kind in conversation, and generous in action with the poor, giving, but never taking from them; and paying for whatever his band took with much more regularity than did the officers of the Spanish troops.

Consequently he was advised by some peasant or other of the approach of every foe, of every ambuscade of the troops, of every movement they made; and he finally escaped them all, keeping two forces, which might almost be called armies, at bay—the one on the Roman confine, the other on the Neapolitan—for more than a week.

He then threw himself back on the mountains of Abruzzi, where by keeping himself in the most inaccessible places, with his men scattered in the most opportune spots, and regular sentinels stationed and guards distributed, he had invariably the advantage over the enemy.

Indeed, whenever the troops mustered courage to approach his strongholds, which he was in the habit of changing frequently, they were sure to return considerably diminished in number, and without the satisfaction, not only of killing, but even of seeing one of the robbers whose arquebuses from behind rocks or the shelter of forests and thickets had so sure an aim.

Six months passed—the soldiers were worn out.

The Spanish officer, who first led them on the useless hunt, was dead in consequence of a wound received from the robbers.

Winter approached, which is felt in all its rigour on the lofty bleak mountains of the Abruzzi; the commissaries, with their men on the other side, had long since returned to their homes at Rome; and the Viceroy's people now went to theirs at Naples.

After these transactions, Marco Sciarra was deemed all but invincible; his fame sung in some dozen of ballads, strengthened his *prestige* in the eyes of the peasantry; his band was reinforced, and he was left to reign a king, at least of the Abruzzi, and undisturbed for many months.

It was about this time that the robber-chief's life was ornamented with its brightest episode.

Marco and his merry men had come suddenly on a company of travellers on the road between Rome and Naples.

The robbers had begun to plunder, and had cut the saddle-girths of the mules and horses of the travellers, who had speedily obeyed the robbers' order, and lay flat on the earth, all save one, a man of striking and elegant appearance.

"Faccia in terra!" cried several robbers in the same breath, but the bold man, heedless of their menaces, only stepped up to Marco, their chief, and said, "I am Torquato Tasso."

"The poet!" said the robber, and he dropped on his knee, and kissed his hand; and not only was Tasso saved from being plundered by the mere mention of his name, but all those who were travelling with him were permitted to mount their horses and continue their journey without sustaining the loss of a single scudo.

A very curious proof this, that a captain of banditti could form a juster and more generous notion of what was due to the immortal, but then unfortunate poet, than could princes of royal or imperial lineage.

The Viceroy was stung to the quick by the failure of his expedition, of whose success he had been so certain, that the Court of Spain was given to understand their kingdom of Naples had nothing more to fear from the incursions of banditti; that the head of Marco Sciarra would soon decorate one of the niches in the Capuan gate.

But Miranda was a man of energy, and in 1590 he renewed his attempt to exterminate the robbers.

Four thousand men, between infantry and cavalry, marched this time into the Abruzzi, under the command of Don Carlo Spinelli.

As the Abruzzese peasantry saw this formidable army enter their pastoral districts by Castel di Sangro, and traverse the mountain flat, "the plain of five miles," they whispered, "The will of God be done! but now it is all over with King Marco!"

Marco Sciarra, however, had no such fears, but came boldly on to an open battle.

With his increased forces he threw himself upon Spinelli in the midst of the Viceroy's troops, which were presently disordered; he wounded with his own hand the proud Don, who turned and fled, but so severely wounded, that he was well-nigh leaving his life in the mountains whither he had gone to take that of Sciarra.

The soldiers followed their commander as best as they could, leaving the robbers the full triumph of the field.

Marco Sciarra's courage and audacity were now increased a hundredfold.

He fancied he could conquer a kingdom; he invaded other provinces, and marching across the mountains of the Abruzzi, he traversed those of the Capitanata, sacking, without meeting with opposition, the towns of Serra Capriola and Vasto.

Nor did he stop here, for he descended into the vast plain of Apulia, and took and pillaged the city of Lucera, a very considerable place, situated near the edge of the plain.

The Bishop of Lucera, who fled for refuge to one of the church towers, was unfortunately shot as he presented himself at a window or loophole to see what was passing.

Without being molested by any attack of the government troops, Marco Sciarra's band leisurely returned from this extensive predatory excursion, loaded with booty, to their Abruzzi mountains, which overlooked Rome, where their enterprising chief renewed his league with the banditti in the States of the Pope, and encouraged them by the flattering picture of his splendid successes. But he had allies more important and dignified than these.

The politics of states now became mixed up with his fate.

Alfonso Piccolomini, a nobleman by birth, but one of the many desperate revolutionists Italy has been fertile in the production of—a rebel to his Sovereign the Grand Duke of Tuscany—had fled Venice, where he obtained service as a soldier of fortune in the army with which that Republic was then waging war with the Uscocchi.

This man was enchanted with the stand Sciarra had made against the Pope and the Viceroy, neither of whom, at the time, was in good odour at Venice; and he induced the crafty senators to wink at his corresponding with and favouring the bold Abruzzese, if he did not even do more, and (working on their jealousies of the power of the Spaniards and of the Pope in Italy) persuade them to assist the outlaw themselves with money and arms.

Marco Sciarra was every day gaining importance and strength by these manœuvres, when a curious change took place.

Here I entreat attention to the vindictive feelings, the utter want of principle, of decency, that marked the proceedings of princes and potentates in Italy in those days.

The Grand Duke of Tuscany, entertaining the most revengeful feelings against his rebel subject, made it a matter of embassy and degrading supplication to the Venetians that they would not only dismiss from their service, but drive out from their states, Alfonso Piccolomini.

But Piccolomini, it was replied, was a man of talent, and as a soldier they were well satisfied with his services.

Marco Sciarra, the Abruzzese (he did not blush to propose a brigand!) was a better man of the two to carry on their wars against the Uscocchi, rejoined the Duke, who did all he could to make them substitute him for Piccolomini.

The Venetians, however, turned a deaf ear to these representations, and the Tuscan refugee could defy the wrath of his sovereign as long as he enjoyed their protection. But in an evil hour Piccolomini returned a haughty, if not an insulting answer to the Capi or heads of that mysterious, sanguinary government.

The Senators of Venice were almost as vindictive as the Duke of Tuscany; they dismissed him from their service and drove him out of their states, when he fell into the snares laid for him by his own sovereign, who put him to a violent death.

The Oligarchy of Venice then thought of Sciarra, and sent to invite him to their service.

He was to prosecute the war against the Uscocchi. But Sciarra, for the present, turned as deaf an ear to their proposals as they had at first done to that of the Grand Duke's, and remained where he was—the lord of the Abruzzi.

He was not long, however, in finding that in the death of Piccolomini, who had so materially assisted him, he had sustained a severe loss, and Sciarra's fortunes were still more overcast when Pope Sixtus died and was succeeded by a better or more active pontiff, Clement VIII.

The new Pope shared all the feelings of the Viceroy of Naples, as far as regarded the banditti, whom he determined to extirpate in his states.

To this end he despatched Gianfrancesco Aldobrandini against them, with a permanent commission.

By a simultaneous movement, a large body of the Viceroy's troops entered the Abruzzi.

The command of this, with absolute power, was given to Don Adriano Acquaviva, Count of Conversano, a nobleman of courage and very admirable prudence.

The first thing he attempted, and without which little indeed could be done in that wild country of mountains and forests, was to conciliate the affections of the peasantry, who had been so insulted and oppressed by all his stupid predecessors in office, and the soldiery, that they could not but wish well to their enemies, the robbers.

The Count, therefore, abstained from quartering his troops in the villages; he imitated the conduct of Sciarra, and made them pay for whatever they consumed; he listened to the complaints of the aggrieved, and at last he so gained on the affections and better principles of the peasants, that they conspired with him for the extermination of the very banditti whom they had so often guided and concealed.

With them as guides, the soldiery had now a key to the mysteries and recesses of the mountains and forests.

Thus deprived of the protection of Piccolomini, pressed by Aldobrandini on the one side and by Conversano on the other, Marco Sciarra was fain to reflect on the tender made to him by the Venetian Senators, and finally to accept the rank and service they offered him.

They must still have thought him and those he could bring with him well worth having, for they despatched two galleys of the Republic for their conveyance.

In these ships Marco Sciarra embarked with sixty of his bravest and most attached followers, and, turning his back on his native mountains, sailed up the Adriatic to Venice.

As soon as the Count of Conversano was informed of the robber-chief's departure, he blessed his stars that the kingdom was quit of so dangerous a subject, and, thinking now his business was over, returned to Naples, where the Viceroy received him in triumph.

But the expatriating bandit left a brother behind him in the mountains of the Abruzzi; and Luca Sciarra in due time gathered together the scattered bands and commenced operations anew with considerable vigour.

Meanwhile, Marco and his men, who in their quality of subsidiaries served the Venetian Republic very much to its satisfaction, corresponded with their former comrades at home.

Marco's glory could not be forgotten.

The soul of their body was at Venice—everything of importance was fomented by him, and he frequently employed his "leaves of absence" in visiting them, and leading them, as of yore, in the more hazardous of their enterprises.

He had now been heard of so long—his deeds had been so desperate but successful, he had escaped so many dangers, that people concluded he must bear "a charmed life."

His long impunity might almost have made him think so himself, when, landing one day in the marches of Ancona, between the mountains of the Abruzzi and that town, where the Pope's Commissary Aldobrandini still remained, he was met by a certain Battimello, to whom, as to an old follower, his heart warmed;—with open arms he rushed to embrace him, and received a traitor's dagger in that heart.

Battimello had sold himself to Aldobrandini, and received for himself, and thirteen of his friends, a free pardon from the Papal Government for his treachery.

For some years after the death of Marco Sciarra, there was a pause in his profession, whose spirit had expired with him.

Other times brought other robbers, but his fame has scarcely ever been equalled—never surpassed.

FRANCATRIPA.

——o——

From the details, concerning the Calabrian banditti, of our countryman, who was only accidentally a passive eye-witness, or brought near the scenes of their exploits, I must beg the reader's attention to details still more interesting, to adventures wilder and more extensive, which I have gathered from a French source—i. e. from "Lettres sur les Calabres, par un Officier Francais." *

The author of this valuable little volume was no less than three years in the country he describes.

He had not been three days before he found the whole of a French soldier's business there to be a chase after robbers; and, indeed, with a few short intervals of repose, the whole of the three years was spent in hunting brigands.

The first brigand chief he came in contact with near Rogliano, about five leagues from Cosenza, was Francatripa—a man eminent in his way and the terror of the whole country.

When closely pressed, this robber was accustomed to retire for awhile to a great distance from the scene of his murderous depredations; but as soon as pursuit was over, he suddenly re-appeared and again carried desolation through the province.

By placing himself upon the heights that commanded the usual lines of communication, he constantly harassed the French couriers, in order to get possession of their despatches, which he sent off to Sicily.

His presence kept the troops in a state of perpetual exertion, the more painful, because it was generally attended with no advantageous results.

A company of French voltigeurs, of the twenty-ninth regiment of the line, had to cross the high mountains of the Syla to proceed from Catanzaro to Cosenza.

This company lost its way, and in an evil spot, for it was near the village called Gli Parenti, a favourite haunt of the brigands, who shared their plunder with its inhabitants; and Francatripa himself was there.

Fearing to engage the French openly, the atrocious mountaineer had recourse to an odious stratagem.

Meeting the company before it entered the village, he represented himself as the commander of the militia, and said

* This excellent work has been lately published in London, under the title of " Calabria during a Military Residence of Three Years "

he came on the part of the commune or village to offer refreshments to the troops.

The officers, ignorant of the country, accepted the invitation without distrust, and suffered themselves to be conducted by him to a large mansion, where confiding in the feigned cordiality of their perfidious hosts, they were improvident enough to cause the arms of the troops to be piled on the ground in front of the door.

To inspire the soldiers with a still greater sense of security, Francatripa and his villanous associates pressed them to take with them refreshments for the march; and just at the moment they were preparing to resign themselves to repose, a pistol-shot fired from a window was the signal for a general massacre.

The three officers, seated together in the saloon, were instantly despatched.

A shower of balls from the adjacent houses and from every approach to the spot left no point of retreat open to those unfortunate soldiers, of whom not more than seven succeeded in making their escape.

The French, never backward in avenging atrocity with atrocity, immediately sent off a strong detachment, with orders to burn the village of Gli Parenti to the ground, and to put every soul found within it to the sword.

They found, however, nothing but empty houses, which became a prey to the flames, the reflection of which, far spreading across the mountains where its inhabitants had taken refuge, suggested new feelings of maddening hate and revenge on the part of the Calabrians.

Not long after, the author of the letters was informed that the scouts of Francatripa had made their appearance in the neighbourhood of his quarters at Rogliano, and, at night, that the captain himself and all his *commitiva*, or band, had lodged themselves among the ruins of their native village, Gli Parenti.

"The French commandant instantly determined to take the brigands by surprise, and we set off, about eight o'clock at night, with a detachment of a hundred and twenty men, and two confidential guides.

"Gli Parenti, situated four leagues from Rogliano, is separated from the latter place by a deep ravine, through which flows a torrent that is always much swollen at this season of the year.

("It was on the 28th December).

"To avoid passing near the village, it was necessary to take a great round, and occupy a certain part of a forest, through which the brigands might endeavour to escape.

"This movement was seconded by a company of the battalion, which had received orders to take up a position by six o'clock in the morning within a short distance of Gli Parenti, and guard all the outlets on that side.

"The dawn of day was the moment fixed upon for making a sudden and unexpected attack, from which a successful result was confidently anticipated.

"A cold, but very bright night favoured the march of the detachment, which followed a beaten track in the middle of a wood, but on quitting it to approach the ravine we experienced considerable difficulty in passing through some very thick underwood, where every object was immersed in darkness.

"Before daylight we came to a hill, at the foot of which Gli Parenti is situated.

"Some musket-shots fired from the opposite side led us to imagine that the attack was commenced in that quarter.

"Accordingly we marched in quick-time, and with the more ardour, as we hoped to surprise the notorious bandit, and destroy his horde.

"But he had made his escape by three in the morning, thus baffling all our projects.

"The shots which had seemed to announce the presence of Francatripa, were fired at some peasants whom our soldiers took for brigands.

"One of these peasants, or brigands—terms which in this country are nearly synonymous—being wounded in the leg, and fearing our men intended to put him to death, discovered the magazine of provisions on condition of his life being spared."

TALES OF BRIGANDS

AND BANDITTI.

[DICK NICHOLSON RECOGNISES THE LADY IN BLACK.]

RED GAUNTLET, THE BANDIT; OR, THE BLACK MOUNTAINEERS.

BOOK II.—THE BLACK CHATEAU.

CHAPTER XV.

THE BLACK CHATEAU.

LET us now enter the Black Chateau.

All was very peaceful and quiet. The building was in the shape of a square, having in its centre a square opening, surrounded by arched cloisters.

Dotting this square opening were many tombstones; no name upon either of them, but each marked with a cross. Some of these crosses were upright, but many more had sunk on one side, appearing as though they wished to creep into the ground, and be at rest with the sleeping body beneath.

It was now even-time, and, hark! a quiet, tinkling bell, crying, as plainly as any mere bell can:

"Come to pray—come to pray!"

Then quiet, slow footsteps; and if you look into the cloisters, you will see shoals of monks, with clasped hands and bent heads, slowly moving on to a certain door.

Not one took any notice of the other—each man might have been totally alone for all the evidence he showed of being aware that he was not alone.

They chiefly appeared to be strong and healthy men, in the full vigour of life; but there were some aged and weary men amongst them, already stooping towards the ground, as though they courted death and burial.

What a peaceful scene!

A quiet old monastery, with the monks trooping to the old chapel, there to say their vesper prayers.

Meanwhile, let us go to the room of the abbot.

He was a powerful-looking man, and by no means unhandsome, if be excepted a certain squareness of jaw, which did not add to his fine appearance by any means.

He was clothed alone in the serge sack-like habit which monks wear as their sole attire, for they wear nought else, winter or summer, beyond this serge robe.

He had thrown open this dress, and it was to be seen that his hairy throat and breast betokened great, giant-like strength, which accorded well with the fierce determination of the face.

Before him stood a monk, with folded hands and meek expression of countenance.

The following conversation passed between them:

"Have all my orders been obeyed, my son?"

"They have, holy father."

"Have means been taken to secure, sooner or later, these rich Englishmen?"

"Yes, holy father."

"When?"

"One to-night."

"By whom?"

"Brother Anselmo, holy father."

"Send the Brother Anselmo to me."

"He has not yet returned to the monastery, holy father."

"When he does, let me see him. Where is the Englishman to be taken?"

"At the top of the cliff, holy father."

"Good, my son. Inform the brotherhood that all things go well. We have amassed large sums of money, and are amassing more each day. Soon—very soon—the land will be once more wrested from the power of the friends of the hated Garibaldi."

The monk bowed.

"Leave the room, my son."

Again the monk bowed.

Left to himself, the holy father placed his head in his hand, and so remained for some time.

Had any watchful eyes been there, they might or might not have seen the quaint head of the carving of some fantastic being upon the wall assume a kind of life which it had not possessed before. And had the watchful eyes regarded more closely, they would have discovered that this change in the face was due to the fact that the hollow eyes of the quaint statue were filled with watchful sight.

The abbot was being watched.

For some time he was motionless.

Meanwhile the bell had ceased tolling to prayer, and the noble sound of the organ had replaced it.

Never once moved the abbot.

Nor did he start or change his position when the chanting of the evening service began.

Yet suddenly he moved as the words came upon him—"Blessed are the dead—if they be holy—blessed, thrice blessed are the dead."

"To die," he murmured—"to be at peace!"

Then he paused. Then followed these sentences:

"Shall I let her sleep? Dare I awake her? Dare I refrain from awaking her? To sleep—to be at peace! I love her! She sleeps! She is at peace, yet she must be awakened! No, I dare not die! Yet if I live, she must! I would that I were stricken dead!"

Then he waited, as though he anticipated the fulfilment of his will.

Then he spoke again.

"She must be awakened!" he said.

He goes to the door, and listens.

He starts—'tis but his own heart beating with fear.

Then slowly he went to another part of the room, raised a hanging, touched a secret spring—a huge stone moved, and discovered a passage.

Into this he passed, still watched by the eager eyes set in the carved figure on the wall. The stone rolled back, and again the quaint carved face on the wall became blind as the dark watchful eyes left the stone orbits.

Then the room was deserted.

CHAPTER XVI.
THE TRANCE PARTIALLY FULFILLED.

WHEN Nicholson came to himself again, he staggered to his feet.

All was dark.

But a something told him that he had but to run forward, and he should reach his destiny—the Black Chateau.

On, then, he went, and his instinct did not betray him, for lo! after a time, still moving on in the darkness, his outstretched hand touched something before him—a smooth, polished surface.

He knew it was the Black Chateau.

And as though the bright goddess of the night was determined to help him to a confirmation of this hope, the moonbeams broke out, and behold! his eyes fell on the black marble surface of the walls.

"It is here!" he said.

And now looking up, he saw a faint light streaming from a window about thirty feet from the ground.

"She's there!" he murmured.

And he had no doubt on this point.

But how was he to reach the room?

Oh—will, and pluck, and energy will carry a man through almost anything.

By the light of the moon, he saw that a clump of trees grew near the wall against which he was standing, but none of their branches touched the building.

For a moment he was baffled.

The next he knew what to do.

Up the nearest tree he climbed—an easy matter to him, who could go hand-over-hand up a rope sixty feet as it hung.

He therefore soon reached the level of the window, and peered in.

And by the light of several wax candles, he saw that his dream, or trance, was realised.

For a moment he was so giddy that he felt as though he were about to fall.

He was about six feet from the window, the air blowing freely between him and the unbarred window level with his eyes—the wind that whistled and hissed in the branches as though it was mocking him.

This is what he saw.

On a bier in the centre of the room lay a female form clothed in pure white—her form.

About the quiet dead several wax candles burnt, and at the summit of the bier stood a huge crucifix of deadened silver.

Ha! a man enters.

The man of the trance.

There was the monk's habit, and there as it opened in front, owing to the man's movement, he marked that the man was beautifully dressed.

He knew what was to happen, and therefore he took his measures.

He did this. You know if you climb up a thin pole it will heel over with you. Well, so will the branch of a tree.

Up he went, caught his branch, made it heel over with his weight, and so it stooped down to the window-ledge, which grasping, away flew the branch off to its place, leaving Nicholson forty feet from the ground, and clinging to the carved work of the window-sill.

He could not now retreat.

His only action was to enter the room.

Nor did he long hesitate on this point.

He saw the subtle-looking villain dressed in a monk's cloak over divers colours—he saw him pour the essence of the trance between the lips of the apparently dead woman, and, as the quiet form moved, sat up, and as the evil-looking yet handsome man cried, "Mine—mine at last!" Nicholson crashed in the window and leaped into the room.

"Hold!" he cried.

Then followed a brief but decisive struggle.

A moment, and the abbot had torn a knife from under his monkish garb, and had rushed at his unlooked-for assailant.

What was he to do?

He was quite unarmed. His assailant held sharp steel.

But his ready right hand again stood him in good need, for it encountered the heavy silver crucifix, weighing about twenty pounds, and in a moment it was being wielded in his arms—it, the emblem of peace, a formidable weapon directed at the abbot's head.

The struggle was soon ended.

Could the abbot's knife have reached the young Englishman's breast, his friends in Naples would have heard no more of him; but the cross is longer than any knife—Italian or otherwise; and before the abbot could reach him, one of the arms of the holy emblem had buried itself in the abbot's right temple, and he fell to the ground weltering in blood and vanquished in the very moment of his supposed victory.

He had very carefully looked after the door.

He had not thought of the windows.

"'Tis he!" cried the fair creature he had saved.

She was clothed in grave-clothes, and about her lovely face was wrapped that hideous linen band which distinguishes some sects of nuns.

"Dorolie!"

"I am Dorolie!"

"And what will you call me?"

"Deliverer!"

"Who are you?"

"I am the daughter of a patrician."

"And why do I find you here?"

"The tale is too long to tell here! Ha—he has moved!" And she pointed to the abbot.

"No; he is still."

"Is he dead?"

"No, senseless."

"What is to be done?"

"I will fly with you from this place, dear Dorolie!"

"Fly—how?"

"Nay, I would beat down whole hordes of monks!"

"Monks? Here there are no monks!"

"What are they?"

"Brigands."

"Brigands?"

"Yes, the most desperate band of brigands in Italy. This much I have found out."

"And who is he?"

And he pointed to the senseless man upon the ground.

"Their leader."

"Their leader? And I have not killed him! Dear me! I am not so useful to society as I thought I was!"

"He is not fit to live!"

"Doubtless not; but I cannot kill him while he is on the flat of his back, and while he is senseless."

"True, for you are a noble-hearted man, yet he were well dead!"

"And is the whole place a nest of brigands?"

"Yes."

"How came you to know that?" asked Nicholson, suspiciously. He was already playing the part of a jealous lover.

"I was forced to learn it."

"How?"

"Have you a right to ask me that question?"

"I saved your life!"

"True—I will tell you!"

"I listen."

"I will tell you—not who I am—yet—but——"

"But?"

"I am willing to fly with you, for I believe such to be my destiny!"

"Perhaps. How know you this man a brigand?"

"I repeat I will not say who I am; but this much you must know—I was placed in a convent on the other side of the hill which adjoins this monastery—the Black Chateau, as it is called. The nunnery is called the White Chateau."

"Go on, Lady Dorolie!"

"Having entered the convent, I learnt——"

"Have no fear—I hear patiently!"

"That the body of nuns were infamous."

"How so?"

"There is a gallery leading under the rock, and——"

"Enough! You need tell me no more, lady!"

"Yes, I need tell you this—that I learnt with horror what kind of place it was into which I had been thrust, and fought with all my power against it!"

"Brave woman!"

"But need I tell you that when once a nun has passed the wall of her convent and taken her vows, she is dead to the outer world—her cries are not heard, and her life is lost,—for good or for evil, the convent is her blessing or her curse?"

"Say not blessing, lady, when a woman closes upon her heart all the great and rapturous joys to which woman is born!"

"Right, good signor—doubtless you are right!"

"Nay, has not destiny protested against your incarceration?"

"Let me tell you, senor, that I did not seek to enter the convent—I was forced!"

"By whom?"

"By my father."

"Wherefore?"

"Wherefore! You do not know the land in which you find yourself. Here too often a proud father casts us into a convent to hide his poverty,—he cannot afford to give his daughter a fitting dowry, and she is therefore buried in a convent."

"But I thought a nun was received into her convent only with money."

"True; but the family of a poor lady will always subscribe to get her out of the way into a convent, while they will not pay to gain her a dowry."

"Why so? Why not give for one as well as the other?"

"Because the marriage of the young and poor lady would not reflect so much honour upon her relations as her entry into a convent."

"So they sacrifice her to their vanity?"

"Too often."

"And cannot the young lady protest?"

"Only to heaven!"

"Poor things!"

"And heaven, hearing them, takes them to its breast, good senor!"

"Or heaven, in its own beneficent way, directs, even in a dream, a foreigner to come and rescue one of its most beautiful creatures from destruction! But how came he to know you so as to lead to the marvellous scene I have witnessed?"

"I will tell you—you, senor, whom I saw in a dream—you, who have come from the far distant England to save me, and to teach me gratitude!"

"So, we saw each other in the dream, did we?"

"Yes. I have said a subterranean passage passes from the Black Chateau to the White Chateau. He cast his cruel eyes upon me!"

"It is ever so—guilt always covets innocence."

"I defied him, and the abbess learning that I was about to try to make my escape, I must have been poisoned. All I know is that, as yesterday's sun set, having drunk some water, which tasted particularly brisk and fresh, I felt drowsy and inclined to sleep. I slept and slept until this hour, when the abbot awoke me in some mysterious manner, and you broke in through the window and saved me! And if all my gratitude——"

"Nay, Doro, if all thy love!"

And then they rushed into each other's arms, and their happiness, even in the midst of all that danger, was sublime.

Suddenly, however, she cried :

"The abbot has moved again!"

"Nay, it was but the flickering candle-light upon his face!"

"Indeed?"

"Indeed! But what is to be done?"

"I do confide wholly in you."

"Tell me—do you know this place?"

"Once—for I was brought here much against my will——"

"Do you know your way back to the White Chateau."

"Yes."

And she pointed to a part in the wall, which Dick examining, he found a knob, which being pressed, a panel moved back and betrayed a secret passage.

"That is it," she replied. "I remembered the spot because while I and the abbess were here alone—I wondering why the superior of the convent had brought me to this place—he came by that way; and when the abbess said, 'It is dangerous,' and I fainted, we left by that same way."

"What if there are other springs?"

And, taking one of the lights, he went quickly round the room.

Nor was he disappointed.

Near the ground, and hidden from sight, he found a second knob, and this touched, a portion of the stone wall itself moved on one side and revealed a cell, apparently, from its circular form, a floor of a tower.

"See," said Nicholson—"a mattress, bread, and water, evidently prepared for a prisoner."

"For me, doubtless," replied Dorolie.

"No doubt. But I will change the prisoner."

"What mean you?"

"I mean, dear lady, that one of the very few ideas I ever had in my head has just entered it."

"Nay, do not jest, dear senor."

"No. It's the quality of an Englishman to jest when he is in danger and to be very solemn indeed when he has every opportunity of enjoying himself. Such is English life."

"What do you suggest?"

"You say this place is a nest of brigands?"

"One of the most dangerous in Italy."

"Then there is danger for us."

"Great danger."

"Alas! dear lady, we have no ropes, or I would soon show you how to escape danger. I am half a sailor, and in no time I would have clewed up a rope and slidden down it from that window with your dear self in my arms! And we would have given the Black Chateau bad luck and good-bye, leaving the rascally lot to wonder what was the matter, until we could get to the government ear, and bring down a swarm of soldiers upon their ugly nest!"

"Alas!"

"But no rope is to be had."

"What do you purpose doing?"

"Listen. You can get back to the convent?"

"Yes."

"Do so—and wait patiently. All will be well."

"But you. Can I leave you in this terrible danger?"

"You must—for we may be surprised at any moment by one of the horrid band."

"True."

"Hence I have kept this great silver crucifix in my hand, so that any villain that had entered had at once followed his master into the kingdom of insensibility."

"You make me tremble, senor; and yet your every word makes me adore you more and more !"

"I will tell you what I will do. I will assume the abbot's garb—we are about one height—and run the risk of what must follow. At all events, you will be safe."

"I safe, when you are in danger? Nay—are we not one ?"

"You make my heart beat, as the new life of spring, when the winter has passed, seems to throb through all nature."

"Ha!" she suddenly cried. "I hear some one approaching !"

No. It was a false alarm.

The doors did not open.

"Quick," he said—"begone !"

Then a woman's pity seized her.

"What will become of him ?"

"I shall imprison him where he meant to imprison you—doubtless no sound can be heard through the wall."

"No—I am sure not, because in all nunneries and monasteries there are cells, called voice-killers, so that when the inspectors come from government, they do not hear the cries for liberty."

"Impossible !"

"Yes."

"But the muster-roll is called ?"

"Yes—but the one who answers to the name of the poor creature in the silent prison is a deception."

"Why are they thus imprisoned ?"

"Nay—I cannot answer. Rather let us tend this poor man."

And now behold a beautiful sight.

The woman whom the brigand was about to destroy, and the man whom he endeavoured to kill, stooped down and stanched the wound on the wretch's temple.

And now Dick, raising the insensible man, stripped his monk's cowl and dress off the body, and carried the form into the cell and laid it comfortably on the bed, then he closed the secret spring, and put on the cowl.

Being the same height and breadth as the conquered man, he looked the same when he pulled the cowl down over his face.

"Go," he said. "Now I hear footsteps !"

She turned to flee.

Then they both hesitated.

Love prompted both—they flew once more into each other's arms, spite of the approaching steps.

Then she touched the spring.

'Twas time, for as the secret door closed upon her, the plain every-day door opened.

Two men stood on the threshold.

One was one of the brigand monks—the other a stranger.

"Holy father," said the brigand, "here is a blessed brother benighted, who seeks shelter here."

"He is welcome," said Dick, in muffled Italian.

"Your blessing," says the wandering monk, kneeling.

"Pax vobiscum !" whispered Dick. "Remain here, brother."

Then, bent on escaping, he motioned the way from the abbot's room.

CHAPTER XVII.

ST. GEORGE IN PERIL.

THE capture of the bandit and the mysterious disappearance of Dick Nicholson set Marriott and his friends wondering. St. George proposed a council of war.

"Where the douce Dick can be is a mystery inexplicable," he said. "He cannot have been taken by the banditti, or we should have heard from him."

"Has his absence anything to do with the masquerade?" suggested Stuart Linn.

"Perhaps. He was in the garden with Nicola. By-the-way, did you see Nicola?"

"The peasant girl with the short dress?" inquired Marriott.

"A very short dress," added Linn.

"I am not particularly artistic," Marriott said, seeing that St. George reddened, "but I admire dimples, especially in the knee. Nicola's knee put me so much in mind of Sybil."

"Confound you! I did not ask you to look at her!"

"A fellow does that kind of thing without invitation, Oliver. Sybil did not ask me to look at hers—but there they were."

"How do you account for the phenomenon?" asked Stuart Linn.

"What phenomenon?"

"That the eye is sure to wander to the object when the object is appertaining to a lady's foot."

"It is magnetism," Marriott said—"some of that Odic force Dick talked about when he told that story of the doctor."

"I liked that story, but I didn't believe it," said St. George, willing to turn the subject from Nicola and her limbs.

Not that he objected in general to the banter gentlemen are apt to indulge in on such subjects, but it did not, to him, seem right to talk of Nicola in such a way.

"Did you see old Scamp-and-Satan when you escorted Nicola home?" asked Linn, returning to the subject, much to Oliver's chagrin.

"No, I didn't; and I tell you what, don't speak of Nicola in that way, for I don't like it! The girl saved my life—she is good, real and sound at heart, and though she has taken a sort of fancy for me, I would rather cut off my right hand than do her a wrong!"

"What do you intend to do, then?" asked Marriott. "I saw you kissing her."

"It's one of those troublesome affairs into which a fellow is apt to drop before he knows it. There is something naturally sinful in our composition, I think—and women are nearly as bad—but, because a girl is poor and pretty, and infatuated as it were, a fellow need not be a rascal and take advantage of her—I wouldn't if I could help it!"

"That's a good proviso, but I would bet ten thousand to a fifty that you run away with Nicola!"

"I won't—I wouldn't be such a cowardly brute. I can't marry her, you know."

"Yes, you could."

"But it would not be the correct thing—such bits of business never come to good. She is beautiful enough, but the breeds would not mingle well, and my family hate plebs; she would only be miserable."

"It would be a *mesalliance*."

"I should not care for that. I would rather have Nicola with her genuine simplicity, than a giggling piece of fashionable silliness."

"Don't you think a mistress is happier than a wife?"

"I think nothing of the kind. I think that those who do think so ought to be choked with their own damnable sophistry. Women were not created to be wanton toys for a man's amusement."

"But you cannot marry Nicola."

"Certainly not. A fellow owes some duty to society. He must, or should, respect its customs and its rules."

"It has no rule against a villa out of town, as a kind of birdcage for a pretty stray bird. Fashionable women do not object to you as a husband."

"That's no reason why you should go to the warm place with a few extra sins to answer for."

"But you can't leave Nicola behind."

St. George pondered.

"I tell you what," he said—"I shall do just as I like. Perhaps I'll buy some den out here, and settle down with Nicola. I don't see why I should be compelled to keep a big house and lots of expensive company for the sake of something we call society. Perhaps I shall marry Nicola—perhaps I shall run away with her—perhaps I shall do neither. I haven't made my mind up, and I hate hurrying myself. Let's talk about Dick, and see what's to be done."

"And about the bandit. What will they do to him?"

"Shoot, behead, or hang him."

"Not if I can help it!" said Marriott. "We will find out where his prison is."

"I know—Duke de Marcosi is the governor."

"So much the worse for Leon," said St. George. "A cowardly foe is sure to be cruel in his triumph. It was something glorious, though, to see the bandit fight. How the soldiery fell back! I made sure he had done for the duke."

"The duke is one of Satan's favourites, and Satan helps his own."

"Leon will escape and kill him."

"Satan?" inquired Marriott.

"No, you donkey! The duke!"

"Very well; we will help him to escape."

"How?"

"I don't know yet, but a way is sure to suggest itself."

"You believe in destiny?"

"A little. Fate will fight for him."

Just then there came a knock at the door.

"John," said Stuart Linn. "Come in!"

"It's Jack," said Marriott, and it was Jack.

"Well, Jack?" said the viscount.

"There's a fellow downstairs, viscount—he won't go away. I have offered to fight him, but he won't fight."

"And he won't go?"

"No, viscount."

"What does he want?"

"To see you, viscount."

"What is his name?"

"Something hard, viscount. It isn't English."

"What did he say, Jack?"

"He said, 'Tell your master that Labian the Corsican would see him. Tell him that Leon wishes Labian to see him.'"

"Show him up, Jack. He is a good fellow—faithful to his master."

When Jack heard that, he went to the hall, where Labian waited.

"Go up," he said. "The viscount will see you. When you come down, I have a bottle of wine—wine, you know, none of your Italian stuff that gives you the gripes."

Labian smiled gravely and mournfully. He was thinking of his master, and Labian loved his master.

"Well," said Marriott, kindly, as the old man entered, "what can we do, Labian?"

"Help my master, senor."

"With my best power. How can we help him?"

"Senor, let me go to him."

"How can we do that, Labian?"

"Senor, you have power—you have high friends whose influence none in Naples dare resist. The Duke de Marcosi is governor of the prison."

"So we have heard, and regret it. If we can get you permission to go to him, how will that help you?"

"It will help him, senor. There is a passage, subterranean, from the prison to Convent St. Lucia. I know where it is and how to find it."

"Well?"

"I can tell him."

"Then?"

"He will escape."

"Good," said Marriott. "It shall be done, Labian. By noon to-morrow I will have obtained an order granting permission for you to visit him. I will accompany you, as an Englishman and a man of rank. They will not venture to search me. He will need weapons—implements by which to sever his bonds."

Labian's eyes sparkled.

"Thanks, senor—noble senor! I know the count had a friend!"

"Several, Labian. The marquis, here, and Mr. St. George, —they will do as much as I shall."

"Senor, I should not doubt them, but Count Adrian sent me to you."

"When?"

"When they were taking him to prison. 'Go to the viscount,' he said, 'and he will help you.'"

"So I will. To-morrow at noon you will find the order ready."

The Corsican spoke his gratitude, and withdrew.

"A faithful old fellow that," said St. George. "He will look after his master."

"Where are you going?" asked Linn.

"To look for Dick."

"So am I," said Linn.

"I," said Marriott, "shall stay to watch the welfare of our friend the bandit."

"Right. And now about Dick. I don't feel particularly uneasy, because he is not the sort of man to get into trouble. But to me it seems clear that if it were all right he would have come back before. Where shall we look for him?"

"What is the most probable cause of his absence?"

"He has been captured by banditti."

"Or made an assignation with the black lady of the masquerade."

"That is it," said the marquis. "And though, of course —though I don't believe that wild story he told us—I have heard of the Black Chateau. Besides, the ninth day has passed, and he may have gone on the search for the spirit of his dream."

"Bosh!" said St. George. "It's the banditti. I shall go to the mountains."

"And I to the Black Chateau," said the marquis.

One hour later saw St. George wending his way towards the mountain inn. Nicola saw him from her window, and went down to meet him.

Scampia Zatani stood by scowling. The brute was doubtful as to St. George's purpose with his daughter, and, savage as the brigand innkeeper was, he loved his daughter, and would have died on the rack rather than have seen her lose her purity.

"You need not glare at me, old fellow," said St. George— "I sha'n't hurt her. Shall I, Nicola?"

By the trustful way Nicola upturned her eyes, it seemed she thought not.

"Whither go you?" she asked.

"To the mountains, in quest of my friend."

"Beware of the brigands, signor!"

"Never fear! I have my pistols. I shall hunt about till night, and if I don't come back, send and tell the viscount."

That was all he said, but he took a moment when Scampia was not looking to kiss Nicola, after which he went away.

Watching him ascend the mountain, Nicola distinctly saw a dark form creep stealthily after him. Quite as distinctly she saw that the dark figure carried a long knife bare.

She was a fearless girl—daring by nature, and more than daring in defence of the man she loved. He was in danger; she knew that to cry out and warn him would be useless, for the figure would hide, and St. George, laughing at her fears, would know nothing of his peril.

So she took her father's gun, and followed.

Nicola only arrived in time.

And then, but that she was defending St. George, even her courage would have failed as his had done, for she saw the dark figure strike Oliver down, and she had but a moment to set the muzzle of her gun against the ruffian's head.

He gazed round, knife in hand, to meet the levelled weapon that kept him at bay. His dagger glittered, and his eyes were demoniac.

The brigand who had tried to kill St. George was Cospoletto or his phantom.

(To be continued in our next.)

THE BRIGANDS OF CALABRIA.

The French, with the vigour and unscrupulousness of a military government, might, at a later period, and indeed did, materially put down brigandism in Italy; but one of the fruits of their first invasion was a temporary state of society particularly well adapted to the renewal and increase of those associations.

The Republican armies spread themselves over the Piedmontese and Milanese territories, preaching liberty and equality.

The enviable equality in the eyes of the poor and ignorant orders of the Italians was that of property; and when they saw their instructors, the French, frequently confounding the *meum* and *tuum* in public matters, they were too apt to follow their example in private ones.

Many of these men, moreover, were shamefully used by the invaders, and driven to desperation.

Many, perhaps, in the north of Italy as in the south, detested the French and the French system generally.

Among the northern Italians there was, indeed, considerable national spirit, and, in the absence of energy in the Government, certain daring individuals thought, by throwing themselves into the mountains and deep valleys, they might check the invaders by a species of guerilla warfare; and proving too weak for such an operation, they were still strong enough to turn brigands, and these supported themselves for awhile on the plunder of the foreigners, and of such as had meanly submitted to their sway, forgetful of their religion and their lawful sovereign.

Several trials at the period prove that men thus found an excuse for or justified their offences.

Such a defence could hardly obtain in any court of justice, but among the simple mountaineers and peasantry the plea seemed reasonable and almost honourable.

It is worth while to remark, in passing, that the French, with their new Republican doctrines in Italy, were generally well received by the superior class of burgesses, lawyers, physicians, &c., of the great cities, and even by many of the nobility, whose importance and rights their system was to annihilate; but from the mass of the populace, properly so called, even of the great towns, and from the peasantry—the oppressed classes, according to their creed, whose condition they were to improve, and whom they were to admit to the *droits de l'homme*—they never found favour.

The French, I am aware, attributed this to their brutal ignorance and superstition; but they themselves showed a woful ignorance of human nature when they expected the poor Italians would take an interest in what they did not understand, and at once throw off all the feelings and prejudices of ages, and renounce their nationality at the apparition of a novel and unsightly idol—the red cap of Liberty.

To the men whose hatred of a foreign invader and whose political feelings led them at this time to brigandism must of course be added, what was probably a still more numerous class,—those men naturally bad, who availed themselves of the disordered state of the country and other things incidental to war, and those whom that war deprived of their habitual means of existence.

At a later period the introduction of the tyrannical conscription was another source of lawless adventure.

Desperate deserters not unfrequently took to the mountains, and preferred living by robbing in their own country, to following the French eagle to rob in Germany, Spain, or Russia.

These bands had generally but a short duration, and though I have heard of the exploits of their leaders on the spot, in the pass of the Bocchetta behind Genoa, about Gavi, in the mountains of the Riviere, and other points of the Apennines, I retain nothing very peculiar or striking; except the Evan Dhu-like remark of one of them when placed before the French military tribunal at Turin.

He had been addressed in what he considered an insulting tone; he raised his arm, made a step forward with his fettered leg, and darting a glance of fire on the officers, he said:

"Per Dio! se fosse nelle mie montagne non parlareste così!"

"By heavens! if I were in my mountains again, you would not speak to me in this manner!"

But it was in the south of Italy, where men have always

been more fiery and lawless; it was in the Abruzzi, and still more particularly in Calabria, the "land of the mountain and the"—brigand, where the French did what Pompey boasted he could do by a stamp of his foot—raise whole legions.

These regenerating conquerors had penetrated as far as Naples; the army had run away, the King and Court had run away; only the poor despised lazzaroni of the capital had made anything like a bold resistance to the entrance of the invaders into the capital, and a puppet, by some degrees more ridiculous than the national Ponchinello, had been got up under the title of "La Repubblica Partenopea."

King Ferdinand, however, for that time had not resigned himself to a long sojourn in Sicily.

He knew the antipathy of the populace of his dominions to the French, which was much more vehement than what existed in the north of the Peninsula; he was aware, also, that though his soldiers had proved cowards, there were plentiful elements of bravery and daring, especially among the mountaineers of Calabria and the Abruzzi, which the breath of fanaticism could kindle to a flame; and he sent over to them, not a general but a priest—the celebrated Cardinal Ruffo, who effected one of the most extraordinary counter-revolutions of modern times.

No sooner had the Cardinal raised the Bourbon banner at the extremity of the Calabrias, than at the call of legitimacy and holy faith (Ferdinando e la Santa Fede!) thousands flocked to it, and swore to purge the kingdom of Frenchmen and Jacobins, and restore their lawful sovereign.

Among these multitudes were some who were already nothing more nor less than brigands; but they had arms in their hands, were daring, active, and better acquainted with the country than any other class, and these were not times for the Cardinal to be very particular in the choice of his instruments.

He enrolled them, and marched forward, gradually swelling his bands with tributary streams that dropped in from the mountains.

Some of these were pure enough, and only propelled by a simple spirit of loyalty; but it is too notorious to be denied that many of these Calabrains were banditti, or now acted as such, favoured by the state of things, and afterwards became robbers en regle.

The march of this most irregular army, headed by a priest—a prince of the holy empire—was signalised by blood and plunder.

Wherever a town had shown any attachment or subserviency to the Republicans, the Santa-fedisti made it run with blood, and murder and plunder were not always confined to such sinful or obnoxious places.

Soon their shout of "Viva la Santa Fede!" (Long live the Holy Faith!) was heard before the Neapolitan capital, where it was echoed by the lazzaroni and the rest of the populace, who rushed out with enthusiasm, that amounted to madness, to join the Cardinal's standard.

The French retreated, and shut themselves up in the castle of Sant' Elmo, where they soon capitulated; but the city became one scene of plunder, destruction, and butchery.

Calabrians and lazzaroni were absolute masters of it for many days.

They did not leave a palace or a house, whose owners were suspected of Jacobinism or Republicanism (they knew no distinction between these two) unplundered.

Unhappy the man, in those days, that did not wear a pigtail! for a tail was their political criterion.

King Ferdinand wore a tail, all the Santa-fedisti wore tails; but the French did not, and all the Neapolitans, who had cut off theirs, were unredeemable revolutionists, who deserved to have their heads cut off.

The madness and ferocity of their hate, in some instances, went to such horrid extremes, that, I have been informed on good authority, they were seen to tear out their victims' hearts, and eat them in the public square, before the royal palace.

All this wholesale robbery and murder was performed to the tune of "Viva la Santa Fede!"

"It was curious," said an old Neapolitan nobleman to me, in describing those events, "to see the evil force of example.

Men of the lower orders, who had been all their lives quiet, honest fellows, who would not have given a blow nor robbed anyone of a grano, now joined the general brigandage, as if they had been all their lives robbers by profession!"

These scenes of horror were chequered, as they always will be where a semi-barbarous horde and a mob are the actors, by much that was ridiculous and laughable, if the spectators had had any heart for laughing a la Don Juan.

A party of the plunderers and Jacobin-hunters one day placed a cannon before the strong and obstinately-closed gate of the palace of the Prince d'——, to force it open.

Through their ignorance and confusion, they so fired it off that they did not burst the gates, but swept down several of their companions, whose Calabrian and lazzaroni blood besmeared the walls of the building, whilst the recoil of the gun killed or maimed several others.

On another occasion they seized a gentleman who was on the wrong side of politics, as far as the tail went, but who had prudently provided himself with a false pigtail.

When the caudal visit was paid, and the capillary appendage found in its proper place, they were going to let him pass on as a faithful subject of his Majesty King Ferdinand, but a prying dog of a Calabrian caught hold of the tail, and it came away in his hand!

Here then was a decided Giacobbo, who merited death; but whether it was that they had some respect for a man who affected a virtue though he had it not, or whether they were in a funny humour, they determined by acclamation that he should be let off, after eating his tail.

Prayers and remonstrances were vain; they thrust the pigtail in his mouth, and with shouts of laughter were trying to force it down his throat, as Fluellin made Pistol swallow the leek, when a more orderly body of counter-revolutionists came up, and saved him from a curious process of choking.

As they were dragging along another of their prisoners, the worthy old Cavalier di ——, a man who ate his maccaroni all his life without one revolutionary or political inspiration ever interfering with his digestion, they kicked and cuffed him in the most hearty manner, bawling at him as he went along, "Giacobbo! Giacobbo!"

"Non sono Giacobbo, ma Giobbe, Giobbe, sono Giobbe!" * said the old man, turning round his patient, suffering countenance upon the mob, who, at length touched by his tranquil, venerable appearance, and by his repeating that he was a Job to bear their treatment as he did, liberated him.

He lived many years to tell this story and this piece of allusive alliteration.

It was almost as unfortunate to be convicted of speaking French as to have no pigtail. A dear friend of mine, who commenced an extensive experience of the blessings of revolutions and foreign invasions at an early age, was well-nigh paying dear for this accomplishment.

He was accustomed to speak French with his father, a native of Switzerland, whose maternal language it was, and this principally led to a visit from the Calabrians, who plundered the house, and carried father, mother, and son before Pane di Grana, one of the chiefs of the counter-revolutionists, and a ci-devant brigand.

My friend has introduced this incident in a work of fiction, that contains much that is true, and decidedly the best account of the troublous times of which I am speaking, with an admirably-drawn character of Cardinal Ruffo.

It is thus he describes Pane di Grana, and the curious tribunal of that robber chief :—

"Under the arched vestibule of the convent of Monte Santo, the massive gates of which were thrown wide open, sat Pane di Grana, a Calabrian chief of some consequence.

"This man, it was said, had been a bandito for several years, and had infested the high-roads of Calabria, where he had, of course, shared a proportion of the misdemeanours of people in his condition.

"He had plundered, and probably shot, the unfortunate

* Giacobbo was the Neapolitan for Jacobin. Giobbe is good Italian for Job.

travellers, whenever he met with resistance, but only, as *he* considered, in fair action; for the rest, he was not sanguinary nor cruel.

"He was a middle-aged man, rather short, strongly and squarely built, inclined to corpulency, of a dark complexion, and with a plain, countryman-like countenance, the expression of which had nothing repulsive.

"On the present occasion he was dressed in a short green jacket of velveteen, a red sash, and leathern belt holding a dagger and a pair of large pistols; he wore high riding-boots, and a low, slouched hat, with a red cockade on one side, and a tin image of the Virgin in front, stuck in the hatband.

"He was seated on a long wooden bench, resting his back against the smoky walls of the building; some firelocks, in better order than those the insurgents generally carried, were piled against the wall opposite, and a tattered, soiled white flag was furled near them.

"These were the head-quarters and tribunal of the chief.

"His men were quartered in the convent refectory and dormitory.

"A few straggling monks, of the Carmelite order, scared away first by the French unbelievers, and little better treated now by the defenders of the faith, had taken refuge in some obscure recess of the vast building, and left the rest at the disposal of the champions of King and Church, who sometimes plundered both the one and the other—by mistake."*

Another celebrated insurgent chief at the time, half-brigand, half-royalist, was the priest or Abbe Proni, whose rifle levelled many a fugitive French republican.

My friend had also the fortune, or misfortune, of an interview with him, which he thus pleasantly describes in a letter to me:—

"In November, 1799, after the horrors of the revolution and counter-revolution of Naples had somewhat subsided, I left the city with my father, on our way to Rome and Tuscany. Boy as I was, the scenes of pillage, violence, and devastation which I had witnessed had made a deep impression on my mind, and I felt relieved as we left behind us the last suburbs of that blood-stained capital.

"But we had not yet done with the insurgents and their feats.

"We arrived early in the evening at Mola di Gaeta, and were ushered into the large dining-room of the locanda, the windows of which look on the beautiful gulf and the distant islands of Ponza and Ventotene.

"We found only one person in the room seated at table.

"He was a stout, square-built man, with a sunburnt countenance, looking something between a country priest and a farmer.

"He had apparently just eaten his dinner, and was engaged with his dessert, which consisted of a small dish of *pignoli* (the pine almond) and a flask of wine, and I was much struck with the nicety with which he picked, one after the other, the diminutive kernels between his big, broad, and not very clean thumb and index.

"I had an unpleasant recollection of the large sprawling hands of the Calabrians who had a few months before invaded our quiet dwelling at Naples, destroyed or carried away our movables, and taken us before their chief to be tried for our lives.

"The association of my ideas was unfavourable to the dark stranger, and I was glad to see him, after both his plate and flask were empty, rise and leave the room without saying a word, though not without having cast upon us several scrutinising glances.

"But our passports were regular, and we had duly delivered them to the landlord.

"After the stranger was gone, my father asked the waiter who that *galantuomo* was.

"The man first looked at the door to see that he was fairly gone, and then in a sort of whisper he said, *l'Abate Proni.*

"Now, this was the name of a celebrated chief of the insurrection in the Abruzzi, who, after hunting the French and their partisans out of his mountains, had effected his junction with the Army of the Faith under Cardinal Ruffo, and contributed to the re-conquest of Naples.

"Not another word was said; we had in the same house a formidable neighbour, a man whose name had struck terror and spread destruction from the shores of the Adriatic to those of the Mediterranean.

"But he was now in the regular service of King Ferdinand, and bore the royal commission as colonel.

"We slept quietly at the inn, and on starting early next morning, my father understood that Proni had left in the night on some expedition connected with his Majesty's service!

"Three-and-thirty years have since elapsed, and Proni has long been dead; yet I have still before my mind's eye the dreaded insurgent chief seated at table, quietly picking his *pignoli*, in the dining-room of Mola di Gaeta.

"We arrived early next day at the villanous-looking town of Itri, perched on the mountain of St. Andrea.

"I almost wish Lady Morgan, who felt so horrified at the appearance of the place, and thought she saw a *bandito* lurking within the threshold of every house, could, without suffering any bodily harm, have seen it as we did then.

"It was, or rather had just been, the head-quarters of Fra Diavolo and his band, many of whom still remained behind.

"The narrow, steep, roughly-paved street was strewed with wrecks of carriages, chaises, caleches, and other vehicles, once belonging to the unfortunate French commissaries and other agents, and their Neapolitan partisans, who had been waylaid and murdered at this very place, after the retreat of the French army.

"Bodies of carriages, wheels, axletrees, &c., were heaped up against the corners of the ruinous-looking houses.

"We were told that about seventy carriages had been thus served.

"What had become of the travellers in them we did not inquire—it was easy to guess.

"In the midst of this delectable scene we remained for three hours, because some part of our own carriage having broken in the ascent of that abominable mountain, we were obliged to have recourse to the Itri blacksmith, who was not very expeditious or skilful.

"The fear of being benighted before we reached Terracina, in a land swarming with banditti or insurgents, for these were synonymous words in the heyday of their triumph, kept my father in continual anxiety, which, however, he thought prudent to dissemble.

"I remember the locanda of Itri, and its bare, smoky walls, desolate hearth, and worm-eaten table and chairs.

"At last the carriage was got ready *come Dio volle*, and we started again down the hill, in perpetual fear of breaking down.

"We passed the custom-house of Fondi, where we saw for the first time on the road something resembling regular soldiers; and late in the evening reached Terracina, glad to have escaped from a land of cutthroats, and reached the comparatively pacific dominions of the Holy See.

"There was then no talk of banditti in the Roman States; they had all gone over the border to help their brethren of Naples."

The restoration of Ferdinand, which had been thus curiously effected, did not last long.

In 1806, the French again took the road to Naples, and the Bourbon and his Court again fled to Sicily.

The Government now established, so far from being a Republic, as on the former occasion, was a Monarchy more absolute than that of old Ferdinand; for the French had submitted to the military despotism of Bonaparte, and Napoleon had willed that his brother Joseph should be King of Naples.

The usurped monarchy, however, prospered better than the Republic; it was better suited to the Neapolitans; it was sustained by an excellent French army, and by the *now* continental supremacy of Napoleon.

(*To be continued in our next.*)

* Anselmo: a Tale of Italy. By A. Vieusseux, Author of "Italy and The Italians," &c &c.

TALES OF BRIGANDS
AND BANDITTI.

I Warn & Strike

[THE KING DISCOVERS HIMSELF TO THE BRIGADIER.]

RED GAUNTLET, THE BANDIT; OR, THE BLACK MOUNTAINEERS.

BOOK II.—THE BLACK CHATEAU.

CHAPTER XVIII.

HOW TO CATCH A BRIGAND.

OVER there in Naples, you can't tell who is spy and who isn't.

The pretty girl who sells you a bouquet; the gentleman who bows to you as you hand him a paper; the man who makes your bed—for it happens in Italy, to make a bull, that all the maid servants are men; your landlord; your landlady; your smiling lady waitress,—each and every one may be a police spy, and they may not be known to each other as police spies, even though they are in the same family—in the same house.

Often there is no harm in this spydom, especially since Victor Emmanuel has been King of united Italy. But it is an unpleasant feeling to know that you may be spied upon by those for whom you have some liking.

Here in London a spy would unquestionably get chucked out of window the moment he was suspected and couldn't clear himself; but in Italy, if you chose to indulge in suspicion, you would have to doubt everybody.

Therefore the Italian waits till he is sure of his spy, and then he has no mercy on him.

The poor wretch gets acquainted with the sharp end of a long knife in double-quick time.

Such is life in Italy.

You will now, reader, allow me to conduct you back to the palazza in which you first made acquaintance with Dick Nicholson.

There he is, fanning himself with a *Times* newspaper, drinking cup after cup of tea, and altogether in a heated and flushed condition, while his sunburnt face testified to his exposure to the sun.

"A devil of an adventure!" says Dick—and took another cup of hot tea, for in your warm countries an Englishman always finds a cup of hot tea the coolest thing to drink in the way.

That is to say, it makes him perspire, and then he is as cool as a cucumber.

A tap at the door.

"Come in!"

And in came Jack—Fighting Jack, as he was beginning to be called in Naples—with a grin on his face like that of the proverbial Cheshire cat.

"Master, yere's another on 'em."

"Who?"

"A Hightalian."

"What does he want?"

"Why, pitching out o' winder!" and here Jack grinned again.

"What does he want?"

"A thrashing."

"That's your opinion. Does he want to see me?"

"Very much—more than you would, master, if you saw him."

"How do you know?"

"Because he reminds me, for all the world, of a black billy."

"And what's a black billy?"

"Why, a black beadle, to be sure! How ignorant you are, master!"

"Perhaps I am—send the gentleman in."

The gentleman was not good-looking, and, to confess the truth, he did remind one generally of a black beetle, to say nothing of the fact that he smelt generally like a kind of back kitchen.

"Master," whispered Jack, "shall I wait outside to polish him off?"

"No."

"Or pick him up with a bit o' paper and chuck him in hot water?"

"Get out!"

"All right, gov'nor," and out Jack went with a horrid grin on his face.

"Well?" asks Dick of his visitor, who was dressed in black that had turned russet—"what do you want?"

"You."

"The devil!—why?"

"You are necessary to the Government."

"What do you mean?"

"You have discovered a certain brigand of whom we are in search, and have been for some time."

"Who are we?"

"His Majesty's police."

"You'll pardon me the strength of the remark when I say d—n his Majesty's police!"

"Sir—do you know that I could take you up for that remark?"

"Oh—and are *you* aware I could knock you down for talking of taking me up?"

"Sir, the police should be respected!"

"Then the police should respect themselves. Now, what is this about a brigand that I have discovered?"

"This morning, at daybreak, you were overtaken by a country cart, in which were two men."

"Yes."

"You asked for a lift."

"And got it."

"You were dressed in a monkish habit over your own dress."

"Yes—it was cold, so I wore it. An ugly kind of Inverness cape!"

"The men asked you where you got it."

"Yes; for here in Italy everybody asks everybody else all manner of questions."

"And you told them you had been taken prisoner by a brigand in the shape of a monk."

"Yes—a man with two legs, a couple of eyes, and a nose—something like any other man. Do you want any more information, policeman?—shall be happy to give it you if I can."

"You must put the brigand in the hands of his Majesty's officers."

"Thanks—his Majesty's officers may put their own hands on the gentleman!"

"Sir Nicholson!"

"No, I'm not—I'm a plain mister, policeman, though I don't see what you have to do with my private affairs—d'ye hear?"

"I do, senor."

"And I suppose one of the gentlemen in the country cart was one of the infernal spies that spoil this lovely land?"

"Possibly."

"Then now I'm going to tell you, mate, exactly what I told them—and put it in your pipe and smoke it after."

"I listen—and let me tell you, senor, that up to this time I only know of the affair."

"That's an awful temptation—because, you see, it suggests that if you were chucked out of window, there would be an end to the matter, and I should be at peace, which, on the whole, would be a great blessing."

"For you, or for me?"

"Both. Now listen. Last night I received a letter."

"Where is it?"

"Well, it wasn't addressed to you, friend policeman, and at present it is in ashes. I went whither it asked me—found a monk."

"What was he like?"

"A good deal like another monk—equally ugly! He told me to follow him."

"Why did you?"

"Because I did, and the end of it was that we had a fight on the edge of a precipice, and we both went over. I was saved, and he wasn't—that was another difference."

"Go on."

"Yes, I will, but don't *you* go on like an undertaker! Be cheerful. Where I was I didn't know—except that I was on the broad of my back—very flat. I got up, saw a building before me, and——"

"And?"

"And there I met with my adventure."

"You mean there was the monastery in which the brigand monks had their home?"

"Yes; you've hit it, and I should say you haven't hit many things in your life."

"Describe the monastery?"

"Thanks—I don't write books."

"What was it like?"

"For all the world like a building."

"You are insolent, senor."

"Why, who ever could be civil to a spy, who pokes his

ugly head into your house, and turns your home into his own?"

"I must have the description, senor."

"Senor, you won't! I don't like brigands any more than I do spies, but I never will turn spy—so do you own dirty work! You know, from no help of mine that I intruded, that there is a band of brigands within a run of Naples, who pass as a band of monks—perhaps they are monks who have turned brigands—I don't know. But you'll get no more from me—you won't. I am no spy. Make the best use of what you've got out of me by a side-wind while I was being brought home in the cart."

"Senor, do you know you could be thrown in prison?"

"Well, don't throw me hard, and whatever you do, give me clean straw, and polish up the window, for I hate dirty glass."

"But I won't inform."

"Devilish kind!"

"But I'm sure you will help the Government to arrest a notorious robber."

"In a fair way, yes. I suppose one must have some kind of admiration for a brigand, because he is always risking his life, for if he didn't risk his life he'd be a coward; so, for his own sake I'd try and have a brigand arrested, provided you shot him off at once, and didn't torture him in gaol!"

"Senor—this monk-brigand—the chief, I mean—devotes himself to the capture of all Englishmen he can put hands on."

"Why, what harm have they done him?"

"Not any; but he knows they are rich, and he will make them pay rich ransoms."

"The rascal!"

"Now will you help to arrest him?"

"Yes; in a fairish sort of way."

"I have thought of a way."

"Ha, then I doubt if it be fairish!"

"This night, the false monk will make one at a grand gala and ball given by the Princess Tolabola: this we know—nothing more. We don't know his appearance, age, height, &c.—we know nothing of any peculiarity by which the scent might be found. We are completely in the dark."

"You are," said Dick, laughing, "if you expect him to be at the gala given by the princess—what's her name?"

"Tolabola."

"What a name to go through the world with! No, your monk-brigand will *not* appear at the gala, I think."

"Why not?"

"He has taken to repentance, and has locked himself up in a narrow cell. Ha, ha, ha!"

"Senor, the information possessed by his Majesty's police is perfect."

"Very well—perfect. So he is to come—and why?"

"He is supposed to scan the countenances of a certain English lord and his lady, so that he may know them again, and catch them when he has a chance."

"Poor dear lord and lady! What is his name—the lord's, I mean?"

"I scarcely remember. Spikywiky, I believe."

"Ha, ha! I know the beauty!" continued the Englishman—"superb! And his wife would bring all her diamonds with her—the foolish woman!"

"They are to be at the *fete*, senor."

"And the diamonds, too, and the brigand-monk! Ha, ha! Well, what do you want me to do, friend policeman?"

"Point him out."

"It is an ugly thing to do."

"'Tis your duty, senor."

"Well, if it's only to save my lady's jewels, I'll be there."

"But in disguise."

"How?"

"If he saw your face we might lose the game."

"What do you want me to dress up as?"

"A monk."

"Oh, ah—thanks! I've had enough of that!"

"Listen, senor! At our *fetes* and balls here in Italy, one monk is always allowed to solicit the guests for alms for the poor. The monk in question always wears his hood down, so that his face cannot be seen, and thus you can go about quite unobserved, and so mark your man."

"Mark him—what with?"

The officer waived the joke past him with the air of a man who was giving his orders, and continued:

"You will then inform me. I shall be there, and my men will arrest him."

"You are quite sure he will be there?"

"Quite. But why do you laugh?"

"I'm afraid he is confined to his room."

"No. The information obtained by his Majesty's police is always perfect."

"What will you bet that he will be there?"

"This diamond ring."

"Good! Give him to midnight, and if by that time he has not turned up, why, the ring is mine."

"Yes," said the eager Italian.

"Bah! What fools you Italians are! You are betting against yourself! You Italians don't understand betting. Don't you see that you are bribing me with your rubbishing diamond ring not to see him?"

"Oh, no! You English gentlemen are generally honourable."

"Well, that's a compliment, anyhow! And so I'm to come as a monk? I shall never be able to walk like one. Well, I'll pretend to be lame. Well, what am I to do then?"

"You will go about with the cup for collecting the money, and crying, 'Pity the poor—pity the poor!' and shaking up the money you have got, and looking at all of them you see until you catch your man. Then you will pass on without showing that you know him, and come to me."

"Well, you talk deucedly like giving your orders! I'll come! I've got my monk's dress, you know; but where is the begging-pot?"

"Here."

"Ho! ready, eh?"

And he took a kind of cup of silvered copper, hanging from three chains, meeting in a handle at the top.

"Let's shake it up!" said Nicholson, dropping some silver into it. "Well, that's no end of a row!" he continued, as the coin rattled.

"You will be there, senor?"

"Oh, yes!—if it's only to save my lady's diamonds! Can't let my lady have her diamonds go—'twould be a loss to old England!"

"Good!" said the police agent, who got up, bowed, and left the room.

"Ha! But I don't half like your looks, though! Well, I'll go! It will be rare fun—rare!"

Then he fell into a fit of musing. What should he do to gain Dorolie—for was she not still in danger?

Then the thought crashed in on him that if the brigand-monk were caught that night his Dorolie would be safe; and thereupon he almost regretted that he had locked the monk up so very safely.

"'Gad!" he thought, "if they don't find him he'll starve, unless I bring the military down upon the place. Shall I? No—at least, I'll wait for the gold."

That evening he sallied out in the monk's dress in which he had quitted the black chateau, the escape from which we have not detailed for the simple reason that it was so simple. All that happened was this—the monastery was open to any wayfarer to step in and rest and eat bread, after the manner of all monasteries, and so all Dick had to do was to walk out.

Well, now he was walking to the palace of the princess, and inwardly laughing as he saw the more superstitious of the people, as he passed, bobbing down as he went on. He raised his hand, and blessed 'em, every one—something after the manner of Lord Dundreary and his "Bless you—bless you!" in the play.

When he reached the princess's, all was gaiety and delight.

"Faith," thinks Dick, "I shall have enough to do here—to go about and see all these faces!"

"Pity the poor—pity the poor!" he said, and began shaking up the begging-pot.

In came bits of silver, while some brute, more charitable than rich, dropped in seventeen bits of copper.

"Confound it!" said Dick. "It will be like a portmanteau if things go on like this!"

"Pity the poor—pity the poor!"

More copper, and more silver; but no sign of the brigand-monk.

"This is hot work," says Dick to himself; "but I suppose a monk mustn't go up to the table and ask for a tumbler of champagne. No, it wouldn't be decent. Pity the poor—pity the poor!"

Suddenly, after an hour of this work, and when thoroughly tired, he was seated in an alcove of flowering plants, and, resting the charity-pot on the ground, he felt a touch on the shoulder *through* the plants, then a voice:

"Don't turn round!"

"Why not?"

"I am the police agent. Have you seen him?"

"No more than I do you."

"Many guests have not yet arrived, especially the principal. Keep your eyes about you."

"I will. Don't want 'em to go astray. But what am I to do with all this copper and silver money?"

"Give it to me."

"Thank'ee,—it's for the poor."

"I'll see it given."

"You will when you see *me* give it 'em—not before! Heavy as it is, I'll carry it till it gets the weight of a sack of coals before I put it into your hands. Be off! When I see him I'll come back here. Ha! here comes a visitor! Pity the poor—pity the poor!" and he shook up the pot.

"D-d-damn 'em!" said the gentleman who approached, using the English language—"they are all poor here!"

"Don't, my lord—*don't* swear!" protested the lady walking with him. "I shouldn't care if it were fashionable—but fashionable it is not!"

"Jingo!" says Dick to himself—"Spikywiky and his wife, and she's got every one of the family diamonds on—poor dear!"

And indeed my lady passed, one blaze of diamonds all over her neck and chest.

"Ha!" thinks Dick—"well, if my friend can get out of the strong box and come here and pocket those diamonds, then he would find 'em worth more than my lady, though she *is* a fine woman, which nobody can deny. Here comes somebody else. Pity the poor—pity the poor!"

For another hour Dick went on at this work, and still no success, and he was just thinking of giving up all hopes of success, when the police agent passed him, and said some more guests had arrived.

Off Dick went after the new guests; and when another hour had passed he was quite disgusted, and turning off, he made for a little room in which he saw there were no guests, only half-a-dozen gilded and crimson waiters, waiting to be asked to run here or there at the pleasure of the guests.

Into this room he went, sat down, put down his money-pot, and was about to indulge in a yawn, when there before him, in a magnificent uniform, blazing with diamonds and various orders—there was the man himself, no doubt. There was a patch of flesh-coloured plaster on his temple, where he had been cut with the crucifix on the previous night, and very pale he looked, as was quite natural after the blood he had lost through the encounter.

The brigand was walking with a fair lady, the very type of aristocratic loveliness.

He was so astounded, and so little accustomed to the ways of Italy, where everybody thinks twice before he speaks once, that he did not prevent himself calling out:

"Ha, the brigand!"

The next moment he repented of his confidence.

As we have said, the room was deserted but for the footmen.

There was a rush at him by the footmen; and, before he could offer any defence, muffled as he was by the monkish garb, a table-cover was thrown over his head, he felt his hands and neck seized, and then he was lifted up.

"Caught!" he thought—"was in their nest! Here's a business! Who *is* he? Lent his servants, no doubt, to the princess, and they are all brigands, every one—every one!"

Then he felt himself lowered—say ten feet,—then he heard the splashing of water.

"On a boat!" thought he. "Are they going to drown me?"

Then the boat moved, and as it did so, the pressure on his throat, from a cord, it seemed to him, was so great that he lost his senses.

Meanwhile, the police spy came up, and saw the pot of money on the ground.

He turned pale, and sat down.

"He has been captured!" he said.

And, as one of the resplendent footmen approached with a flagon of wine and a glass, he asked:

"Where is the monk?"

"Senor, the monk has left the room."

"How?"

"Suddenly the blessed brother dropped his money of charity, and ran from the room, and was lost in the shrubbery of secret flowering plants. Will the senor drink?"

"Yes."

The footman filled him a glass of wine.

Now, his Majesty Victor Emmanuel's police may be very clever, but they don't know everything—for instance, the gentleman in question had no idea who in reality was the magnificently-dressed footman who tendered him the wine.

"Any more, senor?"

"No more."

The footman bowed and retired.

Seven minutes after that, a terrible cry was heard through the halls of the princess.

A hurried cry, a quick mutter of information, and all learned that a guest had been found seated on a sofa in the little crimson and gold room, and that he was dead.

He was the police inspector.

"Died by the visitation of heaven," said the doctor who sought to find the cause of his death.

There was not the least evidence of poison.

CHAPTER XIX.

HOW BRIGANDS CATCH KINGS.

THAT same night, and within two miles of the Black Chateau, a very animated scene was taking place, to which we must now draw the attention of our readers.

About forty soldiery were seated outside a little inn on the mountains, and drinking and clicking cups.

They were quite sure that they were going that very evening to catch a good batch of brigands. They were singing, laughing, and chattering, as your Italian soldiery ever will, when a couple of soldier-like men rode up and dismounted.

"What is this—what is this?" asked the elder of the two, possibly the father of the younger, for there was twenty years difference in their age. The younger was moderately good-looking, though a reddish moustache did not tend to reduce the extreme pallor of a naturally pale countenance.

The elder of the two was unquestionably extremely ugly. He had fiery-looking, ferrety eyes, his cheek-bones were high, and his red beard shot away on each side of his face like a cat's whiskers. Indeed, some people say, for he is a well-known character and is seen daily, that he squints. Certainly he has got what is called a "celestial nose." In other words, it looks upwards at the point.

The two gentlemen were quite unattended, and themselves called for a bottle of plain wine, a crust of bread, and a slice of sausage.

The younger spoke very little; the elder had the conversation all to himself.

"Well, brigadier—well," he began to the officer in command of the soldiers. "So you're brigand-hunting, are you?"

"Yes, senor," said the officer, a little drily, for in no land does your military officer, who never thinks small beer of himself, accept the conversation of an apparent nobody with much eagerness.

"And here's to your success!" says the unknown.

"Thanks, senor!"

"What! Won't you drink with me?" asks the unknown.

"No."

"The devil!"

"You will allow me, senor," says the brigadier, "to assure you that I don't think you are quite so ugly as *he* is painted."

And hereat the younger of the two strangers burst out into an uproarious scream of laughter.

"Papa," says he, "I have often told you you were very ugly, but this is the first time you have been *subjected* to hear such a statement from anybody else."

"But we can't help our make," says the brigadier, smoothing a handsome moustache.

"Ha, and you wouldn't if you could!"

"The women *do* admire me," said the brigadier.

"Well, they come to court me," said the ugly red man.

"Do they?—I don't admire their taste!"

"And what is more," said the red-haired man—"depend upon it you would be very glad to come and see me if I asked you."

This "if I asked you" was said very drily.

The brigadier shrugged his shoulders, and, not deigning to answer, he turned his back upon the red-haired man, and said to his men:

"Come, my fellows, put yourselves together—quick, or this batch of brigands may escape us!"

"Pardon," said the ugly man—"may I join you?"

"No."

"May I ask you where you hope to find your brigands?"

"No."

"You are polite—what are your brigands like?"

"As like the King's soldiers as you are like the King!"

"Then," said the younger of the two strangers, "I trust, brigadier, that your men are picked, or the brigands may get the best of it!"

"Silence!" yells the brigadier—like most vulgar jacks-in-office.

"Nay, brigadier," says the officer next in command, for amongst each other, officers, and even men, in all French and Italian soldiery, are far more familiar than similar ranks in England—"nay, brigadier, the stranger speaks well, and though that be more than he looks, he deserves a civil word."

"Brave sergeant," said the ugly man, "you deserve a bit of silver on your breast!"

"Ha!" replies the sergeant—"p'r'aps some day the King will give me a medal—when I've fought for him."

"Hope so!" says the ugly individual.

"Silence!" adds the pompous brigadier.

Whereupon, the ugly red-haired man took something from his pocket and put it in the brigadier's hand.

Only a bit of parchment.

But it made a vast difference in the brigadier.

"Senor," said he, "I didn't know you were an officer and my superior. I salute you."

And up went his sword.

"What a fellow that brigadier is!" muttered the sergeant. "What a sneak! Do believe he'd kiss the King's great toe, if the King 'ud let him!"

"Well, my name's Rufus," said the stranger—"may I join the expedition?"

"Command it, colonel, if you like," said the brigadier, again saluting, and looking very respectful.

"No; you have had your orders to command. Well—I'm ready."

And in about five minutes the little company were silently penetrating into the mountain fastnesses all about the spot.

This procession had gone on about an hour, when the whole company came to a simultaneous dead stop, as they heard a chanting some distance away.

"Ha, monks!" said he who had called himself Rufus.

"Good!" said the brigadier. "We are approaching a valley,

colonel, which has no outlet but this, and it is in the valley in question we know the brigands to be. These monks will inform us if they have seen anything of unknown men about."

"Hum!" said the old sergeant who had already spoken.

The chanting now came louder, and as the soldiery filed on one side of the road, there came in view, as was seen by the moonlight, a number of monks, all with their hands crossed, and all singing delightfully through their noses.

"Good fellows—good fellows!" said he who was called Rufus. "Brigadier, go forward and question the leader of the holy men."

The brigadier went forward.

"Here—you!" he said to the leader.

"Peace be with you!" replied the leader of the monks.

"Holy man—holy man!" said Rufus, in an edified manner.

"Have you seen any men pass this way?"

"Verily, yes."

"What kind?"

"Men of whom we would say that they looked evil-minded, and like unto cut-throats, but that we are men of peace and charity—therefore I will but say they were not so well-favoured in the countenance as some men we have seen."

"Good—very good!" says Rufus.

"How many of them were there?" asked the brigadier.

"A wicked score—Heaven pardon me for calling them wicked!"

"O-o-o-oh yes!" said all the other monks.

"They went that way, over the left mountain—good night, my brothers!"

And the leader of the monks led off another chant.

Meanwhile the brigadier returned to the head of his company, and, addressing the colonel, he asked what was to be done.

"'Tis *your* affair, brigadier, not mine. Were I to answer, I should say—let the holy men pass, and carry arms to 'em."

"Hum!" said the sergeant.

"Well—well—well?" asked he who had called himself Rufus of the sergeant.

"If the brigadier asked me, and *I'm* second in command, I should say it was our orders to search everybody; and *I'd* turn the blessed brothers inside out—colonel and brigadier!"

"Nonsense!" said Rufus—"what, after the holy men have put us on the track?"

"The King would search them," says the sergeant.

"He *couldn't!*" replied Rufus. "He has got too much respect for the church. Brigadier, tell the holy men to go on, and tell your men to carry arms to the blessed brothers."

And thereupon the monks set up a louder chant, which was quick, with something like laughing notes in it; and as, at the command of the brigadier, all the men sank on one knee and presented arms, the monks moved on, and, raising the thumb and two forefingers, they began blessing the soldiers.

"Present arms?" says the sergeant. "I'd a d—d deal sooner present arms—fire!"

"Benedicite!" says the monk.

And Rufus took off his cap and bowed low.

And when the monks' voices were lost in the distance, the order was given to move forward quietly.

And it was in consequence of this quiet march over the mossy ground that, after a quarter of an hour's stamping, they heard a noise from high up.

"Ho, soldiers! Help! I'm tied! Brigands!"

"Bless me!" said Rufus.

And five minutes after, when the peasant had been released, and told his tale, Rufus blessed himself again.

For said the man:

"The brigands caught me, and would have killed me, only once I saved one of their wives, so they only bound me, and then they all put on monks' cloaks and hoods, and marched away!"

"Oh!" says the sergeant—"why didn't I fire?"

"Great powers!" says Rufus, "and I saluted 'em!"

"And for thee," said the sergeant, "*thou* art a fool, colonel as thou art, and a greater fool than the brigadier, great fool as he is, for *he* was in command of the expedition! And if I knew your name, and if I could tell tales out of school, I would report ye both to the King, who is no fool!"

"Faith," says Rufus, "the King is as great a fool as I am!"

"Peace!" here says the brigadier—"stand back, sergeant!"

And he laid his hand on him.

"Hands off!" says the sergeant, pushing in return.

"What! Strike your superior officer?" screamed the brigadier. "Men—fire!"

The men, not daring to disobey the brigadier, especially as he was in the right according to military law, were raising their carbines against their comrade, when Rufus roared:

"Stop!"

"No, colonel!" said the brigadier. "You have no voice!"

"As much as the King has—and *I* am the King!"

And, flinging back his coat, he showed a glittering star,

The men now recognised the King of Italy in Rufus, and in the younger, Prince Humbert, the heir to the Italian throne.

"Not a word of this adventure! Can the brigands be followed?"

"Sire!" cried the humbled brigadier, "the brigands have by this time reached half a dozen roads."

"Well—well! This was a bad bit of government on my part—respect for the church did it. Brigadier, be a better soldier and a kinder! As for you, sergeant, you have taught the King a lesson. I give you an ensigncy, and I hope to see you a captain, and I promise you the Order of Merit for having played teacher to his Majesty. And now, as the game has flown, suppose we all go back, and let his Majesty pay for some wine."

(*To be continued in our next.*)

THE BRIGANDS OF CALABRIA.

(*Continued.*)

THE mass of the nation was, however, disaffected; many men of different classes of society, from the Marchese Palmieri to the apothecary who blew up the house of the French minister of police, the execrable Saliceti—from the dismissed *employes* of the late Government to the poor fanatics of Bourbonism and Santa-Fede-ism, the lazzaroni—remained in the capital, disposed to plot, and ever ready to communicate with their friends in Sicily, and the emissaries the restless Queen Caroline was continually despatching to them.

Calabria was as loyal and as lawless as ever.

King Ferdinand proposed to Cardinal Ruffo that he should throw himself a second time in those provinces, and repeat the experiment of counter-revolution in which, six years before, he had been so successful.

But the Cardinal had seen the horrors of civil war; the difficulty, the impossibility of restraining within proper limits the violent passions he had so well known how to excite; he excused himself to his Majesty, saying: "That this was a game only to be played once in the course of one's life!"

All entreaties were vain; the Cardinal would not a second time face the earthly Pandemonium.

The Queen, however, and her partisans tried to do what he had done without him.

But the country was occupied by formidable forces whom the Calabrians had not the discipline or other military means to meet in the field; the great towns and the wealthy proprietors pretty generally adhered, some out of affection, but more through fear, to the new system; a middling class was indifferent as to whether King Ferdinand or King Joseph pocketed the taxes they were obliged to pay; and few indeed remained to treat with, when some months had passed, save the populace who hated the French, and the bandits who had gained such laurels under Cardinal Ruffo.

But with these the Queen did treat, and that incessantly, sending them commissions and uniforms, and occasionally arms and small supplies of money.

These robbers corresponded with others in the different mountainous districts of the Principato, Basilicata, and the Abruzzi.

Of the latter some were driven by the French from their haunts, and obliged to fly across the mountains and wilds of Calabria, where they joined their correspondents, and some were suppressed, sent to the galleys, or executed.

The last fate befel no one so notorious as Fra Diavolo, whose name and fame, as I have mentioned, are still fresh and vigorous among the Neapolitans.

This man, after long setting both civil and military authorities at defiance—after having long impressed the people with a notion that he was endowed with ubiquity, for he seemed to be here, there, and everywhere, almost at the same moment—after several bold encounters and hairbreadth 'scapes innumerable, was at length foully betrayed by some of his own friends and accomplices, and marched off in the midst of a troop of French gendarmes to Naples.

Neither the harsh treatment, the terrible fatigue he was made to undergo on his march by the soldiers, who were all mounted, nor the prospect of certain death, could break this man's spirit.

He taunted them with the recollection of the numerous occasions on which he had fooled them, and told them they never would have caught him but by treachery.

As he approached the capital, thousands flocked out to see him.

Loaded with chains, worn down with fatigue as he was, many turned pale and trembled at the sight of Fra Diavolo.

The luxurious King Joseph, who was taking his pleasure at Portici, was also curious to see the man who, for many months, had filled his kingdom with his renown, and very unfeelingly, as it seems to me, ordered that he should be brought out to him.

Fra Diavolo had walked many miles in his road to death, but without any of that regard we are accustomed to pay to criminals in such circumstances, and was at once made to turn back on the road to Portici.

When he arrived there, he was promenaded under a balcony of the Royal palace, whence Joseph satisfied his curiosity, and then ordered him to prison and execution.

But where one robber fell into the hands of the French, fifty Frenchmen fell by the knife or the ambushed shot of the banditti.

The army of occupation could maintain themselves in the large towns, and traverse certain open parts of the Calabrias, but only as an army—a small detachment was almost sure to be destroyed.

A staff officer of the French army informed me that on one occasion, being tired of moving along with the infantry and artillery, and seeing a free country, as he thought, between him and the town to which he was going, he set off alone at a canter.

He had not gone half a mile, when a bullet whizzed past his head.

His canter was converted into a hard gallop; but though he had only about *three* miles now to perform, as many shots were fired at him in the interval, without his ever being able to see from whom they proceeded.

To the desperate men whom the Queen had not hesitated to employ as the asserters of her royal cause, and justice, and legitimacy, were soon added hosts of others whom the oppression and insolence of the French, or the hope of another speedy and successful counter-revolution, induced to take up arms and throw themselves *en campagne*.

The French called them all by one name, whether political

partisans or professional robbers; all were brigands, and treated in the same summary manner when caught.

It is true that at length the two classes were almost confounded in one, and that unfortunate politicians had no resources left them save those of brigandage; but many a fiery Calabrian merited not the name at the commencement of the struggle, and at no time indeed must the wholesale executions of the French be taken *au pied de la lettre* as including only banditti.

On their side the Calabrians were accustomed to hold the French as robbers, and not entirely without reason.

"I ladri siete voi," said a Calabrian prisoner to the military tribunal of Monteleone. "The robbers are yourselves! What business have you here, and with us? I carried my rifle and my knife for King Ferdinand, whom may God restore! but I am no robber!"

The English, who now preserved Sicily from the grasp of the French, meditated a descent on the coast of Calabria.

This intelligence was conveyed to the bands in that country, whose confidence and daring it immensely augmented; and when, in an astonishingly short time after, General Stuart landed and gained the brilliant victory of Maida, the Calabrians looked to nothing less than the expulsion of the French from the whole kingdom.

Many who had remained quiet declared themselves at this period; and a very available guerilla warfare, to be carried on by thousands of hardy Calabrians, might have acted in concert with a strong invading army from Sicily.

But owing to the circumstances of the time, the victory of Maida was rather brilliant than useful; the English had not force sufficient to follow it up, and after humbling the overweening vanity of the French, they returned to Sicily.

The troops of Napoleon, column after column, now poured into Calabria, where the fate of the Bourbonists and the banditti seemed to be decided.

But there were mountains and secret dells, forests and impenetrable morasses, to offer a retreat to desperation, while the outlaws had in themselves the resources of local knowledge, activity, and of a cunning altogether wonderful; and many thousands of the foreign troops had to leave their bones to bleach in the Calabrias before the satellite sovereignty of Napoleon could make a dubious boast of subjugation.

Indeed, more men fell in what they called " *ces guerres de brigands*," than in campaigns with which the French decided the destinies of whole kingdoms.

We may sigh for the fate of many a brave and amiable victim, for many a youthful conscript dragged from his home, perhaps in a country foreign to France, to die in Calabria by the bandit's knife; but these men made part of a system for which we can have little sympathy as a whole.

At the same time the evils that befel the peaceful population were heartrending.

Now the French shot them as being suspected of leaguing with the outlaws, and now the outlaws slaughtered them under a doubt that they informed against them to the French; whilst in many instances, the mere fact of their having admitted the foreigners, too strong to be resisted, into their houses, and given them those refreshments they durst not withhold, was enough to consign them to the destruction of vengeance.

When travelling through the country ten years after the melancholy events, I was shown a deserted farm-house in the plain of Sant' Eufemia.

It stood in an isolated spot.

"You see that masseria?" said my guide; "it was occupied in the time of the French by an honest and industrious *colono*, who had a wife, five children, and his old mother living with him. He had some dealings with the French commandant of the town, and this excited the rage of the brigands who were swarming in the neighbourhood. One night these villains broke into the house; the cries and shrieks of its inmates were so dreadful, that they were heard by the French sentries as far off as the town. A strong guard marched thence, and when they reached the masseria, they found the colono, his wife, his old mother, and little children, not only dead, but hacked to pieces. There were no traces of the

brigands, but it was well known, and *why*, they had done it. They had carried off all the wine and provisions from the house, as well as a mare from the stable."

I believe the Calabrians are not afraid of ghosts, yet the scene of those atrocities had never since been inhabited.

One half of the door and portions of the window-shutters still remained; the former, as we passed, was flapping to and fro with the breeze of a windy evening.

In another part of the country my guide showed me a "roofless cot decayed and rent," and blackened with smoke.

To this, according to his authority, some French soldiers had tracked a brigand, or one whom they considered as such; it was his paternal home, where his father, mother, and a brother lived, and who, instead of turning him out to the soldiers, or to certain death, closed their door, and prepared to defend him as best they could.

Without any consideration for the innocence of the rest of the family, some of the soldiers crept to the back of the dwelling and set fire to it.

But even when they felt the flames gaining upon them, the Calabrians would not give themselves or their relative up to the tender mercies of the troops—they stayed where they were, and were all burned to death.

The cruelties exercised on both sides sharpened their mutual hatred and revenge, until they waged war on each other with infinitely more than the ferocity of wild beasts.

The relations of the horrors I heard when travelling through the country, did more than confirm the accounts which have been given by Mr. Elmhirst, an officer of the British Navy, who was an eye-witness of much that he describes.[*]

"In the centre of the town of Monteleone," says that gentleman, "there is a prison set apart for brigands of the most daring and unequivocal description; and at this time it is full of these unfortunate men. Fresh captives are continually brought in; but the daily executions prevent the place from being too much crowded. They seldom experience the least mercy, but are condemned with merely the shadow of a trial: it is, in reality, martial law by which these men are sentenced, and the executions are conducted solely by the military. At the distance of a mile east of the town is a gallows, which is never without two or more suspended from it. It is usual to execute them early in the morning, and they are left on the gallows, *in terrorem*, until the following morning, when they are taken down, and thrown, with the whole of their clothes on, into a large pit, dug near the spot: their place is then supplied by others."

Mr. Elmhirst goes on to relate that from the frequency of these executions, men's minds seemed to become horribly familiarised to them, and that very rarely a few idle spectators were collected on such occasions.

The brigands, almost to a man, died courageously, some of them being known to embrace the gallows, as their sole deliverance from insolence and oppression.

Without preparation, with no friend to soothe them, with no priest allowed to assist and console them in their last moments, they were generally dragged with unfeeling, indecent hurry, to the Golgetha, amidst the reproaches and insults of the soldiery.

They were hung up, without having their shoes or hats taken off, or any covering over their faces; and as they were turned off, they were fired at by their merciless executioners, not to lessen their sufferings, but from mere spite or wantonness.

"For none of those I saw," says Mr. Elmhirst, "were shot in a vital part, but had musket-shots through their legs, &c., which would rather protract than diminish their torture."

He had the curiosity and nerve to examine the large pit near the spot, into which, day after day, the remains of the brigands were thrown as though they had been very dogs.

"This vault was very deep and spacious, yet was it almost full of these hapless victims.

"On lifting up the cover from its mouth, the spectacle that

* Occurrences during a Six Months' Residence in the Province of Calabria Ulteriore, in the Years 1809, 1810, &c. By Lieutenant F. J Elmhirst, R. N.

presented itself was horrible beyond description, and the stench and heat almost insupportable.

"A promiscuous heap of human bodies, in different positions, some having their feet upwards, others their legs and arms extended, &c.

"The adjoining ground, also, was full of graves, which being of a very inconsiderable depth, the bodies had occasionally been disinterred by dogs and other animals, and the surrounding fields were overspread with human bones and the fragments of garments.

"For the first two or three years, all the brigands that were taken in the province were brought to Monteleone, and shot in a valley near the springs which supply the town with water; in consequence of which, the inhabitants abstained, for a long time, from using it, and went to a rivulet at a considerable distance.

"They complained of the inconvenience, and as the French themselves participated in it, and were likewise desirous that the fate of their victims should be more ignominious, they erected the gallows, and the bones at the former place of execution were collected and burned."

There was a second prison in Monteleone, where six British seamen, who had been taken prisoners with Mr. Elmhirst, were confined for some time.

That gentleman, who visited it every day, on account of the poor sailors, described it as being the most filthy and horrible of gaols; yet, here the French had confined, with women and children of the peasantry, who had been suspected of favouring and carrying supplies to the brigands, many individuals of respectable situations in society, who were too much attached to their allegiance to serve the oppressors of their country.

Our countrymen, who had been shipwrecked, and had thrown themselves on the coast of Calabria, in a country occupied by the enemy of Great Britain, only to escape death, were well-nigh owing their release, during the first days of their captivity, to the outlaws.

They were detained in the little sea-port of Bianco, when the appearance of four Sicilian gunboats threw the whole neighbourhood into alarm, for it was understood that they came from Queen Caroline, with provisions and ammunition for the bands outlawed by the French, that existed in great force in the difficult and lofty mountains a little to the north of Bianco, which place had lately suffered severely from an attack.

It was now expected that the Sicilian boats, which had each twenty or thirty soldiers on board, would land their men under cover of their guns, and that by signals, the mountaineers would descend and form a junction with them on their landing; in which case Bianco could have offered no available resistance.

"In this emergency," says Mr. Elmhirst, "we were far from being a desirable charge, as the inhabitants knew the brigands were acquainted with our being in confinement, as well as with the circumstances of our detention, which would be an additional incitement to them to make the attack, for, could they effect our rescue, the achievement would not only be creditable, but advantageous to them.

"An incident occurred on the following day which convinced me they had projected the attempt.

"At ten in the forenoon, a man of respectable appearance rode up in a great hurry to our residence; and, unmindful of our being in quarantine, passed the sentinels (who were Neapolitans), came within the prescribed bounds, dismounted immediately, and addressing himself to me, asked several questions about the number of our guards, &c.

"The arrival of the intendant of Bianco, who owned the vineyard where we were confined, and whose house stood on the opposite hill, about three quarters of a mile off, put an end to his inquiries.

"The intendant presently dismissed our visitor, and informed us that he was one who lived in the neighbourhood of the brigands, had two brothers attached to them, one of whom was in Sicily, the other in the mountains, and was himself of doubtful character.

"The extraordinary conduct and appearance of this man

fully convinced me that he was an emissary of the mountaineers, sent with the view of ascertaining our situation, and to devise the best plan of liberating us, and conducting us to their retreat.

"In the evening our guard was doubled; in the night patrols were continually going their rounds, and the sentinels were on the alert, and evidently in great alarm.

"One of them, a youth, told me that he was in principle a brigand or royalist (for the terms were now synonymous), and would readily embrace the first opportunity that presented itself of declaring for his original and rightful sovereign."

The very next morning, notwithstanding that the term of their quarantine had not expired, Mr. Elmhirst and the six English seamen were suddenly hurried off, under a numerous escort, to the large town of Girace.

On their way they saw a good proof of the intelligence that existed between the men on the mountains and those from Sicily.

A number of the brigands were assembled near a house on the declivity of the hills, and one of the gunboats was lying-to, on the coast, just opposite to them.

"No place, however near a town, was safe from them, as they concealed themselves among the rocks and bushes by day, and from those retreats sprang unawares on the heedless and defenceless passenger; so that it was usual for a person, even if he had to go but half a mile from his residence, to be well armed, and have one or two armed companions. The capuchins alone escaped their violence."

From Girace, our honest tars were soon marched through this land of brigandism, across the rugged Apennines, to Casal Nuovo.

At this town, Mr. Elmhirst saw evidences of the French oppression, which so directly tended to swell the number of the disaffected and the bands of outlaws.

The contributions, civil and military, were levied with the utmost rigour—with the bayonet at the breasts of those who had to pay them.

A French officer unblushingly showed him a silver crosier, which he had seized at Girace, from a priest, as an equivalent for some arrears he was unable to obtain.

The clergy, from their comparative affluence, their known dislike to the present order of things, and, perhaps, more still from the philosophic intolerance of these conquerors of the new school, were most frequently subjected to extortion.

The churches themselves were not spared.

"These were mostly stripped of their plate, ornaments, and everything else of value; and the only consolation left to the priests for their real losses was a few relics and frivolous pictures, which their worthlessness, not the veneration of the French for such things, had preserved."

The effect of these proceedings alone, on a people so attached to their priests and their churches, and church finery, as the Calabrians, may easily be conceived.

The French soldiery, moreover, made very free with the women, and no people in the world are more sensitive and jealous than the poor Calabrians on this head.

The same licentiousness on the part of the French, and the same feelings on that of the islanders, who very much resemble the Calabrians, had, centuries before, led to the memorable Sicilian Vespers; and though there was now no such successful massacre *en masse*, many a Frenchman paid with his life for those excesses and irregularities which, of all things, were most insupportable to the Calabrians.

But there was yet another curse at work to alienate their minds and drive them to madness.

This was the conscription, or forced impressment for soldiers, which the French introduced wherever they established themselves.

Many young men, who were not desperate enough to turn brigands, passed themselves off as priests, or as candidates for the priesthood. For as none of the laity, capable of bearing arms, whatever might be their rank or condition, were exempted from those arbitrary visitations, this was the only expedient left.

(*To be concluded in our next.*)

TALES OF BRIGANDS

I Warn & Strike

AND ROBBERS.

London: E. Harrison, Salisbury Court, and all Newsagents everywhere.

[A QUEEN TO THE FORE.]

RED GAUNTLET, THE BANDIT; OR, THE BLACK MOUNTAINEERS.

BOOK II.—THE BLACK CHATEAU.

CHAPTER XX.

A QUEEN TO THE FORE.

THE reader must now consent to be carried away some distance—thirty miles from Naples, and once again into mountain fastnesses.

But, if these are brigands, they are indeed gentlemen of that persuasion who are inclined to be very industrious, for all about and on every side most remarkable works are in progress.

The scene is a kind of cave, and about thirty men are hard at work.

No. 8 —In this number is commenced an original Story, entitled, "Hawk's Eye, the Phantom Robber."

A strange scene, for the whole place is ruddy with the glow of the furnaces, and each face looks as though washed with fierce blood.

What are they—coiners?

Here and there is a furnace, and every now and then a magnificent stream of brilliant metal is poured into given receptacles.

No, they cannot be coiners in the real sense of the term, for the metal which is flowing is unquestionably silver—silver such as flows in any mint.

Such a hammering, and filing, and scraping, and banging as was never heard before.

Some of the faces at work were very far from villanous, and actually, there in one corner was a priest, with his dress tucked up, and working away with a fine graver.

It was to this individual that one of the gang, a very strong and powerful man, spoke.

"Is Regina coming to-night, father?"

"Yes, if all her horses are not tired."

"The men always work the better when Regina looks at their labour."

"She will soon be here, depend upon it, for 'tis impossible for her majesty to stay away."

At this point a great crash was heard, and, as the sound fell upon the ears of that working party, all sound of employment stopped—guilty employment unquestionably, for the red of many faces turned pale as that sound was heard.

Some rushed out from the open-mouthed cave in which they were working, and then the cause of the noise was plainly to be seen in the shape of a broken carriage and a couple of dead horses.

The thing was evident. The carriage had pitched over the edge of the precipice, and lay a perfect wreck at the bottom of the ravine.

"A traveller," said one of the band.

"Yes—and travellers tell tales."

"Not with their wizens cut; and those, except ourselves, who see our mint, don't usually spend any of its money."

"Is the traveller in the carriage?"

"If so, he is quiet."

And here all doubt as to where the traveller was became dispelled by a voice from above.

"Down below there! Where's the postillion?"

"Ah, senor! Are you the senor traveller?" asked one of the band.

"I travelled, but I don't know how to continue the journey."

"This way."

"Don't see the path."

"A man shall be sent up to you."

"With a rope, if you please, for I've had so many adventures lately that I begin to fancy that, though I may be a cat and have nine lives, I've lost them all, and the tenth time will be slaughter! The man by all means, and the rope!"

"Beppo, assist the foreigner—he is a foreigner and a fool, by his accent."

Up the brigand, or rather coiner, went, and by a way known only to himself.

"Ho, senor! This way!"

"Where's the rope? I tell you I'm quite sick of adventures!"

"Take my hand!"

"Is it clean?"

"Ay, senor, for I work!"

"Ha—here goes!"

And never a word more said the Englishman until he was on solid and certain ground once more.

"What are you?" asked he who appeared to be the leader.

"A man!"

"Don't be impertinent!"

"Impertinent? Well, that's a queer word for a brigand to apply to a gentleman!"

"What country?"

"Well, the sun never sets on the dominions of my Queen!"

"Ha, an Englishman!"

"Yes—not ashamed of it! Quite the other way, in fact!"

"One of the curst Garibaldians!"

"Yes—helped to hurrah when he came into London!"

"You shall never hurrah at him again!"

"Why not? Going to cut my poor tongue out?"

"No; but try an experiment!"

"What?"

"Why, whether you have any brains or not, by trying to blow them out!"

"Thanks!"

"What! not afraid?"

"Look here, my man—an Englishman may be wanting here and there, and perhaps he may be too fond of singing 'Home, Sweet Home,' but when he has got to die—though I don't give up hope—p'r'aps I've another life—why, he doesn't waste time in trembling."

"Ho!"

"No; strange—isn't it?"

"Shoot him!"

"Good Gad!"

Out came three fellows, each with as ugly a gun as a man could carry.

"Not time even for a prayer, I suppose?" said the Englishman.

"If you like."

"Bah—I sha'n't be shot!"

"Make ready!"

"'Gad, this seems like it!" says the Englishman.

"Present!"

"More like it still!"

"Hold!" cried a voice—a rich, clear, feminine voice.

And the sound caused the guns to be grounded.

They recognised the voice.

Then there was a leap of a horse, and a couple of men rushed forward as the animal, clearing a low piece of rock, came on the open before the cave.

The rider was a fair, dashing woman, in a kind of military costume.

She looked very brave and handsome.

A woman with whom one would not care very much to quarrel.

And as the whole of the coiners turned upon marking the appearance of this lady cavalier, one man rushed to the bridle, the second held the stirrup, and almost before this had been done, the lady was on the ground.

"What does this mean?" she said.

"An Englishman," said the leader of the gang, as though this were a complete apology.

The lady turned to the Englishman and said:

"You were in danger."

"Yes; but I knew I should be saved."

"Ha! Englishmen should not travel in the Italian mountains, since they helped my great enemy."

"Is it possible, lady, that you have an enemy?"

"Yes."

"Who?"

"Garibaldi."

"Indeed?"

"Yes; he drove me and my husband from a throne."

"Bah!"

"Foot!"

"I suppose," said the Englishman, "that you were a queen of some brigands, and now you are not?"

"Perhaps so; but the agitation you have undergone—first of being pitched from the edge of the rock, and then of being shot—may have made you feel in need of refreshment. I am about to have a little chocolate. Will you join me?"

"With pleasure."

The queen merely looked at one of the coiners (the work was again going on inside the cavern, and the noise was almost deafening), and the man turned away with a bow.

Then another coiner approached.

"When will your majesty inspect the coin of the realm which we have finished?"

"When her majesty has had her chocolate, and has had

some talk with this English gentleman. Englishman, have you a cigar? You English always seem to have the best cigars in the world."

"Yes, Regina."

"Ha, you know my name!"

"Nay, you look a queen."

"Smoking? Ha, a good cigar! Got a light, Englishman? Ha, good fusees! And see, here comes the chocolate!"

At this point a table was brought out—the service of chocolate being in crockery-ware.

"Pardon there being no silver," she said to the Englishman, "as she took a seat, "but we can turn our silver to far better use. Sit down."

She was a sharp, clear-brained looking woman, but she did not mark the chief of the coiners talk on one side to one of the most villanous-looking of the gang:

"You see the Englishman? The moment you can, shoot him!"

"I will—I swear it!"

And pulling a dirty little leaden saint from his pocket, he kissed the precious relic.

"Sit down, Sir Englishman. Good!" she continued, as he did so. "Now, I've saved your life, therefore I think I may claim your confidence."

"I swear, lady, never to reveal——"

"Nay, I don't want an Englishman to swear, I can take his word—for though I know the English have been my worst enemies, I respect their honour. Who are you?"

"Dick Nicholson."

"Why in Italy?"

"To work out an adventure."

"How came you to be here?"

"Last night I was kidnapped. Since dawn I have been joggled on a horrid mule's back until within three hours since, when I escaped."

"How?—I suppose you were kidnapped by brigands? How did you escape? We should have made you pay a handsome ransom. Is your chocolate sweet enough?"

"Quite sweet enough. But I am sorry to hear you say we —I'm sorry to hear you are a brigand, for I was falling in love with you."

She laughed.

"In love with me? You had better find something better to do. Have you no love of your own?"

He hesitated, and then he replied:

"Yes."

"And meanwhile you would amuse yourself with me? However, you hadn't the face to lie and say you had no love! That proves you an Englishman! You English gentlemen, whether rich or poor, never lie. Well, you want to get back to Naples?"

"Yes, but the carriage, which I got after I escaped from the brigands——"

"Ah, you did not tell me how you escaped!"

"Well, I was on my mule, and lifted myself off in the dark by the low branch of a tree. The mule was surrounded by scamps, some one of whom must have seen me had I jumped off. So I hauled myself quietly up into a tree, and on they went without the least idea of what had happened."

"Capital—ha, ha, ha! You shall have my carriage to go back to Naples in. Nobody will stop that, you may be certain."

"What! you have a carriage?"

"Yes; I'm handsome enough for one—am I not? You are complimentary."

"You are handsome enough for anything."

"No; not handsome enough to keep a throne after I'd got it! By-the-way, I'm sorry you will have to leave the carriage before it quite gets to Naples, or they might not let it come away again, and might force you to speak!"

"I have given my word!"

"Yes, but a prison! What then?"

"I never would speak!"

"Well, well—we won't run the risk—the carriage sha'n't go to Naples."

"Good—but who are you?"

"I will trust you—I am the ex-Queen of Naples."

"You?"

"Yes."

"And here the queen of brigands?"

"No; not brigands—our cause wants money, and these men are coining the money we want in imitation of the money of King Victor Emmanuel."

"Is it possible?"

"Quite possible—certain. All the royal plate, every bit of silver we can get, and every bit of gold is turned, here, into money bearing Victor Emmanuel's head, and we mean to try to get back our crown."

"Pardon me, Regina—for your sake I wish you may get it! Yet I am sorry you have spoken, madame, for had I not known your rank, I might have tried to kiss you!"

"Good Heaven!" said her majesty, "there is no telling to what lengths these English will not go! There—there is my hand, and good night!"

He kissed the pretty hand of one of the most dashing women that ever rode a horse, and accompanied her to the cavern.

"I go to order you my carriage."

"Your majesty is too good."

"Bah!"

And with a laugh she was gone.

And now again Dick's blessed luck helped him, for suddenly there was the report of a firearm, mixed with a flash of lightning and a roar of thunder.

And down from one of the rocky heights fell a man, still holding a gun.

"Cospetto!" said the chief of the gang. "You are spared, Sir Englishman, for the lightning killed him as he took aim, and saved your life! Heaven guards you—why Heaven should, seeing you are a heretic, I know not—but you are safe—quite safe!"

"Thanks," said the Englishman—"and be quick with that carriage, for the sooner I get back to Naples, the better shall I be pleased!"

CHAPTER XXI.
STUART LINN'S TALE.

THE three friends—Stuart Linn, Oliver St. George, and Marriott—had really quite enough to do to wonder where on earth Dick Nicholson had got to again. It appeared to them as though their friend had passed into a state, first of appearance and then of disappearance, for which they could not in any way account.

Where was he? They saw him at the masquerade in the extraordinary costume which the police had almost compelled him to adopt; and suddenly he appeared to go out—not of the house, but to go out altogether—to be extinguished— and the friends could gain no tidings of him, for the simple reason that the only man who could give information— the police agent—had been poisoned at the ball by one of the abbot-brigand's servitors—poisoned, as the reader knows, so deftly that the man had no time even to call for help.

Then followed that extraordinary adventure in the mountains, in which the three friends partook, and which certainly did not end in the discovery of their friend Dick Nicholson.

Then the three were back at their hotel, as wise as when they started in quest of their friend.

"Tell you what," said Marriott—"I doubt if we can do any good. Depend upon it, Dick will turn up in his own time!"

And here Fighting Jack, putting in an appearance, said to Marriott:

"Beg pardon, my lord—was passing, and happened to hear about Mr. Nicholson. Can I be of any service?"

"Oh yes!" said St. George.

"What shall I do?" asked the man, moistening his hands.

"Put a pair of handcuffs on, and keep them on till your master tells you to pull them off again!"

"Werry good," said Jack—"they won't hurt by waiting. Beg pardon, my lord, but there's something else."

"Well?" asked Marriott.

"Please, my lord, somebody's come."

"Who?"

Jack grinned.

"Well?"

"That dook!"

"What duke?"

"Poodlywoodly!" replied Fighting Jack.

"Do you mean Tikeypoodle?"

"That's the duffer!"

"How do you know?"

"Saw his blessed man Tummis, my lord, going to meet his master and his master's mamma up in the mountains.

"Ha!" replied Marriott, as he wondered what could have brought the stupid duke, who has a fictitious name here, but who is quite well known in English aristocratic circles—"I wonder whether we shall meet."

"Beg pardon, my lord, but——"

It was Jack speaking again.

"Well?" asked Marriott.

"May I duck him?"

"What—the duke?"

"No—only Tummis!"

"Certainly not!"

"What a world this is!" said Jack, turning up his eyes—"what a world, when a feller like me ain't allowed to duck a feller like that! Sitch is life—and—my lord!"

"Confound you!" replied Marriott—"why don't you say all you have to say and be off?"

"Well, my lord, somebody else is come."

"Who?"

"The general!"

"Moffatt?"

"Yes, my lord."

"Is it possible?" said Marriott, looking serious—not because he had the least vestige of fear in his composition, but simply because he knew he could never fight with the father of his dear Sybil, and therefore he feared an encounter in which he must get the worst by his being compelled to refuse a general satisfaction, and by his being compelled to endure, for the same reason, any insults the general might heap upon him.

"I had better be off," said Marriott, looking up, "for if I meet him I know not what may be the consequences!"

St. George and Linn nodded their heads in the affirmative, but Jack shook his from side to side in the most negative manner.

And that he was a spoiled servant is evident from the fact that Marriott, instead of telling him to get out, repeated his word of inquiry:

"Well?"

"My lord, don't run! He's going up in the mountains to meet Toodlypoodly, and p'r'aps when he's there——"

Jack grinned.

"Well?"

"They'll be kept there for the good o' their healths. They say the mountain air is werry fine. Tummis won't like it; and, my lord, I'm pretty well sure as they'll all be took—Toodlypoodly, his ma, old Moffatt, and Tummis—the whole bilin', because——"

Here Jack roared outright.

"Well?" asked Marriott.

"Because I've tipped the office. Don't my lord know what 'tipped the office' is? Well, it means I've passed the word on to a dark friend of mine, and—and I'm pretty well sure he'll pass the office on, and that the whole bilin' 'll keep in the mountains."

"You rascal!" cried Marriott—"do you think I would allow General Moffatt to be caught by any scheming on your part? Get me a horse directly!"

"What for, my lord?"

"To seek the general out."

"Beg pardon, my lord—he's gone!"

"I'll go after him!" cried Marriott. "He may be my enemy, but that's no reason I should be his!"

"Bosh!" replied St. George. "Let him be taken—let all

of them be taken! It is but a question of money. If *you* go, *you'll* be taken, and next time Red Gauntlet will not be such a fool as to give ransom back again. Stop here. Take it cool. Perhaps we shall want all we can muster for Dick Nicholson. It is only a question of money. Sit down. You might as well expect a dairy farm-keeper to kill his milch cows as to suppose a brigand will kill a rich enemy. Tikeypoodle and the rest will only have a few uncomfortable nights, and then all will be well with 'em."

"True," replied Marriott, and turning to Jack, bade him "get out" in rather a surly voice.

Jack only grinned—he knew he was master of the situation.

"Beg pardon, my lord, but——"

"Well?"

"Somebody else is come!"

"Bless me," broke in St. George, "has all the world come to Naples?"

"Who?" asked Marriott.

"Why, she!" says Jack.

"Who?"

"*Miss* Moffatt!"

"Sybil!" bawled Marriott.

While Jack laughed, as though he knew he should get the victory over his master.

"Take me to her!" he continued. "I mean—you, sir," he continued, subduing his tone, "where is Miss Moffatt staying?"

"Please, my lord, I put it on a bit—the young lady don't arrive till to-morrow morning."

Marriott dropped back on his chair.

"Any more news?"

"No, my lord."

"Yes, there is—there's a fiver for you—a five-pound note for your information."

"Thanks, my lord—and now I'll clear out!"

And he did.

And then followed an eager and animated conversation as to Marriott's prospects in event of the general and the duke being taken prisoners, and the lady left utterly unprotected in that foreign city.

"She sha'n't be long unprotected," Marriott said—"or I shall not be alive!"

"Take it easy," said St. George, "exactly as I advise that we shall take it in reference to Dick. Depend upon it, we can do no good—at all events, yet awhile. Now, you, Marriott, try and forget Sybil, or try to try and forget that dear creature, and let us all wait for Dick until to-morrow. And meanwhile—to drown time—suppose you, Stuart Linn, Marquis of Leith, tell us why you are in Italy? We know why Marriott is in Italy—why Dick is here—and you know *I* am here because Nature is always showing herself in her best dress to me, a painter. Well, why are you here?"

"Mine is a strange tale," said Stuart Linn; "and as you have not heard it, hear it:—

"I belong to one of those old families who always possess some drear secret which weighs them down.

"In one that I know of there is a fear that a railway porter may prove himself the real earl, and so overthrow them.

"Only recently a great duke died, who was no more the duke whose title he bore than I am. He never married, for when the real heir discovered the fraud and came to the duke, it was arranged that this false duke should retain the title upon condition that he gave the real heir a great income, and that the false duke should never marry—so that the real heir or his children should one day come into the title and estates.

"The false duke kept his enforced word.

"He never married; and when he died the real heir took possession, simply as though he followed his uncle by right after that uncle was dead.

"In our family our source of worry is one that we need not hide, though heaven knows it is not one of which we can be in any way proud.

"It is this:—

"My forefathers for ages have been jealous, and for a very singular reason.

"All the recognised Linns have always been remarkable for a tuft of white hair on the head. Sometimes this tuft is in front, sometimes behind, sometimes on the summit of the head, but most frequently it is found behind the right ear.

"At once you can divine the cause of jealousy in the husbands.

"Whenever a Linn was born, and no signs of the white tuft of hair appeared, then the father grew jealous, and the son was not looked upon by the reputed father as his.

"Charming state of family things, wasn't it?

"More than one Marchioness of Leith has died of shame of the insult and doubt her lord cast upon her.

"For my part, and in my generation, if once I·fall in love and marry, my wife may have a baker's dozen, and every child may have every hair as black as a coal, and I shall not complain—I'm too plain-sailing; and besides, I mean to give her no cause to be tired of me."

"Good!" said St. George.

"Capital!" added Marriott.

"To get on," continued Linn. "Imagine my horror when, some few months ago, my wet nurse, who had been ailing for some months, came to me with this fearful confession on her lips.

"By the way, she had been born upon our estate, as her father's grandmothers had been born before her.

"She told me that my father, when dying, had been nursed by her, and that to her—an old family servant—he admitted that I—I—had an elder brother—or rather one that was born of my mother. He would have taken my place as the heir to the estates and title, but he lacked the fatal wisp of white hair in the midst of his baby-black hair, and my father doubted.

"The old nurse went on to tell me that the child was put away—that my father would hear no explanation—declared for the credit of the family that no child without the fatal white wisp could inherit the estate; and so the child was put away—sent abroad—sent here to Italy.

"My mother, it appeared, yielded, but drooped away, and soon after I was born she died.

"My father never married again, and I was looked upon as the only son his wife ever had, for my elder brother, as I am convinced he was, had been born away down in the wilds of Lincolnshire, and not a soul knew of his birth beyond half a dozen.

"'You,' my nurse continued, 'were born secretly in the same way; and had you not possessed the white wisp of hair, you, also, would never have been heard of in the world. The white wisp you had, you were acknowledged, and remained the heir-apparent, and succeeded to the estate.'

"'But, woman,' I replied to her, 'my father, when dying—when it was evident there was no one else to whom he could confess but you—confessed his wickedness to you, did he not?'

"'Yes,' she replied, 'to me alone. It was down in that very same old place, the castle in Lincolnshire, where your elder brother had been born. There it was he died—I alone in the room with him. He had been ailing, but had been up all day, pulling about his library. Suddenly he came to me and said what I have told you.'

(To be continued in our next.)

THE BRIGANDS OF CALABRIA.

(Concluded.)

"UNDER the mask of resignation," says Mr. Elmhirst, "the Calabrians, with spirits naturally haughty, dark, and vindictive, cherished the most inveterate hatred and meditated the most violent designs; looking forward with a malignant pleasure to the moment which would afford them an opportunity of gratifying their resentment and revenge."

From Casal Nuovo, the English prisoners were marched still further up the country, towards Monteleone.

On their way they stopped at Loriana, which town, a few weeks before their arrival, had been attacked and pillaged in the night by the brigands, of whom there were parties in the adjacent mountains, consisting of from fifty to three hundred, all well armed, and some of them, who were probably under the guidance of partisans from Sicily, even disciplined and provided with field-pieces.

The baronial palace did not escape plunder.

The robbers, however, committed no acts of cruelty on the inhabitants, some of whom, indeed, were more than suspected of being spies of the banditti, and of having given them notice of the most favourable opportunity for making the incursion.

I have mentioned the importance of a pigtail at Naples a few years before.

It appears the Calabrians still retained the same predilection.

"I had scarcely entered my quarters at Loriana," says Mr. Elmhirst, "when a countryman came in, who, seeing that my hair was cut close, observed in an angry manner to those present, "that I had the appearance of a Frenchman, and, had he met me alone, he should have treated me as one."

The Senza-Capelli (without hair), or croppies, as they were termed, were considered by the brigands to be revolutionists, or partisans of the French, and they exercised on them the greatest and most unheard-of barbarities.

They frequently scalped or otherwise maimed them.

Sometimes they cut off their ears and fingers, which the unfortunate sufferers were compelled to eat; and on the heads of many who were without queues, they sewed the tails of sheep, by way of furnishing them with such appendages, and in that condition dismissed them.

So that everyone who regarded his personal safety took care to preserve an exuberance of hair; the more of it he had, or the longer queue, so much the more he was esteemed loyal, or an enemy to the French, and thereby escaped outrage.

In the neighbourhood of Monteleone, owing to the more accessible nature of the mountains there, the ravages of the brigands were considerably restrained.

But this was, perhaps, still more owing to the circumstance that one of the chiefs of the banditti had deserted them, and was employed by the French, who had promoted him to the rank of captain, and appointed him, with a company of soldiers, to act against his former followers and comrades.

The name of this renegado, who soon afterwards came to a violent end at the hands of those he had betrayed, was Andrea Orlando.

He was, what several of the bandits were not, a man of the meanest extraction, but bold, artful, and enterprising. Acquainted with all their secret retreats and habits, he without compunction hunted his former associates through the mountains with the most lamentable success.

"All that could not be taken prisoners were shot, and in that event their heads were cut off, and brought into the town, fixed on forked sticks, where they were exhibited in the most frequented parts, the bloody trophies of barbarity and perfidy."

As Mr. Elmhirst was one morning at the prison where the English seamen were detained, "an elderly man, who supported a numerous family on the profits of a little shop and wine-house, and who was remarkable for his industry and honesty, was brought in a prisoner, and half dead.

"He had been to a village at the foot of the mountains to purchase wine, and was returning home with two small casks on an ass, when he was met soon after daylight by a party of Orlando's men, who, suspecting him to be connected with the brigands, immediately conveyed him to the gallows, and were preparing to hang him, when he was fortunately recognised by a person who happened to be present, and reluctantly spared from death.

"After a day's imprisonment he was examined and liberated.

"This trifling circumstance proves the wretched state of this country.

"It was by a mere accident that this innocent man was rescued from death; and without doubt, many suffered in that manner who were equally guiltless."

We must follow this interesting authority yet a little further, as Mr. Elmhirst saw more of the state of brigandage in Calabria, when at its height, than any other Englishman whose travels I am acquainted with.

This officer, after several months' captivity, was liberated, and took his route through Calabria from Monteleone, to reach the English head-quarters at Messina.

He again travelled with a strong escort.

Just before he left Monteleone, a brigand chief, famed for his courage and dreaded for his cruelty, but extremely beloved by his band, was made prisoner at no great distance from Maida, and conducted to a neighbouring castle.

His followers were determined to effect his deliverance or revenge his death; and a short time after, they boldly attacked a village, at which a French colonel and his family, attended by a small escort, had taken up their quarters for the night.

With a trifling loss the robbers succeeded in carrying off the whole to their retreats in the mountains, and immediately sent notice of the affair to the commander-in-chief, accompanied with a declaration that if any violence were offered to their captive leader they should instantly retaliate it on the colonel and the soldiers.

In consequence of which an exchange was effected, as creditable and advantageous to the brigands as it was mortifying to the French, who had long wished for the destruction of their prisoner.

On his journey at Seminari, Mr. Elmhirst found that the town and neighbourhood, though protected by several companies of soldiers, were kept in a continual state of alarm by two parties of brigands.

They were commanded by Ronca and Oezzarro, two chiefs celebrated for their talents, courage, and daring enterprise.

The former was said to be supported by Queen Caroline, from whom he received supplies of ammunition and clothing; and he frequently passed over to Messina, in spite of the vigilance of the French, who had offered a large reward for his head.

A little further on, at the pass of Salano, a young Frenchman (a son-in-law of General Partheneau) in command there, informed Mr. Elmhirst that a few days before he received a formal message from this same chief Ronca, threatening him with an attack on the village—that robber's native place.

The French had good stone barracks; they kept to their arms all night and reposed by day, and Ronca had not yet kept his threat or his promise.

Ronca's breaking his word was, however, not so bad as the manner in which his message was sent to the officer.

His band met a poor peasant on the mountains, and having cut him in several places with a knife, and tied his hands behind him, they made him the bearer of Ronca's letter.

The poor fellow had arrived at the French post covered with blood.

Mr. Elmhirst was not to be freed from the horrors of brigandism and atrocious warfare as long as he remained in that country; for at the village of Campo, at the very extremity of Calabria, within three miles of the Straits of Messina, and only seven miles from Sicily, whither he was going, he saw a French lieutenant return with the bleeding head of a robber-chief, called "Il Rosso," from the redness of his hair—a man of audacious courage and enterprise, who had long defied all the efforts of the French Government to destroy or take him.

But at last he was betrayed by some of the peasantry who occupied some lone houses at the foot of the mountains where the robber used occasionally to resort.

It was in one of these houses he was surprised by night.

The soldiers who surrounded it summoned him to surrender.

Il Rosso knew too well what would be his fate, and resolved, though he might not be able to effect his escape, to sell his life dearly.

From the window of the lone house he shot one of the soldiers dead; he then rushed out, wounded two others, and had some prospect of distancing the Frenchmen by his speed in running, when a bullet from the musket of a sergeant of the party overtook him, and brought him to the ground.

He was not, however, dead.

When the soldiers came up, he begged they would put him out of his misery.

They did so with their bayonets, and then cut off his head, which they carried to quarters as a trophy.

HAWK'S EYE, THE PHANTOM ROBBER.

CHAPTER I.

A VILLAIN'S SOLILOQUY.—FIENDISH THOUGHTS.—THE SERPENT ON THE HEARTH.—A LAST ADIEU.—TWELVE O'CLOCK.—THE CHAMBER WITH THE IVY ROUND THE WINDOW.—THE CLIMBER IN THE MASK.—THE ASSASSIN AND THE SLEEPER.—THE RED DEED IN THE NIGHT.

ON a dreary December evening, in the days when fierce civil strife raged throughout the land, when Prince Charles Edward Stuart fought for the throne of his ancestors, two horsemen rode slowly towards the gate of Falcon Grange.

The Grange stood then near the heath of Finchley, and was the home of Sir Bruton Falconer, a steady adherent to the reigning power.

He had but two children—a daughter and a son, and, sadly for him, his boy, the pride and hope of his declining years, had forsaken the cause to which his father gave allegiance, and gone over to the champion of Prince Charles.

This caused bitter feeling between sire and son. The stern old man could not forgive his boy, and forbade him the house until he should abandon the Pretender's cause.

Albert Falconer would not do that. He had drawn his sword for the prince, and for the prince he kept it bare till the disastrous battle scattered the prince's army, and left King George firmly seated on the throne.

The Stuart soldiers scattered then, knowing there was no hope of mercy from the King.

Albert, who had taken an active and prominent part, would certainly have suffered, but for a strange adventure.

His cousin, Bertram Falconer, was an officer in the King's troops, and on the day of battle the cousins met as foes.

Seeing that all was lost for the prince, and not wishing to kill one of his own kindred, Bertram disarmed Albert, and took him prisoner.

Bertram's share in the battle brought him under the especial notice of the Duke of Cumberland—the butcher who revelled in blood, and could admire those who shed it without stint.

Bertram had done that. He took to fighting and to carnage as naturally as a lion's whelp takes to prey.

So the duke, riding over the field, saw Bertram stay his red sword when about to strike a rebel, and asked why.

"Give me his life," said Bertram, in reply, "and I will kill ten rebels in his stead!"

"Ten for one?" laughed the duke. He could laugh while brave men fell dead and dying in gory heaps. "Very well; but why spare him?"

"He is my cousin, you royal highness, and his father is a faithful gentleman to his Majesty."

"Let the rebel live, then! Do with him as you will."

Away rode the duke. The cousins, standing as foemen on the battle-field, looked at each other gravely.

"The cause is lost," Bertram said, "but your life is safe, Albert. Let us be friends."

Albert could not say nay to the man who had saved him.

"And as you belong to me," said Bertram, "I shall give you back to your father as a present from his Grace of Cumberland; and he should be grateful, for he might have had the same present, but given to him without a head, and from the scaffold."

"Never!" said Albert. "Had you not taken me I would have died on the field!"

"In place of which, you will come home."

"I have no home. I am an exile—proscribed and disinherited!"

"You will be reinherited, and as for the proscription, leave it to me. When the duke spoke, he did not, of course, mean that you were forgiven; and were you seen, the probability is that you would be shot without a question being asked."

"I know it," said Albert, gloomily.

"But I can see the duke, and get him to make his half promise a pardon—he will do it for me."

"Thanks, Bertram! You are generous, for we were not friends."

"I was never unfriendly with you, Albert. But come—mount, and leave the field with me."

They left the battle-plain together, and the lapse of some few days saw them journeying homeward in company.

In consideration of the young rebel's kinship with Bertram, the duke sentenced him to exile only.

He was to leave England within seven days.

These seven days were granted that he might see his father and his sister, after which he was to depart, under pain of death.

Severe though the sentence was, it was gentle mercy in comparison with some.

But to Albert the thought of leaving home was bitter.

There was a maiden whom he loved, and whose father being, like Sir Bruton, a loyal man, forbade his daughter to even think of Albert Falconer, the rebel.

But Margaret Sedwyn loved him too well and truly to forget him on her parent's bidding. She clung to the hope that he would return and be forgiven.

The dreary December evening came, and with it the two horsemen to Falcon Grange.

The few wayfarers they passed looked wonderingly at the pair. A rebel and a King's officer riding side by side was uncommon.

Bertram was the first to dismount. Albert sat in bitter meditation, thinking of his banishment—of Margaret and his father.

The voice of Bertram roused him.

"Come, Albert! Things might have been worse. Come to your sire, who is waiting to welcome you."

The old man stood in the hall with open arms, ready to receive the son whose sudden presence dissipated all his father's anger.

Bertram, seeing them embrace, smiled—with pleasure, as it might have been, but for a handsome face Bertram had not a pleasant smile.

Perhaps his close, dark beard gave his countenance the grim, half-savage look that always was upon it when he smiled.

"There goes the disinheritance!" thought Bertram. "So I predicted when Sir Bruton made the will in my favour. I never built upon it, so shall not be disappointed."

His smile seemed to give him the lie. His manner was very frank and cordial when Sir Bruton turned and greeted him warmly.

"It is to you I owe this happiness!" he said—"noble, generous Bertram!"

"Don't praise me, uncle. I did no more for him than he would have done for me. I had some trouble with the duke, though, before I could get him to make Albert's sentence simple banishment."

The old man staggered.

"Banishment? Why, that is worse than death!"

"Nay, uncle—the world is wide, and Sir Bruton Falconer can choose his own place of residence."

"So I can," said Sir Bruton, calmed by the suggestion. "Where Albert goes I will go!"

Bertram smiled again.

"My chances are increasing," he thought. "The old man is going to spend his money abroad. Bertram Falconer will not grow rich by his generosity."

"Well," he said aloud, "make your own arrangements, but do not overlook the fact that seven days are the limit, and after a long ride I am hungry, so let's have dinner!"

"Seven days?" repeated Sir Bruton. "The time is short—I cannot prepare for travel by then, but will follow with your sister."

"My sister?" cried Albert, eagerly. "Where is May?"

"With her aunt, the Marchioness of Cripley."

"I will ride over to-morrow, then, and see her," exclaimed Albert. "Dear little May,—she will be glad to see me safe and at home!"

"So she will," said Bertram, smiling as he went out—"very glad! What a lot of happiness I have made, and what a good fellow I must be!"

The smile on the handsome, dashing soldier's lip was very ugly as he reached his chamber, and, going to the window, looked out upon the Grange.

It was a curious building. Evidently the right and left wings had been distinct structures, and the centre portion connecting them was a more recent addition, which altogether made an immense and quaint, if not attractive building.

The walls of the left wing were covered from the ground to the top with ivy. So were the walls of the right wing.

It was in the right wing Bertram stood now.

Sir Bruton's chamber was in the left wing, exactly opposite.

The window of Sir Bruton's room seemed to be the centre-point of Bertram's observation.

He did not move his eyes from it while he stood and mused.

"A noble fellow I must be," he said, "and really ought to admire myself! See how happy I have made my uncle and my cousin! I saved his life, when, had he died, I should have had a very excellent chance of being a rich man! But bah! what is fortune?—dross, &c! What is dross to a soldier, whose sword shall win him fame?—nothing, certainly!"

His smile was worse than ugly now.

"But I like it," he added, after a pause; "and so that I can grow rich without my sword, my sword may rust and rot in its scabbard. Carve my road to fame and fortune, decidedly, but it is easier to carve with a dagger than a sword!

"And where is the difference in the act, since the act is killing? I win fame and fortune by slaughtering men in the field, but I must set more than an ordinary amount of blood running before I get rich by it. Here a single dagger-drive will clear my path as by a magic wand!

"And after I have been so generous as to save my cousin and only have him banished—after I brought him home and reconciled him to his father—no one will imagine that I slew the old man!

"Especially if I do it when the time for the proscribed to depart draws near. Let me see—the old man's death would not benefit a banished man, whose right of inheritance of course is forfeited. Then there is May—my cousin May—a beautiful young girl, fair, and full of fire and passion. It were maddening desire to think of her until I can make sure. She has a lover, I believe. I am sorry for him. I must get him out of the way."

Bertram Falconer was thinking all this while. He smiled, and hummed part of a battle-song.

Then he lit a cigar, and, still thinking, unpacked his valise, from a secret pocket in the lining of which he took a peculiar stiletto.

It was very thin, and curved.

He struck the point lightly into the table, and raised his hand.

It could be seen then that the hilt came away, leaving the stiletto quivering in the wood.

"That will do," he said. "It is a useful little article—does its work quietly—makes no mess, and leaves no trace. I like anything sure and secret;—this is."

He slid the deadly blade back into the hilt, then examined the weapon carefully.

It was a fit weapon for a man who could make murder a trade, and smile while thinking of his victim.

In construction it was altogether singular.

It was hollow—the point as fine and keen as a needle's.

The hilt acted as a sort of sucker to the tube of the blade, so that, supposing the blade to be driven into a human body, the hilt would suck up and retain the blood caused by the puncture, while the blade itself would remain in the wound.

"My cousin will go to see his sister to-morrow morning," he said, "and perhaps return with her at night or the next morning. Now, if I were to meet them on the road, and tell them the old man had been found dead in his bed, there would be a panic. Albert would ride home, and I should follow with May.

"Should I? Not if the cavern that was the haunt of my old associates is where it was! I wonder if any of my old associates are left, or whether this Hawk's Eye, the new robber, has scared them all away?

"And I wonder who and what Hawk's Eye is? Would it be my interest to know him, or have him hunted down? He is a demon, people say—a phantom. I don't believe in phantoms, or there would be a few to haunt me!"

That very instant, and while Bertram was gazing at the chamber in the ivy wall, a silent horseman came like a black shadow up the avenue.

Bertram's blood went cold with a sudden chill of fear.

The rider wore a mask, and the horse he rode was black.

A long red cloak gave a mystical appearance to his martial figure, and his whole appearance brought with it a strange, weird sense of terror.

The footfalls of his charger made no sound. There was not the faintest clank of sword and spur, yet the horseman wore both, and they seemed to touch each other as he rode.

It was night—a dreary and a cold one, and a white sleet lay thickly on the ground.

Bertram, watching the silent horseman, felt a new terror.

The black, mysterious charger left no footprint on the ground.

Still gazing against his very will, Bertram saw the horseman pause beneath the window of Sir Bruton's chamber.

Then he raised an arm, and, pointing to the room with an awful gesture, made a motion as of stabbing.

This he repeated thrice. His eyes, glittering like stars, held Bertram spellbound.

The wintry moon threw the shadow of horse and rider on the ivy, and as Bertram watched, the black horse and the silent master merged gradually into the shadow, and the shadow faded.

It was no delusion. Bertram rubbed his eyes and tried to think it fancy, but the mysterious thing had been so palpably before him that he could not but be convinced he had seen a supernatural visitor.

"Psha!" he said, after a pause—"it is some trick of my disordered brain, put out of shape by the forecast of the deed I meditate! Phantom or not, I shall do the red work before to-morrow night has gone!"

The morrow passed.

Night came.

Albert was away. He left early in the morning to visit his sister and return with her the following day.

The only occupants of the Grange then were the baronet and his nephew, Bertram.

The servants were domiciled in the extremities of the wings, at such a distance from their master's room that he had an alarm-bell fixed in case of housebreakers or fire.

He had no guard against the serpent on the hearth—no shield against his sister's child, whom he had fed, and loved, and nurtured.

The good old gentleman retired in perfect security, and happy, because thinking of his children, with both of whom he would go abroad and build a home where he could live with his exiled son.

He confided all his plans to Bertram.

Bertram listened and responded with his usual grave, steady grace—a manner that won him the respect of his seniors.

For Bertram the baronet made generous provision, and Bertram was grateful for it.

He pressed his uncle's hand quite affectionately when they said good night, and each retired to his chamber.

Sir Bruton to rest—safely and happily, he thought. There was the alarm-bell within reach of his hand—a faithful watch-dog lay outside his chamber door.

Another dreary night it was, drizzly and cold, with just enough moonlight to show with painful distinctness the sombre sky and cheerless earth.

Bertram opened his window as the bell in the Grange clock-tower chimed the midnight hour.

The solitude and silence were intense. Not a leaf to fall, not the twitter of a bird to raise an echo in the air, not a living thing in sight, and every member of the household at rest save one.

This one, Bertram Falconer, with a mask upon his face and the curious stiletto hidden.

He was going to climb down the ivy wall, trusting to his steady hand and foot for safety.

There was just a chance that did he steal down the long corridor he might be seen by some one of the servants. There was more than a chance, then, even if were not seen, he would be stopped at the door, for friend and foe were alike to the faithful dog at night. He thought only of his master, and unless his master called none dared enter.

So Bertram climbed down the ivy.

He reached the ground in safety, though it was a perilous journey.

Not so perilous, however, as the second part of his task, when, by the ivy, he had to climb up to the window of his victim's chamber.

But that, too, he accomplished.

As he began to climb, the winter wind began to howl, and drowned the rustling of the ivy leaves.

He reached the casement—a pretty Gothic lattice, so insecurely fastened that a slight push opened it, and the assassin stood within the room.

There lay the old man, sleeping placidly; and he was dreaming, for he murmured in his sleep.

But his dream was peaceful, for his face was calm, and upon his lips there was a smile.

A grey-haired, kindly gentleman he looked, with snowy linen draped about him, and one quiet hand resting over his heart.

"My boy Albert," he murmured, "come back, and forgiven! We shall be happy! And *my* May—my fair-haired darling—so like her mother—we shall be happy!"

"He is very easy in his mind," smiled Bertram, drawing his stiletto, and adjusting it carefully in the hilt, "and so he is in a fit state to die!"

"Brave, generous Bertram!" murmured the sleeper again.

"Confiding uncle!" said the assassin; and with pitiless deliberation he moved the hand from Sir Bruton's heart.

The baronet did not wake—he did not move or groan, but a quick, spasmodic sigh broke from his lips, and his eyes opened to look their last upon the masked face of his murderer as the stiletto went into his heart.

Right in to the hilt it went, and the hilt, being withdrawn, brought out a little jet of blood.

The stiletto itself remained in the tiny aperture it had caused. Its presence did not show. A last faint bead of blood came slowly on the skin, and this the assassin wiped away.

Then there was no trace of the crime. The baronet looked as though he had died while asleep. No one, looking at him, would have suspected the deadly little steel.

"Dead!" said the assassin. "One out of the way!"

Just then the dog howled sadly at the door. The sound startled Bertram, and he went to the window.

He had got one foot on the ivy, when a sudden darkness grew beneath him. A cry of terror came to his lips, and his hair rose.

The silent horseman—the black phantom—was waiting for him by the ivy wall.

(*To be continued in our next.*)

TALES OF BRIGANDS AND ROBBERS.

I Warn & Strike

[BERTRAM FALCONER DISCOVERS HIS MYSTERIOUS VISITOR TO BE IMPALPABLE.]

HAWK'S EYE, THE PHANTOM ROBBER.

CHAPTER II.

THE FIGHT WITH THE PHANTOM.—BRANDED ON THE BROW.—A
STRANGE MYSTERY.—A MIDNIGHT RIDE.—A MEETING ON THE
HEATH.—HAWK'S EYE, THE ROBBER.—THE CAVE.

BERTRAM had not heard it come, nor did he hear it now,
though there beneath him it stood, black and motionless.

A phantom.

The Phantom Robber, about whom he had heard, and
whose existence he had doubted.

He could not doubt now.

There was the thing in all its silent terror, sitting his sable
steed.

The red cloak looking like a shroud of blood.

His weird, unearthly eyes glistening like stars of fire.

A sword gleaming in his spectral hand, and round this sword blue lines of light, circling like flame.

"What is it?" Bertram asked himself, in a hoarse whisper, as he still clung to the ivy on the wall. "No fancy, for I have seen it before, and there it is now! Waiting for me," he added, with a shudder—"waiting for me!"

Now came the question—

Should he go down and face the wordless terror?

Perhaps to meet some wild and horrible fate from its hands—perhaps be hideously mangled by the inhuman, fearful object.

Or should he retire to the chamber he had just left?

He thought of the pale corpse lying on the bed, and shuddered at the idea of going to confront it again.

There was the alternative—

To go down and face the phantom,—

Or go back and face the dead.

His fear left him shuddering, without power to move hand or foot.

What should he do?

But while he hesitated, the ivy was yielding and breaking away from the wall.

A few moments, and he fell heavily to the ground, face forwards to the phantom.

The phantom raised his hat.

"If, by that position, you mean to salute me, I thank you!"

"What do you want? Are you a reality, or merely a creation of my disordered brain?"

"I exist!"

"Wherefore?"

"I serve a purpose!"

"And what?"

"I force upon men who have sinned remorse for sin, so that they become useful by warning other people how wretched sinning becomes!"

"Do you know, then, that I——"

He stopped.

The phantom pointed up to the room.

"I know!"

"How?"

"Because I am what I am!"

Bertram felt as though in a kind of vice, from which he could not free himself—or, rather, he felt to be in that state when we are neither asleep nor awake, and have no power to move, while a terrible sense of oppression overpowers life, and makes it a dread.

"Am I ever to see you again?"

"Yes—me or my double!"

"Your double?—who is he?"

"That you will learn!"

"And why are you here?"

"To brand you!"

"How brand me?"

"To mark you with the brand of being mine! Ha, that was good!"

This last remark was addressed to an act of Bertram's—an act nothing less than his suddenly unsheathing his sword and making a pass at the terrible visitor.

It passed through the murky form as it passed through the air about him.

For Bertram Falconer was one of those men who can only experience fear or dread for a short time, exactly as there are men so free from the ability to feel pain that some have been known who, being defied to do it, have chopped off a finger or a thumb; so there are human beings with whom courage could scarcely be called a virtue, for the simple reason that they cannot understand cowardice.

Therefore, Bertram, overcoming that nameless horror with which he looked upon the phantom, at once fancied that perhaps but a deception was being played upon him, and endeavoured to satisfy himself by quickly drawing his sword and making a pass at the unknown.

As it has been said, the sword passed but through air.

"Good—very good!" cried the phantom. "You are a fit subject for the brand!"

For a moment Bertram again trembled, but again that odd, impassive courage which cannot comprehend danger, and therefore is destitute of the pride of courage as defying danger, took possession of him, and he stood defying the phantom.

Suddenly, as the phantom struck up his hand, Bertram felt a sharp pain upon the forehead.

"What is this?" he cried.

"I have the power to brand you—you are branded!"

Again, for a moment, he trembled, and then again he looked up.

"How branded?—with what?"

"Branded by me," replied the phantom, "and by my power!"

Bertram put his hand to his forehead.

"I feel nought!" he said.

"But the brand of Cain is there!" replied the phantom—"the shape of the flaming sword which, brandishing, the avenging angel held in his hand when he smote down satan—when he followed Cain from land to land!"

Bertram was a _____ man, and the dread of a shameful mark upon his forehead was far greater than his fear of the power which _____ there.

"What! am I to bear the mark of your accursed brand wherever I go?"

"No, for _____ wherever you went, men would know and _____. No—the mark is there—ever, but will be seen only by men, and then of a bright red colour, when there is murder in your soul. You are to do good in the world by proving the misery of wickedness—the _____ mark. But only when you are about to _____ flaming sword appear upon your forehead! _____"

"Stay!"

"Well, you see I am obedient," replied the phantom.

"When shall I see you again?"

"In good time."

"Say when."

"When I am wanted."

Then, rather, he was gone. He did not retreat or fall back, but he and his form _____ to dissolve into the shades of the night.

"So, gone! I breathe again."

Not one thought had he of the murdered man gradually growing rigid and ghastly in the room above—not one vestige of pity had he for the _____ dead. He left staring with the death-stare at the _____ room _____ found by his servants in the morning.

All he thought of in connection with the matter was this—he wanted the baronet out of the way, and he was out of the way, and he thought no more of what he had done than he would have thought of killing a rat.

Many people would have killed a rat with far more compunction than Bertram could in killing a holocaust of human beings.

Nor let any reader envy him, for, if he could feel no repentance, he could experience little pleasure—exactly as a man who is not depressed by a wretched November fog never enjoys a pure scene over a bright sea as does the man who would be horribly depressed by a London November day; so, if Bertram could not feel repentance or grief, he could never experience joy.

In fact, life to him was one dead length of monotony. He found no change day after day for years on weary years.

Before mounting his horse, he looked about, and, seeing nothing more of the phantom, he literally almost forgot that encounter, and as he rode away, he said:

"Now for the others!"

Then—horror!

He felt the hot shape of the flaming sword upon his forehead.

Yes, he had *thought* murder, and the brand of the phantom was visible.

"I will call it a scar," he cried to himself, as the hot, throbbing pain passed away—it was hot but momentary—"I will call it a scar, and he who doubts my word shall—ha, again!"

For once more the hot, flame-like feeling was upon his forehead.

On he rode, and for an hour, when suddenly he pulled rein.

In spite of the clatter of his own horse's hoofs, he heard the approach of a couple of horses in the direction in which he was proceeding.

"They are here!" he muttered.

And then again he felt the burning pain in the forehead.

But upon this occasion he paid only slight attention to it. Again his natural temperament was exerting itself; and having experienced some fear at the awful phenomena of the brand, he was already accepting them as matters of course and in the daily current of his life.

For such it is to be callous—hard-hearted.

He waited patiently until the approaching riders reached him, turning his horse into the deep shadow of a tree, and thence watching.

As the couple approached, again the brand scorched his forehead, for he marked the one of the two stoop down and kiss the other—that other being a young and charming girl of about seventeen.

Suddenly Bertram started forward.

"Good even, Cousin Albert, and you too, fair May, though there is little time for courtesy!"

"Be of good cheer!" said Albert Falconer, turning to the fair girl that accompanied him, and who sat in the saddle as though she had been born to ride—"be of good cheer—there is no danger!"

"There is much!" said Bertram.

"Indeed?" asked Albert.

"The government are upon you! Let them once lay hands upon you, and you are a doomed man!"

"But, cousin," cried Albert, "you forget the government promise—seven days for preparation."

"The promise has been rescinded," said Bertram, "for the government can at times act cruelly."

"Then my liberty is not worth a moment's purchase."

"I fear not," said Bertram, gravely.

"And you have ridden out in the night-time to warn me not to approach the castle—the dear home of my youth—because it is in the possession of armed men. Is that so?"

"It is."

"Then, good cousin, you are indeed to be loved!"

"Nay," returned Bertram; "you but increase my honest acts. You must fly the land at once!"

"And you, dear May," cried Albert—"will you follow me?"

"To the ends of the earth!" she replied, sweetly.

"Nay, it must not be!" replied Bertram. "Together you would be known; and you, May, who love your dear brother so deeply, would be the cause of his destruction."

"Oh no—no—no!" she cried, entreatingly.

"Albert," Bertram continued, "you must fly by yourself, and leave all to me. When the King has ceased to be angry, I will let you know; and I—I will obtain your pardon!"

"What of May?"

"Leave her to me—she shall be in safe keeping."

"And my father—is he well?" asked Albert.

Bertram smiled gravely, but the brand heated upon his forehead as he said:

"Your father, dear youth, suffers no pain."

"Then, if he is well and you will guard my sister May, I can flee to foreign lands without a heart so heavy that it will break with its own weight."

"Go—go," cried Bertram, with mock eagerness, "or it may be too late!"

"Good-bye, my darling!" said the brother—"better times are in store for us; and let us trust in Bertram!"

"I do indeed!" said May.

And she looked confidingly in Bertram's face.

"Albert," Bertram continued, "have you money?"

"Yes—a sufficiency."

"So much the better."

"Good—good-bye!" Albert returned.

And so saying, he moved his horse's head, fleeing, and

leaving his sister in the hands of her unknown but direst enemy.

So—again the heat of the brand as he thought—"The baronet is dead, his son is at full flight, and in a day she, the daughter, shall be my promised wife. Then, as the estate and castle are forfeited to the government by Albert's treason, shall not I, marrying the daughter, obtain a grant of all the lands?"

It was only when the sound of the fugitive's horse's hoofs in the distance had died away that he spoke.

"You do not fear me, Cousin May?"

"Why should I, Cousin Bertram?"

"Because most women are afraid of me."

"Ah! but I am of the same blood as yourself. I do not fear myself, therefore why should I fear you?"

"Lady May, have you ever loved?"

"What a question! Yes."

"But I mean seriously?"

"Yes," she replied, smiling, in spite of her fear that her brother might not get safely away from the land in which he was judged to be a traitor—"yes—I love you!"

His countenance flushed.

"Indeed!" he cried.

She smiled again, for when we are good and kind it is astonishing how we can put away our grief, and appear smiling and serene.

"Cousin, let us ride fast."

He stopped at an inn after both had trotted their horses some miles, and then only was the halt for a short time.

Then they passed into a thick and sombre forest.

"Cousin Bertram," she said, as they entered under the dark trees, "this is not the nearest way to the castle."

"Yes, darling, it is," he replied, "for those who are accused of treason, for going by the road may lead to your apprehension—and mine also."

She said no word for a few moments, and then, looking up, she marked the red brand on the forehead.

"Bertram—Bertram!"

"Yes?"

"There is such a strange mark on your forehead—'tis a flaming red sword! What does that mean?"

"Nought—a scar for past valour. Is your horse safe?"

"Quite. Do we pass any houses in this district?"

"Yes, not far from here."

No other word was spoken until they reached the opening of a wide cavern.

There his real nature cropped out.

"This," he said, with sudden passion, "is your bridal chamber!"

"What mean you?"

"I mean that this night shall be so terrible to you that, when the morning's light appears, you will be glad to shrink from very shame to my bosom!"

"Ha, you are our enemy!"

"I hate you, May—yet I love you!"

"And my brother?"

"Him I detest!"

"And my father?"

"Him I abhor!"

"What will you with me?"

"I desire that you promise to marry me, and in all things bow to me as though you were my wife!"

"Your wife, Bertram, I never shall be—never!"

"I will compel you!"

"I defy you!"

"Your father is dead!"

Perhaps he hoped that this threat would lay her at his feet.

So far he was right, for she reeled from the saddle, and, had he not have caught her, she must inevitably have fallen to the ground.

This, then, was the climax of his scheme—to force May to marry him, so that he might have a colourable application to government for the gift of his cousin's confiscated estate.

He had planned well his plot.

And now it was that he leaped off his horse.

As he did so, he caught her in his arms and kissed her.

"Ha! Bertram, your forehead, in touching mine, has burnt me!"

"It proves the heat of my passion! Do you accept me as your husband?"

"No!"

"No? I say you shall! Acceptance will be less terrible than force!"

"You may kill me, Bertram—you cannot conquer me!"

"We will see, fair cousin!"

Then he leaped at her.

"You love some one?"

"Yes," she replied.

"Who is it?"

"Nay, I will not answer."

"I will learn—after our marriage!"

And he approached her, but her screams for a few moments arrested his proceedings.

Yet, with a fearful leap, he grasped her in his arms.

"All is lost!" she cried.

"No!"

It was a voice at the entrance to the cavern.

For a moment Bertram trembled.

There stood the phantom.

The same figure in all its parts.

Then his anger rose; and although he had once before committed a similar act, the only result being that his sword passed through the air—now, to his astonishment, he found resistance.

"Do you live?" he asked.

"Yes," replied the new comer.

"Whence come you?"

"No matter!"

"What do you seek?"

"The protection of that lady's purity!"

"Are you a man?"

"Yes, and a good swordsman! Come on, ruffian as you are!"

And now the swords were crossed, while the poor lady remained trembling.

(*To be continued in our next.*)

RED GAUNTLET, THE BANDIT; OR, THE BLACK MOUNTAINEERS.

BOOK II.—THE BLACK CHATEAU.

CHAPTER XXII.

STUART LINN CONTINUES HIS NARRATIVE.

"'And why did you not repeat to the family solicitor what you had heard?' I asked her," continued Linn.

"She replied:

"'He died almost within ten minutes of what he said, and his last words were: "Tell Stuart to find his brother; and if he have the white wisp—if it has come—(and here he kissed the printed leaf of a book he held in his hand)—tell Stuart to give all to his brother, and let the world know all."'

"'And why did you not? My father has been dead years!'

"'Nay,' the old nurse continued to me—'I had called you the young lord all my life, and I could not bear that you should give up all to some stranger whom not one of us had ever seen!'

"'Miserable woman,' I replied, 'to neglect a dying man's commands!'

"'True!' she said. 'And now I know that I am dying myself, I know how wrong I was; and here I am confessing to you as he did to me.'

"'Where,' I asked her, 'is the print my father was holding in his hand?'

"She replied by giving me a key and a small leather-coloured desk she was carrying, and——"

"Well?" asked St. George; and he and Marriott had been so engrossed in the extraordinary revelation made by their friend that they had scarcely moved during its recital.

"That very night *she* died!

"I have often felt as though it was a kind of judgment dealt to her—as though it had been said that as she had done, so she should be done by."

"And what did the desk contain?"

"Various information the poor woman—who had sinned against the dead for my living sake—had picked up about the family, but most importantly, the piece of printed paper.

"No sooner had I read it than I comprehended the cause of my father's repentance.

"Had he not read that page of an old book of the time of Charles the Second, he would have died true to the tradition of his family, without endeavouring to make that atonement to his firstborn which he did strive to make, and which I shall strive equally to complete."

"What said the bit of printed paper?"

"It was an anecdote concerning our family.

"It appeared from it that in Charles the Second's time a son had been born without this white lock of hair, and that he had been put away privily because of its absence, and that then the father had no more children.

"As the years went on his heart yearned towards this child, and, seeking him out, he found that in the course of years the white wisp of hair had grown, and was plainly visible exactly in the centre of his forehead.

"My father read this chance print, and so only learnt this fact in the family by opening a book.

"In the family this bit of its history had been hidden for fear, if it were known, that at some future time a Leith might be weak enough not to disown a son or daughter born without the white wisp; and, from what I have learnt, it is only too evident that he of our family who was thus brought to inherit the estate, and from whom my father was descended, was quite willing that this peculiarity in reference to the wisp of white hair should be hidden, although he himself had suffered by this peculiarity not being known, so that the public honour of the family—the white wisp being publicly known in his time—should never be tarnished."

"And the long and the short of it is," said St. George, "you are here in Italy to find this elder brother?"

"Yes."

"Do you think you shall find him?"

"Don't know."

"Got many particulars?"

"Not many."

"What are they?"

"Nay—you will allow me to keep them private."

"Very good. And now tell me, if you find this brother, and if *he* has not the wisp of white hair, will you acknowledge him?"

Stuart Linn laughed.

"Well," he replied, "I get out of that family difficulty very handsomely, for you see I can only begin to identify him by the fact of the white wisp—I shall have no stings of conscience on that point. If the white hairs have not grown with his growth, why, I shall not cease to be the Marquis of Leith—for I can only identify him after I see that precious lock of white hair."

"Well, but I never saw the white lock in your beautiful head, dear boy," said St. George, eyeing his friend's shortened locks.

"My dear boy," Linn retorted, "have you ever seen a lady of the markets pulling off the outer shells of walnuts?"

"Yes; but what has that to do with the matter?"

"Much. You will have marked that the juice stains her hands a dark brown, which would go a dark black if the lady of the markets did not wash. Well—they make walnut pomatum, and I buy it, and patch over the white lock—it's behind my right ear when I'm not at home down at the castle. If down there and they were to miss the white lock behind the ear, why, they would think the family was ruined. Finally, I hope that I shall find this brother of mine—if I find him at all—in a few months."

"Have you got a clue?"

"Yes; or rather, I shall have."

"When?"

"In a few days."

"Can I be of any use?" asked St. George.

"Well, that's a compliment to yourself, old fellow, anyhow. Can you be of any use? Well, I suppose any man can if he tries. If you mean—can you be of any use to me in the matter? why, perhaps you can, and I'll let you know how."

"Thanks!"

"And now for a time," continued Linn, "let us say no more about the family honour. For my part, I should like to have my head shaved and wear a wig, I am so heartily ashamed of the white wisp of hair."

"But, Stuart," said Marriott, "I think I can see some doubt in your face. Make a clean breast of it, and let us know all about it."

"Well, I will. There's another legend in the family."

"And what is it?"

"This: Where a brother has been eliminated from the family in this way, he has frequently become the enemy of him who stands in his place, and so he and the brother in possession of the estate will become enemies, neither knowing the other to be his brother. Ay, and on more than one occasion death has ended the enmity—death of one at the hand of the other!"

"How horrible!" cried St. George.

"Yes, to talk about," replied Stuart Linn. "But I do not apprehend anything horrible—at least, not always, for we live in the nineteenth century, and I can't—I cant believe in all these superstitions, while at other times I cannot resist their influence. Ha! what was that?"

It was a glass upon the table before them, and without being touched it snapped and fell into several pieces.

Stuart Linn turned pale.

"'Twas like an omen," said St. George.

"I pray heaven it was not one!" said Stuart Linn.

He remained pale—very pale.

But the silence was soon broken by hurried footsteps and a hurried entrance.

The door broke open.

"Dick Nicholson!"

"Himself!"

"And where the deuce have you sprung from?"

"From inside a carriage."

"Whose?"

"A queen's! Ha, ha, ha! And heaven bless her for the loan of it!"

CHAPTER XXIII.
THE ESCAPE.

ON the following day, almost at daybreak, Labian was seen outside the palazzo which the four English friends occupied.

He had lain in his cloak watching for the day—that day upon which he, helped by the English gentlemen, was to endeavour to set free Red Gauntlet from the prison in which he lay, and the governor of which was his mortal enemy, the Duke de Mareosi.

But, according to promise, Marriott could only keep his promise at mid-day.

Our readers have no need to ask us where he was up to that hour,—he was seeking for Sybil Moffatt.

And he had found her, and the delightful interview he had had with that dear young lady had made his heart as light as the Italian sky under which he had found her.

But now he was to aid in the rescue of Red Gauntlet, who was lying waiting his trial upon charges which would unquestionably involve his death if found guilty, and that he would be found guilty, if once he was tried, was very certain. Marriott was quite right when he said that his rank would enable him to procure a pass to visit the prisoner, while it would equally prevent him from being searched.

Had the minions of the Duke de Mareosi searched him, they would have found a very beautifully-tempered steel crowbar, made in three pieces to pack easily, and a couple of sheet files, so delicate that, together, they did not weigh an ounce.

Marriott carried the crowbar thus—one piece up each arm, and the third down the front of his waistcoat, the whole securely fixed, so that no chance of falling should ruin the enterprise.

Thus provided, off they started.

"Are you sure you know what to do when you get into the prison?"

"Yes, senor. I know the very cell in which my dear master is hidden. Once there, he will soon be far away from the ugly Duke de Mareosi."

They were now approaching the prison, and therefore Labian, as a servant, fell behind the viscount.

The prison janitor having been summoned, they were soon on the wrong side of the jail door, and then it was that Mareosi came upon the scene.

He bowed very low to the English lord, and himself offered him a chair.

"You have the order to visit the criminal, Red Gauntlet—or by whatever name he calls himself?"

Marriott bowed, and, without a word, gave the paper.

"Who is this?" asked the duke, pointing to Labian.

"An old servant of the prisoner."

"Servant?" said the duke, disdainfully. "You mean a fellow-criminal!"

Labian started, and if it had not been for his master's sake, he would have given the duke a little lesson.

"Well," replied Marriott, "let him be what he may, I am going to ask your grace to allow the poor man to remain, and attend upon his master, as he calls him?"

"The government cannot afford to pay to keep prisoners in servants. We, here in Italy," he continued, ironically, "are not so rich as you in England."

Marriott bowed.

"I will pay for him."

"You take great interest in the prisoner," the duke said, sharply.

"Because I maintain that you have mistaken your man. You have captured, not Red Gauntlet, but a man who is like him only."

"Bah!" said the duke.

Marriott was about to give a quick answer, but he knew how much depended on his coolness, and therefore he continued:

"The question is, can I, by paying, set this poor man near him he loves most in this world."

"Most—except his father!" said Labian, in a smothered voice, so that the duke could not detect his words.

"Yes, you can, my lord, by paying."

"Very well, then. Let me at once see the prisoner, as you call him, and have the pleasure of telling him I have procured the attendance of his servant."

"Stop, my lord!" said the Duke de Mareosi. "There are a few formalities to be gone through before you and your companion can pass into the prison!"

Marriott reddened.

"This man is not my companion, my Lord Duke de Mareosi, although I am proud to know him—I am indeed, for he is faithful, which is more than are some folk. What are the formalities?"

"Searching."

"Search me, if you like," said Marriott, "but I should certainly have considered that my rank would have exempted me from such a humiliation."

"My lord," said Mareosi, "if you insist upon your rank, I can but yield, for I am bound not to search a noble if he protests on the score of his nobility; but I should have thought that you, an Englishman, would not have objected to be searched, if only to prove, after the manner of your countrymen, that you have nothing to conceal."

"In a general way," replied Marriott, "I should not object to be searched, but to-day I do, and urge my rank as my prerogative."

Marcosi bowed, and, as he smiled sardonically, he continued :

"And your companion—is his rank so elevated that he must not be searched ?"

"Search me !" said stout old Labian, standing forward defiantly.

And search him they did, and so minutely that one would have supposed they doubted the poor old fellow's finger-nails.

"Done ?" he asked, at last.

"Pass—both !" said Marcosi, contemptuously.

Marriott took no notice, but passed quietly on.

He walked several paces before Labian, and so the little procession reached the cell.

But no sooner was the door open than Labian pushed past, and catching his master in his arms, in the eager Italian manner, their faces came side by side, so that, if the serving-man had any secret to whisper, he had whispered it almost before the jailers were aware that he had leaped forward into the cell.

He had whispered :

"The senor has weapons for your release !"

Red Gauntlet was therefore on his guard—thoroughly on his guard.

And now, as Labian fell back, Marriott approached, and as his broad back was set between him and the prisoner, he brought out the ends of those two pieces of the crowbar, one of each of which was concealed up an arm of his coat.

Red Gauntlet comprehended what was meant in a moment.

"Am very sorry to see you in this plight, my dear fellow !" he said, holding out both hands.

It was a risky moment.

The next instant he felt the two pieces of steel gliding down the sleeves of Red Gauntlet himself.

But there were now the sheet files and the third piece of the crowbar to convey to the brave prisoner.

Red Gauntlet was very heavily chained hand and foot, so that, without the files, the crowbar was but a mockery.

"Thanks, dear friend !" said Red Gauntlet. "Whatever happens, I am glad to know that I have friends ; and whether I live or die, escape or fail, I thank thee heartily !"

And he glanced meaningly and smilingly at the friend who had brought him the means of escape.

"We shall pull you through, I've no doubt !" said Marriott.

"You will do your best, I am sure," replied Red Gauntlet, again a meaning look on his face.

"Time is up, senor !" here said the jailer. "No visitor, not being the relation of a prisoner, is allowed to remain more than a minute in the cell."

Again Marriott looked meaningly at the prisoner, and again holding out his hands—in the palm of each there being a sheet file—again they shook hands.

The files slipped down the sleeves and clanked against the pieces of the crowbar, but the sound was not marked by the janitors. If they heard it, they mistook it for the jingling of the prisoner's chains.

But now there remained the end bit of the crowbar, without which there could be no chance of escape.

How was it to be removed from the breast of the waist-coat ?

There it was, peeping up from amongst the silken folds of the neck-tie.

But it could not be grasped.

Marriott had purposely pushed it up, so that the prisoner might see it.

And Gauntlet *did* mark the steel, but it was another thing to obtain it.

Already the bits of crowbar up the sleeve of his coat,

together with the files, prevented him from much movement, or the danger of discovery would have been imminent.

"And," thought Red Gauntlet, "let me not be rash in my eagerness to escape, or I may involve him in my ruin."

"Time is up, senor !" repeated the head jailer, this time speaking a little imperiously.

"Yes, yes !" replied the Englishman, slipping down the end of the crowbar, and turning as though about to leave the prison —"good-bye !"

He had this idea—to turn to the door, then turn back as though to say once more "good-bye," and then to effect the passing of the steel to Red Gauntlet.

But brave old Labian saved them from that trouble.

"Pardon, senor," he said to Marriott, looking straight at the place where the iron had been seen, showing his teeth and biting—"pardon—but though I know the senor is far my superior, let me thank him for his goodness in bringing me here to the side of my old master, whom I love ! Let me take his hand, and, as I do so, let me bow low down, in testimony of my gratitude !"

Marriott saw the scheme.

"Certainly, my dear fellow !" he said, smiling. "Come here !"

Labian came, bowing low.

"Take my hand."

And Marriott offered his right, pushing up the end of the iron as he did so.

Old Labian took the hand in both of his, and bowed.

Now, Marriott being tall and broad, he totally covered the performance Labian went through.

This was nothing more nor less than simply biting the end of the iron and drawing it forth.

Then he clapped his hands upon his face as though weeping, turned away as though to conceal his tears, shook his shoulders as though repressing a number of unmanly sobs, and quietly slipped the apparatus down the inside of *his* waist-coat.

So, crowbar and files were in the cell with the prisoner.

And Labian, who knew the way to move, was with him to help him.

And now that Marriott saw all was right, his natural spirits returned, and he said :

"I wish I could help you, friend."

"I am sure you would if you could."

"But here you are."

"Here I am."

"And here I suppose you must stay."

"Yes—here I must stay !"

And at this point Labian turned more away, and sobbed in a manner so much like a laugh that it sounded like hysteria, and one of the jailers, a man with a little of the milk of human kindness—just a drop—offered to come and pat him on the back.

An offer which Labian refused in very quick time, for the operation might have "joggled" the crowbar to the floor.

"Good—good-bye !" said Marriott.

"Addio !" replied Red Gauntlet ; "and—and—and if we never meet again——"

At which point both hid their faces, one in his hands, Marriott in his handkerchief, and Labian went hysterical again.

"Lead me out—lead me out !" said Marriott.

And this being done, he spruced himself up, said " Thank you !" and went away with the consciousness of having done a not bad day's work.

Leaving Red Gauntlet to escape.

And this is how Red Gauntlet, aided by old Labian, prepared to escape.

This is what they had to do.

They had to bore through the wall of the prison in which they were confined, when they would find themselves upon a terrace ; then they had to let themselves down a well about twenty feet deep, then through another ; then they had to cross a ditch and scale a wall, for a change. When arrived at the top of this wall, they had to get down on the other side, where the subterranean way to the monastery of St. Cecilia, known to Labian, would be at hand, and there they would be safe.

Now, all this appears to be very hard and impossible work, but when it is remembered that others imprisoned have broken their way out with a rusty nail and a bit of cord, why, it may readily be understood that, with a crowbar to supplant the rusty nail, a deal of time would be saved.

It was so.

But they had no rope.

Marriott and Labian had both forgotten the rope.

What was to be done?

Necessity is the mother of invention.

Labian knew the exact way they were to take, for once, as a sentry, he had learnt every fraction of the way, and therefore he knew exactly what was wanted.

Twenty feet of rope to get down the first wall; another fifteen to get up a wall about thirteen feet high, and with which the descent could be made on the other side,—in all, thirty-three feet of rope at least, and say forty.

Well, the escape began.

In twenty minutes the sheet files, the very best of their kind, had cut through the fetters which chained down the well-made limbs of Red Gauntlet.

Then they began to make their ropes.

Their coats they tore into strips; but, that their material might be made stronger, Labian took off his leather waist-coat, and cut it with a pocket-knife into fine strips.

The cloth of their coats and the strips of leather were then plaited together, and a stout rope made, only it was ten feet short when it was completed.

"Oh," said Labian, "ten feet short!"

"What say you now, stout Labian?" asked Red Gauntlet.

"I say this, good master—we must take six feet off the first rope, and drop from the end, and then take four feet from the second rope, up which we have to climb the second wall; and pull up to it with our hands,—by that rope we are to drop on the side of the second wall. The four-feet drop will be nothing—will it?"

"Right!" said Red Gauntlet. "Now to try the strength of the rope."

He flung it round the bar of the window.

"Now, then, hold on at it!" said Labian.

And he was about to perform this operation, when a warning clanking at the door told them their jailers were on the alert.

A moment, and all the leather and cloth rope was bundled into a heap, and the two prisoners had prepared to appear asleep.

"Ho! wake up there!" said the jailer, bringing in the bread and water which was alone the fare of the prisoners—a fare which was not that instituted for prisoners at Naples under Victor Emmanuel's reign, unless it was for refractory prisoners.

De Marcosi gratified his malicious spirit without infringing the law, by stating that all the prisoners were refractory—every one.

"Where are your coats?" said the surly jailer.

"Under us," said Labian.

And this was strictly the truth, as they were lying on them; but he did not add that they were reduced to the shape of ropes.

"Oh! Why have you taken them off?"

"Because we found them more comfortable as they are than as they were."

"Oh, well, here is your bread and water, and may you enjoy it! You won't get nothing more for weeks, so you had better make up your minds to like the flavour!"

"Thanks!" said Labian.

The door clanked.

"Now, good master, eat. 'Twill give you strength for the coming fight for liberty."

"You are right!" said Red Gauntlet.

And never a word was said until every scrap of the black bread and every drop of water had been consumed.

It was then getting towards sunset, and no time was to be lost in making preparations for the escape.

They had their *first* stone to loosen.

And anybody who wants to know what that means, had better try to get his first brick out of the middle of a wall.

The fourth and fifth bricks almost fall out.

The third is easily removed.

The second offers some difficulties.

But the first is indeed a tussle.

The crowbar had to be chip-chipped against the edge of the stone, until all the mortar was removed some three inches into the heart of the wall.

And this was no light work, to say nothing of the danger of being heard, and an inquiry being made.

(To be continued in our next.)

THE BANDIT MURDERERS.

In a charming villa, situated in a truly romantic country, but at a considerable distance from the high-road, Baron M. was accustomed to spend the summer. His mansion, built on an eminence, was perfectly adapted to his fortune.

It was a spacious building, elegant both within and without, and displayed a good style of architecture. It was about two hundred paces from the village.

Business obliged the baron to take a journey of a few days. His wife, a young and beautiful woman, scarcely twenty years of age, remained at home. He took with him two of his best servants, and two others were left with the baroness.

No violation of the public security had ever been heard of in that part of the country; and as the baroness did not belong to the timid portion of her sex, the ideas of danger were far from entering her mind.

The second evening after the baron's departure, she was just stepping into bed, when she heard an alarming noise in an apartment near her chamber.

She called, but received no answer.

The noise, screaming, and confusion grew louder every minute.

She was at a loss to conceive what could be the matter, and hastily putting on a light garment, went to the door to discover the cause.

What a horrible spectacle presented itself!

Two of her servants, half naked, were extended lifeless on the floor; the room was full of strange and ferocious-looking men; the baroness's chambermaid was kneeling before one of them, and, instead of the mercy she implored, received the fatal stroke.

No sooner did the door open than two of the barbarians with drawn swords rushed towards it.

What man, not to say what woman, would not have been struck with the utmost terror, and have given up life and everything for lost?

A loud shriek of despair, a flight of a few paces, a fruitless entreaty for mercy, would probably have been the last resource of many thousands.

The baroness, however, conducted herself in a different manner.

"And are you come at last?" exclaimed she, with a tone of heartfelt joy, and advancing towards her two assailants with a haste which highly astonished them both, and fortunately stopped their uplifted weapons. "Are you come at last?" repeated she. "Such visitors as you I have long wished to see."

"Wished!" muttered one of the assassins. "What do you mean by that? But stay, I will——".

He had already raised his cutlass, but his comrade averted the stroke. "Stop a moment, brother," said he; "let us first hear what she would have."

"Nothing but what is also your pleasure, brave comrades. You have made charming work here, I see. You are men after my own heart, and neither you nor I shall have reason to repent it if you will but listen for two minutes to what I have to say."

"Speak! speak!" cried the whole company.

"But be brief," added one of the fiercest of them, "for we shall not make much ceremony with you either."

"Nevertheless, I hope you may, if you but grant me a hearing. Know, then, that I am, to be sure, the wife of the richest gentleman in this country; but the wife of the meanest beggar cannot be more unhappy than I am. My husband is one of the most jealous and niggardly wretches on the face of the earth. I hate him as I hate the devil, and it has long been the most fervent wish of my heart to get out of his clutches, and at the same time to pay him off all old scores. I should have left him many a time, had I been able to contrive how to escape. All my servants were his spies; that fellow, whose business you have done so completely, was the worst of them all. I am scarcely twenty-two, and, as I flatter myself, at least not ugly; if any one of you chose to take me along with him, I should have no objection; I would accompany him, no matter whether to the woods or to the village ale-house. Nor shall any of you have reason to repent of sparing my life. You are in a well-stored mansion, but it is impossible you should be acquainted with all its secret corners. These I will show you, and if I do not make you richer by six thousand dollars, then serve me as you have done my chambermaid."

Robbers of this kind are certainly villains, but nevertheless they are still men.

The wholly unexpected tendency of the baroness's address, the unaffected tone with which she spoke, the more than ordinary beauty of a young, half-naked female, altogether produced a powerful effect on men whose hands were yet reeking with the blood they had shed.

They all stepped aside and consulted together in a low tone for some minutes.

The baroness was left quite alone, but she betrayed not the least wish to escape.

She heard two or three thus express themselves:

"Let's dispatch her, and the game will be up!"

She, however, scarcely changed colour, for the opposition of the others did not escape her acute ear.

One, who was probably the captain of these banditti, now advanced towards her.

He asked twice or thrice whether they might absolutely rely on the truth of what she had said; whether she actually wished to be released from her husband and go with them; and whether she was ready to resign her person to one of them—to himself, for instance—during the few peaceful nights they could enjoy?

Having replied in the affirmative to all these questions, having not only suffered the warm embrace of the robber, but even returned it—for what will not necessity excuse?—he at length said:

"Come along, then, and lead us round. The devil trust you ladies of rank, but we'll, however, venture for once. But let me tell you beforehand, that, were you ten times as handsome, this weapon shall cleave your skull the moment we observe the least disposition to escape or to betray us."

"Then it will be safe enough; and were this the only condition of my death, I should outlive you all, and even the wandering Jew himself."

The baroness smiled as she pronounced these words; hastily snatched up the nearest light, as though she had been as anxious as any of them to collect the plunder and be gone; conducted the whole company through every apartment; opened unasked every door, every drawer, and every chest; assisted in emptying them and packing up the valuables; joked with the utmost vivacity; jumped with indifference over the mangled bodies; spoke with the familiarity of an old acquaintance to each of the horrid troop; and willingly aided, with her delicate hands, in the most laborious occupations.

Plate, money, jewels, clothes, and other valuables were now collected together, and the captain of the banditti was already giving the order for their march, when his destined bride suddenly caught him by the arm. "Did I not tell you," said she, "that you should not repent making a friend of me and sparing my life? You may indeed have your fling in places that you find open; but 'tis a pity that you cannot so easily come at treasures that are somewhat more concealed."

"Concealed! What? Where is something more concealed?"

"What! do you suppose that among coffers so full of the most valuable effects there are no secret places? Look here, and you will be convinced of the contrary."

She pointed to a secret spring in the baron's writing-desk. They pressed upon it, and out fell six rouleaux, each containing two hundred dollars.

"Zounds!" cried the leader of the robbers. "Now indeed I see that you are an incomparable woman. I will keep you for this like a little duchess."

"And perhaps better still," rejoined she, laughing, "when I tell you one thing more. I am well aware that you must have had spies who informed you of the absence of my tyrant; but did they not tell you of the four thousand guilders which he received the day before yesterday?"

"Not a syllable; where are they?"

"Oh, safe enough, under half a dozen locks and bolts! You would certainly not have found them and the iron chest in which they are deposited, had it not been for me. Come along, comrades; we have finished above-ground, and now we'll see what is to be done under it. Come along with me, I say, into the cellar!"

The robbers followed, but not without precaution. At the entrance of the cellar, provided with a strong iron trap-door, a man was posted as a sentinel.

The baroness did not take the least notice of this.

She conducted the whole troop to a vault at the very farthest extremity of the cellar.

She unlocked it, and in a corner of this recess stood the chest she had described.

"Here," said she, giving the captain the bunch of keys, "here, unlock it, and take what you find as a wedding gift, if you can obtain the consent of your companions as readily as you have gained mine."

The robber tried one key after another, but none would fit.

He grew impatient, and the baroness appeared still more so.

"Lend me them," said she. "I hope I shall find the way sooner. Indeed, if we don't make haste, morning might overtake us. Ha! only think—the reason neither of us could unlock it is clear enough. As welcome as your visit is to me, yet I have no scruple to confess that the unexpected arrival of so great a pleasure has flurried me a little. I have brought the wrong bunch of keys. A moment's patience, and I'll soon set that to rights."

She ran upstairs, and presently they heard her coming down again; but she went more slowly, as if out of breath with the haste she had made.

"I've found them! I've found them!" cried she at a distance.

She was now within about three steps of the sentinel placed at the entrance of the cellar, when she made a spring at the wretch, who as little expected the dissolution of the world as such an attack.

A single push with all her strength tumbled him down the stairs from top to bottom.

In a twinkling she closed the trap-door, bolted it, and thus had the whole company secure in the cellar.

All this was the work of a single moment.

In the next she flew across the court-yard, and with the candle set fire to a detached pig-stye.

The watchman in the neighbouring village, perceiving the flames, instantly gave the alarm.

In a few minutes all the inhabitants were out of their beds, and a crowd of farmers and their servants hastened to the mansion.

The baroness waited for them at the gate of the court-yard.

"A few of you," said she, "will be sufficient to put out this fire, or to prevent it from spreading. But now provide yourselves with arms, which you will find in abundance in my husband's armoury: post yourselves at all the avenues of the cellar, and suffer not one of the murderers and robbers shut up in it to escape!"

Her directions were obeyed, and not one of them escaped the punishment due to their crimes.

THE FORESTERS' FEAST. IN THE OLDEN TIME.
With an early number will be Given the companion Picture, printed in Colours, entitled, THE FORESTERS' FÊTE OF THE PRESENT DAY.
London : E. Harrison, Salisbury Court, and all Newsagents everywhere.

TALES OF BRIGANDS AND ROBBERS.

I Warn & Strike

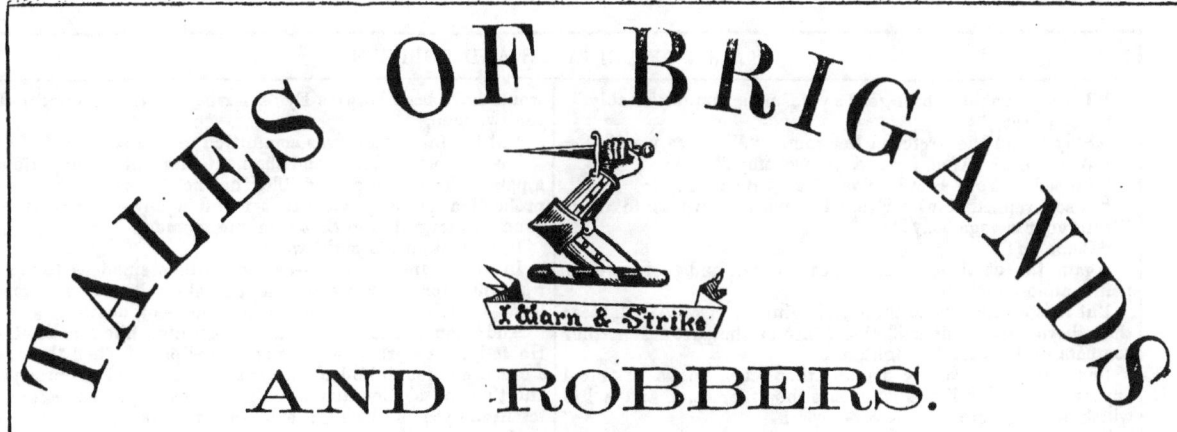

[CRITICAL POSITION OF LADY MAY.]

HAWK'S EYE, THE PHANTOM ROBBER.

CHAPTER III.

THE DUEL.

THE two men were face to face.

Two strong men, hating each other, as they knew, each man by the gleam in the eyes of the other.

Each man held his sword steadily pointed at the breast of his rival, and there between them was the helpless Lady May.

"Is it a duel to the death ?" asked Bertram.

"To the death !" was the answer.

And as the men thus spoke, they advanced a step to each other.

"Are you a good swordsman ?" asked Bertram, calmly.

"As good as hope can make me !" replied Hawk's Eye.

No. 10

"Then you should be a good swordsman, unquestionably."

"Let us see!"

"Stay," said the wretched Bertram. "Who are you?"

"Who am I? Well, for one, your enemy!"

"Indeed! Your sword quivers," said Bertram.

"If so," replied Hawk's Eye, "it is with eagerness to drive it into your savage body!"

"Come on!"

Again the combatants neared each other, and their swords' points almost touched.

But it is a remarkable thing in beginning a war with steel that there is an unmistakable desire on the part of neither combatants to begin the fight.

But once the warfare begun, then each blade of steel appears to gain a life as it touches the other steel, and a life which is ever increasing—ever—ever!

So it was with them.

They hesitated until their steel touched, and thereupon they were eager.

Meanwhile, there was the Lady May standing between them, hands clasped, eyes dilated, and her whole form trembling.

"Gentlemen, I pray you be merciful—if not to yourselves, to me!"

But men, when they have swords point to point, cannot listen even to the voice of the woman they love, for if they but turn an ear—nay, only lend an ear—their attention may be drawn away from the fight, and in that moment this or that man may lose the fight in question.

She soon saw that her intercession was worse than useless—that it was even dangerous—and therefore she turned away; and, hiding her face against the wall, with sickening hope and eager despair she waited for the awful issue of the fight, upon which so wholly depended her future.

Now the encounter began in earnest, and reallest earnest.

Bertram was the first to thrust, and certainly, had his thrust taken effect, Hawk's Eye would never have got over the result.

But, happily, Hawk's Eye did not belie his name. He saw the approach of the weapon, threw it on one side, and then, in his turn, thrust at his opponent. Unhappily, he saw the approaching thrust in his turn, and he guarded it, and was saved.

The two men then began in real earnest to beat each other down. Sometimes one got the advantage, and sometimes the other, but they were marvellously well skilled, both of them, in the sword, and therefore, for some minutes, the fate of the battle was quite undecided.

Now, they say in swordsmanship that three rules prevail. If both of you are very splendid swordsman, it depends upon some precautious ruse upon one of you, or else the ability to wait and be patient, which gains the victory. If, on the contrary, you are a moderately-good swordsman, and your opponent is ever so little your superior, you are sure to lose; while, if your opponent is a perfect swordsman, and you know nothing about the weapon, the probabilities are that you may be run through; but, at the same time, it is not unlikely that you may give him a wound, and perhaps even one to the death.

But in this case the men were equally good swordsmen, yet neither fought well, for the simple reason that neither was cool. Bertram Falconer was enraged with hate of his opponent—Hawk's Eye was excited by fear for his lady-love in event of failure, and dread of the effect upon her of seeing any blood spilt whatever—blood rushing from the veins of either men or both.

For five minutes nothing was heard but the fearful yet exciting sliding of the swords one over the other, interspersed with little clashes as a pass was made and the other man met it with a parry.

Parry and thrust—thrust and parry. So it continued for five minutes, when the lady, turning round and screaming slightly as she fancied she saw her lover wounded, gave the victory to the enemy.

Had she kept her face hidden, undoubtedly the victory would have been Hawk's Eye's, for he was the less angered of the two men.

But the misfortune was committed as she screamed.

He trembled, turned, and the next moment he experienced a pain so horrible—so terrible, that he had no power to comprehend anything beyond that awful agony,—the Lady May even was forgotten in that supreme moment.

In an instant his sight went.

In that same instant—as his brain seemed as though it was being torn from its temple, the skull, by some ravening bird—he felt that this was the summons of death.

And then a cold feeling came upon him, like a bath of ice. He fell, as it were, down a deep precipice. Then there was a crash, as though he had reached the bottom of the precipice; and then, as a thousand waving torches appeared before his tortured eyes and brain, there came a blank.

He knew nothing more.

This was the state of the case.

The enemy's sword had passed through and behind his left ear, a great nerve had been cut, intense pain had been caused, and a deathly faint was the result.

Lady May had not so far moved.

Horror froze her into iciness, and it was only as she heard Bertram say: "Dead,—one enemy the less!" that she drooped, and, melting like the ice-bound cataract when the loving sun of spring pours upon it, forward and down she fell upon the still and unresponding body, and she also for a time forgot the miseries of her fate.

"He dead and she senseless!" said Bertram. "All works well for me!"

And, lifting up the dead weight of the Lady May, he carried her forth to the entrance of the cave.

Before doing so, however, as she lay powerless on the ground, a horrid light filled his eyes, his lips parted, and colour spread over his face.

"Shall I?" he said. "Opportunity serves me well, and henceforth she would be mine irretrievably, and Falcon Grange and all its broad lands would be mine!"

Then he looked at the prostrate figure near her, and some little remains of a good conscience resting with him, he said:

"No, not here!"

And, as we have said, he raised the Lady May, and carried her forth from the cave.

His patient horse stood neighing and pawing the ground.

Bertram stroked the animal, and then raised himself and his burden into the saddle.

But he then learnt that to carry a dead weight in the saddle is hard work.

Carrying off a living woman, she clings to you, her great enemy, to save herself from falling; but, senseless, she has no power to comprehend her danger.

"This is heavy work," said the villain—"more than I bargained for! I must get me a coach. Again, it may kill her, and then what would become of Falcon Grange and the estates? Albert may be an outlaw, and he may be dead; but the estates, as those of a traitor, would be forfeit to the King; and I am not sure that I am so well thought of at court that the King should give me the estates."

Then, as he rode on, he remembered that there was a posting-house not far away, and for this he determined to make, in the hope of obtaining a coach, which should save him from the danger of losing the Lady May.

But suddenly he remembered something, and, with a start and shudder, he turned his horse's head, and rode straight back to the cave—straight to Hawk's Eye's noble black steed, which was tied to a neighbouring fence.

"No, no!" says Bertram. "If the horse is seen here, attention may be attracted, and the old cave may be searched, though not once in a year does a human being set foot in it, for there is a fear that it is haunted. If the horse be removed, then what is there to show any human being has been here during the night? There will be no evidence—yes, the hoof-marks. Well, the poor boors about here—the wretched country people who neither read nor write, their fine task-masters declaring it would injure them—they will suppose that they are the marks of the phantom horseman. If the horse be let go, then all will be safe! No one will visit the cavern—bats and ravens, foxes and badgers—nay, even the nauseous beetles of the land,—nay, even the very ants will be my friends, and eat off mine enemy from the face of the earth—even his very bones shall be gnawed into nothingness!"

So murmuring, he untied Hawk's Eye's noble steed with one hand, as he held the Lady May before him with the other.

And as he did so, the moonlight increasing, he saw that his enemy's horse was a magnificent animal, sheeny and splendid, bright-eyed and keen.

"Ha, a finer horse than mine! Well, the dead ride not on earthly horses; therefore, I, not being dead, will take him as a guerdon of victory!"

So saying, he caught at the bridle, and was about to draw the horse away with him.

But Brilliant—that was the name of the horse—must now have found it time to interfere, for, with one plunge, he reared himself on his hind legs, struck out one of his fore feet, and as with one of them he caught Bertram a blow on the mouth, with his teeth he bit upon the right arm of the would-be thief, and tore away the leather sleeve which alone protected Bertram, and fortunately, from a fearful bite.

As it was, the blow of the hoof smashed Bertram's lips fearfully, and the jutting blood fell upon the white clothing of the unhappy Lady May.

Such men as Bertram can pass into a state of rage in a moment.

Almost as he felt the blow, he let the bridle go, and, this done, his wicked right hand leaped at his sword, still wet and red with the blood of Brilliant's master, with the full intention of burying the same wickedly-used weapon in the heart of the good steed.

But, as though the horse knew what was coming, he shied away, gave a low and defiant neigh, and galloped off at a pace which quite defied anything like pursuit.

But Bertram's rage was too great for caution.

A moment, and one of his saddle pistols was in his hand—a report followed, and then a crash.

The bullet had but hit a neighbouring tree.

The horse Brilliant answered with another neigh—distant and defiant.

"Curse me!" cried the miscreant. "What have I done? I may have alarmed the neighbourhood! Well, well—I will say I had an encounter with a highwayman, who has stolen my lady's horse! But what if she revives and attempts to speak?"

He hesitated for a moment.

"Ha," he said, "I have a remedy for that! *She* shall not speak! I will defy her to betray *me!*"

Then he listened.

"Good! His horse is fleeing from him at a good sixteen miles an hour! All goes well—very well! His body is left to my friends—the beasts, birds, and creeping things of the forest! When next I return to the cave that I alone haunt, not even his skeleton shall offend my sight! So now for my lady here, and my scheme!"

He turned his horse's head, and set off at a gallop, for the night was passing away, and in a couple or three more hours daylight would be upon him.

His lips pained him very much, and as he raised his hand to his face, he found that they were much swollen.

Then he perceived that he could not speak plain.

"This will not improve me," he said; "but I doubt whether aught could make my lady hate me more than she does, and, therefore, I need trouble myself little on that score!"

On he rode for about an hour, and then he found the house for which he was seeking.

One twinkling light alone saved it from utter darkness.

"Ho—ho! Inn, there! Inn!"

And he beat with the pommel of his sword at the echoing oaken door.

After a pause, the window at which the light was to be marked was opened, and a feeble voice asked:

"Who have we there?"

"A traveller," replied Bertram, "who needs the pity of all good men."

"How so? 'Tis a strange time for travelling."

"Maybe, necessity compelled."

"What have you there in the saddle?"

"A lady."

"A lady?"

"Ay; we have been attacked by a highwayman. My dear lady here, my wife, has been thrown from her horse, with which the villain has made away. And here am I, a most unhappy gentleman, with my dear wife senseless in my arms, myself wounded, for my lips are shapeless with a blow from the butt-end of our assailant's pistol, and I am almost broken-hearted!"

"And your purse?" asked the cautious innkeeper.

"The highwayman took it, good mine host."

"Ha!" said the cautious host, "then your honour can-not——"

"Pay? Oh, yes; I have another purse under my coat. Quick! come down at once, and open the door!"

"As the lightning is quick!" said the host. "And a very clever gentleman you must be to carry two purses, for I heard your honour's money chink."

Down went the window, the light vanished, and the next minute, after much clanking and shooting of bolts, Bertram and his still senseless burden were shown, thanks to the influence of the chinking purse, into the very best room mine host had in his house.

The landlady came fussing about the poor Lady May.

"Your dear lady seems very ill—lay her carefully on the sofa. You, Dolly and Polly, run for my salts, and, Nancy, burn a feather before the dear lady's mouth! Ah, sir, your dear lady——"

And then the landlady stopped suddenly, for she saw that Lady May had no ring upon the third finger of the left hand.

Bertram saw the weak point in a moment.

"Ah," said he, "you may judge to the cruelty to which we have been subjected, when I tell you that the rascal even took my wife's wedding-ring!"

The landlady comprehended *that* in a moment, and, as apology for the horrid suspicion she had formed, she bobbed a low curtsey, and said:

"Ah, your honour is a great gentleman, as I see by your words—and, Dolly, fetch his honour some water to wash his honour's lips with! What a wretch, to steal a wedding-ring! He should be put in a large basket, your honour, and dipped in a pond till death did for him, hanging being too good for a man as could steal a wedding-ring, your honour! Ah, look —your dear lady is a-coming-to!"

This was the fact.

The poor lady was regaining her senses, owing to the care bestowed upon her.

The eyelids began to quiver, and the lips to tremble; then movement came into her hands, and at last the lovely blue eyes gazed oddly at all around them.

Suddenly they marked Bertram, and then a sudden fear came upon the face.

Bertram saw his danger, and said:

"Leave the room, all of you! I want to speak to my wife!"

"But——" said the landlady.

"Leave the room!" he repeated, in a loud, thundrous voice, that admitted of no denial.

And they obeyed him, for your masses are generally afraid of your thunder-voiced people.

"Lady May!"

"You here—and I—alone in this room?"

"Lady May, would you save your lover?"

"Save him?" she cried.

"Ay, save him!"

"Is he not dead?"

"No."

She uttered a cry of joy, and then, catching at Bertram's hand, she kissed it.

Yes, she, the pure Lady May, kissed that villain's red right hand.

" And he shall live as you decide."

" Where is he ?"

" That is my secret. Suffice that he is my prisoner."

" What conditions do you make ?"

" I do not kill him because to let him be dead, and my power over you through him would cease ! No—he lives !"

" What are your demands ?"

" Is your love true for him ?"

" As the loadstone to the north !"

" Then your love is unselfish ?"

" As any earthly passion can be !"

" Then prove it !"

" How ?"

" By sacrificing yourself for *his* sake !"

" How so ?"

" If you refuse to marry me, he dies !"

" Ha ! you would turn his life against his very happiness ?"

" Yes."

" Bertram—what have I done that thus you should treat me ?"

" Nought—I love you !"

" Strange, your way of loving ! If I love and am sacrificial, how happens it that *you* love and are selfish ?"

" Because I have a greater passion in me than love !"

" Is that ambition ?"

" Yes—undying, unending ambition ! The estates of Falcon Grange *shall* be mine by my marriage with you ! Once let me own them, and I will seek to be a good man ! I will aid your brother—help your lover, unknown as he was to me until to-night ! But until I gain the old family acres and mansion, I am as satan himself !"

" You horrify me ! Why not be good and simple in your life, Cousin Bertram ?"

" My ambition—my ambition !"

And here the landlady tapping at the door to make inquiry if the dear lady wanted any attention, Bertram continued :

" Mind, May, no attempt to defy me ! If you betray me, your lover dies ! Perhaps you also may have to die, that the estates may be mine ; and mine they shall be, even though I tear the King's consent from his Majesty ! So be on your guard !"

Then Bertram opened the door.

" Good madam," he said, " my lady desires that we depart at once. Have you a coach ?"

" The finest in the parish, I warrant me !" said the hostess. " But will not the dear lady wait till the blessed sun gets up ?"

" What say you, my lady ?"

For a moment she was unable to make any reply.

" You see," he continued, " my lady has not yet recovered the shock of meeting with that rascally highwayman. Collect yourself, my lady—what say you ?"

" I—I say, my lord, as you say," said the unfortunate young lady.

She had committed herself now to his command that she should appear to be his wife.

He stooped and whispered :

" If *now* you say you are not my wife, I will say you are *mad*, and I will have you bound in the carriage !"

The shock was so terrible as he said these words, that again she fainted.

But this time she soon recovered—almost without the assistance of the friendly landlady—and then she tremulously signified her desire to set off as quickly as possible.

" Your word is law with me, my lady," said Bertram, bowing low.

Ten minutes passed—they were in a coach, and had left the posting-inn behind them.

CHAPTER IV.
THE REVIVAL.

Turn we now to the cavern where lay, stark and cold, the body of Hawk's Eye.

Nothing moved in the cavern.

But after a time there was the galloping of a horse heard nearer and nearer, until it stopped outside the cavern.

Then came a low winnying—such a noise as a horse makes when he is pleased to get back to his stable, and his favourite ostler is bringing him his feed of corn.

Then there was a sniffing.

Then came another winny.

And now the horse, with careful steps, entered the cavern.

Had Hawk's Eye had his senses, he would have known by the very tread that the approaching beauty was Brilliant.

Up came the horse to where his master lay upon his back, his arms outstretched.

Winnying, sniffing, with ears laid back, and each step felt for before it was taken, Brilliant came to his master's side.

Then he stooped down, sniffed, and uttered a cry, which appeared to be expressive of pain.

Then he began steadily licking his good master's face.

Well, whether it was the warmth of the tongue or the motion again put Hawk's Eye's blood in circulation, or whether it was some peculiar sympathy between horse and man, it is certain that gradually Hawk's Eye returned to life.

And, strangely enough, it was just about this time that the Lady May was returning to a sense of her wretchedness.

And, lest our readers should fancy this vivification, or coming to life again, as quite impossible, they will allow us to explain how Bertram had naturally fallen into the error of supposing that he had slain his enemy.

We have said Bertram's sword severed a nerve behind the left ear. Now, the severing of a nerve behind the left ear is not a wound sufficient to cause death, but it causes so horrible a pain that nature, unable to endure it, compels the sufferer to faint, and so dead is this fainting that positively the heart ceases to beat, and the body is quite without motion.

And if means are not taken to revive the sufferer—for this awful agony appears to pass away during the unconsciousness, and only a dull pain remains—death probably ensues.

Possibly Hawk's Eye would have died of sheer want of attention.

But his brave Brilliant saved him.

Saved him !

Up he rose, a little weak and staggering, but with no more sense of pain than that caused by the cutting of a finger pretty deep.

Nor had he lost a table-spoonful of blood.

In a moment he comprehended all.

" Good horse — bravo Brilliant !" he cried, patting the animal's neck, and the creature answered with far more love and sweetness of tone than you will find in many a human being.

" Good horse—you have saved *me*, and now you must save her !"

And, as though the horse knew what was said, he pawed the ground impatiently.

" Fine fellow !" replied Hawk's Eye.

And so saying, he leaped into the saddle, feeling a little giddy, and that was all.

Then once more, the fresh, cutting air, which you only feel when a horse is galloping under you, came upon his cheeks, and brought the colour upon them.

" I shall save her," he said—" I feel I shall save her !"

And away he bounded towards the road.

Suddenly a thought came upon him.

He had no money !

" I shall find some on the road," he thought, gaily. " Anyhow, I have not yet taken from the road one tenth part of what the King of England has taken from me in confiscating my estate. And if ever I get back my estate, I will return all I have taken—every penny ! But rather now let me alone think of the dear Lady May, my sweet mistress !"

And calling to Brilliant, who had no need of either spur or whip, he galloped still more rapidly.

And happily in the direction whence the coach was coming which was occupied by the Lady May and Bertram.

About twenty minutes, and Hawk's Eye heard the coach approaching.

"Ha! they must go on their way lighter-pursed than now they are."

The coach came nearer.

Then a scream.

A cry for help.

He knew the voice.

May's!

Does the reader guess the rest?

Bertram wanted to make assurance doubly sure, and as they travelled, he sought to place her wholly at his mercy and as he had command over her heart by her love for the supposed imprisoned lover, so to command her utterly by her sense of shame.

But her cry was answered.

A few moments, a quick gallop, and the coachman was flung from his box, the horses were turned over into the ditch, and as Bertram, who certainly did not lack bravery, leaped from the coach, Hawk's Eye was ready for him.

(To be continued in our next.)

RED GAUNTLET, THE BANDIT; OR, THE BLACK MOUNTAINEERS.

BOOK II.—THE BLACK CHATEAU.

CHAPTER XXIV.

RED GAUNTLET EFFECTS HIS ESCAPE.

STOUT old Labian kept singing while the crowbar was at work, though this manœuvre could hardly be called successful, for, though the thud of the pick was not heard, the song was distinctly discernible, and the head jailer, being of a musical turn of mind, and knowing Labian was not a real prisoner, suddenly opened the door, and told Labian, if he liked, he might come in the guard-room and tip them a stave.

But the two had time to fall upon their straw again, Red Gauntlet pretending to be half asleep, while Labian continued his song lustily.

"Ho, mate," says the jailer, "you sing lustily!"

"Do you sing?" asked Labian.

"No, mate, but I like a song."

"Then I'll begin again."

"Come to the guard-room—you can sing there!"

"Can, but won't! Be off, jailer—you are intruding on our privacy!"

"So, that's the way you treat an invitation?"

"That's the way I answer it."

"Good! I'll not ask you again!"

"Don't want you to!" replied Labian.

"There you may stop!"

"So you say!"

"What do you mean?"

"*What* I say!"

"Sing away till the rats eat you, my man!"

"Thanks!" said Labian—"obliged! Good day!"

"Ugh!" said the jailer, and went.

Then the thudding began again, and so did the singing.

"That's a man of bad taste," said the head jailer to another. "He prefers to sing out of my company rather than in it."

"Ah!" said the second jailer, "what a world it is—ain't it?"

And it was about an hour afterwards, and when the dusk had arrived, that the first stone fell upon the ground.

Once again they were visited, but Labian was equal to the occasion, for, marching up to the jailer, so as to distract his attention, and standing before the lantern, so that its light should not fall upon the broken wall, he promised the jailer that he would come and sing next day, if he could find his voice in the prison, and then apologised for having refused to sing before.

"Don't mention it!" said the jailer. "Come and sing now!"

"No, Senor Jailer—I have been singing too much—to-morrow."

"Good! Now give me your hand!"

Now this was too much for old Labian.

However necessary it was to deceive, he could not shake hands with a prison jailer. But how was he to get out of the proffered courtesy? Very easily—'twas no trouble for Labian.

"No, senor," said he—"I do not deserve it. Wait till to-morrow, and I will then do myself the honour to take it, if you can then offer it to me."

"Certainly will I—certainly! You are a fine fellow! and I've just slipped a fine sausage into your bread! To be sure, it is another prisoner's, and he had paid handsomely for it; but I can easily say the money or the sausage was lost. So good night to you, if you won't take my hand!"

"Senor, I am not worthy," said Labian.

And when the door was shut, Labian said:

"Now, can we fairly eat the sausage, knowing it to be stolen?"

"'Twill digest, Labian—eat away!"

"And you?"

"No—I can't, for I'm the man's prisoner."

"I've two minds to throw it away, though it is true it smells very finely."

"Eat it—'twill aggravate him the more to learn he gave you a supper than to find that you flung it away!"

"Oh, Madonna," replied Labian, "what sinners we are—great sinners!—we can always find excuses for ourselves!"

And thereupon he bit into the sausage.

The meal done, and the night quite come, Red Gauntlet began their escape.

The wall was soon slipped through, the ropes collected on the outside, and the crowbar carefully stowed away inside the leather gaiter of Labian's right leg.

They now found themselves on a kind of platform, about eight feet wide, and bordered by a battlemented wall, which had a fall of twenty feet.

To fix the rope of cloth and leather round one of the battlements and make it tight was a very simple operation.

But they knew that a sentry might pass, and the hole once seen in the wall, the alarm would be raised.

They had therefore to put the stones back, as nearly as possible like to what they were before, ere Marriott's trusty bar had begun its work, and then they had to sweep up the fallen and crumbled mortar into a heap in a shadowy corner.

"Master, go you down by the rope first."

"Why?"

"Because I am the heaviest, and might break it."

Red Gauntlet laughed lightly.

"I know you to be too unselfish to wish me to risk a danger which you could take upon your shoulders. You have another reason—what is it?"

"This, master—many a heavy man has held on to and lowered himself by a rope which has broken directly afterwards with a lighter man, the fact being that the heavier man has strained it. Go down first."

"Well, I promise."

"And I want another promise, master."

"What is that?"

"It is, that if *I* fail and fall, you continue your escape. You can do me no good if I fall, while away from here you can, I believe, be of great public service. Do you promise this?"

"Yes, I do, but with much pain."

"'Tis well, master. I have your word, and now one

hearty shake of the hands, master—it may be the last—before we begin."

"Willingly."

There were tears in old Labian's eyes as their hands parted.

"Now begin, master."

Red Gauntlet, without a word, slung himself over the battlement and began the ugly descent, hand under hand.

The rope strained, old Labian on his knees meanwhile, but it did not break.

When Red Gauntlet reached the end of the rope he dropped.

"Confound it!" he said, as he reached the ground and fell from the shock of the distance he had fallen—"more than six feet!"

It was.

Labian had not counted the quantity that had gone round the battlement.

Then Labian came down.

He reached the ground with a run, for he was not less than within three feet of the end of the rope when it gave way and landed him on his back.

"Well," said Labian, "I got half-way down before I fell, I think, and, master, I do believe the crowbar broke my fall!"

"Ha!—but is the crowbar broken?"

"Blessed saints, I hope not!"

And he examined the crowbar in double-quick time.

No—so far all was safe.

They had now reached a terrace, bounded on each side by a wall.

Now, with the apparatus they had with them, it would have been far easier to scale the wall, at the top of which was a sentry-walk built upon arches, these arches being backed by the wall under which they were now standing.

But Labian knew that a sentry was walking continually along this terrace, and that, therefore, it was safer work to dig through the second wall than climb it.

Oh, that *first* stone!

They were three hours before they got it out. To be sure, they had to desist from their labour every time a sentry passed—about every ten minutes; but it was hard, hard work.

The removal of the other stones, to enable them to pass, was soon effected that terrible first stone once was extracted, and then they crept through, to hear the sentry overhead tramping along and bawling out, "All's well!" with the air of being quite sure that all *was* correct.

Crossing the roofed stone corridor over which the sentry was passing, they came to the archways built upon a rugged rock, which latter led down to a wide moat, filled with blackish water.

To slip through this moat was a necessity.

"Labian!"

"Master!"

"Shall we want the crowbar again?"

"No."

"Then leave it—the weight might break you down."

"Pardon, dear master—can't leave the old crowbar behind us! I love it too much for the good turn it has done us!"

"Well, as you like."

So Labian swam with the yet unused rope round his waist and the good crowbar down his leg, and no sooner had he emerged on the other side of the moat than he whispered that that was the most one-sided swim he had ever had in his life.

And it was as Red Gauntlet plunged into the water that he felt once again free.

"Liberty—liberty!" he cried, as he spurned the water on each side of him—"once again I feel I am no longer a prisoner!"

Once on the other side of the moat, they had but to get on the other side of a third wall, and then they would be comparatively free.

The wall in question was the boundary of the prison, and was quite unguarded—quite.

"Now, friend crowbar," said Labian, "you shall do another sort of service."

And tying the end of the rope firmly round the steel bar, he began to swing the end backwards and forwards.

"Master," said he, "the water will make our rope stronger, and our crowbar is not so greedy of rope as the battlement was—la, there she goes!"

And, as the old fellow spoke, up the iron flew in the air, and, plunging in amongst the branches of a tree on the other side, swung round and round, so as to form a safe fulcrum upon which to depend.

"You first again, master."

"As you will," said Red Gauntlet.

And catching the rope, and putting his knees to the wall, he soon raised himself to the top, where, hauling himself by the rope, he caught a branch of the drooping tree, and there remained for Labian to get up, when the rope would have to be shifted to the other side of the wall.

Up came old Labian, very steadily, so that he might be as gentle with the rope as possible. Only as he reached the top did he give a jerk, as he said:

"The rope knows its duty, and don't break."

When it did instanter, near the branch, and the next moment Labian would have been "down again," probably with a broken back, when Red Gauntlet, true to his word, would have had to continue his escape alone.

But Red Gauntlet saw the danger.

He caught Labian's right hand with his right hand.

Feeling himself, however, being drawn by Labian's weight over the wall, in a moment he changed his scheme.

Still holding the tree branch, he flung himself on the opposite side of the wall, and there was Red Gauntlet hanging on one side and Labian on the other, clinging together by their right hands.

"Labian!"

"Master!"

"What's to be done?"

"Ha!"

"Can you raise yourself?"

"No,—I'm so stout I can scarcely get my legs to the wall!"

"What can be done? If I rise, my lightened weight will pull me over."

"Master, let me go, and escape yourself."

"Never!"

"Your promise, master."

"Do you command me?"

"I must."

"Then——"

"Ho!—SAVED!"

This was Labian's little remark.

"What is it?"

"My foot's found a resting-place where a stone has fallen out."

"Saved indeed!" said Red Gauntlet, as he felt the awful weight upon his wrist relax.

By the aid of his branch, he was soon on the wall again, and, still keeping hold on the old attached servant, he very soon had him up on the wall also.

"That was a breather, master!"

"Yes. Ha!—what was that?"

"A sentry!"

"Who goes there?" thundered a voice from the terrace.

No answer.

"Who goes there?"

Still no answer.

Then the challenge was put for the third and last time a soldier on guard must challenge before he fires.

"To-woo—to-woo!" said clever old Labian.

"Ha, ha!" laughed the sentry—"an old owl! All's well!"

"All's well!" was repeated by a sentry further away.

And again Red Gauntlet and Labian were safe.

"We must climb into the tree," said Red Gauntlet.

"Yes, for I must have my crowbar, master."

And up the old fellow climbed after Red Gauntlet.

One more danger, and they were safe in the subterranean passage.

As they reached the ground, a savage dog was there, apparently waiting for them.

"Ha, he's about to bark!" said Labian, and then the dog was silenced.

"What a crowbar this is!" said Labian. "It has stopped that cur, now, from giving the alarm. If ever I get a drawing-room, I'll hang this bit of steel over the fire-stove. Now, master, run through the bit of moonlight!"

They had just begun to run, when a loud voice was heard:
"Broke jail—broke jail!"

A gun was fired.

Another.

Then a bell began quickly tolling, and lights began to appear all over the battlements, and, to crown all, the wounded dog recovered his senses, and began to join in the riot.

But by the time the guard had arrived at the spot where the wounded dog still lay yelping, Red Gauntlet was safe; for they might hunt all over the open land about as much as ever they liked, but they dreamt not of looking *under* it for the escaped prisoner.

Not once did the chase relax during the night, but bloodhounds and men, cavalry and infantry, all in a heap, could not find a trace of the fugitives, who—not forgetting the crowbar—were by this time safely lodged in the monastery of St. Cecilia.

The Duke de Mareosi nearly strangled himself with passion,—but that did not hinder Labian from making a handsome meal, nor Red Gauntlet from dropping into the sleep he so much needed.

"And now I'll to sleep too," said Labian, "and with my new sweetheart in my arms. And if ever woman has been truer to me than my old crowbar, why, so much the better for me!"

CHAPTER XXV.

TIKEYPOODLE.

THEY had seventeen boxes with them, four portmanteaus, and a hat-box. They had had more when they started for England, but as at every place where they had stopped thirty porters had seized hold of a parcel apiece and carried it to his own particular continental hotel, why, no wonder, when they got into the mountains near Naples, they had only twenty-one and the hat-box.

They were the Dowager Duchess Tikeypoodle, and the present duke, her precious son.

Tikeypoodle was fair, fluffy, and foolish; very tall, very thin, and weak in his legs. The only strong thing about him was his stare, and his whiskers, which were long, fluffy, and weak. They were yellow in colour, very weak,—so that one whisker would blow behind his head, while the other was tickling up his eyes, which were of a watery, blueish-greyish green.

He wasn't lovely, but he was amiable.

The dowager, his mamma, was tall and severe, had eyes like gimlets, a nose like a beak, a mouth like a bite, and a chin so square that it looked like the corner of one—a square.

She was a woman with no nonsense about her, and if she had been condemned to be hanged by mistake, in place of somebody else, she would have said:

"This is inconvenient; but, if it can't be helped, kindly bury me decent. And if it can be done, I should prefer a silk rope—rose colour."

She was a strong-minded woman indeed, and, in fact, they would not have had the twenty-one boxes remaining if it had not been for the dowager "ma," who no sooner saw a box being carried off than she charged at the delinquent with a huge umbrella like a mast tied up in a sail, and drove the sharp end in his back, when the poor devil dropped the box, swore in foreign language, and rubbed himself, while the dowager mamma chucked the box on to the heap.

Well, there they were in Italy and a carriage of the country—they inside, and all the luggage wobbling on the roof like a load—which it was.

The carriage pulled up at an inn.

Scampia Zatani was the name over the door.

Out came the innkeeper, bowing as innkeepers do to carriages.

"Ma, what an ugly brute!" says Tikeypoodle.

"Hold your tongue, Tikey!"

"But——"

"Put your whiskers in your mouth—that generally stops you!"

"Yes, ma."

He did it.

"My good man, we request to stop here—can we?"

Tikey pulled his whiskers out of his mouth to say this:

"Ma, don't!"

And then he bottled himself up again.

"Yes, my lady," said Scampia, with that grin of his which made him much more horrible than he was by nature—that was bad enough.

"Ma, look at him!"

"Put your whiskers in your mouth, Tikey!"

"Yes, ma."

He did it.

"My good man," said the dowager mamma, "we will stop. But there are no brigands about, are there?"

"Brigand, my lady—what is that?"

"Thought the man was a fool! An Italian, and don't know what a brigand is! Tikey, take your whiskers out of your mouth!"

"Yes, ma."

"Man, take my umbrella!"

And the dowager ma shot her gingham at Scampia so sharply that an eye, if not two, was certainly in danger.

"Lift me out!"

Scampia tried to do it, but down they both went together.

The dowager ma was up again in a second.

"Knew the man was a fool! Can't even look after a lady! Man, look to the luggage—twenty-one boxes and things, and a hat-box."

"Take care of the hat-box!" bawls Tikey.

"Tikey, put all your whiskers in your mouth directly!"

And the dowager sailed into the inn as though it was a palace, and her own.

Now, Tikey ought to have immediately followed the dowager ma, and he was about to do so, having once more pulled out his whiskers—one immediately flew up into his weak eyes.

But he was arrested by the appearance of Nicola.

Weak as his eyes were, he had force enough in them to tell that she was beautiful.

"Goodness gracious giminy!" said the Duke Tikeypoodle.

Nicola gave him a neat little curtsey.

"Do—do come and kiss me!" said Tikey.

Whereupon Nicola gave him another little salute, and tripped away.

"Very fine gal! Never saw a finer in—in Wotton Wow! Don't care a bit for Sybil now—not a bit!"

"Tikey—Tikey!"

"Coming, mamma!"

"Directly! And put your whiskers in your mouth!"

Now, the dowager mamma and the duke had not been in the place above a quarter of an hour, when a new arrival startled the propriety of the rascally little inn.

The man who appeared was well known there.

"Leon!" said Scampia.

"'Tis I!"

It was indeed Red Gauntlet.

"We thought you were in prison!"

"I was. You have just had arrive an English gentleman and lady?"

"Yes, senor."

"And?"

Leon looked meaningly as he said this, and Scampia, lowering his voice, gave some information.

Leon laughed lowly.

"I can pay part of my debt of gratitude to Marriott at a more early period than I could have expected. So, this Tikeypoodle is his rival, is he? Well, where there is no bridegroom there can be no bride. We will see how my lord will like the mountains; while, as to madame, his mother, she need not fear that her charms will get her into mischief,—she has but to look at any one of my men for any of them rather to run a mile from her ladyship than after her."

"But, senor, how know you all these particulars?"

"Suffice that I do know them."

"Enough, senor."

"Show me into the room where they are."

"Senor, she told me if I did show anyone in, she would fling me out of window."

"Of your own house? That's happy. Nevertheless, show me in."

Leon, as we will call him in this chapter, entered the aristocrat's dining-room with all the most possible politeness.

The dowager ma immediately looked at the water-jug, as though she should much like to fling its contents over the two men at the door.

"Pardon, my lady," said the innkeeper, "but this is the only room."

"We hired it!"

"But this is a gentleman."

"No,—or he would not have intruded upon me—a lady."

"Ma," said Tikeypoodle.

"Put your whisk—no, don't,—you're dining."

"My lady," said Leon, in good English, "I beg your pardon!"

"Oh, if you speak English, I offer you part of our dinner."

"Thanks,—I am hungry."

The dowager ma was in five minutes most gracious and condescending—the strange gentleman being such a charming person.

"Travelling, my lady, on the Continent for the good of your health?" asked Leon.

"No—for the good of my boy."

"Ma!"

"He is to be married."

Leon's countenance changed.

"Does the lady love him?"

"No—but that does not matter!"

"Does it not?" he asked, his fine countenance becoming quite radiant with indignation.

"No—she will love him all the better, for he is a dove!"

"Is he, indeed? But suppose the poor suffering girl loves somebody else?"

"Then she must learn to know better, for I couldn't have any improprieties after her marriage. My son is a very fine young man."

"You dear ma!"

"And very clever."

"Indeed?" asked Leon, scarcely concealing his scorn. "How is he clever?"

"Clever?—I'll tell you, though I wouldn't if you did not speak English, you know. But you're a foreigner, and you do speak English, and therefore you must be a fine fellow. Ha, ha!—if the brigands fall upon us, they won't find what they expect!"

"What is that?"

"Money."

"Oh, nonsense!" says Leon. "You English don't travel without money."

"No, no,—we travel with lots of it! Excuse me if I put my whiskers in my mouth—ma makes me do it so often when she won't have me speak, that it has become a confirmed habit—yes."

"Indeed!—where do you put your money, my lord?"

"Where?—lor, I'm sure—an artful customer, I am! The brigands will never find out, and you may swear I shall never tell one of 'em where it is. Guess!"

"In the lids of the boxes?"

"No!"

"In the writing-desk, done up like note-paper?"

"No!"

"Where then?"

"Ha, ha, ha! I'm *lined* with money!"

"Lined?"

"Yes—my coat's lined with bank notes—that is why I always wear the same, though I've got seventeen in the boxes."

"Thanks for the hint," thought the student Leon; "with this money I can fly with Lulalu, and when once my distracted country is again in order it shall be returned, and they are too rich to miss it. Some other brigand would seize it, did I leave it. Again—her ladyship and my lord must be kept in the mountains until Marriott has made Sybil his for life. This is my work."

But openly he said:

"So, my lord, you wear your money as a coat-lining?"

"Yes, it looks a shabby coat for me, Tikeypoodle, don't it? Why, it's worth more than any coat you ever saw. Knew you was a gentleman, or wouldn't have told you. Got seventeen more coats, but can't wear 'em because of the lining in this, —beautiful coats—lovely! Got more coats than socks. You see, one of the boxes that was stolen had all my socks in it, and we can't only wear English socks, though, at least in ma's case—and *she* fainted—it was stockings, and——"

"Tikeypoodle, put your whiskers in your mouth, my son!"

"Yes, ma."

"The fact is," continued the lady, "we lost all those useful articles of apparel to which my son referred rather coarsely —for him. I myself had to go about like a—really, like a Scotch person. I caught cold."

"It was terrible," said the student, with a smile, "that so fine a woman should suffer so much!"

The dowager ma bowed.

"I was a fine woman in my time," she said, "as this will prove," she continued, taking a miniature, set with diamonds, from her square-breasted dress.

"Diamonds?" said the student, unguardedly.

"Yes—diamonds. They are to be reset for my daughter Sybil, when she becomes the duchess."

"Ma."

"Don't take them out! Keep your whiskers where they are!"

"Yeth, ma."

"Diamonds!" said Leon, as he thought that he would be the bearer of the diamonds himself to Sybil—"what are diamonds?—mere stones! But a beautiful woman—great! It shall never leave me!"

"But, I say," says Tikey, pulling his hair out of his mouth, "they're worth two thousand!"

"Never shall it leave me!" says Leon.

"But, my dear sir, the diamonds?" cries my lady.

"And do *you* dare, madame, to speak of diamonds in connection with this fair face? It shall never leave me! But, my lady, I will take the worthless diamonds from the priceless gem they now contain. For it—it shall never leave me!"

"Lor, don't you go it!" said Tikeypoodle.

"Really, sir," said the dowager ma, "you are very flattering, and if the portrait of what I once was is in any way attractive, keep it."

"I will—I will!" said Leon, and he popped it in his pocket.

"But the diamonds, dear sir?"

"Are yours, my lady; but no hand but this shall remove the priceless ivory from its worthless case!"

"But——"

Here, however, they were interrupted by the entry of Tummis, my lord's man—a regular West-End upper servant, whose disgust at all things continental had been such that he now went perpetually about with a sour look of disgust on his countenance.

"My lord!" said he.

"Well, what is it, Tummis?"

"They won't give me a bit of beef, my lord!"

"What have they got?"

"Only fowl, my lord."

"Well, eat that!"

"Can't, my lord—never eat no fowl, my lord!"

(*To be continued in our next.*)

THE FORESTERS' FEAST, IN THE OLDEN TIME.

With an early number will be Given the companion Picture, printed in Colours, entitled, THE FORESTERS' FETE OF THE PRESENT DAY.

London: E. Harrison, Salisbury Court, and all Newsagents everywhere.

TALES OF BRIGANDS
AND ROBBERS.

I Warn & Strike

[ALBERT FALCONER ATTACKED BY ROYAL TROOPS.]

HAWK'S EYE, THE PHANTOM ROBBER.

CHAPTER V.

ALBERT'S HEART SMITES HIM.—HE TURNS.—HIS FEAR TO ENTER THE HOUSE.—HE CLIMBS THE IVY.—HE ENTERS THE ROOM.—HIS HORROR.—SUDDENLY A NOISE.—HE FLEES.

ALBERT FALCONER we left, tearing away from home, country, and the dear lady of his love, Margaret Sedwyn.

On went his good horse for two leagues—for six long miles—and then his pace slackened.

For have you, reader, ever gone a long, long journey away from home, and away from all those you love? If so, you know how, as the miles increased in number, your heart sank lower and lower.

What, then, would it be if you were going away for *life*—exiled for life?

No. 11.   [THE RIGHT OF DRAMATISING IS RESERVED..]

Ah! *that* is a kind of death which is almost worse than real death, for that is passed in a moment, and is nothing like so terrible as you many think, if you have never seen death. If, on the contrary, you have seen more than one or two human beings die, you have seen what peace, and calmness, and real sleep mean.

Do you not remember, you who have had this experience, how beautiful and calm the dead face, however pained it may have been until the good sleep came—do you not remember how happy the face remained for half an hour—nay, a whole hour after the last weary and tired sigh had passed happily away?

But exile—it is a million deaths.

And so Albert drew rein, and, as the horse took to walking, each step appeared a mile further away.

And so, after doubt and doubt, *he turned.*

Back to the dear old house—back to the good Grange where he had been born, and where lived the father to whom he had been so recently reconciled.

On, I tell you, he rode, hard back to Falcon Grange.

But when he drew near the Grange his heart failed him.

Exile is terrible—but imprisonment is worse than exile.

What if the King's people were on the watch for him?—what if he but returned home that his dear father might have the agony of seeing him seized and carried away to prison?

For a few moments, when the old Grange had come in view, he was half minded to turn again, not from any score of fear, but because he dreaded the pain he might cause Sir Bruton.

But his heart did so leap with pain at once more turning away from the old house, that he determined, come what might, that he would see his father.

Suddenly he remembered the old ivy against the wall—like a ladder always there, and ready to the hand and feet of the climber.

Why, the very ivy seemed to whisper *home* as the breeze shook the leaves above him.

"Father!"

He had climbed up to the window, and, to his surprise, found that it was open, for Bertram had not closed it while escaping after his bloody work.

No answer—for how could the dead answer?

"Father!"

Then a kind of panic seized him, and, leaping into the room, he again called his father.

No answer.

But suddenly he heard in the distance approaching hoofsteps.

As he remained listening, the hoofsteps rapidly approached the Grange—so rapidly that he felt sure that whoever the cavaliers might be, their destination was his father's house, because such a pace could not be kept up for any length of time.

What if it were several of the King's people come to arrest him, supposing him still to be at the Grange?

With sudden trepidation, he drew his sword from its sheath, and so roughly, that he broke the buckle of his sword-belt, and the belt itself fell to the ground.

The noise the sheath and belt made in their descent was quite unnoticed by himself—quite—so great was his agitation.

"Ha!" he thought, "they are now passing round by the west front. Would I could see them! But, from this point, it is quite impossible! Who are they?—who are they? What if they are the King's people? If I remain, my father will have the pain of seeing me arrested! Yet I cannot—will not go until I have again spoken to my dear father! Father—dear father!"

So speaking, he approached the bed, stretching out his hands as he did so.

And he came against the cold face of the dead man.

"Oh God!"

The exclamation was terrible; but, tender-sounded as it was, 'twas as deep a prayer as any heard that night. It was a quick, sharp, entreative prayer that the father might not be dead.

He, being a man of action, then shook the dead man, and the weight and the stubborn yielding of the body told him—a soldier used to death—that life had indeed passed.

"My father—and dead? Thank Heaven, we were friends! Dead—and how? Would that I had a light that I could see his dear features! But I dare not call for help, though in the house in which I was born, for I know not who are under its roof. And when I am calling for help I may be arrested—arrested! I dare not risk this, for who now stands between dear May and the world? Then again, I must not forget that were I a prisoner Margaret might fade away. No, I must be free—I must be at liberty! Ha! what's that?"

It was an approaching light, the rays of which came under the door of the chamber.

"A light! Then must I flee, never to see my father's face again! Yet I can kiss it—kiss it with the love and reverence of a loving son!"

So saying, he stooped and kissed the cold face.

Ha! could he but have known who was approaching, he need have had no fear. Could he but have guessed how terrible his flight would be construed, he would have remained and suffered a hundred deaths as a traitor rather than stirred a step.

But this was not to be.

"Ha, the light is nearer the door!" he thought, for he had kept his eyes fixed upon the door even when he was stooping towards the dead father.

So saying, he fled. Better—better a thousand times had he stayed.

And so sudden was his flight, that he fell over some article of furniture in his eagerness to reach the window, dimly seen as a square piece of something less profound than the darkness.

He was up again in a moment and at the window, and the next he was clinging to the ivy—and cautiously, too, for the impetuosity with which he leaped from the window had torn several feet of the rich, dark-green growth from the old wall.

"Did the light enter the room?" he asked himself, "or was it my fancy? Did I hear a scream, or was that also pure fancy?"

Still, he continued his way down the wall, and rapidly reached the ground.

His patient steed was eagerly waiting for him, and noighed gaily when his master approached.

A moment, and he was on the good horse's back, and the animal leaped forward as though he knew Albert's life depended upon his—the steed's—good efforts.

Away he sped, never dreaming for one moment that he was about to be accused of parricide—that they would say he had slain his father.

CHAPTER VI.

END OF THE ENCOUNTER BETWEEN HAWK'S EYE AND BERTRAM.— THE LADY MAY'S RETURN HOME, AND WHAT SHE SAW THERE.

THE encounter between Hawk's Eye and Bertram was not of long duration, for Hawk's Eye was cool, and upon Bertram was great fear.

"Alive again?" he cried, and as he spoke he himself felt his sword quiver in his hand.

"By the good fortune of war," said Hawk's Eye, "I have not yet been dead!"

"I left you for dead."

"A mistake. Give up the Lady May!"

"Rather my life will I give up!"

"Then come on!"

But as we have said, Bertram was in no fighting cue. One—two passes made at Hawk's Eye, and away went Bertram Falconer's sword shimmering overhead in the faint moonlight.

"My life is at your disposal!" said Bertram.

"It is not worth disposal."

"Fool!" cried Bertram. "Do you think I will accept mercy at such hands as yours?"

"You certainly will, whether you like to or not, unless you object to the Lady May stepping from the carriage."

"I do!"

"Then——"

"No more bloodshed!" cried the Lady May, and, summoning all her fortitude, she leaped from the carriage, and then it was for the first time she recognised by whom it was that the carriage had been stopped.

For a moment she fancied she should go mad, but happily at the next she persuaded herself that he, her dear one, could not have been killed in the cavern, but had fallen only wounded, and that he had recovered, and had been sent by some good and precious chance to her protection.

"George Blake!" she cried.

"Oh, his name is George Blake, is it?" said Bertram.

For Bertram was one of those men who could feel no sentiment of generosity for good done him—for mercy shown him. He never spared any man or woman, and therefore it can readily be understood that he despised at heart anyone who could show mercy or kindness. Hawk's Eye, then, once having pardoned him and given him his life, his idea at once was rather to plot how he could injure his benefactor than feel grateful towards him for his goodness.

Now there are such men, and you meet them in every street.

He set the name George Blake down in his mind.

"Let the Lady May pass!"

A black shadow passed over Bertram's face.

He stepped on one side to let May pass, and as Hawk's Eye welcomed her, Bertram leaped at the man who had given him his life, designing to possess himself of the weapon.

But Hawk's Eye was in preparation, although welcoming his dear lady to his arms, and all Bertram gained was a stab in the arm.

"By the sword," cried Hawk's Eye, "don't, good Bertram Falconer, say I, Hawk's Eye, wounded an unarmed man! If the man go to the water and jump in, he drowns himself; but you know the old tale—if the water come to the man, then the man drowns not himself! Had my sword gone to your arm, I might be blamed, but, as your arm came to my sword—why, blame yourself!"

"Curse you!" cried Bertram, as he bound up his slight wound with his handkerchief. "This comes of my having spared you in the cavern! Had I thrust my good sword through your black heart half-a-dozen times——"

"You would have done so six times more than you did! As for your curses—curse away! Your words don't hurt me, and they may delight you!"

May whispered him not to anger Bertram.

"Anger him, dear May?" he continued. "What matters the anger of a chained dog? This is his bondage!"

And he raised his sword.

Then, turning to the defeated man, he continued:

"I see your horse has followed the carriage, ridden by a varlet from the inn. Tell the varlet to get down."

The man riding the horse called for no other notice. Off he jumped from the saddle, as though it had suddenly taken to boiling.

"Thanks! A brisk lad!" continued Hawk's Eye. "My Lady May, I must pray you to do your best in your cousin Bertram's saddle for the next mile. After that, I promise a side-saddle, and more safety for you."

"I would ride bare-backed," she whispered, "to escape from him, believe me!"

And as she spoke, he lifted her into the saddle.

As he did so, Brilliant, Hawk's Eye's gallant steed, caused some commotion.

For Bertram, still plotting how he could take the life of the man who had spared him, suddenly caught up a huge flint lying in the road, and, taking a deadly aim, cast it with all his force at Hawk's Eye, whose head was now partially turned from him as he lifted the Lady May into the saddle.

But Brilliant, as though he saw what was about to happen, and meant to prevent it, suddenly dashed forward from the spot where he had been waiting with the utmost patience and motionlessness from the moment Hawk's Eye left the saddle, and intercepted the passage of the flint, which struck against his body with a dull, dead sound.

The good horse shook all over with the force of the blow, and indeed the wound made with a sharp edge of the flint at once began to flow.

Bertram comprehended in a moment the attempt that had been made.

"Miserable wretch!" he said. "What! again you are ungenerous!"

"Not to myself!" said Bertram.

"Listen to me! You are such a wretch that it is more merciless to let you live than take your life! Live to repent, if you can—if not, to die as you have lived—unworthy the name of a true man!"

He turned away as Bertram, now struck to the very heart of his vanity, cowered upon the ground. He then jumped upon Brilliant, and, taking the bridle of the second horse, he led it away at a trot.

"Hear him—how he curses!" said Hawk's Eye, as they rode away.

He was cursing savagely and loudly.

But they were soon out of hearing of the wicked man's weak rage, and then the following conversation took place between them:

"Oh, my dear May!" said Hawk's Eye, "how can I explain the delight I feel at again seeing you—at being the fortunate man who has saved you from worse than death!"

"Oh, my dear George!" she replied, "do not estimate too highly the service you have done me, for I estimate it only as you have served my father and my brother in saving me from the fate to which this villain destined me, and again in saving me to be yours—and yours only!"

"Oh, what joy," he returned, "to hear you speak thus!—what delirium of pleasure to know that you still love me, in spite of the fact that such doubt and dark bodings surround my life!"

"What has become of you of late? Your letters I have received, which have told me you are well, have given comfort to my heart! But I have suffered a world of uneasiness in wondering why you have abandoned the life you have always led, and have taken to this secret style of existence! What does it all mean?"

"It means what you may not yet learn, dear May; but in good time, believe me, all will be well—quite well! In the meantime, rather let us consider what is to be done with your dear self."

"Nay," she returned, "I will not yet cease to question you. How was it that, after I had left you in the cavern, as I thought, dead—how was it that you so suddenly appeared before me?"

"I was but stunned by the fall, and I soon regained my senses, helped thereto by my good steed Brilliant. But tell me—whither were you travelling when I arrived so opportunely to save you?"

"Towards the Grange with Bertram, who had taken Albert's place, for as Albert, my dear brother, and myself were riding to the Grange, Bertram met us—warned Albert to fly, as the King's people were in pursuit of him; and this Albert did, leaving me with Bertram; then followed—what you know."

"Enough, dear May! Let us think no more of such a wretch!"

"And yet I am dismayed when I remember that in battle Bertram really saved Albert's life!"

"May be; but depend upon it he is an arrant villain; and did he save your brother's life, it was but to gain by it, believe me!"

"Indeed, I believe you speak the truth, although what you say does not agree with facts, for I know my father had disinherited Albert, and willed all his lands to Bertram, and so it was until Bertram reconciled my father and Albert, and thereby Bertram lost his chance of the estate."

"Depend upon it, nevertheless," continued Hawk's Eye, "whatever he did was the action of a villain!"

"I fear you are right!"

"See—there is the place I spoke of! There we shall find a side-saddle, and then, dear May, we must gallop, and by a roundabout way, for, though I have said nought, I am anxious, for we have come so slowly, owing to your not being able, of course, to ride quickly without a proper saddle, that we may be overtaken, and——"

"And what, George? You cannot—cannot mean that your present life is so terrible that *you* are in danger of arrest?"

For a moment Hawk's Eye did not reply, then he said:

"Dear May, pray make no inquiries further! In good time you shall know all!"

Here he pulled in his horse, and turned to a cottage by which they had stopped.

As he approached the door, it opened without any summons on his part, and as, after half-a-dozen moments, he returned, carrying the side-saddle, it closed noiselessly after him.

To lift Lady May to the ground, remove the ordinary saddle from Bertram's horse, and fix the other in its place, all took up so little time, that Lady May felt that there were pressing reasons why he should not remain within chance of pursuit.

But, rapid as were his movements, they received one interruption on the part of Lady May herself, who suddenly screamed.

"What is it, May?"

"Nought—but I am nervous. 'Twas only your Brilliant licking my hand!"

The good horse had stepped up to her as though he knew her to be a friend of his master's, and had licked her hand—a little attention for which she was not at all prepared.

A few moments, and they were again in the saddle.

"Whither now, dear my lady?" Hawk's Eye asked.

"Home," replied Lady May—"home!—the fittest place for me, dear George; and again, I experience an extreme desire to see my father. It appears to me as though I had not seen him for a very long period. 'Tis a strange fancy, but one over which I cannot get, let me seek to do so as much as ever I can."

"'Tis strange! Then, to the Grange, dear May!"

"And you will enter with me, dear George, for you know that you are almost as welcome there as I am?"

"No," Hawk's Eye replied, after a pause—"I cannot stop beneath the roof of the Grange! I would that I could!"

"Why—why not?"

"Dear May, rest contented you must with my assurance that all will be well in the end! Now for a quick gallop!"

Brilliant did not want telling even once to gallop, and so good was his example, that Bertram's horse, mounted, as the reader knows, by Lady May, tried his best to keep up with him.

The hoof-falls of these animals it was that Albert heard while in his father's chamber of death.

Unhappy youth! The King's people were not near the Grange, and had he remained, his very presence would have saved him from the suspicions which were inevitably to fall upon him.

The very sounds which should have been to him the heralds of joy caused him to lead to his own destruction.

The reader will recall that Albert heard the hoofs pass round the Grange, and that then, after a few minutes passed in taking his leave of his dead father, he made for the window, and in doing so, stumbled, and afterwards imagined that, while rising after his fall, and rushing to the window, he was bathed in light for a moment or two.

This was no imagination. It was reality.

The Lady May, having parted with Hawk's Eye at the entrance of the Grange, and she having paused for a moment to hear him gallop away—and her heart died within her as the sound faded away in the distance—she turned her horse's head to find one of her father's grooms waiting to take her horse.

"Good evening, miss!" said the man.

"Good evening, Evans! Where is my father?"

"Retired to his room for some time."

"Help me off!"

"Yes, miss," said the man, suiting the action to the word. "Mr. Bertram's horse, Miss May, is it not?"

"Yes."

"Shall I wait for Mr. Bertram, miss?"

"Do you expect him?"

The man looked at his young mistress with absolute stupidity.

"Do you expect him?" she asked, assuming a calmness she certainly did *not* feel.

"Why, wasn't that Master Bertram, miss, who rode away just now, leaving you at the Grange gate?"

"No—put the horse in the stable!"

The man touched his hat and shook his head doubtfully. How could he help it? He could scarcely avoid thinking something was wrong, for here was his young mistress come home late in the night on Master Bertram's horse, the steed he, Bertram, always rode himself, and which he never lent, while an unknown horseman accompanied the lady to the gate, and then rode away, "as though," said the man, to one of the stable-men, "the very devil were after him!"

No wonder the poor Lady May herself became suspected.

Entering the house, the Lady May at once called for a lamp, and proceeded to her father's room.

It was the rays of light proceeding from this lamp which alarmed Albert Falconer.

Then it was that he started forward and stumbled, and the noise it was which he made in this operation, which, giving the alarm to the Lady May, caused her to start forward and throw open the room door—a very easy operation, for Sir Bruton was a brave man, and never would sleep with his door locked.

As she entered, flooding the room with light, she saw *him*, her brother, and the sudden shock was so great that she, with a slight scream, let the lamp fall.

It was immediately extinguished, and in the following darkness Albert made his panic-stricken escape.

Ah, had he but turned or spoken to her!

For her part, she for some moments lost consciousness; but, quickly recovering herself, she staggered to the door, and called for another light.

For some moments she was not heard, and in that time Albert was making his escape at the most rapid gallop.

When, however, her calls were heard, the servants at the Grange assembled in the most rapid manner.

A dozen lamps and other lights streamed into the room.

"Father!" said May.

Of course he could not reply.

"Father!"

Then, taking something like an alarm, she approached the bed, and touched him on the cheek.

"Close the window," said May—"my father's cheek is quite cold—doubtless due to the night air entering."

The servants had remained crouching near the door, but at this order one of the foremost moved towards the window, and, in so doing, kicked against the sword-belt which, it will be recalled, Albert had unconsciously let fall upon the floor of his father's room, after he had drawn his sword in anticipation of an attack by the King's people, whom he supposed were advancing towards his father's room, knowing him, Albert, to be there.

The man stopped and picked it up.

And having closed the window, he returned to the group of domestics, and taking up the belt, said:

"Master Albert's belt—he has been here."

"Father!"

Then suddenly she trembled.

But she turned as the man approached her.

"My lady, here is my young lord's belt—Master Albert's—which I just found upon the floor."

"Then it was no fancy," she said, speaking aloud, but with no idea that she was giving utterance to her thoughts—"no fancy! I saw my brother as I entered the room."

Fatal—fatal words!

Suddenly, the man who had brought the belt cried:

"Why, lord in heaven, Sir Bruton is dead!"

"Dead?" cried they all at the door.

"Dead?" echoed May.

Lights came rushing forward—a flood of illumination poured upon the countenance.

Dead beyond all doubt, as they all distinctly saw.

Dead—pallid skin, glazed eyes and helpless, fallen under-jaw.

As for the Lady May, she was too paralysed to speak or to faint—to faint, and fall into that merciful state which saves us from madness.

"Who did it?"

The servants turned, to see Master Bertram standing near them.

He looked not any the handsomer for his crushed lips—due to the blow Hawk's Eye had given him.

Who had killed Sir Bruton?

The servants looked in accusation at the sword-belt.

Bertram, who, finding the Grange house door open, had entered, and so come upon the scene—Bertram approached the horror-stricken but conscious May.

He whispered.

The servants thought he was whispering of the heir to the house, so they fell back.

"May," he said, "you are in my power again, and safely! Your brother has been here—they will think he murdered him! And if you oppose me—defy me—if you do not think even as I think, I will prove you an accomplice of your brother, *and send you to the gallows!*"

CHAPTER VII.

THE ENCOUNTER WITH THE KING'S TROOPS.—THE FIGHT NEARLY LOST.—HELP.—ALBERT SAVED.

THAT same night, when all these adventures were occurring, and about half an hour after Albert Falconer had fled from his father's house with the suspicion of his very sister following him that he had committed murder upon their father—that very same night a party of the King's people—about half-a-dozen cavalry, in the command of a sergeant, one Teddy Smithson—were on the road after Albert Falconer.

The Government, for some unknown reason, had thought fit to order the immediate arrest of that gentleman, and Teddy Smithson and his men were the result.

"The time has come," said the sergeant. "I am quite dead certain as now I'm going to make a hit. To-morrow, at ten, I shall be a famous man!"

"Ha, sergeant," said Bill Somers, in answer, "you've been going to be a famous man next morning at ten for a werry long while, and, for all that, every morning at ten you are just what you were yesterday morning at half-past nine."

"What was that?" asked the sergeant.

"Nothink not at all," said Bill Somers.

"Anyhow, I'm your superior officer, Private Somers!"

"I knows that, sergeant, but I don't aspect to be anything at ten o'clock to-morrow morning, do I?"

"How should I know, Private Somers? But this here I *am* aware of, as I feel the time is come, and that to-morrow morning I shall be some one."

"How do you mean some one?"

"Why, different nor what I am now."

"How different, sergeant?"

"Private Somers," said the sergeant, "you are a fool, and ought to get a cracked head!"

"Think you've got one!" muttered the private; but he did not say so aloud.

"Think, sergeant," asked another private, "as we shall take the traitor prisoner?"

"No, I don't!" said the sergeant.

"Then," asked Bill Somers, "how is it you expect as you shall be famous to-morrow morning at ten?"

"Ha! that's because you don't foller me as I follers myself," replied the sergeant. "You asked me if I thought as how *we* was agoing to take him prisoner. Well, I've a firm conwiction as he will be taken, and I've a firm conwiction as you won't take him; for I've a firmer conwiction still, as I, Sergeant Teddy Smithson, will have the honour of taking the traitor myself, and getting all the honour; so, at ten to-morrow, I shall be different to what I am to-night—I am sure o' that!"

"Ha!" said Bill Somers, "and where are *we* to be all the time?"

"That," said the sergeant, "I ain't got a conwiction about; *I* don't know where you will be; but of this I am sure, as to-morrow morning I shall be different to what I am to-night."

"Anyhow, sergeant," said Somers, "hope your head won't ache!"

"Ha! draw rein!" said the sergeant.

This was done, and in a moment the clatter of the hoofs ceased.

And thereupon the sound of a horse in the distance, galloping hard, was to be remarked.

"That's him!" said the sergeant.

"How do you know?"

"I've a conwiction!" said the sergeant.

And, however doomed the sergeant might be to disappointment at ten o'clock on the following morning, it is very certain that in that case his "conwiction" was right.

The horseman before the military party was Albert Falconer.

On the party went, and on Albert continued; but when half-a-dozen horses are pursuing one, it is half-a-dozen chances to one that the single horse is better than the six.

In the case under consideration, one of the privates found his horse break down under him.

But Albert Falconer's was the second to break down, and to his horror he found his pursuers gaining upon him.

At last, hearing the sound increase, like some brave animal brought to bay he turned upon his pursuers.

At once he saw that he had five pursuers to contend against. Now, perhaps even a brave man may fairly tremble when he sees that he has five men for enemies at one and the same time.

So he stopped, and on they came.

"Yield!" yells the sergeant—"yield, in the King's name!"

"Never!" cried Albert; "neither in the name of any man or devil, king or not!"

"Steady, my men!" growled the sergeant. "He must be taken alive, or the Government will put black marks against us, for it looks as though traitors were butchered when they are shot down. So, steady!"

"Ay, ay," said Will Somers—"think of to-morrow morning at ten!"

"Sir," said the sergeant to Albert, "we are five to one, and that is more than the bravest Englishman can fight against, when the five happen to be Englishmen—so do it with a grace, sir, and be a respectable prisoner."

"On guard!" yelled Albert, lashed by despair into rashness; and so speaking, he rushed at the whole posse.

Bayonets were in a moment pointed, and the sergeant's sword was out of his sheath.

Down went one of the soldiers in a moment, wounded in the right wrist.

There were now four enemies.

"To-morrow at ten!" whispered the sergeant, and adding to his men, "Leave him to me—wound his horse—get him on his pins!"

Then the sergeant rushed, sword in hand, on Albert Falconer.

Now, there can be no doubt that the sergeant, helped by his best men, would very quickly have had the victory, if that can be called a victory where one Englishman is overcome by five Englishmen; but unfortunately, as a bayonet-thrust brought Albert's horse upon his flank, rescue came in the shape of a horseman who dashed in amongst the soldiers like a whirlwind —like a stream of lightning.

The soldiers were not prepared for this attack.

A moment, and the stranger's sword had leaped into the breast of the horse of the soldier nearest to him, and this animal, roaring with pain, kicked out at the next nearest horse, who made no more to do but buck-leapod,—that is, jumped clean off the ground, flung his rider over the hedge, and took the road to London at the rate of at least twenty miles in a short hour.

Two soldiers and the sergeant remained.

(*To be continued in our next.*)

RED GAUNTLET, THE BANDIT; OR, THE BLACK MOUNTAINEERS.

BOOK II.—THE BLACK CHATEAU.

CHAPTER XXV. (*Continued.*)

"WELL, starve!" says my lord, very sharply.

"Think I shall, my lord, if I stop here much longer; and, my lord, can't get a comfortable cottage loaf!"

"Try what they have got."

"And, my lord, I want a silver fork."

"Oh, Tummis!—well, I wish you may get it!"

"And, my lord, there is two monks in the kitchen—which I never could abear and won't abear—and please, my lord, I I want them monks turned out!"

Here Scampia, appearing at the door, explained that the monks in question were a couple of poor Benedictines, who craved shelter for the night, and who were to be put in the loft.

"Yah!" said Tummis.

"Well," said my lady, "it's very inconvenient to have monks bothering one's servants; but if it must be, it must be; and, Tummis, it shall be considered in your wages, Tummis."

"Thank you, my lady!" said Tummis, with a relieved face, for, to confess the truth, this was the seventy-eighth promise of a similar kind which had been made to the valet since he had been on the Continent to oblige his lord; and, as he knew his strong-minded lady was a woman who never broke her word, he calculated that when he got back to England he would be paid sufficient, in consideration of his continental martyrdom, to set him up in a small public-house, where he might drink himself to death as soon as he thought fit.

"Tummis!" said Tikey.

"My lord?"

"Get out!"

"Yes, my lord!"

Tummis went.

"My lady," continued the innkeeper, "requires to retire to rest early—is it not so?"

"Yes, my good man. Tell my maid to come in an hour."

The maid was the individual Tummis contemplated marrying, and making the landlady of the little inn. Perks was her name, and *she* had complained of the Continent even more times that Tummis, and *she* had likewise been promised to have it considered in her wages.

Imagine the hour past, and the dowager ma and the Duke Tikeypoodle preparing for bed.

All the inn is asleep—fast asleep, and the two monks have been shown to their garret.

Even the inestimable Tummis and the perfect Perks have left off complaining that the foreign bedsteads haven't four posts, and all is quiet.

Quiet? Softly!

If you go to the loft where the two monks are supposed to be sleeping, to your immense astonishment you will find them wide awake, and talking in very low tones.

Hear what they say.

"Our chief says the lady is to be brought to the Black Chateau."

"An ugly old woman—isn't she?"

"Uglier than a rusty screw—reminds me of nut-crackers! But she is worth her weight in gold, for she is rich!"

"And the Englishman?"

"He is to be killed."

"Why? Could not he be ransomed also?"

"Ay, yes—but the ransom of both the mamma and her boy is to be set upon *her* head, and so the chief can have the pleasure of getting the ransom and vengeance at the same time!"

"Why does he want to kill him?"

"Because an Englishman played him a trick but a few

nights since. You remember when we found him in the wall cell of his own chamber, with his head stove in?"

"What are our orders?"

"To go to the middle window of the first floor—that over the signboard—and opening it, strike a light, when the chief, knowing all to be quiet, will approach with a ladder and ten of ours, and the inn will be in our hands."

"Why ten men?" asked the other.

"Because old Scampia Zatani is to be polished off!"

"How so?"

"Know you not he is a brigand who doesn't belong to us?"

"Ay—they say he belongs to Red Gauntlet's band, and our chief dare not attack one of Red Gauntlet's band!"

"There you make an error."

"How so?"

"Our chief is determined to destroy Red Gauntlet's band!"

"Why?"

"Red Gauntlet is too good and kind."

"But how is this to be done?"

"Why, one of Red Gauntlet's band, whom Red Gauntlet supposes to be dead—and it is wonderful that he is not, for you or I would have been done for with half he went through, —this rascal and traitor, whose head I pity after he has done his work—for our chief of the Black Chateau knows what to do with a spy—this man will betray the band of Red Gauntlet in fragments, and Red Gauntlet is to be delivered up, to the Duke de Mareosi. And this time, depend upon it, he will not get out of prison, for he will never enter one!"

"How is that?"

"He is to be shot as soon as caught, and his head taken for identification to the duke!"

"Nice job!"

"Very—and to-night's work is the beginning of it! To-night old Scampia Zatani is to fall—and that will be the first blow at Red Gauntlet and his band! Red Gauntlet and our chief cannot live longer in the same district. One or the other must die, and our chief has no desire to begin his long sleep yet awhile!"

"The house is quiet. Shall we begin our work?"

"Yes. We have to pass through the room in which Nicola sleeps."

"I should like to give her a kiss as we pass!"

"Refrain, for it might lead to our having to kill the pretty Nicola, and our chief especially forbids that to be done, as he has a fancy for her attendance upon him at the Black Chateau after to-night's work is over!"

"We shall have the soldiery down upon us quickly."

"No, not at all. Here is the plan. After the inn is overcome, and all killed in it but Nicola and my lady, it is to be fired, and it will be supposed that a conflagration only has occurred, and all have perished in the flames."

"Ha! but Nicola and my lady?"

"Nicola—a few days passed—will possibly be able to make no confession, for our black chief soon tires of his fancies, and you know he is merciless; and as for my lady, she is to be trapped in her bed-room, and she will be led to believe that she was rescued by brigands, who, being brigands, will desire her ransom. She will have no idea that the house was entered and set fire to by brigands."

"A goodly plot!"

"Is it not?" said the other. "And now, as all the house is quiet, let us to work with all possible caution."

"Good!"

"You know what is to be done in the event of our being surprised before we can give the alarm?"

"Yes; I am to play the sleep-walker, because I am the

stupidest, and to play it have only to stare and move forward, while you are to pretend to be following me, to save me in case of my moving near danger as a sleep-walker, and explain that you do not attempt to wake me when I have one of these sleep-walking fits, which you are specially ordered by our dear abbot to watch over, because it may be dangerous to do so. Then, while you are talking, I am to awake, start with amazement, and ask where I am. Then you are to pray heartily that I am safe. I am to follow suit, and every soul in the inn will be taken in. We shall be marched back to our loft, in which we sleep because of our monkish humility; and then all is to begin over again; and again, if we are disturbed, I am to play the sleep-walker, and you my guardian."

"Good—you know your work well."

"A rare master for a plot is our black chieftain—is he not?"

"Yes. Now to work."

Meanwhile, poor Tikeypoodle had gone to bed, and so had his mamma, without the slightest idea of danger from any one quarter, and not the least idea had they that from *three* quarters danger threatened them.

Three quarters.

First, Red Gauntlet, who had no idea of taking life—that he scorned; his scheme was to get what he wanted, intending some day to return it, when once he came into his possessions —only to take from the rich. His intention was to possess himself of my lord's well-lined coat, and my lady's diamonds.

Then, secondly, there were the two monks—the scouts of the brigand band of the Black Chateau.

And, thirdly, there was Scampia Zatani, who, totally oblivious of any attempt upon his life, had made up his mind to secure all the luggage of my lord and my lady, send it off across-country in a waggon, and then have fits of fainting next day at the discovery that his dear customers had been robbed in his highly-respectable house.

Poor Tikey!—he never would have taken such pains to see that Tummis took pains in frizzing his whiskers and hair, and he never would have called out so sweetly through the wall, "Good night, ma!" had he had the least idea of danger.

As it was, he went up to sleep as peacefully as a snoring lamb.

Poor dowager ma!—*she* never would have so peacefully dropped her wig on the looking-glass, and taken out her false old teeth and put them in a tumbler of water, and never would she have answered her son and hope so cheerily, "Good night, lovey, and go to sleep, like a good boy!" had she had the faintest idea that she was to be awoke by a rascally landlord looking after her luggage, a couple of brigand monks, and also the redoubtable Red Gauntlet.

She would have screamed until the whole of Naples had heard her and come to her rescue.

As it was, *she* went to sleep with a mild snore, and a ba-a-a, like a dear old sheep.

All was quiet in the house, and most of them were awake— wide awake—except the English party, for Perks had at last jerked herself to sleep, and Tummis had fallen to slumber, calling Italy a haltogether beasly hole.

Scampia Zatani had gone to bed, to keep up appearances.

But *he* had not gone to sleep.

"Heaven help me!" says Scampia, getting up; "and if Heaven does, I'll promise to live on the proceeds, and keep an honest man all my life—if I can! But the flesh is weak!"

Well, he was just nearing his door as Red Gauntlet neared *his*, for Leon had a bed-chamber in the house.

He had no idea that Scampia would venture to do brigandage on his own behalf.

So things were looking comfortable, and the chance of a row was imminent.

But there was another person awake, and that was Nicola.

The fact is, she was dreaming awake of St. George, and wondering whether he was wondering about her.

Then she wondered whether he ever thought of *her* as a wife, and then she wondered if ever she thought of him as a husband, seriously.

And then she wondered whether she was pretty enough to be his wife.

And to settle this point, she determined to get up and have a good look at herself in the little glass on her dressing-table.

Now, it was just as she had struck a light, and had begun to look at herself in the glass, that the two monks approached the room by a small passage, and, quietly opening a door, they came upon the young and beautiful Nicola, admiring herself in the glass, and making sweet faces at herself therein.

Now, perhaps the reader has often, in the course of his or her life, experienced the desire to laugh exactly at that moment when he or she ought to be most solemn.

So it was with the studpider of the two brigand-monks— the one who was to play the part of sleep-walker in event of their being disturbed.

The moment he saw the pretty sight of Nicola making pretty faces at herself in the glass, he broke out with a hearty, "Ha, ha!"

Nicola turned, and must have seen them as the wiser of the two clutched his companion round the neck.

But unfortunately she upset the candle, and was plunged in darkness.

But she had emitted a scream, which awoke my lady in the next room.

"What is the matter?—murder!" yelled the lady.

And my lord, waking at the sweet sound of his ma's voice, cried:

"Ma, dear, is it tooth-ache—is it?"

"Is it murder?" yells the dowager ma.

"No," said Nicola. "I——"

"Is it fire?" asked my lady.

"Ma, dear," yelled Tikeypoodle, "I feel cold all down the back!"

"Is it thieves?" asked the dowager ma.

"So please you, my lady," Nicola returned, "I thought I heard something."

"What?"

"A—a laugh!"

"Rats!" said my lady.

"But it was a laugh!"

"Rats!"

"But rats can't laugh, my lady!"

"Rats scampering!" replied my lady. "Good-night, Nicola —bless you—bless you! Tikeypoodle!"

"Yes, ma. I'm cold all over now!"

"Go to sleep!"

"But——"

"Go to sleep, and don't talk any more!"

"But——"

"Hush!" said the dowager ma.

And then the house was silent again.

Nicola crept to bed in the dark, once more thinking of St. George, and supposing that "my lady" must be right, because she spoke so positively—so *very* positively.

"Shall I go strangle her?" asked the sleep-walking brigand.

"No, idiot!—didn't our chief bid us make her a prisoner?"

"But suppose she don't go to sleep again?"

"Gag her!"

"True—I didn't think of that. What a man of brain you are—almost as good as our chief, who is a great man!"

Now, Nicola's scream had frightened Scampia back into his room, and even Red Gauntlet determined to wait another quarter of an hour.

A few minutes, and the inn was again quite quiet.

A little while, and then they heard Nicola's soft breathing. She had fallen asleep thinking of St. George.

"Hadn't I better scrag her?" whispered the sleep-walking gentleman. "We can can easily tell the chief it was an accident!"

"No—when the chief says a thing, he means it! Were anything to happen to Nicola, *you* might meet with an accident, and though *I* don't think much of your head, it doesn't follow that you are of my opinion as to its value!"

" What a man you are !"

"Hush !"

And then they commenced crawling over the room.

They moved very lightly, for they were accustomed to the work, and passing their time as monks, of course they were accustomed to go barefoot.

There was not a sound as they crossed the room.

And the leader, with the same wonderful noiselessness, opened the window, which, like all windows in Italy, opened like a door, and he stepped out on to the portico, whence, as the reader knows, he was to give the signal to the Black Bandit of the Black Chateau.

Now, the two rascals had scarcely got their footing upon the portico, when Scampia Zatani, bent upon his errand, came slowly into the room—very slowly. Perhaps he would have moved much faster had he had the slightest idea that Red Gauntlet was not more than ten paces behind him.

But the old proverb tells us that " where ignorance is bliss, 'tis folly to be wise."

Well, things were in this position, when there was suddenly such a flourish upon a military bugle as made the very echoes wake up.

As for my lady and Tikeypoodle, they were both on the floor, as though each had had a bedfellow very good at kicking.

Then there were some hurried footsteps, and then—bang! a gun was fired not twenty paces away from the inn, and apparently at it, for, almost simultaneous with the shot, there was a yell and the crashing of broken glass.

This, mingled with Nicola's scream—Tikeypoodle yelling " fire—fire—fire !" as though calling to a file of soldiers—and the dowager mamma springing the rattle which she always had under her bed—made altogether a frightful clatter.

Somebody then rang a bell, a dog began to howl, and even a donkey in the stable joined in.

"Hoy—hoy !—house—house !"

Scampia Zatani rushed to the window, and flung it open.

"Why, what means all this?" he bellowed. "Who are you, firing at an honest innkeeper's house in the dead of the night? Who are you ?"

"Soldiers !"

"What do you want ?"

"Open house—open house !" bawled twenty voices.

"This is a respectable inn," said Scampia.

"No doubt," replied a voice—"we say not to the contrary !"

"And all here are respectable."

"No !" replied the voice.

"How—how ?" bellowed the innkeeper. "Dare defame my virtuous inn, and I'll have you trounced !"

"Why, fool," said the voice, "there were men trying to enter your house when we came up !"

"The saints preserve us ! Were there ? What were they like ?"

"House—house—open house !" bawled the voices.

"Si, si, senor ! See—lights are lighting, and I will let you in ! But who could expect your excellencies at such an hour ?"

"Brigand-hunters hunt at all hours !" replied the cheery voice from below, as again cries of "House—house !" arose.

And now lights appeared all over the house, and Scampia, going downstairs, unbarred the door, which had been fastened as carefully as though he were indeed the honest landlord he pretended to be, and in swarmed—not a company of brigands, as the reader may have anticipated, but a posse of soldiers, headed by that same outspoken gentleman we have already described—Victor Emmanuel, the King of Italy.

Again he had sallied out, and joined a party of soldiers, intent upon brigand-hunting, and without betraying his rank to them, for his Majesty is of a very adventurous turn of mind, and loves nothing better than running himself into danger.

Not a soul of the soldiers knew the King was with them.

They took the personage for nobody beyond a captain who had joined in the hunt for the simple love of adventure.

It was his quick eyes which had marked the two figures in the balcony over the door of the inn, and he himself had given the order to fire.

"Upstairs—upstairs !" cried the King. "I heard a scream when the rifle was discharged ! We must see into this !"

"Bless us all the saints, captain !" cried Scampia. "There could not have been brigands trying to get into my poor house !"

"Then, brigands, my good man, were certainly trying to get out of it !"

"Nay, nay !" replied the landlord—"no dishonest men ever entered my house !"

"Indeed !" replied the King—"that is more than *I* can say of mine !"

"But I am such a respectable man !" whined Scampia.

"Then the more likely that disrespectable men should try and take you in. There—that is the window—the centre one !" his Majesty continued, for he had led the little army upstairs, having taken the light from the trembling hand of the scamp Scampia, and pointing to the window through which the two monks had passed.

The King went to the window, and opened it.

"Hallo ! What have we here ?"

"*Domine dirige nos !*" said a voice.

And the King, poking the candle out of window, said:

"Hallo—two monks ! Ha, wherever there's a monk, there is mischief, and here are two of them ! What's the matter ?"

"*Domine—domine—domine !*" said the monk who had already spoken, and who was kneeling and supporting the other, who was apparently senseless, and who was certainly on the flat of his back.

"Speak out !" said the King.

"*Domine dom——*"

"Pull 'em in !" said the King.

And the soldiers, nothing loth—for soldiers have always been the enemies of monks—pulled the two monks in, for all the world as though they were pulling a couple of teeth out.

"Oh lord !" said the monk.

"What are you doing here ?" asked Victor Emmanuel.

"Rather ask," said the monk, "what have you done, you man of blood !"

"Why, bless us and save us !" here struck in Scampia. "How came you here ? We left you both in the loft !"

"Ha," said the monk—the other was on the ground, still senseless, but there was no sign of a wound about him—"you left us in the loft, but wonderful are many things. I am Brother Ignatius, and that is Brother Anselmo, and a very pretty condition have you brought Brother Anselmo to !"

"Well," said the King, "why were you moving about like cats on a roof in the middle of the night ? Is the man hurt ?"

"He may not be wounded," said brother Ignatius; "but think of his feelings !"

"How got you from the loft to the balcony ?" asked Scampia. "Answer me that !"

Brother Ignatius turned up his eyes.

"Brother Anselmo walks in his sleep. Like a good brother, I watch him when he sleeps, and if he walks, I walk too. This is my duty. I never wake him unless he is in danger, for fear the shock might kill him !"

"Ha, ha !" said the King, "but when he was in the balcony *he was* in danger. Why didn't you wake him ?"

"So please you, you didn't give me time !" replied Brother Ignatius, with a quiet twinkle in his eyes; "but you banged away like the man of blood you are !"

"Oh," said Victor, "and what's the matter with him now ?"

"He has fainted."

"Fainted ? So have I and mamma, for the last five minutes !" here said Tikeypoodle, marching in, done up in a blanket, and with his head in a towel to hide the curl-papers.

"Here, ma—como here !"

(To be continued in our next.)

With an early number will be Given the companion Picture, printed in Colours, entitled, **THE FORESTERS' FETE OF THE PRESENT DAY.**

London: E. Harrison, Salisbury Court, and all Newsagents everywhere.

TALES OF BRIGANDS AND ROBBERS.

I Warn & Strike

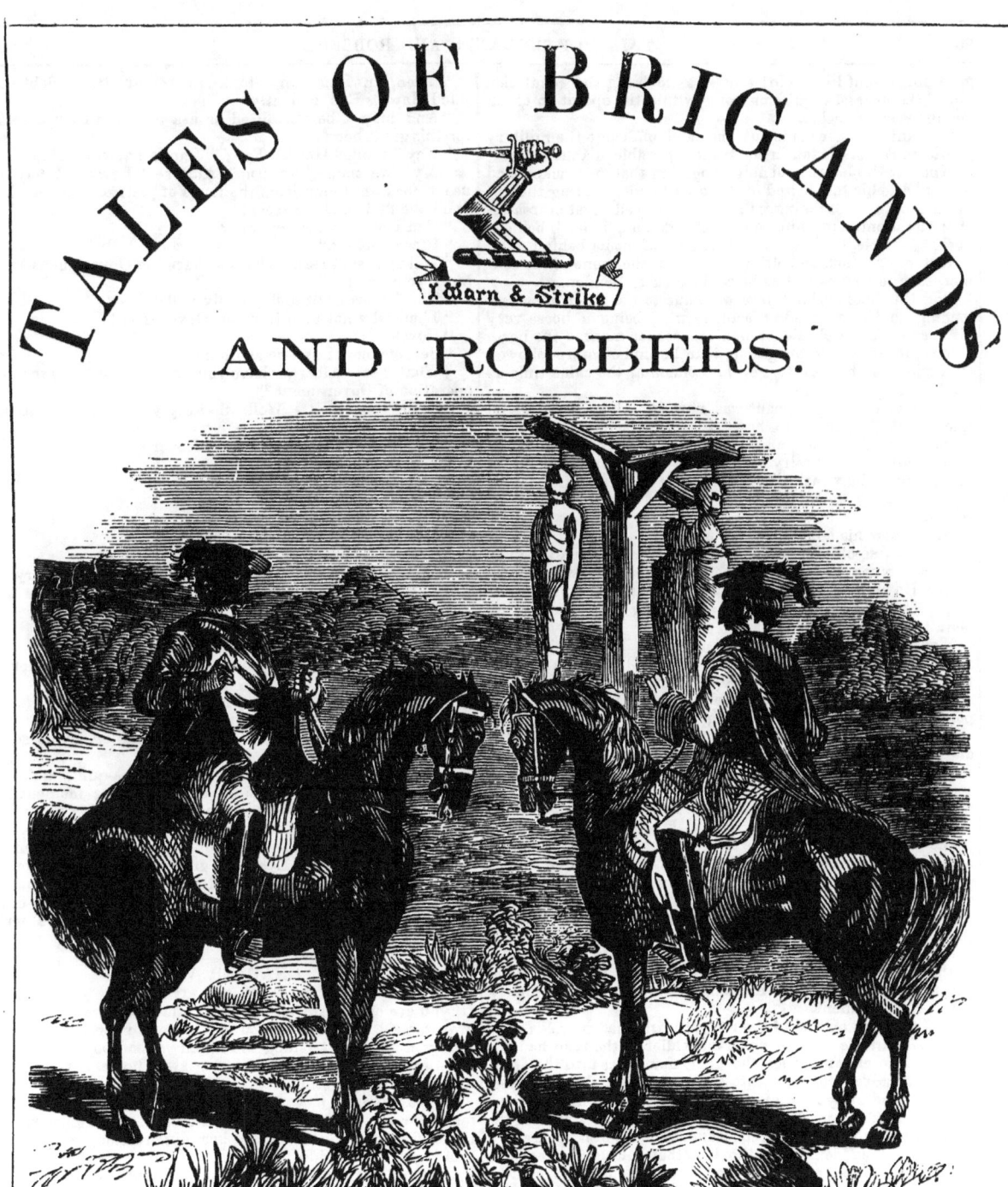

[THE ROBBER AND HIS PHANTOM.]

HAWK'S EYE, THE PHANTOM ROBBER.

CHAPTER VII.—(Continued.)

THE sergeant did not remark the new comer—all his efforts were directed to overcome the traitor, and inasmuch as the remaining two soldiers in a state of warfare (for of the other two, one was quite sure he was in a damp, unpleasant ditch, and was trying to get out of it, while the other had not the least idea where he was)—as the remaining two soldiers in a state of warfare had been told by their superior officer that he did not want their active interference in making the rebel a prisoner, and as they saw the new comer was an enemy, why, they set to work instanter to demolish him.

But it was a fair fight, for it was *not* two to one, because the stranger's horse counted as one, he was so clever; whereas the soldiers' horses were simply animals—mere brutes.

"Wheel, Brilliant!" said the new arrival, and round the

good horse went like a christian, so as to bring the regulation tail of the nearest regulation horse within the operation of cut one in swordsmanship.

Brilliant's master made cut one, and off came the military gentleman's horse's tail in the neatest possible manner.

Whereat the horse, probably imagining that a cracker had been tied to his tail, bolted off towards London, taking the bit in his mouth, and, taking no heed of the yells and entreaties of the gentleman in uniform on his back, and, indeed, being a horse of mettle, excited, by the sounds of hoofs behind him, to further exertions in bolting away from the scene of the conflict, and getting as fast as he could back to London.

Now the hoofs behind him were due to the other horse belonging to the remaining soldier, who, being a horse very military as far as obedience went, no sooner marked the horse before him taking to the gallop, than he immediately followed suit, and tried his best to get to London at the same time as his leader.

The unfortunate sergeant was now left alone, and had he known what he ought to have been about, he would have dashed from the saddle, and have done the combat on foot.

Our advice to cavalry sergeants is this: never to fight on horseback while wearing spurs—it leads to mischief.

An unlucky touch of the spur, and the horse veered round.

Albert saw his advantage in a moment.

As for the other man—the rider of the horse called Brilliant, and whom it need not be said was really Hawk's Eye—as for Hawk's Eye, he was too brave a man to help either of a couple of men who appeared to be fighting upon equal terms —quite upon equal terms.

Well, Albert, seeing that his enemy, by his horse's movement, had put him at a discount, did not take advantage of that to run him through the body, as many a meaner-hearted man would have done, but suddenly holding his sword by the point with the left hand, passing the sword thus held to his right hand, he used the weapon as a mallet, and fetched him a quiet crack on the back of the head.

Now, this would have sent the sergeant—who would now certainly have on the morrow morn a something which he had not been possessed of on the previous day, in the shape of a handsome large bump on the back of his head—this, we say, would certainly have sent the sergeant over his horse's head to look after his men; but his horse getting poked up at this point by the private on the ground objecting to being trampled on, and in consequence punching the horse's stomach with a one, two, three, up the luckless sergeant's steed went, and up the sergeant went clean into a tree by the roadside.

And he did not come down again, owing to his being forked at the waist between two branches of the said tree, in a manner that certainly broke his fall, but which was singularly far from convenient.

And to make an end of the sergeant, who had now *certainly got a rise* in the world—when the soldier in the road had recovered himself, and when the gentleman shot into the ditch had so far advanced back into civilisation as to have scraped so much mud away from his uniform that he once more looked about half like a man; and when the two horses bolting to London had turned back in consequence of the first apparently being struck suddenly with the idea that bolting was not the proper thing, and came to a dead stand, the other obediently following his example, of course; and when all the privates had been looking about for their sergeant for hours, and come to the conclusion that he must have gone up so much in the world that he had leaped clean out of it—when, we say, all these things had come to pass, and it was quite ten o'clock in the morning, the sergeant came to his senses, and put out this little remark :

" Good morning, mates !"

" Oh lord !" said they all.

" Will you kindly pick me down ?"

And hard work it was.

The sergeant did not expect a rise in the world for a month.

But to return to Hawk's Eye and Albert Falconer.

" Sir," said Albert, " I owe you my life !"

" Then, sir, I am happy to know you are in my debt," replied Hawk's Eye, gallantly.

" And may I be permitted to ask to whom I am indebted for this great boon ?"

" Nay," replied Hawk's Eye ; " I am a nameless man."

" My own name," returned Albert—" I swear I may not use it, for I am flying from the fangs of justice, some of which you have delivered me from !"

" Can I help you in any way ?"

" I fear not, sir."

" Tell me," said Hawk's Eye—" have the Government taken away your estate ?"

" The Government undoubtedly will."

" Then why not take from the Government ?"

" How so ?"

" Become one of us—be as I am."

" What !" said Albert, " have you lost your estate by the kind operation of Government ?"

" Something like it. Well, what say you ? Will you become a knight of the road ?"

" I a highwayman—I, Albert Falconer ?"

" You Albert Falconer ?"

" That is my name."

" The brother of the Lady May ?"

" My sister's name is May."

" And you belong to Falcon Grange ?"

" I do."

" And you are now in full flight from the military, or rather were, when our friends here stopped you ?"

" You speak quite truly."

" Then am I your devoted servant !"

" Wherefore, good sir ?"

" Because I owe you devotion and my life ! Whither go you ? Abroad ?"

" I fear I must, for England is not safe for me."

" I trust I shall persuade you to remain in England. Ha ! One of the soldiers is moving. Quick !—leap on my horse !"

" And you ?"

" Ho !—one saddle must do for both of us—quick, quick !"

Brilliant gave a low neigh, and the next moment the two men were upon horseback, and were clattering away from the scene over which Sergeant Teddy Smithson hoped to reap so much honour by ten o'clock on the following morn.

But before Hawk's Eye had given Brilliant the word to gallop—and Brilliant never asked for any other inducement— he had flung a handful of silver into the road, calling out— " There, if I've given you one good thrashing, there's something to get a good wetting to make up for it."

CHAPTER VIII.
DOWN BY THE RIVER.

IF you are on the swiftest horse in the whole world, and you are stopped by a river, you may depend upon it that if the man you may be pursuing is but only a bad boatman, he will get away from you, in spite of your swift horse, if you are not a better boatman still.

In like manner, if you are a very capital boatman, and the man you are pursuing leaps to the bank, and limps away on the back of the most wretched horse in creation, you will lose him if *you* cannot ride.

Now, all this means to say that highwaymen always had a *station* on a river-side, in order, when pressed, to abandon one element—the land, and to take to another—the water.

These gentlemen had double the chance then of escaping.

And well the gentlemen of the road knew of these advantages.

The reader will, therefore, be amiable enough now to accompany us to the Anchor of Safety, a sufficiently-meaning name, down by Wapping.

The Anchor of Safety had not a nice name, even in that far from nice neighbourhood.

The landlord himself, Hans Schwincks, was in himself a libel on the place. It was not that he squinted that was the objection—it was how he squinted. It was not that his eyes appeared to be calling in upon each other, and not so much with the desire of asking each other how they were, as of bowling away at each other until one or the other was done for; but the great objection lay in the fact that these orbs of Hans's (one was a chocolate colour, and the other tea-greenish and coffee-hued) appeared to gimlet you through with the kind inquiry, "Ha, mein got, how zall I do for *you*, mein herr?"

He was about the worst villain in all Wapping, and he certainly would have got called Mugs, only his own name of Schwincks was such a satire upon his murderous eyes that no name could have been an improvement on his own.

Schwincks had got his name and house up owing to some schnaps, so strong and smoky, that it had got the name of "gunpowder;" and so Schwincks's customers would ask, not for schnaps hot or cold, but a go of gunpowder hot with—meaning hot and sweet schnaps and water; or a turn of gunpowder cold without—meaning schnaps just as it came from the bottle.

And, as a kind of further praise in favour of this liquor, which Hans sold at a slapping price, although it paid no duty, for it dropped up the river in ugly little Dutch boats, and was sunk in places where Hans's people were sure to find it—they pretended to be fishing (for there were fish in the Thames then)—as a kind of further praise of the ungodly schnaps, all the other liquors in the house were called milk, whatever it was. Gin was satin milk, and rum was seedy milk, and usquebaugh was smoky milk—a name due to the smokiness of the liquor.

So that a stranger was considerably surprised at the drinks he heard called for—certainly half a pint of smoky milk did not sound like a relish.

Schwincks was helped in his business by a young lady called the "Angel"—a name applied in gentle satire of her personal qualities, for when she and her dear papa, who was Schwincks himself, stood together, and especially when they looked at each other, they appeared to be endeavouring to out-ugly each other.

She had not a good temper, but, as she herself said, "how could she help her temper?"

Her mother had never been known at the Anchor of Safety. It appeared, if you took Schwincks's word for it, that he had had to fly from Amsterdam in consequence of the head burgomaster's beautiful daughter falling in love with him; so he fled, brought the beauty to England, and left Dutchland behind him.

There were people who said that Schwincks had had to flee his native land in consequence of a difference of opinion with the authorities in reference to a certain case of jewels, and that the beautiful bride was really a violent young woman, who had fallen in love with Schwincks's diamonds rather than himself, and came away with him, after having punched and pommelled him into a promise to marry her.

Then she made him keep his word.

He soon got tired of her, but it took fifteen months for her to get tired of Schwincks; and then, when she did leave him, she left behind her a tribute of affection in the Angel, called at that time Sarah Jane.

She left their daughter, but not the jewels, for you must know only one-third of those sparklers were sold to set the admirable couple up in business, and then the dear wife took care of the rest, promising Hans that, if ever he referred to them, she would "pound" him.

He never did; and when she bolted at the end of that fifteen months, taking the sparklers with her, after the first hour of rage he thought the price cheap at which he had got rid of his loved one.

But as the years went on, he gradually forgot all about her shrewishness, and so at last—after thirty years were past, and Sarah Jane was beginning to be afraid that she should be on the shelf of single-blessedness—Hans always referred to his wife as though she had been an angel come down from above to bless him for fifteen months, when she had gone back again like a blessing—he never referred to the diamonds.

The Cherub—as the angelic Sarah Jane was called even more frequently than Angel, and as we will call her here—had tried to captivate every handsome gentleman of the road who, in the course of his professional career, had had occasion to trouble the Anchor of Safety.

But never an offer had she had—that is, of marriage.

True, she would never listen to any man who was not a fine, good-looking fellow, and that may account for much of her want of success, for whereas an ordinary fellow would have perhaps ventured to tackle Miss Schwincks, seeing there was a prospect, when Hans had drunk himself to death, of the ownership of the Anchor of Safety, it was not likely that a Paul Clifford or a Gentleman Jack would be given to make eyes at such a prospect.

The ownership of the Anchor of Safety was a pleasant lookout, but the Cherub was a horrid pill to swallow with it.

The Cherub had one good quality and one bad one—the first was a fatal facility for falling in love with every fine man that she saw, and the second quality was an extremely and and hopelessly greedy love of his Majesty George the Second's portrait in its yellowest condition—we mean stamped on a golden guinea.

And between these two qualities the Cherub was frequently grounded, for whenever she fell in love, the way in which she tried to prove her affection was by immediately offering to negotiate a loan with the handsome fellow without *any* security, as the quickest way of walking into his affections.

Well, the handsome gentlemen took the loans, and sometimes they returned them, but when the Cherub proposed, which she always did, the handsome gentleman always ran away, at which point she ever dropped into a stiff fit, and yelped for an hour.

Then she made love again, got refused again, and had another fit.

This had gone on for ten years, and all that time she had made the ugly men pay all the expenses to which she was put by the fine fellows.

She said she had been much tried—you should have applied to the ugly fellows to learn how much the Cherub had tried them.

On that particular night when Hawk's Eye had saved Albert Falconer from a lodging in the Tower of London, poor Cherub had been suffering hugely, for a gentleman had made love to her, borrowed no less than fifteen pounds and a crown-piece, had also run up a long score, and had then run away, leaving a line behind him to say that she was "a nut-cracker-faced old fool!"

Then she had fainted, and being bumped up into consciousness by her father insisting upon her paying the gentleman's bill, she did so, and then had a quiet convulsion all to herself.

Then she came-to, put her hair in order, took a quiet glass of gunpowder cold without—neat, in fact, for in that way she was a *neat* party—and then she came into the one large room at the Anchor of Safety, determined to make some of the ugly ones make up for the fifteen pounds before the week was out.

She had been in the room where she played barmaid for some half-hour, when was heard the peculiar summons which always had to be sounded on the door of the Anchor of Safety before it was opened to anyone desirous of entering.

"Ugly or fine-looking?" thought the Cherub, as she poured some October ale into a customer's cocked hat instead of his pint brimmer.

The door was opened, and the person who entered did not satisfy the dear Cherub's inquiry in a moment, for actually his cloak was well up over his face, and his hat well down over his features.

"Tall, at any rate," she said to herself.

"Mine good master—vat duff yer want?"

"Rest," said the stranger.

"And der pass-vord?" asked Hans—"Mein got, vere ist der pass-vord?"

"Did I not knock properly?" asked the stranger.

"A beautiful voice, certainly!" thought the Cherub; "and there is a great deal in that—a great deal."

"Can I sleep for an hour or two?" asked the stranger.

Hans looked at him after the usual fashion, as though he was debating in his own mind how he should best like to kill him, and then he replied:

"Yah—you can have der best bed!"

"Thanks!"

And so speaking, he dropped the cloak and raised his hat.

The Cherub gave a little scream.

How handsome he was, she thought.

And his good looks saved him, for had he been ugly, he would unquestionably have gone to the best room at once.

But he was good-looking, and was saved—at all events, for a time.

The Cherub rushed forward, and giving a look at her father, which this latter knew how to interpret as "Do, and it will be much the worse for you, Herr Schwincks," she said to the stranger:

"Good sir, can you not sleep here in this room until your friend comes?"

And she gave him such a meaning look, that if he had been an ordinary man it would have knocked him down at least, and perhaps it would have done him more harm still.

As it was, the stranger, being strong, felt grateful for the obvious warning that was in her words, and he replied:

"Madame, I can sleep anywhere, and I have need of sleep, I assure you, if only for an hour; but, ah me! how could I sleep in the presence of a lady?"

Down she went with a curtsey—so deep, that she nearly carried herself off her own legs, and with a gratified air, only a little damped by the tittering she heard through the room, she said:

"Oh, your honour flatters!"

And she felt that loved a man she never had so much before, and she began to contemplate how much money she had in the old stocking upstairs, which she could lend him.

"Would he would take me with the gold!" she thought.

It did not strike her that his honour could change the gold, and get rid of it altogether, while as to herself, she was like a bad penny, and would continually keep on hand, unless chucked away.

"I am very tired," said the stranger.

"Sit, then," said the Cherub, showing all the teeth she had left, and they looked more like milestones than a set, so many of them had either been pulled or dropped out, or more generally knocked out while having rows on her own account at the Anchor of Safety, or interfering when her reigning favourite was attacked.

"Thanks!" said the stranger, as he seated himself. "Can I have anything to eat?"

"Oh," said the Cherub, looking as though she could eat the visitor, "I'll see to your honour's supper myself!"

And she did, Schwincks himself looking on, and muttering: "Goot himmel—what a gal mein gal is!"

And the Cherub was good enough to sit down and eat with the stranger, who certainly looked upon this performance as a liberty.

He had no idea that actually she was doing this for fear of poison; this was so, and so desperately was she in love with him, that actually she was devoted enough, the dear, to run the risk of death for his sake.

To be sure, she felt almost certain that her father would not be such a brute as to allow her to poison herself, and that, therefore, he would rush forward if anything was wrong, and hence the reason she ate what the stranger ate.

But how could she be *sure* of Schwincks?

However, affectionate love is sweet, and so she ate as the stranger ate.

But he was not very gallant, for he nearly fell asleep over his plate.

"Your honour is very sleepy?"

"Yes, my dear maid—can I sleep at once?"

"Lie there, your honour," she replied, pointing to a sofa. And then she added, "Your friend will soon be here—will he not?"

"I trust so."

And without a word more, the stranger flung himself upon the sofa pointed out to him, and, putting his hands under his head, almost in a moment he was asleep.

Now, unfortunately, this way of placing his hands brought into view a handsome diamond, about the size of a large pea,

and which the stranger wore on the third finger of his left hand.

The position of this ring had caused the poor Cherub a horrid pang, for she had asked herself:

"Is he engaged?"

But hope is a blessing, and she began wondering if he would give it to her, should he propose, as no doubt he would.

The diamond, however, completely deprived Hans Schwincks of anything like any good feelings he might have, for diamonds had been his ruin all his life; they had brought him so many times near the halter, and once quite up to the altar.

"Mein himmel!" he said—"I must have it!"

And then he persuaded himself that, as the stranger only had the pass-knock, and not the pass-word, he, Hans, might do as he liked with him.

But there was the Cherub protecting him.

"Mates," said Hans, to a tableful of the most villanous-looking men in the room, "we must send him to sleep!"

"How?"

"Suppose we all sit down on him together!"

"Ha, but didn't you hear o' that case over there in Paris, where the lag was set over with small poisoned spikes, and how, when they went to settle the bloke, the points ran in 'em, and they all died raving mad?"

"I don't believe der tale!" said Hans.

"Then there's the Cherub," said another.

"Yah—I'm going to give mein dear fraulein a good dose!"

And thereupon up Hans got, the sparkle of the diamond completely overcoming him, and, going to a certain bottle, he filled a glass, flew at his dear daughter, put the hug on the Cherub from behind, and, as she yelled, "Pa-pa-pa-papa!" down her scraggy throat went the liquor.

She gave three kicks and a yelp, and then she was as fast asleep as the traveller himself.

She did not wake so soon as he did, however, for it was as Hans and half-a-dozen of his rascally friends moved towards the sofa upon which the unknown lay, that this latter suddenly opened his eyes, and, without betraying any fear, asked:

"Has my friend come?"

"No, your honour!"

"Ha—I think I had better get to bed! Is there a boat dropping down the river to-morrow morning?"

"Your honour," said Hans, with a grin—"your honour shall certainly go down the river in the morning, believe me!"

The old rascal meant that the tide would carry his body down with it towards the sea.

"Thanks! Where is the bed-room? If my friend calls, wake me."

"Who is your friend?" asked Hans.

"I doubt whether I am permitted to say," replied the stranger.

At which Hans whispered to himself:

"The shroud beadstead is der one for him!"

Then he bowed and led the way into a near bed-room.

The bedstead was a heavy-looking piece of furniture—something like a hearse, if like anything except itself; the sheets, however, looked very welcome and refreshing.

"I sha'n't undress," said the stranger, pulling off his boots, in which operation Hans stooped and helped him, "for the moment my friend arrives, I shall accompany him down the river."

Hans smiled as his face was stooped over the stranger's boots, which he thought would make a capital Sunday pair.

"Good night!"

And the stranger flung himself upon the bed.

"Asleep already," said Hans—"den der sooner he vill be asleep for good! Down der river he vill go!"

The landlord then left the room.

(To be continued in our next.)

RED GAUNTLET, THE BANDIT; OR, THE BLACK MOUNTAINEERS.

BOOK II.—THE BLACK CHATEAU.

CHAPTER XXV. (*Continued.*)

THEREUPON the dowager duchess appeared with her head in a pink petticoat, and a counterpane trailing after her like the tail of a comet.

"I shall write to the *Times!*" said her ladyship. "I won't have my rest broken in this way for nothing! I certainly shall write to the *Times!*"

"Do, ma!"

"Tikey, put your whiskers in your mouth! Why, what ugly vagabonds!" suddenly her ladyship continued, as her eyes fell upon the two monks, both of whom were uglier than monks in general, and monks never were celebrated for being handsome.

"They *are* ugly—so ugly," continued the King, "that I think their very looks call for a search-warrant! Sergeant, search them!"

And it was at this point that Brother Anselmo came to his senses, and sat up on the floor, and looked about him as though he had just been shot from the moon, had fallen upon earth, and couldn't comprehend it at all.

"Where am I?" he said.

"I am here, dear brother!" said Ignatius. "You know me?"

"Brother—Brother Ignatius!" yelled Brother Anselmo, as though the sight of him were joy indeed. "Now indeed I am safe!"

And he hugged Brother Ignatius as though he had not seen him for years, and was the dearest friend he had in the world.

"Who are all these people, Brother Ignatius?" asked Brother Anselmo, meekly, and looking round at the soldiery.

"Brother Anselmo," the other monk returned, "don't be afraid! They are men of blood, but they shall not harm thee while I am here to fight for thee!"

"What do they want with us, Brother Ignatius?"

"They want to search us, Brother Anselmo!"

"What's that, Brother Ignatius?" asked Anselmo, trying to look innocent, and, in reality, looking, if anything, far more evil and cut-throat-like than he did before.

"There, enough of that!" said the King. "'Tisn't the coat makes the monk! Ransack them!"

"Oh, holy Mary!" yelled Brother Anselmo, as the soldiers began pulling him about, "and blessed St. Catherine, and St. Ann, and St. Cecilia—come and help us!"

"Hang it," said the King, "call upon the saints—don't entreat ladies to see you searched, brother! Search away, my men!" the King continued to the soldiers.

And they were nothing loth.

The poor monks were nearly turned inside out.

Nothing was found to implicate them in any way.

Their leader, the Black Bandit, was a clever man. His bandits, when playing the monk, never had the sign of a brigand about them—not a knife under the frock was one of them allowed to wear.

Only one difficulty could the Black Bandit never get over.

It was this.

Every monk must have a round patch shaved away on the top of his head.

Now, to appear monks, each of his men had this mark of monkhood.

But the misfortune was, that when his men put off the gown and cowl, and took to the jacket and the brigand's gun, they could not grow hair with which to cover the patch on the top of the head.

And thus it was that it became known to the authorities, by the capture and shooting of several of the band, that there was a monastery somewhere about, in which all the monks were brigands and monks by turn.

"I don't like the looks of you!" said the King, when the search had been completed, and nothing had been discovered that could in any way inculpate the men. "To what order do you belong?"

"The Black Benedictines."

"Black enough!" said the King. "Where are you going?"

"We are begging friars," said Ignatius.

"Where did you come from yesterday?"

"From the north," replied Brother Ignatius.

"Then, as you are wandering friars, and come from the north, you can tell us where you slept last night."

Brother Ignatius started, and then he saw he had done wrong thus to betray himself, for he noticed the keen eyes of the King upon him.

"Where did you sleep?"

"At an inn called the Golden Fleece."

"Good. If you *are* monks, you can prove it to-morrow; meantime——"

"Meantime?" asked Ignatius, threateningly.

"Meantime," his Majesty continued, "you are prisoners!"

"Oh, saints save us!" said Brother Anselmo.

"Prisoners?" added Ignatius, morosely.

"Yes, prisoners—to be treated well, but prisoners."

"And what if we don't to-morrow answer your questions?"

"Well, you will keep prisoners."

Now, Ignatius knew that it was a rule of the Black Bandit's, and one there was no gainsaying, that if one of the band were taken as a monk, he should never betray the Black Chateau, for that would have brought the Government down upon the horrid building.

In fact, Ignatius saw that, by the keenness of the captain, he was ruined, and he determined to take his vengeance.

Remember, he had no arms.

"Prisoners?" he repeated.

"Yes—but as monks are plain livers, and profess to live only to pray," said the King, with a laugh, "why, you will not miss sumptuous fare, while you can pray as well on the inside of a wall as the outside!"

"Take care!"

"What of?"

"This!"

In a moment, the feigned Brother Ignatius had leaped at a soldier standing by his side, had torn his side-arms—the bayonet—from his belt, and——

As the bayonet was thrust at the King, an explosion was heard.

Suddenly Ignatius stopped, leaped in the air, blood poured from his mouth, and then he fell heavily—dead—upon the floor.

"A good shot—a good shot!" said the King. "Whose work?"

The soldiers made way.

And there stood, silent and passive, Red Gauntlet.

"Were you the man?"

"I was."

"Who are you? Give me your hand!"

Red Gauntlet bowed, but did not take the proffered hand.

"I am nameless," he said.

"Make a name."

"'Tis easier to lose one."

"Have *you* lost one?"

"Ay, sir."

"Regain it."

"I have enemies!"

"Conquer them!"

"They are too powerful."

"Are you afraid to try?"

"*No!*"

And Red Gauntlet's head was proudly raised.

"Well, you are a brave man!"

"I am glad I saved your life."

"Why glad?"

"Because you are a brave man!"

"Well answered! Can you be helped?"

"Thanks—only the King could help me!"

"Well, suppose *I* am the King!"

"Nay, sir, you jest!"

"'Tis true, I never saw the King; but I swear to you, every man I have spoken to knows his Majesty."

"If all you know spoke of me to the King, the King would be deaf!"

"Nay—I know one whom he would hear."

"Who?" asked Red Gauntlet.

"Yourself!"

"You are very confident."

"Oh—I know the King as well as any man."

"You can do me no good."

"Quite sure?"

"As sure as though I was the King myself!"

"He is not so handsome as you are. But listen. You have saved my life, and I don't care to remain under an obligation that I can repay, though I know how to be grateful. Let me speak to the King for you. I promise you—I dare promise you that he will grant your request."

"His Majesty *could* not grant my prayer."

"How so?"

"Because his Majesty could not violate the law."

"Ha—you have offended the law?"

"Ay; because the law offended me!"

"That is strong language," said the King.

"I thank you for your good intentions, sir," continued Red Gauntlet, "but you can do me no good—no good whatever."

"Nonsense! Take this ring!"

"Wherefore?"

"Take it! There you have——"

"I see, it is a Masonic ring," said Red Gauntlet.

"Yes. When you are in your deepest trouble, send it to the King!"

"Why, what claim have I on him?"

"More than you think for!"

"And why should *your* ring be so precious?"

"You are polite."

"I am plain-spoken."

"And his Majesty likes plain-spoken men, I assure you—much. Well, will you promise me, in your greatest need, to send the Masonic ring to his Majesty?"

"I do not promise."

"Why not?"

"I do not care to promise, for my own sake."

"Then promise for mine!" said the King, laughing.

"Why?"

"Because I am sure, whatever you are, and whatever you may have done, that you have the making of a good subject of the King's in you."

"*I promise!*" said Red Gauntlet.

"That's the best day's work you've done," said the King. "And day it is, for here is daybreak!"

They turned to look at the daybreak.

But when the King turned again, bent upon addressing the mysterious stranger, Red Gauntlet had disappeared.

CHAPTER XXVI.

A MYSTERIOUS DEATH.

THE scene is the exterior of a cottage fixed in the side of a precipitous mountain.

All is still.

It is sunset.

Look, there, before the door, stretched on the sward, is a great form.

It does not move.

It had not moved for hours.

It was all alone.

Mark it.

An old—old man, with white—white hair.

No expression in the eyes, no expression in all the face, beyond the awful blankness of death.

The sunset and the black shadows stole up the hill-side and darkened the face.

Yet no one came.

Hour after hour—all still.

The hoarse cry of the wolf in the plain below was heard, the cry of the owl was heard on the night air, yet still the great form lay undisturbed before the door of the cottage.

At last, and it was midnight, two forms might have been seen stealing through the night—illuminated only by the faint, dim light of the stars—towards that mountain but unoccupied home.

These two were, the one a young man, the other a stanch, strongly-built, elderly man.

The younger, as he approached the cottage, said in a whisper to his companion:

"No light! 'Tis strange! He who ever kept a light burning to welcome me!"

Approaching nearer, he called:

"Father!"

Alas! there could be no answer; for, had there been sufficient light, it could easily have been seen, by the resemblance of the living face of the approaching young man to the features of the ghastly dead, that they were of the same blood.

"Father!"

And he approached nearer the house.

All was silent.

And then, in nearing the house, he almost trod upon the dead and upturned face.

By-the-way, the hands were crossed upon the breast. It appeared as though their possessor had known the great deliverer, King Death, was at hand, and that he had been prepared to meet him.

Yes, the son almost stepped upon the upturned face of the father.

The son approached the house, still calling, when, suddenly, a terrible cry arose from his companion, the elderly man, who had the previous moment stumbled over something.

"'Tis he—my old master! I need no light to know his features! Master—master, 'tis I, your old servant, Labian, who calls! Hear me—hear me!"

Alas! he was past all earthly hearing.

"Labian, what say you? My father on the ground?"

He flung himself down on the sward.

"Labian, how cold my father is!"

"Very cold—very!"

"What ails him?"

"I fear, good master, that which will one day ail us all!"

"Dead?"

"DEAD, Red Gauntlet!"

The son fell forward, happily insensible, for a time, to the horror of his grief.

He was now wholly an orphan.

Let us pass over the hours that elapsed before Red Gauntlet was able fairly to look his misery in the face.

Then the following conversation took place:

"Labian, we will bury my dear father beneath the willow tree he loved so well. Shall we?"

"Nay, Red Gauntlet, you are now my sole master. As you will *I* will; where you go *I* go; my fate shall be your fate; and your death, if you die first, shall be the summoning of *me* to the grave! I am Labian, who is thy servant, master!"

"And my friend. How did my father die?"

"I fear foul play, although we have examined him, and found no wound."

"Possibly poison," murmured Red Gauntlet.

"At all events," answered Labian, "the Marcosi's great opponent is dead. The Marcosi need never fear your father more."

"But the Marcosi must never know that my father is dead."

"No—no—no!"

"Nay, he cannot have died by poison. The Marcosi apart, my father had not an enemy. Natural has been his death, I am sure, for the Marcosi did not know of my father's hiding-place."

"I don't know that, Red Gauntlet."

(*To be continued in our next.*)

BANDIT LIFE IN CORSICA.

THE following account of bandit life in Corsica we extract from an interesting work entitled "Wanderings in Corsica:"—

Although the Corsican bandit never lowers himself to common robbery, he holds it not inconsistent with his knightly honour to extort money.

The bandits levy black-mail; they tax individuals, frequently whole villages, according to their means, and call in their tribute with great strictness.

They impose these taxes as kings of the bush; and I was told their subjects paid them more promptly and conscientiously than they do their taxes to the imperial government of France.

It often happens that the bandit sends a written order into the house of some wealthy individual, summoning him to deposit so many thousand francs in a spot specified; and informing him that if he refuses, himself, his house, and his vineyards will be destroyed.

The usual formula of the threat is—*Si preparasse*—let him prepare.

Others, again, fall into the hands of the bandits, and have to pay a ransom for their release.

All intercourse becomes thus more and more insecure—agriculture impossible.

With the extorted money, the bandits enrich their relatives and friends, and procure themselves many a favour; they cannot put the money to any immediate personal use—for though they had it in heaps, they must nevertheless continue to live in the caverns of the mountain wilds, and in constant flight.

Many bandits have led their outlaw life for fifteen or twenty years, and, small as is the range allowed them by their hills, have maintained themselves successfully against the armed power of the State, victorious in every struggle, till the bandit's fate at length overtook them.

The Corsican banditti do not live in troops, as in this way the country could not support them; and, moreover, the Corsican is by nature indisposed to submit to the commands of a leader.

They generally live in twos, contracting a sort of brotherhood.

They have their deadly enmities among themselves too, and their deadly revenge; this is astonishing, but so powerful is the personal feeling of revenge with the Corsican, that the similarity of their unhappy lot never reconciles bandit with bandit, if a Vendetta has existed between them.

Many stories are told of one bandit's hunting another among the hills, till he had slain him, on account of a Vendetta.

Massoni and Serafino, the two latest bandit heroes of Corsica, were at feud, and shot at each other when opportunity offered.

A shot of Massoni's had deprived Serafino of one of his fingers.

The history of the Corsican bandits is rich in extraordinary, heroic, chivalrous traits of character.

Throughout the whole country they sing the bandit dirges; and naturally enough, for it is their own fate, their own sorrow, that they thus sing. Numbers of the bandits have become immortal; but the bold deeds of one especially are still famous.

His name was Teodoro, and he called himself King of the Mountains.

Corsica has thus had two kings of the name of Theodore.

Teodoro Poli was enrolled on the list of conscripts, one day in the beginning of the present century.

He had begged to be allowed time to raise money for a substitute.

He was seized, however, and compelled to join the ranks.

Teodoro's high spirit and love of freedom revolted at this. He threw himself into the mountains, and began to live as bandit.

He astonished all Corsica by his deeds of audacious hardihood, and became the terror of the island.

But no meanness stained his fame; on the contrary, his generosity was the theme of universal praise, and he forgave even relatives of his enemies.

His personal appearance was remarkably handsome, and, like his namesake, the king, he was fond of rich and fantastic dress.

His lot was shared by his mistress, who lived in affluence on the contributions (*taglia*) which Teodoro imposed upon the villages.

Another bandit, called Brusco, to whom he had vowed inviolable friendship, also lived with him, and his uncle, Augellone.

Augellone means *bird of ill omen*—it is customary for the bandits to give themselves surnames as soon as they begin to play a part in the macchia.

The Bird of Ill Omen became envious of Brusco, because Teodoro was so fond of him, and one day he put the cold iron a little too deep into his breast.

He thereupon made off into the rocks.

When Teodoro heard of the fall of Brusco, he cried aloud for grief, not otherwise than Achilles at the fall of Patroclus, and, according to the old custom of the avengers, began to let his beard grow, swearing never to cut it till he had bathed in the blood of Augellone.

A short time passed, and Teodoro was once more seen with his beard cut.

These are the little tragedies of which the mountain fastnesses are the scene, and the bandits the players—for the passions of the human heart are everywhere the same.

Teodoro at length fell ill.

A spy gave information of the hiding-place of the sick lion, and the wild wolf-hounds, the sbirri, were immediately among the hills—they killed Teodoro in a goatherd's shieling.

Two of them, however, learned how dangerously he could still handle his weapons.

The popular ballad sings of him, that he fell with his pistol in his hand and the firelock by his side, *come un fiero paladino* —like a proud paladin.

Such was the respect which this king of the mountains had inspired, that the people continued to pay his tribute, even after his fall.

For at his death there was still some due, and those who owed the arrears came and dropped their money respectfully into the cradle of the little child, the offspring of Teodoro and his queen.

Teodoro met his death in the year 1827.

Gallocchio is another celebrated outlaw.

He had conceived an attachment for a girl who became faithless to him, and he had forbidden any other to seek her hand.

Cesario Negroni wooed and won her.

The young Gallocchio gave one of his friends a hint to wound the father-in-law.

The wedding guests are dancing merrily, merrily twang the fiddles and the mandolines—a shot!

The ball had missed its way, and pierced the father-in-law's heart.

Gallocchio now becomes bandit.

Cesario entrenches himself.

But Gallocchio forces him to leave the building, hunts him through the mountains, finds him, kills him.

Gallocchio now fled to Greece, and fought there against the Turks.

One day the news reached him that his own brother had fallen in the Vendetta war which had continued to rage between the families involved in it by the death of the father-in-law, and that of Cesario.

Gallocchio came back, and killed two brothers of Cesario; then more of his relatives, till at length he had extirpated his whole family.

The Red Gambini was his comrade. With his aid he constantly repulsed the gendarmes; and on one occasion they bound one of them to a horse's tail, and dragged him so over the rocks.

Gambini fled to Greece, where the Turks cut off his head; but Gallocchio died in his sleep, for a traitor shot him.

Santa Lucia Giammarchi is also famous; he held the bush for sixteen years; Camillo Ornano ranged the mountains for fourteen years; and Joseph Antommarchi was seventeen years a bandit.

The celebrated bandit Serafino was shot shortly before my arrival in Corsica; he had been betrayed, and was slain while asleep.

Arrighi, too, and the terrible Massoni, had met their death a short time previously—a death as wild and romantic as their lives had been.

Massoni was a man of the most daring spirit and unheard-of energy; he belonged to a wealthy family in Balagna.

The Vendetta had driven him into the mountains, where he lived many years, supported by his relations, and favoured by the herdsmen, killing, in frequent struggles, a great number of sbirri.

His companions were his brother and the brave Arrighi.

One day, a man of the province of Balagna, who had to avenge the blood of a kinsman on a powerful family, sought him out, and asked his assistance.

The bandit received him hospitably, and as his provisions happened to be exhausted at the time, went to a shepherd of Monte Rotondo, and demanded a lamb; the herdsman gave him one from his flock.

Massoni, however, refused it, saying—"You give me a lean lamb, and yet to-day I wish to do honour to a guest; see, yonder is a fat one, I must have it;" and instantly he shot the fat lamb down, and carried it off to his cave.

The shepherd was provoked by the unscrupulous act. Meditating revenge, he descended from the hills, and offered to show the sbirri Massoni's lurking-place.

The shepherd was resolved to avenge the blood of his lamb.

The sbirri came up the hills in force.

These Corsican gendarmes, well acquainted with the nature of their country, and practised in banditti warfare, are no less brave and daring than the game they hunt.

Their lives are in constant danger when they venture into the mountains, for the bandits are watchful—they keep a look-out with their telescopes, with which they are always provided, and when danger is discovered they are up and away more swiftly than the muffro, the wild sheep; or they let their pursuers come within ball-range, and they never miss their mark.

The sbirri, then, ascended the hills, the shepherd at their head; they crept up the rocks by paths which he alone knew.

The bandits were lying in a cave.

It was almost inaccessible, and concealed by bushes.

Arrighi and the brother of Massoni lay within; Massoni himself sat behind the bushes, on the watch.

Some of the sbirri had reached a point above the cave, others guarded its mouth.

Those above looked down into the bush to see if they could make out anything.

One sbirro took a stone and pitched it into the bush, in which he thought he saw some black object; in a moment a man sprang out, and fired a pistol to awake those in the cavern.

But the same instant were heard the muskets of the sbirri, and Massoni fell dead on the spot.

At the report of the firearms a man leaped out of the cave—Massoni's brother.

He bounded like a wild goat in daring leaps from crag to crag, the balls whizzing about his head. One hit him fatally, and he fell among the rocks.

Arrighi, who saw everything that passed, kept close within the cave.

The gendarmes pressed cautiously forward, but for a while no one dared to enter the grotto, till at length some of the hardiest ventured in.

There was nobody to be seen; the sbirri, however, were not to be cheated, and, confident that the cavern concealed their man, camped about its mouth.

Night came.

They lighted their torches.

It was resolved to starve Arrighi into surrender. In the morning, some of them went to a spring near the cave to fetch water—the crack of a musket once, twice, and two sbirri fell.

Their companions, infuriated, fired into the cavern.

All was still.

The next thing to be done was to bring in the two dead or dying men.

After much hesitation, a party made the attempt, and again it cost one of them his life.

Another day passed.

At last it occurred to one of them to smoke the bandit out like a badger—a plan already adopted with success in Algiers.

They accordingly heaped dry wood at the entrance of the cave, and set fire to it; but the smoke found egress through chinks in the rock.

Arrighi heard every word that was said, and kept up actual dialogues with the gendarmes, who could not see, much less hit him.

He refused to surrender, although pardon was promised him.

At length the procurator, who had been brought from Ajaccio, sent to the city of Corte for military and an engineer.

The engineer was to give his opinion as to whether the cave might be blown up with gunpowder.

The engineer came, and said it was possible to throw petards into it.

Arrighi heard what was proposed, and found the thought of being blown to atoms with the rocks of his hiding-place so shocking that he resolved on flight.

He waited till nightfall, then, rolling some stones down in a false direction, he sprang away from rock to rock, to reach another mountain.

The uncertain shots of the sbirri echoed through the darkness.

One ball struck him on the thigh.

He lost blood, and his strength was failing; when the day dawned his bloody track betrayed him, as its bloody sweat the stricken deer.

The sbirri took up the scent.

Arrighi, wearied to death, had lain down under a block. On this block a sbirro mounted, his piece ready.

Arrighi stretched out his head to look around him—a report, and the ball was in his brain.

So died these three outlawed avengers, fortunate that they did not end on the scaffold.

Such was their reputation, however, with the people, that none of the inhabitants of Monte Rotondo or its neighbourhood would lend his mule to convey away the bodies of the fallen men.

"For," said these people, "we will have no part in the blood that you have shed."

When at length mules had been procured, the dead men, bandits and sbirri, were put upon their backs, and the troop of gendarmes descended the hills, six corpses hanging across the mule-saddles—six men killed in the banditti warfare.

If this island of Corsica could again give forth all the blood which in the course of centuries has been shed upon it—the blood of those who have fallen in battle, and the blood of those who have fallen in the Vendetta—the red deluge would inundate its cities and villages, and drown its people, and crimson the sea from the Corsican shore to Genoa.

Verily, violent death has here his peculiar realm.

TALES OF BRIGANDS AND ROBBERS.

I Warn & Strike

[PERILOUS ESCAPE OF MARGARET SEDWYN.]

HAWK'S EYE, THE PHANTOM ROBBER.

CHAPTER IX.

THE MEETING WITH THE PHANTOM OF HIMSELF.—THE COMPACT.—
THE WARNING.—THE GOOD-BYE.

ÉNTERING the great room, Hans gave one look at the still snoring, beautiful Cherub, and then whispered to three hideous-looking rascals:

"Go down, and give him der gentleman more bed dan him thinks for!"

The men nodded, and slipped down a dark staircase.

But they had scarcely disappeared when one of the company, going to the sofa to lie down, found under his hand a something which, picked up, made him leap.

"Hans!"

A moment, and Hans comprehended.

He looked at what had been found, yelled, and called:

"Shtop der machinery!"

At that moment a heavy knock came at the door.

There was a wonderful buoyancy in the heart of Hawk's Eye as he rode away after seeing the Lady May safe within the doorway of Falcon Grange. And if any of you want to know exactly the state of his feelings, allow me to recommend you to follow his example in some one of his many ways —I mean, do some good which, while you do it, puts you in some danger, and more especially, which may put you to the risk of your life.

Then you will understand how it was that his heart was so light as he rode away from Falcon Grange—albeit he rode into danger—albeit he rode away from the dear lady of his love; for, believe me—the man who writes to you—the man who does his duty cannot wholly be unhappy; for if he does his duty, however wretched he may be in his own life, he has done some good for somebody else, and that will be enough to give him a sense of satisfaction which, in the midst of all his own wretchedness, will save him from despair.

Believe that. It will be all the better for you. Nothing can make a man happier than in making others happy.

Now, that is the truth indeed.

So Hawk's Eye rode away with a heart as blithe as that of a boy of sixteen; and let me tell you that there is not a man from the top of Scotland to Land's End in the county of Cornwall but would be glad to have a heart as light as that of a boy of sixteen, when he is a boy as happy as a boy ought to be.

He had parted with Albert Falconer a short time after they had parted with the King's people—say, about an hour.

And this is what he had done for the brother of the Lady May:—

He had given him first a password.

Secondly, a sign.

Thirdly, the address of the safe inn down by the river.

Fourthly, a hint how to knock at its door.

Now, Albert Falconer quite forgot the password, which was for that week "Wolf," and hence the danger he incurred when he got entrance to the Anchor of Safety, for if a man knocked at that door in the only way that would gain him admittance, and then could give neither the password nor the sign of any individual who was a great patron of the Anchor of Safety, Hans Schwincks was to understand that the visitor had been sent with sufficient knowledge to get him into the inn, but only with enough to get him past the threshold, and that he was, in fact, a *victim*, sent with the mode of getting into the inn, and nothing more—his ignorance being really to mean, "Kill him—he is worth murder."

Now, unfortunately, all that Albert remembered of the various directions given him by his good protector was the name of the inn down by the river, and the mode of knocking at the door.

That of the password "Wolf," and of the sign or token, he recalled nothing.

Had he recalled either, he would have been far safer at the Anchor of Safety than—outlaw as he was—he would have been at any other spot of English ground.

Old Hans Schwincks naturally supposed he was a Jacobite fugitive, wherein he was right.

As for the Cherub, she being sent into a seraphic sleep, she had no power to prevent what was to happen in the shroud bed-room.

Now, it will be remembered that upon Schwincks seeing a certain something which had been found by one of his rascally lot on the sofa where Albert had been lying, the effect was so great that he immediately called upon his people to "Shtóp der machinery."

Now what was this talisman which could change so obdurate and savage a nature as that of the old Dutch rascal Hans Schwincks?

This was simply a bead—the sign given by Hawk's Eye to Albert Falconer.

And this bead was the sign which, possessed by anyone, saved him at the Anchor of Safety, and guaranteed him utterly from danger.

The bead was exactly the counterpart of a *hawk's eye*, and it was known throughout the whole fraternity of the knights of the road as the promise—nay, the certainty of safety from all of the craft.

There were three dozen of these beads, and whoever received them carefully guarded them, and returned them to their rightful owner the first time he was seen.

Not once had either of these beads been lost.

The three dozen, and always the three dozen of beads.

And Hawk's Eye was asked for an account of the people who had carried his sign.

Woe be to the man who could not prove that he had done aught but good to him who had been the bearer of that sign!

Therefore the reader may judge of the old rascal's fears when he saw the hawk's-eye bead looking at him, as it were, as though it were accusing him of murder.

Well he might call upon them to stop the machinery.

Poor devil! before his men got to the "machinery"—which we will take an early opportunity of describing—and need we say that it referred to the "bridegroom bedstead," as the shroud bedstead was sometimes called—before his myrmidons could reach the wheels and springs, old Hans Schwincks had rushed at a schnapps bottle, and—if we may be allowed the pun—had "schnapped" it up.

And as he did so, the Angel, the Cherub, the Seraph, the beautiful being who had been christened Sarah Jane came to, or, rather, it appeared as though something had hit her in the back and shook her senses alive again.

The beauteous being opened her eyes, squinted until she must have seen half-a-dozen candles for every one in the great room, and committed herself to this remark:

"Where—where—where is my own—my beautiful one? Oh—oh—oh, ye have not torn him from my grasp?"

"Goot job for him if er have!" said her brute of a father, and then, deeming probably he had no further use for the schnapps bottle, which he had now quite emptied, and to be sure of which he had shaken it four times in an inverted state over his extremely ugly mouth—why he flung it at the Cherub.

Luckily, it did not hurt her much, as it only struck her on the knuckles—a little attention which caused her to use a word we will not sully our pages by repeating.

In fact, she repeated the word.

It was not at all characteristic of a cherub.

But we must leave the Anchor of Safety to look after itself, and return to Hawk's Eye, who is gaily prancing along the road, and quite as happy as any gentleman or knight on or off the road.

He was still at the gallop when he thought he heard a gallop behind him; and as the thought came across him, he noticed that Brilliant's ears were laid back upon his head in the most evident fright, while his eyes were starting backwards, as though he saw a horrible sight.

A moment, and Hawk's Eye's sword was in his royal right hand; and as he did so he wheeled Brilliant round.

The next moment, seeing a horseman before him with his sword drawn, he made no more ado, but, putting himself at the guard, he cried:

"Come on!"

No answer.

"Who are you?"

Still no answer.

"Begone!"

The still horseman did not move.

But no sentiment of fear overcame Hawk's Eye so far.

"Why do you remain?"

Still the horseman was motionless.

"The road is wide enough for both, and it has two ways. Choose your own way, and I will take the other. I am in no humour for bloodshed, for I am happy."

Slowly and gravely, the horseman before him raised his hat, and courteously saluted our hero.

"Why do you salute me with that courteous air?"

No answer.

"Because I said I was happy? That could scarcely be."

Again the silent horseman raised his hat and saluted Hawk's Eye.

"This is impossible to comprehend," continued Hawk's Eye. "Have you business with me?"

Again the silent horseman saluted Hawk's Eye.

"Then, why do you not speak?"

The phantom laid his right hand upon his mouth.

"If you would speak, and will not speak—if you seek me, and, finding me, do not utter a sound—you are incomprehensible, and, methinks, a savage; therefore, good night!"

And, saluting the silent horseman in his turn, he gave the word to Brilliant—who had been trembling very much, and sniffing affrightedly at the nostrils of the horse before him,—and away the good horse went.

And then it was that the gentleman of the road began to feel the less chivalric portion of his nature arise, for he heard the galloping once again of the silent horseman behind him.

Suddenly he turned.

"Sir," said he, "so far I have been courteous; but if you force me, I can be far from amiable and obliging. It appears you are going this way. I will turn."

Hawk's Eye turned.

Again he heard the offensive galloping behind him.

Now his hot temper was fairly aroused, and turning, he cried:

"On guard, sir!"

And, without more ado, he thrust at the unfortunate stranger.

Horror! His sword passed through the form before him as though nought was there.

Then a soft voice was heard:

"You have struck at me, and I may speak."

"Great powers! I felt a pain at the heart!"

"'Twas even so."

"How know you that?" asked Hawk's Eye.

"Because you must feel what I endure."

"I tremble!"

"Thou hast no need, good Hawk's Eye, to tremble when I am near thee!"

"No?"

"No. Tremble rather when I am far away from thee!"

And now, the light about them increasing in a most mysterious manner, Hawk's Eye discovered this horrible fact—that creature before him was made in his—Hawk's Eye's—own image—*his own image!*

The gentleman of the road began to tremble; and believe us, readers, however brave the man may be, there is not one of us who could meet such an apparition and be fearless.

To be fearless of such a horror would prove us base and bad indeed—most infamous and bad—most hopelessly wicked, beyond all question.

Why, as Hawk's Eye began to tremble, even Brilliant below him began to quiver, just as though the very creature himself had detected his likeness in the horseman's steed.

And perhaps Brilliant had. Who knows? May not a horse have the power of knowing and thinking as well as a human being? Why should he not, pray?

And now the following conversation took place between the phantom—for it was the Phantom Robber, and no other appearance—and Hawk's Eye.

"Why do you seek me out?"

"Because I am thy other self."

"My other self?"

"I am thy shadow."

"Have all men shadows such as you are?"

"All."

"This I have never heard."

"Few men see them."

"Why am I singled out to see my shadow?"

"Nay, this is what you may not learn."

"And shall I never learn?"

"Perhaps at some future time."

"And when shall that be?"

"When the time comes to learn."

"How shall I know?"

"Then thou wilt learn."

"And why do you appear before me?"

"That I may warn thee."

"Am I in danger?"

"Yes."

"From an enemy?"

"Yes—your greatest."

"Who is he?"

"Canst thou not guess?" asked the phantom.

"Bertram Falconer?"

"No."

"Man or woman?"

"Man."

"Do I know him?"

"Very little."

"Shall I ever know him?"

"Not much."

"How shall I know him to be my enemy?"

"Only by watching for him."

"How will he appear?"

"As such an enemy ever appears to all men."

"How is that?"

"As his greatest friend."

"Nay, phantom, begone, for you would teach me to dread all men."

"Nay, I only teach thee to dread one."

"The one enemy, do you not mean, phantom?"

"I do, oh man!"

"And yet you will not tell me who this one is?"

"Yes, oh man, since thou art not wise enough to learn for thyself!"

"Who is he?"

"Nay, lay not thy hand upon thy sword, for by the sword thou canst not conquer him."

The great drops of cold sweat were now upon Hawk's Eye's forehead, and he looked the picture of terror—the example of despair.

"Who—who is he, good phantom? You speak in such a gentle voice that I do think that thou must be my friend."

"I am thy friend, and would be more thy friend."

"How so? How can I make thee more my friend?"

"By being more thine own."

"And how can I be more my own friend than I am?"

"By learning who is your enemy."

"Who is that?"

"Once more—can you not guess?"

"No."

"Does not your heart tell you?"

"No."

"Think."

"I have no power to think."

"Ask thyself."

"I have only power, oh phantom, to hear!"

"Hear, then!"

"I hear."

"The greatest enemy thou hast is the greatest enemy each man has—HIMSELF!"

"Himself? Then——"

"Yes—thy greatest enemy is THYSELF!"

"I mine own greatest enemy?"

"Beyond all doubt."

"And why do you tell me this?"

"That thou mayst subdue thine enemy."

"How shall I do this?"

"Nay, that thou must learn."

"What is the road?"

"Ask thy heart."

"I have no power to ask my heart, with you, dread phantom, before me!"

"Why am I a *dread* phantom?"

"All phantoms are dreadful."

"To the wicked only."

"But are they not terrible?"

"Why should they be? Man makes them terrible only

Think you they could exist except by reason of the divine will?—and think you that the divine will can work wickedness?"

"No, no," cried Hawk's Eye—"never!"

"Then never fear phantom more, good Hawk's Eye!"

"I will strive to believe your words."

"Ha, thou art already, then, a better man!"

"Thank heaven!" said Hawk's Eye.

And a kind of echo of the words was heard in the air.

"But why—why, oh phantom, do you specially appear to *me*? Why do I see my shadow, and no other man see his?"

Hawk's Eye quite forgot, in his agony and mental agitation, that he had already asked this question, and been answered.

"I answered you before," the phantom continued, in a deeply-melancholy tone—a tone of such combined mournfulness and sweetness that it was quite indescribable—"but I will answer you at greater length."

For a moment the strange being—it was no longer a *terror*—was silent, and then he began:

"All men are haunted by their second self, but to very few is it permitted that they shall be so fortunate as to see their other selves, and to listen to them, and to be helped and saved by them. *But* every man has that other self near him, and he is the nearer the more the man tends to do good,—he is the further away from him in exact proportion to his tendency to do evil. Some men can never be permitted to see their other self—others must. Some court their phantoms—others dread them; and yet both these sorts of men may have no idea that a phantom of each of them exists."

Hawk's Eye trembled again, for *he* had never had any conception of such a shadow of himself being in existence.

"Why you are visited, and not other men, is a matter that you shall learn in due time, and when of yourself you have done those things which shall lead to such a knowledge; and through you, perhaps, some day, man will learn that he has a double which leads him to goodness, if to goodness he will but be led."

Hawk's Eye bowed.

"Listen! Henceforth I am ever of and with thee!"

"Why?"

"Because I am of thee."

"Terror!"

"No—be not terrified. When you think good, I shall do good."

"Yes."

"When you think evil——"

"Will you do evil?"

"Yes."

"Then, if I only think of murder?"

"I, acting for you, shall do murder."

"Then I dare not even think of killing?"

"No, or I shall kill."

"Then my thought is not free?"

"Do not think of murder," said the phantom, gently.

Hawk's Eye bowed.

"List! Whenever you rob a bad man, you will be successful."

"Yes."

"When you rob a good man, you will fail."

"I comprehend."

"Give to the poor."

"I always have."

"Give more."

"I will."

"It is the best money you will spend."

"I will take heed of what you say."

"When you want me, call for me."

"I will."

"But never call for me unless you are in extremity."

"I will not."

"Whenever you can save yourself, do so."

"I will not fail, good phantom—depend upon that."

"All that you can do for yourself you must."

"I always have done so."

"A good rule, Hawk's Eye, and one few men care to follow. I shall never *help* you unless you are in danger——"

"I thank you, phantom!"

"And——"

The phantom stopped.

"And?" asked Hawk's Eye.

"And you are worthy of being helped."

"I will be worthy."

"Take from the wicked."

"I will."

"'Twill teach them, by their own sufferings when they lose, how they have made others suffer when they robbed in a *safe* way, and did not risk life, and, worse, *liberty*, on the road."

"I will obey."

"You swear?"

"I swear!"

"Swear!" was echoed through the air.

"In good time, Hawk's Eye, you shall learn why *you* amongst men are chosen to have revealed to you your other self."

"I will patiently await the time."

"'Tis well! And now—good-bye!"

"Good-bye!" was mournfully echoed through the air, and the sad words appeared to die away, hissed by the varying currents of the atmosphere.

"Good-bye!" said Hawk's Eye.

And he was alone—quite alone.

The phantom horseman and the phantom horse had melted into thin air even before the echoing air had ceased to play with those words—"Good-bye!"

"Strange—more than passing strange!" said Hawk's Eye.

"Has it been all a dream?" he asked himself, after a moment's lapse.

He put his hand to his forehead. His brow was still steeped in perspiration.

"No—no dream!"

"No—no dream!" he repeated, as his hand fell upon the reeking neck of his steed, Brilliant, for that fine arching line was also wet with the dew of fear.

"So, being gone, I breathe again! Come, good Brilliant—we are mortal once again, and so, a gallop, my brave boy!"

And away horse and man bounded over the breezy heath.

(To be continued in our next.)

RED GAUNTLET, THE BANDIT; OR, THE BLACK MOUNTAINEERS.

BOOK II.—THE BLACK CHATEAU.

CHAPTER XXVI.—*(Continued.)*

"DEAR father," continued Red Gauntlet, mournfully, "it is best for thee that thou didst not know that thy son was the terrible Red Gauntlet. I grieve for thee as dearly as ever son grieved in a manly way for father; and yet—Heaven pardon me!—I feel a secret sense of relief in knowing that I can never pain thee by the knowledge that I am a bandit—that I can never make thee flinch by the remembrance that I love still the daughter of thy foe, and that the great ambition of my life is to make her mine!"

"Let us bury him before the sunlight falls upon him again, after the custom of your family," whispered Labian.

It is a custom in Italy that no more than twice shall the sun go down upon an uninterred corpse, and in some families only one daylight is allowed to shine upon the stark body,—ere the second day be come, the stilled form is laid in the tomb.

This custom has led to several burials during life.

So the son rose with heavy heart, and he and Labian, by the light of one poor lantern, began digging a deep grave below the willow tree, the leaves whispering softly as the work went on.

Ere daylight—before the second day's sunlight fell upon those stilled features—the good Duseanelli had been wrapped in the military cloak he had worn when a young man, and when he had fought the battles of his country, and the ground had been softly piled over him, and the turf relaid.

Then Red Gauntlet flung himself upon the grave at full length, and wept and prayed with all the fervour of a little child.

Poor faithful Labian turned away, feeling that it would be impious to look upon such grief and prayer, and kneeling down himself—for he felt the need of prayer—he became motionless.

So things were when the cold, bleak daylight came upon them.

Then, as the old man knelt upon the ground where the dead body had lain, his eyes streaming before him, lo! in the strengthening light, he saw that on the white door-post of the cabin which made him start.

"Master!"

There was no response.

"Master! Red Gauntlet!"

Red Gauntlet did not reply. He lay with his hands clasping his head, and upon one of his fingers was the Masonic ring the King had given him.

Again Labian called.

And then, with a shudder, Red Gauntlet raised his head.

"Master, come here!"

Red Gauntlet got wearily up, and came to where the good servant, Labian, was still kneeling.

"What is it?"

"Look!"

Labian's right-hand index-finger pointed to the white post on one side of the cottage door.

"Writing!"

"Yes, master; and whose?"

"My father's!"

"Your father's, though his hand was growing weak when he wrote it."

"My father's handwriting!"

And, stooping, he kissed the written words.

"And, see! here is the piece of chalk with which those words were written."

"My father!"

"Nay, Red Gauntlet; kiss not the words away ere you have read them!"

This Red Gauntlet had nearly done; but they managed, after some pains, to read as follows:—

"I AM DYING. I HAVE HAD A SECRET. YOU ARE NOT——"

There the writing stopped.

Evidently the poor father, suddenly dying, and all alone in that mountain home, had endeavoured to tell his son that secret which he had died without transmitting.

"My old master could not have been poisoned."

"No; and he was permitted to know death was coming, although he was not permitted to tell that secret."

Who was the "you?"

Undoubtedly Red Gauntlet.

And what was it he was not to know?

What?

So ran the message—

"I am dying. I have had a secret. You are not——"

Then—DEATH!

CHAPTER XXVII.

HOW ST. GEORGE SETTLED UP WITH COSPOLETTO.

OUR English friends, being together in the viscount's part of the palazzo, were having a rather serious discussion—each had a little trouble of his own.

"I tell you what it is, old fellows," said St. George, with a lazy sort of energy, "I think we have had enough of this kind of thing."

"What kind of thing?" asked Marriott.

"Getting mixed up with brigands, and having lots of fights, and playing the devil generally. I shall toddle back to England."

"When?"

"When I've got Nicola."

"Got Nicola?"

"Yes—to marry me."

His friends opened their eyes wide with surprise.

"I shall!" said Oliver, seriously. "She is beautiful enough to be a duchess. She is a lady by nature. A little education will make her all right—and I am fond of her."

"Bravo!" said Dick Nicholson. "That is brave and honest!"

"But how about the family?" asked Marriott. "They will cut you!"

"Let them! I want nothing of my family, and, for the sake of my family, I certainly am not going to marry a pale-faced bit of affectation while such a girl as Nicola is to be had. Besides, she loves me!"

"Then marry her," said Stuart Linn—"I should, if the case were mine."

"So should I," said Dick Nicholson. "Wouldn't you, Marriott?"

"I would."

"That's settled, then," St. George said. "So I vote a move homeward. We cannot, of course, go till we have seen our bandit friend out of his trouble. A noble fellow Red Gauntlet is!"

"Do you know, I was struck by a curious thought respecting him," said Dick Nicholson.

"Indeed!"

"I don't believe he is an Italian."

Linn started, and asked:

"What then?"

"An Englishman."

"An Englishman?"

"Yes. Study him when next we see him. He has English features, is altogether English in his style, and his accent is the purest Saxon I ever heard."

The idea made Stuart Linn reflective.

"We will go back all together," he said; "but let what we have to do be done before we go. I want to find my brother."

"And I to get Dorolie from the convent," said Nicholson.

"And I to run away with Sibyl," said the viscount. "So I propose we help each other."

This was agreed.

"I shall go to old Scamp-and-Satan's place to-night," said St. George. "It strikes me Nicola is not safe there. The brute of a Scampia is nothing but a bad old brigand, and his inn is a rendezvous for sharky company."

"Perhaps she will not come with you," suggested Dick.

"It is more likely that she will. I am anxious, too, for the last time I passed the place I am certain I saw Cospoletto there."

"Cospoletto? Why, he must be dead!"

"He ought to be!" said St. George, more sternly than he was wont to speak; "and the next time we meet, it is more than likely that he will be. So suppose you help me to bring Nicola here?"

"Very well," said Dick; "then we can have a go in at the convent for Dorolie."

"Then I shall run away with Sibyl," said Marriott.

"Then I shall find my brother," said the marquis. "I shall look at every fellow's head I see, till I find one with the white tuft of hair."

"Certainly an original way of looking for a brother," observed St. George, "but the best to be adopted under the circumstances."

That night, much to the astonishment of Scampia Zatani, St. George presented himself at the door of the mountain inn.

The house was closed. The hour was not late, and it was therefore evident the innkeeper did not want any more customers that day.

"He must have a house full," thought St. George—"the old sinner would never shut his house while he had a chance of getting a customer. I should like to see who is inside!"

He kicked again—he had kicked several times before.

"Hullo!—house!" he said. "Scamp-and-Satan! Hullo!"

A little window over the door opened, and the shaggy head of the innkeeper appeared.

"Senor?" he said, respectfully.

"Open the door!"

"Senor, the house is full."

"Is it?"

"Quite full, senor."

"Then turn somebody out to make room for me," said St. George.

"Senor, it is not possible."

"Open the door—I'll kick it in if you don't!"

"Senor——"

Just then St. George caught sight of the pretty face of Nicola at an upper window.

She made a supplicating gesture, imploring him, as he understood it, not to go away.

That was enough for St. George.

"Once more," he said—"open the door!"

"Senor," said Scampia, "I cannot!"

"Then here it goes!"

And there it went, for Oliver took a step back, and, with one powerful kick, sent the door flying from its hinges—taking it completely out, in fact, and leaving nothing but the broken lock and shattered bolts.

He heard a savage oath. The door had gone against somebody, and that somebody, not being prepared for the visit, went on his back and hurt himself.

This somebody was a brigand, his face half concealed by a hideous growth of hair, and more than half concealed by a hideous patch over his eyes.

Evidently he recognised St. George as a man made sacred to the brigands by the friendship of Red Gauntlet, for the dirty hand that went by instinct to the long knife in his belt left it again.

He got up, and limped away into a room where sat a number of such gentlemen as himself.

The sudden advent of St. George startled them. They were playing at cards, drinking bad wine, swearing in vile Italian, and gaming for stolen money.

"Don't let me disturb you, gentlemen," said the Englishman, walking in with the utmost unconcern. "Pray proceed with your pastime."

Several oaths were uttered, with significance to him, more dirty hands went to long knives, and St. George was in danger.

He saw it.

"If," he said, quietly, "you forget that I have the protection of Red Gauntlet, be kind enough to remember that I have my own. See these?"

From each pocket of his coat he produced a revolver capped and loaded.

This gratifying sight had the effect of calming the company. The dirty hands relinquished their holds of dagger-hilts, and the savage oaths were changed for humble apologies.

"Twelve very excellent little friends these!" St. George said, "each weighing a quarter of an ounce, made of the purest lead, and shaped conically; but they make ugly little holes. Try one?"

He put a revolver playfully within an inch of the ugliest brigand's ugly nose. The ugly brigand went back, upset his chair, and rolled over.

"Very well," said St. George—"don't have it without you like! Have a gallon of wine and poison yourselves."

"Good, senor Englisse!" said the brigands.

"That's it. Here, old Scampia, bring a lot of wine!"

"Senor Englisse, bravissimo!"

"Thank you! Now, then, old Scampia!"

The innkeeper stood before him, scowling.

"I am going to stay here for the night," said St. George, walking into the private room, and seating himself comfortably before the fire, "and send Nicola to me."

"Senor, she is not at home."

"Don't lie!"

"Senor!"

"Don't lie—I saw her."

Scampia muttered an oath.

"She has retired to rest, and will not come down to-night, senor."

"She has not retired; and she shall come down!" said St. George, resolutely. "No trifling, old man—I came here to see her."

"Senor!"

"Devils!" St. George could be energetic when he got into a passion. "Look here, old man. I want to take the girl from this foul sink of crime. She is worthy a better place—a better father. Send her down to me, and I shall ask her if she will come with me—to be my wife, Scampia."

The innkeeper's cheek went livid.

"Malediction!" he muttered, in a whisper. "You would take her from me?"

"I would—I will! She loves me. I will give her an honourable name, and take her where she will in time forget the scenes of crime that must have marred her childhood, and would destroy her. Is the prospect so bad that you scowl at it?"

"Senor, you would take her from her father!"

"Could you wish her a better fate? Or would you rather see her the mistress of some brutal bandit?"

Scampia did not reply to that.

His dark face underwent a darker change, and the evil expression faded, and the sinister light left his eyes.

"Stay to-night, senor," he said. "I will place my best chamber at your disposal. See Nicola in the morning, and if she consents, I have no objection."

"Very well; but I will see her to-night."

"For her sake, senor, do not. Think of these," he indicated his brigand customers. "I am obliged to keep her from their sight as a wolf would guard its young from the hunter."

"Very well. If that is why you will not let her come, I have nothing to say against it. Not that they should touch her with so much as a look—there would be some scattering of brains if they were to attempt it. So in the morning be it."

"And the senor will have my best room?"

"No, the senor will not—the senor will stay here by the fire."

"The senor will have wine—my best?"

"The senor will see you hanged first! I have a flask of good old cognac here. You can bring some water, though."

Scampia bowed and withdrew.

The determined aspect of his unwelcome guest had evidently subdued him.

But there was a devilish glimmer in the innkeeper's eyes as he said to himself:

"He would take her from me—he will not drink my wine —he will not have my best chamber, so I cannot poison him with wine, nor kill him while he sleeps. But it is not always safe to drink water!"

St. George, sitting by the fire smoking one of his own cigars, fell to musing.

"The old ruffian means mischief!" he muttered. "But, by Jove, he had better not try it! I would send a shot through him!"

He shut the door, remarking casually, as he did so, that the bolts were on the outside.

"Odd, rather," he commented, "but brigand innkeepers do odd things. Now he is letting his guests out; then, I suppose, he will come back to me."

He was right. Scampia got rid of his customers—not, however, till he had had a long, muttered conference with one or two of them at the door.

This conference warned St. George. He knew it, for he had quick ears, and perfectly understood Italian.

"A pretty little plot," he said, smiling, "to wait for me as I go home, and plant a random shot into me from an ambush. Folly!"

He seemed rather to like the idea, for he was quite affable when Scampia entered with a flask of water.

"Is it clean?" he asked.

"Senor, it is filtered."

"Thank you. Good night!"

Taking the hint, Scampia made his exit. St. George saw his eyes glisten on his jewellery.

"He would like to have them," thought the Englishman—"my watch, rings, &c. He had better try and get them—he would get some of these instead!"

St. George drew his revolvers and laid them on the table, stirred the fire, took from another pocket a miniature edition of Byron, opened it at the fourth canto of "Don Juan," began to read, and to think of Nicola.

He finished the fourth canto, and began the fifth, still thinking of Nicola. Then he felt thirsty.

So he produced his flask. It was a good-sized one, holding about a pint, and was full of the finest cognac.

Some of this he poured into a glass, then he smelt the water Scampia had brought him.

Evidently he did not like the water Scampia had brought him. There was a decided upturning of the nostrils, and a look as though he had made a discovery.

"Thought so!" he said. "What an old fool to think I should not find it out!"

The water was poisoned!

Scampia had not calculated upon the effect it would have by mingling with spirit. St. George poured some of the water into the brandy, which began to scatter and bubble, and finally turned green.

St. George emptied the glass, rinsed it with brandy, then poured in a small quantity, which he drank with as much gusto or as large an amount of unconcern as though he was at his own fireside, instead of being under the roof of an old rascal of a bandit, who had tried to poison him.

We are bound to believe St. George did not like the old rascal of a bandit any the better for the attempted experiment.

He lit another cigar, went on reading the fifth canto of "Don Juan" and thinking of Nicola till he felt drowsy.

The drowsiness increased. Sleep stole upon him unconsciously, and he subsided into a dreamy doze; but, with instinctive caution, dosed with his hand upon his pistols.

He was a light sleeper. A very slight sound awakened him.

It was that of the bolts of his chamber door being slid gently into their sockets.

He got up a slight snore, but he listened.

He heard a stealthy footstep steal away, and listening still, heard it steal towards——

"By heaven!" he said, "towards Nicola's room!"

He was on his feet in an instant, had drawn a sharp and powerful dagger-knife, and begun to work at the wood which covered the sockets of the bolts.

The wood was old and rotten, the knife was keen, and the wrist that worked it strong, so in a very short time, and without noise, out came the sockets, and a gentle push opened the door.

He went back to the table, took up his revolvers, put one in his pocket, and, with the other in his hand, crept softly up after Scampia Zatani.

Into Nicola's apartment went the bandit innkeeper, pausing at the door to look back, lest he should have been followed.

St. George crouched back in a turn on the narrow stairway. He did not wish to be seen just yet.

Scampia went in and shut the door. He locked it—the Englishman heard the key turn.

The blood went hot through St. George's veins then.

In her room! She so young and beautiful—he a hardened ruffian, to whom crime was pastime. Did he mean to *kill* her that she might not become the bride of a Saxon?

St. George went hot and cold at the thought.

"Perhaps," he said to himself, "the old brute is fond of her, and is going to say a kind of farewell. But why did he lock the door?"

A low cry startled him and made him quicken his footsteps

—he dared not go too quickly, for, though he had taken his boots off, the stairs creaked with his every step.

The low cry was repeated, but this time as though muffled.

St. George's chief thought was now to be in the room. That Scampia meant mischief now was a firm conviction.

So out came the strong, sharp knife again, and Oliver went to work on the wood outside the socket of the lock. Like the wood on the door beneath, it was old and rotten, and was soon cut away.

St. George listened while he worked, and listening, he heard this muttered, in the harsh, guttural tone of Zatani:

"And so you love the Englishman, my pretty Nicola, better than you do me?"

Then the sweet, low voice of Nicola:

"Father, you terrify me!"

"Do I? Shall I tell you a little secret, Nicola? It is interesting, though it may terrify you more. I am not your father!"

A scream from Nicola.

St. George, opening the door an inch or two, saw the brown hand of the grey-haired ruffian on Nicola's bust—a white, lovely bust, burning and heaving with indignation at the outrage.

"Not my father?" said Nicola, trying to cover her bust again.

"Not her father!" thought St. George, fingering his revolver. "Then I shall have less remorse in killing him."

"Not your father," said Scampia, glaring like a greedy wolf at the beautiful form trembling on the bed; "but I love you very much, and you will never leave me, Nicola, for to-night you will be with me as my bride."

This revelation, so sudden and astounding, and coupled as it was with words of a purpose so infamous, well-nigh took from Nicola the power to move. But she saw her danger—saw the unholy fire in Scampia's eyes—felt his hot breath on her cheek, and his eager hand upon her bust.

"Oh!" she said, "spare me! I have been to you as a child! Do not destroy me so utterly, body and soul!"

"I have watched you grow in beauty day by day," said Scampia, in a voice thick with passion, and in a language for which, in its rude poetry, the Italian peasant is remarkable, "and longed eagerly for the time when I could tell you no parental blood stood in the way of my desire. Your parents died here—killed by brigands—and I saved you, that you might be mine. And now the time is come. You need not struggle. I shall stab you if you do, even if I have to possess you while you die!"

An awful thing it was to see this man, whose hair was grey, and whose soul was black with foul and fell desire—an awful thing to see with what brutal force he held the girl down, heedless of her struggles and her prayers.

And she must have fallen—the morning would have seen her a thing of shame, dishonoured and polluted by her father and her mother's murderer—but a saviour and an avenger was at hand.

St. George took three great, rapid strides across the room. He set aside his pistol, not wishing to scatter the old man's brains, or dabble his grey hair in blood; but the Englishman's strong hand went up and caught the bandit's throat in an iron grip.

Scampia turned. Nicola huddled the coverings over her, and hid her scarlet face. She heard a heavy, dull crash—a heavier fall. Scampia had gone to the floor, with his face half broken in by one tremendous blow.

He rose again—staggering, blood-blinded—and feeling for his knife, drew it, and rushed forward, to be stricken down again.

St. George's blood was up. He loved Nicola dearly, and woe to him who would have destroyed her.

"Help!" shouted Scampia, as he fell. "Kill the Englishman!"

Help came—half a dozen savage brigands, with COSPOLETTO at their head, and all eager for the Englishman's life.

"Ah!" he said, with dangerous calm, "my old friend Cospoletto not dead yet! But now——"

He stood unflinchingly before the gleam of many knives, as

his foes rushed upon him in a body. He took deliberate and steady aim at the first, and the first was Cospoletto.

The pressure of St. George's finger on the trigger, then the flash and the report, and crashing through Cospoletto's forehead and his brain went a bullet. Out gushed the blood, and like an ox—staggering amid a deluge of gore—went the bandit on his face, dead.

Another and another shot, and with each shot fell a brigand, slain.

The Englishman made short work of them now. A pile of bodies lay in confusion round him, and blood ran down the stairs.

Out of the six banditti only one was left, and he crawled away with three bullets in him. He had a rifle, which he fired at St. George; but the ball missed, and went through the heart of Scampia Zatani.

Another shot from St. George finished the last bandit there. Poor Nicola had fainted, sick with terror, long ere this took place; and she was senseless quite when, lifting her half-nude and beautiful form from the bed, St. George folded her in his strong arms, and bore her from the tragic scene.

CHAPTER XXVIII.

HOW THE DUKE OF TIKEYPOODLE LOST SIBYL.

St. George carried Nicola right from the mountain inn to the palazzo, in the city of Naples.

It was a long way; but, being a burden of love, she was light to him, and he did not feel at all fatigued; and he was stopped by the Neapolitan police. He had wrapped Nicola in his coat, but it did not altogether hide her state of nudity; and the sight of a man spattered with blood, in his shirt sleeves, and carrying a girl evidently taken in her night-dress from her bed, was enough to arouse their curiosity.

The chief of the police asked the meaning of the strange scene.

St. George answered him briefly:

"Go to the mountain inn," he said, "and see what has happened there. I am Oliver St. George, staying at the Palazzo St. Jaco with my friends the Marquis of Leith, Viscount Marriott, and Mr. Nicholson. If you want to ask any more questions, come in the morning."

And on he went, leaving the police marvelling at his manner, and admiring the pretty legs of Nicola.

The viscount, Dick Nicholson, and the marquis were considerably astonished by the advent of their friend.

They were sitting up over a game at cards, and smoking a late pipe, when he entered with Nicola.

"Hallo!" said Dick, glancing alternately from his blood-bespattered friend to Nicola's legs, "there has been the deuce to pay, with a vengeance!"

The game of cards was broken up incontinently, the pipes laid aside, and all stood looking at St. George and the yet lifeless figure in his arms.

Oliver walked straight to the fire, before which stood a couch, on which he laid the girl, and knelt by her side.

"Strip one of the beds," he said, "and bring the covering here. Don't go away. When she comes to, let her see she is with friends."

He was obeyed. The viscount ran to one of the bed-rooms, and returned with his arms full of blankets, with several counterpanes and a lot of sheets trailing behind him.

He had a very fair load altogether:—a bolster under one arm, two pillows under the other, and a huge feather bed skilfully balanced on his head.

"Here you are," he said. "Tuck the lady up, then tell us all about it."

St. George did not reply. He took his coat from Nicola, and so left displayed a form that made his friends envy him. It was not a time to stand upon false delicacy. He knew that his companions would think more of Nicola's distress than of her beauty; or if they thought most of her beauty, it would not be with an unmanly or unholy sense.

But there she lay—beautiful and statuesque—pallid, and

with her white drapery clinging to the outlines of her form—one fair breast peeping from her open robe, and the other heaving softly beneath its covering. Her limbs were bare from the knee, and for some little way above, and those who saw them thought them wonderful.

St. George wrapped Nicola in the blankets as tenderly as he would have done a sleeping child. Then he bent his ear close to her breast, to note the pulsations of her heart.

Her breathing was low and regular now—she had passed from her swoon into a peaceful sleep.

When St. George discovered this, he kissed her gently, but with passionate love.

"Dear little Nicola," he said, "I wish I had run away with you a month ago."

"Had a fight?" asked Dick. "Are you hurt, old fellow?"

"No."

"You are smothered in blood," said the viscount.

"Look quite sanguinary," said the marquis.

"It's a bad mixture out of six or seven brigands," said Oliver, answering them all. "I had a fight—killed old Scamp-and-Satan, and a lot of them."

"Killed her father?"

"Her father! Bah! The old ruffian murdered her parents years ago. Had I not saved her from him to-night, to-morrow morning she would be fit for nothing but to kill!"

His friends shuddered.

They could feel what a fate that would have been for her—what a blow for him.

St. George gave Nicola to the care of the female domestics, and went to bed to rest after his fight.

The night passed.

Morning came.

In the morning, while the four friends were at breakfast, Jack made his appearance.

Jack had a very bad black eye.

"What's the matter?" asked the viscount.

"Please, sir," said Jack, "it was Tummis."

"Who?"

"Tummis."

"And who the deuce is Tummis?"

"Tikeypoodle's wally, sir."

"Jack."

"My lord?"

"You ought to be ashamed of yourself."

Jack looked hurt, especially about the eye.

"What for, my lord?"

"To let Twankydoodle's Tummis give you a black eye."

Jack's face brightened.

"I doubled him up!" he said, "made him swallow six of his own teeth, knocked his left eye into his elbow, and spread his conk all over his face!"

"His what?"

"His conk."

"What the dickens is conk?"

"His sneezer."

"Eh?"

"Smeller."

"Smeller?"

"Conk, sir."

"Jack."

"My lord?"

"If you don't tell me what you mean, I shall kick you all the way downstairs!"

"Yes, my lord."

The way in which Jack took the threat was sublime. He was six feet and several inches; but had he been ten times his own size, he would have let his slim, gentlemanly master kick him downstairs without murmuring.

Not that Jack took kindly to kicking. He could have smashed any six foreigners before breakfast, and would have hit the Pope, if his holiness had lifted his toe against him.

But his master was sacred. Jack would have died for the viscount.

(To be continued in our next.)

TALES OF BRIGANDS AND ROBBERS.

I Warn & Strike

[HAWK'S EYE'S STRANGE ADVENTURE AT MIDNIGHT.]

HAWK'S EYE, THE PHANTOM ROBBER.

CHAPTER X.

THE RESOLVE OF A LOVING WOMAN.—MARGARET LOCKS HERSELF
IN WITH DANGER.—HER DEFIANCE.—ESCAPE.—THE IVY WALL.

WE must now introduce our reader to dear Margaret Sedwyn,
the lady-love of Albert Falconer.

Tell you what she reminded one of—a field daisy. She
was candid and simple, loving and fresh as that open-hearted
little flower, which hides away not from the sun, but closes
from him when the great luminary is too ardent, and which
shuts up from the rain after catching enough to kiss and
fondle in its white little arms, or say leaflets.

She was a confiding, charming lady—neither retreating

nor audacious; and, indeed, just such a woman as every good fellow who reads this chapter deserves to have.

She was not the kind of woman to flop down on a fellow and make his life a burden to him; nor was she so audacious as to make the man who loved her feel ashamed of her.

In fact, she was that perfect woman who, while she recognises in man one who is placed on the earth to be her guide and help, is not at all inclined to drop down upon him as though he were made to carry a wife through life.

She was a lady always blithe and happy, if she could be, and ever desirous of making the best of everything; therefore, she was not devoid of courage.

Now, it need not be said that such a good sort of lady was exactly one who would weep rather for her lover when punished, than for herself at losing that lover.

Therefore, it need scarcely be said that, when she learnt Albert was to be exiled, she wept—not so much for herself as for him, for she knew it was hard indeed to leave one's native land, to speak a language unknown and harsh upon the lips.

Now, it will be remembered that it had been permitted by the Government that Albert Falconer should be allowed seven days in which to make his preparations for quitting England. It will also be remembered that Albert suddenly learnt that these seven days had been rescinded—that even the permission given him to leave England was withdrawn, and that the royal troops had been ordered to effect his arrest.

It will also be in the recollection of our readers that it was intimated that the main cause of the change on the part of the Government, as represented by the Commander-in-Chief, was due to the machinations of Bertram Falconer himself, who, desirous of obtaining the estate for himself, had endeavoured to prove to Sir Bruton that he had done all he could for Albert; whereas in fact Bertram Falconer was the greatest enemy Albert Falconer, his cousin, possessed.

There could be no doubt upon this point.

It will also not have been forgotten by the reader that Albert returned to the Grange, and entered it by the ivy-grown wall, and so entered the room where his father really lay dead.

He had returned yearningly to his dear home, to take one last farewell of a father whom in the course of nature he would never see again; and the reader will recollect that the consequence of that loving action on his part was that the Lady May, his sister, going into her father's bed-room, identified her brother as the man who leaped from the window; nor will it be forgotten that Albert dropped his sword-belt in his hurry, and that this belt being recognised as his, a conviction of his guilt as the murderer of his own father flashed horribly upon the minds of all then and there present, at the discovery of that damning piece of evidence.

So far we had advanced when we left that branch of the tale. Nor shall we continue that line of our narrative at the present moment. Suffice it to say that even the Lady May —the purest and most single-hearted of her sex—could not wholly battle with and keep down the idea that her father had been destroyed by his dear and only son.

For evidence is so dreadful a thing.

Sir Bruton had retired to bed an hour or so previously, quite safe and in health, and then he was found murdered—foully murdered; and the Lady May admitted seeing a man escape from the window.

Who but this man was the murderer?

Why did he fly if he were not conscious of being an evil-doer?

Alas, poor Lady May! She could not understand—how could she?—that he feared, in her lighter approach, the advance of soldiery.

How could she know that?

Had she been accused of believing her brother a murderer, she would have repelled the accusation with scorn; but, in her heart of hearts, a little voice kept whispering her: "Who —who, if not his own son—killed thy father?"

In vain she asked herself—"Why should he kill his dear father?—what motive could he have in so doing?" Nay, it was his *ruin*, for while Sir Bruton was alive, he would, as an adherent of King George II., hold his estate, and there-

fore he could afford to send Albert money while he was in exile; whereas, on the other hand, were Sir Bruton dead, his successor being proscribed, the estate would go to the Crown, unless the Crown thought fit to give it to the next male heir in the line who still clung to the cause of King George.

But, although all these truths pressed themselves upon the aching brain of the Lady May, and although she would rather have died than have admitted she thought her brother guilty of being a parricide, nevertheless, that still small voice kept whispering to her: "If *he* did not kill him, who did?"

But let us leave this branch of our tale, and return to the fair lady, Margaret Sedwyn.

She had no idea that Albert Falconer had experienced the cruelty of the loss of the seven days given him in which to prepare to leave England; and, indeed, all through the evening of that eventful night—the whole events of which are still not yet in the possession of the reader—she was anticipating his arrival at her father's house.

But when eleven o'clock had arrived, she became fearful of what was happening, and, not being the kind of woman who would feel piqued at the non-appearance of a lover, and feeling certain that something unusual had occurred, she said nothing to either of the family—either father or mother, brother or sister—but quietly going to the stables, she ordered her horse to be saddled.

"Lor, miss," said the man, "you be joking!"

"I am not."

"Which horse?"

"The fastest."

"Why the fastest, miss?"

"Because I don't want to be caught."

"Well, miss, I'm an old servant of the family, and you don't suppose as I can allow you, my young lady, to start off by yourself at near midnight nobody knows where on the fastest horse in the stable so that you shall not be caught?"

"Yes, you will, Tom White!"

"No, miss."

"But you know I'm a sensible girl."

"Ay, miss, we all know that."

"Very well, then—saddle the horse."

"On one condition."

"What?"

"Why, that I saddle another, miss, and ride behind you."

"No."

"Then, miss, you can have no horse."

"You refuse?"

"Yes."

"Then listen to me. I once saved your wife's life."

"Yes, miss, the Lord He knows you did."

"And now you take *mine* from me?"

"Take your life? Why, miss, I'd lay mine down—ay, and my only boy too, afore I'd do it."

"Then saddle the horse."

"When will you be back, miss?"

"Perhaps never."

"Perhaps?"

"Perhaps soon. Come, saddle the horse."

"Miss, I dare not. What would master say to me?"

"He shall never know you had a hand in it."

"Why, do you think I could hold my tongue and let him die of grief, thinking you were dead, when I could tell him you had gone away from your good home, in the dark of the night, like some thief, miss? No, no, no!"

"Mr. Tom White, you listen to me!"

"Yes, miss—like a dog."

"You know we are told to leave father and mother, and cleave to the man whom we call husband?"

"Good Lord, my lady! You don't mean to say you are married, and I as nursed you when you was so high!"

"Yes, but I've grown; and remember I've nursed you and your wife, and saved her life."

"I don't deny it, miss, for one moment; but I—I *can't* let you have the horse."

"Now listen here. You, Tom White, because I speak of leaving my home, don't think that my heart is not bleeding at the idea."

She laid her hand upon his shoulder, and he felt it tremble. But he did not want to be told she was a true-hearted woman.

She was.

"But, miss——"

"Listen to me. I have determined to accompany Mr. Albert Falconer in his exile abroad. Poor fellow! he will be alone, whereas my father and mother have my brothers and sisters to keep them company. No, I am determined to go away with him and marry him."

"But, miss," continued the stanch old servant, "why not tell your father and mother of your intentions?"

"Because I am convinced they never would sanction my plot, and, meanwhile, the poor fellow would go away and be wretched."

"True, miss."

"Then saddle the horse."

"No, miss."

"Look here," and she showed him a purse—"here is all my own money, and all my poor little jewels. Most certainly I shall go. If not on horseback, by foot; and if I am overtaken and brought back, and die of a high fever or a broken heart, Tom White, what do you think your heart will say to you when you remember that I saved your good wife Polly?"

"Oh Lord, miss, take the horse, in the name o' charity!"

"Then saddle him quick."

"But—but, miss, I may tell the squire half an hour after you are gone?"

"No."

"An hour, then?"

"No."

"Two?"

"No."

"Well, say two and a half?"

"No—nor three, nor four."

"Say five, miss?"

"No. They think me gone to-bed, and they will have no fear or worry until to-morrow morning, when they will miss me, for I am always down first, and then you may tell them, Tom White, as soon as you like."

"Thank ye, miss."

"Only you need not take the trouble."

"How's that, miss?"

"Because they will know by that time, for I have written a letter, and they can read, you know."

"Well, miss, you've fixed me so as I can't get out of it, and here goes to saddle the horse. But you'll let me go with you?"

"No. How could you, if you give me Calloon, the fastest horse by two miles an hour in the stable? You would be bumping the saddle all to no purpose."

"Well, miss, you are a young lady! I only wish as my only girl shall be such a ripper!"

"All right! Saddle Calloon."

Three minutes after, she was away, galloping hard from the home of her youth.

Ay, but after she had given her hand to kiss to the old groom, Tom White, she rode round by the house, and kissed the door.

She was a brave-hearted girl—ay, and as tender-hearted as any in the county.

Then away she went.

And the reader has already seen her tactics.

Good darling!

She knew that her people at home could do without her—she knew he would be alone in a foreign land, and so, though she had not offended the Government, she determined to share Albert's extradition; and she was so good-hearted that she would not even cause her people the pain and suffering of parting from her.

For she had quite made up her mind to accompany Albert, *if he would let her.*

If he would let her!

What a condition!

As though the lonely fellow would not be only too heartily glad of her dear solace and bright heart to go with him into the sad foreign land.

So away she galloped.

Nearing the Grange, her heart began to beat half with hope and half with something like shame; for, all said and done, and taking all the circumstances of the case into consideration, it was a serious thing for a young lady to go and say to a gentleman:

"Sir, you know you cannot ask me to marry you, seeing that it would be selfish in you to do so, and therefore I have come to offer myself to you."

'Twas audacious.

But she never faltered. She knew he never—never would ask her to marry him, a poor exile, and so she meant to offer herself.

Indeed, as she neared the Grange, she put Calloon on to a harder gallop, as though she could not rest until she had told Albert her resolve.

She leaped from the horse almost before he had ceased to be in motion, and, fixing the bridle round an iron railing, she made quickly for the door.

No light, but, to her surprise, she found it open.

And now it is necessary to explain how it was that she had found the door open.

When Margaret reached the Grange, Albert had escaped from it about half an hour.

What had occurred in that half-hour was this:—

Bertram had ordered all the servants to leave the room, and, when they had done so, he and the Lady May remained in the room with the dead.

What then occurred?

The conversation that ensued will have to be detailed at another time; but this is certain, that the servants heard Bertram Falconer lock the closed door.

They listened.

Nothing for a time was heard.

At last a cry.

It was the Lady May's voice.

Then again silence.

Then the door opened.

"The Lady May has fainted," they heard him say. "Bear her to her room at once, and use the usual restoratives. As for you men, three of you ride off, each one to one of the nearest doctors. Three more ride off—one to the Lord of the Manor, the next to the nearest magistrate's, and the third to the colonel at head quarters at Finchley."

He spoke to them like their master.

And somehow they appeared to recognise in him a master.

Then, having seen the unhappy May carried from the room, and having heard the clatter of the half-dozen horses bearing away his messengers for doctors, magistrates, and military commander, he strode to the late Sir Bruton's library, situated against the bed-room in which Sir Bruton lay stark and horrible.

Bertram had quite overcome all fear of the dead man, and, being hopelessly and utterly wicked, the memory of the phantom had now passed away.

"Bring me some port," he said.

And never a word spoke he until the wine, a huge flagon, was placed before him.

Never a thought thought he until he had swallowed a great draught of the wine.

Then he thought, and wickedness—sheer wickedness.

He wanted a companion—some easy-virtued woman, who would smile upon him, and with her laugh and smile lighten the heaviness of his evil.

Then he felt the brand of the flaming sword upon his forehead.

No fear felt he, only *rage* that it was there—horrible rage.

He leaped up, and looked into the glass. There it was—red, and in the form of the sword of fire.

"CAIN—CAIN!" he cried—not with shame, with anger.

This meant, "Cain once more—Cain again."

Then he flung himself upon his chair, again refilled his huge glass, and seized and possessed himself of the good liquor rather than drank it.

Poor wretch! There was no human being in all England more wretched than he in this, the very hour of his triumph—the hour when he felt that the Falconer estate was his.

For had he not spoken with the Lady May?

Then, again, his eager thoughts reverted to a companion, and again he felt the hot shape upon his brow.

This time he felt that he was proud of the mark, since it told him that he was powerful to commit another sort of crime than that with which he had already stained the night.

Aye; but although he was then and there proud of the mark upon his forehead, he had drawn the thick, black, short curls he wore over it, so that no one could see it, and ask him what the sign meant.

Now, in the eagerness of the servants to fulfil their messages, it was very natural that the Grange door should be left open.

And so Margaret found it.

She was the promised daughter of the house.

She entered.

No lights.

Not a soul to be seen.

"I will go to Sir Bruton's library," she said. "Sir Bruton will assuredly be there."

She knew the way about the house quite readily.

On she went, her heart beating lightly, for she little wotted of the tragedy the mansion contained.

Her hand is on the door.

She enters.

She sees a figure with its back towards her.

Dazzled by the light of the lamp, as it falls upon her in passing from the dark passage to the well-lit room, she does not recognise the form of the man before her.

He obviously marks her *not*.

She shuts the door.

She turns the key.

Still the figure takes no notice.

She takes the key from the lock.

She flings it over the head of the form, and as she does so, she says:

"Sir Bruton, I've locked myself in with you! You wicked rake, you, to have a lady—young and pretty, too—in your library!"

Then she screams.

The key is on the table before Bertram, who, at the sound of a woman's voice, has roused himself from his half-drunken doze, every vein in his body heating; and who, clutching at his hot throat with both hands, turns to meet the companion he has sighed for.

She saw her danger in a moment, for she recognised Bertram Falconer.

How eagerly she looked at the key, as it lay on the table.

Perhaps, had she made a dash at it while he was recovering his drunken senses, all would have been well; but she was too paralysed with horror at the danger into which she had thrown herself to be able, for a moment, to decide upon any course of action.

Meanwhile, hot-breathed Bertram was trying to rise from his chair, and endeavouring to get together his senses sufficiently to pay attentions such as he thought were charming.

"Come here, pretty one!"

"Sir!"

"Come here, I say! There's a place for you on my knee; and a handsome knee it is, too!"

"Do you know to whom you are speaking?" she asked.

And by this time she experienced a burning desire to know where Sir Bruton was, and why Bertram was installed and drinking in the most private room in the whole of Falcon Grange.

Of course, as she had passed into the house without being seen by any of the household, and as she had made her way to the library because she knew the house as well as that in which she had been born, she could not be aware that poor Sir Bruton—for the presence of whom, in her present danger, she so much desired—was dead and terrible in the room

towards which she glanced, she feeling certain that help would come from that quarter.

"Come, pretty one," he said, not answering her question, but fortifying himself with another bumper of port, "don't be unkind. Here is my handsome knee growing cold waiting for you."

"Sir, do you know to whom you are speaking?"

"No, my beauty; but knowing that you came to me and flung the key of the room at me, I suppose you think more of your name than anyone else thinks of it."

"Sir—Bertram Falconer!"

"Ha, you know my name!" he said, startled for a moment; but then, tossing away the thought of hesitation which the dignity with which she spoke created, he continued: "Well, come here, and tell me your name. I'll kiss you, if you do."

"Sir, do you know what I am?"

"I can guess. Come—come, girl, no prudery. If you think to gain by that you are mistaken. Come, do you hear and make yourself welcome. I'm sure I'm doing my best to welcome you."

"Where is Sir Bruton?"

"That is more than I can say."

"Is he not at the Grange?"

"What is left of him."

"Left of him! What do you mean, Bertram Falconer?"

"By my faith," he answered, "you appear to be far more familiar with my name than you care to be with me."

"Is—is Sir Bruton dead?"

"Ay, as the last year."

"Oh, no, no—impossible!"

"Why impossible? He was no more than other men, and, like other men, he has taken the long journey."

"When did he die, Bertram?"

"Bertram, without the Falconer! By Heaven, you hussy, you make a pretty fellow's blood boil, Sally, or Polly, or Nanny, or whatever you may call yourself—what *do* you call yourself? I won't ask what the fellows call you."

"My name is Margaret."

"Madge, you mean, and a devilish pretty name it is, my lass! Come and whisper your name in my ear, and I'll kiss you."

"Where—where is Sir Bruton's dead body?"

Bertram pointed to the inner room.

"There," he said; "but let the dead look after the dead. Come you here—drink, and let us sing."

"Wretch! Would you dare sing within a room's length of the uncle who so loved you?"

"Hullo, my lady! You seem to know all about the family. Ha, I suppose you came to know more about it! Well, well—here is my knee, still getting colder and colder."

"Sir, you asked me just now what I was. I have scarcely power to speak, so terrified am I by the news you give me of Sir Bruton's death. Whether you speak the truth or not I am unable to say; but, accepting what you say to be veracious, I need not say that the news is overpowering, especially to me."

"Hey-day—did the old man keep a darling?"

"I therefore ask, Mr. Falconer," she continued—"nay, I demand—that you at once give me the key I flung to you—supposing you were Sir Bruton—and let me pass."

"Ha, if I were Sir Bruton, you would not want to go!"

"No."

"Then, by all the powers above or below, you shall think me to be Sir Bruton!"

And, so saying, he leaped up, and lurched towards her.

In vain she pressed against the door; she had imprisoned herself only too securely.

At her he came, his hat tipped over his eyes, and his sword clanking over the ground.

He caught her by both arms.

"Do you know me now?" she said, as he came up with her.

"I know you are a woman, my pretty one."

"I am Margaret Sedwyn."

"Margaret Sedwyn?"

"Yes—your cousin's affianced wife."

"Ha!" said Falconer; and he had the grace to fall back a pace or two.

"Oh, Bertram," she said, "how can you be so cruel? Do you forget that we were children together, and that you always promised to fight for me and take care of me? How can you be so cruel?"

"Margaret, I——"

"Yes, you have been drinking; but you will be yourself to-morrow, when we will talk again. Give me the key."

He went to the table, took up the key, but did not give it to her.

"You've grown a pretty woman, Madge."

"Bertram—Bertram—how can you talk in this fashion, so near your dead uncle? And—and where is Albert?"

"Ha!" and his eyes began to lighten up—"if Albert were here, you would not fence him off, would you?"

"He is my affianced husband—where is he?"

"In full flight. His seven days' permit for preparations has been rescinded, and he is now possibly nearing the boat which will bear him away from England, never more to be seen by you."

"Unless I follow him," she said, as she felt her limbs trembling, and she feared she should fall.

"Follow him you may, dear coz, but you have got to leave this room first—then you may, as soon as you like. Faint away, if thou likest, at the loss of thy lover—I will catch thee!"

She saw the danger of insensibility, and stood bravely facing him.

"Bertram Falconer, if you approach me one step, I will alarm the house."

"No screams can be heard from here. Sir Bruton so loved quiet—that you know, no one better—that there are three swing doors in the corridor leading to the body of the hall. You might scream—'twould but be a loss of breath. Ha!"

For she had made a rush at a bell-pull which she knew would only have been used by Sir Bruton when in immediate want of servants; for she knew Bertram was quite right when he referred to the impossibility of her screams being heard.

"Look here, Madge!" and so speaking, he took from his pocket a knife, and cut the bell-pull away far above her reach. He then lightly flung the end of embroidered velvet to her.

"Come and look at Sir Bruton."

"No, no!"

"Ha—you fear that you should faint! Certainly, the old scamp would be of more use than he has ever been in life."

"Oh, Bertram—Bertram!—if you ever loved me——"

"Love?" he said; and as the word came from his mouth, his face was suffused with the red shadow of Hades itself. "Love?" he cried. "That word has ruined you!"

She saw that entreaty was useless—that gentle pity had taken flight, and wickedness reigned supreme within him.

Locked in the room, and by her own action.

Her voice deadened by the very doors she had opened and let close behind her.

Alone, with a merciless man.

She knew there was no time for words.

As he lunged at her, she flung the heavy chair near her before him, and as he, still clumsy in his movements, from the effect of the drink he had taken, but sufficiently sensible of his purpose—as he fell over the chair, she ran with much speed past the swinging, red-velvet-covered door, into the bed-room where lay the baronet.

The next moment, as the darkness of the room surrounded her, she felt that he was following her.

"Come, my gipsy!" he cried. "I have loved you from the time when I was a boy. Many is the time you have made me suffer for your coldness, and now you shall pay off the old score!"

Horror! A drunken man, with outstretched hands, seeking for a woman that he may destroy her, and in the presence of the very man whom he had murdered!

This is what unbridled wickedness will bring a man to.

The room was fortunately large, and this was in her favour, for stooping behind one of the curtains of the death-bed, and on the side furthest from the door at which she had entered, she remained for a time thoroughly concealed.

But he was not to be foiled.

On he came, and then, as by the faint light streaming into the room she saw him stumbling towards the bed, and then grasping over the still body of the good uncle he had, when alive, so slavishly sought to please, she felt her senses finally leaving her.

She knew that she could not much longer endure the strain upon her brain.

"Ne'er mind, my beauty—the lamp will show your prettiness as well in this room as the other, and you will look all the prettier if first I take a look at old quiet here!"

And thereupon he stumbled back into the room, and the next moment she saw the light moving in the library, whence she had escaped.

As she saw that, she made a determination to rush at him as he entered, beat the lamp from his hand, and so plunge them into safe darkness. But her fear was this, and it prevented her putting that scheme into operation—

What if, as she rushed forward, he dropped the lamp and leaped at her?

What—what could she do?

Then she screamed slightly. It was an ejaculation of hope. She remembered the ivy-grown wall below the window.

Dangerous. Yes, certainly, but a less danger than that she ran.

"It is as though," she thought, in that instantaneous way in which we do think in moments of great danger—"it is as though Heaven itself had prompted him to teach me to climb the old ivied wall when we were children."

A moment, and she sped rapidly towards the window.

And this speed served her, for it so startled him that as he approached her he let the lamp fall, and the room was plunged in total darkness.

Now, all the world knows that if your eyes are near a great light, and it is suddenly extinguished, for some moments you are quite incapable of seeing anything in a less light than that which has suddenly ceased to give its illuminating power. Therefore, it is evident to the reader that as the lamp carried by Bertram was extinguished by the shock of its fall, he was unable to see what was taking place in the chamber of death.

Now, Margaret had reached the window, and, thinking rather than saying a hurried prayer, she committed herself to the safety of the rare old ivy green, much more true and stanch than the man from whom she was escaping; and it was as her fair head disappeared below the window-sill that his eyes grew sufficiently accustomed to the dim starlight that filled the chamber to mark her mode of escape.

With a terrible oath, he leaped towards the window.

"Lass," he cried, "the longer the hunt, the more the hunter is pleased! So—you've the start, but you're not yet out of the wood!"

She was now hanging by the ivy, and slowly letting herself down the wall.

As for Bertram, the wretched man, too eager to be cautious, literally leaped over the sill, and the consequence was that the ivy broke away from the wall, and peeled over with him upon Margaret Sedwyn.

She clung to the wall.

She heard a swish past her.

Then a jerk.

Then all was still.

"Bertram!" she said.

And far below she heard him mutter a half-indistinct oath.

This again nerved her to oppose him with all her power.

She felt in the mass of ivy-growth before her, and found an opening in it, after the lapse of some moments.

Then a fear came across her.

He had torn away the ivy from the window in his fall, and how, therefore, could she reach the window?

Then she would have to descend, and again meet him.

No—she would rather, she said to herself, cast herself down than again put herself in his power.

Fortunately, however, the atmosphere brightened a little, though the moon did not break forth from behind the watery banks of cloud which enveloped her, and she saw that at the side of the window the ivy-growth was quite sufficient to support her.

So gradually she once more reached the room whence she had escaped.

Then she called to him again.

There was no response.

But her fear predominated.

She well knew that window, and its means of being made safe from an intruder.

She closed the shutter and barred it.

Then, and only then, her overstrained brain yielded, and in the chamber of death she fell prone to the floor, and lay as quiet as the dead form itself.

(*To be continued in our next.*)

FRA DIAVOLO, THE NEAPOLITAN BANDIT.

FRA DIAVOLO's real name was Michel Pezza.

He had already rendered himself celebrated by his murders at the time when the French made the campaign of Naples, commanded by Championnet.

He then harassed the rear of the French army, organized bodies of insurgents in Calabria, directed a vast conspiracy against the French, and did them considerable mischief. He was born at Itri (Terra-di-Lavoro), and in his youth had been a goatherd.

He afterwards turned monk, entered a convent, and there assumed the name of Fra Angelo.

His bad conduct, however, caused him to be expelled from the convent, after which he retired to the mountains and devoted himself to the commission of every crime.

He lived by plunder, and every day of his life was marked by a murder.

He headed a band of smugglers, and spread terror and desolation throughout the country.

The Government of King Ferdinand condemned him to be hanged, and a price was set upon his head.

But Queen Caroline, the wife of Ferdinand, was a woman who knew how to turn the worst things to useful account.

An amnesty was concluded with Michel Pezza, and he was appointed to the command of a corps formed of freed galley slaves, who were to attack the rear of the French army from Foudi to Carigliano.

While the French were engaged in taking Gaeta and Capua, Fra Diavolo established himself at Itri, his native place, where he was signalized by the commission of all sorts of atrocities.

Travellers were murdered, and every inhabitant of the place who was known to be possessed of any property was mercilessly plundered and put to death.

Itri was soon occupied solely by the agents of Fra Diavolo; and numerous travellers on their way from Naples to Rome, hoping that the town, being a military station, would afford them a secure resting-place for the night, retired to their beds, but never rose again.

The art which was employed to banish suspicion from the minds of the victims was remarkable.

The entrance to the neighbouring villages was guarded, and the night travellers advanced with full confidence to the place where certain death waited them.

Those who were induced to enter the houses of Itri never came out again alive.

General Olivier had at that time the command of Gaeta.

Being informed that there was a party of banditti at Itri, he sent thither a Polish regiment commanded by a young officer of his staff, who, regarding the expedition as a fair opportunity for distinguishing himself, exposed his life with almost chivalrous courage.

He succeeded in expelling Fra Diavolo from Itri, and driving him into the woods.

But the brigand was no less brave than his adversary; he re-entered Itri, and was again attacked by the Polish regiment.

A frightful conflict ensued, and Fra Diavolo inhumanly massacred all the prisoners who fell into his hands.

A little chapel, situated near the bridge, was the scene of many atrocities.

At length Fra Diavolo and his followers were once more driven to the mountains. But no sooner had the military withdrawn from the path leading from the road between Naples and Malo di Gaeta, than two thousand insurgents again showed themselves.

General Olivier sent to meet them two squadrons and a detachment of Polish troops, who dispersed them, and took possession of Itri.

Fra Diavolo then abandoned Terra di Lavoro and fled to Calabria, which once more became the scene of his atrocities.

By future generations, it will perhaps scarcely be believed that Fra Diavolo enjoyed the marked favour of the King and Queen of Sicily.

Queen Caroline sent him a bracelet, set with her portrait, and he held the rank of Major in the British army.

Yet he had previously been condemned to the gallows, and a price had been set upon his head.

Salicetti called to mind these facts when Fra Diavolo was arrested in 1808.

Massena assured me that the influence of this extraordinary man was immense during the occupation of Naples by the French; for the inhabitants of the mountains in which he habitually dwelt, being as savage as himself, joyfully followed a chief who led them on to pillage and murder.

One honourable trait is recorded of Fra Diavolo.

Having effected his landing at Itri, through the fault of General Girardin, who left that part of the coast undefended, Fra Diavolo massacred during the night all the inhabitants who resisted him, and made the rest prisoners.

Two ladies, the wives of officers of the second Swiss regiment, were made prisoners, and were conducted by Fra Diavolo and his brigands to the mountains.

Some time afterwards, he sent them to Naples, having previously required them to give him a certificate, stating that they had been treated with due respect.

The two ladies, on their part, requested to have a copy of the certificate, countersigned by the brigand himself.

Fra Diavolo was arrested at Salerno, by an apothecary's apprentice.

This was a miserable conclusion to his career.

He was conveyed to Naples, where the scaffold was erected for his execution before any measures were taken for his trial, for, observes Salicetti, "Nothing more was necessary than the condemnation of the most just and equitable King Ferdinand and his Queen Caroline."

It is a curious fact that the English, whose ships were continually cruising before the Bay of Naples, sent a flag of truce to demand the liberation of the British Major Michel Pezza, threatening, if this demand should be refused, to make reprisals on all the French and Neapolitan prisoners who might fall into their hands.

It would appear that Salicetti's watch was a little too fast for the above demand of the English. He replied that he knew of no major in the English service who had been made prisoner by the troops of his Majesty King Joseph; but that, if the individual alluded to was a bandit, who held no commission, who had no character, either political or military, and who was known in the country by the name of Fra Diavolo, he had been hanged the evening before, in pursuance of an old sentence pronounced upon him by the tribunals of King Ferdinand.

Such is the true history of Fra Diavolo.

RED GAUNTLET, THE BANDIT; OR, THE BLACK MOUNTAINEERS.

BOOK II.—THE BLACK CHATEAU.

CHAPTER XXVIII. (*Continued.*)

"SMELLER is conk, my lord," said Jack.

"And what is conk?"

"Sneezer, my lord."

"And what the deuce is sneezer?"

The marquis nearly choked himself with half a muffin. Dick Nicholson stirred his coffee with a roll in mistake for a spoon. They could not see for laughing.

"His nose, my lord."

"So you broke Tummis's nose, did you?" said the viscount, much gratified.

"Yes, my lord."

"What for?"

"Because he said that Susan said that Miss Moffatt said she loved the Duke Spikeytoodle, and didn't care for you a bit."

"Who is Susan?"

"Miss Moffatt's maid, sir."

"And what did you say?"

"Told him he was a liar, sir, and hit him a drive in the head."

"That was quite right; and here is a sovereign for you."

"Thank you, my lord; and here's a letter for you."

"A letter!"

The viscount snatched it eagerly.

"From whom?"

"Miss Moffatt, sir."

"Here's another sovereign, Jack."

"Thank you, my lord."

The viscount read the letter.

It ran thus:—

"DEAR CECIL,—

"Do save me. Papa is going to make me marry the Duke Tikeypoodle to-morrow. Only think of it! How dreadful! I shall die, if he does!

"Ever yours, in grief,
"SIBYL."

"Die if he does!" said the viscount. "I would wring his neck, and make him swallow his whiskers! I should like to catch him at it!"

"There's some more," said Jack.

"What is it?"

"The major-general swears he will eat you, my lord!"

"Very wicked of him! Where are they going to be married?"

"In the chapel in the mountain, my lord."

"Very well. Jack, here's another sovereign."

Jack pocketed the third sovereign, said "Thank you," and then said:

"Please, my lord."

"Well?"

"I ran away with Susan."

"Eh?"

"Yes, my lord. She's downstairs in the hall."

"What are you going to do with her?"

"Marry her, my lord."

"Go downstairs, you reprobate!"

Jack went down, grinning, to tell Susan how nice it was.

"Perhaps somebody will suggest what is to be done," said the viscount, looking round. "The Duke of Stikeytoodle is to marry Sibyl to-morrow, and the major-general is going to eat me!"

"That's if you get in his way," said Linn.

"Which I certainly shall. The fact is, there will be a row. But I shall take Sibyl from Crikeyloodle, without the remotest doubt."

"Don't see how it's to be done," said St. George. "It's a different thing to such a case as Nicola's. I had only to deal with a lot of brigands, whom I could shoot down without mercy. You will have to deal with an English gentleman and officer."

"To say nothing of Tikeypoodle," said Dick Nicholson.

"Bah!" exclaimed the viscount. "I shall not flinch. The chapel in the mountain shall be the scene of a lively little drama, or I am much mistaken."

"We are with you, whatever it is," said his friends.

"Thanks! But, much as I value your help, there is one who could do me more service."

"Who is it?"

Just then Jack re-entered to announce Leon, the student.

"There is your answer," said Marriott. "He who can help me most is——"

Red Gauntlet entered the room.

His noble face was sad and pale.

"I have come to say farewell, gentlemen," he said; "to thank you for much kindness done; and to tell you that, out of the many I have met in my strange career, there are none whose memory will be remembered with greater pleasure than yours."

"To say farewell!" said the marquis. "Why, where are you going to?"

"Out of this land," replied the bandit student. "It has lost its beauty, for the valley of my mountain home is changed into a sepulchre."

"What has happened?"

"My father lies buried there, where he was happy; for he was happy, though blind and exiled."

"Your father—dead!"

"My more than father, though the Count Duseanelli had no natural claim to the title of father from me. I knew no other. My earliest childhood was spent with him. He loved me always, and I shall love his memory."

"Not your father!" said Stuart Linn.

"No. And I am not even an Italian, though it is the land to which my heart clings."

"Not an Italian!"

"I am an Englishman."

"Ah!" said Stuart Linn, and he looked anxious while waiting to hear more.

"The story is strange," said Leon,—"strange enough to make you smile; but it is somewhat sad. I am the son of an English peer."

Linn listened more intently than ever.

"There was an old tradition in our family—a tradition in which, for many generations, our ancestors had strict belief."

"A tradition!"

"That all the lawful children of the house should be distinguished by a peculiarity."

"A peculiarity!" echoed the marquis.

"A tuft of white hair. If a child was born without this, there was a doubt upon his mother, and the child became an outcast. I had no white tuft. My mother was doubted, and she fled, seeking protection of the Count Duseanelli, who adopted me. That is the story, gentlemen."

"Not all of it," said Stuart Linn. "There was another son—a younger one—who, in your absence, inherited the title. He loved the brother he had never seen, and came to Italy, seeking him."

"Ah!" said the bandit, "if this were true? I cannot prove my story, for I do not know my name."

"Your story is proved true," said Stuart Linn, with his hand upon his heart. "I am your brother!"

The two men looked an instant at each other. It was wonderful to see how much the same thought and the same wish made them alike.

Then they sprang into each other's arms.

"This accounts for our all liking you so much," said St.

George, when the meeting was over. "But, I say, what's to be done? You must not be a bandit any longer."

"To-morrow I leave my band," said Leon. "But I shall want them till then, though not for plunder."

"What then?"

"Revenge and love! The Duke de Mareosi lives, and Lulalu is in a convent."

"What would you do?" asked Stuart of his brigand brother.

"Kill him, and rescue her!"

"Rescue her, and forgive him."

"You forget my southern teaching," said Leon, with a calm smile. "An Italian cannot forgive. He is my foe—my rival! He shall die!"

"You will face him single-handed?"

"I would not lose an atom of my vengeance! I shall face him foot to foot, and slay him!"

"Then we must travel, to get you out of the way," said Stuart, "or you will be hotly hunted."

"Fear not," said Leon; "I shall escape. "To-morrow, if you would see a spectacle worth remembering, be at the gates of the Convent St. Agatha."

"Otherwise called the White Chateau," said Stuart Linn.

"The White Chateau."

"Well?"

"Lulalu is there. This White Chateau is a pandemonium of vice and cruelty—a seeming refuge, and a sanctuary for innocence; but, in reality, a place for its destruction. The convent has subterraneous connection with the Black Chateau."

"The Black Chateau!"

"Whose abbot is Doctor Montena, the brigand monk—a wretch who must have had his soul from satan."

"Doctor Montena!" said Dick Nicholson. "I know the man, though I did not recognise him. He has, as you say, a satanic soul. And Dorolie is in the Black Chateau."

"Dorolie is a lady whom you love?"

"It is so."

"You would rescue her?"

"With my life."

"Come with me to-morrow, then."

"We will all go!" cried St. George. "By the way, I took Nicola from the inn last night."

"I have heard of it," said Leon, quietly. "You killed seven of my brigands."

"By Jove, they would have killed me if I had not!"

"Nicola is safe now?"

"Quite. She is with me."

"We are doing our work," said Dick. "St. George has got his bride—Linn has found his brother. Now what remains to be done?"

"The rescue of Lulalu, and De Mareosi's death," said Red Gauntlet. "That is my work."

"Mine," said Dick, "is to rescue Dorolie, and settle up with Doctor Montena."

"Mine," said Marriott, "is to take Sibyl from his Grace of Pikeyboodle, and be eaten by the major-general. I like the latter part of the arrangement. You can help me in that."

This was to Red Gauntlet.

"Call me Leon," said the student. "It is the name given to me by my adopted father. I love it for his sake, and like to hear it from my friends."

"Then you can help me, Leon?" said the viscount.

The bandit bowed.

"What is the case?" he said.

The viscount told him.

"Leave it to me," said Leon, "and there shall be some uninvited witnesses to the wedding in the mountain chapel."

And so there were.

The morning came—

The morning of Sibyl's wedding with his Grace of Tikeypoodle.

His grace had never felt so happy in his life.

He sneaked about after Sibyl like a poodle tike, and eyed her as though he could have eaten her.

His Grace of Tikeypoodle was a very nervous gentleman.

Every time any person looked at him he blushed, and every time he thought of Sibyl he trembled.

The duke gnawed the ends of his long whiskers, and thought of the coming happiness, till it was the hour for starting for the chapel in the mountain.

The chapel in the mountain had been chosen because the Duke Tikeypoodle and his sage mamma both had an idea that, should Marriott hear of the intended marriage, he would not let it be performed quietly.

Moffatt, the major-general, had a similar conviction; so to the chapel in the mountain they went.

Sibyl very pale, and in fear, but not entirely destitute of a faint hope that the note sent by her to Marriott would have effect.

A few of the English residents were invited as witnesses, but they went privately.

The major-general was in full uniform, and wore his sword.

"Damme, sir!" he said to Tikeypoodle, who was dreadfully afraid of his prospective father-in-law, "we might meet some brigands! Damme, sir, and if we did, why, damme, sir, they should see what a British major-general could do!"

Tikeypoodle tried to feel valiant, and failed. The marriage was a very serious undertaking, and as the morning wore on, his heart kept getting nearer to his mouth.

Sibyl avoided him as much as she dared, and clung about her stern old father.

Perhaps, in his heart, the major-general felt sorry for the sacrifice he was about to make to pride and mammon.

His daughter, beautiful and innocent as she was, was far too good for the thing that had a title and extensive whiskers, and was called Tikeypoodle.

The chapel was reached at last; the priest, an English clergyman, was at the altar; and Sibyl, paler than marble, was led forward by her father.

She looked round wistfully. The chapel was filled with mountain peasantry—quite picturesque fellows—with their pretty, brown-skinned, bare-legged mistresses and wives.

The major wondered what the deuce they wanted. He did not think anyone knew of the wedding.

Questioning the clergyman, he learned that a monk had just been preaching to the people, who now were staying out of curiosity to see an English wedding.

The service began. Sibyl abandoned hope, and looked round despairingly at last, as the duke took her hand, and knelt by her side.

The service progressed till the minister had to make the usual question if anyone had aught to say against the union.

He made the inquiry, and in the pause that followed came a rich, clear bugle-note.

Thrilling through the air, its echo swept through the mountain air and floated to the chapel roof.

A hundred echoes answered it.

All gazed round in surprise. The interruption came like an answer to the minister's words.

Sibyl, looking round with the rest, saw a strange commotion at the chapel door.

This was guarded.

Again the bugle-cry was repeated.

This time it found an echo within the chapel.

"Proceed with the ceremony!" said the major-general. "No trickery shall interrupt it now!"

"Save me!" Sibyl cried. "Oh, Cecil, where are you?"

"Not here yet!" said a voice from among the peasantry—"but he will be soon!"

And the speaker, who had seemed a young peasant, dropped his goatskin cloak, and stood out in a rich and fanciful attire.

There was a RED GAUNTLET on his right hand.

"Major-General Moffatt," he said, advancing and taking Sibyl's hand, "in the name of my friend, Cecil Viscount Marriott, I forbid this ceremony!"

The major-general's hand went to his sword.

"Damme, sir! who the deuce are you?"

"Ask these men," the stranger said—"they will tell you!"

(*To be continued in our next.*)

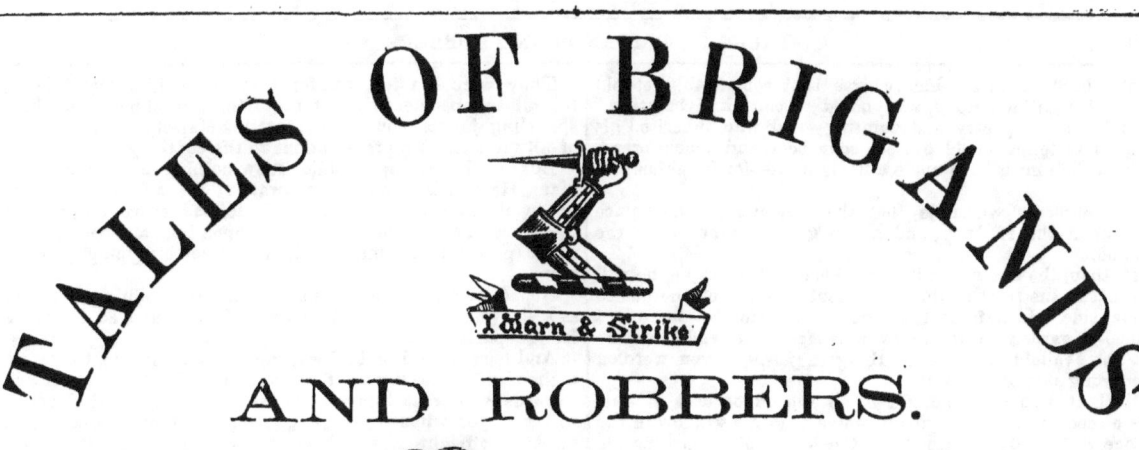

TALES OF BRIGANDS
I Warn & Strike
AND ROBBERS.

[THE FRANTIC APPEAL.]

HAWK'S EYE, THE PHANTOM ROBBER.

CHAPTER XI.

THE ROYAL PRINCESS AND THE ROPE LADDER.—THE MISTAKE.—
THE PRINCESS'S ALARM.—THE CONCEALMENT.—THE DISCOVERY
OF THE ROYAL WARRANT.—THE KING.—THE ORDER OF THE
GARTER.—THE APPROPRIATION.—THE COMING OF THE REAL
LOVER.—THE DUEL.—THE ESCAPE.

IF you go down Pall Mall until you come to St. James's
Palace, and then turn to the left by the first royal gate you
come to, you will have Marlborough House, the residence of
the present Prince of Wales, on the left, and the east wing of
St. James's Palace, ever the state residence of the Kings and
Queens of England, on your right.

At the time at which this story is written, the royal occupant of St. James's Palace was that remarkably stupid King, George the Second, who hated " boetry and bainting " —as he called poetry and painting—and who inherited his father's taste for putrid oysters, sour beer, and black bread, all of which must have made a lively meal—for breakfast, let us say.

The observer will note that the windows of the palace look upon the roadway, and at no great distance from the ground.

If, then, the observer will carry his eyes further on, he will see that in the front of the whole southern face of the palace —that side which faces the park of St. James's—there is a walled-in garden—a wall quite twelve feet high, and therefore one not available for a mild thing in *jumps*, if you were on the wrong side of the wall.

Well, it was on the night of all the adventures of this tale already related, that about twelve o'clock a window in the palace was stealthily raised, not the least noise marking the operation, and a fair hand was waved from the opened portion.

Now, just at this moment, who should pass the gate where the sentry was on duty, but Hawk's Eye.

And why was he there?

We will tell you.

After that terrible interview with his own phantom, he rode hard from Finchley to London, intending at once to make for the Anchor of Safety down by the river, have an interview with Albert Falconer, and see what was to be done.

He had a plan to submit to Albert, which he hoped would obviate the necessity of that gentleman going abroad; but he had determined upon this: that, if Albert rejected his offer —and of this offer we will at present say nothing—that he would provide that unfortunate gentleman, the brother of his dearly-loved May, with means to live either in France or Holland in a quiet but gentlemanly manner, until times were improved with him—until either the Stuarts returned to England—happily they never did—or the King thought fit to grant a pardon to all who were engaged in the rising of 1745, the date to which our story especially refers.

But having made this good resolution, Hawk's Eye became considerably overcome when he remembered that actually he was out of funds—that positively he had not five guineas to offer Albert.

Now, it must be felt that to start a gentleman off to foreign parts with only five guineas in his pocket is what may be called a twopenny-halfpenny way of doing the thing.

And as Hawk's Eye never did anything in a twopenny-halfpenny way, why, the result was that he made two determinations more.

The first was not to go to the Anchor of Safety, where he supposed his friend to be quite anchored in safety—for how could he know? He would forget the sign until he had money to give him.

The second was to get that money in next to no time.

So he turned Brilliant's head to the west end of town, and, baiting that splendid animal at a certain stable he wotted of in the neighbourhood of Charing Cross, he started in the direction of the park, fully intending to ease some swell going home of his treasures, in the shape of a diamond-hilted sword, or some trifle of that kind.

Because, as you must know, highway robberies rarely took place in the parks, owing to the danger, for, after a certain robbery some years before, it was arranged that upon a given bell being rung at any of the park gates, it was an intimation that a robbery had been just committed, that notice had been given at the nearest gate, and that in all probability the thief was in the park itself.

Then all the gates were closed, and everybody found within them taken into custody.

Now, this was a capital arrangement, only they had never caught a thief—ay, to the night when Hawk's Eye was approaching the park.

The general public knew nothing of this pretty arrangement for catching a thief in the park, and it was put together chiefly on the King's account, for, to confess the truth, George the Second was a coward, and a vain one, for he never would walk out without being loaded with diamonds.

They were his torture, for they made him fear thieves, for all the people knew of the King's weakness for these sparkling jewels; but wear them his Majesty would, in spite of all ministerial representations to the contrary.

But, if the general public knew nothing of this arrangement, Hawk's Eye was quite aware of the affair. He would not walk innocently up to the gate, and there be pounced upon, searched, the diamonds found upon him, and be marched off to prison in the midst of half a dozen strapping guardsmen.

No, Hawk's Eye could vault over the iron railings as readily as a six-year-older over the nursery fender, and so he made for the park.

And here a word on highwaymen. At all events, they were a thousand times better than burglars, for these latter are cowards who break into your house of a night, and if alarmed, will kill you when you are unarmed, defenceless, and just awoke in affright, or, at all events, bewilderment, out of your sleep.

Whereas, the highwayman rode up to you while you were awake, and he had a very handsome chance of being spitted with somebody's sword, or of his head being blown off his handsome shoulders by half a dozen of somebody's bullets.

No, there's no comparison between a burglar and a highwayman. The first is a sneak, who, when he gets into quod, comes the hypocrite, kids the " howling cove," as the clerical gentleman is called, and gets his ticket-of-leave.

Whereas, the highwayman was brave, defiant, and went, at all events, to the scaffold with a brave look on his face, and generally a new bunch of ribbon on his left shoulder, and another bunch of handsome flowers stuck in his coat.

Well, Hawk's Eye went on, and had just reached that gate of St. James's Palace to which reference has been made, when, by the faint light of a bleared old oil lamp in the palace court-yard, he saw the window go up.

He stopped.

He did not see the sentry at the gate carry arms to him.

Then from out the window there came a fair hand, which was waved.

"At me?" asks Hawk's Eye, of himself.

[And this chapter is quite a sermon upon the danger of the right people being late; the wrong people are then sure to get into the right people's places.]

"At me?" thinks Hawk's Eye.

And then, being a very gallant gentleman, he raised his handsome three-cornered hat, and made a truly elegant bow.

"All right, my lord!"

"What?"

It was Hawk's Eye said "What?"

He looked up, and saw the sentry squinting at him as only a sentry carrying arms can squint.

"The devil!" says Hawk's Eye.

"Pass, devil, my lord!" says the sentry.

"What?"

"Yes, my lord," whispers the sentry, "that's the password—the devil. It was the King as give it. You're to time to-night, my lord, and there's her Royal Highness a-waving her royal hand in the usual royal manner."

"Oh, indeed!" said Hawk's Eye.

And looking up again, once more he saw the white hand waving welcome as well as any white hand could do it.

"Oh, very well!" said Hawk's Eye.

For he felt that where treasure was wanted, a palace was the place in which to find that acceptable kind of thing.

He marched past the sentry, who now squinted more vilely than before.

Hawk's Eye laughed.

The squint was so horrid.

He had no idea the handsome sentry was squinting after the ordinary two guineas he got every night when "my lord" came.

Hawk's Eye laughed loudly.

"My lord's merry to-night!" said the man.

"Yes—yes!" said Hawk's Eye.

He passed on.

Flop—flop!

He saw nothing at first.

And no wonder.

For the rope ladder was exactly the colour of the wall against which it dangled.

"'Tis a curious adventure," thought Hawk's Eye.

And here the voice of the sentry was heard in a strained whisper.

"Get in the sentry-box, my lord—yere comes the royal carriage."

Scarcely had Hawk's Eye time to rush into the sentry-box than a carriage, all blaze and gilding, dashed in at the gate.

He looked for the ladder.

It had vanished, and the window was down—nor was any little white hand to be seen.

A clatter and noise—the King just home from the theatre, leaning heavily on his people, and talking bad English in a low voice.

Then the carriage came back, evidently much lighter than it had been, and the sound of its wheels died away in the distance, going towards the royal stables.

"All right, my lord!"

And by the light of the bleared oil lamp, Hawk's Eye saw that the sentry had marched up to him, and he also noted this remarkable thing in the sentry, that the hand not occupied in holding his musket was being held in the shape of a scoop, and as near Hawk's Eye's nose as the huge palm could be held.

Hawk's Eye understood.

He took a guinea from his pocket, and pressed it in the sentry's palm, and then he raised it and laid it on another part of his hand.

"Thank ye, my lord, for *both !*"

He thought there were *two*, for if you press a coin on the hand, and then dexterously lift it, the victim will still suppose he has got the metal.

And as the next moment the sentry began looking on the ground, Hawk's Eye saw that his bait had taken.

"Why," says the man, looking on the ground, "where the devil——"

"Ho—ho!" whispered Hawk's Eye. "Take care, sentry, you are using the password."

"Beg pardon, my lord, but——"

"There's the ladder," said Hawk's Eye.

And he went to the swinging rope ladder, tried it to see it was safe, and then began mounting it.

And the last thing he saw as he stepped over the sill of the window was the sentry looking about for the supposed lost guinea, and swearing to himself like a ruffled old house-dog.

"Dear my lord!" said a soft voice, and then Hawk's Eye felt himself in the soft embrace of what was evidently a young woman.

She shut the window down as she spoke.

"Madam !"

Then there was a scream.

"Madam !"

"Who are you ?"

"A gentleman, I trust."

"How came you here ?"

"Why, by the rope ladder, lady—you yourself helped me too."

"I am lost !"

"Nay, lady, you are found. Prythee, are you some pretty wench who belongs to the household of St. James's, and waiting for an ardent visitor ?"

"Sir !"

"Pardon."

"How dare you insinuate ?"

"I don't—I merely suggest."

"Who are you ?"

"As I said, a gentleman."

"What is your name ?"

"That I refuse."

"Do you belong to the palace ?"

"No, but I wish the palace belonged to me."

"Are you a courtier ?"

"No."

"Then, how came you to be able to pass inside the palace gates without the password ?"

"I had the password."

"Nay, you speak falsely."

"The *devil* I do, lady !"

She screamed.

"You must be a courtier, and you are here to confound me, and to betray me to the King ! You have come from his Majesty !"

"*Parbleu*, madam !" said Hawk's Eye, "nothing of the kind ! I am here to batray you in no manner of way ; and as for coming from the King, the fact is, I should be very glad to find my way to the King his Majesty, and have a little talk with him."

"On what subject, my lord—are you a lord ?"

"I am lord of all I survey, when I am at home."

"Do not trifle with my feelings. Do you know who I am ?"

"I know you have the sweet voice of a woman, and I seek to learn no more."

"You are not a libertine ?"

"No, for I love."

"Whom ?"

"She I love."

"Her name ?"

"No name."

"Do I know her ?"

"Faith, I hope, lady, she doesn't know you, for I should not care for my Lady May—ha, I meant not you should hear her name—to know a damsel who flings rope ladders from a palace window to gentlemen passing by chance along St. James's Street at midnight, and who has a sentry in her pay, or rather the gentleman's, for I gave him two guineas, on the word of a gentleman."

"Lady May ?"

"Well, that *is* her name."

"Lady May Cavendish ?" asked the lady, in an angry, sharp voice.

"No."

"Lady May Marymore ?"

"No, my lady—for I suppose you *are* a lady, since you take me for a lord."

"Lady May Pottenay ?"

"No—nay, my lady ! I am sure you do not know my May !"

"Whoever she may be," cried the unknown, "she has endeavoured to subject me to disgrace, and when once I learn the real name of your Lady May, I will be revenged upon her !"

"*You* revenged, my dear lass," said Hawk's Eye—" you, who are probably some serving-wench trying to pique my curiosity and my passion ? Bah ! My Lady May has little to do with my being here ! I pass the palace gate—I see a window raised, a white hand waved—a thick-headed sentry pretends to take me for somebody else—and here I am !"

"Sir !" cried the lady, imperiously.

"Am I not right ?"

"Do you mean to say that absolutely your being here is chance-work ?"

"I do, dear creature !"

"Impossible ! You say so in order to foil me in learning who this enemy of mine is—this Lady May—for I will find out, happen what may ! Nay, you shall not escape by the window !"—he had made a movement that way—"for I will order the sentry to fire upon you—I will, upon all my earthly hopes !"

"Thanks ! If I must be shot down by a sentry, I trust it will not be by such a chuckle-headed noodle as the one who has passed me within the boundaries of the palace !"

"Then you will not dare to escape ?"

"No."

"You are not afraid ?"

"No—not I, lady ! Rather *you* should be afraid that you admit a strange man by a window and a rope ladder into the palace of the King of England !"

"You are audacious !"

"I am plain-spoken !"

"What do you seek?"

"Candidly—when I saw your token I was looking for money."

"You are poor?"

"I am not rich."

"Why are you poor?"

"Either the King, or the King's ministry—or all of them—robbed me of all I had."

"And?"

"And I confess I should like to repay the little obligation by robbing the King and every minister he has—and the better dressed they were, the better I should like it!"

"You are a wit," said the lady.

"No, I am a——"

Here he stopped.

And his silence was judicious.

"Take this," said the lady.

She gave a something into Hawk's Eye's right hand.

By the peculiar feel of the object, he knew it was composed of diamonds, and, taking it to the window, he saw even by that faint light that the bracelet—for it was that kind of jewel—must be worth some hundreds, if not a thousand or so of pounds.

"Faith of my fathers!" he thought. "This can't be a serving wench, unless she has been dipping in the royal caskets!"

"Madam," he said, returning, "I thankfully accept your offer, but I pray I may know to whom I owe the loan—for I will not take it as a gift. Some day, he who speaks to you will be a recognised and rich gentleman, then the Jew who will hold this jewel in pledge for me—and for which I shall pay the Hebrew handsome interest—then the Jew will yield me the bracelet, and I shall seek to place it upon the arm whence you have taken it. So, lady, your name! Never once shall it pass my lips."

"I am the most unfortunate of ladies."

"And the name of the most unfortunate of ladies?"

"Why do you seek to know it?"

"That I may know the name of my benefactress."

"I am—my name is——"

The unknown had proceeded so far in a low tone of voice, and then she suddenly merged into anger.

"Ha," she cried, quickly, "I know now why you seek to know my name! The Lady May who has employed you to betray me has not told you whom you were to betray, and you would know my name in order that you might protect her from my vengeance!"

"I swear——"

"Swear! Forbear, my lord! You are the Duke of Casselton!"

"I would to Heaven I were!"

"The Earl of Dorset?"

"No."

"Lord Carringly?"

"No."

"Sir James de Burgh?"

"No."

"You shall not leave this place until I have seen your features!"

"I swear you sha'n't!"

"Why not?"

"Because then, at some future time, you would identify me by seeing me with my Lady May; and, by the tone of your voice, I fear you could be merciless."

"I will——"

But here a peculiar whistle was heard, which caused the unknown lady to tremble, and utter a cry of evident fear.

She ran to the window.

There was the sentry, with his mouth wide open, for all the world as though he had come to have a tooth taken out—a tooth very far back in his head indeed.

"Your Rial Highness!" he gasped.

"Well—well?"

"Yere he is again!"

"Who?"

"My lord!"

A scream was the response.

And it so astounded the sentry, that his musket fell to the ground, the noise causing an extraordinary sound for a palace.

"Where is my lord?"

"Outside the gate, your Rial Highness, pretending to be drunk, and waiting your commands, your Rial Highness, for I knowed as one had got up the ladder already"

"Augustina!"

The voice was very low and mild.

It came from a tall form standing near the sentry.

He had advanced silently, and must have heard the last words uttered by the sentry.

"My lord!" she cried, with a faint scream.

Then, recovering herself, she said:

"My lord, wait a moment!"

She turned quickly.

"Sir," she said, bitterly, to Hawk's Eye, "I am in your power!"

"Be sure I shall not use it!"

"Then you will obey my commands?"

"Nay, if you are in my power, lady,"—he had not heard the title 'Rial Highness,' or rather '*Rial* Highness,' given by the sentry—"it is not for you to command."

"I entreat!"

"And I will obey upon one condition."

"What is it?"

"That you swear never to seek to know whom it is I have referred to when I mentioned the Lady May—and perhaps I have assumed a name——"

"I swear!" she said, eagerly.

"And that if you ever learn that, you will not persecute her because of this night's work, with which she has had nothing to do."

"I swear—I swear!"

She spoke quietly, and with no evidence that she felt he was binding her by the most solemn obligation it is in the power of man to make to his fellow-man.

"Then, I am at your service."

"Quick—here—behind this sliding-door!"

And as he moved in obedience to her request, he heard the soft voice say:

"Augustina!"

"Great Heaven!" thought Hawk's Eye; and his sudden discovery was so great that he let fall one of his gloves. "Is the Bavarian Princess now at the English court?—and who in her own land bears such a name for implacability? She must never know my Lady May!"

"Quick—quick!" she cried.

"Your Royal Highness!"

"You—you know my rank?"

"I guess it."

"Then I *do* command you to obey!"

"Augustina!"

Again the voice.

"Augustina!"

Then the panel was shut upon him.

A half minute, and he heard a step in the room.

Then the sound of a deep, sweet embrace.

Then words of love.

"By the faith of my fathers, 'tis lucky I had my mask on!—or she would have seen my face, and I should fear for my May if once that implacable Princess saw her leaning on my arm! Ha, I hear his words! How he loves her!"

Then he waited a moment.

Then he thought:

"Nay, no gentleman will willingly listen to the words of another gentleman—and he obviously is one—when the latter thinks himself alone with the lady of his love! But here am I boxed up, and cannot avoid hearing. Faith, I may hear more, for she dare not put him on his guard!"

Then he heard a sudden, low cry.

"What ails you?" he heard the Princess say.

"Nought, your Royal Highness," was the reply.

"Nay, say not Royal Highness to me, dear my lord and husband!"

"Husband?   Faith, 'tis time for me to be off!"

"Why do you not speak?"

The ardent lover had evidently become silent.

"What has vexed him?" asked Hawk's Eye.

And then he heard the Princess imprint a soft kiss upon a cheek.

"By my faith, I trust that there is a way out of this hole, for I care not to assist at a love scene!"

So thought Hawk's Eye.

And, so thinking, he moved off.

Suddenly his hand touched a hard substance

"Wood," thought Hawk's Eye.

Well, if wood, it yielded.

"A door," he thought.

On he went.

Put out his hands on each side.

"Ha, a passage—a wall on each side!"

Took ten steps forward.

"Ha, a door that doesn't yield! But there must be a spring, or what would be the use of the door?"

So he began feeling about for a spring.

He thought he was making his search very silently.

He was not.

For a certain personage, in a dressing gown, and a devil of a bad temper, remarked, in a low voice:

"Tam de rats—tam de rats!"

"Now, the words sound like those of mine host Schwincks, of that noble hostelry the Anchor of Safety."

But how could *he* be in a palace? much less could he be at St. James's and the Anchor of Safety at one and the same time.

No, it was not Meinheer Von Schwincks.

Who was it?

His Majesty King George the Second, by the grace of God, according to the coin of the realm, Prince of England, Ireland, Scotland and France, and ever defender of the faith.

"Tam de rats!" said the King.

And thereupon Hawk's Eye made, quite unintentionally, a little more riot.

"Tam 'em ten tousan times!" said his Majesty.

His Majesty was locked up in his room for the night.

Two bolts, a chain, a bar, and a very big lock, with the key turned twice.

Four bars upon each of the windows.

The King was awfully afraid of being interrupted.

More noise.

So the King took up the poker.

What the King intended to do with the poker is more than a subject of his descendant can say; but, in all probability, he meant to go driving away at the wall with the poker's point until the rats had ceased from troubling, and the King was able to go to rest.

But just as his Majesty, who was dressed for the ball (whence he had but recently returned)—if we except the dressing-gown in the place of the crimson velvet coat his majesty had been wearing—just as his Majesty came near the wall, a sliding-door opened.

"Der teufel!" said his Majesty.

Never once had his Majesty known of the secret passages of St. James's—for the House of Brunswick had but just come to England, and knew nothing before of its palaces.

Never would George have gone to bed in a room with a secret passage leading from it to nobody know where.

And, in fact, nobody would care to go to bed under such doubtful circumstances.

Well might his Majesty say, "the devil!" for there in the door-way, with the yawning blackness behind him, stood a tall figure, the face of which was masked.

"Who are you?" asked the King.

"A visitor."

"And what der teufel have you come in that way for?"

"Because I couldn't find another.! May I come in?"

"Donner und blitzer—how shall I help it?"

"That means may—thanks!"

And Hawk's Eye raised his hat courteously.

"What is your name?"

"Your Majesty would not know it."

"What was your fader's name?" asked the King.

"How should I know?—'tis a wise son that knows his own father!"

"Take off that mask!"

The King still kept hold of the poker.

"No, for then you would know my father's son."

"Do you know who I am? Mein got in himmel!"

"Yes—the King on earth—how are you?"

"How dare you speak to your King thus?"

"Beg pardon! Suppose I say I am a Jacobite!"

"Then you are a traitor, and I could have you beheaded—nay, hanged!"

"How so?"

"I have only to call to the sentry in the passage."

"Don't!"

"'Don't' to the King in his own palace?"

"Yes."

"Why 'don't?'"

"Because number one is the first law in nature, and I should quiet you!"

"Would you kill me?"

"No. I said quiet you—so that I had time to escape!"

"Vretch!"

"Whatever your Majesty pleases! Hard words break no bones! I want money!"

"Do you—you wagabones?"

"Yah!" said Hawk's Eye.

"And suppose I haven't any?"

"Well, there!"

And Hawk's Eye pointed to the Order of the Garter at the King's knee.

The motto, *Honi soit qui mal y pense* was worked in diamonds of no small size.

All the world knows of the origin of the Order of the Garter.

A certain King of England picked up a lady's garter, which a certain Countess of Shrewsbury had let fall, and, presenting it to the lady, his Majesty said : "*Honi soit qui mal y pense* "—in English, "Evil be to him who evil thinks"—for at the time English Kings were much above speaking plain English; and he added that, before long, many thousands would be wishing for the Order of the Garter.

He was right; and that was how this King George the Second came to be wearing that garter on the night when Hawk's Eye paid him a visit, the motto being spelt in the most expensive manner—that is to say, in diamonds.

"Vot?" said his Majesty. "You was take mein jarter?"—for when his Majesty lost his temper, he missed what English he had as well.

"You can get another jarter."

"Vretch!"

"You said that before! Don't let me keep your Majesty out of bed, though I am bound to say your Majesty don't look very sleepy, seeing your Majesty's eyes are as wide open as though they were about to start from your Majesty's head—still, I dare say your Majesty would like to get between the sheets."

"Willain!"—his Majesty always mixed up his v's and w's.

"Yes, I am—to take your Order of the Garter, and then take my leave!"

"Suppose I call the guard?"

"I shall bark!"

And out came from Hawk's Eye's pocket a little pistol.

Down went the poker, and as it fell upon a china vase, and this in its turn crashed upon the marble hearth, there was no end of a row.

The alarm in the corridor was immediately taken.

The sentry knocked at the door.

"Majesty!"

"Give the alarm!" said Hawk's Eye, putting his pistol so near the ear of his Majesty of Great Britain that his Majesty of Great Britain felt the cold air about the steel—"give the alarm, and they shall have something to be alarmed about!"

"Vould you blaugh me brains out?" asked the King.

"Yes, provided your Majesty has any brains to lose, which I doubt! However, it would settle the question!"

Another hurried knock.

Then again the voice.

"Majesty!"

"Answer, or I must!"

The King went to the door, the pistol following him, so to speak, as a dog keeps his eye on his enemy, and then his Majesty said:

"Vot is it?"

"Majesty, heard a smash—thought Majesty ill!"

"No, I'ms werry vell! Go to der teufel with you!"

"Yes, Majesty!"

And then the step of the huge soldier was heard tramping away.

"There, you schwine," continued the King to Hawk's Eye,

"you have made der King of Inkland" (such was the black title he gave our England) "tell one lie!"

"Yah!" said Hawk's Eye; "but I should say that since he has been crowned, der King of Inkland has told two lies—and perhaps three."

"Yah!" screamed the King; "you should be scoltcht."

"What's that?" asked Hawk's Eye.

"There," said the King, who certainly was not an arrant coward, and flinging the Order of the Garter at his visitor; "there, you schamps, take it!"

"I say, Majesty, don't fling my property about. If it was your own you might do as you liked, and I wouldn't interfere."

"Go along! What are you looking at my table for?"

(To be continued in our next.)

RED GAUNTLET THE BANDIT; OR, THE BLACK MOUNTAINEERS.

BOOK II.—THE BLACK CHATEAU.

CHAPTER XXVIII. *(Continued.)*

RED GAUNTLET pointed to the peasantry. With one voice they said:

"Red Gauntlet—our chieftain—Red Gauntlet!"

"The dweadful bwigand!" exclaimed Tikeypoodle, trying to hide himself behind the altar. "Good gwacious!"

The major-general was a brave man. He felt all the soldier and the Englishman rise in his breast as he divined the situation. He was surrounded by a horde of brigands—for such the seeming peasants were—and he was confronted by their chief.

The major-general's friends were in extreme terror.

The ladies, who had heard much of banditti atrocities, trembled and grew faint. The gentlemen went pale, but not with fear. They were few against the many bandits, but each would have died for his fair countrywomen.

The guests and the banditti stood back, ranged on either side of the chapel.

The minister remained at the altar, book in hand, and quite calm, as though the sacred place in which he stood kept fear away.

Sibyl stood with the bandit chief. He had said he was Cecil's friend, and, bandit though he was, there was in his manner, in his bearing, and his looks, a truthful nobility that prompted her to trust him. His attitude was graceful and statuesque, and he confronted with wondrous quietude the fierce glance of the major-general.

"You are an English gentleman," he said—"a brave soldier, used to command, and to be obeyed. Such a man should be noble."

"Demme, sir!"

"Keep your sword in its sheath, good sir. There are fifty men around, each of whom has his hand upon his pistol. A motion to injure me would be fatal to yourself."

"Demme, sir!"

"Is it right," Red Gauntlet asked, "to give this girl, your own and only child, to such a thing as that? See how beautiful and young, pure and innocent, gentle and submissive; and then look at him, a shirking, titled cur—a disgrace alike to his manhood and his rank. Is *he* fit to have a soldier's daughter for his bride?"

He pointed with unutterable scorn to his grace, who, seeing the red hand singling him out, began to tremble at the knees.

"Demme," said the major, looking at Tikeypoodle, "I don't think he is!"

"Then why force her to have him?—why choose him in preference to the viscount?"

The major-general was not prepared to answer, and while

the bandit chief waited a reply, Marriott returned, accompanied by his friends.

"Major," he said, advancing frankly, and offering his hand, "give Sibyl to me. She loves me—look!"

He opened his arms. Sibyl went to him, and Tikeypoodle gave a howl.

"Would you part them?" asked Red Gauntlet—"and for him?"

He pointed to the duke again, and the duke gave a second howl.

"Come, major," said Stuart Linn, "be generous. Let the marriage go on with Cecil for bridegroom. We will go back to breakfast with you."

"And I will give a wedding gift," said the bandit.

He took from his breast a magnificent necklace and massive cross of rubies and diamonds.

"Wear it in memory of me," he said, dropping it gracefully over Sibyl's head, so that the necklace encircled her fair throat, and the cross slid to its resting-place on her breast. "Major-general."

"Sir."

"Do you consent?"

"I suppose I had better," growled the veteran, "though my daughter won't be a duchess after all."

"She will be the wife of a gentleman," said St. George, "and not of a Tikeypoodle!"

"Your consent is worth just twenty thousand pounds," said Red Gauntlet.

The major stared.

"That being the sum I should have exacted as ransom for yourself and friends," the bandit continued; "so you may look upon that as a dowry."

"Demme!" said the major-general. "Then it is a good thing I consented."

The Duke of Tikeypoodle had left off trembling by this time, and was keeping very close to his mother.

"What shall we do with him?" asked Red Gauntlet.

Tikeypoodle howled again.

"Let his mother take him home," said the Englishman.

And his mother took him home.

"Now let the ceremony proceed," said the major-general; "and, viscount, take the girl, since I must forgive instead of fight with you."

So that is how Tikeypoodle lost his bride; and the brigands gave a great cheer as Cecil the viscount and Sibyl, Lady Marriott, went from the chapel.

"We are nearing the end," said Stuart Linn. "St. George and Marriott are done for. Now for the bandit monk and the White Chateau!"

CHAPTER XXIX.

THE ATTACK UPON THE CONVENT.—RESCUE FROM DEATH.—THE KING'S GIFT.—PARDON OF RED GAUNTLET.—CONCLUSION.

THE secrets of convent life have been so frequently revealed to the public that the existence of such a place as the White Chateau is no longer a matter of doubt or disbelief.

In such places, where all that is diabolical in monkish craft has no restraint, debauchery and moral ruin is carried on to an appalling extent.

Lulalu was comparatively safe. The child of a noble house, with powerful friends, and relations high in power, she was beyond the reach of the daring and sinful bandit monk, Doctor Montena.

But she had been received into the convent with strict injunctions that she was never to quit its walls, save in the custody of her father, the Luali, or of her lover, the Duke de Mareosi.

So, then, she was in a lonely cell, watched and guarded noon, night, and day.

As with the novices who required most rigorous care, her cell was built in the wall, the door being so constructed that when closed it looked like part of the wall itself.

With Dorolie it was different. She was one of the many orphans whose friends or parents, not being rich enough to give them such a dowry as is necessary to be given to a husband of high birth, pay a small sum to have them hidden from the world for life in a convent.

What becomes of them there is a matter of indifference.

They are out of the way, and the secrecy of the whole proceeding precludes the possibility of any strange information reaching the outer world, except by accident.

A girl like Dorolie, going into the convent in childhood and inexperience, makes easy prey for the subtle wretches who make religion a cloak to cover most damnable sin.

Her beauty had fired the heart of Montena—he determined that she should add one more to his list of victims.

She was too pure, in spite of his infernal teaching, deep sophistry, and passion whispered in the guise of scripture. He would have taught her that such sin was no sin; but her heart said nay.

Up to the time when she was rescued from him by Dick Nicholson, he had tried many a time to overcome her scruples, but without success.

How he was baffled that time we already know. He was released from the prison cell into which Dick thrust him by another monk as sinful as himself.

Meanwhile, Dorolie had sought protection of the Lady Abbess, and she, whose sanctity was like Montena's, a mask for vice, was too careful to let this be seen, so Dorolie was safe for a time, and lived hoping that her dream-love would come to her again.

On the day of Sibyl's wedding with the viscount, and while Red Gauntlet, with his brigands and his English friends, was marching to the White Chateau, a visitor arrived at the convent gate.

It was the Duke de Mareosi, his purpose being to see Doctor Montena.

He was admitted.

The Lady Abbess, a fair and somewhat handsome lady of perhaps thirty years of age, was with Montena when the duke was announced. The Abbess was a mere cipher in the hands of Montena; his power over her was extraordinary and complete.

"Of what we have been speaking we will have more anon," the doctor said to the abbess; "but Dorolie shall be mine!"

The abbess retired as De Mareosi entered. The duke had evidently heard the last words.

"A brave resolve!" he said, his dark eyes flashing keenly on the monk's fine face. "This is a rare and safe place for the growth and care of beauty, Doctor Montena!"

The bandit monk smiled.

"Have you come for the daughter of Luali?" he asked.

"I have come because I am tired of the world," said De Mareosi, with a sneer. "I would dwell in peace in the cloister—and," he added, "near Lulalu."

"What dowry will you bring?" asked the doctor, catching the other's sinister meaning.

"One worthy such a novice. The mysteries of priestcraft are worth learning."

"They are indeed."

"When should I reach the honour of receiving confessional?"

"When it would please your grace."

"To-night, then."

"And whom would you choose for penitent?"

"The daughter of Luali!" replied the duke, with a wild flash of the eye.

"But is there not danger?" the doctor asked.

"Bah! Women rarely tell such tales, but keep the secret of their passion and their shame. Besides, she is my affianced bride, and there is no other way of winning her."

So the diabolical plot was arranged.

That night, De Mareosi, disguised as a monk, was to be introduced by the Lady Abbess to the cell of Lulalu.

And the night came.

Lulalu, thinking of her lover—the outlaw, Count Adrian—and praying as she nightly prayed for succour, saw the opening door, and the Abbess entered, followed by a monk.

"A reverend father, my child," said the Abbess, kindly, "whose exhortations will, I trust, soften your heart to a parent's will. To-night is the last of your novitiate, and you will consent to wed the Duke de Mareosi or take the veil, and say farewell for ever to the world."

The words went chilling-like into the heart of Lulalu. She bowed her head, and when she looked up the abbess had gone.

She was alone with the monk.

Lulalu knew not yet of the crimes committed in the convent, and looked upon the visits of her confessor without fear.

But an instinct roused her to recoil from this new priest. His cowl was closely drawn, and she could catch only the faintest glimpse of his face in the dusky shadow of the hood.

The eyes were evil in their glitter; the voice, though subdued, quivering with a passion that made her dread a danger she did not comprehend.

"Daughter," he said, softly, "hearken to me! I plead with a parent's voice that you will obey his decree, and wed De Mareosi."

"Never! Rather eternal misery in this living tomb—rather death!"

"Is there still in your heart a sinful yearning for the outlaw—the brigand?"

"I love him, holy father!"

"Cast out his image—forget him!"

"Never! While I live I am his—only his!"

"This is sinful, my daughter."

"Heaven forgive me, then!"

"I come with prayers from your sire and your lover. They implore you, for your sake and for theirs."

"I cannot say that which would be perjury in the sight of God. Rather let me die sinless in the cloister than wed one whom I cannot love!"

"This is your final decision?"

"Final—unalterable!"

"Then let us see what can be done to alter it," said the monk, with a change so sudden in his voice that the girl started, with a shriek.

The cowl and cloak were flung aside, a firm hand gripped her wrist, and, sick with terror, she recognised the dreaded face of De Mareosi.

His purpose shone in his eyes—quivered in every lineament of his face. Had it not shone in these, his words would have rendered it beyond a doubt.

"The cloister, if you like," he said, "but not to my despite. I have set my heart upon you, and mine—mine in honour or mine in shame—you shall be!"

"Help!" she shrieked—"help! Save me—Heaven save me! Adrian—Adrian!"

"Shriek," said De Mareosi, in savage triumph—"call and cry in vain!"

In her mad battling, she twisted her hand in his hair, and wrenched his head aside. The sudden pain forced him to let her go.

Retreating to the wall, she stood panting like a hart, and he, pausing before he seized her again, was startled by a wild uproar in the convent.

"Lulalu—Lulalu!" shouted a voice. "Speak, that I may find you!"

"Adrian!" she sobbed, with a glad cry; and then De Mareosi stopped her mouth with his hand.

"Let him come," he said savagely, as before, "but he shall find you dead or I have triumphed!"

She could not cry out again, though her lover's voice called again, and yet again. The cruel hand upon her lips choked her voice.

The door in the wall was shut, and so her cell was hidden. She heard the tramp of feet rushing by in eager search.

De Mareosi exerted all his strength to hold her motionless, lest the sound of a struggle should be heard.

In spite of the compression on her lips, Lulalu uttered an exclamation. Red Gauntlet was knocking at the wall.

"The place is full of devilish mystery," he said, "and she is hidden somewhere here. The convent shall be torn down stone by stone until I find her!"

De Mareosi threw Lulalu across his knees, drew a dagger, and set the point against her breast.

"Never his, if not mine!" he said. "Should he find the door, you die!"

"A lever here!" the voice of Red Gauntlet cried at that moment. "The wall is hollow here!"

The point of Mareosi's dagger pierced Lulalu's bosom.

A sharp cry of pain she gave, then with a sudden twist broke away, and caught the wrist of the hand that held the dagger in her teeth.

"Malediction!" he said, and the dagger fell, just as, with a mighty crash, the stone door yielded, crushed in by a powerful blow from an iron bar.

The bandit stood in the opening, his red hand grasping the bar, and his eyes glimmering with terrible fire on the face of his foe.

Lulalu reeled, and fell into his arms. He pressed her to him, kissed her, and turned to Labian, who stood beside him.

"Take her," he said, in a strangely deadly voice. "The Duke de Mareosi—my rival—my foe—is here!"

While speaking so he was resting on the bar. Having done speaking, he raised and swung the ponderous weapon high above his head.

De Mareosi drew his sword to oppose the awful descent. He was appalled by the aspect of his avenging foe, and uttered cries of terror as he thrust at him vainly with his sword.

Three short, quick cries, like the sharp bark of a dog recoiling from the lash, were given as he retreated to the wall.

And all the time he retreated, this fearful bar kept its deadly level.

So terrified De Mareosi was, that at last he dropped his sword, and sinking on his knees, clasped his hands above his head, and said:

"Mercy!"

The answer to his appeal was stern and brief:

"Pray!"

"Mercy!"

"Pray!"

He could not.

He could not speak, except to ask for mercy, and huddled up in terror in a corner, crouching, pallid, trembling, and covered in a cold sweat from head to foot, he shut his eyes, and shrieked in horror as his doom descended.

Heavy and swift it came, sinking with a dull, horrible crash into the traitor's skull, and with a spattering and splash of blood and brain, out went De Mareosi's life.

The bandit's smile was grim and stern as he gazed at his fallen foe. He let the heavy bar fall from his hand, as though, in taking that one life, the weapon had done enough.

"Dead!" he said. "I thought vengeance would come. I never thought I could slay a fellow-creature and feel so little remorse."

He turned from the sickening spectacle, and took the senseless form of Lulalu from Fabian.

The bandit drew a short, strong poniard, and held it with the blade turned up his wrist; he raised his bugle to his lips, and blew a war note.

"I warn before I strike," he said; "but after I have warned, let my foes beware!"

And there were foes in plenty. The brigand monks were up and in arms, and the Luali, who by this time had heard of the intended attack upon the convent, were there in swarms.

So the fight stood. The banditti against the bandit monks and the Luali, the two latter outnumbering the first by three to one.

But the ones were better than the threes.

With such men as Red Gauntlet, St. George, Dick Nicholson, the viscount, and Stuart Linn to lead them, the banditti were more than a match for their numerous foes.

The fight raged hotly.

Dick Nicholson went in search of Dorolie, whose name he called, and as he called it a mocking laugh rang out behind him.

He turned to see the devilish face of Doctor Montena, in whose hand blazed a lurid torch.

"Seek her in the funereal pyre!" yelled the doctor, waving the torch madly. "The secrets of the Black Chateau shall find a red and fiery tomb!"

He rushed away.

Following the torch, Dick dashed after him, breaking through the struggling throngs till he neared the convent stair.

This was guarded by an iron door.

Leaping through the door, Montena laughed again, and dashed the door back to its fastening ere Dick had time to follow him.

There was heard a laugh and a shriek.

The laugh from Montena, the shriek from Dorolie.

Dick shook with agony at thought of Dorolie's peril.

(*To be continued in our next.*)

TALES OF BRIGANDS

I Warn & Strike

AND BANDITTI.

[THE DUEL ON THE THAMES.]

THE RED DWARF.

CHAPTER I.

THE NIGHT RIDER.—THE SHRIEK FOR AID.—THE LADY AND HER RIVAL.—TWO TO ONE.—THE FIGHT.—THE STRANGER.—THE PURSUIT. — SILVER JACK TO THE RESCUE. — A MOONLIGHT CHASE.—ON THE THAMES.—THE STRUGGLE IN THE WATER. — A BULLET THROUGH THE BOAT.—SINKING! SINKING!

THE night was beautiful—the sky quite clear. Bright stars were twinkling, and the song-birds made sweet music in the hedgerows.

The hour was midnight! The bell of old St. Paul's tolled out the solemn tidings, waking deep, spectral echoes far and wide.

In a green lane on the outskirts of the city stood a solitary horseman in the shadow cast by a giant tree. The steed was motionless, the rider evidently on the alert.

There was no doubt as to his profession—not a question as to his purpose in such a lonely spot at this lonely hour.

A red mask hid his face.

By his side hung a long, curved sword, its steel scabbard glittering in the starlight.

In the holsters of his saddle was a pair of heavy pistols—not handsome but serviceable weapons.

Another pair, slightly made, silver mounted, and elegant of shape, were in his belt.

The rider himself—a young athlete, graceful in limb, and full of leonine strength, sat his splendid steed in a manner that told he was an accomplished equestrian.

Horse and master were models of their kind.

"Out two hours and not a traveller yet!" the rider muttered, with an air of discontent. "One would think the very devil had emptied all the pockets in London, and frightened the good citizens into staying within doors!"

He patted the glossy neck of his beautiful bay charger, his white fingers playing with a pistol's silver butt the while.

"Another month of such dull work," he went on, "and I should feel inclined to sell out and retire! The hardest thing would be to part with you, my Lancelot, and the rest would not fetch much!"

Caressing his charger's silken mane, he bent his ear to listen for a sound.

None came.

"Not much to be done now!" he went on, twisting his brown moustache. "I think King Charley must spend all his money on his mistresses. I should like to meet his Majesty this night—not even his royalty would save his purse!"

"Steady, Lancelot—so—what, comes some one near?—right, brave lad! Your ears are sharper than mine—they are longer, too, and that is something!"

He smiled and drew his sword; his horse had detected an approaching sound—his ears were straightened and bent forward.

The horseman could see nothing yet—his gaze was strained intently on the road.

Sight and sound were satisfied together.

Then came the shadowy forms of two men mounted, and evidently in rapid pursuit of something.

What that something was our friend on the bay charger could not see yet.

A moment more.

Then came a cry—a girl's scream of terror, and, seeming to come from amidst the feet of her pursuers' horses, there ran towards him like a hunted fawn, a lovely girl, who threw herself upon her knees.

"Save me!" she cried—"save me!"

The rider took the mask from his face and thrust it into a side pocket.

"Save you, lady!" he cried—"ay, were your pursuers ten instead of two! Come here!"

He had extended his hand to assist her to his saddle—he had not time, for the horsemen were upon him.

The girl clung in terror to his saddle. He touched her with a reassuring glance and rode a step forward.

"Gentlemen," he said, advancing sword in hand, "the hunt is over for to-night. The fawn has a place of refuge and a guardian!"

"'Sdeath!"

The elder of the two persons spoke.

Both were masked, but it could be seen that one was a man of middle age, powerfully built, and wearing a strong, black beard.

"'Sdeath!" he said, and drew his sword.

His companion had a figure of almost effeminate grace. About his being a court beau of the first water there could be no question.

He drew his weapon also, and, with his companion, paused before the stranger who confronted them.

They found, however, the single rider was not the kind of man to attack without some consideration.

He sat very quietly watching the two, with something like a smile on his handsome face.

"'Sdeath!" he echoed. "And if that is what you want, you can get it by following this lady!"

"Perdition, man!—would you stand in our way?"

"Were you the demon! See, the lady here wants succour."

"The girl is witless, Sir Stranger!" cried the elder, with the impetuous rage that he had seemed inclined to use at first. "She has broken from her bounds, and we followed to save and restore her!"

"How like a lie that sounds! Come, lady, speak; your form is beautiful enough to win belief had your tongue no sweetness. Who are these?"

"Alas! good sir, I know not. I stood out on the terrace of my father's house, when I was seized by him, and had not time to give a cry, but was borne hither on his horse, till but now, the sight of you giving me hope, I broke from his grasp and fled!"

"Sweet lady, have no fear. Not much trace of the witless there, my hero of the abduction!" he said to the elder man, who gnawed his nether lip angrily.

"Witless or no," he said, "the girl is ours. If you value your life, stand aside and keep your own counsel!"

"If I value life. I do so well that I stand here to show it has some value. Were I a rat, a fox, a wolf, or any coward, wretched brute of prey, I might stand back to save my life; being a man, my life is hers!"

"At him!"

The younger one commenced the attack; he dashed with inconceivable rapidity and force at the lady's champion.

Who met him well.

"Step out of danger's reach!" he cried to the girl. "Away till the fight is done; or—the thought is better—fly, while I keep the way!"

"Noble sir, I should be lost—the road is strange to me."

"Stay, then. How—two to one! Well, come! You, sir, who handle your weapon like a soldier, should put it to better work than this!"

Though the two weapons pressed him hard, he gave way no inch—nor did he for an instant lose courage.

He found the elder stranger a formidable antagonist. The younger would not have given him five minutes' play had they been alone.

The elder needed all his care in fence; nothing but his skilful horsemanship enabled him to compete with both.

Anxious to be rid of one, he backed suddenly, and so drew himself out of range.

Then as suddenly he leaped forward. His sword, flashing swift as lightning, struck the younger cavalier, who staggered in the saddle bleeding from the arm.

His sword dropped.

"Are you deeply hurt?" the elder asked.

"Deeply—but no matter."

"Can you ride?"

"Ay."

"Then do so with the girl. I will keep this man!"

Hearing this plan to deprive him of the lady, her champion did his best to defeat it.

But his best was not enough.

Opposed to a man of iron strength, a grim, stern man, to whom fighting seemed but pastime,—he found himself fully occupied, and altogether unable to thwart the other's strategy.

He tried desperately—rained blows like hail upon the other's sword and struck out showers of fire—but the man stood it like a rock, and seemed to revel in it with a kind of fierce, ironical joy.

"If 'tis not to be done now," he said to his companion, "the chance is gone, and such another may not be. Pass now—quick!—away!"

He bore upon the lady's champion like a battering ram, forcing him, in spite of his horsemanship and skilful fence, to give way.

Only for an instant—but in that the work was done.

The poor girl had been clinging to the saddle till the animal, plunging, threatened destruction. Then she went back, but kept as close as she dared till the elder of her enemies spoke. The young one dashed past the combatants, and seizing her with his unwounded arm, swung her up before him.

"Away!" the elder said, and the abductor spurred onward.

Her thrilling shriek for aid maddened her champion—he struck desperately at his herculean foe, and beat him back—then turned to follow the fugitives.

The other took a pistol out.

"Not so fast," he said, taking aim; "the sport must not be spoiled so soon. Stop!"

And deliberately he fired at his late opponent's head.

He had aimed too well. The brave man staggered and rolled to the ground. His adversary, without staying to see what hurt he had inflicted, was riding on, when Lancelot caught him by the hand with his teeth.

The stranger uttered a savage oath as the horse let him go. The hand was bitten nearly through.

"Good, Lancelot!" murmured the fallen man. "I shall know him should we meet again."

The words were within a little of settling his fate for ever.

The stranger, in the act of riding by, paused with his hand upon the butt of a second pistol.

"To be known," he muttered—"that would be the Tower and the axe. So!"

Out come the pistol—his finger went to the trigger.

"Yet to kill a man for a fear," he said, "were the act of a cur. Besides, it would dim some pretty eyes to see the gay and gallant SILVER JACK still and dabbled in his death-sleep. No!"

He replaced the pistol, and rode after his companion and the fair captive.

"The hand bleeds," he muttered, "and there is venom in a horse tooth. This will be a case for surgery, which I hate. Meanwhile, a bandage will do good."

A delicate white kerchief was thrust carelessly in his belt. Drawing it forth, he bound it over the bitten palm.

"A pretty, scented trifle, surely never so badly soiled before," he cogitated, in a tone of self-mocking bitterness peculiar to the man. "This dropped upon the road would have been a clue to the way she came. I knew the danger of a slight token in such a case, so I picked it up. Now its use rewards me for my care."

He rode rapidly in the direction of old London Bridge, near which he overtook his companion and the girl.

"What of him?" asked the abductor.

"I left him on the road with a bullet in him."

"Then he will not follow, you think?"

"I think he will not."

"What is in your hand?"

"His horse's teeth were, not long since. But of that no matter. Ride on, or the precincts will be closed, the sentry gone, and then we shall not reach Whitefriars to-night."

"Will the ferryman be at his post?"

"The man who has been punctual ten nights is not likely to fail us on the eleventh. On!"

"Who comes behind, colonel?"

The elder man looked back.

Horsemen were galloping full speed towards them.

"When they come close enough we shall see," replied the colonel. "But I think, Lord Smedleigh, it were not prudent to stop for the exchange of courtesy."

"A thousand devils, colonel! One is the man who wounded me!"

"Silver Jack," said the colonel, calmly. "He will kill my lord some day. The man he fights one day to hurt, he fights a second to slay. Beware of him!"

"Malediction! Who is the other?"

"Young Allan Buckhurst, if my eyes may trust the moonlight and the distance. 'Tis he! By St. Michael, Lord Kylo Smedleigh, we are likely to lose the fair Madaline after all."

"Not living—by the stars!" exclaimed the wild young reprobate. "I have set my soul upon her, and will be no longer cheated! Come, colonel, ride you first, and wait with the ferry."

"Give me the lady, then. Your horse is but a palfrey, and carries double badly. Mine would take a son of Anak and go easily."

"Nay."

"Tush! your arm is wounded. Or keep her if you will, and lose her for the silly fancy of keeping her unclasped by another's arm. You need have no jealousy of me, Lord Kylo—I have that within which is proof even against such beauty as hers."

"What is the charm?" asked Kylo, doubting.

"Satiety—the soul's sick surfeit—the throeless chill that follows passion's glut. I have outlived humanity, and changed."

"Into what?"

"A demon, it may be; and I do not so much evil as I did before."

"Scoffer—sceptic!"

"Boy!" said the colonel, with a grim laugh. "But look! Our friends ride well, and here is the ferry."

They had crossed London Bridge at headlong pace, dashed through the uneven road, and stood by the ferry opposite the shore of Alsatia.

A boat stood in waiting. Its attendant, seeing them coming, sprang in, and made all ready.

Another man stood near, waiting for the horses.

"Now, in—and quickly," said the colonel, leaping from his horse, "or young Buckhurst and his companion will be upon us soon. My bitten hand with your perforated arm would make the contest not too equal. The girl is senseless, and the quieter for it. In, Lord Kylo! Now an oar for each. Pull!"

The boat shot from the steps out into the water. Lord Smedleigh and the colonel each pulled an oar with the hand he had unwounded. The ferryman used a pair.

They were not twenty yards from shore, when Allan Buckhurst and Silver Jack reached the ferry.

They had come so soon in pursuit because of this:—

Young Buckhurst was Madaline's lover; and very often, when her sire was sleeping, the girl would steal out to the terrace to pass a few sweet moments of innocent love with Allan.

He was not her father's choice, and therefore dared not go in open day.

A maiden so bewitching in her loveliness as Madaline Catemass had many suitors, but encouraged none.

Lord Kylo Smedleigh loved her madly. He was a rich and extravagant boyish profligate, determined in his desires, and scrupling not at anything to gratify them.

So, having wooed Madaline and been rejected, he resolved upon the course by no means unfrequently resorted to in those days of our merry monarch Charles the Second—her abduction. Once away from her father's roof, Lord Kylo trusted to his persuasive powers to reconcile her to her fate.

She might be his wife, or mistress, as she chose, but his she should be.

Hence the present night's work.

He had set a spy to watch to learn the signal—that given by Allan Buckhurst brought Madaline to the terrace. Having learned this, Lord Kylo went, disguised, gave the signal, and Madaline, thinking it was her lover, knew not her error till she found herself being borne away in his arms.

He had the colonel with him to assist in case of interruption.

The rest, so far, we have seen, with the exception of how young Buckhurst and the gallant robber Silver Jack came to be together in pursuit.

That was occasioned thus:—

Silver Jack was not wounded by the colonel's bullet. It had grazed his head and stunned him for a moment.

Then, though shaken by the fall, he felt himself unhurt, and rose to remount his horse and follow in pursuit.

Just at this instant Allan Buckhurst came thundering on in pursuit, having heard from Lord Kylo's spy what had happened.

He saw Silver Jack in the road.

"Hast seen two horsemen with a lady pass?" he asked.

"Seen—and tried to stop them! Who are you?"

"Allan Buckhurst, her lover. Accept my best thanks for your chivalry. Tell me which way they rode!"

"Yonder way. I will ride with and show you. I have set my heart in the lady's cause, and her rescue may be work enough for two!"

Allan grasped his hand.

"A noble friend! Your name?"

"No matter that. I have no name, save as occasions need, yet, for the nonce, you may call me Captain Blake."

"Then, Captain Blake, for your brave help I have more than thanks anon; and since you are with me let us ride!"

"Forward, then!"

So they rode in pursuit, and were at the ferry before the colonel, with Lord Smedleigh and their captive, were more than a hundred yards from the shore.

Several boats were moored at the ferry, fastened to a water post by strong rope.

A cut from Captain Blake's keen weapon severed the rope and set a boat drifting at liberty.

Both left their horses and leaped in.

Some few night wanderers, attracted by the strangeness of the scene, had gathered round.

Blake recognised one of the bystanders.

"Look to our horses," he said "Take them to the haunt in Lambeth."

"All right, captain."

Blake seized a pair of oars.

Allan took another pair.

Both could row well.

The little craft sped like a bird over the dark tide.

The other vessel, encumbered by greater weight, and with two of its rowers partly maimed, did not make such pace.

"They near us, my lord," the colonel said.

"Curse them!"

"We shall have to fight them Such men are not kept back by curses."

He drew his pistol as the other vessel drew near.

"What weapons have you?" he asked of Smedleigh.

"One pair only."

"Give them to me."

It was done.

"And now, if my crippled hand spoils not my aim, this will cause a check."

A flash, and the bullet sped, passing within an inch of Allan's ear, but touching neither.

Less than twenty rapid strokes brought pursuers and pursued together.

The colonel fired another shot.

He missed again.

The last weapon he reserved.

Neither he nor Lord Kylo did anticipate the daring act on which young Buckhurst resolved.

The boats were stern and stern.

A desperate fight with swords ensued, and then Allan relinquished his oars and threw himself into the water

"Look out," said the colonel—"he has us!"

He had.

A dive took him beneath the boat.

Up he came, seized the gunwale, and, by an effort of main strength, almost overturned the craft.

The colonel and Madaline were thrown out.

Lord Kylo righted the boat by a miraculous accident.

Allan and the colonel both made for one object—

The girl.

The sudden plunge into the water restored her to consciousness.

She clutched at and clung to Allan.

He had a heavy pistol grasped by the barrel.

The colonel came at him savagely.

"The girl!" he said, gripping her arm. "Yield her, or we sink together!"

For reply he received a terrific blow from the pistol butt.

He let go.

In making the blow, Allan had to throw his arm out of the water, the consequence being that he sunk with Madaline.

He rose with her again, separated now from the colonel by a few yards.

The ferryman found his whole time employed in keeping the boat steady.

The colonel was half stunned, and had grasped it to save himself.

Lord Smedleigh would have joined the action, but he was kept in check by Silver Jack's pistol being directly levelled at his head.

Allan swam with Madaline back to the boat.

Jack helped them in, and pulled away.

"Rescued," said Buckhurst, kissing her tenderly—"rescued!"

"Not yet," yelled Lord Kylo, in savage spite at being baffled. "This to kill you, or sink altogether."

He fired.

The ball passed through the boat, and the water gushed in.

Meanwhile the ferryman had assisted the colonel to his boat again.

"That was good," he said. "The boat will sink. They will not let the girl drown."

He was right.

"Sinking," said Allan. "Devils that they are! Cling to me, Madaline, dearest! We will swim for it."

He clasped her to him as the boat filled and went down, leaving them in the water.

Here a difficulty arose.

Silver Jack could not swim.

He would not say so, lest Allan, in staying to save him, should lose Madaline.

But Buckhurst saw it.

"Keep cool," he said.—"your hands down—your head thrown back—then you can float at ease, and I, having reached the shore, will come back for you."

"Will you?" said Kylo. "Come, colonel, we have him now."

Silver Jack obeyed the instructions, and found that he could keep himself from sinking.

Allan swam bravely.

The colonel's boat started in pursuit.

It soon reached the fugitives.

Kylo stood up. He grasped an oar, and struck twice at Allan, stunned him, and saw him sink with Madaline.

Then the colonel leaped in.

He was not altogether pitiless, and he took an oar with him.

"Cling to this," he said, forcing it into Allan's hand, "you are a brave lad. I do not want to see you die. I only want the girl."

He tore Madaline from Allan's arm, and swam back to Kylo's boat with her.

Allan clutched the oar dizzily.

The blows had nearly knocked his senses out, and only very dimly he saw the vessel glide away with Madaline in the arms of Lord Kylo.

Over the water towards the desperate locality of Alsatia it went, directed by the colonel to the back of a dark house overlooking the river.

The colonel gave a peculiar signal.

Silver Jack saw a water gate open in the bottom of the wall. The boat glided in—Madaline clasped in Kylo's arms, the ferryman rowing, and the colonel sitting like a fiend in the stern.

The gate closed.

Allan had gone senseless by this time, but he clung to the oar with the tenacity of a drowning man.

"In the Red House," said Silver Jack. "She is lost, if we do not save her soon. What, ho! a boat, there—my friend is drowning! Rescue—rescue!"

(To be continued in our next.)

HAWK'S EYE, THE PHANTOM ROBBER.

CHAPTER XI. (Continued.)

HAWK'S EYE's sight was fixed upon the table near at hand.

And upon what on the table?

On a paper on which was written the name "Albert Falconer."

Quite forgetting the danger he ran, he laid down the pistol and took up the paper.

In a moment he was absorbed in a contemplation of the contents of the document.

So, by it, Albert Falconer's title to the estate of Falcon Grange was confiscated, and the heritage was to descend on Sir Bruton's death (society had to wait till the morning before it was to learn that Sir Bruton had done with the world) to *Bertram Falconer.*

Then followed the Order for the complete outlawry of the unfortunate Albert, declaring, after the barbarous manner of that barbarous time, that after a certain date, any liege subject might shoot down the said Albert Falconer, and for that deed be considered—not a murderer, but a good citizen.

And so absorbed was Hawk's Eye in the perusal of this document that he did not mark the King's manœuvres.

First his Majesty poured a glass of wine over the nipple of the pistol which Hawk's Eye had laid upon the table.

Then his Majesty slipped off his shoes.

Then the King walked as lightly as he was able—and even then his was the step of a small elephant—towards the door.

Good.

One bolt undone.

T'other bolt undone.

Down went the chain.

Up came the two bars.

Still Hawk's Eye was deep in the study of the document.

There was now only the lock to unlock, and then his Majesty could bolt, and put the stalwart sentry outside between him and danger.

But even Kings can't have it all their own way.

The lock creaked.

Hawk's Eye looked up.

And all was over with the King's escape.

One bound, and Hawk's Eye was at the door.

But the sentry had heard.

"Majesty!" said he.

The King was in too great a rage to answer.

"Answer, your Majesty, as you value your own safety!"

"All right, sair, werry comfortable!" said the King.

And the sentry, growling "All's well!" again began his tramp.

Hawk's Eye deliberately bolted the door.

"Majesty, you are not a man of honour!"

"What else do you want?"

"The paper!" which he still held in his hand.

"Why?"

"For a purpose."

And he put it in a pocket.

"Schamps!"

"I've picked up this Order of the Garter, your Majesty; and I do hope you have not shaken any of the diamonds out; and off I go! But, your Majesty, I must have a fair start. Will your Majesty give me your royal pocket-handkerchief?"

"What! are you a common pocket-pick?"

"No—no; but I must gag your Majesty."

"No!"

The King saw he must obey, and was glad at any rate to get rid of his unwelcome visitor.

So he threw the handkerchief at Hawk's Eye.

But when our hero, advancing to gag the King of England raised the fair square of cambric, the scion of the House of Brunswick caught Hawk's Eye a swingeing spank of the face.

"Thanks!" said Hawk's Eye, "you make me blush—at all events, on one side of the face!"

"But, you schamps, I'll—woof!"

For at that moment Hawk's Eye clapped the royal handkerchief over the royal mouth.

And very quickly tied it behind his Majesty's head.

Hawk's Eye now took the cord which bound his Majesty's dressing-gown.

But this was too much for the King.

His Majesty tore off the handkerchief.

"Wretches—is you going to hanggen me?"

"Hang your Majesty? Bless your Majesty, I would not take the trouble—not I. And again, I am not the common hangman—am I? To be sure, I am a Jacobite; and as a Jacobite I ought to be glad to do for your Majesty in any way; but if your Majesty gave up your crown, why your Majesty has a son, and he, I think, is not quite so charming as yourself. No, your Majesty, I'll not hang the King of Inkland. I'll only truss him like a turkey, and tie him up."

"Vell, be quick," said the poor King, who had never suffered so much take down of his royalty in all his life before.

Hawk's Eye was quite polite enough to be quick. In one little half minute his Majesty was gagged and tied in his royal chair by means of the silken cord of his gold-embroidered dressing-gown.

Then Hawk's Eye prepared to decamp.

Four strides, and he was at the secret door.

Up went his hat.

"Your Majesty—good-bye."

The King nodded his head.

"Heaven bless you!"

Smack—that was the secret door closing.

And there the King was—a most unroyal-looking personage, under the circumstances—bound with his own royal dressing-gown cord in his royal bed-room, and swearing to himself a few royal oaths as he reviewed his position, and knew he must remain in it all night, and be found like a trussed turkey in the morning.

CHAPTER XII.

THE REMEMBRANCE.—THE ENCOUNTER.—THE DUEL.—THE DOUBTFUL ESCAPE.

MEANWHILE, Hawk's Eye, having closed the sliding-door upon himself, found that personage (himself) in total darkness.

What should he do?

He could scarcely return to the chamber where he had left the Princess. What was to be done?

Done?

Why, try and find another secret door; for as a man of common sense, he thoroughly well knew that where there is one secret door, there is generally a score.

So he determined to try for a door somewhere, and by it seek the means of escape.

Two conditions favoured him.

The King was safe from giving the alarm until the morning. That was the first favouring condition.

The second was this: He had the password for the night to and from the palace—"The Devil"—a password that the very King himself had given, and which the soldier at the palace gate had very naturally supposed Hawk's Eye possessed when he used the two words quite inadvertently.

He had turned one or two corners, and was silently asking himself whether he was or was not going the way he came, when a terrible thought struck him.

The document! He had taken this one from a number on the royal table, and left the rest!

The next morning the King would find out what paper of

those laid for him to read and sign was missing, and then, getting a copy of it, he would associate his midnight visitor with the name *Albert Falconer* in the missing paper!

"Great Heaven!" said he, "I shall have done my dear Albert an irretrievable injury. Let me return and seize the other papers!"

But he was so confounded by his terrible discovery that turning, so to speak, he lost himself, and in the darkness had no idea which way he had to turn.

At last in despair he went straight before him—holding out his hands like feelers, that they might give him warning of any door or wall he was approaching, and to prevent an alarm being given by his striking heavily against such obstructions to his progress.

Of this he was sure—that whatever way he went, he was safe to meet with a door.

Of course, he was quite right so far.

And he came upon the door suddenly.

He listened!

No sound!

Then he felt for the spring he knew he should find.

Gently the door opened!

Ha!—a drawing-room hung with yellow satin—a claret velvet carpet on the floor!

For these things he saw by the tender light emitted through a rose-coloured glass to a lamp standing on a gilded table.

At first he saw no one!

There was a row of windows—and neither the shutters nor blinds doing service, Hawk's-eye was enabled to see that the room opened upon the palace garden running parallel with the park.

And, indeed, he saw the park and oil-lamps beyond the highish wall enclosing the royal gardens.

"Good!" he thought. "I can escape by the garden, or I'm no man!"

And he stepped into the room.

Very lightly—but the Princess Augustina was listening for the lightest footfall, and she heard one!

She had been buried in a large easy chair, the back of which being towards Hawk's Eye, he had no power to mark that the room was occupied.

"You, my lady!" he said, in a whisper.

"Hush!" she replied.

There was great alarm depicted in her face.

"You have saved me, lady!" he said, flinging himself upon his knees.

"Hush! Begone!"

Her terror was very great.

"Madame, you are afraid of some one? Let him be whom he may, with your permission, I will protect you!"

"Nay; you could do me no greater injury than to protect me—unless it were a greater injury to injure him."

"Him? Where is he?"

"Hush!—do you hear a footstep?"

"No."

"Begone, oh! begone—as you came!"

"Are you in danger?"

"I fear I am not safe!"

"And do I gather that *I* am the cause of your danger?"

"Yes."

"Then I will not go—rather will I suffer imprisonment and what may come—what must come—after imprisonment if once the door of a jail turns upon me. Rather will I run that risk than place one of my mother's sex in danger—although quite inadvertently—and then leave her to battle alone with her danger."

"Leave me—'tis the only way in which you can help me. Hark! Do you not hear a footstep?"

"No."

"He has gone to seek you."

"Ha, you fear a man?"

"Yes—and a jealous man."

"He is—is what to you, dear lady?"

"He is——Nay, I dare not say—dare not, here in this palace!"

"Why is he jealous of me?"

"You dropped your glove in escaping."

"Ha! and he has found it?"

"Yes, and seeks in the room itself your presence."

"Then I *will* remain!"

"I pray you, go! It may cost you your life!"

"'Tis of less value than mine honour."

"For *my* sake go!"

"I will."

And again he flung himself upon his knees.

A white, angry-faced man, standing with the raised door-curtain of one of the doors in his hand, heard those words—saw that action.

(*To be continued in our next.*)

EXECUTION OF A BANDIT IN CORSICA, AND HOW AN ENGLISHMAN WOOED AND WON A LOVER OF BRIGANDS.

——o——

THE Place San Nicolao, the grand promenade of the Bastinese, assumed a strange and busy scene on a splendid morning some few years ago.

A bandit was to be executed.

The executioners were busy erecting the machinery of death —the fatal guillotine.

A body of carabineers were stationed ready to protect the executioners in case of any revolt amongst the crowd that hovered round the spot, conversing in low and murmuring tones, as every now and then they glanced at the preparations going on to launch into eternity one of their country-men.

Seated on a block of wood near the dread instrument of death was a beautiful young woman, her long, silken tresses of raven black hair flowing over her white and well-shaped shoulders. With a wild, dazed look she watched the workmen as they silently pursued their grave occupation.

"Why so sad, my fair daughter of the sunny south?" exclaimed an Englishman, as he contemplated the young being before him.

Startled from her reverie, the young Italian looked up in the face of the speaker with surprise. Observing the stranger's eyes riveted upon her, a blush mantled to her brows as she perceived her scarf had fallen from her shoulders and left her throbbing bosom exposed. Hastily gathering her scarf around her, she arose from her seat, and would have walked away had not the stranger detained her.

"I beg you will not depart, fair lady, without deigning me a reply. On my honour! I meant no offence. My heart felt sympathy for your grief, and my lips could not be silent. I am an Englishman and a stranger in this country, but if the son of one nation can befriend the daughter of another, it is his duty; for are we not all brothers and sisters in this world of many tongues?"

The Englishman's words, spoken so feelingly, made a deep impression upon the Italian, and, touching the tender chord within her heart, stretched to its utter tension until now, caused her to burst into a flood of tears.

The uncontrolled grief of the Italian, and the distinguished appearance of the Englishman by her side, attracted the attention of some women, sailors, and workmen, who, up to this time, had been lounging about on the quay, smoking their little chalk pipes, and forming quite a picturesque group with their brown jackets hanging half on and off, their broad breasts bare, and red handkerchiefs negligently twisted round their necks.

To be surrounded by such a company was not in accordance with the Englishman's notions of reserve, and caused his fair companion to tremble with emotion.

Gazing upon the numerous inquiring faces intently watching him, the Englishman exclaimed:

"My worthy friends, this young lady would thank you all to disperse, as she would wish to explain to me the cause of her grief, in which I feel deep interest."

"Cause of her grief!" cried one of the women spectators, her eyes flashing forth fire of jealous hate. "Why, it is through love for Bracciamozzo, the bandit that is to be beheaded this day; but of what use is all her sorrow?—he loved her not. I was his idol, and I glory in the love of such a hero."

As the woman was speaking, a deathly pallor overspread the countenance of the young Italian; she trembled violently, and, clinging to the Englishman's arm for support, said in notes of sad and silvery sweetness:

"Senor stranger, for mercy protect and lead me from this crowd!"

A feeling of delight thrilled through the Englishman's breast upon being thus appealed to by the fair form by his side.

Placing his left arm tenderly around her waist, politely lifting his cap and bowing to the spectators, he addressed them in their native language.

"Fair daughters and brave sons of Italy, so renowned for heroism and noble deeds, permit me to escort this trembling maiden to her father's home!"

These words and the gracious manner in which they were spoken created a feeling of respect in the crowd, and the Englishman and his companion left the quay unmolested.

When they had proceeded some distance from the promenade they entered an olive grove, where the Italian withdrew her arm from that of the Englishman's, and seating herself upon a bank, said:

"Senor, I thank thee from my heart—a heart almost crushed and dead, as memory recalls the bright and sunny past so overloaded and darkened by the present and the future—oh! mercy—mercy, the future is still more terrible!"

"Speak not thus sadly; you so young, so free from all appearance of guile, will surely recover the shock that now so overwhelms you with a grief out of sympathy I fain would know!"

"Painful as the task is, still, senor, for the kindness you have shown me, I will briefly tell you the cause of my sorrow."

Seating himself by her side, the Englishman listened attentively to her simple narrative.

"I am the only daughter of humble but respected peasants. Being left much to myself, I grew up with wild and romantic notions of brigands, whose deeds of daring I had often listened to with rapture, as the minstrels would relate them with all the impetuous ardour of my countrymen. Filled with admiration for the brigands, I sighed to be the wife of one, and with delight would picture to myself the life in the mountain fastnesses, dreaded by the wicked rich and tenderly loved by the poor and weak—whom noble brigands especially protect."

"My fair friend, methinks you formed a wrong estimate of the said brigands," said the Englishman.

"Alas, to my sorrow, yes," she replied. "For now in six short months my dream of pride and joy, and my love, like a bud rudely snatched from its stem, are cast to the ground withered and dead."

The hum of many voices was now borne towards them, and a visible shudder ran through the Italian's frame.

"Mercy!" she exclaimed, "it is the procession. Farewell Bracciamozzo—farewell! May the saints look with pity upon thee, for though you never knew my love for thee, still you were the idol of my thoughts by day and sweet companion of my dreams in slumber!"

Burying her face in her hands, she remained silent and absorbed in grief.

The Englishman, respecting her sorrow, stepped aside, and as he looked forth, a singular spectacle met his view.

A troop of gendarmes were proceeding towards the quay. Amongst them he perceived a singularly handsome young man with bronzed features, curly black hair, and a face pale as death, made more conspicuous by a fine dark moustache.

His eye, like that of tiger's when the thirst for blood was coursing through his veins, was calm and still. Behind his back his left arm was bound; the right was broken off near the shoulder. His bearing was upright, and he walked firmly. Several monks, called the "Brothers of Death," in hooded capotes, leaving nothing but their eyes free, gleaming spectrally out through the little opening, were muttering in hollow tones to themselves.

A priest stood on each side of him—one holding a large crucifix before him. A black coffin, with death's head and cross rudely painted in white, came last. Slowly this strange and ghastly procession moved along.

The young Italian during this time remained sitting with her head covered over with a handkerchief.

Curiosity upon the Englishman's part caused him to inquire of an Italian sailor the meaning of this procession.

"The young man you saw between the priests was Vecchio Bracciamozzo, the bandit, going to be executed for killing Malaspina, the physician," replied the man, with a nonchalant air.

"Vecchio! Why call him so, for that means the old one, whereas he was young?" said the Englishman.

"True, senor; but though Bracciamozzo was young in years, he was old in dealing death, for he had killed ten men!" exclaimed the Italian, with evident admiration.

In Corsica, nobody despises the bandit; the people look upon him in the light of an avenger for some personal family injury—the origin of bandit life arising from the ancient custom of the vendetta—that is, the exacting of blood for blood.

"Tell me, man," said the Englishman, "had the bandit now preparing for execution any family wrong to avenge?"

"No," answered the Italian, "Bracciamozzo had no family wrong to avenge; but during the time when the celebrated Massoni was at the height of his fame, and the idol of the peasantry for the daring deeds he had done and the dire vengeance he had inflicted upon those who had insulted a relation of his, the young Bracciamozzo conveyed to him the means of subsistence when he was hiding from the sbirri in the mountains. During these visits he became so intoxicated with Massoni's adventures that, out of mere caprice, he shot a man, took to the bush, and became a bandit; and never was there a more daring one—he would fight like a tiger. When the sbirri sought him for this last act, he bravely defended himself, and it was not until they had shot his arm off that he could be taken. Ah, me! he was a brave fellow, and only twenty-three years old. Had he lived, what deeds he might have done! But I must hasten on, senor, for I would not lose the sight of seeing such a hero die for the best barretto in Corsica."

Bowing to the Englishman, for politeness is universal to the Corsican, he hastened after the funeral procession.

The Englishman returned to his fair companion, and gently touching her shoulder, said:

"The road is now clear of all persons; shall we proceed to your home?"

"Home!" she cried, "to meet the angry glances of my friends, and the upbraidings of my parents, from whom I fled this morning, heedless of their entreaty and request, to the grand promenade, there to gaze, for the last time, upon the loved features of my brigand lover! No, no, I cannot bear it."

"Surely they will have pity on you, and forgive the passion that had taken possession of your mind—a passion arising from the light in which a bandit's life is held amongst your own people. Come, let me be your mediator."

For some time she appeared irresolute, but at last yielded to the Englishman's request.

On their way to her peasant-home, they spoke but little. A feeling of pitying love took possession of the Englishman's breast for the light and beautiful being by his side.

"Why not?" he murmured to himself. "She is but a child, and this fleeting passion—more romantic than real—will pass away, and in another country, surrounded by fresh scenes, she may forget the past, and learn to love me, purely and honestly for myself alone."

With these thoughts in his mind, they arrived at a pretty cottage.

As they approached the door, an elderly man and woman came towards them.

"Beatrice, poor child!" exclaimed the woman, as she clasped the almost fainting form of the young Italian to her heart. "We thank the Saints that you have returned."

Then, gently disengaging herself from her daughter's embrace, she curtseyed to the stranger, and continued :

" Accept a mother's prayers for protecting our child from harm this day."

" And a father's, too, noble stranger," added the old man, as he fondly kissed his daughter, " for we have heard of your kind attentions to our child ! Step inside, sir, I pray you, and honour me by taking a cup of wine."

" Cheerfully, my good friend," answered the Englishman; " and, if I might crave a favour, I would ask permission for the fair Beatrice to join, for, however bright and sparkling the wine, its charm is doubly enhanced when partaken of in the company of youth and beauty."

" Your gallantry is only equalled by your kindness, senor, and, having returned our daughter to us, with gratitude we grant the boon you ask. Beatrice, my child, hasten in with thy mother; the senor and myself will follow."

The peasant and the Englishman viewed for a few minutes the beautiful scenery that surrounded them, then entered the cottage, and found Beatrice and her mother, who had in the meantime spread a light repast for them.

(To be concluded in our next.)

RED GAUNTLET, THE BANDIT; OR, THE BLACK MOUNTAINEERS.

----o----

CHAPTER XXVIII. *(Continued.)*

" HELP—ho !" shouted Dick Nicholson. " Something with which to batter down this door."

A huge form rushed past him.

It was Jack, with his big arms bare, wielding an iron bar much bigger than the one with which the bandit had slain De Marcosi.

" Here we are !" said Jack. And, swung by his mighty arm, the ponderous bar went crash against the door.

Broken like a bandbox by the single blow, the last entrance yielded.

" Now," shouted Jack, " in we go !"

Then he recoiled.

The devilish laugh he heard, the appalling sight he saw, chilled him as it chilled Dick Nicholson.

When the broken door went down in splinters, it disclosed a red chaos behind—a fiery pile—a funereal pyre—on the summit of which stood Doctor Montena with Lulalu in his arms and a dagger in his hand.

The dagger was at her breast; a thin streak of blood trickling down its whiteness showed that in his deadly purpose he was desperate.

" Devil !" shrieked Dick—" let her go ! "

" Ha, ha, to death, or with me—Doctor Montena has sworn !"

" Then he dies a liar !" said Jack, and the iron bar, sent with terrific force and deadly aim, went from his hand.

Swift as a thunderbolt it whizzed on its way, and the point, striking Montena's forehead, dashed completely through his skull, literally impaling bone and brain.

His short, wild shriek of pain was like that of a dying tiger. A black cloud of smoke shot from the lurid pyre as he fell dead into its depths with Dorolie.

The brave Jack sprang forward, but the foot of Love was quicker, and instantly the pale face of Dick shone through the glare of flame and fire. He was in its very midst !

But he found Dorolie locked so tightly in Montena's clasp that it needed all his strength to break the death-clutch. Then, as though she were no weight, he leaped with her from the hideous vortex.

" Hurrah !" shouted Jack. The thoughtful fellow had run for a bucket of water. " Let's put you out ! Away, there !—escape ! The convent is on fire !"

He dashed the water over the burning garments of Dick and Dorolie as a crowd of terrified girls burst from their cells.

The fight was over—the terrible approach of something more dread than human foes had stopped hostilities.

" Beat back the brigand monks, but save the women !" shouted Red Gauntlet. " I have warned—now I strike ! Death to the brigand monks !"

He was obeyed. His Black Mountaineers drove back the cloaked bandits of the Chateau, but the women were taken out alive.

All but the Abbess. She loved Doctor Montena, and would not go without him.

Jack tried to save her. She broke from him, and ran to where she had seen the doctor disappear—his form lay in the yet burning pyre.

" Don't, mum—don't !" said Jack. " It's the wrong thing to do !"

With a wild, shrieking laugh, she dashed the broken door to in his face. He heard the crash of the falling pyre as her weight descended upon it.

The fight was over—the convent was in flames. To have followed the fated woman would have been madness, and Jack turned to escape with the rest.

The monks were driven back, to die the doom they so richly merited.

Red Gauntlet with Lulalu, Dick Nicholson with Dorolie, and the rest, escaped.

The convent burned till not a trace of its dark existence remained.

Outside the burning walls a party of the King's guard, with the King himself at their head, were mustered.

Waiting for Red Gauntlet.

He saw the King and heard the cry :

" The bandit—the bandit !"

" Here !" he said, going forward, and he put the Masonic ring into his Majesty's hand.

The King knew the token.

" Ho !" he said—" what would you ?"

" Your pardon."

" For what ?—for whom ?"

" Red Gauntlet !"

" Why," said the King " since I promised, I must keep my word. But you will promise in return——"

" What ?"

" To be a bandit no longer."

" I have already promised that," replied Leon, " to my brother, to my friends, to my bride, and to my King."

" Then go !" said the King. " I can retire with my guard, and may Italy never know a worse outlaw than Red Gauntlet."

" It was for Italy," the bandit said, " that I became a brigand. I have been faithful to my country and its monarch."

" So you have," said the King, and he rode away.

Red Gauntlet was pardoned.

In the great world of London, in the very centre of its beauty and its fashion, may be seen a fine, dark gentleman, with a gentle wife and a fine, lovely child. He is known as Lord Linn, brother to the Marquis of Leith, and few who see him would suspect that he was the recent terror of Italy—Red Gauntlet.

St. George is very happy with Nicola, and Marriott with Sibyl. Even the major-general softens when a little grandson pulls his white whiskers, and thanks his lucky stars that his white whiskers are not pulled by a juvenile Tikeypoodle.

These strange adventures would never have been told but for the kindness of the gentlemen who have subscribed their names.

The story is their own, though we have told it for them, and we now express our grateful sense of the deep obligation under which we are to the reader, and to

" Oliver St. George,"
" Cecil Viscount Marriott,"
" Dick Nicholson,"
" Stuart Linn, Marquis of Leith,"
And
" Lord Leon Linn," some time
" RED GAUNTLET, THE BANDIT."

[THE END.]

TALES OF BRIGANDS

AND ROBBERS.

I Warn & Strike

[LORD KYLO SMEDLEIGH IS SHOT IN ESCAPING FROM THE RED HOUSE.]

THE RED DWARF.

CHAPTER II.

A BOAT FROM SHORE.—THE RED HOUSE IN WHITEFRIARS.—CLAUDE DUVAL IN THE TIGER'S DEN.—THE ALSATIAN.—THE SPY.—A SNARE.—THE HANDKERCHIEF.—"WHO GOES THERE?"—THE FALSE PASSWORD.—THE SHOT.—A DOOM OF DEATH.—"HOLD, HOLD, FOR YOUR LIVES!"—A FRIEND.—THE WORD IN TIME.—RED DWARF THE ROBBER.

THE cry was heard.

Yet, though by this time there were many spectators gathered on the banks, watching the extraordinary scene, not one ventured forth to save the drowning man, until a slight, well-built youth, with a bold, brilliant eye and dauntless aspect, stepped forward.

"There is a cry of rescue," he said, with a faint female accent in his tone—"a fellow creature drowning! Who is with me to give aid?"

An irresolute, hesitative pause of silence followed.

"Why, truly, a brave set!" and the boy's lip curled in scorn. "Art afraid of the Black Colonel and his den of death—the Red House yonder? Why, were he ten times black, I would save his victim in his very teeth!"

And all gallantly dressed as he was—booted, spurred, and brave in rich lace and richer velvet—he dashed into the water and waded to one of the boats yet drifting out.

Without waiting to ask again for some one to accompany him, the boy took the oars and rowed like an aquatic athlete.

"He will come back slower than he went, and he take to interfering with the Black Colonel," muttered one bystander, whose chief characteristics were swarthiness and dirt. "Many a braver cub lies rotting in the river's slime for daring less."

With which cheerful observation he pulled his huge slouched hat over his shaggy brow, and turned aside to watch the boy's progress.

Few men of mature age could have been so prompt and cool.

He saw at a glance that to attempt to get Allan Buckhurst into the boat without help would be an impossible task.

So he did not wait to try.

His boat shot like an arrow past the white face and nerveless form rocking slowly with the sluggish heaving of the waves.

Then he reached Silver Jack.

"In!" he said, steadying the boat, as Jack, needing no second invitation, clambered dexterously over the side. "And no words now. Keep your thanks till your friend is saved."

"Brave youth!"

"Tush! Be careful how you lift him in, or the double weight will overtax my strength. Fortunately the rowlocks are good and will bear the pressure."

He drew the oars in deep, and held a back-water stroke against the current with all his might.

This kept the boat quite still while Silver Jack lifted Allan in.

"Is he hurt much?" said the boy.

"Not much lasting injury, I hope, but badly for the time."

"See—he recovers already! We make a wet crew, and no merry one. What is the cause, good masters?"

"You saw it from the shore."

"The latter part only—the ending of the fight, and disappearance of the Black Colonel. What mischief has he now afoot?"

"The worst. He and the felon courtier with him have carried a lady from her home."

"Against her will?"

"By treachery."

"Shame on their cowardice! The fair that cannot be fairly won is better let alone. This gentleman?"

"Is her lover."

"I think I know his face."

"His name is Allan Buckhurst."

"Ay, then do I know him. Master Allan, a loyal son of a disloyal father. Who is the lady?"

"Madaline Catemass."

"She—the witching, golden-haired one for whom the silken Buckingham sighs in vain, and our jovial King himself looks longing at? St. Paul, but there will be mischief! Why, his Majesty would rather give his right hand than offend Sir Stuart Catemass."

"Are you at Court?"

"I am his Grace of Buckingham's page. My name is Claude Duval. Yours?"

"Captain Blake."

"A tale, that, for the ancient marines," laughed the duke's page. "I have free entrée to the Precincts, and in Alsatia's Sanctuary have seen a gallant whom some call Silver Jack. Ha!"

"Why, lad, you are right; and, since you know me, we can trust each other."

"And help each other. I am a boy, but my hand has felt a sword-hilt. The lady must be rescued."

"As, with your aid, she may be. Hear you that, Master Buckhurst? Here is another friend—a true one, for he saved your life, and now promises to assist in the rescue. How goes it with you?"

"Better, good and true companion—much better! My head swims yet, but my scattered senses are coming back."

He rose to a sitting position, and warmly thanked the page.

"Now," said the boy, "if out of my young head you will take counsel, you will find it good. The lady is in the Red House."

"The Black Colonel's fearful abode!" shuddered Allan. "Then she is lost indeed!"

"Fear not. We shall soon be on the track. Misfortune throws us into strange company,—so sayeth the proverb, and it is truth with you. Here are—a—a Captain Blake and a graceless page ready for adventure. I am not unknown in the Sanctuary, and the captain is no novice. Trust me, we shall save her yet."

"Could I but hope so!"

"Could you doubt?" said the boy. "See—we are at the back of Whitefriars, and we can enter. By the fairest lady in the Court—and she shall be nameless yet—I am like a water-rat—wet! Some fighting would make me dry."

He seemed to enter into the spirit of the adventure as much out of some reckless devilry of nature as out of native chivalry.

By this time they had reached a place where the dark shadow of Whitefriars threw its gloom upon the Thames. Duval sprang out first, regardless of his handsome boots, which sank knee-deep into the mud.

The others followed.

They had to traverse a narrow way, down which a safe passage was a matter of extreme doubt.

The inhabitants of Alsatia were of a character that rendered seclusion a necessary, and every outlet and inlet was guarded well.

So well, that before our three adventurers had proceeded far, the dark way was darkened still more by a burly form, and a voice came, saying:

"Who comes?"

"River rats," said the page, promptly, "with venom in their teeth! Who keeps the way?"

A hoarse laugh and the ominous click of a pistol preceded the answer.

"A ratcatcher?—so!"

The "so." was followed by a cry of agony, and the bullet intended for the page's head went harmlessly into air.

The ratcatcher fell.

Blood bubbling from his lungs.

"What is done?" asked Allan, quickly.

"Nothing, more than my sword is soiled! Pho!—the carrion has a bad odour!"

The page sheathed his sword.

He had run the Alsatian through.

"You have killed him!" said Silver Jack.

"I think so," the boy said, coolly; "my weapon is sharp, and the hilt stopped against his button. His own fault. He should have recognised the password!"

"Cool!" thought Silver Jack. "If he begins like this, we shall hear more of him anon."

Then he drew his sword, as did Allan Buckhurst. The cry given by the dying ruffian had been heard, and the gleam of coming torches told the three adventurers that others of the fraternity were not far away.

"We must run for it," said the page—"once in the Tiger's Den, we are safe."

"The Tiger's Den?"

"Ay—a place by no means new to you, Captain Blake; and, if report says truly, a rendezvous for strange people."

"What people, Sir Duval?"

"I' faith!" laughed the boy—"knights unchartered by the King, but familiar to the road—gentlemen of mysterious means, gained, as the malignant would assert, by desperate work. One thing is certain, HE has been seen there."

"He!—who?"

"Red Dwarf."

"Ha! Red Dwarf?"

"The night terror—the mystery—the demon himself, if hearsay may be believed."

The face of Silver Jack underwent a change.

"Is he feared, then?"

"Is he feared? Sweet innocent! What man is there but would not shun the road did he think to meet the monster?"

"Is it a truth, then," asked Buckhurst, "that this thing of dread haunts the waysides of our land—he whose deeds are said to be so terrible?"

"Who says so lies!" said the boy, warmly. "Red Dwarf is no cowardly slayer of his kind—no creeping, crouching plunderer who hides in the dark to strike his prey behind! I met him once."

"You?"

"Not long since, Captain Blake."

"When?—where?"

"Not long since, captain, as I said; but the story is for another time. The present hour is one when 'tis valour to use the heels and save our swords till wanted. Here are the torches and their bearers. Come!"

He led the way down a turn more narrow and darker than the first, as a crowd of ruffians, bearing lights and naked weapons, made for the spot where lay their slain companion.

"How the brutes howl!" said the page, listening to the cries of rage that followed the discovery of the body. "Presently they will be after us!"

This was true.

The footsteps of the three adventurers were deeply marked in the mud.

Some rapid tramping and savage oaths sounding close behind told the fugitives they were being pursued.

They came quickly; but the boy and his companions knew the way well. At least, the boy and Silver Jack did. Allan followed, trusting all to them.

He only thought of one thing—the rescue of Madaline.

Keeping the distance in advance they had gained by the delay made while the ruffians were howling over their fallen comrade, the three adventurers dashed into a tavern of forbidding aspect.

A stranger would have hesitated before entering. Claude Duval and Silver Jack were known there.

Silver Jack especially. He was one of the most remarkable highwaymen in Charles the Second's time.

His adventures on the road, at home and abroad, while following the fortunes of Madaline and her lover, have yet to come.

They dashed into the tavern.

Somebody who stood in the way went with a smash against somebody else. Both, getting up, swore vigorously.

When his companions had entered, the page shut and barred the door.

"What, my merry comrades!" laughed the page, as the two gentlemen who had been overthrown grasped their swords menacingly—"using profane language and emptying scabbards for me? Nay!"

"Our wine is spilled!" grumbled one; but he let his sword drop back.

So did the other.

The Duke of Buckingham's fearless page was a favourite—and with good cause.

Never a rusty throat went thirsty during the time of his visit.

"Your wine is spilled? Well, have some more. What a row there is outside!"

There was indeed.

The comrades of the man found dead were battering at the door, eager for revenge.

The man who stood behind the bar—a giant stunted in his growth, and broken into a huge, misshapen dwarf—paused in retailing liquors to his thirsty customers, and asked:

"What's the matter?"

"Nothing," said the boy; "only some fellow—one of the Black Colonel's men, I think—would not let me pass through. I gave him the password——"

"Well?"

"He got in the way of my sword, and it went through him—that is all!"

"Who is your companion?"

He pointed to Allan Buckhurst.

"One for whom I can answer," said Silver Jack.

"Good!—come in here."

The dwarf beckoned them into a room behind the bar.

They entered.

"One of the colonel's men?" the giant dwarf said; "and other of the colonel's men wanting to come in? Well, we will see them!"

This with a grim smile.

He took a ponderous battle-axe—keen and sharp like a razor at the edge—and went to the door.

He opened it.

He had a magnificent voice—this giant dwarf—and a noble face, with large black eyes like smouldering fire. Had he not been so misshapen, he would, in limb, and body, and in beauty, altogether have been an herculean Apollo.

He was known as "The Tiger."

Because he was so terrible when roused—because his wrath was so full of terror to its cause—his strength so mighty and destructive.

So now, when he went to the door, even his crew of ruffian customers left their liquor, and waited, with bated breath, to see what was to come.

A pause at first.

He stood by the open door, and in the opening a crew of evil faces, all eager to rush in for their prey till they saw the dwarf standing quietly there resting on his gleaming axe.

"What do you want?" he asked.

His voice was like subdued thunder.

None of the ruffians, who had been so eager, found courage to reply.

Only one man, extremely behind the rest, said:

"He who killed our comrade!"

"Why did he kill your comrade?"

The dead man had not told them. So that little circumstance remained unknown.

And no one answered till the same man, yet more extremely in the rear, said:

"The slayer and his friends are in here."

"Well?"

"We want them."

"Come in and take them, then," the dwarf said, quietly—"there is not much in the way."

Not much! Only that powerful form, like a crouching tiger, and the heavy axe, with which he could cut a man in twain at a blow.

"Come in," he repeated, with grim irony. "There are the gentlemen who slew your comrade."

He pointed with his left hand to Silver Jack and Allan Buckhurst, who stood with the gallant page not far from the door.

The Alsatians declined to enter.

"They are ungracious," said Claude, "not to accept this cordial invitation."

"I think them wise," said Silver Jack.

Allan Buckhurst said nothing. He had caught sight of a man at the door, and wrapped round the man's hand there was a blood-stained handkerchief.

It was not the blood that attracted Allan's attention—it was a crest and two initials in the corner.

Buckhurst gave a cry, and leaped past the Tiger.

"Madaline's kerchief!" he said. "Ho! stay him there!—the man with the wounded hand!"

But the man was gone. Allan, impetuous and brave, would have followed.

The Tiger held him back.

"'Twas the Black Colonel," he said, lowly, "or some one sent by him. A ruse—a snare—to lure you on to sure destruction."

"But Madaline?"

"Shall be saved. Come back with me."

With an easy effort of his giant strength, he drew the young cavalier from the entrance. Then he closed the door.

None of the mob who had been so eager tried to open it. There was a chance that the first one who went in might get hurt.

The dwarf led the three adventurers to a private room.

"Now listen," he said. "I like brave men, and I would serve you. To prove this, I will show you how to reach the Red House."

"But Madaline? She is in momentary danger."

"In a few minutes you can be with her. Look!"

He pulled aside the carpet, and disclosed a trap-door. This he raised.

"That is a secret way to the Red House—a subterranean way hitherto known only to myself. Go cautiously—be on the alert, and have no fear. The mysteries of the Red House are not mysteries to me. Men call this a tiger's den; that is a lair of bloodthirsty wolves. But there—good swordsmen can take care of each other. Should you need more assistance, use this."

He placed a silver whistle in Allan's hand.

"Your generous interest in my cause is kind."

"'Tis not," said the dwarf, with a singular smile—"I shall ask requital soon. I want a promise now."

"A promise?"

"A sacred oath. If, through me, you save your mistress, swear that you, in return, will do anything I ask."

"I swear!"

"Pause before you take the oath—I may ask too much."

"No—were it my life! Let me save her!"

"Go, then!—here is a lantern. At the end of the first flight of steps you will find a passage—at the end of that there is a vault. The doors will be open as you descend; but you must pause on the third stair, which revolves on pressure from the front. Turn it three times—that will open the doors."

Allan and his companions listened with deep attention.

"Scan the cellar walls carefully. You will find a brick in which a small piece of granite seems to have been left during process of making. Press the piece of granite hard with your thumb, and the back of the vault will open. Then you will find another vault. But do not stay to look at what you see. Touch nothing—say nothing while there. Walk through to the wall at the end. Tap seven times, and an opening will disclose to you a passage. Proceed along that, and you will find yourself in the Red House."

"Thanks! If I save Madaline, I shall not forget you!"

"You will not," said the dwarf, with a significance that made Allan's blood run for a moment cold. "That you will save her is a matter of no doubt. The room in which she will be confined is the second one above the water. You might reach it from the Thames had you a cat-like way of climbing, but you would not descend alive. One of the Black Colonel's men is lying in a boat in the water-gate, waiting to shoot anyone who may go up or come down."

"Then we will not try that way," said Claude. "Come, Captain Blake, and you, Sir Buckhurst, lead the way. I long to begin the adventure. It is ten to one that we shall meet some of the colonel's men on the stairs."

"Then there will be a fight," said Silver Jack.

"Which would betray all," said the dwarf. "Should you meet again, give the password."

"What is it?"

"Mystery to-night."

"Mystery to-night. I shall remember."

He had good cause to remember. The password had been given to the Tiger by one of the Black Colonel's men, who acted as spy to the terrible dwarf.

But the man, a traitor to both when it paid him, had betrayed the Tiger. He gave a false password.

Down the cavernous steps went Allan with the light, followed closely by his brave companions.

All were very careful to remember the instructions as to the secret ways.

They went safely through both vaults, but as they passed the second all shuddered.

There was indeed good need for the Tiger's caution that they should not look to see what might be seen.

Some tokens—grim, bloody, and horrible—of fearful deeds.

Allan shaded the lantern. He felt sick at heart.

"Now, caution!" he whispered, as they stood in the passage of the Red House. "Keep watch here—I will go to Madaline."

He went lightly but rapidly up the stairs—his hand ready to use sword or pistol, as occasion came.

It came soon.

Silver Jack and the page, keeping watch below, heard a cry, and following the cry a human body came tumbling downstairs.

A dead man.

Allan had given the password. The man now dead, recognising it as false, had tried to stop his way. Allan slew him.

Then in he went to the chamber where Madaline was held in captivity.

He did not stay to think. Action was all at such a time. The sounds of a struggle, and of Madaline's voice praying for mercy and for help, reached his ears.

Crash, and the door was open.

He peeped in. Saw two struggling forms—Madaline and Lord Kylo.

Allan leaped at Kylo like a leopard.

He would have brained the profligate or made a hole in his heart, but Lord Kylo, objecting to either process, let go his victim, and escaped by the window.

A rope hung there.

Allan, following to strike or shoot Smedleigh, heard a pistol-shot, a cry, and a splash.

Lord Kylo had disappeared.

The Alsatian set to watch in the water-gate had heard the noise of a man descending, and, obeying his orders, fired at him.

Lord Kylo sank into the dark waters of the Thames.

"Madaline—Madaline!" said Allan. "Dearest, you are saved!"

She ran to him with a sob of joy.

He had spoken too soon.

There came the sound of a desperate conflict on the stairs, where Silver Jack, having been attacked by the colonel's men, was doing gallant work, but could not do enough to stay the entire gang, some of whom swarmed like wild cats up the stairs.

The Black Colonel came first.

"Bring out the girl!" he said, sternly. The intruders *kill*!"

He himself tore Madaline from Buckhurst, and his bravoes set upon the youth.

Brave as Allan was, he stood no chance against a score of deadly knives, but he fought madly for liberty and Madaline.

He must have died,—he was stricken to the floor, and a ruffian was kneeling to slay him, when an awful voice rang out the words:

"Hold—hold, for your lives!" and an awful form leaped into the room.

Even the Black Colonel recoiled in terror, as his men, retreating back, exclaimed, with quaking hearts:

"THE RED DWARF!"

(To be continued in our next.)

EXECUTION OF A BANDIT IN CORSICA, AND HOW AN ENGLISHMAN WOOED AND WON A LOVER OF BRIGANDS.

(Concluded.)

BEATRICE, nervous and agitated from the scenes of the morning, merely sipped a glass of wine with the stranger, thanked him in a trembling voice for his kindness to her, bade him farewell with a blush, and retired from the room with her mother.

"A good gentleman, and a handsome one too," said the old lady as she led Beatrice to an inner room. "Would that you had seen him earlier. But there—there," she continued, as she saw her daughter's flushed face, "your father and I have determined never to mention the past, and hope you will endeavour to forget the dream of youthful passion."

"Never, whilst I am in this spot, mother. Can you not send me away—anywhere, so that I escape the scenes so painful to my memory?"

"Though our means are scanty, still will we do our best to engage your mind with other objects, so that we may restore peace to your mind!"

Whilst the mother of Beatrice was planning how to send her daughter away for a time, the Englishman was in deep conversation with her father.

"My meeting with your daughter this morning," said the Englishman, "was purely accidental; but it has left an impression upon my mind that will never be obliterated, and given rise to an idea that, with your permission, I would cheerfully carry out."

"Name it, senor; and if in my power to grant your request, I shall do so with pleasure."

"For years past I, like your daughter, have been in love with an ideal being—a creation of my mind. For the purpose of finding the real of my ideal, I have travelled round the world in vain until this morning, when I beheld your daughter, in whom, through her sad but sweet melancholy, created by a highly-sensitive and romantic mind, I immediately recognised the being I could love. 'Tis strange, but life itself is strange. Having ample means at my disposal, I would wish you to place her in a convent for one year, where she could receive the best education possible; at the end of that year I would return, when, if she was thoroughly free from the influence of her fancied love, and no other passion had taken possession of her heart, and she would return the love I entertain for her, I would marry her and introduce her to the nobility of England."

"Senor, you surprise me," exclaimed the peasant; "knowing the fatal passion of my child and her humble origin—to make me such an offer is beyond my conception."

"Still 'tis true, and on the word and honour of a gentleman I am willing to pay every expense, leaving it to you to carry out my views without mentioning to your daughter my intentions. No, leave her heart free. Did she know what I was doing, gratitude might tell her she ought to love, and this I do not wish."

"Senor, I will obey your instructions," responded the peasant.

"In this pocket-book," said the Englishman, "you will find sufficient to pay all demands; and now, my friend, farewell for one year, remember. But stay—in case of death, 'tis well that I should know your name."

"Nicholo Sclavoli."

"Nicholo Sclavoli, I have written in my book," said the Englishman. "Now, your address—where to send a letter, I mean?"

The peasant considered for a few moments, then replied:

"Should any accident befall you—and may the saints protect you from all harm—a message or letter would be received for me at the cloister of San Antonio. And your name, senor?"

"Remains unknown until the realization of my hopes respecting your daughter. If her answer is Yes, then you will know who I am; if No, let the past be buried in oblivion. And now, my friend, farewell! Mind, not a word to your daughter."

"Farewell, senor; your secret shall be sacred."

Leaving the cottage, the Englishman bent his steps towards the hills, and then gave way, in the sunny air and hermit loneliness, to the refreshing solitude of nature.

From this spot, so tranquil and calm, he returned in the evening to the promenade, where in the morning a brigand's blood had been shed. What a contrast was presented to his view!

Not a trace of the morning's dread work was discernible—fashionable women of Bastia, maidens and youths were promenading, laughing and chatting most gaily. The sea was beautiful and calm; the fishermen, floating in their little skiffs with twinkling lights, were singing, and the notes, borne upon the evening breeze, sounded sweetly and lent a charm to the scene.

"I almost repent me of my morning's work," said the Englishman, "for these Corsicans are but butterflies after all; but time will show the result, and to-morrow I return to England."

The parents of Beatrice, upon the departure of the Englishman, conversed together over his strange request, and decided to send away their daughter the next day.

On the following morning they acquainted Beatrice that, according to her wish for a change of scene, they had arranged for her retirement to a convent for one year.

Beatrice received this intelligence with pleasure, and in a few days entered the home of religion with a grateful heart and subdued spirit.

Twelve months soon passed away, at the expiration of which time the Englishman returned to Nicholo Sclavoli's cottage.

Nicholo Sclavoli had faithfully carried out the wishes of the Englishman, who learnt with pleasure that Beatrice was quite an altered woman, the love of learning having entirely absorbed all other feelings.

The next day, according to agreement, she returned home. The Englishman wooed, and was accepted. They were married in the church in which Beatrice had been christened. Well providing for Sclavoli and his wife, the Englishman with his bride returned to England.

They are now residing at the West-end of London; and the peasant girl—the romantic lover of Bracciamozzo, the brigand —is a welcome guest of the nobility and royalty, the secret of her history and name of the English nobleman being known only to a few.

HAWK'S EYE, THE PHANTOM ROBBER.

CHAPTER XII. (Continued.)

HAWK'S EYE kissed the unknown's hand, and was arising, when she trembled.

"Hush! Now you hear the footsteps—do you not?"

"No—he does not!"

It was the man standing in the doorway that spoke.

"Charles!" cried the wretched woman, and turning, buried her head in the chair in which she had been sitting when Hawk's Eye made his appearance.

"Who are you?" asked the stranger.

"Faith, who are you?" asked Hawk's Eye—"you who frighten a woman?"

"I do not tell who I am," said the stranger.

He was a noble-looking man, but with a fierce cast of countenance.

"Then, so far, we are of one opinion," said Hawk's Eye, "as for some time past I have had great objection to telling those I meet who I am; somehow they are amiable enough always to wish to know who I really am. I never tell them."

"Are you noble?" asked the stranger.

"Yes—in a small way."

"I see you carry a sword."

"Yes."

"Can you use it?"

"Yes—in a small way."

"Draw!"

"Pardon, I never draw a sword in a lady's presence."

The stranger turned towards Augustina, and speaking haughtily, he said:

"Leave the room!"

"No—no—no!" she cried.

"Leave the room!"

"Pardon me," said Hawk's Eye, "but are you under the impression that you are talking to a dog?"

"No—I am addressing myself to—— but it has nought to do with you who she is! Draw and defend yourself!"

"Who are you?" asked Hawk's Eye, "who violate the first rule of knighthood by calling on a man to fight before a lady?"

"Assuredly I am a greater man than you."

"Then I'm not sorry, seeing what you are capable of, that I'm a less distinguished man than yourself."

"Ha!"

The unknown's sword had leaped from its scabbard, and it would the next moment have been in Hawk's Eye's heart, had he not felt sure that whatever the title of the man before him, he was no gentleman, and would take any advantage to which he might see his way quite clearly.

Hawks Eye's sword swinged against it, however, and so far he was safe.

"Gentlemen—gentlemen," cried the Princess, "be merciful to me if not to yourselves! Let your swords part company, I pray you!"

"You hear what the lady says?" urged Hawk's Eye.

"I take no heed!" and the gentleman thrust at his opponent.

"Decidedly you are not so good a gentleman as you are a swordsman!" said Hawk's Eye, as, making a thrust, the other parried it.

Now there is no knowing how long this encounter would have lasted, for the antagonists were equal, and therefore there is no saying who would have become the victor.

But two circumstances ended the strife.

The first was an accident.

The second—no accident; but the King's very best intention.

The accident arose in this way.

The eager stranger, pressing on at Hawk's Eye, intending to drive him in a corner, fell over a hassock, and snapped his sword upon the ground.

He stood at his enemy's mercy.

"Gad, there's an end of the duel," said Hawk's Eye, "for two men can't fight with one sword, unless, indeed, I break mine, and so we carry on the pretty performance with the points for weapons!"

"Gentlemen—gentlemen," cried the Princess, "will you not comprehend that Heaven itself has stopped the duel—that it cannot continue?"

And at this point the intention quite put an end to the impending continuation of the duel, for at this moment the palace alarm bell began to peal, and the sound of the sentries calling to each other in alarm was distinctly heard.

The Princess screamed.

And as though this was the signal for what was to follow, the door was broken open, and there appeared, surrounded by guards, the King.

Before the King or his party could see what was to be seen in the room, Hawk's Eye, ever ready and alive to danger, had made up his mind what to do. He had not five seconds in which to make up his mind.

A turn—a leap—and he went crash through window and window frame, the wood and glass making a sound like the report of firearms.

He knew he was only on the first floor, and as he leaped he hoped there was grass below.

"Treason!" bellowed the King, as his Majesty heard the sound.

And then, by this time, the royal personage having become accustomed to the light of the room, for he had broken his way in from a dark passage, he saw the strange nobleman.

"So there you are, schamps!" he said, looking at the stranger.

"Do you speak to me, George Guelph?" he asked.

"Vat—you thought to tie your King up!"

"You my King? I deny you!"

"Treason—but you didn't tie your knot tight enow!"

"I tie thee, George Guelph? I would not touch thee!"

"Highty-tighty!" cried the King—"still as brave as ever!"

"As ever were my fathers!"

"Vell, vell—you're a fine man, but one finer morning you shall hang!"

A scream, and with a cry of pardon, the Princess fell at the King's feet, happily for a time unconscious of the extreme misery that surrounded her.

The King now, for the first time, saw the lady, for, as the room was burst into, she screened herself entirely from view.

"Augustina!" cried the King.

"Seize that man!" he cried.

The soldiers did so.

"Ay," replied the stranger; "but, before Heaven, you cannot truly keep the right you have stolen from me!"

"Stolen—I—the King? Who are you?"

"I am——"

The stranger stopped.

"Well?" asked the King.

No reply.

"Take him to prison—to prison with him!" cried the King.

"Ay, but thou canst not imprison my soul, usurper!" cried the stranger.

And as the soldiers approached him he struck them back.

Then he led his captors from the room.

He was a prisoner, but he looked like a conqueror.

When he was gone, the King suddenly started.

"Blessed St. George!" he suddenly cried. "'Tis—'tis——"

Then he stopped.

"Fetch me some brandy!" he said to one of those near him.

But before he could get it he sat down.

And, truth to say, before it came his Majesty had fairly fainted away.

CHAPTER XIII.

HOW HAWK'S EYE ESCAPED.—BACK AT THE ANCHOR OF SAFETY.— AN ARRIVAL IN TIME.

THE reader will now be amiable enough once more to come back to the Anchor of Safety, which we left at the moment at which old Schwincks—having looked at the pass amulet that had been picked from the floor, and where it must have fallen from the hand or pocket of the sleeping Albert—called out: "Stop the machinery!"

It was at this moment that the angel—the beauty—the perfect one of all her sex (need it be said we refer to Schwincks's most beauteous daughter?)—came to herself, with a frightful gurgle, and said:

"Where is he? where am I? Who is he? who am I? And where are we now?"

We were directly in a mess, for so excitable were the feelings of the blessed old Schwincks, that, at a blow, he wasted two quarts of beer in a gallon can all over her lovely shape.

This little bit of treatment brought her round wonderfully.

"I'm better now!" she said.

Which information her amiable pa immediately responded to with a huge bottle.

Had it hit her, she would unquestionably have been worse again, poor dear.

Meanwhile, the men had rushed to the bed-room to which old Schwincks had consigned Albert Falconer; and there arriving, they uttered a combined token of regret, for the machinery had done its work.

And now it is necessary to explain this extraordinary bedstead.

The Anchor of Safety, you must know, was built of wood, was very shallow, and had no back premises, so to speak, for the simple reason that the river was on one side, and the street on the other.

Now, wood will carry sound very rapidly; and if you are just outside a wooden house, and somebody screams inside it, or calls for help, hear it you are bound to.

So at that rascally place of entertainment—where, for " so much," they would as soon knock you over an enemy, or knock you over for him, as draw either of you a mug of ale—they had one or two mild ways of quietly disposing of an unwelcome guest, or a guest who was sent in order to be disposed of.

If the victim would not go to bed, he was just drugged, and then sat down upon. This was a very convenient way of disposing of the poor fellow, because there was no blood to show what had happened.

Old Schwincks, who had certainly never been born to be drowned, was much too clever an old rascal for any mistake of that sort. Old Schwincks would say: "Let us have not never by no means never no *blood!*" And so, if the gentleman could not, or would not, go to bed, he was sat down upon, when he hadn't the least chance of crying out, and was disposed of comfortably.

However, Schwincks did not look upon a victim in the light of a gentleman if he would not go to bed and be killed comfortably.

It was much better to go to bed.

The bedstead of destruction was a heavy oak one, with four curious, ridged bedposts.

The machinery was as follows.

All of a sudden the centre of the bed collapsed, sank down, covered up the individual upon each side, and quietly smothered him.

This done, he was packed in a huge box, with shot or heavy stones, and in full and broad daylight he was shipped on board a barge from the wharf next to the Anchor of Safety, and carried down the river, where the cargo was pitched out, the weight of the stones or shot in the box sinking it for ever in the ooze and slimy clinging mud which forms the bottom of our river Thames.

Such was old Schwincks's chamber of state, and a very pretty chamber it was.

As the reader knows, the machinery had worked when the men rushed into the room.

Fortunately, one of them knew the counter-operation, and worked the treacherous bedstead into the semblance of an honest four-poster.

There he lay upon his bed, dark and convulsed in the face. Albert showed no evidence of life.

As far as he was concerned, death had done its worst.

They brought him into the great room, and laid him down before the fire that was burning.

And now the angelic one, getting over the agony of the bottle, which had caught her on the funny bone, and had apparently, as far as she was able to judge, made her poor arm sing—the Cherub rushed forward, and bursting into tears, gave the still form one kiss on the forehead—murmured "I am a widow once more!"—and then, with all the goodness of heart that she really possessed, although she had been brought up in such a place, surrounded by such people, and was the daughter of such a father—she must have got her goodness from her mother,—she proceeded to "fetch the martyr to," as she called it.

But the solemnity of his face did not change,—it was as still as though it meant to go with that awful expression on it to the day of judgment.

All was useless.

"Dead, mein Got!" exclaimed Schwincks—"dead as Pharey after he'd been at de bottom of de Red Zee for six weeks! And what, mein precious life, sall de captain say?"

As though in answer to the inquiry, there was a summons at the door.

"Mein Got—*him!*"

There was no need to tell one of the men present to open the door.

Half a dozen had already done so, and there stood Hawk's Eye.

He in a moment saw what had happened.

Without a word, almost without a glance bestowed upon that rascally troupe of rascally things—for who could call them men ?—he walked rapidly to the prostrate form, looked searchingly at it, and as a gleam of hope appeared upon his face, he threw off his coat and devoted himself to the work of restoring the brother of her whom he loved with all the strength of his own life.

But before we proceed further, the reader should be informed of how Hawk's Eye happened to be there.

It cannot have lapsed from the memory of our readers that, seeing himself in danger in the palace of St. James's, when the King gave the alarm, he leaped at a window, and carried it away, frame and all.

Hawk's Eye knew that his life was forfeit if once he was taken; and, indeed, he felt pretty certain that the angry King himself might call him to account with his royal sword; therefore in a moment he came to the conclusion to dash at the window.

It was his only chance of escape, and he felt that he could but die.

One thought in his mind—May,—one name engraved upon his heart—her name in his mouth—he leaped at the window, and went crash through it.

A moment falling, and then he felt himself caught.

" A tree."

He knew it.

So far he was safe.

But the soldiery were unquestionably in search of him, and he felt that his position was very little altered for the better.

Now a diversion in his favour was created by the sudden exchange of words between the King and the gentleman whom the Princess Augustina had called Charles.

Those few moments were really his safety.

The King standing near the window, and too much astonished at the sight of this gentleman to give the grenadiers orders to fire, gave Hawk's Eye time.

The grenadiers knew their orders and duty too well to dare to pass before the sacred person of his Majesty without his Majesty's permission, and therefore they waited the word of command, during which time Hawk's Eye was effecting a comparative retreat.

There was enough light to show him that the trees swept round the whole of the garden, and he knew enough of the locality (and anyone who reads this paper may satisfy himself of the accuracy of this description, for there the palace and grounds of St. James's remain *exactly* as they existed in the time of our hero, with the exception of the cutting down of some trees)—Hawk's Eye knew enough of the locality to be sure that if he could work round to the wall which divided the palace from the Mall which lies between St. James's Park and the palace of that name, he would then be able to effect his escape.

But how was this to be done ?

He knew that if he remained in the tree he should be fired on, and he felt equally certain that if he descended either a similar fate or imprisonment awaited him.

Therefore, he slung himself from branch to branch into the next tree, and so on to the next; and it was as he found that the fourth tree was farther away than the others that the King arrived at the window.

"Vere is de blackguard?" screamed the King. "Shoot him to vite!"

His Majesty meant "bits." But though he could not speak English, he was King of Great Britain and Ireland, and at his coronation had been declared King of France, after the manner of Kings of England for hundreds of years.

At the royal command the grenadiers arrived at the window, and the next moment a dozen bullets crashed into the tree and towards the ground.

"Vere is he?—vere is dar teufel?"

His Majesty meant "devil."

Now, the teufel, having no idea of being shot down if he could conveniently help it, had, as judiciously as possible, made for the wall skirting the Mall.

But he had to *fall* from the third tree to the fourth.

He was awfully shaken—but now his danger was half over. Reaching the wall, he ran along it, and so came to the point whence the wall ran parallel with the palace.

And by this time the King, half dancing with rage and nearly dropping with fright, was yelling:

"Shtop him, der teufel! Five shillings to whoever shall shtop the rascal, who have stolen one of my jarter, worth mooch monies. Shtop him!"

It was all very well for the King to say "stop him;" but unfortunately that was not to be done, so far.

But there was one clever grenadier, and he did not remain a grenadier all his life; in fact, quite without trying to get a reward, he made enough this night to get his discharge and set up in a public-house in a small way. This grenadier, being a sharp fellow, saw that the man escaping from the palace would leap from tree to tree; and so, taking advantage of the excitement, he ran round by the east entrance, and came to the corner of the wall at which Hawk's Eye had now arrived.

"Brayvo!" said he.

For Hawk's Eye took the leap from the wall to the first row of trees in the Mall.

He caught the extreme ends of the branches of a tree. They yielded, creaked, kept him up for a moment, and then, having broke his fall, broke themselves.

However, he caught at the branches below him, and so saved himself from a fall of at least twelve feet.

And he reached the ground bruised, and for a moment overpowered to see a grenadier's musket pointed at him.

"Stop!" cried Hawk's Eye. "Don't blow my brains out while I'm on the ground—let me stand up!"

"Ha! to give you a chance—eh?"

"No! I swear I'll only leap at you if you don't shoot me —a prisoner I won't be!"

"Bah!" said the soldier—"don't be afeerd! I enlisted to fight battles, not to march fellers that can climb, and are one to all a regiment, to prison. Be orf; *I* ain't going to earn His Majesty's five shillings!"

"Do you let me go?" asked Hawk's Eye.

"Yes."

"Your hand!"

And then it was that Hawk's Eye slipped into the man's hand a jewel that he thought he never could part with.

It had been his mother's.

But his life was saved—he had nothing else, for he forgot the Order of the Garter in diamonds, and he was grateful.

"Ha! a button to remember yer by!" said the grenadier— "well, anyhow, you are a brave one, you are! Which way are you going?"

Hawk's Eye pointed to the east.

"All right! I'll fire the other way when you have turned the corner!"

Hawk's Eye had reached the corner and turned from danger as he heard the gun fired.

No one followed him, and he knew the grenadier had kept his word.

For him to get a horse in any part of London and at any time was common; and, therefore, he was soon at the Anchor of Safety, to which hostelry we will now return.

Hawk's Eye stooped rapidly by the side of the senseless Albert, and then began one of those extraordinary scenes which so few of us witness—very few. Hereby is meant the witnessing of that wondrous power some very few men have of commanding the soul and will of others.

Scarcely had Hawk's Eye been about the prostrate man three minutes than that amiable but horrid Cherub vowed that there was some colour in the poor martyred Albert's face.

She spoke the truth.

Gradually as Hawk's Eye continued his ministrations, so gradually did the colour come back into Albert's face, and exactly in proportion to the increase of colour in the prostrate man's face so the countenance of Hawk's Eye himself became livid.

Such was the curious fact.

And at last Albert's mouth quivered, and with a great sigh he was once more alive.

"He lives—he lives!" cried the Cherub, at which point of enthusiasm—which Old Schwincks, believe us, was heartily glad to witness—that low Dutch brute testified his disapprobation of the remark by flinging a chair at his only child with such good aim, that though it only barked her poor shins, she was afraid for a few moments that both her legs were broken.

"Done for!" she said, and fell to her mother earth without consciousness.

Certainly the angel's was not a happy life—by no means a happy life.

But there—she would have changed it if she could, and had that lover she was perpetually trying to find have turned up at last, probably she would have made him a better wife than many a handsomer woman would have made, and no doubt the poor man would have been very decently done for.

"Quick," said Hawk's Eye—"a light—some ice, if you can get any, and a bed!"

"Not the machine bed!" screamed the Cherub, coming-to apparently to say it, and then fainting again.

A few moments and Albert was placed in a bed which the fair Cherub herself used, and therefore there was no danger, for as she was useful to Old Schwincks he had no desire to get rid of her.

For some time Albert Falconer wavered between life and death, but after a time the wondrous light of knowledge came into his eyes, and he recognised Hawk's Eye.

"You, who have already been my friend?"

"Yes," said Hawk's Eye, "and who now hope to be your companion. Egad! I had little expectation, some half-hour since, of ever hearing you speak again."

"How so?—what has happened?"

"What has happened? What has not?"

"I am still bewildered. Where am I?—I—oh, that horrid nightmare—that terrible dream!"

"Faith, it was no nightmare—it was fearful reality! How came you not to follow my instructions?"

"Ha, I forgot them! And upon my word, you appear to have introduced me to a charming inn—a very charming inn!"

"You did not present the bead I gave you?"

"Faith, I did not!—but what happened?"

"Happened?" cried Hawk's Eye. "Tell me, for curiosity's sake, what do you remember from the moment that you got into that accursed bed downstairs?"

"I will tell you. I was lying awake, wondering what would become of me, when I felt the bed yielding under me. But this idea immediately gave way to the supposition that the feeling was but the effect which we all sometimes experience, that of floating down as we fall away to sleep. But the next moment I became conscious of my error. The bedstead appeared to—to close in upon me. I endeavoured to rise, and not being able to, I supposed for a moment that I was suffering from nightmare. Doubtless you have suffered from that horrible distemper?"

"Yes, I have," said Hawk's Eye.

"But the next moment," cried Albert—and, as he recalled the horror of that moment, he was so overcome that Hawk's Eye feared he was about again to lose his senses; however, by an effort, he recovered himself, and continued— "but the next moment I *knew* I was being stifled. Oh, the horror of that moment! A sudden awful singing in the ears, as though my brain were sounding my knell!—a sudden redness before my starting eyes, as though I had been plunged into a sea of my own blood!—and then my throat felt as though seized in the blood-red, hissing hot hand of the demon!"

"All this I have suffered," said Hawk's Eye. "But peace, my dear Albert, followed—did it not?"

(*To be continued in our next.*)

TALES OF BRIGANDS AND ROBBERS.

Learn & Strike

[DISCOVERY OF LORD KYLO SMEDLEIGH'S BODY.]

THE RED DWARF.

CHAPTER III.

THE RED DWARF TO THE RESCUE.—A FRIEND IN NEED AGAINST A HOST OF FOES.—THE RED DWARF FOILS THE BLACK COLONEL.—THE MASTER-SECRET, WHICH PROVES THAT "KNOWLEDGE IS POWER."—A WHISPERED WORD, AND ITS EFFECTS.—MADALINE'S DOOM AVERTED BY THE RED DWARF.—THE ESCAPE FROM THE DEN OF INFAMY.

"Ay, the Red Dwarf, or the Tiger, if you like that name better. You little expected to see me here, my swarthy colonel, black in heart as you are dark in feature!"

"Still our foe, then, in every plan we form!" said the

colonel. "Methinks you have well earned your name of the 'Tiger,' since you spring here, with hate and fury in your eyes, ready to worry those who would like to call you friend. There is still a compact between us, remember."

"A compact!" sneered the dwarf. "What! to drag innocent maidens from their homes, and murder those who defend them?" pointing, as he spoke, towards Allan, who was pinioned in the grasp of the Black Colonel's men. "Did our bond of fellowship extend to that? Release the youth, ye knaves!" exclaimed this mysterious being, as he strode towards the colonel's hirelings, who looked towards their master, awaiting his instructions.

At a sign from the colonel, the youth was set free.

"You are at liberty to go," said the colonel, motioning Allan to depart.

"Oh, no, Allan—no!" cried Madaline, who was still held in the iron grasp of the colonel. "Leave me not in the power of these lawless men!"

"Did you think for one moment I could act the part of such a craven?" answered Allan. "Beshrew me for a coward if I leave your side, even though they strike me dead at your feet!"

And as he spoke he strode up to the colonel, and, shaking his fist in the reprobate's face, exclaimed;

"Let go your hold of that lady, if you are a man!"

A shout of derisive laughter was the only answer the colonel vouchsafed the youth, who, stung to madness by the taunt, would have thrown himself upon his enemy, had he not been restrained by the powerful grasp of the dwarf.

"Bide your time, young sir!" said this mysterious being. "The fruit is not ripe for you to grasp at present; leave it to me!"

This was said in a low tone, intended only for Allan's ear.

The youth fell back a step or two, and waited to see the upshot of his strange friend's visit.

The colonel raised the half-insensible form of Madaline in his arms, and made for the door.

But before he could pass through it, the Red Dwarf sprang before it, and barred his passage.

"Down with your fair burden!" cried the dwarf, in a terrible tone, flashing his broad rapier before the colonel's eyes, "or the Tiger's teeth will not be half so sharp as his steel, which I now point at your treacherous throat!"

The colonel fell back a step or two, undecided how to act.

Allan had placed himself by the dwarf's side; and though they only numbered two against a score, their adversaries saw they had men of determination to deal with, ready to fight unto the death.

"Cut them down, boys!" exclaimed the colonel, dragging Madaline to the other end of the room, and urging his associates to attack Red Dwarf and Allan in a body.

The ruffians rushed to second bidding, but rushed like a pack of hungry wolves upon the men they thought certain of making their victims.

"Hold off, ye mongrel curs!" shouted a stentorian voice from the passage.

And before the colonel's satellites advanced another step, Silver Jack bounded in at the door, followed by young Claude.

"A murrain on ye for a parcel of cowards!" said Silver Jack. "A score against two is treacherous and hellish work! I'll make another on their side, before I'll see you do it!"

"And I another," added Claude, ranging himself by the side of his friends.

"Hot-brained fools!" cried the colonel, "even as we now stand, we are more than five to one! Of what avail, then, is your resistance? Let me depart with the lady freely, or, by St. Anthony, we'll carve a way through your bodies!"

This threat, however, had no effect on the four brave men, who, with their eyes flashing as brightly as their swords, still barred the advance of the colonel and his mercenaries.

But, on a sudden, Red Dwarf lowers his weapon, and calls on his companions to do the same.

"Do you fall from us, then?" asked Allan, with marked contempt in his voice as he put the question.

"You're a strange-looking varlet!" said Claude; "and truly your conduct seems of a piece with it, now that you m can to show the white feather!"

"The white feather!" indignantly retorted Red Dwarf. "Take heed I do not pluck your own from the cap you wear, for venturing such a remark!"

"Then why do you lower your weapon?" asked Allan Buckhurst, "when it should be raised to rescue the best and fairest girl in merry England?"

"Oh, do not abandon me, for pity's sake!" exclaimed poor Madaline, striving in vain to release herself from the firm grasp of the colonel, who laughed aloud at her fruitless efforts.

"The dove in the talons of the kite is not more secure than you are in my grasp, for you see even the dreaded Red Dwarf abandons you to your fate, and will see you the mistress of the gay and gallant Lord Smedleigh!"

"Ho, ho, ho!—how we may be deceived!" laughed the Red Dwarf, or the Tiger, as he sometimes chose to designate himself. "What? did you think I lowered my weapon because I feared you?" said the Tiger, sheathing his sword and going boldly up to the colonel. "No; it is because I wish to settle this business without shedding blood, if I can!"

"I have already told you that you can do so. All you have to do is to call your men off, depart from this house, and leave the fair Madaline in my keeping."

"There you are reckoning without your host; for when I leave here with my friends the lady leaves also!"

"Psha! A foolish speech—a vain boast, which you know it is impossible for you to carry out."

"Indeed? Be not too sure."

"And by what miraculous means will you accomplish this?" asked the colonel. "Have you a reinforcement at hand?"

"No; neither do I need one."

"Some witchcraft, perhaps; or potent spell of evil, perhaps?" laughed the colonel, with mocking derision.

"No; neither by witchcraft nor spells shall I attempt to gain possession of the fair Madaline; but by simply whispering one single word in your ear, my distant colonel!"

The colonel and his myrmidons laughing upon hearing Red Dwarf's speech; and Allan, Claude, and Silver Jack began to doubt the sanity of their new ally.

The dwarf, casting upon them a look of meaning, as if to restore their confidence, approached the colonel and whispered a word in his ear.

What made this reprobate colonel start as though bitten by an adder, and turn of an ashy paleness, while his strong frame shook with terror?

We shall learn that in due time.

"Well?" inquired the dwarf, with a laugh of triumph, "shall we cross swords, or depart in peace, taking the lady with us?"

"You know I dare not refuse you," muttered the colonel between his clenched teeth, growling like a chastised cur.

"What, colonel? You dare not refuse him, do you say?" exclaimed several of the colonel's followers in a breath. "Is the prize we have so hardly fought for to slip through our fingers so easily?"

"Peace—peace, my brave lads! You have earned your pay in this business, and shall receive it. It's the money, not the girl you want—is it not so?"

"Well, yes, that's the point," growled the hirelings.

And upon the colonel assuring them they should receive it on the morrow in good broad pieces, they put up their weapons and turned their backs upon their antagonists.

The sudden turn which affairs had taken, filled Madaline, her lover, Silver Jack, and young Claude with surprise. Red Dwarf, taking Madaline gently by the hand, led her to the side of Allan Buckhurst with a look of triumph, exclaiming as he did so:

"The Tiger saves the lamb from the clutches of the wolf!"

The fair Madaline, once more by her lover's side, and rescued from a fate far worse than the most cruel death would have been to her, knelt in thankfulness at her preserver's feet and blessed him through her tears.

"Rise, girl—rise! You would not kneel to one like me if you knew all!" exclaimed Red Dwarf, gently raising her.

"But you have done a good deed, and I owe you a lifelong blessing for it!" cried the grateful girl.

"And I, also!" said the overjoyed Allan, as he pressed to his heart the loved girl who had passed through so many dangers.

But how would both of them have shuddered, could they have foreseen the perils that were still in store for them!

How true it is that the veil which covers the face of futurity is woven by the hand of mercy.

"In the fiend's name, who can he be?" whispered Claude Duval to the equally mystified Silver Jack, as he looked at the Red Dwarf from top to toe with a curiosity not unmixed with fear.

"In faith, you might as well ask my horse, Lancelot, who he is, as seek to learn that news from me," replied the highwayman. "They say a friend in need is a friend indeed, and, by my hopes of a full purse, the lovers have found it so."

"And we also, I take it; for most of us would have been mangled food for the fishes to-night, but for our strange friend's mysterious power over the black colonel and his cut-throat band."

"Before my friends and I take our leaves," said Red Dwarf to the baffled colonel, "I'll trouble you for the *true* password, if you please. There's honour among thieves, they say—so let there be the same between——"

Before he could finish the sentence, the colonel exclaimed rapidly:

"Silence! The password is 'Moonlight and Midnight!'"

"You are acting fairly by me?" asked the dwarf, as if he partly doubted the colonel.

"I tell you I have given you the true password, and no other."

"It is well, and I'll trust you; although I may as well inform you that what *I* know others know—and if the Red Dwarf should happen to be missing through any *accident*—you understand me—your head would be remarkably unsafe upon your shoulders, my bold colonel!"

"I tell you I have acted fairly as regards the password—let that content you."

"It shall for the present. So adieu, my gallant *friends*, and see you let Red Dwarf and his friends pass out from here unharmed and unmolested!"

"Go!" exclaimed the Black Colonel. "For to-night you and your friends are safe."

Then, muttering to himself:

"But no longer!"

He led the way to the water-gate, where a boat was moored.

Red Dwarf saw his friends safely in it, then stepped in himself.

As they were putting off, another boat crept out of the shadow of the building, containing a single man, who, with his slouched hat pulled over his brow, made for the boat which contained Red Dwarf and his companions.

"The password!" demanded this mysterious sentinel

"Now, then, to prove whether the colonel has dealt fairly with us!" thought Red Dwarf, as he sought for the hilt of his sword.

"The password, or I fire!" cried the sentinel, as his boat neared theirs.

"Moonlight and midnight!" exclaimed Red Dwarf, with his weapon ready for the attack in case of treachery.

But the sentinel merely answered:

"Good! Pass on!" and retreated back in his boat to the spot from which he had emerged.

Perceiving that no obstacle was opposed to their departure, the Red Dwarf took the oars in his hands, and, with powerful strokes, rowed for land.

The Black Colonel and his band noted their departure from the window which overhung the river.

"Well," exclaimed Hal of Hockley—a reprobate and cut-purse; the colonel's head man in his various schemes of villany—however you let that girl escape—for whose capture Lord Smedleigh offered so much—is a mystery to me!"

"Why need I study Lord Smedleigh now? No doubt he has met his fate in the river below. I heard a cry and a splash as my lord tried to escape by the window: and no doubt our sentinel, Geoffrey the Alsatian, thinking one of our victims was escaping, fired upon him, and he fell below into the water."

Such, as we have seen, was the case.

But was it Lord Kylo Smedleigh's lot—libertine and gambler that he was—to meet his death by drowning?"

We shall see.

CHAPTER IV.

THE REVEL DOWN THE RIVER.—THE DUKE OF BUCKINGHAM'S TOAST.—THE LIBERTINE'S CAROUSAL.—A QUARREL AND ITS RESULTS.—TWENTY AGAINST ONE.—ATTACK OF THE PROFLIGATES ON SIR STUART CATEMASS.—DEATH STARES A BRAVE MAN IN THE FACE.—THE CRY OF TREASON, AND TIMELY ARRIVAL OF OLD ROWLEY.—SIR STUART'S ESCAPE DOWN THE RIVER.—DISCOVERY OF LORD KYLO'S BODY.

IT was a night of high revelling at Hampton Court.

Charles, the Merry Monarch, as he was beginning to be called, was surrounded by his libertine companions, and the fair and false mistresses, who led him captive by their charms and meretricious arts.

The song and jest went round, the dice-boxes rattled, and the wine-glasses clinked with foaming bumpers, as some reigning beauty was toasted by her ardent admirers.

Mistress Eleanor Gwynne, no longer Nell the orange girl, was then in the plenitude of her power, and showered her gifts of money and place on all who had succeeded in basking in her almost royal favour.

Daylight appeared, and still the revel lasted.

"Fill to the brim, my roystering gallants!" cried the gay and witty Duke of Buckingham, who headed a party of revellers as boisterous as himself.

"Fill, I say, and drain your glasses to the fair lady Madaline, the daughter of Sir Stuart Catemass, the noble cavalier who graces with his presence this festive board."

A loud cheer followed this announcement, and the revellers uprose and drained their glasses.

As Sir Stuart listened to their prolonged shouts, his heart sank within him.

He had good cause for alarm.

Whenever the dissolute Buckingham toasted a lady, her ruin mostly followed.

Madaline was the only daughter of Sir Stuart, and, being deprived of a mother's care—for the day she was born her mother died—her father naturally looked upon her with even more than a father's usual love.

He idolised the child, whose name seemed doomed to be polluted when uttered by the ribald lips which had just pronounced it.

All sat down expecting Sir Stuart would respond to the great honour which they imagined they had conferred upon him.

Often had he been rallied by King Charles and his courtiers as to his daughter's absence from court.

But nothing could induce him to allow his daughter to mingle with the unprincipalled train which thronged the court of his reckless and dissipated sovereign.

Like Lord Kylo Smedleigh, the Duke of Buckingham had marked Madaline for his own, little knowing Lord Smedleigh was his rival.

But had he even known it, it would not have prevented him prosecuting his object—nay, it would rather have whetted his sensual appetite.

The duke guessed the cause of Sir Stuart's silence, but was too wily to let the baronet perceive he suspected it.

Buckingham's object was to gain an interview with Madaline. He had never seen the maiden, and, without he employed stratagem, saw little hope of doing so, for whenever he was seen approaching Sir Stuart's mansion, Madaline had strict orders to keep in her chamber until the duke had taken his departure.

"Beshrew me, sir," exclaimed Buckingham, as Sir Stuart Catemass still kept his seat, "your silence shows but little courtesy to your friends when your fair daughter is toasted by them!"

"My lord," answered Sir Stuart, "my daughter will never mix in court revels or public pageants, like many of her sex. I have marked out quite a different course for her. She is a fair flower that will flourish better in the shade than in the sunshine of your favour. Still, I thank you for your compliment, in my daughter's name, although she will never know it has been so *honoured*."

The sneering tone in which the last word was uttered did not pass unnoticed by the duke, who vowed in his heart to be revenged upon the father through the daughter.

"Pray stay, my lord!" said Buckingham, as he saw Sir Stuart rise to depart. "By the mass, I wish your daughter well, and deem it a cruelty that you should coop up the maiden to mope her life away like a nun in a convent! Bring her forth into the world without fear! If I give you my word she shall be safe, will it not be sufficient, and equal in weight to my royal master?"

"Oh, quite equal to *his*!" replied Sir Stuart, at the same time muttering in an under tone: "Neither of your words are worth a groat!"

This last remark was overheard by Sir Pierrepoint Lucy, a boon friend and companion of the libertine Duke of Buckingham.

"Treason—treason!" cried Sir Pierrepoint, laying his hand upon his sword and addressing Buckingham.

"What raises your ire thus?" asked the duke.

"The remark that fell from Sir Stuart's lips!" answered the gallant. "I have sharp ears for a sharp remark, and when I hear you and your Majesty's words set down as not being worth a groat, methinks it is high time for a loyal man to speak!"

"Sir Stuart Catemass, unsay those words!" exclaimed Buckingham, growing red with anger. "Dare you speak thus of his Majesty and his friends?"

"You are not his friends—no, not one of ye!" replied Sir Stuart, the truth getting the better of his discretion. "Ye are more truly his enemies, helping to make old England a hotbed of vice, instead of the fair and noble land it should be!"

A cry of rage and vengeance burst from the whole of the half-drunken cavaliers at those words—tables were upset, wine was overturned, and a score of rapiers flashed from their scabbards upon hearing the rash words of Sir Stuart.

But Sir Stuart Catemass was a brave man, and his rapier was drawn as soon as theirs.

"Down with the malcontent!" shouted Sir Pierrepoint, as he advanced upon the offender, who, with his back against the wall, stood his ground like a lion at bay.

"Make the dog eat his words!" cried a half-drunken cavalier, advancing upon him.

"Take heed—the dog has teeth and can bite sharply!" answered Sir Stuart, presenting his rapier full at the throat of the speaker, who, stumbling over a chair as he was advancing, would have assuredly been impaled on the point of Sir Stuart's sword had not Sir Pierrepoint plucked him back.

The rage of Buckingham at being so openly defied knew no bounds.

"Cut the traitor down!" he shouted. "Death to the puritanical cur, who miscalls his royal master and the court of King Charles!"

"Aye—death, death to the varlet!" cried the cavaliers in a body, as they began to close round Sir Stuart so as to hem him in.

Looking from right to left, like a wild beast at bay, Sir Stuart Catemass looked around him in vain for a helping hand to aid him.

He saw no one but enemies.

A dozen swords were pointed at his throat.

His time had come, then, and a murder was to take place where a few moments before all was enjoyment and good-fellowship.

He thought of his only child—his Madaline.

What would become of her now?

Dishonour would await her in the first place, and a broken heart in the second.

These agonising reflections flashed through his mind with the rapidity of lightning.

For a moment his courage failed him, and for his daughter's sake he begged for mercy and lowered his sword.

A mocking burst of fiendish laughter from his half-drunken and maddened opponents was his only answer, as they rushed on him like a pack of hungry wolves.

It was then that Sir Stuart Catemass, seeing that his foes were bent upon his death, resolved to die like a brave soldier that he was, sword in hand.

He struck down the range of swords that were pointed at his breast as though they had been reeds, and for a moment his drunken adversaries recoiled.

But only for a moment.

Headed by the infuriated Buckingham, they charged Sir Stuart in a body.

The foremost of his assailants, urged on by those behind them, were thrown forward with a violent shock, and Sir Stuart, losing his balance, fell to the ground.

Half a dozen rapiers were raised to pin him to the earth.

But at this moment a commanding form stepped from behind the arras near where Sir Stuart Catemass had fallen, and exclaimed:

"Hold your hands, I command you, and fall back!"

"The King!" exclaimed the cavaliers, as every sword was lowered and every hat was raised as they bent the knee to their sovereign.

"Why, the foul fiend seize ye all!" cried his Majesty, who, to say the truth, was not a whit more sober than the rest, "do ye call yourselves Englishmen to worry a single man thus? Fall back, I say, or, beshrew me, but I'll place every man of ye in the Tower!"

He raised Sir Stuart as he spoke, and even the bold Buckingham was awed for the moment by his royal master's words.

But Buckingham speedily regained his self-possession, and put on his usual plausible manner.

"My liege," said he, "we were but defending your good name from insult."

"And did it require so many to do that?" replied the King. "Oh, Buckingham—Buckingham, a petticoat is at the bottom of this brawl, as usual!"

"I protest, your grace——"

"You can save yourself the trouble, my lord, for I was behind the arras, and heard all. Sheath your sword, my Lord of Buckingham, and you, gentlemen cavaliers, do the same. I will pour oil upon these troubled waters, and settle this matter after my own fashion."

"I am glad to see your Majesty is setting us so good an example by becoming so moral on a sudden!" said the audacious Buckingham, in a supercilious tone.

"Say rather that I am becoming just. A truce to your follies, my Lord of Buckingham, and don't seek to possess every woman you hear of with a fair face. If Sir Stuart Catemass wishes his daughter to remain in security, let her remain so, and unmolested. Mark you that, on pain of my sovereign displeasure!"

Seeing his Majesty was in a firm mood, and visited with one of those eccentric fits of justice which sometimes possessed him, Buckingham promised strict obedience to his royal master's commands; but still vowed within his heart to gain the maiden, by fair means or foul, however long he might have to wait for an opportunity.

"I would be alone with Sir Stuart Catemass for awhile, gentlemen," said the King, bowing ironically to the cavaliers. "Await me in the banquetting hall. I'll soon rejoin you."

The duke and his roystering companions bowed and left the apartment; many of them had been sobered by the incident we have related, and were heartily ashamed of their share in the transaction.

King Charles, being alone with Sir Stuart, motioned him to a seat, and with his own hands filled him out a goblet of wine from one of the neighbouring flagons, which stood upon a table close at hand.

"Come, that will give you a rouse, man!" said the jovial King; "and, by my word, I should think you needed it; for, had I been in your shoes, I should have reckoned that my last hour had come."

"In faith, your Majesty, such were indeed my thoughts, and I have little doubt but they would have been fulfilled but for the opportune arrival of your Majesty."

"It was indeed opportune, as you say. I saved your life, and their credit as Englishmen. I know Old Rowley, as they call me, is a sad dog in many ways, but, odds fish! he'll never stand by and see one of his subjects put out of the world with a score pieces of cold steel. Drink up the wine, man, and I'll put you in the way of reaching home safely, without a chance of your again falling in with your hot-headed friends."

"Believe me, your Majesty, the words I used towards my assailants bore no disrespect to your Majesty."

"Tut, tut!" said the King—"I am well assured of that! You and your family have ever been reckoned amongst our most loyal subjects, and it is that knowledge which makes me anxious to serve you. Follow me!"

Doing as he was desired, the King led the way behind the arras whence he had entered.

A dark passage led them to a secret door at the end of the corridor, where the rays of a feeble lamp gave sufficient light to discover a small entrance in the opposite door of black walnut which faced them.

The King tapped at this door gently, and one of his confidential pages appeared.

"Conduct Sir Stuart Catemass to his mansion. You know its locality, I trow?"

The man bowed in reply, and signed for Sir Stuart to follow him.

Sir Stuart knelt and kissed the hand of his royal master, and followed his guide, who closed the door behind him, and led the way down a flight of stone steps which led to the water's edge.

Here they entered a boat which was in readiness, and the guide, fixing his oars, rowed up the river.

They proceeded in silence, the noise of the distant revel growing fainter and fainter as the boat bore them onwards.

The sun, which had not long risen, poured fourth a flood of golden light across their track.

An object in the water, which rose suddenly to the surface entangled in some weeds, caused Sir Stuart to give a cry of alarm and horror.

It was the form of a man.

Another moment, and he recognises the features.

They are those of Lord Kylo Smedleigh.

To start up and seize a boathook at his feet was the work of a moment, and, aided by his companion, Sir Stuart Catemass drew the body of Lord Kylo Smedleigh into the boat.

(To be continued.)

HAWK'S EYE, THE PHANTOM ROBBER.

CHAPTER XIII. (*Continued.*)

ALBERT hesitated a few moments before answering the question of Hawk's Eye, and then, in a low tone of voice, said:

"Yes, a few ghastly moments, and then peace came. The horrid sound in my ears became the sweetest silence in the dear world—the sea of red became like a beautiful green sea, in which I floated calm and in peace. And then, as I forgot all my troubles—my sister, my danger, myself, even my dear Margaret—I drifted away into what must have been death—death unquestionably, the peace-giver, if all death is such as that I experienced; death, dear Hawk's Eye, from which you have rescued me, and for which I thank you, not because I am glad to live for myself, but for my sister's sake, and for the sake of my dear Margaret!"

"Good!" said Hawk's Eye. "And now, what do you intend to do?"

"Make for Holland. Where I shall then go I know not."

"My dear Albert—if I may call you so——"

"You may indeed!"

"You do not know me; and the Fates decree that for some time you must not know who I am,—suffice it to know that I am not what people think I am."

"I am quite willing to wait, dear Hawk's Eye, until you are willing to speak."

"But are you determined to go to Dutchland?"

"What can I do here in England, where I am hunted for being true to the cause of an unfortunate King; while all here in England, if they did not uphold the being who is on the throne, would be punished for want of the very loyalty for which I am now to be outlawed?"

"If you are an outlaw in name, why not in deed?"

"How do you mean?"

"If your country turns against you——"

"No—no," said Albert, "my dear country does not turn against me—it is a few human beings in that country—the rich and powerful—those who swore fealty to one King and who now uphold another."

"Albert—apart from what I really am—do you guess what I do?"

"No."

"I take from the rich to give to the poor."

"Ha!"

"I keep little, and I have money of my own at times. Further, I have been robbed of all by the Government, and I mean to take back from the Government!"

"How so?"

"All highway robberies are repaid for by the Government."

"Ha! And that is the way in which you make the Government repay you what it has taken?"

"Yes. Will you join me?"

"I would, and yet I dare not. I do not fear Tyburn Tree, but I fear for my sister."

"Never fear, Tyburn will never claim us!"

"Bah! it may."

"Then let it!"

"True!"

"True!"

And the men clasped their hands.

"And now, who are you?" asked Albert.

"Wait," said Hawk's Eye.

And as he spoke, Albert Falconer thought he heard a strange sighing sound in the chamber.

CHAPTER THE LAST.
HOW THE KING ENDED IT ALL.

As Hawk's Eye spoke, there was a sound at the door—a summons, hasty, imperious, and savage.

"A spy!" said Schwincks.

And almost before he had said it there was a second summons.

"Open!" roared a voice—"open, in the name of the King!"

"Mein Got!" said Schwincks, and well he might, for the summons meant that the military were about to quarter in the Anchor of Safety.

"Good mein Got deliver us!" said Schwincks, and the Cherub, at this point, breaking out:

"Oh, my pa! I trust they won't injure a hair of his venerable head!"

Schwincks found himself compelled to fling at the Cherub a two-legged stool, which barked the beauty off both her arms.

Again the summons.

"Open, or the door shall be forced!"

"Wait—wait!" yelled Schwincks. "Don't—don't hurt neither an honest man nor an honest man's door."

Ha! a score of soldiers, and led by a captain and another man—a pale, cadaverous, and wicked-looking man.

A moment, and a voice cried:

"Bertram."

The pale man turned.

"Ha, Albert, we expected to find you here! We came for you."

"What do you mean?"

"I mean that I, Bertram Falconer, am a true gentleman and a loyal subject of his Majesty King George, and that, having obtained information that you were here, I am here to arrest you."

"Forsworn wretch!" cried Albert. "And do you really seek the arrest of one of your own blood?"

"I am no traitor."

"Thou art, to all, even to the King; for here I declare, in the presence of these gentlemen, that you—you, Albert Falconer, aided my escape from the pursuit of the military."

"Ho! so this is my return for having been for a moment weak and disloyal?" replied Bertram, turning to the soldiers. "Sirs," he continued, "I admit that for one moment the pity I felt as the blood relation of this misguided man," pointing to Albert, "led me to violate my duty to my King. I did aid him to escape the first pursuit of the royal troops; but after he was gone, I knew the wickedness of which I had been guilty, and therefore I then felt degraded by the wickedness of which I had been guilty. But while truly repenting of my disloyalty, I obtained information which enabled me to reach this place in time to repair the wrong I sought to do his Majesty, whom, I pray Heaven, will pardon me! If the King refuses me grace, then Heaven above be merciful to me!"

"Thou art an arch hypocrite!" cried Albert. "'Tis but a few hours since you aided me to escape from the pursuit of the military, and therefore you could not have had time to learn whither I was going—nay, I scarcely knew myself. You well know you have had spies at work, and that they have done your work; and I tell you, Bertram Falconer—you who have supplanted me of name, birthright, title, all worldly advantages—I tell you I would rather be myself, I, who am perhaps destined to a scaffold, than be you; albeit all your plans have been successful, and you are free—for your *soul* is in bondage!"

"Peace," cried Bertram, with sudden rage, as he felt the truth of the remarks levelled at him by his cousin—"peace! I have been helped in my work of arresting you almost by a miracle, for I lay stunned and near death at the foot of the ivy tower."

"The foot of the ivy tower?"

"Yes—and strength was given me to come here."

"The foot of the ivy tower! Ha, ha! Who could climb down and fall might have climbed up before. Ha! you had all to gain by Sir Bruton's death—all, when *I was disposed* of. So, by my outlawry I *was* disposed of. My father was angered against me, and your star was in the ascendant. But you augured it might not always be that Sir Bruton should hold his favour to you; and so you sought to clench it. I see all; Sir Bruton dead, and you once proclaimed heir, I had no further chance. Sir Bruton dead, and you having forced the Lady May, my dear sister, to marry you, the Government would be still less inclined to give me back my lands, should an amnesty be proclaimed. Sir Bertram, cousin mine, *you* murdered my father, Sir Bruton!"

A low-murmured cry spread through the room, and Bertram fell back fearingly.

As he did so, a small "something" fell from the breast of his coat.

Albert immediately took possession of it.

"And see, here is the weapon, doubtless—a delicate destroyer of life, truly!"

"Soldiers, do your duty—arrest Albert Falconer!"

The captain in command gave the order also, and the red coats were about to advance to take possession of Albert, when a sudden exclamation from Bertram again arrested their movements.

This was caused by the fact that Hawk's Eye had suddenly stepped from a spot, where his face had been shadowed, into the full open view of the light in the room.

The reader will in a moment comprehend what had happened.

Bertram confounded the *phantom of the man* with the *man himself*.

"Again I see you."

"No."

"Did I not see you some hours since?"

"No."

"You are phantom, and I exorcise you!"

And so saying, Bertram took his sword from his sheath, reversed it so that the handle became crucifix shaped, and cried:

"Satan, avaunt!"

"Bah!" cried Hawk's Eye. "If I were a phantom, and the minion of satan, think you, such a wretch as you are, could fright me away? No—no, Sir Bertram Falconer!"

Now Bertram, with all that cunning and cruelty which distinguished him, had, in a moment, determined to test whether the form before him was phantom or human being.

In his own wicked but certainly brave mind, he was quite convinced that a mere shadow was before him, and as he was half savage, animal-like in his bravery, he felt but little fear of danger from a mere phantom.

"Does not the flaming sword upon your brow burn?" asked Hawk's Eye.

These words served to convince Bertram that it was indeed only a phantom that stood before him, for did not the phantom only a few hours before place there the red mark of Cain, and who, therefore, but the phantom could know anything at all about the matter?

He did this therefore:

He had reversed his sword and held it in his left hand. He had therefore but to catch the handle with his right hand, and in a moment he was armed.

A glinter of the sword, and the rascal had made a pass at Hawk's Eye.

But it was *Hawk's Eye*, and hawk's eyes are sharp. There was time to draw the sword and, by a dexterous turn and movement of the body, parry the thrust as the second sword left its sheath.

Bertram, feeling the resistance, was in a moment powerless.

The shock was so great to find the phantom a material thing that the effect upon him was the exact of that upon the German student who was suddenly convinced of the supernatural.

In the case of the German student the young scholar evidently protested against ghosts, and vowed that he would fire at any ghost that should appear to him.

A ghost appeared to him.

He fired a pistol.

The next moment the ghost laughed, and held up a bullet between his fore-finger and thumb.

The revulsion of feeling on the part of the student was so great, that he fell dead.

And yet in that case all was only a joke.

The ghost was a fellow-student, who, hearing the other's determination, had first extracted the bullet, and then played the ghost.

Now, in Bertram's case, his horror was so terrible to find the supposed phantom a living thing like himself, that the shock half paralysed him.

There he stood.

Knees bent in; head fallen forward.

The man was half dead.

And now Hawk's Eye approached.

"I am," said he, and then he whispered in the wretched Bertram's ear.

That ended it.

The terrible shock was culminated by the name whispered in the man's ear.

A sudden tremble, a shock, a rush of blood over the face and neck, a reddening of the very eyes, and, with a convulsive plunge, down fell Sir Bertram—

Dead !

A few moments, and then comparative peace was procured.

"And such a *fine* man, too !" said the howling Cherub.

As far as *she* went, it mattered very little what was a man's moral worth. If he were a fine man, who would have looked well as the Cherub's husband, she was always ready to howl if he came to grief.

"He was not Sir Bertram very long !" said Hawk's Eye, as he and Albert stood, hand in hand, looking on the dead man.

"No; and so much the better for him, for he could never have been happy," replied Albert.

"Never," Hawk's Eye returned. "His life would have been his greatest punishment, as life is the greatest punishment of all evil-doers."

"True."

And now their conversation was interrupted by the approach of the captain in command of the royal guard. He said to Albert:

"Sir Albert, I grieve that I must arrest you."

Albert bowed.

"Believe me, all my interest shall be used at court to obtain your reprieve; and, indeed, I may add that his Majesty is supposed to be not at all inclined to be ill-disposed towards the rebels."

"I am glad to hear that, for my sister's sake rather than my own," said Albert, and whose hand was the next moment gratefully taken by Hawk's Eye.

And now the arrest of Sir Albert was again interrupted by shouts in the street, and a gentleman, in a great state of excitement, rushed in.

"Hooroar—hooroar !" he roared. "The Jacobites are safe ! There is a royal proclamation out granting a general amnesty to all traitors !"

"But how am I to believe this ?" asked the captain.

"Here," said the intruder. "I tore this copy of the proclamation down from the gate of St. James's Palace, and it is signed by the King."

"Then," said the captain, taking the paper, "at all events I have somebody to arrest. Not you, Sir Albert, for I take upon myself the responsibility of restoring you to liberty ; but *you*," he continued, turning to the luckless herald.

"What for ?" asked this one.

"For seditiously tearing down a royal proclamation," replied the captain. "However, don't be alarmed. I daresay his Majesty will spare your life too, and perhaps let you off altogether."

"Thankee !" said the herald, looking, however, very ruefully at the soldiers as they surrounded him.

"And when you are at liberty," said Albert, "for the good news brought to me, I will make your fortune."

"Thankee, Sir Albert," said the herald, and this time he spoke far more cheerily than before.

"I could not tell you before, Sir Albert," continued the captain; "but I had private reasons for knowing that a gentleman—a prince—was secretly in the palace, with the full endeavour to obtain this proclamation, and as he was, and is, the husband of the Princess Augustina, and answers for no further rising on the part of the Stuarts, why, his Majesty must have at once acceded to him just after your escape from the palace. Sir George Blake," turning to Hawk's Eye.

"You, Sir George Blake ?" cried Albert.

"Yes—the Jacobite Sir George Blake. Now you comprehend the effect of my name upon Sir Bertram, for you know the old superstition in your family that when a Falconer drew sword upon a Blake, a Falconer must die !"

"True," said Albert.

"And the superstition in this case came true, because he died of his own fear. Fear we need not, for we can never draw swords upon each other, Albert."

"My brother !" cried Albert, as they flung themselves into each other's arms.

But as this embrace took place, Albert found that Sir George or Hawk's Eye trembled.

"What art thou ?"

Hawk's Eye was looking at what to all but him appeared vacancy.

He saw the phantom of himself.

"I am come," said the phantom, in a gentle voice. "I say farewell. You are safe, and need my help no longer. Remember always I came do good, exactly as all phantoms come. Good-bye !"

"Stay."

"Good-bye—good-bye !"

As the words lessened in sound the form dwindled.

It was gone.

Again Albert asked:

"What art thou ?"

"'Twas but a *thought*, my Albert," he said—"'*twas* but a *thought !*"

Well, my tale is done.

Need it be said the Lady May married Hawk's Eye, otherwise Sir George Blake?

Ay, that she did; and their children had far darker, more piercing, and more splendidly hawk-like eyes than their cousins, the children of Sir Albert Falconer and his lady, once Margaret Sedwyn.

Their families last to this day.

Ay, and so do the descendants of their horses, Brilliant and Calloon.

Well, we have done—have we not?

No.

The Cherub married at last a very ugly man; but then, as the Cherub said, nobody could see how ugly he was, for you must know he was a *coal heaver*, and so always went about under a kind of mask.

Poor Cherub !

She always cherished the memory of old Schwincks, her father, whose death she never forgave herself, for she was ever contending it was her fault.

The fact was, that as that inestimable man stood at the riverside door of the Anchor of Safety, he flung another bottle at the poor Cherub, and with such viciousness, that he jerked himself backwards into the river, down to the bottom of which he went like several stones.

And there was an end of him.

And now, good-bye !

[THE END.]

BLACK GOLPHO, THE BRIGAND; A CONFESSION.

BLACK GOLPHO had a short but tyrannical reign as "King of the Brigands." It was a "reign of terror," not only to the strangers who fell into his hands, but equally so to the band of ruffians who hailed him as their chief, and who acknowledged no law but his will.

Golpho's confession of how he became a brigand was found in his cell, shortly after his death. It was taken possession of by the father confessor, and for many years has been kept as secret as a priceless treasure, but at last it is offered to the public as one more history in the calendar of crime.

* * * * * *

I was born in Germany, and continued with my parents until I reached the age of twenty-three.

An accident in my youth had so severely injured my face, that I was almost hideous.

Men shunned me, and women seemed afraid to look upon me. This contempt so wounded my pride and soured my nature, that, although I was poor, I could not stoop to seek employment, by which I could support myself.

Soon after I reached my twenty-third birthday, I saw an

loved a peasant girl named Florilla, who was also loved by a forester, or ranger, called Holbert, a man of handsome appearance, and in every way a formidable rival.

I clearly saw that I could not, by fair means, overcome my enemy, I therefore did that which thousands have done before me—I resorted to stratagem, and strove by presents to win the favour of my beloved Florilla.

How to support this was my greatest anxiety—there seemed but one way, and that was by theft.

My home was on the borders of a dense forest; I soon therefore took to deer-stealing, and all the gains I procured from my adventures I poured lavishly into the lap of my smiling lover.

A severe edict was issued against all trespassers on the forest laws, and so secretly was I watched by Holbert that I soon found myself trapped, and detected in the very act.

I was tried, found guilty, and sentenced to a fine, the payment of which ruined my parents, and ultimately caused my father's death.

Holbert triumphed—for I was beggared, and Florilla knew how I had obtained the presents which I had enriched her with.

Pride, jealousy, and rage were in arms within me. Want set the wide world before me, but passion and revenge kept me close to the borders of the forest still.

A second time I became a deer stealer, and a second time was I detected in the crime, this time also by my hated rival. I was then sentenced to one year's chastisement. I suffered it without a murmur, and went back again with a full knowledge that absence had only cherished the attachment which I had felt for Florilla. For her I felt that I would work; necessity with iron hand bent my stubborn pride, and I sought for labour, but contempt met me every time I appealed.

I was chased by scorn from one door to another, until, almost mad, I was forced back to the forest and thieving. My unlucky stars, for the third time, led me into the power of my bitter and vigilant enemy, who at last heard me sentenced to be branded, and then have three years' hard labour in the fortress. They passed, and my chains fell off, but I was no longer the same Golpho.

The current of my life was turned. I went into the fortress an offender, but I came out a villain.

I had been thrown into the company of more than twenty convicts, two of them murderers, and all the rest notorious thieves.

They jeered me if I would not mix with them; they sang songs which at first horrified me, but which I soon learned to echo—no day passed over without my hearing the recital of some profligate act, or the concoction of some audacious villany.

At first I avoided these men, but I could not bear to be left alone; I saw not one kind face—the gaoler even denied me the company of my dog, so I needed that of men, and thus became accustomed to the only company allowed me.

I became an altered man. I rapidly learned all the villany they could teach me, and before I left, could surpass many of my teachers.

I came out, and I felt an unquenchable thirst for revenge—revenge against all men, for all men had injured me.

I gnashed my fetters with my teeth when I beheld the bright sun rising up against the battlements of my prison, and the bird that perched itself upon the grating of my window seemed to be only mocking me with its triumphant song of liberty. Then it was that I vowed hatred—undying hatred to everything that bears the image of man. I have tried hard to keep my vow!

Tired with revenge, immediately I left the prison I bent my steps towards where I was born. My heart beat quick and high as I saw the little spire rising out of the trees, and the recollection of all my troubles and sufferings aroused my faculties from a terrible, dead slumber of sullenness; they set every wound bleeding afresh, and jarred every nerve in my frame.

The clocks were striking the hour of vespers as I reached the market-place; the crowds were bending towards the church door, and I soon saw that I was recognised, for every-one seemed to shrink from coming near me.

I turned into a wood-yard near the church, and waited until it was going to be locked up, then I stole out to seek a shelter.

In turning the corner of the yard I saw Florilla coming towards me: her eyes met mine, and the expression that passed over her features I shall never efface from my memory. Other human faces I cared not for—their contempt and hatred was natural; but that face to frown so fiercely—it seemed more than my brain could bear; she shunned me as she would a pestilence; she appeared even to fear me; then I felt the last link snap—I was alone—uncared for, and not caring for any one living being—for even my mother was dead. Then it was I thought I would die by my own hand, but my infamy had buried my pride and vanity, so I lived on, determined that while I lived I would do evil. Previously I had sinned more from levity and necessity, but now I resorted to sin from free choice and for my pleasure.

I took to the woods, and slew every animal that came near me, and got them sold outside the barriers, living wretchedly in the meantime, scarcely spending any money, save for powder and shot, for months. I lived thus, fearing nothing, for I was well armed, and felt certain about my aim.

One morning I had hunted a stag for more than two hours, and began to despair of my booty, when suddenly I perceived the animal exactly at the proper distance for my gun. My finger was on the trigger ready, when my eye caught sight of a hat lying on the ground a few paces in front of me.

I looked carefully around, until I saw a figure lurking behind a massive oak. It was taking deliberate aim at the stag.

I could scarcely believe my sight for a moment, but looking steadfastly at the form, I saw plainly it was Holbert.

A deadly coldness crept through every limb as I fixed my eyes on him. There stood a man—and the man above all others in the world whom I hated—there he stood, within reach of my bullet.

By a sudden impulse I raised my gun—my arm shook, my teeth chattered, I could scarcely draw my breath; for one instant I held my gun, wavering between the man and the stag.

For one moment conscience struggled with revenge, but the demon triumphed, and my rival fell dead before me!

I rushed towards him, and stood speechless over the corpse, and then, forcing a wild laugh, I drew him into a thicket, with his face upwards. The eyes stood stiff and staring upon me.

As I looked on him I felt horrified at the deed I had committed, and which had been done so suddenly—so entirely from the irresistible impulse of the moment that I could not conceive how I had become a murderer.

I was still standing over the corpse, when I heard the sharp crack of a whip and the creaking of a fruit waggon going through the wood; this aroused me to the sense of danger—I turned to fly, when I suddenly remembered that Holbert had a watch, and also that I needed money to pass the barriers.

I knelt upon the earth, and took the watch and all the money from his pocket, but a strange feeling came over me; I did not wish to rob, but to be revenged; it was to feed my passion of hatred towards my personal enemy that I had slain him; so, throwing back his watch and the money, save one piece for the barriers, I went away right down into the depths of the forest.

All through the wood I wandered slowly on, and not till the sun rose high in the horizon did I lay myself upon the grass and try to sleep; but sleep would not come to my eyelids. Conscience haunted me with horrible visions, and with a yell of terror I awoke, and started to my feet.

I drew my hat over my eyes, and was rushing instinctively along the line of a small path into the very heart of the wild wilderness, when a rough, stern voice, directly in front of me, called:

"Halt!"

I lifted my hat from my eyes, and looking up, beheld a tall, savage-looking man advancing towards me with a ponderous club in his right hand.

(*To be continued in our next.*)

TALES OF BRIGANDS AND ROBBERS.

I Warn & Strike

[RED DWARF ENLISTS A NEW COMRADE.]

THE RED DWARF.

CHAPTER V.

SIR STUART CATEMASS SAVES FROM DEATH HIS WORST ENEMY.—THE GOOD SAMARITAN AND HIS EVIL GENIUS.—THE BLACK COLONEL'S SECRET MISSION TO LORD SMEDLEIGH.—THE PLAN LAID TO SACRIFICE THE FATHER AND ENTRAP THE DAUGHTER.—THE JOURNEY BY NIGHT TO ALSATIA.—THE ROBBER'S DEN, AND WHAT HAPPENED THERE.

WITH the aid of his companion, Sir Stuart Catemass placed the inanimate form of Lord Kylo at the bottom of the boat, and placing his hand on the breast of the young libertine, found that his heart still beat.

"He lives!" exclaimed Sir Stuart. "Let us pull for land with all our speed, and procure assistance."

Landing near the Abbey of Westminster, Sir Stuart, leaving the insensible form of Lord Kylo in the charge of the man who had accompanied him, made for his residence in search of assistance to convey his insensible charge beneath his own roof, until a skilful leech (as medical men were termed at that period) was procured.

"Heaven be praised! You have returned!" exclaimed Musgrave, Sir Stuart's valet, with fear and anxiety depicted on his countenance. "Is my young lady with you?"

"With me?" answered his master, the words trembling on his tongue as he put the question. "Is she not in her chamber? I left her there when I departed last night."

"True, my lord, you did so, I can bear witness; but shortly after you had taken your leave of her, and bidden her good night, I thought I heard her lattice window open, and my young mistress walking on the terrace, then I heard a scream, a cry for help, and going to her chamber, I found it empty."

"My daughter gone!" exclaimed the nobleman, in tones of agony. "Cowardly varlet that you are! Did you not follow and seek to obtain traces of her?"

"I did, my lord; myself and the other servants went in every direction in search of her, without success."

"What can this mean?" cried the distracted father. "Has my daughter been taken from me? or has she eloped of her own free will? But no, no—I can't think that, for I indulge her every wish, and she had but to ask and have. Oh, if she has indeed acted deceitfully to me, it will break my heart!"

Trying in vain to repress his anguish, this strong, brave man gave vent to his feelings, and wept like a child.

"Have I turned driveller?" at length he exclaimed, dashing the tears from his eyes, and standing erect. "I'll not believe her ungrateful until I have proved her so. Quick, varlet, my horse! and send your fellows to assist the wounded gentleman from the boat at the terrace steps. Let them place him in one of the best chambers, and fetch the most skilful leech this city boasts! Away!"

Musgrave hastened to execute his orders, the horse was brought, Lord Kylo conveyed into the house, and Sir Stuart, giving the strictest orders that he should be well looked to in his absence, rode rapidly towards the heart of the city, his heart torn with conflicting emotions at the sudden disappearance of his beloved and only child.

Little thought he, that the man he had rescued from a watery grave was the treacherous foe who had struck his heart such a cruel blow.

The reprobate Lord Kylo Smedleigh, lay struggling for many hours twixt life and death, but at length the usual restoratives prevailed and all danger was past.

Half unconscious, the young libertine, as he muttered incoherent words, greatly betrayed his treachery towards the daughter of the man under whose roof he was being so kindly tended and cared for.

"The girl must be mine—mine!" he cried; "if not, she shall not live to be the bride of another! Look to her well, colonel—bind her, gag her, anything to stop her cries!"

The servants who listened to this little imagined he was speaking of their young mistress. Affairs of gallantry, as they were then called, were so common, and abductions so frequent, that they only imagined his lordship was thinking of one of his numerous intrigues which had gained him so much notoriety in the dissipated circle in which he moved.

When reason resumed her sway, Lord Kylo began to reflect on his position.

Suppose Madaline's father should learn the truth, return with his daughter, and call him to a strict account!

Was the girl rescued, or still in the power of the Black Colonel and his myrmidons?

If so, his best plan would be to join them, and make off to the continent with the girl for whom he had risked so much. He rose from his couch, dressed himself, and was framing some excuse to leave the house, when Musgrave, Sir Stuart's valet, entered with a letter addressed to him, which had just been left at the hall door for Lord Kylo Smedleigh, and marked private.

His lordship started as he gazed upon the superscription, for he recognised the writing of the Black Colonel. When Musgrave had withdrawn, he hastily broke the seal and read as follows:—

"My Lord,—I have heard of your rescue from the Thames. I fancy that neither you nor I are doomed to perish by drowning. But beware how you play your cards! The dove has escaped from the hawk's nest, her mate also. The Red Dwarf defends them. At present I cannot choose but yield to him. Meet me as soon as possible after you receive this, at our old haunt in Alsatia. Be wary, for we are in danger."

Madaline had escaped, then—Allan Buckhurst also.

"Matters are beginning to look cloudy," muttered the libertine, as he thrust the missive into the fire which was burning in the grate.

He knew Sir Stuart Catemass had powerful friends, and dreaded the vengeance which would fall upon him, should Madaline arrive while he was under her father's roof, and denounce him as being the chief agent in her seduction.

Some plan must be formed, some loophole carved out by which he must escape suspicion, even though it cost him half his fortune.

A sound of horses' feet in the courtyard below made him start from his reflections.

Had Sir Stuart fallen in with his daughter?

Was Allan Buckhurst also with him?

He ran to the casement and eagerly looked out.

To his great relief he saw Sir Stuart was accompanied by two of his servants only, and, by their looks of disappointment, he guessed their search had been fruitless.

Where, then, was Madaline?

Where her lover?

Had the Black Colonel and his band again fallen in with them?

He scarcely dared hope that this would prove the case, and hearing footsteps approaching the chamber, he threw himself on the bed as though he was still weak and exhausted from his immersion in the Thames.

Sir Stuart Catemass entered the room with a deep sigh, and threw himself into a chair by the bedside.

Lord Kylo feigning sleep, still watched under his apparently closed eyelids the demeanour of the baronet.

"Gone—gone!" he heard him mutter. "I fear she has become a prey to the spoiler, who bears her far away from her father and her home."

Lord Kylo gave a heavy sigh as though he had just awakened from a heavy sleep.

"How fares it with you, sir?" asked Catemass, little think ing that the cause of all his misery lay before him.

"Somewhat better," whined the hypocritical libertine. "But is it that seems to distress you so much?"

"My daughter—my Madaline!" exclaimed Sir Stuart Catemass. "She has been borne off by villains—for I cannot bring myself to think she would willingly abandon me; and every inquiry I have yet made regarding her has been in vain."

"Borne off?" cried Lord Kylo, raising himself on the couch as though the information astonished him. "I grieve to hear this, and yet I do not marvel much, after what I have seen lately."

"What have you seen lately?" echoed Catemass. "Explain yourself! Do your remarks apply to my daughter's conduct; if so, tell me at once what you mean by the words you have just uttered."

"Pray calm yourself," replied the artful hypocrite. "Heaven knows how I sympathise with you in this matter! I long dreaded this, yet feared to tell you. I now perceive it was a mistaken kindness on my part."

"Lord Smedleigh, do you wish to distract me with these words, which strike upon my heart as sharply as though you pierced me with your dagger. To the point at once, I entreat of you—nay, I *demand!*" exclaimed the agitated father, as he rose from his seat, and struck the hilt of his sword.

"Fair and softly, sir—fair and softly!" said Lord Kylo, rising from the bed, apparently with great difficulty. "I have no doubt, under the blessing of Providence, we shall be able to trace her."

"Indeed!" cried Catemass. "What makes you think so?"

"Because I am tolerably well assured I know the gallant who has deprived you of your treasure."

"What—you know him?" exclaimed the baronet. "Quick—quick—tell me his name, and from King Charles will I obtain justice on the villain, even though I seek it at the foot of the throne!"

"Well, then, his name is Allan Buckhurst."

"Allan Buckhurst?"

"Even so."

"What, the son of that traitor, Martin Buckhurst, who perished on the scaffold?"

"The same."

"You amaze me! Quick—quick! Explain this, or I shall go mad with rage at the infamy and dishonour which I see hovering over my good and ancient name!"

Lord Kylo's plan was to get Catemass to follow him from the house before his daughter arrived there, for he well knew Madaline would make her way home the moment she was enabled to do so, and by her testimony clear Allan from all complicity in her abduction, and denounce the guilty parties who had so boldly planned their schemes for her downfall.

"By Heaven, you seem to hesitate!" cried Sir Stuart, as the libertine paused for a moment, while the thoughts we have just narrated passed through his mind.

"Hesitate? Not I, Sir Stuart. I was but arranging my scattered thoughts—a ducking in the Thames is not the best stimulant to a man's intellects, and I wish to be as near the truth as I can. This, then, is what I have to tell you:—During the past month, while passing down the Thames in my barge to a friend's villa, I have seen a light shine from a lattice window in your mansion. This seems to have been placed there as a signal, for no sooner did it appear than a boat used to push off from the shore, and steer towards your terrace steps. Urged by curiosity, I watched, saw a man—whom I afterwards discovered to be this Allan Buckhurst—secure his boat to the wall; then the light would disappear from the casement window, and your daughter step forth on the terrace to meet her lover."

"The traitress!" muttered Sir Stuart Catemass, as his frame shook with rage.

Lord Kylo saw that he had gained his first point, which was inflaming the baronet's mind against young Allan Buckhurst.

"To think that a child on whom I lavished all a father's fondness should deceive me thus!" cried the half-distracted nobleman.

Then pausing for a moment, a sudden thought struck him, as he quickly turned towards Lord Kylo, and put the following question:

"How is it, my Lord Smedleigh, you never took the trouble to acquaint me of these meetings between my daughter and her villain of a lover until now? You say you have known of this during the last month. Methinks you would only have been acting the part of a man and a friend to have mentioned this to me at the time. Why did you not?"

This question for a moment seemed to stagger the hypocrite; but he speedily regained his assurance, as he answered, in the blandest voice possible:

"I was not aware these frequent meetings were clandestine. Allan Buckhurst might have been your daughter's accepted lover, for aught I know to the contrary. Seeing them trying to elope together was the first suspicion I had that all was not right. I did all in my power to prevent their escape, received a slight wound on the head for my pains from one of his accomplices who was lying in ambush, and fell into the river, from which you so kindly rescued me. Well, well, perhaps, for the future, it will be the best for every man to mind his own business, and not interfere in that of his neighbour, even though he sees a villain about to carry off his only child."

This plausible and artful speech completely threw Sir Stuart Catemass off his guard.

He had hitherto no very favourable opinion of my Lord Smedleigh; but this pretended kindness of the libertine's towards his only child, Madaline, at once disarmed all his suspicions, and he blamed himself for entertaining such harsh thoughts towards the young man, thinking he was not so very bad, after all.

While these thoughts were passing through the mind of Sir Stuart Catemass, the crafty hypocrite, Kylo, had also his reflections.

He knew, if Madaline's father ever proved the falseness of the lying statement he had just made to him, his life would pay the forfeit, for Sir Stuart was one of the most expert swordsmen of the period, and Lord Kylo was only brave when he had a brace of bullies to back him.

His great point, then, must be to escape from the vengeance of Sir Stuart, who, he feared, sooner or later, would become aware of his baseness from some source or other.

Then another thought struck him.

Suppose he could get Sir Stuart silenced—*silenced for ever!*

He had plenty of daring associates who would undertake the deed, if well paid.

It might be done in a street brawl.

"Or," muttered the traitor, "in Alsatia. Yes, that is the spot, if I can but lure him there. If so, the Black Colonel and his men will soon make short work of him."

Sir Stuart, absorbed in grief, was pacing the chamber undecided how to act.

No doubt the fugitives were on their way to France, and by this time far beyond his reach.

"Not so," said Lord Kylo, as Sir Stuart mentioned his suspicions to him; "I think I have a better clue than that."

"You have?" he exclaimed.

"Be patient, Sir Stuart, I only say I think I have; and after all I may be wrong."

"Speak—speak!"

"Well, then, I have of late seen this Allan Buckhurst much in company with a disbanded trooper, a notorious character, of whom you have no doubt heard—he is called the Black Colonel."

"Indeed!—is it possible he is leagued with a villain such as he is?"

"Why not—what desperate means, or what villanous companions, will a man not league with to gain his ends?"

"True—true!"

"Now, if this colonel is at the bottom of this business, of which I have hardly a doubt, I think we can get on the runaways' track."

"Indeed!—how so?" eagerly demanded Sir Stuart.

"I suppose you wouldn't spare money to effect the rescue of your daughter and the capture of Allan Buckhurst?"

"Spare money? I would give half my fortune—nay, the whole of it, to know my daughter was safe and pure once more in my longing arms."

"Then I will go with you to the colonel."

"What!—do you know where to find him?"

"I think so. I once did the knave a service by saving him from the pillory and whipping-post, and he promised, if ever I required a service, he would perform it for me. I will now go with you and claim that promise."

"My kind—my good friend!" exclaimed Sir Stuart, wringing, with gratitude, the hand of the lying hypocrite. "Let us lose no time."

"Not a moment; I am most anxious to depart," replied the wily traitor.

And so he really was, for Madaline and her lover might return at any moment, and his scheme of treachery be blown to the winds.

"Quick—quick! I will order horses for us!" said Sir Stuart, urging him to depart. "But where shall we find the man you speak of? Will our journey be a long one?"

"Not very. No horses will be required. We will go on foot."

"The place?" demanded Sir Stuart.

"Alsatia," replied his pretended friend.

Brave as he was, Sir Stuart Catemass gave a start and turned slightly pale at the mention of that fearful locality, into which few cared entering alone.

"Surely you don't hesitate—*you*, her father—if I, who am only her friend, am ready to accompany you? Besides, there is really no danger while I am with you. I know every signal and password in the place, and will guarantee your safety with my life. Ay, ay!—I will see you are safely kept!" muttered the libertine to himself.

"I should be a coward were I to hesitate another moment," replied Sir Stuart.

They proceeded to the courtyard.

"I will leave word with the servants where we are going," said Sir Stuart, about to address his valet, Musgrave.

"Not for the world, Catemass! You know what servants are; the knaves might get tattling to the neighbours. No doubt Allan Buckhurst has his spies still lurking about to watch our movements; and if they were informed of them, it might throw us off the scent."

"True," said Sir Stuart, whose love for his child and eagerness for her recovery blinded him to the artful plan Lord Kylo was weaving for his destruction.

Taking no heed of the servants, Sir Stuart Catemass left the mansion with his pretended friend, and, passing along the banks of the river, they made their way towards the heart of the City of Westminster.

Evening was closing around them as they passed under the shadow of the Abbey.

Two men emerged from the gloom and watched them, following their footsteps with stealthy tread.

"A couple of brave gallants!" said one of the ruffians, for such they really were.

"Did you not notice the gold chains about their necks and the rings upon their fingers?" asked the other.

"I did," replied his companion. "Let them only walk on a little further, and they shall soon change hands."

"And their purses to boot," said the other.

"Not only their purses, but what there is in 'em," silently laughed his companion, with a grim attempt at joking.

Marking well the onward progress of their intended victims, the ruffians followed in the wake of Sir Stuart and Lord Kylo.

As the latter turned down a dark alley in the Almonry, which they had now reached, the two fellows who were dogging them pressed close to their heels.

Their intention was to trip them up in the first place, then rob, or even murder them, if needs be, in the second.

The foremost ruffian, springing on Sir Stuart, tried to cast him across his knee, and, by so doing, to hurl him to the ground; but his lordship, who, during the time he had been following Lord Kylo, had been listening to the stealthy footsteps behind him, and, knowing the dangerous locality they were in, was prepared for the worst.

Therefore, the moment he felt a hand upon his shoulder trying to grasp it, he swung himself suddenly round, and, being a strong and powerful man, hurled his antagonist against the wall of an adjoining house with a force that seemed to shake the crazy tenement to its base.

The other ruffian, who had marked Lord Kylo for his prey, soon had the libertine at his mercy; but, in the short struggle which took place between them, the mask which the fellow wore fell to the ground, and Lord Kylo recognised his features.

"Hold your hand, Geoffrey!" he hastily cried, as the ruffian plucked forth a gleaming knife and raised it above his head. "Don't you know your friends?"

"Friends?" echoed the fellow.

"Ay. I am Lord Kylo Smedleigh!"

"His lordship!" cried Geoffrey, in confusion, raising Lord Kylo to his feet. "And to think, now, I shouldn't know you! But the night is mortal dark, and who'd have dreamt of seeing you this side of the Abbey at this hour?"

"Help, Geoffrey—help!" cried Hal of Hockley, Geoffrey's companion, for he it was who, now being pinned against the wall by the iron grasp of Catemass, shouted for assistance as he saw his lordship unsheath his sword and level it at his throat.

"Tarry, my lord—these are friends!" interposed Lord Kylo.

"Friends, forsooth! Methinks they make themselves known in a strange fashion then!" replied Sir Stuart Catemass.

"They are but the means by which we shall gain our ends," rejoined the false friend.

Then turning to Geoffrey, he asked him if the Black Colonel was to be seen that night.

"Well, that all depends upon who it is that wants him," answered Geoffrey, looking towards Sir Stuart, who, upon hearing that no danger was now to be apprehended from the two worthies, had released Hal from the iron grasp in which he had held him.

"I'll answer for my companion," returned Lord Kylo, pointing to Sir Stuart; "so lead the way to your chief without more words on the matter."

He nudged Geoffrey unobserved as he spoke, and the fellow, guessing Lord Kylo had some stratagem to work, gave him to understand that the colonel was to be met with at the usual place, to which he would conduct them both, if they were so willed.

"Truly are we, my good Geoffrey," said Lord Kylo, "so lead the way, I say."

Ducking an awkward, slouching bow to Sir Stuart Catemass, and making a rough apology for the error into which his comrade had fallen, Geoffrey led the way down the entry, followed by the others.

Hal of Hockley seemed anything but pleased at the turn affairs had taken.

He had marked Sir Stuart down for plunder, and he had not only been foiled in the attempt, but remarkably well shaken and bruised into the bargain.

But a secret sign made to him by Lord Kylo assured him that something was about to happen conducive to all their interests, so Hal kept his hand on his dagger and waited to see what turn events would take.

It struck him that, perhaps, after all, the stranger was to be their victim.

In this surmise Hal was not far wrong.

Geoffrey, after numerous windings and turnings, stood still beneath the wall of a ruined building, and, with a dagger, which he took from his vest, removed one of the bricks from the wall in question; thrusting his arm into the orifice thus made, a sharp click was heard, as if a string had been touched or a bolt drawn, and, to his astonishment Sir Stuart saw a portion of the wall revolve and disclose an opening large enough for a man to enter.

Geoffrey led the way, and the others followed.

Hal stooped down by a heap of rubbish which faced them as they stumbled in, and, producing a flint and steel, he proceeded to strike a light.

This accomplished, he lighted a small lamp, which seemed ready to his hand, and motioned to the others to follow him.

Sir Stuart Catemass then saw that the portion of the wall which had moved aside to admit them from without was enclosed in a frame of iron, connected with which was a spring lock, which could be touched from without by removing a brick, as we have already seen.

At this moment a chill of misgiving crossed the heart of Sir Stuart, and he paused.

Lord Kylo noticed this, and bade him keep a stout heart for his daughter's sake.

These words recalled his confidence for the moment, but still he thought he detected a kind of sneer in the way the other spoke.

Still he kept his hand on the handle of his rapier, ready for the worst.

He did not so much misdoubt Lord Kylo as he did the two villanous-looking fellows who were conducting him he knew not whither. Yet, if it led to the recovery of his daughter, he felt ready to brave any danger.

They paused in a ruined court-yard, in the centre of which were the ruins of a huge stone fountain, the waters of which seemed to have been long dried up.

Geoffrey, seizing a stone ring in one of the flagstones by the fountain's base, raised the stone and disclosed a flight of wooden stairs, which looked crazy, and rotting from the damp which appeared to rise from below.

"Descend," said Lord Kylo, pointing after Hal, who had gone first with the light.

"No," said Sir Stuart, "I will remain here. Send this Black Colonel, as you call him, to me, and what is to be arranged can as well be done here as below."

"Not it!" growled Geoffrey. "The colonel does not dance attendance on anyone. If he is worth consulting, he is worth seeking. He has escaped from too many traps that have been laid for him to venture above ground unless we give him the word there is no danger in doing so. And how can we say that when we do not know who you are?"

This seemed to be a reasonable excuse, and Sir Stuart followed without any further remark.

The steps terminated in a long passage paved with stone. A dim lamp suspended from the roof disclosed a range of doors on the right hand, and on the left he saw, to his horror, a number of tombstones at the heads of various banked-up graves.

He could not help starting, and uttering an exclamation of surprise as they met his view.

"Don't be alarmed, Sir Stranger," said Hal, remarking the start of horror which Sir Stuart gave. "This is a burial-ground, where all we brave lads hope to rest. Better to lie there than swing upon a gibbet—eh, my lord?"

Sir Stuart made no reply, but again asked to see their chief.

"Have a little patience, my lord; we are just about to take you to him."

He unlocked an iron-bound door as he spoke, and they all entered what appeared to be a huge stone kitchen. A fire, composed of a lot of old lumber, was burning on the hearth, and seated around it were at least a score of the Black Colonel's band, drinking, dicing, and quarrelling.

All started to their feet with oaths and a cry of alarm as the new-comers entered.

"Fear nothing," said Lord Kylo, throwing some gold pieces towards them; "you know me as your friend, and the cavalier who accompanies us will prove your friend also."

Perceiving that the money seemed to make a very favourable impression on this motley group, Sir Stuart took out some gold pieces also, and begged their acceptance of them.

They were eagerly grasped, and the health of the new-comer was toasted with acclamation.

"What now, ye devil's birds?" roared a voice, which seemed to proceed from a room at the end of the kitchen.

"That's the colonel, just risen from his sleep," said Hal.

"Away, and tell him I am here," said Lord Kylo, "and seek some conference with him!"

Hal did as he was bidden, and Sir Stuart and his supposed friend awaited his return in silence.

In a few moments Hal returned, saying that the colonel wished to speak to Lord Kylo Smedleigh.

"He wishes to know who you are before he admits you to his presence!" explained the artful libertine. "I'll pave the way for you, never fear!"

"Quick, then, and let us come to business, for I can promise you I have no liking for this place!"

"Nor I," returned Lord Kylo; "and were it not to serve you I would not have been here!"

Sir Stuart Catemass thanked him, and the traitor, entering the colonel's chamber, left his lordship pacing up and down waiting his return.

In a few moments Lord Kylo returned, and, saying the colonel would be happy to confer with his lordship, beckoned Sir Stuart to follow him.

He did so, and on entering the Black Colonel's chamber he beheld the man he had come to seek reclining on a rude couch at the end of the room, looking as though he had just slept off some drunken orgie or midnight revel.

"Approach, my lord," said the colonel, motioning Sir Stuart Catemass towards him, as he rose to a sitting posture on his couch.

As he did so, he pulled what appeared to be the handle of a bell, depending from the ceiling.

By this time Sir Stuart was about half-way across the apartment, when suddenly, with a loud crash, the flooring parted beneath his feet.

With a cry of despair, Sir Stuart Catemass was precipitated into the yawning gulf, his head seemed to strike against some hard and rocky substance, and his senses left him.

CHAPTER VI.

THE LOVERS MEET ONCE MORE, BUT ONLY TO BE PARTED BY THEIR SUPPOSED FRIEND THE DWARF.—THE MYSTERIOUS JOURNEY.—APPEARANCE OF THE RED DWARF'S BAND.—THE SECRET CAVERN, AND WHAT BEFELL ALLAN BUCKHURST THEREIN.

THE RED DWARF having reached the shore with his rescued friends, was overwhelmed with thanks both by Madaline and her lover.

But the mysterious being who had saved them seemed heedless of their expressions of gratitude, and, waving his hand with an air of authority, desired them to desist.

Taking Silver Jack and Claude Duval aside, he whispered earnestly with them for a few moments, took a ring from his finger, gave it to Silver Jack, who received it with a low bow as he gazed on it, touched his hat with an air of respect, and took the road towards the Strand, followed by young Claude.

"Again I thank you a thousand times, generous stranger, for your gallant aid, and will now depart with this fair lady, so that I may place her again beneath that roof from which she was so basely and treacherously taken."

"Call on my father, Sir Stuart Catemass, whenever you will," said Madaline, as she felt her heart throb with gratitude towards the mysterious being who stood before her, "and no reward will be considered too great for him to bestow upon you! Farewell, worthy man—farewell!"

"No, no—we part not yet!" said the dwarf, placing himself before them.

"What is it you mean?" asked Allan, in surprise.

"Do you not remember swearing to me that if I saved your mistress you would in return do anything that I might ask?"

Allan started as he remembered swearing to do so.

"Did I not say, 'Pause before you take the oath, for I may ask too much?'" said the dwarf.

"You did," replied the bewildered Allan.

"You also said you would peril your life to save her, did you not?" inquired the dwarf, pointing to Madaline.

"What does this mean?" asked Madaline, a vague feeling of terror stealing over her. "Surely you are not a man of evil deeds to require any desperate service at the hands of this generous young man?"

"Whether my mission is of good or evil, I am not permitted to tell. Time will prove that; but before we part, Allan Buckhurst and I must be better acquainted!"

Sounding a low note on a small silver whistle which he carried round his neck, a number of strange-looking men formed a circle around them as if by magic.

Two carriages also appeared on the road at the same time.

Madaline was forcibly yet respectfully conducted into one of the vehicles by two of the strange men, and driven off on the instant.

Allan was suddenly seized by two others, who blindfolded him, led him into the remaining carriage, and he was driven in a contrary direction.

He sprang to his feet, intending to leap from the window.

"Sit still!" cried the dwarf, who was by his side, as he grasped his arm and pressed a dagger against the young man's bosom.

Allan reflected a moment, and saw the folly of resisting.

He could only marvel at the strange turn affairs had taken.

After proceeding, as it seemed to Allan, for about half an hour, the carriage suddenly stopped, and he was led through what he supposed to be a garden by the sound of his footsteps on the gravel, and the scent of numerous flowers which cast their odours round him.

Suddenly he heard the ripple of a river.

A thrill of horror shot through him as he thought they were again taking him back to the Red House.

He was instantly conducted into a boat, which in a few moments, urged on by the powerful strokes of the rowers, grated against what struck him as the steps of some building, into which he felt himself urged by the firm grasp of the Red Dwarf.

"To your knees!" exclaimed the dwarf to Allan, in a tone and manner which plainly indicated he was not a man to be trifled with.

Allan, seeing that to disobey was useless, did as he was ordered.

Red Dwarf then suddenly plucked the bandage from his eyes, and he looked around.

He was surrounded by a number of men cloaked and masked. In one of their hands they held a lighted torch, in the other a dagger.

"Friends," said the Red Dwarf, raising a poniard over the head of Allan, "behold our new brother!"

(To be continued in our next.)

THE NEAPOLITAN BANDITTI.

On one of the last evenings of a residence in Naples, I visited the grand lion of the soil, Vesuvius.

The sun was too fierce for an excursion over the five miles of fiery sand that have scorched the cuticle from so many a fair cheek of my countrywomen.

I took a boat, and found the benefit of my prudence in at once escaping the death of St. Lawrence, and hearing an infinity of Neapolitan gossip from my Lazzarone. But as we rowed under the little promontory that makes a rude landing-place to Portici, he insisted on my hearing the story of a pile of ruins that lay, covered with the green beauty of wild flowers and of rich climbing plants, on a commanding point of the shore.

There (said he, with somewhat more of gravity than I expected from his bold and jovial visage)—there was the palace of the Conde Florestan de Alcantara. When I was first in his service, they called him a hermit, and I know not what; for never was there a man who more hated the fools and knaves of Naples. But of that there was an end, like all things besides.

Suddenly news came of the old king's death, and of the arrival of the Duca di Santa Croce, from Sicily, along with the new king, as his chief minister.

This intelligence gave my lord new life. He became instantly another man.

He went to Naples in a few days; and from that time the Alcantara palace was a round of entertainments.

I never saw so complete a change in man. I could scarcely remember the fierce brow and bitter lip of the Conde in the country, in the gay countenance and brilliant manners of the Conde at Naples.

Our palace was the constant rendezvous of the first personages of the state; we had all the ambassadors, all the beauties, all the artists, all the distinguished strangers.

Why was there no Condessa? was the question of everyone; and, undoubtedly, if bright looks and noble offers could have established the daughter of the first names in the kingdom in the Alcantara palace, it would not have been long without a female head of the household.

But an extraordinary personage, of whom the Neapolitans talk, and with good reason, to this day, now came to check our festivity.

The Conde had, like all other grandees of his fortune, palaces or villas in different parts of the coast; and, as the weather changed, or the wind shifted, or it suited his humour, or possibly the still more changeable humour of some fair lady of the court, we all hurried from one to the other, at a moment's notice. But, after a whole summer spent in those ramblings—to-night in Naples, to-morrow night in Calabria, the night after on the shore of Tarento, and the night after here in Portici, as if we wore wings—intelligence began to be spread of the return of Joachimo d'Imola, or Il Florentino, or Il Diavolo, the name that belongs by right of highway to all our great men who dislike paying taxes, have

a taste for collecting the public money, and scorn to die in their beds.

This fellow began to molest our movements prodigiously.

A mule laden with plate, a dozen hampers of Monte Pulciano, or a case of guitars, was sure to fall into his hands every time; and, in fact, we seldom made a journey without paying a royal price for leave to change our prospect.

The Conde laughed at these losses for awhile, and said that as robbery was the original trade of the country, strangers like him were the natural prey, and that, if every rogue in Naples were sent to the galleys, we should have the most crowded fleet, and the thinnest court, of any kingdom under the sun.

But Fra Joachimo's proceedings at length began to have their effect.

In this very palace of Portici, the Conde had assembled a party of the nobles.

We had three days of feasting and gambling. The Conde played high, as was the custom of his class; but he played fair, which was not the custom, and he lost accordingly. His money was spent magnificently on all occasions, but at play it flew.

On the last day of the week there was to be an entertainment surpassing all the rest; a general invitation was sent to every distinguished personage for twenty leagues round. All was as showy as possible. Dancing, singing, and masquerading, were the order of the night; but, as some of the peasantry had spread rumours of Joachimo's band having been seen crossing the Apennines in the course of the week, I was ordered out with the gamekeepers to clear the road of stragglers. We might as well have saved ourselves the trouble.

While we were beating every hedge along the high-road for banditti, as if they had been hares, and turning every sound into the blowing of horns or the firing of carbines, Fra Joachimo had quietly walked into the palace with a party masked, taken his supper in the coolest style, and then, marching up to the table where the Conde was at high play, pulled out a pistol, and transferred every sequin on the table to his pocket.

The same operation was performed in the same moment at every table in the rooms; the surprise was complete: the little resistance that was attempted was soon finished by the sight of half a hundred fierce-looking fellows, armed to the teeth, and taking possession of the doors, while their masquerade brethren plundered the company perfectly at their ease.

Never was there a more thorough purification of the vanities of the flesh!

Away went bracelets and necklaces, drawn from the polished arms and swan-like necks of the fair dames of Naples, with the grace of a master of the ceremonies. Tiaras of diamonds and chains of pearl followed with the same delicacy of touch. Shawls, watches, stars, epaulettes, and purses bade a like adieu to their owners; and, by the time of concluding this new system of *douana*, never were generation of grandees less indebted to ornament.

The banditti took their leave before daybreak; and the first glimpse of dawn saw the whole multitude of the brave and fair flying homewards in all directions, hating pleasure for the first time in their lives, and penitent without the help of a confessor.

This affair made a prodigious noise in Naples; for, if you want to make a noise about anything, there is no contrivance equal to engaging a woman in it; and, if you wish to make it eternal, you have only to give them an opportunity of talking of themselves.

The Conde was indignant at the insult. I had never before seen him in a thorough passion; and this single specimen was enough for me if I lived with him fifty years. He offered enormous rewards for the seizure of the banditti; but they seemed to have sunk into the earth. He spent days and weeks galloping over the country, wherever there was a rumour of their having appeared; but he might as well have been asleep on his sofa.

Fra Joachimo had the claws of a wolf, but he had the wings of a falcon, and we should as easily have caught either in fair field, as this swift-footed amateur of bracelets and necklaces.

But the Conde had his enemies, like all other great men, and they made the most of the disaster; pronounced that the strong box of the palace had been thoroughly emptied by the band; that his bankers looked sullen; that equipages, establishment, and fetes were at an end, and that the illustrious city of Naples was to be honoured with his presence no more.

These stories came flying about the country so thick, that they even reached us on our travels in chase of Fra Joachimo.

The innkeeper at one of the most miserable places where we put up among the hills had the insolence to ask, "By whom his bill was to be discharged," with the addition, that he was beginning to think that "neither master nor man was likely to be troubled with more money than they could manage."

I answered his hint by a lash of my whip, which will make his forehead a sign to all impertinent innkeepers while he lives, and answered his bill by taking that and his words directly to the Conde. He flung me a handful of sequins on the spot, and bade me "pay the scoundrel, and keep the remainder for myself;" but, as I had paid the scoundrel already in the only coin fit for him, I deposited the sequins in my pocket.

The event, however, slight as it was, put a stop to our chase.

"For Naples!" was the order; and to Naples we instantly drove.

Our entry was like an ambassador's, and the Lazzaroni swore by all the saints that the earth never produced such a magnifico. The whole mob of fashion were exactly of the same opinion; and, if popularity were to be measured by eating, drinking, and dancing, the King of the Two Sicilies had not in his dominions a cavaliero so much adored by man, woman, and child.

It had been one of the wonders of the household, that, among all the brilliant figures who flourished at our balls, the Conde had never selected any donna as the object of his particular attentions. He talked, laughed, danced, and made love; but, unluckily, it was alike; and the conjectures of the fair dames were turned upon all kinds of strange modes of accounting for this prodigious breach of good manners. At last they were satisfied that the iron-hearted Conde was not accessible to any of the darts of Cupid.

The Capitano Commandante of Principato Citra had lately made his appearance at court with his Spanish bride. She must, of course, choose a cavalier.

The Conde gallantly offered his services; but the lady's choice fell upon the emptiest coxcomb about the court—a fellow who bore the distinction without joy or sorrow, and followed her to church, to the concert, and the ball-room, with the most becoming punctuality of his profession.

The Conde Florestan laughed at his defeat, and from that moment he had nothing to do but to outshine the world. Always splendid, he became now wildly sumptuous.

He built a palace on the side of Vesuvius, as if in scorn of the chances of eruption, or as if he took for the emblem of his wild career the crater above.

Nothing was heard of but the waste, the luxury, the boundless prodigality of the Conde Florestan.

But his Spanish agents served him well; wealth flowed in to fill up all his expenses, and many a needy Italian prince envied him the possession of those American mines which lighted the chandeliers of the Vesuvio palace.

But play was now his chief delight. He drove gaming to the most glorious excess; no man was welcome who would not play, and few were unwelcome who would. Italy is a nation of gamesters; and he, of course, had full rooms.

But the Conde's inexhaustible purse was the grand attraction, and it bled freely; he seemed even to take a strange delight in losing; he absolutely flung away his money; and, in the delight of the game, buried all his other feelings.

If to one man on earth he had a determined personal antipathy, it was to Capitano; yet that man made immense sums by my master's play, who actually threw the game into his hands; and many a rouleau have I seen flung over to him by the Conde with a smile of triumph, as if he were rejoiced to make his fortune.

The Capitano was a sullen, rough soldier, haughty in his looks and insolent in his language; he had served long in the continental wars, and this was enough to give him ground for merciless contempt of the Neapolitans—army, fleet, and nobles.

The Conde Florestan shared his sullen looks; but he laughed them off, and his purse was too useful to the Capitano to suffer a quarrel between them.

But the bride was a creature of another mould. Among the Spanish beauties who were perpetually crowding to the gay court of Naples, the Capitanessa was beyond all comparison the handsomest, and, I might say, the most unhappy.

In my attendance at the palace, I had often seen the very Lazzaroni round the gate kneel, as if to worship her as she alighted from her carriage. She was in the very spring of life, with a pair of large black eyes that looked like stars, and an expression of face as fine as the picture of a muse; but the countenance of a marble statue was never more fixed in melancholy.

It was only when the Conde passed by, or spoke to her, that life seemed to return, and then it was in bitterness.

Her cheek flushed with indignation, which she took little pains to suppress; and her answer to his language of ceremony was always the language of disdain.

The cause perplexed me for awhile, but a conversation which I overheard let me into the secret.

On one of our masquerade nights, as I lingered under the windows to catch the fresh air of the gardens, two masks came out from the rooms and stood in the balcony.

"I have sought you, Conde de Alcantara," said a female voice, "and sought you to make a remonstrance."

"Your excellency does me too much honour," was my master's answer. "But how can I have offended?"

"No more of this, Conde. The life that the Capitano leads is owing to you; he plays perpetually, and to an enormous amount."

"I was not aware that he had suffered at play. I think Fortune, that smiled on him in the most essential crisis of life, seems not to have refused her smiles even in such trifles as the concerns of the hazard-table."

"Conde, I am not to be deceived. The passion for play has been pampered in him. He has been fortunate, if to be lured to ruin be fortunate. His dangerous propensity might have slept but for his success in your palace; but now he lives only for gaming. Conde, this is your doing."

"Your excellency must always be in the right; but how the remedy may lie in my hands, I am unhappily ignorant. Permit me to say, that, delighted as I should be to attend to your excellency's slightest wish, I can scarcely believe that the Capitano will be satisfied with receiving me in the character of a mentor."

There was silence for awhile; and the Capitanessa seemed to have been weeping; at length she burst forth with a torrent of reproach.

"I know your design well; you are determined on his ruin. You have plunged him into a pursuit from which no man ever returned guiltless. His continual sittings here are observed. His enemies about the king are not idle. His absence from his government has been prolonged beyond royal patience. If I condescend to come under your roof, it is to watch over him—to force him away, if possible—to prevent him, at least, from some act of despair, when he finds that he is undone—for undone he will be."

The conversation then sank, or was broken off by the passing of a group of masks, and I heard no more.

Two nights after, as we were returning from the opera, at the corner of one of the narrow streets that leads from the San Carlos by the Santo Croce gardens, some drunken quarrel stopped the carriage.

The Conde impatiently sprang out to inquire the cause, and mingled with the crowd.

In another moment I heard an outcry; he had been stabbed in the side, but whether by one of the mob accidentally, or by an assassin, none could tell.

All fled instantly, and I carried him bleeding and speechless home.

The wound was all but mortal, and the Conde languished for some days without hope of life. No discovery of the perpetrator of this act could be made; but it excited universal interest, and among the most frequent inquirers was the Capitano—a civility which, by those who knew his iron nature, was reckoned miraculous, but which the multitude not unfairly attributed to his fear of losing a friend who was so useful to his revenue.

During the height of the Conde's fever, the door of the chamber opened one night while I was sitting by his bedside, and a person whom I took for one of the monks of San Georgio appeared, saying that he was come to confess the patient.

I left the room, of course, but waited within hearing.

The confession seemed long; and, fearful that it might exhaust my master, I approached. In the darkness of the chamber, lighted only by a single taper, I was unseen. The confessor's words were those of no monk.

(To be continued in our next.)

BLACK GOLPHO, THE BRIGAND: A CONFESSION.

——o——

THE stranger's size was gigantic, and his face of a dark Italian cast, while there was a fierceness and fire in his eye that would strike everyone who beheld him.

Instead of a girdle, he had a piece of sailcloth twisted round his body and loins and covering him down to his knees: at his side a large, bare knife and a pistol.

"Halt, there!" he repeated, as his brawny hand fell upon my shoulder, and held me with a grasp of iron.

The sound of a human voice had terrified me, but the sight of this brigand gave me heart again. I had reasons to fear a good man, but none at all to tremble before a ruffian.

"Whom have we here?" said the brigand.

"Such another as yourself," was my answer—"that is, if your looks do not belie you," I continued.

"May I be hanged," said he, "if you have not rubbed shoulders with the gallows ere now!"

"It may be so," replied I. "So farewell till we meet again!"

"Nay, stop, comrade!" shouted the huge ruffian, as I strolled away. "Stop, and drink!"

He pulled a tin flask from his pocket and held it towards me.

I went back, took the flask and drank. New strength seemed to flow into my body, and with it came fresh courage to my heart.

There seemed something pleasant in finding a companion of my own stamp.

He stretched himself on the grass, and so did I.

"Your drink has done me good," said I. "We must get better acquainted."

He struck his flint and lighted his pipe.

"Are you old in the trade?" said I, "and has that knife seen much blood?"

He looked sternly at me, and snatching the pipe from his lips, said:

"Who art thou?"

"A murderer, like yourself," replied I. "But only a beginner!"

He took his pipe, which had dropped in his consternation, and, assuming an easy position, looked me full in the face:

"Do you know me?" I asked.

"No!" said he.

"Did you never hear of Golpho?" I inquired.

"What—Black Golpho, the poacher?" he stammered out, harshly.

"The same!" I replied. "Well, then, I am Golpho!"

He seized my hand, crying out:—"Welcome, comrade—welcome! I know thee well, now. I have long reckoned upon having thee among our banditti!"

"Why reckon on me?" I gasped.

"Because the country is full of you. You have enemies—you have been dealt hardly with. Was it because you shot a pair of stags, or boars, that you should be chased from door to door, confined three years in the Castle, and beggared for life? Is it come to this, that a man is less worth than an animal?" replied my comrade.

"Who can alter these things?" I urged.

"Ha!—that we shall see!" was the reply. "But tell me whence come you, and what are your plans?" he asked.

I told him my whole story, and as I finished, he leaped up and dragged me by the shoulder along with him.

"Where will you take me to?" I said.

"Ask no questions, but come along," he replied, and, clutching my arm with the grasp of a giant, he pulled me forward with him.

We had gone on thus far for about a quarter of a mile, the wood becoming more thick, wild, and impassable at every step—neither of us speaking a word—when I started at the sound of a whistle, which my guide was blowing furiously. I looked up and saw that we were standing on the edge of a rock, which hung over a steep, dark, ravine.

A second answered from the bottom of the precipice, and a ladder arose in the air, as if by its own motion.

My guide stepped upon it, telling me to await his return, saying that unless he "tied up the hounds, as I was a stranger, they would tear me to pieces!"

In a few seconds, he ascended, and bade me follow him. I obeyed.

A few yards down, the precipice widened, and some small huts became visible. In the midst of these there was a plot of smooth turf, with about twenty figures around a fire.

"Here, comrades!" shouted my guide, leading me down into the centre of the group—"here, get up and bid Golpho welcome!"

"Welcome, Black Golpho!" shouted all the men and women as with one voice.

Their joy seemed hearty and honest as their welcome, and they made me sit down to toast them in a bumper.

A meal was prepared of many kinds of game, and good wine. We all joined heartily in the repast, the company seeming full of affection towards each other, and goodwill towards me.

I was placed between two females, whom I expected were not great ornaments to their sex, but was agreeably surprised, upon taking a good look at them, to find that they were handsome, young, and very intelligent.

The youngest seemed deeply interested in me, and watched me until I felt there was a mystery between us.

(To be continued in No. 21.)

TALES OF BRIGANDS AND ROBBERS.

Warn & Strike

[SILVER JACK RESCUES MADALINE.]

THE RED DWARF.

CHAPTER VI. *(Continued.)*

WITH one voice, as it seemed, the masked men exclaimed:
"He is welcome !"

You hear ?" said the Red Dwarf to the perplexed Allan.

"I do," replied the young man. "But suppose I refuse to join you? How do I know but you are leagued together for some bad and unholy end ? Methinks it is a cowardly advantage to take over a helpless man, when you force him into a company which may be both treasonous and infamous."

"Our company may be either better or worse, as you suppose," replied the dwarf.

"You speak in riddles," answered Allan.

"I am one myself!" laughed Red Dwarf.

"If you mean to achieve my destruction, you might as well have left me in the hands of the Black Colonel and his gang! You raise up my hopes, show me a prospect of liberty with the maiden I love, and then again sink me into the gulf of despair by juggling tricks like these! Kill me at once, villain!" exclaimed the indignant young man, springing to his feet, "for if I lose Madaline and liberty, of what value is life to me?"

"Thou art a rash boy!" said the dwarf, grasping him by the arm with a giant's strength. "Bide thy time, and who knows what may happen? All is not lost that is in danger, and the darkest night sometimes brings forth the brightest morrow. Go to—go to, prove a faithful comrade, and as far as the Red Dwarf can compass it, the Lady Madaline shall yet be yours."

"Indeed!" said Allan, in joyful surprise. "Then you do not seek to part us for ever?"

"Had such been my intention, I should not have rescued you," answered the dwarf.

"I would I could bring myself to think you are bent on no evil," murmured Allan, perplexed between hope and fear. "Answer me that question, and then my mind will be more at ease."

"I cannot answer you that question. Ours is a band of mystery, and until the proper time arrives, that mystery must be kept; but on one point I can set your mind at rest. Neither myself nor any of my band take human life, except in self defence."

"I rejoice to hear it. That avowal reassures me; but Madaline——"

"Take the oath which makes you one of us, and within the next hour you shall again behold her!"

Allan paused for a moment.

His love for Madaline overcame all his scruples, and he exclaimed:

"I am content to join you; and if I am doing wrong, may Heaven pardon me, for I seek to injure no one!"

"Listen, then," said the dwarf. "Since you consent, you must swear to be ready to do our bidding in any way that I may dictate or point out. You have already sworn to me when we were alone to do anything that I might ask. Now swear also to do the same for my comrades."

As the Red Dwarf finished these words, and before Allan had time to reply, a score of daggers pressed against his breast.

Then as many voices exclaimed in a loud tone:

"Swear!"

"Then I swear henceforth to obey you in the faith and honour of a man, since you promise that I shall see Madaline once again."

"It is well," said the dwarf. "Remove the bandage from his eyes, brothers, also the masks from your own faces; so that you may each know one another when you meet."

Allan looked at his companions as they unmasked, and felt assured, as he gazed at the determined faces that surrounded him, that he was linked with resolute and determined men.

"May you prove a worthy comrade of our band; faithful you must be if you wish to live in safety, for I swear to you on the word of a determined man, that if you ever sought to betray us, our vengeance would reach you—ay, even at the foot of the throne!"

As the dwarf spoke, he led Allan to a grated door, which he unlocked by the aid of a key which he selected from a bunch hanging to the girdle around his doublet.

"Bide your time," said the mysterious being, motioning Allan to enter what appeared to be an excavation in the rock.

"But you promised if I acceded to your wishes to set me at liberty," remonstrated Allan.

He was still doubtful as to how this strange adventure would terminate.

"And so I will. So again I say to you—bide your time."

Seeing it was useless to argue further, Allan entered the cave.

The dwarf locked the barred door at the entrance, and Allan was left alone to ruminate over what had passed and what was to come.

He had sworn to obey the dwarf and his comrades in any stratagem they might wish to achieve.

He felt he had been rash to bind himself thus, but it was for Madaline's sake.

The dwarf's words, wherein he had assured him that neither himself nor any of his band took human life except in self-defence somewhat reassured him.

He was aroused from his reflections by the sound of two well-known voices.

By looking through the bars which formed the door of the cave in which he was placed, he could command a full view of the outer cavern, in which he saw Silver Jack and young Claude Duval surrounded as he had been by Red Dwarf and his comrades, who were raising their daggers over Claude and Silver Jack as if administering to them the same oath to which he had himself been subjected.

"Is civil war again to rage in Old England?" thought Allan, "and have I leagued myself with rebels? My father was beheaded as a traitor, and I believe unjustly. I vowed to my poor dead mother to revenge his death if I ever traced the villains who betrayed him, and may Heaven prosper me as I keep my oath! But then again," exclaimed the youth in a tone of anguish, "who knows but I may be aiding and abetting those who may cause me to die the same death as my poor father?"

His reflections were interrupted by seeing all the torches suddenly extinguished, and the cavern wrapped in total darkness.

Had they forgotten him?

Was he to be left there to perish?

To die perhaps by starvation?

Horrible thought!

As the idea idea struck upon his mind, the cold perspiration of fear for a moment bedewed his brow.

Then, impelled by all the fury of despair, he rushed to the grated door, shaking the bars with all his force, and calling to the Red Dwarf for his liberty and the fulfilment of his promise regarding Madaline.

"If you mean me foul play, despatch me with your daggers at once, nor leave me to a life of lingering agony!" cried he.

As he spoke, he felt his arm grasped with rude force, and a voice cried in his ear:

"Silence! Are you a child that you fear the dark?"

Allan recognised the tones of the Red Dwarf.

"You here?" asked Allan, in surprise.

He knew not whether the dwarf's visit boded him good or evil.

"How could he have entered?" thought the astonished Allan.

He saw him in the outer cavern a moment ago.

That he could have passed through the iron door was impossible.

It was fast locked.

"I can guess the reason of your surprise," said the dwarf; "but had I not as many openings to go in and out at as a rabbit in a warren, the Red Dwarf would have been caged long since. Give me your hand, and follow me cautiously."

The dwarf led the way through a concealed door at the other end of the cave, by which he had entered. This led into a winding passage, and, by the damp odour which prevailed, Allan guessed they were underground.

At length a ray of moonlight struck across their path, and the Red Dwarf's companions, who were again cloaked and masked, stood awaiting them at the entrance.

Before Allan could look around him he was again blindfolded, led to the boat, and rowed by the dwarf back to the place from whence they had at first started.

Leaping ashore, the dwarf secured the boat in its hiding-place, and, taking Allan by the hand, led him along in silence.

"Stoop," said his conductor, as he touched Allan on the shoulder.

Allan did as he was ordered, and passed through an opening covered with ivy large enough to admit two persons.

Following the dwarf, who still grasped him by the hand, Allan suddenly felt the handkerchief plucked from his eyes, and found himself at the spot where he first entered the carriage with his mysterious companion.

"Now go your ways to the house of Sir Stuart Catemass, and let him know the villany of Lord Kylo Smedleigh in its true colours. Take the rescue of Madaline entirely to your own credit, and, if her father does not reward you with her hand, he is destitute of generosity."

"I dare not hope for so much happiness," answered Allan. "But now I know Madaline is safely out of the libertine's hands, a weight is lifted off my heart which once went wellnigh to crush it."

"Go, then," said the dwarf.

"But what if I am again molested?" asked Allan.

"Do not fear that; the Red Dwarf's band have their eyes open, ready to shield your safety and secure their own. Begone."

He pointed up the road towards the city as he spoke.

Allan moved away in the direction indicated.

Still he thought the dwarf's rescue of Madaline merited some expression of gratitude.

He turned to thank him, but he was gone.

All that had passed seemed to Allan like a dream.

The rapid chain of incidents which had occurred during the last twelve hours bewildered him as he thought upon them, and the knowledge that he had bound himself by oath to a band of desperate men did not tend to allay his anxiety.

Still he made his way to the residence of Madaline's father, hoping that the share he had taken in his daughter's release would have some weight, backed as it would be by the intercession and confirmatory words of Madaline, and cause the proud nobleman to look somewhat more kindly on the love which he felt for his only child.

CHAPTER VII.

MADALINE'S RETURN HOME.—THE SCHEME OF TREACHERY UNFOLDED.—THE FAITHFUL SERVANT AND HIS MISTRESS.—THE COMPACT BETWEEN THE BLACK COLONEL AND LORD KYLO.—THE PLAN FOR THE DESTRUCTION OF SIR STUART CATEMASS.—THE MIDNIGHT ATTACK.—THE NOCTURNAL FLIGHT.—THE ENCOUNTER.—SILVER JACK TO THE RESCUE.

THE carriage into which Madaline had been conducted rolled swiftly along the road.

The joy she felt at her deliverance was neutralised by the absence of Allan.

Why had they separated them? If he was still in peril, her liberty would not seem half so sweet.

He had been her firm and trusty champion, and he reigned in her heart as its sole and undivided master.

But then he was of obscure birth, and she sighed as she remembered often hearing her father say that no daughter of his house should ever wed beneath their ancient dignity.

Her heart clung with tenderness to both parent and lover. To lose either would be to forfeit all that made life dear.

"But my father will yield to me when I tell him all—I am sure he will!" thought the sanguine girl. "For what is pride of birth to a life of happiness."

Her reflections were brought to an end by the sudden stoppage of the coach.

A masked man opened the door, and, telling her to alight, respectfully assisted her to do so.

"You have reached the end of your journey," said the man.

"But where am I?" asked Madaline.

"Look around you," he replied.

Madaline did so, and found she was within a few paces of her father's residence.

"You are now safe," said the man. "And bid your father keep a sharp eye on you, for hawks are abroad."

"But what of Allan Buckhurst?" eagerly asked Madaline.

"Fear nothing for him; he is under the protection of the Red Dwarf and his band—of which I am one."

"But is Allan at liberty?" inquired Madaline.

"By this time I have no doubt he is. Ask no more questions, but get thee in, and thank providence you are out of the clutches of the Black Colonel."

"I do most fervently," said Madaline. "But tell me where my father can send reward to the man they call the Red Dwarf for his brave deliverance of me."

"What!—disclose the abiding-place of our chief?" laughed the man. "Make others as wise as ourselves, that they may hunt down the man dreaded by all? No, no, lady; that secret remains safe in the hearts of the Red Dwarf's companions—and he who discloses it dies."

"But you will at least accept some token yourself at my hands for aiding in my rescue?" asked the grateful and overjoyed girl, taking a valuable ring from her finger.

"No, lady," said the man, rejecting the proffered gift; "I am well paid for my services, and to accept a present from you would be to anger our chief. Farewell! May honour and safety ever be with you!"

He sprang into the coach lately occupied by Madaline, and the vehicle was driven rapidly off.

Ringing hastily at the gate-bell, the overjoyed girl looked forward to the surprise she should give her father when she presented herself before him.

But where was that father?

The reader knows, but as yet the daughter was in happy ignorance.

She was so impatient to behold him that she again rang at the gate bell before anyone appeared.

What was the meaning of this? Was her father absent?—the servants also?

At length she heard footsteps approaching, and the gate was opened by Musgrave, her father's valet, who appeared rejoiced as he beheld her.

"Oh, welcome—a thousand times welcome—my dear young lady!" exclaimed the faithful servant, leading the way. "Have you met with my lord? He departed in search of you some hours since."

"And has he not returned?" exclaimed the anxious girl.

"Not at present," replied Musgrave.

"Did he leave here alone?" asked Madaline.

"No, my lady, Lord Kylo Smedleigh was with him."

"Lord Smedleigh!" cried Madaline, a suspicion of foul play crossing her mind. "Did you hear where they were going?"

"I heard Lord Smedleigh caution my lord not to let us hear the destination they were about to take."

"Oh, the villain!—the crafty hypocrite! It is Lord Smedleigh who bore me from my home last night."

"What!—and not young Allan Buckhurst?" asked the astonished servant.

"Lord Smedleigh is the villain, I tell you! Why should you suppose Allan Buckhurst would be guilty of such an outrage?"

"Because my master is led to believe so."

"By whom?"

"By Lord Kylo Smedleigh," replied the servant.

"The crafty knave!" exclaimed Madaline. "Oh, how could my father repose confidence in such a villain? Something seems to tell me he is being led to his destruction."

"The very same thought crossed my mind, my lady, shortly after their departure, so I instantly sent all the servants in the house after Sir Stuart, telling them to trace their master, and see that no harm had befallen him."

"Thanks—thanks, my good Musgrave! I pray Heaven they have overtaken him!"

But they had not, as the reader has already seen.

"And how long have the servants been absent?" asked Madaline.

"It is now some four hours since they departed," replied Musgrave.

"Then their search has been unsuccessful, and I will trace my father even though I again peril my own safety."

She was about to go forth again, when Musgrave forcibly yet respectfully detained her.

"Stay, my lady—stay! Think not, I beseech you, of again venturing forth at this late hour! Wait a little while, I entreat you, and who knows but Sir Stuart may return? The city is dangerous at this time of night, as your ladyship is aware; besides, you might miss my master even as he was hastening home again to see if you had returned."

"True—true," reflected Madaline; and she resolved to abide within for a short time to see if her father really did return.

The actual state of things was mercifully concealed from her for a time.

Had she known the truth, her reason would surely have given way under the blow.

She therefore decided to wait until Allan should arrive, and ask his counsel and advice.

She knew in him she had a firm and faithful friend through every danger.

By Musgrave's advice, she went to her chamber and sought to take a little repose.

How she listened to every sound—started at every breeze—hoping to hear every moment the sound of her father's footsteps!

It was only his absence she mourned. She did not dream of any danger.

Gradually slumber stole upon her, prostrated as she was in mind and body by past events.

She awoke with a start.

A faint cry of alarm from the servants' hall below seemed to strike upon her ear.

She sat up on her couch and listened.

All was still.

She must have been mistaken, so she again courted repose, hoping to be awakened by the sound of her father's voice.

We must now conduct the reader back to the dread region of Alsatia, that we may watch the movements of the crafty Lord Kylo, the Black Colonel, and his base associates.

The Black Colonel saw Sir Stuart Catemass disappear through the flooring with a loud shout of mocking laughter.

"You're safe enough for a time!" cried the ruffian, as the secret trap closed over the prison of Sir Stuart.

"Is he dead?" asked Lord Kylo, looking into the room.

"Not he!" answered the colonel. "But he soon shall be, if you wish it. We don't stand at trifles here, I promise you, especially as regards your lordship's orders, for we know you always pay well and promptly for them."

And, as he spoke, the ruffian held forth his hand, with a look of meaning, towards Lord Kylo, who took the hint and poured some pieces of gold into the desperado's palm.

"The father being secured, now what prevents me gaining possession of the daughter?" asked the libertine.

"Two things," answered the colonel. "In the first place, the Red Dwarf and his comrades; in the second, we don't know the whereabouts of the maiden."

"Think you the Red Dwarf will claim her for himself?" asked Lord Kylo.

"Not he," said the colonel. "I see you don't know the man; he's above such weaknesses, and plays for a higher stake."

"And seems to be your superior, whoever he may be," said his lordship, in a taunting tone, to his friend the colonel.

"More of that anon," said that worthy, with a growl. "Don't make too sure. It's true he has me in his hands as matters stand, but it shall be diamond cut diamond before I have finished with him."

"I should like to know whether the girl has returned home or not, colonel."

"If she has, depend on it she did not go there unattended."

"She won't find her father there—that's one comfort!" laughed the libertine lord, with all the malice of a fiend. "Are you bold enough to come with me, and see how the land lies in that quarter?"

"What end will it answer?"

"Never heed that," said Lord Kylo. "It stands to reason that the house of Sir Stuart will be all confusion at his non-return, and I should like to know what measures his lordship's fair daughter will take in his absence. Let us watch the house."

"First we must be assured we are not watched ourselves. Remember, young Allan Buckhurst is now at liberty, and joined with him are Silver Jack and young Claude Duval, two fiery spirits of the fiend's own breed."

"Why, surely you don't fear them, with your troop to back you?" asked Lord Kylo.

"To tell you the truth," said the colonel in a low voice, "my band are getting mortally dissatisfied of late, and, to hold them in check, I have to divide every rap I get with them, so it will be small profit to me to aid you further."

"Why need they know I require further aid from you? Say your business with me is at an end."

"And then suppose we wanted help from them?"

"Why, then select two or three of the most dependable, and we'll bribe them to keep the secret from the rest of their comrades," said the artful libertine.

"Good!" cried the ruffian colonel, smiting the table at which he sat with his hand. "If I only had your wit, and you had my daring, we might carry the world before us."

"Sink your scruples, then, and come with me," said Lord Kylo.

"Well, I will if you'll make some plausible excuse as to my leaving here with you to my comrades."

"Do you fear them so much, then?"

"Not man to man, or two to one, if it came to that; but there are other means of removing a man out of the world without attacking him openly. And during the last month," whispered the colonel in Lord Kylo's ear, "I have almost dreaded tasting food here for fear of its being poisoned."

"Indeed!" said Lord Kylo, starting. "Had I such suspicions, I'd sell my comrades to the law at the best price, and secure my own safety at any risk."

"Ay, ay: but the worst of it is, I'm not *certain* of what I've been telling you. I've removed others from my path by the same means *I* dread, and that makes me suspicious."

"No wonder," thought Lord Kylo.

"But come at once, and I'll make an excuse to the band as to your leaving here with me."

"But Sir Stuart Catemass, what is to become of him in the meantime?" asked the colonel, pointing towards the boards at his feet.

"Let him remain there and die— die of *starvation*, if you will!" hissed the malignant fiend in the colonel's ear.

Ruffian at heart as this desperado was, he could not help starting at the hellish proposition.

He was about to utter a volley of oaths, and scorn such a proposal, but on second thought he said nothing, and formed his plans in another way.

"You don't seem to relish my plan," said his companion.

"What makes you think so?" asked the colonel.

"Because you started when I broached the plan, and even now you seem irresolute."

"You are mistaken, I was never more decided. Let us go."

They passed into the long chamber where they had left Geoffrey and the others, who were throwing dice for the gold pieces Lord Kylo and his victim had bestowed upon them.

"Hal," said the colonel, beckoning that worthy aside, "a word in your ear. Look to the prisoner who is entrapped in the secret vault beneath the flooring. My Lord Smedleigh wishes him dead, *I* wish him to live *for the present*, that I may have a hold on Master Kylo. This between ourselves."

Hal gave his master a knowing look, and muttered between his teeth:

"I comprehend."

"Lads," said the colonel aloud to the band, as they paused in their play to watch the brief conference between the colonel and Hal, "I shall soon return. A matter of some moment which concerns us all calls me hence. I will explain all upon my return."

Then, motioning to Hal to lead the way, the colonel and the libertine lord left the robbers' haunt by the same way they had entered it, and strode once more into the open street.

While they are making their way from the mysterious windings of Alsatia, let us return to the chamber of Madaline.

She still slept.

But it was a broken slumber, burdened with fearful dreams and strange forebodings.

At one moment she thought she saw her father and Allan in deadly combat, each striving for the other's life.

Then the scene would change.

She fancied herself standing before the altar with Allan, about to become his bride.

Her father was joining their hands.

The priest was about to make them man and wife, when a form, clad in black garments, suddenly took the priest's place and hid him from her view.

The form seemed to approach her father with a sudden spring, and place a fleshless arm upon her dear parent's breast.

Sir Stuart Catemass appeared to fall at her feet lifeless without a word or groan.

Allan sprang forward to seize the dark and mysterious form.

The figure confronting him, threw up the black drapery which concealed its features, and the head of a skeleton surrounded by a blue and sulphurous flame, caused Allan to retreat with horror.

The dark figure plucked a dart from beneath its cloak of sable hue, and aimed it at her lover.

She sprang forward to protect him, and the weapon seemed to enter her heart.

She shrieked aloud with horror, and awoke.

As she did so, the flame of her lamp suddenly expired, and she found it was but a dream.

Yet, at the same moment her scream seemed to be echoed below.

She heard it plainly.

That was no dream, or fancied sound, but a waking reality.

She listened.

She thought the sound might be repeated, but all was silent.

Half dead with the terror inspired by her dream, and the sound she had just heard, she knew not what to do.

Suddenly she rose from the couch, resolved to seek Musgrave, and know if anything serious had happened, and whether any of the servants had returned with tidings of her father.

Feeling her way to the door, she had just placed her hand upon the lock when she heard frotsteps stealthily ascending the stairs.

Her heart beat with joy.

It was her father coming to tell her he was safe and overjoyed at his child's rescue.

"Father—dear father, is it you?" she exclaimed, as she heard the footsteps reach the landing.

"Yes, Madaline," replied a voice, but it seemed a strange one to her ear.

A momentary suspicion of treachery shot across her mind, and she strove to close and lock the door.

But before she could accomplish this, a cloaked form darted into the room, and seized her by the wrist.

At the same moment the moonbeams streamed into the room and revealed the features of Lord Kylo Smedleigh.

"Help, help! Father—Allan—Musgrave! Save me—save me!" screamed the horror-stricken girl.

"They will find a difficulty in doing so," said her remorseless persecutor. "Your father is safely disposed of, your lover far away; and as for Musgrave, the fool, has fallen a victim to his vain resistance."

That was the cry, then, she had heard.

Their faithful servant had fallen defending his master's daughter.

"Villain!" cried Madaline, her womanly indignation rousing her to courage. "Never will I leave this place with you while life remains, or I have strength left to struggle with you!"

Exerting all her strength, she strove to reach the casement to call for assistance from without.

But the libertine dragged her towards the staircase with all his force, and Madaline, feeling her strength fast leaving her, would have fallen insensible on the ground, had he not caught her in his arms.

He descended the staircase with the poor maiden, who was no longer able to resist him.

They reached the hall, upon the floor of which lay the faithful Musgrave, with a sword by his side, no longer able to wield it in the defence of his master's daughter.

Lord Kylo, with his fair burden still insensible in his arms, stepped over the inanimate body, and opened the hall door, where the colonel was waiting without with two horses ready saddled.

The ruffian, a fellow of almost superhuman strength, taking madame round the waist with his left arm, sprang into the saddle with her as easily as though he carried an infant.

Lord Kylo mounted the other horse, and both spurring their steeds, they made for a by-road down by the river side.

"Ha! who are those men?" cried Lord Kylo, as two forms sprang into the road before them after they had proceeded some distance.

"Calm your fears, they are our friends Hal and Geoffrey. Thinking we might require aid, I sent back word for them to join us here. You are welcome, lads," said the colonel, addressing them. "Is the coast clear?"

"No, colonel—no," cried Geoffery in alarm. "Three horsemen come this way—do you not hear the sound of the horses' hoofs coming down the road?"

"I do," said the colonel. "Quick, my lord, let us turn back! This night's work must not be seen by anyone."

Turning their horses' heads, they urged the animals to their utmost speed.

But not before a horseman, closely following at their heels, had recognised them.

It was Allan Buckhurst.

He saw they were bearing away a female form, and his heart's instinct told him that it was the maiden of his love.

"Madaline—Madaline!" he cried, urging his horse to the top of his speed.

His two friends speedily came up with him.

They were Silver Jack and young Claude Duval.

In a moment they guessed how matters were, and drawing their rapiers, swore to aid him in the rescue of Madaline.

Silver Jack being the better mounted of the three, speedily passed Allan, and was the first to reach the colonel's side.

"Release that lady, caitiff!" cried Jack.

"Not by your command!" answered the colonel, making a thrust at him as he spoke.

The thrust was quickly parried, and the highwaymen—one of the most expert swordsmen of the time—made a lunge at his foe, and penetrated the arm which encircled Madaline.

The colonel called aloud for Lord Kylo to come to his assistance; but, looking round, saw that the libertine as well as coward had fled.

As the colonel turned his head, Silver Jack struck the villain down, and caught Madaline in his arms.

All this was the work of a moment.

The next instant Hal and Geoffrey, advancing to their leader's aid, find themselves kept at bay by the gleaming rapiers of Allan and Claude Duval.

(To be continued.)

THE NEAPOLITAN BANDITTI.

THE confession, to which I breathlessly listened, was this:—
"Florestan, I have learned too late the desperate treachery practised upon us both. But this day I heard it from my husband's—my betrayer's lips; in a transport of folly, or absurd jealously or frenzy, he insulted me with charges that he well knew had no foundation [but in his own taunting heart. He detailed the whole long tissue of artifice which separated us in Grenada; which had made me, in my madness, pronounce you the most faithless of men, and, in my still greater madness, believe him capable of truth, fidelity, or honour. With the bitter triumph, less of a man than of a fiend, he showed me the trivial suspicions that I had taken for proofs; the giddy surmises that I had shaped into facts; the whole system of willing deception into which I had plunged blindly, to aid his purposes, and destroy every chance of my own escape. But you do not hear me—you close your thoughts against the miserable being who has come to make a last acknowledgment of her own error, to solicit your last forgiveness, to relieve her burdened—her breaking heart, and to die."

A deep groan from the Conde was the only answer.

I heard loud sobs and wild sighs. In the fear that he was dying, I drew aside the curtain. The stranger was kneeling beside the bed; the cowl was thrown back; but to discover the countenance baffled me—the hands covered it; and, on my making a movement towards my master, the cowl was instantly drawn down, and the figure started from its knees and was gone.

But, whatever my curiosity might have been, it was soon divided by the visits of others equally mysterious, and coming in all kinds of disguises, which, though enough to escape the eyes of the household, were not sufficient to conceal them from mine, sharpened as they were by the first interview.

Sellers of various toys, jewels, or embroidery, chiefly in the dress of females, were perpetually soliciting to see the Conde; and even in his feeblest state, the request was seldom refused.

On those occasions I was excluded.

Those merchants were evidently the bearers of letters and other intelligence, which deeply agitated the invalid.

But all my attempts to shut them out were useless.

The Conde's command was for their instant admission; and I was left to conjecture.

The monk came no more.

But I one day found, flung on the escritoire, a fragment of a letter, with these words:—

"To see you is impossible, if it were not unnecessary. I have ascertained, on the fullest proof, the hirer of your assassin. The attempt will be made again and again until it succeeds. Beware! But if a feeling remain in your heart for one who so deadly wronged you and so fatally wronged herself, make no effort to revenge this crime—make no effort to see me—either would only make me miserable. Farewell, Florestan, and remember!"

The Conde slowly recovered, though he had four physicians of the court to attend him.

But, to complete the cure, he was ordered to remove to his palace at Portici.

The gardens were rich, the prospect was unrivalled, and the air health itself.

But the pleasure had its peril.

Fra Joachimo began to give notice of his movements towards the capital, by the plunder of some house or traveller every night.

The troops stationed to guard the roads could do nothing in pursuit of this extraordinary personage, who seemed to be everywhere at once; and, like honest Italians, they resolved, that, as to waste their time in running after a phantom was folly, the best thing they could do was to pile their arms and go to sleep.

Half a dozen of their patrols were carried off in this condition, arms, accoutrements and ammunition,—before they could find out that sleeping in the face of the enemy was contrary to prudence. But nothing could change the sumptuousness of the Conde's style of living.

He laughed at Fra Joachimo, renewed his fetes with his returning health, and established his hazard table on a more desperate scale than ever.

Gaming had been his pleasure before; it was now his passion.

He sat up whole nights at the table; and losses produced no other effect on him than an extravagance of high spirits.

But the effect was not the same upon all.

The Capitano, in the interval of my master's illness had continued to play, and, unluckily for himself, falling into harder hands than the Conde's, was on the edge of ruin.

When he returned to our fetes, I never saw a man so changed.

The bold, broad visage was dwindled down into narrowness and misery.

Its soldierly bronze was as sallow as if he had been a sick girl; and the voice, whose very sound had been insolence, was broken and sunk into a whisper.

Night after night he played; but fortune had deserted him. In his distress he borrowed of the Conde, and, fast as he borrowed, the loan flew from his fingers.

At length a rumour went abroad that a large sum of money, belonging to the royal treasury of the Principato, intrusted to the Capitano's care, had been unaccounted for.

I saw him on the night when the rumour was first whispered in the palazzo; and if the Capitano had an enemy, that was the night for him to enjoy his triumph.

He played with the madness of a man to whom death or life was in the stake.

On that night I marked the Conde's manner to be singularly disturbed. He was the Capitano's opponent, and as the pile of gold rose before him, he smiled with an expression of fierce delight.

As the stakes doubled, and the game grew at once bolder and more in his favour, his exultation perpetually betrayed itself.

At length one critical throw came.

All gathered round the table.

There was not a whisper among the multitude. Every eye was fixed on the board when the die was next moment to terminate this furious game.

The box was in my master's hand.

I glanced at him as he raised it to make the throw.

His lips quivered, his countenance was burning; and, if ever a prayer was made to the powers of chance or of evil by the eye alone, it was in that wild upturned eye.

The die was thrown.

"Ruin!" howled the Capitano, as with his meagre hands grasping the die he fell backwards on the floor.

"Revenge!" muttered the Conde, as, giving one look of bitter triumph at his fallen enemy, he rushed from the room.

Events of this kind were so common among the higher ranks of the nobles, that the wreck of the unfortunate gamester made no pause in the entertainment; the same ruin was going on at fifty tables through the house at the same time, and, when the summons for supper came, no one thought of the Capitano.

The Conde was in his usual temper, neither elevated nor depressed, but doing the honours of the banquet with the ease and high courtesy of his rank.

Never was there a more sumptuous entertainment, even among the extravagancies of the noblesse; and seldom assembled a party who less thought of care.

In the midst of the festivity, a note was handed to the Conde, and he followed the messenger to his study.

As I passed the door, I heard voices in rapid conversation, and a small window looking into the garden gave me the opportunity of gratifying my curiosity to know the occasion of this unseasonable billet. To my utter astonishment, I saw the handsome and haughty wife of the Capitano kneeling at the Conde's feet. I could catch but a fragment of her words:

"Florestan, you have had your revenge. You have undone my unhappy husband. He deserved your abhorrence and mine. I acknowledge that he had deceived us both—that all my early hopes of happiness were blasted by his treachery."

Her voice was lost in sighs.

The Conde raised her from the ground, and led her towards the casement to restore her by the cool air.

She had been incomparably the handsomest and most superbly attired of the crowd of ladies at the palace during the evening; and, when the Conde drew the mantle from her head, I was actually dazzled with its sudden blaze of diamonds.

But, when she turned, and looked on the single twinkling lamp that lighted the chamber, as if she saw it in some image of her own unhappy heart, I never saw so much melancholy and beauty in the face of a human being. After gazing awhile, she suddenly turned and said:

"Conde, you have heard my misery. I have made my last confession to the ear of man. I may not live long. I must not live long. There is at this hour an impression on my mind that speaks as if it were the voice of a spirit. But I implore you, if you ever remembered me in the long and wretched years that have passed since our parting; if you still do not hate me; if you would wish to think of you in that world to which I am hastening, save my wretched husband!"

The Conde had listened till now, with declining head and eyes fixed on the ground. But, at the mention of the Capitano, he sprang up.

His eyes blazed with sudden fury; he cursed him as his destroyer.

"Save him!—save the cold-blooded traitor! Save him who has made me for years the most miserable of mankind—who has stretched me on the rack of disappointed hope, of degraded honours, of undone love—save the Capitano, save your husband? No! may this right hand perish from my side, if I would not give it—if I would not give fortune, name, and life, to strike him at my feet, and to ring in his dying ear, that I knew his treacheries, and thus at last repaid them!"

The lady, shrinking from his fiery violence of gesture and language, buried her face in her hands and wept aloud.

But suddenly recovering, and dashing the tears from her cheeks, she advanced towards him with the step of an empress.

"Conde!" exclaimed she, in a solemn tone, "you have scorned my entreaty—now refuse, if you dare, my command. From this hour we are strangers to each other. It is my first duty to save my husband from ignominy, wretched and guilty though he be. Your revenge, bitter and deadly revenge, first tempted him to the gaming-table. You alone are answerable for the consequences. You are high-minded, determined, and sagacious: he is weak and worthless, a tyrant and a fool. He has embezzled the money of the state; he has lost it under your roof: this night he has made a desperate effort for its recovery. The sum that he has lost within this hour was the sum which he had gathered to stop inquiry to-morrow, until he should be enabled to repay the whole. I have left him in the agonies of one over whom public shame, perhaps public death, is impending. Refund that money which you have won of him, and entitle yourself to my prayers while I live."

She paused—there was no answer.

"Then, Florestan," she added, in a low, sepulchral tone, "I know what you have been; I know what you are; and I know what you shall be."

She remained with her mysterious eyes fixed on him, her lip compressed, and her cheek pale as death.

The Conde had been leaning against a statue as motionless as itself, but at those words he started, and gazing haughtily on the fair accuser, exclaimed:

"You know what I am? So be it! But who has made me

so? Who flung me from my rank in life? Who drove me, despairingly and undone, into my degradation? Who has made the face of woman hateful to me for life, and the face of man seen only as an enemy or a victim? Who has driven Florestan out into the wilderness as a beast of prey; to run through a career of abhorred life, and to perish in the midst of public execration? Your husband has done this: and now, by every power that exists in the mind of man, he shall rue what he has done! Lady, I am a lover no longer: our only tie is that of mutual misery. Years have subdued all that was fond or feeble in my nature. I have extinguished my weakness in the bitterness of privation, in rapine, in the scorn of the idle and contemptible beings that make up the sons and daughters of greatness in this contemptible land; in the association with the daring, the merciless, and the ruined like myself; and, more than all, in the determination—the solemn, sacred, sworn determination of revenge."

The lovely lady struck her hand on her forehead, as if she had heard her sentence of death. The blow forced an aigrette from her hair, and the diamonds flew sparkling over the floor. She uttered a scream of joy.

"Why did I not think of this before?" she exclaimed; "he may yet be saved!"

She tore the jewels out of her hair; and, with her raven locks disordered, and her hands full of precious ornaments, she rushed to the door.

The Conde made an effort to detain her; but she sprang from him with the fleetness of a deer, and darted from the room.

My master's countenance continued in its gloomy mood. He went to a secretaire, wrote a few lines, with which he despatched me to Naples, late as the hour was, and I saw no more of him for the night.

The nobleman to whose house I was sent was either absent or indolent, and I was kept waiting during the day for his reply.

Towards evening I lounged down to enjoy the cool air at the port.

A crowd of cavalry, round some carriages, were coming along the Stradi di Toledo.

I climbed a balustrade to see what they escorted. To my wonder, I saw several of my fellow attendants tied with cords in the carriages, and at the close of the train, doubly guarded, the Conde.

I was overwhelmed with alarm and sorrow, and followed the escort.

They stopped for a few minutes at the palace of the minister of justice, and then turned off and entered the Castle of St. Elmo.

A confused story soon made its way through the city; but all agreed that the Capitano, returning from the Conde's entertainment, had been stopped by a banditti, who robbed him of a vast amount in jewels; that the story of the robbery had been at first conceived to be a contrivance to screen him from the effects of a charge of embezzlement, but that evidence had suddenly come forward which fixed the plunder upon the Conde de Alcantara!

All Naples was in astonishment; but other intelligence came in rapidly, which made it more than probable that the splendid Count Florestan was one with Fra Joachimo himself.

The clue once given, the discovery was not far off.

That he was a Spaniard of noble family was known; but where his estates lay, by what means his extraordinary expenditure was supported, or how his occasional deficiencies of revenue were so suddenly and profusely supplied, was a national riddle.

Among other recollections that now grew upon the public were his strange periodical absences, his declared passion for wandering among the wildest districts of the mountains, and the mysterious interviews which he held during the time when he was unable to stir from his chamber.

Even his singular personal activity, his power of enduring fatigue, his seamanship, and his skill in the use of the pistol and sabre—at which I never saw his equal—made a part of the general proof.

(To be continued in our next.)

MARTINO; OR, THE BANDIT CHIEFTAIN.

It was on a cold, tempestuous winter's night, that honest Michael and his little family were sitting by their comfortable fireside, talking of the dreaded Martino, the robber-chief, when they were startled by a loud knock at the door. Michael went to the door, and lifted the latch. A fine, tall young man, covered with a cloak, hastily entered, and, accosting Michael, begged his hospitality for the night. Michael readily assented, and bade the stranger take a seat by the fire. A jug of ale was quickly placed upon the table, and the host and his guest soon became excellent friends.

"Young man," said Michael, after a cursory conversation, "have you heard anything of Martino, the noted robber, lately?"

The stranger turned pale, and, in somewhat agitated tones, said:

"Speak not that name again, I entreat you; the mere mention of it ever fills me with terror."

"Indeed!" returned Michael. "Why so?"

"Why, I was once well-nigh losing my life in an affray with one of his desperate gang."

"You surprise me—a man of your height and size attacked by a single robber! Were you on horseback?"

"Yes; but the robber was on foot."

"Pray give us the particulars!" said Michael, replenishing the stranger's glass, and handing it to him.

"They are very brief," replied the young man; "nevertheless, as you appear interested, I will state the circumstance simply as it occurred: "I had been commissioned by my employers to journey to a distant part of the country, many miles from hence. I reached the town in safety, transacted my business, and set out on my way homewards. Nothing particular occurred till I reached yonder forest, through which I had to pass before I could put up for the night. The sun had just sank below the western hills, and the huge oak trees throwing their branches across the roadway, gave—in addition to the solemn stillness of the evening—a gloomy aspect to the scene before me. A feeling of timidity came over me; a recollection of the daring band that infested the forest rushed upon my mind; and scarcely had I assured myself of the security of the valuable property I had about my person, ere a shrill whistle accosted my ear. In a moment after a man rushed from among the trees, and, seizing my horse's bridle, presented a pistol to my breast, at the same time ordering me to dismount. I instantly drew from my breast-pocket a small piece, and ere my antagonist was aware, discharged it at him. Though fired at random, it took effect; releasing his hold, he staggered and fell. My horse was fleet, and started off at full gallop; but the report of the pistol had summoned the rest of the party, and the road seemed literally thronged with them; pistol-balls flew past me in all directions, but, happily, I sustained no material injury; one of the shots slightly grazed my wrist, the mark of which is, you see, still visible."

Here the narrator extended his arm, and, folding back the cuff of his coat, exposed a fearful scar; at sight of which a thrill of horror ran through the little company, and the children of Michael seemed instinctively to cleave closer to each other, and to their parents, as if they foreboded evil.

"But the speed of my horse," continued the young man, "soon conveyed me beyond the reach of their bullets, and I arrived at my destination without any further annoyance."

The clock now struck eleven, and, after a temperate repast, the inmates of Michael's habitation retired to rest.

At an early hour in the morning, the stranger rose, and when Michael and his family besought him to remain he replied:

"After the kindness I have received at your hands, it would afford me equal pleasure with yourselves to prolong my visit; but urgent business denies me the gratification. I must be in Vienna before sunset."

Having thus spoken, the guest took his leave, and departed.

He had not been absent many hours ere the roll of a drum announced the near approach of the military, and shortly after, the door opened, and an officer entered the cottage. Addressing Michael, he said:

"I have orders to search your dwelling for one Martino; and, further, I am commanded to take you into custody, upon suspicion of encouraging the bandit chief."

Michael was quite astounded, and, though at other seasons he was by no means at a loss for language to express himself, in the present instance it was some minutes before he could gain sufficient composure to reply. At length he said:

"Sir, you wrong me! I am utterly ignorant of Martino, and, so far from having encouraged or entertained such a character, the only individual that has crossed my theshold within the last three weeks, besides yourself and the members of my own family, is a gentleman, who, being benighted, sought succour beneath this roof."

"That's the very man," replied the officer. Then, turning to his men, he continued: "Prepare to take this person with you!"

"The very man!" said Michael, repeating the officer's words. "If you will allow me, sir, I will soon convince you to the contrary!"

"I am quite willing to listen to what you have to say on the subject," answered the officer.

"Well, then, sir, as we had been talking of Martino's fearful enterprises just before the gentleman entered, I asked him if he had lately heard anything of him. To my astonishment, he shuddered at the mere mention of the robber's name; I asked him the reason, when he related to us the particulars of an affray with the desperate banditti which infests yonder forest, at the same time showing us the marks of a pistol-shot which had struck him on his right wrist. This, sir, I trust, is enough to convince you that my guest was not Martino."

"It certainly has not that appearance, my good man; notwithstanding, I must abide by my orders."

"And will you take an innocent man from his wife and family, and cast him into prison?"

"I am compelled to do so."

Michael therefore was hurried from his peaceful home, and that night lay in a loathsome dungeon at Vienna.

Martino and his band now became the terror of the whole country, by the success of their depredations.

Robberies and murders were continually committed, until at length the command of some forces was given to Count Alberto, who received orders from the capital to carry the chief there, whether alive or dead.

The first object of the count was to win over by favours the love of the peasantry, whom he knew to be stanch adherents to Martino; but his attempts were vain—they continued true to him who had so often rescued them from the tyrany of their oppressors.

On the morning of the 26th of July, the count drove the robbers from their fastness in the mountains to the sea-shore, where young Martino effected his escape by getting on board a vessel which was bound for Africa.

Though the loss of their commander dispirited the robbers for a time, an increase of numbers soon inspired them with fresh vigour, and they became more formidable than ever.

In the meantime, Michael remained in prison, expecting daily to be condemned as an accessory to Martino.

A plan, however, was formed for his deliverance. The man that attended him in his cell had often listened to his "tale of woe," believed it, and determined, if possible, to deliver him.

Accordingly, he furnished Michael with a small instrument by which he could throw back the bolt of the lock attached to the door of his dungeon, upon which he was to follow a particular track, which the turnkey described as leading directly to the prison yard, from which he could easily escape by scaling the walls.

This was practised with success, and Michael, in the dead of night, found himself once more at liberty, and on the road which led to his cottage.

(*To be continued in our next.*)

TALES OF BRIGANDS AND ROBBERS.

I Warn & Strike

[RED DWARF SAVES THE LIFE OF SIR STUART CATEMASS.]

THE RED DWARF.

CHAPTER VIII.

FLIGHT OF SILVER JACK WITH MADALINE.—THE FIGHT FOR
LIFE OR DEATH.—CLAUDE DUVAL'S MOMENT OF PERIL.—A
FRIEND IN NEED.—THE PURSUIT.—THE MEETING.—THE JOUR-
NEY HOMEWARDS.

SILVER JACK'S first anxiety was to secure the safety of the
Lady Madaline.

Fearing that the Black Colonel's other companions might
be at hand, and by coming to his aid regain possession of the
maiden, the highwayman, sharply spurring his good steed
Lancelot, thought it advisable to secure the safety of his charge.

Calling to his friends to follow him, he galloped up the road, bearing the insensible form across the noble animal he rode, making him at the same time use his utmost speed.

The moment Allan Buckhurst saw Madaline being borne off in the charge of Silver Jack, his desire to follow and guard her from any further danger overcame every other consideration.

Collecting all his strength in one decisive blow, he saw his adversary fall overpowered at his feet, then giving his horse the rein, he was quickly on the track of the friendly highwayman and Madaline.

Claude was now left on the scene of action alone, and to prevent his escape, Geoffrey crept stealthily behind him, and with a knife hamstrung the horse he rode.

Young Claude Duval now found himself in no enviable position.

The young page leaped from the horse's back as he was falling, and was instantly attacked by the ruffian Geoffrey, whose superior strength and longer weapon seemed at fearful odds against his own slender rapier.

To make matters more desperate, Hal, who had been struck down by Allan, rose to his feet.

He had fallen from the force of receiving his adversary's blow on his sword, which he had raised to ward off the desperate blow Allan had aimed at him; he was therefore uninjured.

Seeing that Allan, Silver Jack, and Madaline had eluded them, they turned all their rage upon Claude, who, rapidly growing weak under the exertion he was using to keep off Geoffrey, now saw to his despair that Hal was about to join his comrade in making short work of him.

He felt every moment more incapable of warding off the attack of Geoffrey.

Now that the other ruffian pressed upon him he gave himself up for lost.

"Cowards!" he exclaimed. "Do you call yourselves Englishmen that ye fall two to one upon a man?"

"A man!" sneered Geoffrey. "Thou art yet in thy teens, and before thou canst ever reach the age of manhood, we'll make crow's meat of thee!"

"Ay, we'll teach thee to neglect thy master, the duke's service, to mix thyself up in matters that concern thee not," cried Hal. "Look at our colonel, there, lying wounded to the death in the road," and as he spoke, he pointed to the insensible form of their ruffian leader prostrate and helpless. "Your companions have escaped, but you, my meddling young master, shall pay for all! Upon him, Geoffrey!"

They rained their blows upon the upraised sword of Claude, who, with death staring him in the face, resolved at least to die weapon in hand.

Retreating to the shelter of a tree, he placed his back against it, and resolved to sell his life dearly.

The ruffians pressed him closely; he retreated to avoid a desperate stroke from Geoffrey's weapon, and as he did so, he stumbled over one of the roots of the tree, and fell backwards.

He gave himself up for lost, as he saw the weapons of his assailants within an inch of his breast.

At that moment such a loud shriek of horror and alarm broke from the lips of the Black Colonel, that the ruffians paused in their murderous work, and turned in the direction of the sound.

The colonel, on his knees, was begging mercy from a strange-looking form, who bent over him with a determined air, as he grasped the ruffian leader by the throat.

"It is the Red Dwarf!" exclaimed Hal and Geoffrey in the same breath.

"Strike if you will, villains!" shouted the dwarf to the ruffians who held Claude's life at their swords' points— "strike if you will, I say! But the moment your weapons descend to harm that youth, my dagger shall at the same time find a sheath in the heart of your leader!"

"Hold your hands, Geoffrey and Hal, I command you!" exclaimed the colonel, in a voice of terror and supplication, as he saw the gleaming dagger of the dwarf about to descend —"hold your hands, I say, and spare the youth's life to save mine!"

"Well, since you command us, it must be so," growled Geoffrey.

He and Hal stepped back, and Claude rose to his feet with an emotion of joy, as he felt he had now a powerful friend at hand.

Seeing that Claude was unharmed, the dwarf released his hold of the colonel, who was raised to his feet by Geoffrey and Hal, who had looked upon him as having gone to his last account.

"How is it with you?" asked Geoffrey of the colonel.

"It might have been worse," replied his leader. "It is a wound through my sword arm, and I must have fainted from loss of blood. Take my handkerchief from my pocket, and bind the wound. I have had a dozen such in my time, and take little heed of these things."

Hal and Geoffrey did as they were desired, and the colonel raised himself on his feet to address the Red Dwarf, but, to his astonishment, both he and Claude Duval had vanished.

"Beshrew me if the thought doesn't often strike me that this dwarf is after all little better than one of the fiends of darkness! Not one sound did I hear of his departure, nor of the youth's, who no doubt bears him company."

"You seem mightily afraid of him, colonel," remarked Hal.

"So would you be, if you knew all," replied the colonel.

"Knew all what?" asked Geoffrey. "Can't you let us into the secret?"

"Not at present. All I can say is, those who live longest will see most. Oh that I were free from his accursed influence!"

"But suppose we laid a plan to put him out of the way, and succeeded in it?" asked Geoffrey.

"Why, then a dozen would spring up in his place," answered the colonel. "All I can do is to bide my time, and see what turn affairs take."

"Do you think he knew Sir Stuart Catemass is our prisoner?" inquired Hal.

"Not he," said the colonel. "Had he been aware of it, none of us would have escaped so freely. I believe he has friends even at the Court of King Charles himself, and, from the information he gains respecting my movements, I sometimes believe that some of our band are in his pay."

"Indeed!" cried Geoffrey. "Well, all I can say is it is not myself who has turned traitor."

"Nor I," said Hal. "I'm true to the cause I have sworn to obey, bad as it is. A murrain on all traitors, and a speedy death to them!"

"So say I, comrade," exclaimed Geoffrey. "I hold with you in that opinion to the last."

Whether the two ruffians were sincere in their protestations will be seen in the sequel.

They assisted the colonel into his saddle, and the worthy trio made their way back again into the evil regions of Alsatia.

Let us now see how it fared with Silver Jack and the Lady Madaline, who still continued insensible, as she was borne along in the arms of the highwayman mounted on his good steed Lancelot, who was flying along the road at his best speed.

Silver Jack was making for the mansion of Sir Stuart Catemass.

He imagined the joy with which the father would hail the return of his only child, little guessing the treacherous snare into which the baronet had fallen.

Hark! the rapid sound of a horse's feet.

His pursuers, then, are on his track?

"Let them come," cried Jack, grasping his good rapier. "I'll defend my fair charge to the death!"

Nearer and nearer comes his pursuer—the highwayman's steed was losing ground, oppressed by the extra weight of the unconscious Madaline.

"On, on, good Lancelot!" cried the highwayman, urging the steed to his fastest flight.

Judging by the sound of the horse's hoofs behind him, his pursuer was fast nearing him.

Silver Jack perceived it would be useless trying to reach the mansion of Sir Stuart Catemass with his fair burden.

He turned his head, and saw he was followed by a single horseman only.

"Since it is only man to man, I'll try the issue with him!" exclaimed the undaunted Jack.

He gradually slackened his pace, turned in the direction of his pursuer, grasped Madaline as firmly and as tenderly as though she had been his own child, and awaited the result.

A turn of the road brought the pursuing horseman rapidly upon him.

Oh, joy! It was young Allan Buckhurst!

"Welcome—right welcome!" cried Jack. "We may now reach the mansion in safety. How far behind are our pursuers?"

"We have nothing to fear from them. It is Madaline who is my only anxiety. How fares it with the poor girl?"

He took her hand in his—it was cold as ice.

"Good Heaven! Is she dead?" exclaimed Allan.

"Heaven forbid!" replied the highwayman. "She has only swooned. And no wonder, for the events of to-night would try the nerves of the boldest of her sex. Let us go gently down this by-road. There is a spring close at hand, and, by bathing her temples freely, we'll soon bring back her senses, never fear!"

They walked their horses slowly in the direction pointed out by Silver Jack, and Allan dismounted by the side of a bubbling spring, which sparkled in the moonlight by the hedge where they paused to dismount.

Receiving the unconscious Madaline from the arms of Silver Jack, Allan placed her on the green turf, pillowing her fair head on his knee, while the highwayman bathed her forehead with water from the spring.

In due time, the poor girl gave signs of returning animation.

Her first glance of recognition was fixed upon Silver Jack, as he knelt beside her, chafing her cold hands in his huge palms.

"Allan—save Allan!" she murmured. "They will kill him—they will murder him! And through me—through me! Oh, where—where is he?"

"Here—here, dear Madaline!" exclaimed her lover, as he bent over her and kissed her fair cheek.

"Is it indeed Allan?" cried Madaline, in tones of joy, as she clasped his hands with gratitude. "Oh, now I am ready to meet any danger, knowing that you are once more by my side!"

"There is no danger now, dearest—our pursuers are defeated and dispersed."

"But who is this man?" whispered Madaline to Allan, regarding Silver Jack with apprehension.

The highwayman guessed the question she asked of her lover, and replied to it himself.

"What? have you forgotten Silver Jack, who helped to aid your escape from the colonel at the Red House? Don't you remember me? Ah! I see you do by that look of gratitude," said the highwayman, as Madaline took his hand and grasped it in tenderness. "I never thought I could do so much for womankind till now; but the truth is, you remind me of one I knew before I took to the road—one that I once looked forward to making my wife and calmly sailing down the stream of life with, happy, innocent, and contented. But it was not to be so; she became another's, and I became Silver Jack, the highwayman. But no more of this."

He rose to his feet, dashed a tear from his eye, and advised their getting on the road.

"Take my advice, and don't tarry here another moment," continued Jack. "Place the maiden in safety, and then let us secure our own."

"Is not the danger past, then?" eagerly asked Madaline.

"That's more than we can tell, lady. The Black Colonel's band are as crafty as foxes, and fierce as hungry wolves where they declare war against anyone; but now the Red Dwarf is

on our side, we shall in the future be well able to cope with them, never fear."

"Who is this man they call the Red Dwarf, whose name seems to inspire such dread?" asked Madaline of Allan.

"He is a man of mystery and a man of power, it seems," replied Allan, trembling within himself at the oath he had taken to that strange being. He almost fancied he heard the dwarf whispering in his ear "Remember your sacred oath!"

Allan well remembered its purport.

He had bound himself to the Red Dwarf by a fearful vow, by which he was expected to do anything that dreaded man might ask at his hands.

Concealing his uneasiness from Madaline, he mounted his horse.

Silver Jack transferred his fair charge to the care of Allan, who, placing Madaline on the same horse which he had just mounted, followed Silver Jack as he led the way once more to the high-road, and made for the mansion of Sir Stuart Catemess.

A fearful discovery awaited them when they reached there.

CHAPTER IX.

THE DISCOVERY THAT SILVER JACK, ALLAN, AND MADALINE MADE IN THE MANSION.—THE CAPTIVITY OF SIR STUART CATEMASS.—THE MYSTERIOUS DUNGEON.—THE BLACK COLONEL'S OFFER OF LIFE AND DEATH TO HIS VICTIM.—THE VICTIM'S DOOM.—MATTERS TAKE AN EXTRAORDINARY TURN.

MADALINE's heart leaped for joy as they came within sight of her father's residence.

She pictured the delight with which he would receive her, and the thanks he would bestow upon her deliverers.

She was prepared to praise all to the utmost, and by so doing hoped her father would henceforth regard her lover with an eye of favour.

If that could be accomplished, she had no doubt but his ultimate consent to their union would in time be obtained.

She knew, although her father's pride was great, his love for her was equally strong.

Dismounting from his horse at the gate of the mansion, in order that he might summon the servants, Allan saw to his surprise that the portal was open.

"Truly, madam, you must have a careless set of knaves in your service to leave open doors in these roystering times!" said Silver Jack, as he also saw the gate was unsecured.

Requesting Allan's aid to dismount from the horse on which she had remained seated, Madaline advanced to the gate-bell and rang it loudly.

The summons was unanswered.

With an expression of impatience, Madaline rang again, and with the same result.

What could be the meaning of this ominous silence?

"My father, then, has not returned. Oh, what can detain him?" exclaimed the anxious maiden—"and why is the house deserted?"

"That we must ascertain," replied Allan. "I fear something is wrong. Remain here while our friend accompanies me within."

"No—no!" said Madaline—"I will also attend you!"

"I fear there has been some foul play here," remarked Silver Jack. "Do you think your father's servants would prove treacherous?"

"I do not believe there is one in the household who would betray his trust," replied Madaline.

And she was right.

The servants were absent in a vain search for their master and young mistress.

What had befallen the faithful Musgrave, who was left in charge of the mansion, we have already seen.

"Then this is doubly strange," remarked Allan. "Let us proceed within, and see what we can learn."

"Be prepared," said the highwayman, drawing his sword, and recommending Allan to do the same.

The youth did as he was advised, and led the way inside

the mansion with Madaline, followed by Silver Jack, who, closing and bolting the gate within, muttered to himself:

"If any of the enemy are really inside, they shall not get out again without a struggle for it!"

Previous to this, Silver Jack had led the horses into the court-yard, and left them standing under the shadow of the wall, not knowing how soon they might need them again.

Allan, followed by the others, cautiously advanced, listening for the slightest sound, but none could they hear.

They reached the hall.

The moon, now obscured by clouds, lent no friendly ray, and cautiously, step by step, they, by the direction of Madaline, made for the chamber of her father.

Suddenly Allan, who was in advance of the others, feels the ground slippery beneath his feet, which causes him to stagger.

Striving to recover himself, he loses his footing and falls.

Madaline, with a cry of alarm, thinking Allan was attacked by some unseen foe, clung to Jack, who was immediately behind her, and urged him to assist her lover.

"Speak, lad!—what has happened?" asked Jack, as he placed himself before Madaline as a barrier of defence.

"Beware how you advance!" exclaimed Allan, rising to his feet. "If I mistake not, blood has been shed here, and you may perchance stumble over the body of a murdered man!"

"Ah, it is my father!" shrieked Madaline, dreading the worst. "They have killed him!"

But the moon, at that moment emerging from the dark cloud which had shrouded it in gloom, darted its rays through the long windows on either side of the hall, and disclosed the fact of its being empty.

Hearing voices, the valet, as he lay in an adjoining chamber, whither he had been conveyed by the other servants who had gone in pursuit of their young mistress, uttered a faint cry for help, entreating them, if they were friends, to hasten after his young mistress, who had been forcibly taken from the house.

Madaline, followed by Allan and Silver Jack, made her way into the chamber of the wounded servant, where the rays of a feeble lamp, placed on a chair by the bedside, disclosed the half-delirious Musgrave.

"I am safe—I am safe!" exclaimed Madaline, kneeling beside him and taking his hand. "How fares it with you?"

"Wounded—wounded almost to the death!" groaned Musgrave. "A surgeon, for pity's sake, before I bleed to death!"

Medical aid had already been afforded him, but, half-delirious, he was unconscious of the fact.

"You shall have every advice that money can procure; but can you give me any news of my father?"

"I cannot, my lady—oh, would that I could! I have seen nought of him since he left here with Lord Smedleigh. I sent the other servants in search of him, remaining here alone to take charge of the mansion. Some villains afterwards gained an entrance, and in opposing them I was wounded as you see."

Notwithstanding the terror which seized upon the heart of Madaline as she gazed upon the injured man, she took the lamp in her hand, and made her way towards the chambers of the female servants of the house.

She found them trembling with fear at the cries of alarm, which had penetrated to that portion of the building.

Reproving them for their cowardice, Madaline summoned her maid Cicely, and ordered her to see the wounded man was well tended until medical aid arrived.

Trembling at the terrors which seemed to surround her, the handmaiden followed Madaline to Musgrave's chamber.

The faithful servant had now become more conscious, and remembered being tended by Dr. Alwyn, his master's skilful physician, under whose direction his wounds were dressed.

During the absence of Madaline, Silver Jack and Allan had remained with Musgrave; and, from what they could glean from him, arrived at the conclusion that the Black Colonel was at the bottom of this piece of villany.

Madaline could testify that Lord Smedleigh was the man who had dragged her from her chamber.

But all her sorrows and past dangers seemed as nothing when compared with the fears that beset her regarding the safety of her father.

"I will away at once to the foot of the throne, and demand justice on our enemies!" said the excited girl, about to leave the chamber.

She was gently restrained by Allan, who begged her to be calm until morning broke, when he would accompany her to the King's palace at Whitehall.

"Besides, who knows but we may expect your father's return every moment?" reasoned Allan.

But even as he spoke, his fears seemed to belie his hopes.

Silver Jack had also dark thoughts upon the matter, but out of mercy towards Madaline he kept them to himself.

A loud ringing at the gate bell caused them all to start.

"Perhaps that is my father!" exclaimed Madaline, as she was about to rush from the room to answer the summons.

"Stay, Madaline—stay! Go not alone!" remonstrated Allan. "You are not certain whether they are friends or foes. I will answer the gate. Remain you here."

She reluctantly yielded to his wish, and Allan, beckoning to Silver Jack, crossed the court-yard and made for the entrance gate.

Before they could reach it, the summons was repeated.

"Who is it that rings so loudly?" demanded Allan.

"We are Sir Stuart's servants," said a voice, which Allan recognised as belonging to Gilbert Wyatt, one of the baronet's head serving-men.

Allan quickly drew the bolts of the gate, and Gilbert and the other servants, who had been out with him in the fruitless search for their master, entered the court-yard.

The started as they saw Allan and Silver Jack.

"Fear nothing," said Allan, noticing their alarm. "We are friends. Have you heard any tidings of your master?"

"None. We have searched through the city in vain," answered Gilbert.

By this time Madaline had joined them, and, overhearing the words of the serving-man, the poor maiden burst into a passionate flood of tears, and again relapsed into insensibility.

Allan took her in his arms, and bore her within the house.

Calling for her maid Cicely, he saw her placed upon her couch under the girl's care.

After the exhaustion consequent upon her grief had passed away, Madaline, overwrought by grief and weakness, sunk into a heavy slumber.

Leaving her to "tired Nature's sweet restorer—balmy sleep," Allan went from the chamber to consult with Silver Jack and the servants as to their best course of action.

Leaving them in deliberation, let us return and see how it fared with Sir Stuart Catemass in Alsatia.

Stunned by his fall from the room above, it was some time before his senses returned, so that he could realise his situation.

At length his reason gradually came back, and he found himself in utter darkness.

He rose to his feet, and felt around the walls to discover some means of exit.

But no door or opening could be found.

He seemed enclosed within four stone walls.

His heart sunk with despair as he made the discovery.

Pacing the dungeon with rage and indignation at the treachery which had befallen him, his foot struck against a grating.

He knelt down, and by his touch discovered that it was sufficiently large to admit the entrance of one or two persons.

He tried with all his strength to raise the grating, but in vain.

Then he called for help down the opening, until his voice failed him.

It was in vain.

The echoes of his own voice were the only sounds he heard in return.

After a few moments of reflection, he stooped down again to the grating, and listened.

He fancied he could distinguish the sound of rushing waters.

He shuddered as he thought it might be his doom to be cast below.

But how would his enemies assail him?

From above?

They could easily reach him by lowering a ladder.

Starting with alarm, as the thought crossed his mind, he placed his hand quickly to his side, in order that he might draw his sword.

But it was gone.

Like a madman he paced his cell, distracted at the loss of his liberty and the separation from his daughter.

He suddenly paused, for he saw the glimmer of a light below the grating.

Gradually it became more visible.

It neared the top of the grating, and Geoffrey stepped into the dungeon from below, bearing a lamp.

"Well, my lord, how do you like your quarters?" asked the ruffian.

"Why am I detained here, and treated thus?" demanded Sir Stuart Catemass.

"Because our chief has orders to that effect," replied Geoffrey.

"And you mean to aid him in enforcing them, I presume?"

"I always do what I am well paid for," returned Geoffrey.

"Aid me to escape and I will pay you better than any of your companions ever will."

"Indeed! Then, suppose your lordship gives me a taste of your bounty to begin with!" said Geoffrey, holding forth his hand.

Sir Stuart Catemass placed his hand within his doublet to take out his purse.

But it was gone.

At the same moment he missed the rings from his fingers and the massive gold chain he used to wear around his neck.

"I have been robbed!" cried Sir Stuart.

"I shouldn't marvel at it!" laughed the ruffian.

"You are rogues and villains, all!" exclaimed the exasperated nobleman.

"Of course we are," replied Geoffrey, "and are counted the most expert cutpurses in Old England."

"What is the purport of your visit to me?" asked Sir Stuart Catemass, repressing his rage as well as he could, while he put the question.

"I've come to tell you that you may shortly look for a visit from our colonel, and I warn you to agree in whatever he may propose, for he has been crossed in his plans by some of your friends, and is wounded into the bargain. So beware!"

"Can you give me any tidings of my child?" asked the baronet, in a tone of anguish. "If you have one spark of mercy in your heart, tell me how it fares with her?"

"I daren't do that without the colonel's orders. Here he comes," said Geoffrey, pointing below. "Ask him yourself."

The iron grating was again raised, and the Black Colonel, pale and haggard, with mischief in his eye, stood before the captured baronet.

"Good evening to you, my lord," exclaimed the ruffian leader, making a mock obeisance to his victim. "How do you like your extremely pleasant quarters?"

"Why am I detained here?" indignantly demanded Sir Stuart Catemass.

"Because I and others wish it," replied the Black Colonel.

"They may have paid you well to trap me," said the baronet, "but I may pay you even better if you open the door of my cage."

"Indeed!" said the colonel, the fire of avarice lighting up his malignant eyes. "What will you give?"

"Anything in reason," answered Sir Stuart.

The colonel hesitated a moment.

By naming a good round sum he might be enabled to leave his band in the lurch, escape to France, and live for the future like a gentleman.

"I'll ask enough," thought he, so the selfish desperado coolly demanded the sum of twelve thousand marks from his prisoner.

"Never—never will I yield to such an extortion!" exclaimed Sir Stuart.

"Please yourself," said the colonel; "but I should have thought the pleasure you would have felt at embracing your daughter, who has escaped us——"

"My daughter escaped? Then, well knowing as I do, that she will never rest in her exertions till I am set free, I refuse to pay you one single coin—villain that you are!"

The colonel trembled with rage as he listened to these words.

"Be it so," he muttered. "Be as obstinate as you will, and hear me tell you to your teeth, that I and my band will yet hunt your daughter down, and never rest till we see her in the arms of Lord Smedleigh, who, when he has gained his ends of her, will cast her forth into the streets like the veriest wanton."

It was not in his lordship's nature to bear this horrible boast calmly.

So with a cry of indignant rage he rushed upon his tormenter.

With a terrific blow from his fist, he felled him to the ground.

The dagger of Geoffrey was instantly raised and aimed at the heart of Sir Stuart; but to his surprise, the colonel rose and arrested his comrade's arm.

"No, Geoffrey, he shall not die so easy a death," and the ruffian leader whispered the remainder of his speech into the ear of his associate, who, with a diabolical smile of evil on his countenance, descended, followed by the Black Colonel.

Sir Stuart Catemass again left alone, almost regretted his rashness; but the villain's taunts had roused him beyond control.

He was interrupted in his reflections by the noise of several voices below, and Geoffrey, followed by Hal and two other fellows of the band, sprang up the grating, threw themselves upon him, and he was soon rendered helpless by means of a heavy chain, which they affixed to his wrists.

Hal and his comrades again descended, but quickly reappeared, each bearing a pickaxe and shovel.

They began to break down a portion of the wall, nor paused in their work until they had made an opening sufficiently large for the body of a man.

Looking through the orifice, Sir Stuart saw it communicated with a small vault, even more dismal than the one in which he was a prisoner.

"Is it finished?" asked the Black Colonel, ascending from the grating.

"All is ready," said Geoffrey.

"Finish the work, then," replied the colonel, with a look of hatred towards his victim, "and then join us."

Geoffrey and the fated baronet were left alone.

"If you have a prayer to say, make haste about it," said Geoffrey to Sir Stuart.

"What does this mean?" asked he.

"Why, it means that your time has come! Bricked up in yonder cell, you'll be left to perish there by starvation!"

These cruel words, spoken with all the deliberate coolness of a fiend, struck a chill of terror to the heart of the ruffian's intended victim.

"No—no!" he cried. "In pity's sake, do not doom me to so horrible a death!"

"You are already doomed," coldly answered Geoffrey.

"Since there is no escape for me, for the love of Heaven plunge your dagger into my heart and release me from my misery!"

"Well," said the villain, after a moment's reflection, drawing his knife from his belt, as though he were conferring a favour on his victim—"you shall die here, and be buried afterwards in yonder cell!"

He raised the fated dagger over the prisoner's head; but at

that moment the ungainly form of the Red Dwarf sprang from the newly-made aperture in the wall.

Levelling a pistol at the ruffian Geoffrey, he exclaimed: "Die thou!"

With a sharp cry, Geoffrey fell dead against the wall, and the Red Dwarf, advancing towards Sir Stuart, dragged the astonished baronet after him through the opening.

(To be continued in our next.)

THE NEAPOLITAN BANDITTI.

(Concluded.)

I RESISTED the evidence long, and, when I dared, argued fiercely for the honour of the Conde; but how was I to resist all the world?

The story at length passed away like other wonders of a week.

The Conde lay in chains at St. Elmo; and the Capitano was sent back to his government, where he soon after died.

Two years passed over my head, while I was catching tunnies, or carrying passengers between Sorrento and Naples, with now and then, I will confess, a little smuggling to amuse the dulness of life, and cheer the donnas of Ischia and Capri with rum and coffee. But one wild evening, I carried over in my boat a passenger, whose voice I knew through all her mufflings.

It was the Capitanessa. I found that she knew me too. We steered to the back of the mole.

The wind blew a gale, the rain fell heavily, and there was no fear of meeting any of the custom-house officers.

There never was a finer night for contraband. But we had other things to do.

The lady asked me whether, if I had the opportunity of helping my master to escape, I had the will.

I swore by the bright eyes of my mistress, that to save the noble Conde, if he were ten times Fra Joachimo, I would go through fire and water.

I need not say how the affair was done; but before the clock of St. Elmo struck twelve that night, the wall was scaled, the Conde's fetters knocked to pieces, and he and the lady tilting over the waves, a mile down the bay.

Yet, whatever service I might have done to my bold master, I did but little to the traders and travellers within fifty miles of Naples.

For, from that moment, scarcely a man of them arrived without leaving a pack or a purse on the road.

The old stoppages were child's play to what happened now, every day in the week, and every hour, from sunset to sunrise. It was less like the desire of plunder than of revenge.

The cavalry were sent out to hunt down the banditti, and were always either baffled, or fairly met, and thoroughly beaten. But the chief scene was the neighbourhood of the mountain, and not a philosopher dared look for a pumicestone nor a pilgrim say an ave beyond Portici.

Il Vesuviano was the name of this new terror of the land.

The royal couriers were no longer able to carrry cheese-cake and compliments for the use of the princesses, and the ministerial profits by stock-jobbing were cruelly suspended.

Il Vesuviano went on flourishing more and more.

The veterans of the service walked off to him by whole companies, and their officers were, perhaps, only sorry that they could not follow their example.

The pomp of Il Vesuviano, the pay, the feasting, and the fine clothes of his troops, were the universal talk; and if it had been the time of sending kings about their business, Il Vesuviano might have figured as the founder of a dynasty.

But the affair was now serious, and little less than an army was ordered on the pursuit of this king of the banditti.

I was lying by the mole in the evening, as they marched along the chiaja, and I followed them in my boat along the edge of the bay.

It was known that Il Vesuviano had been seen on the mountain within the last twenty-four hours.

The troops took possession of the passes before nightfall, and the attack was to be made on all quarters at once, by signal from the city.

I lay on my oars, watching the course of affairs, and half inclined to spring on shore and take part with my old master. But how could I be sure that he was on the mountain, or that I could find him if he were?

As I watched eagerly for every sight and sound, I saw the lights hoisted on the battlements of St. Elmo, and immediately after came the rattle of musketry. But a deeper rattle than ever was made by musketry soon echoed over the shore. I looked up and saw a heavy cloud slowly creeping up the crater, and spreading over the sky.

The firing went on as the troops advanced up the road, and they seemed to be desperately resisted. But the lightnings over their heads began to glisten, and the flashes of the engagement were like the light of glow-worms to it.

The cloud now rolled up with great swiftness, and spread over the sky in a thousand branches, like an immense palm tree.

As the darkness increased, every branch became a column of fire.

The roar from the crater was now tremendous, and with every explosion up burst volleys of rock, red as metal from the forge. Vesuvius was in full eruption!

I pushed into the centre of the bay to escape the falling rock, and there—Santa Virgine!—the sight was grand and terrible above all that I can tell.

From Posillipo to Portici, round the whole semicircle of the city, all was as bright as if it were in a furnace.

The sulphur blue of the flame touched everything with a wild and ghastly look. But as is common in the eruptions of the volcano, with the most furious explosion its colour changed, and for some time it threw a golden hue over the whole city.

The castle, the mole, the chiaja, looked as if they had been suddenly sheeted with gold.

The bay was liquid gold; the mountain, the sky, all were covered with this glorious blaze.

I could see the crowds on the roofs and battlements waving their caps, and hear them shouting with delight and wonder at the magnificent spectacle.

But another and more awful explosion came, and Vesuvius shot up a pillar of flame, the whole width of the crater, and which was said to be three times the height of the mountain. The mighty column, ten thousand feet high, was of the deepest colour of blood, and it covered the whole scene with fierce crimson.

All Naples seemed to be deluged with a sea of blood.

I saw the crowd, smitten with horror at the conflagration, which they thought the beginning of the conflagration of the world, rushing away along the shore, and dropping from the roofs and walls, to hide themselves from the coming of the hour of judgment.

The lava now came burning and bursting down to the sea-shore, and some of the villages began to blaze.

I pushed towards Portici, to render what service I could.

As I was rowing round a point of rock, a man sprang into my boat.

"Have you seen the captain?" were his first words.

"What captain?"

"Il Vesuviano. I left him a few minutes ago, making his way down the ravine to the beach."

"Has he beaten the soldiers?"

"How can you ask such absurd questions? Did they ever stand him? We gave them one volley, but they did not like it well enough to make them wait for another. But the lava is another sort of enemy, and Il Vesuviano himself may not be able to make battle against that. Row for the thicket on the right of the point."

I asked no further, but shot the boat among the rocks, and climbed up the precipice.

There, indeed, I saw a tremendous spectacle.

The lava, in making its way to the shore, had been divided into several streams by the ridges of rocks that lined the beach.

On one of those ridges I observed two figures standing, one of them leaning on the other, and apparently hurt.

We bounded over the crevices, and soon reached them.

Their worn-down countenances and wasted forms gave me no recollection of them; but the Conde's voice soon made him known.

He thanked me for my offer of service, but said that he believed he had received his death wound in the skirmish, and, at all events, had no power to move further.

It was the Capitanessa who was by his side!

He implored her to leave him; but she refused, and, bursting into bitter cries, charged herself with having betrayed him to his ruin—with having, in a moment of mad wrath and rash zeal, to save a worthless husband, revealed her knowledge that Fra Joachimo and the Conde were one.

She declared that her only hope now was to die with him.

I proposed to my comrade that we should carry the Conde to the boat; but we had not gone a dozen steps, when the volcano exploded again. The roar deafened us.

A shower of fiery stones fell; and, in my blindness and suffocation, I was flung I knew not where.

When I recovered, dawn was breaking over Lorrento, and I found that I had been thrown within a few feet of the shore.

My first effort was to look for my master and the Capitanessa.

I found them both, but they were lifeless; they had fallen clasped in each other's arms, and had probably died in the fiery blast, and without a struggle.

Their features were, of course, still pale and wasted away, from the anxieties and hardships of their late life; but they had recovered their calmness and noble beauty.

With the help of a monk from a neighbouring convent, I had the rites of the church performed over them; and, with more tears than I ever wish to shed again, I buried the lovely and the bold in one consecrated grave.

MARTINO; OR, THE BANDIT CHIEFTAIN.

———o———

(Concluded.)

WHAT were Michael's feelings when, arriving at the well-known spot, he found, instead of his pretty cottage, a heap of ruins?

The merciless soldiers, after having stripped the place, set fire to it, and thus involved a once happy family in wretchedness and want.

Michael, with a heavy heart, bent his way to that part of the Apennine Mountains which separates Germany from Italy, intending to join Prince Eugene, who was then marching to the relief of Turin.

On his road, however, he fell in with that desperate gang which then held undisputed sway of the renowned Apennines.

"A spy—a spy!" said a hoarse voice, and in a moment the weary traveller was surrounded by the daring band, with their loaded carbines presented at him.

At this juncture a voice cried, "Hold!" and immediately a stranger burst from among the throng. The robbers hesitated, when Godolphin, their leader, commanded them to seize the traitor who had thus dared to interefere with his mandate.

The stranger threw off his cloak, and the robbers gave three shouts; Godolphin started back, and exclaimed:

"Martino!"

"Ay," said the stranger, "who comes to claim his right—the chiefdom of the Apennines!" Then, turning to Michael, he continued, "To you I owe a debt which I can never repay."

Michael stood confounded.

"Do you not know me?" inquired the stranger.

"I do not," replied Michael, in an agitated tone.

"Do you remember," resumed the stranger, "once giving shelter to a benighted gentleman?"

Michael was too much affrighted to reply, for in Martino he recognised the features of his former guest—the individual who had been the cause of all his suffering.

Martino now conducted him to a distant part of the forest, where, after partaking of some refreshment, he called his band together, and announced his intention of absenting himself from them for a month.

Having given the command of his troop to Rodolpho, instead of to the perfidious Godolphin, Martino and Michael journeyed onwards towards Turin.

In three days they arrived at the camp of Prince Eugene, and, having produced their passports, they joined the troops. Early the following morning, the prince led his forces to the gates of Turin.

His first attack having been vigorously repulsed, he put himself at the head of the battalions on the left, and forced intrenchment.

Eugene was taken prisoner in the conflict, which Martino seeing, he rushed among his assailants, and succeeded in bearing the prince away almost lifeless.

As soon as Eugene recovered the shock, he ordered the gallant warrior who had preserved his life at the imminent peril of his own, to be brought before him. As soon as the bandit chief appeared——

"Noble stranger," said the prince, "some wish may lie near your heart which is in my power to gratify; if so, speak freely, and your request shall be granted; but first reveal your name."

Our hero fearlessly obeyed, and exclaimed:

"Martino!"

The officers started back with astonishment.

"Art thou indeed that dreaded man, the leader of a band of assassins?" cried Eugene. "Why, then, art thou here? why art thou not among thy band in the Apennines!"

Martino, no way daunted, exclaimed:

"I come here to serve my king and country; and," continued he, "one wish does lie near my heart which is in your power to gratify."

"Name it," hastily returned Eugene.

"Pardon for one who has suffered wrongfully—bestow that, and your debt is discharged."

"His name?" inquired Eugene.

"Michael."

"Enough!—he is free! but, Martino," continued Eugene, "for the present you must submit to become my prisoner, until I intercede with the king on your behalf!"

Martino bowed, and resigned his sword.

At this moment the friend of Prince Eugene, General Montmorency, entered the apartment. Martino started; his breast heaved convulsively, and he sank upon the floor.

When he recovered himself, he desired to speak with the general; but this was denied him. With the fury of a maniac, he rushed from the chamber, and sought every apartment in the palace; but in none was Montmorency to be found.

In the course of an hour, however, the general returned; and, being informed that the prisoner wished for an interview with him, he entered the room where Martino was sitting.

The latter rose, and, with a trembling hand, presented a small packet to the general. It contained a written paper capable of clearing up the mystery which had so long hung over the birth of Martino.

As Montmorency read, his countenance changed; he looked first at the paper, and then at the prisoner, until at length, unable any longer to contain himself, he burst into tears, and, falling upon the fugitive's neck, exclaimed:

"My son—my long-lost son!"

Recovering himself a little, he continued:

"And yet it grieves me much to find thee thus a branded thief and an outlawed man; but come—come to these aged arms; there shalt thou find a solace for thy troubles, yet how to save thee from thy foes I know not."

A noise from beneath the window attracted their attention; shouts of "Vive le roi!" rent the air. Father and son threw themselves at the feet of their sovereign.

The king held out his hand, and exclaimed:

"Martino, thou art free!"

The herald then read aloud the proclamation of pardon to Martino and to all who should through his influence embrace a military life.

Martino shortly after summoned his late comrades to the border of the forest, where he addressed them in glowing language, and prevailed on each of them to follow his example: they unanimously entered the service of the French monarch.

Michael now returned home; he found his wife and family at Turin, where they had been supported by the benevolence of friends, ever since the destruction of their cottage.

Another and a better habitation has been erected; the wealth which he enjoyed in his youthful days has been restored to him in rich abundance; and oft of a winter's night, over a bottle of wine, he drinks "Health and prosperity to Martino, the late bandit chief of the Apennines."

BLACK GOLPHO, THE BRIGAND: A CONFESSION.

—o—

(Concluded.)

THERE was a muttering among several of the brigand crew; then suddenly my gaunt guide rose, and cried out:

"Brother Golpho, you see how we live here? With us every day is alike. Is it not so, comrades?"

"It is—it is!" shouted every one of the black band.

"If you like our way of life," continued the champion, "strike in with us, and you shall be our captain. I bear that dignity for the present, but will yield to Black Golpho. Am I right, comrades?"

A hearty, "Yes—yes!" broke out from the rest of the band, while the women gave an assent which was quite as welcome.

For a moment I felt as if my brain was on fire—the wine and the joviality of my new companions had influenced my blood.

The world had thrown me like a leper; but here was a welcome.

Good cheer, and sudden honour offered me.

Whatever choice I might make, I knew death was before me; but here, at least, I might sell my life dearly.

Women had spurned me, but now one smiled upon me, and those smiles were like nectar to my soul.

My mind was soon made up.

I walked into the midst of the men, saying:

"I will remain with you, if my pretty companion there wishes it."

She assented, and so I became the lord of a female robber, and the captain of a band of banditti.

Here Golpho's confession ended.

His career can be briefly told.

Once the captain of the lawless ruffians who formed his band, he became energetic in evil-doing, never resting until he had succeeded in some desperate outrage, and had planned a fresh one.

Having become the king of the banditti, so great was his daring, and so extraordinary his exploits, that his name was the terror of the province.

The country was in an unsafe state, and his nocturnal excursions and deeds of violence kept the citizens in a constant state of alarm.

Justice set every device at work to ensnare Black Golpho, and set a heavy premium upon his head, yet he was fortunate enough to escape all attempts at capturing him, and crafty enough to convert the superstitions of the peasantry into an engine of defence.

It was universally given out that Golpho was in league with the devil, and that all his band were wizards.

The ignorance of the people inducing them to believe this, not one could be found willing to come to close quarters with such a fire-and-brimstone enemy.

With the reward offered for him, there was also offered a free pardon to any of his accomplices who would deliver him into the hands of justice.

This made Golpho distrustful of his comrades.

They had received him with great show, but he soon discovered that the veil of brotherly affection was thrown aside, and beneath it he saw lurking paltriness of thieves and harpies.

He despised them, and therefore he ruled them with an iron sceptre.

Golpho at last, tired of the world and disgusted with the selfishness of his companions, sent in a petition to his sovereign craving for pardon, and offering his life and services for the good of his country.

Although this was just at the outbreak of the seven years' war in Germany, the offer was refused.

"Then let justice do her part," said Golpho, "and I will do mine!"

He determined to leave his band, and go to another part of the country.

Well mounted and armed, he one day started off from his old retreat never to return.

He had travelled many miles.

Daybreak was just revealing to him the beautifully mountainous character of the district, when he came to a narrow ledge of rock which formed a natural bridge over a very steep ravine.

Golpho checked his jaded horse for a few moments, and looked down until his brain grew quite dizzy, and a cold chill stole over his frame.

He hesitated, and looked round him to find another road, but could not.

Then shaking himself, as though to raise his courage, he muttered:

"Well, here goes—I can but die once!" and putting spurs to his horse, they started over the fatal path.

The horse was worn out with his long ride, and, missing his footing, falls sidewards, struggles for a few seconds, and then plunges headlong down the ravine, bearing to an almost instantaneous and silent death, Black Golpho, the brigand chief.

A ROBBER OUTWITTED.

—o—

PASSING a gravel-pit, O'Connell said, "That is the spot where Brennan, the robber, was killed. Jerry Conner was going from Dublin to Kerry, and was attacked by Brennan at that spot. Brennan presented his pistol, crying: 'Stand!' 'Hold!' cried Jerry Conner, 'don't fire!—here's my purse!' The robber, thrown off his guard by these words, lowered his weapon, and Jerry, instead of a purse, drew a pistol from his pocket, and shot Brennan in the chest. Brennan's back was supported at the time against the dyke, so he did not fall. He took deliberate aim at Jerry, but feeling himself mortally wounded, dropped his pistol, crawled over the dyke, and walked slowly along, keeping parallel with the road. He then crept over another dyke, under which he was found dead the next morning."

HOW THEY PUNISH ROBBERS IN CHINA.—A piece of bamboo cane is provided, which nearly corresponds with the height of the criminal, and is of considerable circumference. This bamboo being perfectly hollow, admits the passage of a large iron chain, one end of which is riveted round a stake, the other encircles his neck, and is confined there by a padlock; his legs are fettered by a few links of chain.

TALES OF BRIGANDS

I Warn & Strike

AND ROBBERS.

[RED DWARF FINDS A FRIEND AT COURT IN THE PERSON OF THE KING.]

THE RED DWARF.

CHAPTER X.

A HAIRBREADTH ESCAPE.—THE HELPING HAND OF THE INVISIBLE
FRIEND.—THE MASTER-KEY, AND THE USE THE DWARF MADE
OF IT.—THE PERILOUS MEETING IN THE STONE PASSAGE.—THE
CELL OF DEATH, AND THE SKELETON WHICH THE DWARF AND

SIR STUART CATEMASS SAW THERE.—THE VAULTS BENEATH THE
OLD ABBEY OF WESTMINSTER.

RESCUED from the very brink of destruction, Sir Stuart Catemass was completely bewildered at the strange turn events
had suddenly taken.

[THE RIGHT OF DRAMATISING IS RESERVED.]

Who was the strange being that had appeared as if by magic and proved so true a friend?

He was about to pour forth his expressions of gratitude, but the dwarf, grasping his arm, and telling him to be silent, proceeded to make his way from the vault in which they seemed to be enclosed.

Stooping to his knees, the dwarf directed Sir Stuart Catemass to mount upon his brawny shoulders, so that he might reach to the ceiling above their heads.

Sir Stuart Catemass did as the dwarf told him.

"Feel for a small piece of iron resembling the head of a nail," said the dwarf.

Sir Stuart Catemass traced his hand along the ceiling, and his touch encountered a small spike, about an inch long.

"Have you discovered it?" asked the dwarf.

"I have," replied the nobleman.

"Press it from you towards your right hand with all your force," said his mysterious deliverer.

Sir Stuart pressed it as he was desired, and a trap-door suddenly opened above his head.

"Now place your hands towards the left and tell me what you feel there," said the dwarf.

"I detect something like small rods of iron," answered the baronet.

"Pull the one nearest to you with all your force.

Catemass did so, and a small iron ladder unfolding itself, descended to within a few steps of the ground.

"Ascend, Sir Stuart, and leave me to follow."

Doing as he was directed, the baronet found himself in another cell resembling the one beneath.

The dwarf was quickly by his side, by the aid of the iron ladder, which he drew up after him, and reduced it into its original small compass by means of the small joints formed in it at intervals.

Closing the trap-door silently through which they had ascended, the dwarf paused as if expecting some one.

Sir Stuart Catemass was about to ask his strange preserver a question, but he felt his arm grasped with a giant's force, while the dwarf exclaimed in a whisper:

"Not a word for your life! The Tiger, as they call me, is not yet out of the lion's den. Silence, and you may be saved!"

Perceiving that his only chance of escape lay in obeying his guide, Sir Stuart did as he was commanded, and waited with forced composure for the issue.

They were in perfect darkness.

At the end of about half an hour—as it seemed to Catemass—a stealthy footstep was heard outside the cell.

A small wicket in the wall flew open.

"Are you there?" asked some one, who appeared to be speaking in a feigned voice.

"I am," answered the dwarf, in a low tone.

"And not alone?" inquired the visitor.

"Not alone!" echoed the dwarf.

"Be wary, then. To fail now would be certain death, before you could procure aid!"

"Give me that which you promised me," said the dwarf.

"It is here," said the same assumed voice, placing what appeared to Sir Stuart by the faint light which peeped in from the feeble rays of a small lamp without, to be a small key.

"Take this in return," said the dwarf, placing something in the palm of the man. This Sir Stuart guessed, by the slight chink it made, to be gold.

The opening by which their visitor's hand had been thrust in was now closed, and they were again left in darkness and solitude.

Distant shouts of laughter, and the noise of boisterous drinking songs reached their ears, mixed with oaths and altercations.

"Revel away to your hearts' content," muttered the dwarf. "Yours may be merry lives, but they will not be long ones!"

The carousal now seemed to be breaking up; for heavy footsteps staggered along the passages near where Catemass and the dwarf lay in concealment; and drunken voices were heard wishing each other good night, as they sought their various chambers.

At length all was still.

Again the wicket in the wall flew open, and the same voice which had spoken before exclaimed, in a whisper:

"Now!"

The Red Dwarf took from the extended arm which was thrust into the cell a dark lantern. He told Sir Stuart to summon all his courage, for the moment of his escape was at hand.

"Do not fear for my courage," said the baronet—"for the thought of seeing my daughter once again banishes every fear!"

The dwarf turned the rays of the lantern towards a corner of the cell, and a small, arched door became visible.

To this the dwarf applied the key he had received from his mysterious colleague, and the door turned slowly on its rusty hinges.

Closing the door silently behind him, and re-locking it, the dwarf led the way along a narrow, gloomy passage paved with stone.

They had not proceeded many steps, when the sound of advancing footsteps struck upon their ears.

What was to be done? Should they advance or retreat?

The dwarf closed the lantern he carried and drew his sword.

What would Sir Stuart Catemass have given at that moment for a weapon!

They both knew if they were detected there would be no escape for them—no mercy from the Black Colonel and his myrmidons.

Nearer and nearer the footsteps advanced, and a voice in drunken accents hiccuped forth a lewd song of the period.

With a shudder which seemed to strike to his heart and wither every hope of escape, Sir Stuart recognised the voice of the Black Colonel.

He it really was—feverish and half-delirious from the pain of his wound. He had been aroused from his slumber by a burning thirst, and was now making his way back to bed, after having imbibed copious draughts of the smuggled wine which was concealed in secret vaults beneath the building.

To reach his chamber he must pass the Red Dwarf and Sir Stuart Catemass.

Another moment and he would be upon them.

But at that moment the lamp which the colonel carried in his unsteady hand fell from his grasp upon the stone floor, and all was in darkness.

They heard him stoop and search for it in vain.

With muttered curses on the accident, he proceeded to grope along the passage in order to reach his sleeping-chamber.

"If we attack him and try to secure him, he will give the alarm, bring the rest of his fellows here, and our lives will not be worth a straw," thought the dwarf.

Hoping that he might pass them in the dark unobserved, the dwarf drew his companion as close back to the wall as possible, to prevent the colonel coming in contact with them.

But the passage was so narrow, and their enemy's steps so unsteady as he came reeling along, that such a chance seemed hopeless.

At that moment an unexpected event occurred.

As the dwarf and his companion pressed their backs against the wall, it suddenly yielded behind them, and they entered into what seemed to be a large niche in the stonework.

They heard the colonel stagger by, gain his door, and close it.

Feeling more assured of their safety, curiosity prompted the dwarf to look around the hiding-place that chance had so luckily afforded them.

He withdrew the shade of his lantern that he might do so.

"Look here!" exclaimed Sir Stuart Catemass, starting back with a cry of horror, as he pointed to a skeleton extended on the ground.

"Even so would you have perished, had I not come to the rescue!" said the dwarf.

Sir Stuart Catemass felt the truth of this remark, and fervently thanked the man who had so far secured his safety.

"What have we here?" said Red Dwarf, stooping and picking up a rusty sword from the ground. "Let us hope this was the weapon which sent the owner of these bones to his last account, and he did not perish from sheer starvation."

Catemass hoped so too, and shuddered at the thought of the poor victim's fate.

"All again seems quiet," said the dwarf, listening at the entrance of the cell, which was formed of a worm-eaten door, whose rusty lock had yielded without to their pressure. "Take this—it may serve you in self-defence, if matters come to the worst!" and as he spoke, he placed the rusty weapon in the baronet's grasp.

Leaving the cell with stealthy footsteps, they again proceeded cautiously along the passage, pausing every moment to listen.

No sound broke the solemn stillness of the night as they went on their perilous way.

A thick iron gate now barred their passage; but the dwarf, applying his master-key, which had been given to him so mysteriously, caused the barrier to turn upon its hinges, and leave the way open for them.

Re-locking the gate, and placing his lantern on the ground, Red Dwarf drew a piece of paper from his vest, and stooping down, read the writing inscribed upon it.

Sir Stuart guessed this to be a plan of the building.

He was right in his conjecture: for the dwarf, after a moment's perusal of the paper, looked around; and counting five flagstones towards the right hand, stooped down and struck it gently with the hilt of his dagger.

The stone sounded hollow beneath.

Then scraping the dirt from the cracks which surrounded it, he placed his dagger in the crevice, and using the weapon after the fashion of a lever, the stone was raised.

Red Dwarf, holding down the light, saw a long, tunnel-shaped passage, descending, as he conjectured, beneath the building.

Bidding Sir Stuart stay where he was for a time, the dwarf descended the aperture, leaving him alone in the darkness.

Grasping the rusty weapon given him by the dwarf, he determined, in case of attack, never to be again taken alive.

Five minutes elapsed—they seemed an hour to Sir Stuart Catemass.

All was as still as death.

Another five minutes passed, and yet another, and the dwarf did not return.

Should he follow the dwarf unbidden?

He was about to do so, but paused as he reflected the dwarf might have fallen amongst enemies below, and to follow might seal his own fate.

"Yet should the man who has braved so much to rescue me be in danger, why should I not hasten to lend a helping hand?" reflected he.

At this moment he felt his leg grasped as he placed it below to descend.

He started back, but was reassured by hearing the friendly whisper of the dwarf.

"Come," said the mysterious being. "The way lies open before us without further danger. Descend cautiously. I did not bring the light for fear of detection. Pass by me, and go carefully onward, while I replace the stone over our heads."

Sir Stuart Catemass did as the dwarf had directed.

The passage—or tunnel, as it might more properly be termed—became so narrow in its limits, that sometimes he was obliged to stoop, and at others crawl forward on his hands and knees, directed by the light of the lantern, which now twinkled in the distance.

The light seemed to quiver as though the air from without was blowing upon it.

This discovery gave new life to Sir Stuart Catemass, and seemed to promise a speedy escape into the open street.

He was now joined by the dwarf, from whom he learnt that this was the secret way by which the Black Colonel and his band hoped to escape whenever their haunt grew too hot to hold them.

Again referring to his written instructions, the dwarf extinguished the light within the lantern as being no longer needed.

The lamp being put out, streaks of daylight were perceptible at the end of the excavation in which they stood.

Guided by the yet uncertain light, they advanced, and found themselves in a vault beneath the abbey.

Their footsteps scared thousands of rats, who vanished in all directions as the region in which they had been accustomed to reign was invaded by the two intruders.

"Where are we now?" asked Sir Stuart Catemass, unconscious of the locality in which they stood.

"We are in the vaults of the old Abbey of Westminster," answered the dwarf. "Follow me!"

CHAPTER XI.

LORD KYLO'S PLAN TO ESCAPE FROM A DARK NIGHT'S WORK.—THE DUKE DECEIVED BY THE LIBERTINE.—CLAUDE DUVAL IS DISCHARGED FROM THE DUKE'S SERVICE, AND BECOMES A KNIGHT OF THE ROAD.

WE must now return to Lord Kylo Smedleigh, whom we left galloping from the lane. When Claude Duval, Silver Jack, and Allan Buckhurst came to the rescue of the Lady Madaline, he imagined they did not recognise him in the business, and trusted to his confederates not betraying his plans. His first step must be to secure friends at Court, and this he knew could be done by winning over the unprincipled Duke of Buckingham to his interests. He suspected his grace had cast a longing eye upon Madaline, and chuckled to himself as he thought what an excellent scheme it would be if he could throw all the blame of the night's work upon the dissolute nobleman.

He had heard of the quarrel between him and Sir Stuart Catemass at the banquet, and knew his grace of Buckingham bore the baronet no good will.

The disappearance, then, of Madaline's father (whom he imagined by this time to be numbered with the dead), and the abduction of Madaline, could be safely laid to Buckingham's account, who was too powerful for the King to punish, unless his Majesty wished to pull a hornet's nest about his ears in the shape of the swaggering cavaliers who ranged themselves on the duke's side, and almost ruled the Court.

King Charles, therefore, was in a great measure in the hands of these nobles, and many times had to wink at an act of injustice which his naturally generous heart revolted against; but he remembered the fate of his father, and resolved to make himself easy on the throne, and enjoy his licentious pleasures at any sacrifice. Lord Kylo knew all this, and resolved to build his plans upon it.

He reached his house, went to bed, and thought how he should mature his plans.

Of one thing he felt assured—he should meet with no further obstacle in the person of Madaline's father, who was the person he most dreaded.

The next morning he made his way to the duke's palace, and craved an audience.

This was not obtained without much difficulty.

Servants and pages had to be feed before he could get his name taken to his grace, who had just risen, and was surrounded in the ante-chamber by a throng of time-serving flatterers and demireps of the time.

"Well, my Lord Smedleigh, what news? You have been a stranger of late. We heard rumours of your turning Puritan, and forswearing wine, women, and dicing for ever," said Buckingham, in a bantering tone. "Speak! Confess! Is this really so, or have you been belied?"

"One can see by his long face that something grave has troubled him," said Sir Pierrepoint Lucy, who was present. "Kylo has had bad luck in some project, and has come to ask our sage advice on the matter. Speak out, Smedleigh! I think I can promise you every assistance at the hands of his grace. As to my own assistance, you know it is always freely yours."

"What I have to say must be spoken to his grace alone," said Lord Kylo.

"Nay, nay—that's not fair!" cried the other gallants. "If you have come to confess your sins, you should have gone to a priest, and not made your way here to damp our enjoyment with your grievances."

"Well said, friends!" exclaimed Sir Pierrepoint. "Drain this cup of wine, my bold Kylo, and let it unlock your heart."

"I tell you this is private business," said Lord Smedleigh, as he refused the proffered draught.

"Since it is so important, and can only be spoken in private, come this way."

As Buckingham spoke, he rose, and led the way into his private cabinet, followed by the crafty Kylo.

Buckingham threw himself on a couch of rich damask, and motioned his visitor to a seat.

"You can speak now in safety," said the duke. "But be brief, I pray you, for my head is none of the clearest, thanks to last night's Malmsey, and long histories have a trick of sending me to sleep. What is this wondrous secret?"

"It relates to a fair maiden on whom your grace has been pleased to cast an eye of favour."

"Beshrew me if I did not think so!" laughed Buckingham. "Truly, I had no idea you knew my secrets half so well."

"There could not be much secrecy in the matter, your grace, for I was present down the river when you toasted the lady before a party of us, although, as I understand, you have never seen the maiden."

"Do you allude to Lady Madaline, the daughter of Sir Stuart Catemass?" exclaimed the duke.

"I do, your grace."

"Well, go on! What have you to say of her?" eagerly inquired the duke.

"I know that your grace cannot abide being crossed in any project that you may form."

"True. You judge me rightly. Go on."

"And, during the last two days, I have been exerting all my influence to place the Lady Madaline in your power."

"Indeed!" said the duke, with a start of surprise. "And what may be your motive in wishing so suddenly to serve me in the matter?"

This question, put suddenly to Lord Smedleigh, was so unexpected by him, that the hypocrite was staggered for the moment; but he speedily recovered his assurance.

"I wished to ask a favour in return," he answered.

"Ha! I guessed so! There is a wheel within a wheel! Well, I suppose we men of the world always act upon that principle. Proceed with what you have to say."

Lord Kylo then began to tell the artful story he had concocted.

He began by saying how deeply he deplored the insolence of Sir Stuart Catemass at the festive board, when his grace had toasted the Lady Madaline; and that he, Lord Kylo, had no notion of so great a personage as the Duke of Buckingham being openly insulted in the manner his grace had been.

"You speak well, if you speak truly," said Buckingham.

"Of that I will soon convince your grace. And, to prove it, myself and friends carried off the Lady Madaline, in order that we might place her in your hands."

"You did? Where is she, then? Have you got her in safe custody?"

"Alas! no, my lord. Myself and some trusty friends had succeeded in taking her from her father's mansion, but were interrupted and foiled by Allan Buckhurst, who numbers amongst his friends the notorious highwayman known as Silver Jack, and a page of your grace's, who made himself most active in the matter."

"A page of mine? His name?"

"Claude Duval."

"Claude Duval?"

"Even so, your grace; he is leagued with as vile a gang as ever graced the gallows tree—in good truth, he spends half his time with them."

"This, then, accounts for his frequent absence of late. I thank you heartily, my lord, for informing me of this—it shall be seen to. Silver Jack, you say, is the name of the highwayman whose company he keeps?"

"Ay, your grace, and another more desperate character is known to him—no less a personage than a ruffian they call the Red Dwarf—a name which seems to strike terror into the hearts of all."

"I swear by my good sword he strikes little terror into mine. I would I could meet with the rascal! I warrant me I'd learn who and what the fellow is, that he carries on his pranks so boldly! I have never seen the knave. Describe him to me."

Lord Kylo was about to do so, when a respectful tap was heard at the door of the ante-chamber.

"Who is there?" asked the duke.

"Your grace's page, Claude Duval," replied a voice.

Lord Kylo started as he heard the youth's voice; his conscience told him that if they met face to face his coward tongue would fail to substantiate the charge he had made against the page.

"One moment, your grace," said Lord Smedleigh, as Buckingham was about to bid Claude enter—"one moment! Let him not see me here. If he should, he will guess my errand, and, by warning his friends, prevent me placing the fair Lady Madaline in your hands. Cannot your lordship conceal me somewhere until he is gone?"

"Perhaps that will be the better way," said the duke. "Wait in the next chamber."

He pointed to a small door opposite, and Lord Smedleigh left the room.

The knock without was repeated, and Buckingham, rising and opening the door, admitted Claude Duval, who, bowing respectfully, asked if his grace had need of him.

"I have had need of you many times, young sir, during your absence. How is it you leave the mansion at such unseasonable hours, and pass your time with cutpurses and knights of the road?" cried the duke, in a rage.

These words so staggered Claude that he could not reply on the instant.

"You may well hesitate, varlet! I know all! Since when have you been the champion of the Lady Madaline, and who told you to interfere between me and my desires?"

"I know not what your grace's desires may be!" boldly answered the undaunted page.

"Lady Madaline Catemass—what of her?" asked Buckingham, advancing fiercely towards the page, as though he would strike him.

"What of the Lady Madaline Catemass?" said Claude, repeating his master's words. "Why, I helped to defend her from the villain who wished to get her into his hands, and I'd do the same again if I saw the lady in peril."

Thinking he was meant by the term villain, the haughty duke broke forth into an ungovernable rage towards Claude, to the great delight of Lord Kylo, who, from his place of concealment, could hear all that passed.

"Away from my house—away from my service!" stormed the duke, stamping with rage, as he rang for his servants, who hastened to obey the summons, wondering what had happened in their master's apartment.

"Seize this knave and cast him forth into the street!" cried the duke to his menials, as he pointed towards the astonished Claude.

"But what have I done? How have I offended?" asked the bewildered page.

"Cast forth the varlet without further parley!" exclaimed the duke.

The attendants, not daring to disobey, laid hands on Claude.

In vain he begged to be heard; the duke threatened to have him beaten like a dog if he resisted, adding that henceforth he need not look for a character from him.

Bewildered at the strange turn affairs had taken, Claude found himself in the street bereft of a home and deprived of a service.

After he had paused awhile and realised his situation, he coolly observed to himself:

"Well, since the only shelter I had is shut against me, I

must take a new turn in life, as many brave men have done before me—and that turn must be the road."

He pulled his cap over his eyes with a sigh, to conceal a tear of regret, and went in search of Silver Jack.

And this is how Claude Duval, a youth of generous impulses and good intentions, first took to the road.

After Claude had been ejected from the duke's mansion, Lord Kylo and Buckingham had a long conference together, which ended in the duke binding his knavish visitor to secrecy, and promising to go to the King immediately, so that he might obtain warrants for the arrest of the highwayman, Silver Jack, Allan Buckhurst, and the mysterious being known as the Red Dwarf.

Lord Kylo and he left the mansion together. They parted as they neared the King's palace, Buckingham promising to let his false friend know how he succeeded with his Majesty as to getting his sanction for the arrest of the persons we have named.

Lord Kylo went homewards laughing in his sleeve as he thought how easily he had duped my Lord of Buckingham.

The King's servants bowed low as he entered the palace and expressed a wish to speak with his Majesty, and the duke seated himself until he should be sent for.

But who is this coming from towards the royal audience chamber with stealthy steps, as though he wished to quit the palace unobserved?

It was the Red Dwarf!

Buckingham and he had met once before, but on far different ground.

The duke started up with amazement.

The Red Dwarf in the King's palace!

What could be his business there?

Perhaps no other than the assassination of the King himself!

With a cry of alarm, he threw himself upon the dwarf, calling aloud for help.

The servants of the palace quickly throng around him, the dwarf is seized, and the duke, charging them in a loud voice to see he does not escape, is interrupted by the entrance of King Charles, who, addressing the servants in an imperious tone, exclaimed, as he pointed to the dwarf:

"Release that man, and do not harm him at the peril of your lives!"

(*To be continued in our next.*)

FIGOLI; OR, THE BANDIT'S FATE.
A TRUE SKETCH.
———o———

"My lord, this is indeed a sorrowful story."—SHAKSPERE.

THE sun was sinking behind the hills of ——, and the moon was gaining her accustomed ascendancy in the "starry firmament on high," as Sir George Wolfe, with his ward, the beautiful Emma Reynolds, were approaching the peculiarly-picturesque village of Afflours.

"My dear Sir George, had we not better put up at the first inn we come to?—night is fast closing in around us, and in these horribly-infested regions it is dangerous to travel after the sun has set," said Emma to her guardian.

"Dear child, be not afraid; we will desire the postilions to draw up at the first convenient hostelry, and delay proceeding further until to-morrow," replied the guardian.

Orders were accordingly given, and, after a few winding roads had been passed through, the travelling carriage stopped at one of the retired inns in the luxurious country of Switzerland.

Three countrymen were sitting on a rough bench before the door, quaffing a large cup of some apparently delicious liquor. On seeing the carriage stop, they rose, and, with all the politeness peculiar to their country, assisted the landlord and servants in disencumbering the carriage of the luggage.

"Well, host," said Sir George to the bustling landlord, "how can you accommodate us?"

"Signor," replied he, "I am much distressed; all our rooms are engaged, except the one suite which overlooks the hill yonder; it is a pleasant 'department,' but I am afraid it is not a proper one for a nobleman of your station."

"Distress yourself not; we will inspect the chambers, and I doubt not they will suit us," replied the baronet.

"You are very obliging, sir," replied the host, with a profound bow.

Passing through various intricate passages, which betokened that the house was not one of recent construction, M. Babaut, the host, followed by his illustrious visitors, arrived at the chambers destined for their nocturnal abode.

The principal room was of a peculiar shape. A window, of the antique fashion, looked upon the verdant hills of Humley. Exactly opposite was a capacious fireplace, which contained a wood fire, blazing up now, then dropping down exhausted, as if being aware of its feeble existence. In a recess stood a canopied bed, the curtains of which gave a peculiar look of deadness to all around; and although the fire lit up the room at intervals, it added an appearance of gloom and desolation indescribable. The room was tapestried; and when the embers blazed up, they displayed, on the wornout hangings, representations of the ancient history of the ever-political changing state. Immediately adjacent was a room of smaller dimensions than that already described, communicating by folding doors. It also was antique; and, if possible, had a more gloomy appearance than that described.

We will for a time leave the visitors, and listen to the conversation of the occupants of the "common room." The two men who had so politely unloaded Sir George Wolfe's carriage had retired into the "long-room."

"Host, who are these people just come?" said one of the men, whose name was Jacque.

"Monsieur Jacque, I can't say: they are rich, it appears."

"Rich, say you: and from whence came they?" inquired Jacque's companion Rigoli.

"I made no particular inquiries; but here comes one of the servants," replied mine host, pointing to a man certainly the worse for travelling.

Arundel, the servant, as he entered, saluted the host and the gentlemen present in the regular English mode; and, drawing a chair to the fire, said:

"I must have some good liquor after the sort of weather I have gone through. M. Babaut, or whatever your name may be, I'll have summut short."

The host stared in utter amazement; and bowed, as if he did not understand the gentleman's lingo.

"A summut short, I say," said the servant.

"Je ne vous comprends pas, monsieur."

At this unpleasant juncture an English gentleman entered the room, and explained to the landlord what the servant meant.

The strangers had left the hostelry, and none but Jacque and his companion remained as the clock struck the hour of eleven.

"And you say, host, that these men are rich?" said Jacque.

"Yes, monsieur, very rich," replied the host.

"A prize, I suppose."

"Whatever you do, monsieur, remember the respectability of my house."

"Monsieur landlord, you may rely on us. Ferdinand and Ribaut, with twenty men, will be here in ten minutes. You see if all the strangers sleep, and we will not disturb the honour of your good inn."

The trusty host obeyed the recommendation of the bandits. He went round to all the rooms, and found their inmates wrapped in a dead sleep. On the table in Sir George's room lay a brace of pistols cocked, and a sword of goodly dimensions, he fearing the attack of some unlawful band in the plains of Switzerland.

The landlord took the dangerous weapons off the table, and hastened down to the door to await the arrival of the expectant band.

* * * * * * * *

"A pair of pistols and a sword," said the leader of the bandits, surveying the weapons. "Oh, mon Dieu! it is lucky you discovered these; but we have no time to lose—show us the way!"

M. Babaut, with a dark lantern in his hand, led the way to the room of the English travellers.

Rigoli and a few of his friends stole softly into the room, and the remainder waited outside the door; but the cautious landlord had hastened to his chamber, and feigning a sleep, listened all the while to the gangs of the party below.

Jacque had broken open the portmanteau, and Rigoli had helped himself to the before-hidden treasure ere Sir George Wolfe had awoke to discover the situation in which he was.

Perhaps there are few things so unpleasant as waking out of a sleep, and, after rubbing your eyes, to observe a man standing over you with a pistol cocked, and pointed at your head.

With the utmost presence of mind, the gallant baronet, with one blow of his arm, knocked the pistol on one side. The movement caused it to go off, and the contents were lodged in the wall.

Alarmed at the partial defeat of their plans, the bandits sounded a retreat, and one of rather an expeditious nature. The confusion was great; the going off of ready-cocked pistols, the tripping up of one another, would have been a subject of laughter, was it not one of danger.

Our landlord, as in similar cases, was not too soon on the spot. When he did enter the English travellers' room, he stared with an amazement which would have put our best dramatic actor to the blush.

Emma, alarmed, in common with the rest of the inn, at the report, had hastened into the room of her guardian; but, strange to say, no one ever thought of pursuing the bandits, and, as it may be supposed, they got off easily.

* * * * * * *

"Ninety and a quarter, do you say, Mr. Rene?"

"Oui, monsieur," was the answer to the query of Sir George Wolfe, whom we find in the Exchange at Paris about two years after the above occurred.

"Well, then, buy; you say the prospects are fair—buy."

"Monsieur, by your orders I will buy, and for the amount you mention," said the courtier.

Sir George was just going to part from his man of business, when he observed a man on the Exchange of rather a striking appearance.

"Hold!" said he. "Can you tell me who that man is?"

"Monsieur," replied the Frenchman, "I know him not—a stranger, I suppose. He is of rather a droll appearance."

"Adieu, monsieur," said Sir George, breaking away from the courtier, and approaching the droll man; when, to his surprise, he discovered that he was no other than Figoli the bandit!

"Hold, villain!" cried the English nobleman, in no low tone, seizing the marauder of the highways of Switzerland by his arm.

The people began to crowd around him, when he briefly explained to them who the man was whom he held, and desired a "gend'arme" to be called. Figoli was brought before the officers of justice, who sent him into Switzerland, where he was finally tried and shot.

The rest of his desperate band were afterwards taken, and suffered for their offences.

THE ITALIAN BANDITTI.

—o—

IT was towards the close of a beautiful autumnal day that two travellers were pursuing their journey through a track of that luxuriant and romantic scenery with which Italy abounds.

The younger, having the appearance of being about eight-and-twenty, was of tall though compact figure, the expression of whose very handsome features, glowing with health and exercise, was rather heightened than diminished by the tint they had derived from exposure to the sun.

His dress and bearing indicated what he really was—an Englishman of rank.

The other, his elder by some years, was of about the same stature, though of a squarer and more robust make, with a cast of countenance decidedly Hibernian, in which an air of openness and good-humour compensated for whatever it might want of comeliness.

They stood towards each other in the relation of master and servant.

The master, whom I shall call Vernon, had sent his carriage on before him, having determined on performing the latter part of his journey on foot—a resolution adopted rather on the impulse of a somewhat romantic temperament, than in obedience to the dictates of prudence, since the police of the district, at no period very effective, were at the time of which I am writing, in so relaxed a state as to encourage rather than repress the outrages of those predatory bands by which Italy has always, in a greater or less degree, been infested.

Having arrived at the ruin of one of those architectural monuments of its ancient splendour, with which the country is interspersed, Vernon paused to survey the magnificent prospect it commanded.

The setting sun was shedding his parting glories upon a noble stream that expanded to the breadth of a lake in the extreme distance, and pursued its devious course through a thickly-wooded country, in which, for some miles, it was buried from the traveller's eye, and then flowed within a few hundred yards of his feet.

Here and there, among the woodlands, were scattered the castles and palaces of the ancient nobility, and the temples of classic times, lifting their tall summits into the sunshine above the trees, and imparting an air of grandeur to the scene, of which none but those who have gazed upon an Italian landscape can form an adequate conception.

"A fine country this!" exclaimed Vernon, after a long pause, to his attendant, who, as an old servant of the family, was a sort of privileged person.

"Your honour may say that," was the reply; "but to my humble thinking, the sight of an inn, or even an ale-house, would improve it greatly."

"Why, I must confess, Terence," cried his master, "our own prospects would be none the worse for such an addition. I begin to fear we have taken the wrong road."

"A road your honour calls it?" rejoined Terence. "Faith, and it's doubtful I am if any foot but a brute beast's has been upon the path we are treading for this many a day. It's benighted we'll be, anyhow."

"Not quite so bad as that, Terence," said his master, "I hope: you appear to be quite out of spirits on the occasion."

"That's true for your honour," replied Terence, mournfully; "for sorrow a drop of Innishowen's in the bottle."

"Nay, I did not allude to your whiskey-flask; I meant that you look on the dark side of the matter."

"Will your honour see any other side of it by this light?" inquired the man; for the sun had then dropped behind the mountain, and the mists were beginning to come up from the valley.

"But surely," continued Vernon, "some of the buildings we see around us must be inhabited."

"Oh yes!" answered the servant; "I'll be bail for them they are, but it's by them that don't cook thair victuals before they eat them. Troth, and it's a wild place we're in; the more by token that a big fox came out of a bush just now, and may be he did not look up in my face as bould as if he never seen a Christian before in his born days."

"Your eyes were sharper than mine, then, Terence."

"How would your honour see it, and you busy reading the inscription down there? And it's glad I'd been if ye'd lighted on 'Good Entertainment for Man and Horse,' instead of that same."

"If my eyes deceive me not, Terence," exclaimed his master, "that is certainly a light glimmering from a window down in the valley there. Let us make towards it."

"Oh, then it's myself would go after your honour anywhere," was the reply; "but I hope you won't find yourself up to the chin in a bog, as I did, one night, when I'd a fancy for following a light as like that to the fore as two peas."

Regardless, however, of his servant's apprehensions, Vernon pressed forward in the direction of the light, followed by Terence. They were just entering a defile of the valley, when they were startled by a voice commanding them to stop; and, on looking upwards, they perceived the figure of a man standing upon a projection of the rock, in high relief against the twilight sky.

The travellers neither admiring the tone in which the mandate was uttered nor the appearance of the speaker, continued to advance, when the challenger unslung his carbine and presented it. Before, however, he could adjust his aim, he received a pistol-shot in his arm, which dropped useless by his side.

"Put that in your pipe and smoke it," exclaimed Terence, who having been a little in the rear of Vernon, was not at first observed by the robber, and had fired immediately on perceiving the danger to which his master was exposed.

Scarcely had the smoke dispersed, when they were surrounded by a dozen banditti, by whom they were, after a short but severe struggle, secured—not, however, until Terence had wounded another by the discharge of his remaining pistol, and brought a third to the ground with the butt end of it; while his master received a slight wound in the shoulder, a favour which he acknowledged by placing a brace of his assailants on the pension list for life. The travellers were then disarmed, and marched off, in the midst of the band, to head-quarters, to be examined and plundered at leisure.

The reader is mistaken if, judging from what he has seen on the stage, or read in a novel, he imagines the captain of the band to have been a fellow six feet high, with a corsair cast of features, and differing from a hero of the first water in no other respect than his having preferred to make war and levy contributions on his own account, instead of for the benefit of his country. The chieftain to whom our travellers were introduced was a short, bloated man, between forty and fifty, with a red nose, small but fiery eyes, and a countenance whose general expression bespoke him vulgar, sensual, and cruel by nature, and brutalized by intemperance.

The robbers were exasperated at the resistance they had encountered, and disappointed on finding that the property on Vernon's person consisted chiefly of letters of credit, which to them were useless; while their apprehensions were excited by the discovery of the rank of the party on whom they had committed the outrage.

It was under the combined influence of these considerations, any one of which would have decided their fate, that the captain informed the prisoners they must prepare for death, for that they should be shot the next morning at sunrise. It was in vain that Vernon backed his remonstrances by the offer of procuring a ransom to any amount they might name. Their reply was, that any communication they might suffer him to have with the capital for that purpose would be more likely to bring a troop of horse down upon them than the money. The prisoners were then conducted to an apartment, secured by a grated door, before which was placed a sentinel with a loaded carbine.

(*To be continued in our next.*)

THE ROBBERS' TOWER:
A TRUE ADVENTURE.

AFTER a long period of debility, the consequence of a dangerous wound received in the great "Battle of the Nations," fought near Leipzig, I found myself so far recruited in the autumn of 1815, as to undertake a long-planned excursion to the residence of a widowed aunt, who lived, with two daughters, on the family estate of her deceased husband, near the sources of the Elbe, in Bohemia.

I proceeded by slow journeys, and at noon, on the fifth day after my departure from Berlin, reached a small post-town, a few miles from my destination.

Here I heard, with inexpressible sorrow, that my aunt had very recently lost her eldest daughter, a lovely girl of eighteen, by fever.

I had not seen my cousin since her childhood, but my reminiscences of a delightful visit to my hospitable aunt during the happy days of boyhood, were acutely roused by this afflicting intelligence; and to save my bereaved relatives from the agonising necessity of announcing their loss, I folded some crape round the sleeve of my uniform, and, with no enviable feelings, journeyed on to the house of mourning.

About a mile from the little post-town my carriage turned a sharp angle on the road, and suddenly one of the finest prospects in this romantic district burst upon me.

Between the giant stems of a dozen venerable oaks I beheld a wide and fertile vale, through which the infant Elbe was gliding like a silver serpent.

The middle ground was varied by green and swelling hills, crowned with copses of oak and beech, while in the distance towered the vast and awful forms of the venerable Giant Mountains.

On the slope of the highest intermediate hill stood the modern and elegant mansion of my aunt, surrounded by a well-wooded park, above which, on the summit of a dark and frowning rock, appeared the decayed but still imposing castle of my late uncle's ancestors, which retained its ancient and characteristic name of the "Robbers' Tower."

A large portion of this once extensive pile was now a shapeless mass of stones, over which the giant ivy mantled in green and prodigal luxuriance; but the keep, a round tower of vast dimensions, still defied the tooth of time, and threw up its lofty head with Titian grandeur.

During my slow progress up the hilly roads, I recognised many spots, endeared to me by vivid recollections of former enjoyment, but now they suggested no pleasurable associations; my fancy was haunted by the image of the disconsolate mother, and I could find no relief from depressing anticipations but in the hope that my unexpected arrival would afford at least a temporary relief to the mourners.

The afternoon was considerably advanced when I arrived at the house; and my poor aunt, to whom the crape on my arm revealed my knowledge of her recent loss, clasped me in a maternal embrace, and, leaning her head upon my shoulder, sobbed aloud.

Her once full and finely-formed person was wasted with sorrow and want of sleep, and her expressive features wore furrowed with the lines of deep and heartrending misery. She was the living image of woe and desolation.

"Dearest nephew," she said at length, in a low and broken voice, "why did you not arrive three weeks sooner? You would then have found me rich and happy in the possession of two daughters; but it has pleased Heaven, for wise purposes, to sear me to the quick, and to deprive me of a moiety of all I valued in this world; for what has a widowed mother on this earth but her children?"

At this moment entered Julia, her surviving daughter, a beautiful girl of seventeen; but grief had preyed upon her bloom, and her cheek was fair and spotless as her snowy neck, which rose in delicate proportion from the crape handkerchief which shaded her youthful bosom.

She had heard of my arrival, and, while the ready tears started into her large and expressive blue eyes, she permitted me to salute her cheek, but her emotion forbade all audible welcome.

Feeling how premature would be all attempts at consolation, I gradually led my aunt and cousin to talk of the departed Cecilia, and had, ere long, the pleasure to see them more tranquil, and able to speak of her with comparative firmness and resignation.

From their conversation I gathered that she was perfectly conscious of her approaching death, but was nevertheless apprehensive of premature interment, and earnestly besought her mother to have the vault under the large round tower converted into a sepulchre, and to place there her unscrewed coffin in an open sarcophagus.

The tender mother eagerly promised to comply with the last wish of her darling child, and the pall which covered the coffin was daily moistened with the tears of the desolate survivors.

With a view to cheer the spirits of my aunt and cousin, whose health had visibly suffered from long confinement, I proposed a walk round the park. Avoiding the lower road, which led to the sepulchre, I conducted my companions up a steep and well-remembered path, which brought us to a higher level of the castle ruins. Here an agreeable surprise awaited me. When I had played a boy about this ancient pile, all approach to the baron's hall and the apartments in the tower was impracticable, owing to the entire destruction to the lower staircases; but with a view to better security of person and property, in case the not distant tide of war should roll through this secluded district, the baroness had ordered the construction of a staircase terminating in a long corridor, which connected the apartments in the great tower with a fine old baronial hall in tolerable preservation, and accessible only by a small door from the corridor, in consequence of the two grand entrances having been blocked up by large masses of ruin.

In this noble apartment every trace of decay had now disappeared. A new flooring of polished oak, new furniture of massive and appropriate design, and new casements of stained glass which admitted a soft and checkered light through the tall and narrow windows, proved the tasteful application of abundant means.

In each corner of the hall stood a vast iron stove of antiquated form, with the family arms curiously emblazoned; and on the walls hung some large oil paintings, bearing the stains and wrinkles of two or three centuries; but having been recently cleaned and varnished, they were still, at some distance from the eye, wonderfully effective.

The most striking of these were a wolf hunt, drawn with a display of bone and muscle not unworthy of Rubens; two battle pieces from the days of chivalry; and the catastrophe of a mortal combat between two mailed knights. In the last, especially, the artist had produced an effect as powerful as it was appropriate and true.

Observing how much I was struck with this old picture, my aunt told me that a clue to the subject had been found in an old family chronicle, written by the successive castle chaplains. The prostrate knight was the valiant Bruno of Rothfels, who was killed in single combat about three hundred years since by Gotthard, then lord of the "Robbers' Tower."

The dying man was unhelmed, and his life-blood, issuing from a wide gash across his throat, had flowed in torrents over his breastplate. The convulsed features and glazed eyeballs of the wounded man told his approaching death, while his clenched right hand was raised towards Heaven, as if imprecating his adverse fortune, and his left was grasping the blood-stained grass.

I gazed upon this singular picture until I fancied that I saw the sinewy limbs of the wounded knight quivering with convulsive effort, and almost thought I heard the death-rattle in his throat.

When I described to my companions the strange impression which this scene of blood had produced upon my imagination, they acknowledged a similar feeling, and begged me to quit a place they rarely entered, from an invincible reluctance to encounter this painfully effective picture. Returning to the corridor, I observed at its extremity a low arched iron door, secured with a bar of iron and large padlock. Inquiring to what part of the castle it conducted, my aunt informed me that it was the entrance of an old armoury, which occupied the upper floor of a low square tower containing the castle dungeons; and, being massive and fire-proof, she had availed herself of its security to place there some plate and other valuables, until the Austrian deserters and other marauders, who occasionally committed outrages upon private property, had been taken or dispersed by the police.

Above the iron door was suspended another old picture, which immediately absorbed my attention. A young and lovely woman, in the garb of a nun, was kneeling in prayer before a shrined image of the Virgin. A beautiful infant boy lay dead and bleeding at her feet—wild despair and delirious agony spoke in every feature of the kneeling mother, and contrasted strangely with the lifeless, stony look of the image above.

"Good Heavens!" I exclaimed. "What means this horrid picture?"

"It is a portrait of the hapless Leah," replied my aunt, "the daughter of the dying knight in the baron's hall. Her young affections were secretly given to Gotthard, his opponent, who had in some forest feud incurred her father's hatred. Forced by her despotic parent to take the veil, she broke her vows, and fled with her lover to this castle, where she became the mother of a lovely boy; but when Gotthard had long and vainly sought to obtain for her a dispensation from her vows, her wounded conscience preyed upon her reason, and, in a moment of delirium, she destroyed her infant and swallowed poison. The sad tale of her crimes and her remorse is legibly told in that coarse but powerful picture of some old German master. Soon after this tragic event, the hostile knights met in the forest, and the fatal combat ensued which you have seen depicted in the hall. This sad tale is still a popular legend in our valleys; the peasants will tell you that the unfortunate Leah rests not in her grave, and that the shades of her slain father and unhappy husband wander nightly in this castle. It has long been rumoured, too, that the clattering of swords and armour, the chanting of nuns, and the sound of fearful groans and lamentations, have been occasionally heard here at midnight by the shepherds, when seeking strayed sheep amidst the ruins."

During this detail we had retraced our steps, and at the other end of the corridor we entered the large round tower or keep, from which the whole castle derived its romantic appellation.

The spacious circle had been divided into two roomy apartments, of which the outer one had been elegantly fitted up as a parlour of Gothic design.

On the wall hung the portraits of my late uncle, and of the lovely girl whose mortal remains reposed in the vault beneath.

The picture of my cousin had been painted a few months before her death, and represented a blondine, blooming with health, innocence, and beauty.

Her fine auburn hair clustered in glossy ringlets round her angelic features, and a white rose adorned her bosom.

The resemblance to her sister was striking, and would have been perfect, had not the darker eyes of Julia given to her lovely countenance a character of greater intelligence and vivacity.

"That is my sainted cousin," I said, in a voice subdued by emotion into a whisper.

"Such she was, but two months back," replied the agonised mother; and now——"

Her sobs impeded further utterance; and to change the current of her thoughts, I requested her to show me the inner apartment.

Here I found an elegant bedroom of Gothic design, and commanding from three windows in the half-circle described by the wall, successive and boundless views of hill and vale, of the distant high ground in Silesia, and the lofty summits of the Giant Mountains, some of which were capped with snow, and reflected in glowing and rosy tints a splendid sunset.

Fascinated with the picturesque situation of these apartments, and desirous to behold from their windows the glories of a summer morning in this mountain region, I begged permission to occupy this delightful bedroom during my stay.

(To be continued in our next.)

TALES OF BRIGANDS AND ROBBERS.

Learn & Strike

[THE BLACK COLONEL AND HIS COMPANIONS DISCOVER THE DEAD BODY OF THEIR COMRADE.]

THE RED DWARF.

CHAPTER XII.

CLAUDE DUVAL'S FIRST EXPLOIT AS A HIGHWAYMAN.—THE UN-
EXPECTED MEETING.—A PRIZE APPEARS IN SIGHT.—THE ROB-
BERY OF SIR RALPH GRANVILLE'S DAUGHTERS.—THE ANTIQUE

RING, AND HOW IT CHANGED HANDS.—SILVER JACK'S SECRET
RETREAT, AND WHAT HAPPENED THERE.

YOUNG CLAUDE DUVAL, after being so unjustly expelled from
his master's house, began to sum up his means. He had been
paid his wages the day previous, and found he had enough

money to purchase a pair of pistols, a horseman's cloak, a slouched hat of the period, and a black velvet mask. The rapier he wore would still stand him in good stead. All he now required was a swift steed to complete his outfit. And this was the difficulty, for a knight of the road without a horse ran a speedy risk of capture, as all travellers in those days made their journeys well mounted, and well armed also.

A thought struck him.

The stables of the duke were at some distance from his mansion, and the grooms in charge of his late master's horses might not be aware of his expulsion from his Grace of Buckingham's service.

He resolved, therefore, to visit the stables, and see how matters stood.

Throwing his cloak around him, and concealing his features in case he should meet any of his late fellow-servants, who might watch him if he were recognised, Claude took his way to the duke's stables, then situated where Charing Cross now stands.

Going boldly down the gateway which led to the stables, he knocked loudly at the portal.

Barnaby, the duke's head groom, started back at the appearance of a man cloaked and masked, and rudely demanded his business.

"Don't you know me, Master Barnaby?" asked Claude, as he revealed himself, half in doubt as to the reception he might chance to meet with.

"What, is it you, young sir?" said Barnaby, in a tone so friendly that it at once assured Claude the groom had heard nothing of his being dismissed the duke's service. "But what is the meaning of this masquerade?" continued the man. "In verity, I took you for some ruffian of Alsatia, or its neighbourhood."

"I have a purpose in this disguise," answered Claude. "Let us go within, and I'll tell you all."

Barnaby admitted him, and Claude, taking the groom aside, invented a plausible tale of the duke and himself being about to depart on a night ride which must be kept a profound secret; hence the reason of his disguise.

"Therefore, my good Barnaby, saddle his grace of Buckingham's brave steed Rosemary without delay, for our master and I travel many miles to-night," added Claude.

"In that case you will want two horses," remarked the man.

"No, no—only one—only Rosemary; and be quick with him!" answered Claude, trembling with anxiety lest any of his fellow-servants from the mansion should arrive and spoil all.

"Only a single steed!" said Barnaby, in surprise. "Are you and his grace going to ride on the same horse, then?"

Claude saw he had made a mistake. He would fain have recalled his words, and taken two horses instead of one, but the difficulty lay in his disposing of it; one horse would be needed, but two an encumbrance that might probably lead to his detection.

"The fact is, Barnaby," answered Claude, with a mysterious air, "I am not bound to tell all I knew. I was bid to bring his grace's steed only; maybe I am to return for another—maybe not."

Barnaby well knew the strange and adventurous being his master was, and the freaks he was wont to indulge in; he therefore merely remarked it was no business of his, and, leading the way to the stables, saddled Rosemary, and gave the animal into Claude's charge, who quickly sprang into the saddle.

"How now, Master Claude!—what liberty is this you are taking? You should lead the steed of our master, not mount him. If the duke sees this it will anger him."

"Ay, but the duke shall not see it, my good Barnaby," said the audacious stripling, throwing the groom a piece of money as he spoke. "Take that silver crown, and drink success to the future fortunes of Claude Duval!"

Barnaby stooped to pick up the money, which had rolled upon the ground, and as he did so Claude gave Rosemary the spur, and horse and rider were gone.

"That's a mad-brained young knave!" remarked the groom.

"I've heard my Lord of Buckingham say he'd crop the ears of any varlet he caught astride of Rosemary. Well, well, Master Claude knows his own business best, so let him go his own way, 'tis no affair of mine."

So Barnaby went within, and locked the door when the steed was stolen.

"Hurrah!" said Claude. "Well mounted and well armed, I am on the road to become as gallant a highwayman as ever cried 'Stand and deliver!'"

Making for the village of Islington, he rode quickly on the northern road.

Claude's wild and wayward spirit of adventure blinded him to the fact that he was about to launch himself into a career of crime.

To take to the highway seemed to be entering into some way of distinguishing himself, and the rash and impetuous young man fancied that his late master's treatment justified him in taking to the road for his future subsistence.

To go on the highway was, in those days, the last resource of the desperate and depraved of society. For a time they flourished and led a life of riotous enjoyment, but the round of guilt and dissipation was mostly a short one, the highwayman being generally betrayed either by an abandoned mistress or a false friend.

Claude had been bewildered and dazzled by the stories he had listened to from the lips of Silver Jack. All seemed so joyous and exciting in the present, that he never once gave a thought of the gallows-tree looming in the dark future.

But the wood was growing for his gallows—the hemp being twisted for the rope.

Had such a thought ever crossed Claude's mind, it is more than probable that the young man would have paused on the downward road he was taking. But no, the consequences of the illegal acts he longed to indulge in never once struck him. He lived for to-day—to-morrow might take care of itself.

How many have been wrecked on that fatal rock of wilfulness!

Let the youths who read these pages ponder well over before they take the first false step on the road to crime, however tempting it may look, and begin nothing doubtful without well considering the end.

Although the night was dark, Claude's quick eyes perceived a man on horseback coming towards him.

Claude's heart beat wildly as he determined to stop this traveller, and cry "Stand and deliver!"

He drew a pistol from his holster, reined-up his steed by the side of the road, and waited for the traveller's approach.

The advancing horseman was muffled in a cloak which partly concealed his features.

Cantering briskly along the road, he found his way barred by Claude Duval.

"Your money or your life!" exclaimed Claude, presenting his pistol.

The traveller, instead of obeying the order, burst into a fit of laughter, and cried:

"Well done, sir page—boldly said! But how long is it, pray, since you have taken to the highway in opposition to your friends?"

The horseman let fall the folds of his cloak, which had hitherto shrouded his features, and revealed the amused countenance of Silver Jack.

"What!—is it you?" asked Claude, in surprise, "Why, I was expecting a rich booty from you."

"And I was expecting one from you!" laughed Silver Jack. "Why, how comes it you are here? Explain, or we may verify the old proverb that two of a trade can never agree."

Whereupon Claude Duval told Silver Jack the reasons, already known to the reader, which made him resolve to become a knight of the road.

"Well, since you're in for a short life and a merry one, I hope you'll have the courage to carry it through," said Jack.

"Never fear," replied Claude. "Although born in France of foreign parents, in heart, soul, and courage I am as bold in spirit as any thorough-born Englishman in King Charles's dominions."

"Well, we shall see," said Jack. "That's a fine animal you are riding, and says something for your taste in horseflesh; and, if I guess rightly, he is fresh from your late master's stables."

"If you were to guess again you might guess wrong," laughed young Claude.

"Then you declare for a highwayman's life?" asked Jack.

"I'm bound to it henceforth, back and edge!" replied Claude. "Don't fear that I shall be returning with the duke's horse and asking his forgiveness."

"The duke couldn't forgive you now, even if he would, for horse-stealing is an offence that the State ever punishes with death; so, as you're in for a penny, you may as well go in for a pound, for the gallows-tree pays for all."

Claude started as he heard these ominous words, and for the moment it struck him how easy it was to drift into crime, and how difficult to steer out of it."

But, casting aside fear, he exclaimed, in a gay voice:

"Let it be as you say, Jack—in for a penny, in for a pound, and let the gallows-tree pay for all!"

But, though Claude gave utterance to this sentiment so defiantly, he mentally resolved to abandon the highway when he had acquired sufficient money to take him over to his native land and enable him to live there like a gentleman.

False resolve—vain hope! Hundreds of adventurous and lawless spirits have made the same resolve—but, ill-gotten, ill-spent has ever been the result of evil gains.

Their conversation was interrupted by the distant sound of coach wheels.

"Hark!—do you hear that?" asked Jack. "And look at the ears of my horse Lancelot, he pricks them up like a Christian at the sound, well knowing what my practice is in these cases. Stand by, and let's see what fortune sends us."

The sound of coach wheels now drew nearer, and a clumsy vehicle of the period approached them.

An outrider came first, and by the coachman's side another servant was seated. Two servants were also on the footboard behind the vehicle.

Onward they came.

"Stand and deliver!" cried Silver Jack, as he and Claude occupied the middle of the road.

The outrider, spurring his horse, galloped by them, and rode quickly off, exclaiming:

"Help, help!—robbers, thieves!"

Claude would have ridden after the fellow to silence him, but was restrained by Jack grasping his arm and whispering in his ear:

"Stay where you are: he is one of us—our decoy-duck."

This was really the case. The retreating horseman was Nat Kepple, one of Silver Jack's companions, whose motive was to lead travellers on the road where he knew they must fall into his comrade's hands.

No one ever suspected the treachery of this man, who was to all appearances an honest fellow, always ready to protect travellers and give such information as would lead to the identification of the highwaymen, or even give them battle, if needs be.

So, at least, thought the public; but our readers, being let into the secret, know better.

Nat had assisted Silver Jack indirectly in many robberies, telling him when travellers would start, which road they would take, how many they numbered, and how their purses were lined.

Besides, he always described the robber's appearance to be so different from what it really was, that no one ever suspected Silver Jack.

When Nat had galloped off crying for help, the servants in charge of the coach began to show vigorous signs of resistance.

The servant seated by the coachman's side quickly drew a blunderbuss from beneath the box-seat; the other servants drew pistols from their pockets and levelled them full at their assailants.

"Begone, you knaves, and let us pass freely on the road, or we'll fire, and save the country the expense of hanging you!" said the foremost servant.

So formidable an array of fire-arms within so short a distance of Claude's body somewhat appalled him, and he instinctively retreated a few paces.

Not so Silver Jack.

He laughed defiantly at the servant who had spoken, and, instead of retreating, advanced closer to the man, levelling his own pistol.

"Will you keep back?" shouted the servant, with his finger on the trigger of his weapon.

"Not till I've lined my pockets from the contents of yours," said Jack.

"Then your blood be upon your own heads!" cried the man, as he addressed his companions, and exclaimed: "Fire, lads!"

The servants each pulled the triggers of their respective weapons sharply.

"Click!" went the triggers.

But no report followed.

Nat Keppel had provided against that.

While the servants were refreshing themselves at the half-way house, leaving their firearms in the pockets of their great coats in an adjoining room, Nat had made his way unobserved into the chamber, and drawn the charge from every weapon.

Silver Jack had received information of this, hence the boldness with which he had advanced up to the muzzles of the firearms.

"Missed!" said Jack. "That's a bad job, for I assure you my friend and I will not do the same!"

The highwayman, who now saw Claude was again by his side, levelled his pistol at the servants, who fell upon their knees and begged for mercy.

Silver Jack's finger was on the trigger of the weapon, but he did not press it. He had never yet taken human life, and had vowed never to do so under any circumstances.

"See who is within the carriage, and learn how their purses are furnished," said Jack to Claude, who, letting down the carriage window, begged the travellers not to be alarmed, but surrender their purses and trinkets with a good grace, assuring them, if they did so, there was nothing to fear.

The occupants of the carriage were two sisters, Laura and Phillis Granville by name, the daughters of Sir Ralph Granville, an ardent Loyalist and firm friend of King Charles; they were on the road to London to join him, when their journey was interrupted as we have seen.

The appearance of Claude was the signal for renewed cries of alarm on the part of the sisters, who, from the moment they became aware their carriage had been stopped by highwaymen, had given vent to piercing cries for help.

Laura, by far the most timid of the sisters, covering her head with her shawl, appeared as if shrouding herself from the sight of some dreadful being, and fairly shook with terror.

Phillis, venturing to look up at the sound of Claude's voice, saw, to her great relief, that he was not the desperate ruffian her imagination had pictured, for Claude, forgetful at the moment to replace his mask, which he had removed for an instant, suffered his handsome features to be distinctly seen.

"May I trouble you for your cash, watches, and jewels, fair dames?" said Claude, in a voice of insinuating softness. "Yield up those, and I promise, on the true word of a knight —a knight of the road—that no harm shall befall you."

Calmed by this address, so different from the one she had anticipated, Phillis yielded up her purse, watch, and ornaments, urging her sister Laura to do the same.

Keeping her countenance still concealed, Laura did as her sister advised, though not without well noting the face of Claude Duval as she did so.

He received his booty with a low bow, promising they should meet with no further molestation on their journey.

Then, suddenly perceiving the moon was shining upon his face, he replaced his mask to avoid further recognition.

But the sisters had noted it well.

Once seen, it was a face not easily forgotten.

Claude Duval found this out afterwards to his sorrow.

During this, Silver Jack had been exploring the pockets of the servants, who, seeing resistance was useless, suffered the highwayman to do with them as he pleased.

"Well, comrade, what success?" asked Jack.

"By Cynthia, the goddess of the night, never did a minion of the moon meet with better booty in his first expedition!" said Claude, showing the valuables he had taken from the ladies.

"Glorious!" exclaimed Silver Jack, his eyes sparkling as he looked upon the spoil. Then, turning to the carriage windows, he thanked the ladies most ceremoniously for travelling so well provided, assuring them he should be happy to meet with them on a future occasion.

The coachman was allowed to resume the reins, and the servants to resume their seats upon the carriage, as Silver Jack and his companion turned their horses' heads in a contrary direction and galloped off rapidly.

The sisters reached London without meeting with further adventures, and were driven to the mansion of their father, Sir Ralph Granville, who was most anxiously expecting them.

His rage and indignation knew no bounds when he learnt the manner in which they had been robbed of their money and valuables.

He prized, above all other things, an antique ring of gold, in which was set a small diamond of peculiar shape.

This ring Sir Ralph had placed upon the finger of his daughter a week previous. She had just attained her twentieth year, and the ring in question had always graced the hand of a member of the Granville family when they reached a score of years.

Phillis and Laura were the only remaining children of the baronet, and the ring therefore fell to the lot of Phillis, as she was the elder of her sister Laura by two years.

The loss, therefore, of this family jewel incensed the old knight beyond measure, and he vowed to spare neither money nor exertion to discover the perpetrators of the robbery.

The highwayman and his new comrade were in the meantime making for London by a circuitous route well known to Silver Jack.

Being both well mounted, they reached the metropolis nearly as soon as the carriage which contained Sir Ralph's daughters, and divesting themselves of their cloaks and masks, which Silver Jack stowed away in a valise he carried behind his saddle, they made for Blackfriars as morning began to break.

Silver Jack led the way towards the river's bank until they reached a barn-like structure, standing gloomy and forlorn by the water's edge, and, dismounting from his horse, bid his companion do the same.

Claude, leading his horse, followed Jack to the rear of the wooden building. A flight of steps led to a gallery above, which formed a rough kind of verandah, in the centre of which was a small lattice window.

A feeble light was seen burning from within.

"It is the signal," said Jack, half aloud, as he looked up to the casement. "All is safe, then. Good!"

Under the flight of steps which we have described was a strong, rough-looking door, crossed with planks, as though it had been indifferently repaired by some awkward hand.

Pressing what appeared to be the head of a rusty nail, the boards moved quickly aside at Jack's touch, and disclosed a keyhole.

The highwayman took from his pocket a key, turned it within the lock, and the door, turning on its hinges, disclosed the interior of a stable, into which Jack led his horse, telling Claude to follow with his.

Securing the door on the inside, Jack began to groom his horse, and advised Claude to do the same.

"Always praise the bridge that carries you over, and the steed that brings you safely home," said the highwayman, patting the neck of his horse as affectionately as though the animal had been a pet child.

Claude followed Jack's example as regards bestowing the requisite care upon his steed, and, after the horses had been fed and stabled, Jack informed his companion that he had something of particular moment to impart to him on a subject dearer to him than his life.

"Sit down," said Jack, motioning to a bench, "and let me claim your serious attention."

Claude did as he was desired, and Jack took a seat by his side.

"In the first place," observed the highwayman, "let us divide our booty."

The spoil was valuable, and Claude retained for his share the antique ring belonging to the Granville family, of which we have spoken, and a few gold pieces to boot.

Silver Jack had the lion's share as regards quantity, but the ring Claude retained was in reality worth more than all the rest of the plunder.

"Well, that matter's settled," said Jack, "and now for another. I am going to let you into a secret. There is one within this house who takes me for a far different being from what I really am. In fact, I believe her gentle heart would break did she know I was a highwayman."

"I suppose you are alluding to your wife?" remarked Claude.

"No, no," answered Jack, with a deep sigh; "my wife has ceased to exist, but I have a daughter living—a dear girl, in whose welfare all my future hopes and anxieties are centred. But she must never learn she is maintained by robbery, and it is that I may bind you over to secrecy which causes me to name this matter to you. My daughter still thinks me a man of property. I was so once, but she little dreams my fortune is lost, and must never, if I can help it, know the real truth. Let me, then, hear you swear, upon the honour of a man, never to disclose what you know of my doings on the road."

"I swear solemnly and sacredly never to betray your secret to her!" said Claude, grasping his companion's hand fervently.

"Enough," said Jack—"I am satisfied."

"But are you never afraid of being tracked here and arrested?" asked Claude.

"I have always charged Amy—for that is my daughter's name—to place a light in the casement window every night as a signal that no one has been inquiring for me."

"And why does she think anyone might inquire for you?" asked Claude.

"I have told her I was once concerned in some trifling plot against King Charles, our merry monarch, and am in hiding here until the affair blows over. The fond and affectionate girl believes it, and may she never learn anything to the contrary. But come to your sleeping-chamber, for, like myself, you need a few hours' rest before breakfast time; and when we meet at that meal you shall see the only being who is left to love me in the wide world. I have your promise, and feel assured I can trust you."

"Rest satisfied you may," said Claude.

Silver Jack then led the way to a loft over the stable, well filled with hay and straw.

Removing a portion of this from the side of the wall, a door presented itself to view. This Jack unlocked, and made his way up a narrow staircase, followed by Claude.

A door at the head of these stairs opened into a small bedroom, neat, clean, and tastefully furnished after the manner of the time. The hangings of the window and bedstead were rich and substantial, and betokened an air of comfort which Claude was surprised to see.

Bidding him farewell for the present, Silver Jack left his guest to repose, and sought the same rest for himself.

CHAPTER XIII.

THE BLACK COLONEL SUSPECTS HAL OF TREACHERY.—THE TEST AND THE RESULT.—WHAT HAL SAW IN THE SECRET VAULT.—THE STORY OF THE SKELETON.—WHO IS THE TRAITOR?

WE must now conduct our readers back to the foul regions of Alsatia.

The Black Colonel awoke the next morning after the escape of Sir Stuart Catemass and the Red Dwarf with a splitting headache, and the wound in his arm still more painful from his deep potations of the previous night.

He stretched forth his hand towards the wine-flagon, and raised it to his lips, in order to quench his burning thirst, but he found it was empty. Casting the flagon from him with an oath, he arose, and proceeded to dress himself, in order that he might descend below for more liquor.

He had scarcely reached the door, when it was opened from without by Hal, who inquired of the colonel if he knew aught of Geoffrey's whereabouts, as that worthy member of their fraternity was not to be found.

"I have not seen the knave since last night," said the colonel; "but I warrant me you will find him dead drunk close at hand, if you search well."

"I have searched well," replied Hal, "and it strikes me he has left the building."

"He would be cunning to do that without the keys," said the colonel, showing them as they hung at his girdle.

"I marvel much, then, where he has stowed himself. After the deed you set him to do in the vault," answered the ruffian, "he told me he should want me to help him brick up the entrance that we made in the wall for the reception of the baronet's body, but I have seen nothing of him since."

"Oh, he's at rest, safe enough, never fear," replied his leader, who, notwithstanding the unconcerned manner in which he spoke, had certain misgivings as to the safety of Geoffrey.

The thought again crossed his mind that there might be treachery in the band, and himself run a risk of becoming the next victim.

"A truce to your suspicions, Hal," said the colonel, with an air of bravado, "and fetch me another flagon of wine, for my throat's as dry as a lime-kiln, and this wound of mine grips me with pain like a vice. My curses on the recreant arm that dealt me the blow! I would I had him here to make it even with the knave."

Hal knew that wine was the very worst kind of drink that the colonel ought to take in his present feverish state; but being well aware that it would be useless to remonstrate with his leader at that particular moment, he departed on his errand for the wine.

The colonel being left once more to himself, the dread fear of being poisoned again took possession of his mind, and he shuddered within himself as he thought the racking headache which had seized upon him during the last few moments might be one of the first symptoms of the working of some deadly drug, prepared, perhaps, by the hand of the very man who had just left him.

He reflected for the moment, and then thought of a plan by which he could put him to the test.

Hal made his appearance with the wine, looking pale with fear.

"What ails thee, man?" asked the colonel, noting his scared look.

"I have seen that which I would not have looked upon for a thousand marks," answered Hal.

"How so?—what is it you mean?" inquired the colonel, fearing the officers of the law were on their track.

"You know the rich Jew we enticed within our stronghold three years back, under pretence of selling him some diamonds and precious stones which had fallen into our hands?" said Hal, looking round nervously as though he expected to see the ghost of their victim rise up behind him.

"Ay, ay, I remember all about it," replied the colonel, speaking as though the recollection of the fact was by no means pleasant to him; "the fool fell into a trap through his avarice. He had cheated and taken in thousands during his lifetime, and at last he got taken in himself. What else does it amount to? He's buried where no one can ever discover his bones—and there's an end of it."

"I am not so sure of that," said Hal, in the low voice of fear.

"In the devil's name, what do you mean?" thundered the colonel. "Speak out. What has happened?"

"I'll tell you, colonel. I passed the door of the cell in which the old man met his fate, and to my surprise it stood

wide open; urged by curiosity, I looked within, and saw imprinted upon the dust on the dungeon floor the marks of recent footsteps.

"You did?" said the colonel, starting as he listened. "Why, no one save you and I knew where we placed the body. Was the dungeon door forced?"

"No, but the lock had rusted away almost to a powder, as though it had been there three centuries, instead of three years."

The colonel took counsel with his thoughts. He had no doubt but some of his band had visited the Jew's dungeon.

"And who knows," thought the ruffian, "but there may be some deep-laid plot to consign me to the same fate?"

"Drink, colonel," said Hal, offering the wine, "and then come with me to the dungeon and judge for yourself."

"Drink yourself, my good Hal, and tell me whether the wine is to your liking."

Hal hesitated a moment; he fancied there was some meaning in the peculiar manner the colonel spoke. But, then, what harm could there be in a draught of good wine?

The colonel noticed his hesitation, and ascribed it to guilt. But his suspicions were speedily set at rest by seeing Hal raise the flagon to his lips and take a hearty draught.

The colonel followed the example, feeling convinced the liquor had not been tampered with.

The flagon was emptied, and followed by another, over which the mysterious opening of the dungeon door in which the skeleton of the Jew lay mouldering, and the disappearance of Geoffrey, were discussed.

All at once a sudden thought seemed to flash across the mind of the colonel as he started to his feet and exclaimed:

"Who knows but Geoffrey, instead of being able to silence Sir Stuart Catemass, may have met with his match, and got silenced himself?"

"Let us go to his cell and assure ourselves," suggested Hal.

"It shall be done," said the colonel. "Quick, assemble some of the band to accompany us!"

Hal departed to do so, and the colonel armed himself and followed.

He questioned every member of the gang, but none of them had seen their missing comrade.

"Well, even supposing the baronet has made short work with our comrade, we can soon make short work with him in return, for, chained as he was to the dungeon wall, escape would be impossible. Follow me, boys, and if Geoffrey has really fallen a victim in this business, Sir Stuart shall yield us a terrible revenge!"

With a loud shout of approval, the gang followed their leader towards the cell wherein they still expected to find Madaline's father a prisoner.

The colonel applied the key to the lock of the door which led to the vaults below.

It had evidently not been tampered with.

"Soh, no one has passed through here," said the colonel, feeling assured their victim was safe.

Arrived at the stone steps which led to the grating in the dungeon floor, the colonel was the first to mount and unlock the opening.

He sprang into the dungeon, but recoiled, with a cry of rage and disappointment, as the body of Geoffrey met his view extended on the ground, perceiving at the same time that the prisoner had escaped.

The colonel's cry of alarm caused Hal and the others to enter the cell quickly.

They rushed to the opening in the wall, and, looking into the next cell, guessed how their prisoner had escaped.

This was evidently the work of some confederate of the prisoner's.

"There is a traitor amongst us," thought the colonel. "Who is the man?"

The colonel hoped that Geoffrey had only swooned, and might be able to give him the information he desired; but, placing his hand upon the intended assassin's prostrate form, he found that his heart had ceased to beat.

(*To be continued in our next.*)

THE ROBBERS' TOWER:
A TRUE ADVENTURE.

(Continued.)

My aunt appeared to find a gratification in the idea that I should sleep near the tomb of her Cecilia, and willingly consented; promising that she and Julia would join me to an early breakfast in the tower the next morning, and on our return to the house, ordered my old playfellow, Caspar, the gamekeeper, to carry my luggage after supper, to the castle.

Fatigued with several days of travel in a still infirm state of health, I left my aunt and cousin before eleven, and walked with old Caspar to the ruins.

The day had been intensely hot; some menacing clouds in the southern horizon indicated an approaching storm, and, as we ascended the staircase leading to the corridor, the deep, low muttering of distant thunder was audible.

"And do you really mean to sleep every night in the 'Robber's Tower,' major?" said the old man, as he placed my portmanteau, sabre, and pistols, on a chair in the parlour.

"Certainly, my good Caspar! And why not?" I replied.

"I would only say," answered he, "that you must have more courage than I have; and yet a Bohemian gamekeeper is no coward. Many a dark night have I passed alone in the mountain woods, in spite of old Rubezahl and his imps, and the Wild Huntsman to boot; but in this tower I would not sleep alone for all my lady's broad lands."

"What, Caspar," I exclaimed, "an old woodsman like you afraid to sleep where my aunt and cousins slept every night last summer?"

"Ay, ay, major," muttered the old man, "the castle was quiet enough then; but since the death of my Lady Cecilia, strange sights and sounds have been heard here; and you may take my word for it, that the Lady Leah, who murdered her child, is not yet quiet in her grave!"

The old man then lighted my tapers with his lantern, commended me cordially to the protection of Heaven, and departed, leaving me considerably less pleased with my quarters than when I had seen them by the rich and cheering light of sunset.

The consciousness of utter solitude, at such an hour and in such a place, began to infect me with the superstitious fears of old Caspar, and the solemn stillness of the lofty and dimly-lighted Gothic room, interrupted only by an occassional and distant roll of thunder, made me feel something very like repentance, that I had exchanged the modern mansion of my aunt for this old robbers' nest on a mountain crag.

During the struggle which released Germany from the iron grasp of Napoleon, I had stared death in the face too often to fear any danger from human agency, and a liberal education in Prussia had raised me above any apprehension of supernatural sounds and appearances; but as I sat alone near midnight, in this old tower, and recollected my immediate vicinity to the sepulchre, and the baron's hall, the grim picture of the dying Bruno, and the still more appalling portrait of the pallid nun and her bleeding infant, I felt the necessity of banishing from my thoughts a crowd of images which would inevitably murder sleep; and, exchanging my tight uniform for a light dressing gown, I bolted the door, snuffed my candles, and looked around for a book with which to beguile an hour, and induce a more tranquil train of thought.

In a small recess between the windows I discovered a few books, one of which I eagerly opened, and found a collection of hymns, treating upon death and eternity.

I closed it, and opened another, entitled, "An Essay on Death." A third was, "The Solace of Old Age and Infirmity."

This was a most unpalatable collection for a reader in quest of worldly associations; but at length I discovered a small volume, curiously bound in black velvet, and containing more mundane matter.

It was an historical detail of the Order of Knights Templars, printed in ancient black letter, and, according to the title-page, from a rare manuscript of the thirteenth century.

Having been always prone to the study of history, this little book would have been a prize under any circumstances; but as the solace of a sleepless night, in this lonely tower, it was above all price, and I sat down with eager impatience to peruse it.

Opening it accidentally at the chapter describing the ceremonies of the order, I recognised, with surprise and delight, the name of a valiant ancestor of my own, whose deeds shine brightly in the history of Germany's middle ages.

I knew not, however, that he had in middle life become a knight of this order, until I here discovered a detailed account of an imposing funeral service, performed over his remains at Prague in the year 1190.

To be reminded of this great man's death, and to read of his funeral at such an hour, and in such a place fraught with sepulchral associations, were somewhat singular coincidences, and with strong and growing excitement, I read as follows:—

"The temple walls were covered with black cloth, and on a trestle in the centre of the church was placed the coffin containing the mortal remains of the departed knight.

"Nine skeletons stood near the coffin, each bearing a lamp, which threw a dim, religious light over the lower part of the spacious edifice, leaving the higher portion in deep shadow.

"Upon the upper end of the coffin lid lay a chaplet of white roses, below which were the insignia of the order, and the sword of the deceased Templar; and upon a table near the coffin was a skull, surrounded by seven large candle-sticks, moulded like sphynxes, but bearing no lights.

"The Grand Master, followed by seven Knights Preceptors, seven Knights Companions, and seven Squires or Novices, all bearing tapers, and attired in black, with scarfs of crape, now entered the temple, one by one, and silently as shadows.

"They stood opposite to the skeletons and the coffin, and were addressed by the Grand Master, who, in a few words, informed them that the purpose of their assemblage was to hold a judgment on the knight, whose mortal remains were before them.

"'It is midnight,' he continued; 'and the grave is ready. Our brother knight has finished his earthly probation. Let us look back upon his life, and see how he has stood the test. If any of you can accuse the deceased of wrong, let him stand forth and declare it.'

"A deep, unbroken silence prevailed throughout the assemblage, and, after a long pause, the senior Knight Preceptor advanced to the head of the coffin, begged permission to speak, and thus began:

"'Brother Grand Master!

"'Brother Preceptors, Companions, and Novices!

"'It belongs not unto man, but unto God, to judge the dead. He alone can reward and punish—He alone can look into our souls and know our most secret doings. Therefore, brother Grand Master, wert thou to call us even thrice to accuse our departed brother, thou wouldst call in vain, for we are all brethren in Christ our Lord.'

"'It is my bounden duty,' resumed the Grand Master, 'again to ask you. Brother Templars, ye are free members of the order; speak, if ye have aught to speak against the departed.' Again he paused, but the death-like stillness remained unbroken. Then did the Grand Master exclaim, with a loud voice, 'As there is no accuser there can be no judgment! Does no man accuse the dead?'

"And all the Templars knelt down and answered: 'God is our judge.'

"The Grand Master now raised an iron hammer, struck with it three heavy blows upon an iron cross, placed at the head of the coffin, and called aloud, 'Open the gates of Death!'"

I had read thus far when I heard three knocks, which sounded seemingly from the corridor. I started, closed the book involuntarily, and listened long and anxiously, but all was silent.

"It was delusion!" whispered common sense. "My heated imagination carried me amidst the Templars, and the blows of the Grand Master's hammer struck not my outward but my fancy's ear."

Determining to place this probable construction on the mysterious sounds, I again opened the little book, which had laid a strong hold of my curiosity, and pursued as follows:

"And now the Novices rolled up the tapestry, which covered the floor on the left side of the trestle, and behold there was an open grave close to the coffin. Then did the three junior Novices deck the brink of the grave with garlands of red and white roses; and, while they were thus employed, the Grand Master said:

"'Brother Preceptors, give answer to my questions—When will God judge the dead?'

"First Preceptor: On the day of judgment.

"Grand Master: Who will be man's accuser?

"Second Preceptor: His conscience.

"Grand Master: Who his defender?

"Third Preceptor: No one.

"Grand Master: Who will have mercy on him?

"Fourth Preceptor: No one.

"Grand Master: No one?

"Fifth Preceptor: God is our judge.

"Grand Master: Is not God almighty?

"Sixth Preceptor: Almighty and all-just.

"Grand Master: Hear then, brother Templars! God is almighty and all-just; therefore obey his laws.

"Seventh Preceptor: The grave is ready. Commit our brother to his mother earth.

"And again the Grand Master struck the iron cross thrice with his hammer, and the brotherhood knelt around the grave, and kissed the earth in silence."

At this moment I again heard three knocks more distinctly than before, succeeded, too, by a low sound of mingled muttering and lamentation.

I distinguished both sounds with a clearness which no excitement of my imagination could supply, and I observed that the three knocks resembled the ringing sound of iron upon iron.

I gazed in alarm at the door which opened on the long corridor, from whence the noise had seemed to proceed, and with growing horror I now heard a clearly audible and long continued sobbing, like the last struggling breath of a dying man.

At this instant the thunder again reverberated in long echoes from the mountains—the book dropped from my trembling hand—I felt a sudden shivering of the extremities, and all the blood rushed to my heart, which beat with audible violence.

I now fancied that I heard the sound of distant footsteps, and, seizing the candle, I approached the door and listened, but no sound was distinguishable.

"Nonsense!" I exclaimed, assuming an indifference I did not feel. "'Tis nothing but the rising storm-gust, howling in the long passages and wide chimneys of the castle!"

I resumed my book and chair, determined to finish the curious recital, and retire to bed.

The narrative proceeded thus:—

"Then did the Novices remove the coffin-lid, and expose to view the body of the deceased Templar in a white shroud.

"The hands and feet were tied with cords, the temples were adorned with a chaplet of laurel and vine leaves, on the breast lay a golden cross, sparkling with jewels, and on the heart a bunch of fresh-culled violets.

"'Brother Novices,' said the Grand Master, 'give heed to my commands, and answer to my questions. What means the chaplet of laurel and vine leaves?'

"First Novice: It means that man was born to honour and enjoyment.

"Grand Master: Better things await him in a better world. The laurel and the vine decay and perish. Strip the dead of such frail distinctions.

"And the Novices took the chaplet from the temples of the deceased.

"Grand Master: What means the sparkling cross?

"Second Novice: It means that the man striveth after wealth and splendour.

"Grand Master: How does man come into the world?

"Third Novice: Naked and poor.

"Grand Master: Then must he return to his mother-earth, naked and poor as he was born. Strip the dead of such vain adornment.

"And the Novices took the cross from the breast of the deceased.

"Grand Master: Why are his hands and feet bound with cords?

"Fourth Novice: To show that in this life man is the slave of sin.

"Grand Master: Death has overcome the dominion of sin. Release the freed man from his earthly bondage.

"And the Novices did as they were commanded.

"Grand Master: What means the bunch of violets on his heart?

"Fifth Novice: It is the emblem of humanity, and the offering of brotherly love to the departed, who deserved the tribute; because, during life, he was humble and pure in heart. Blessed are such, for theirs is the kingdom of Heaven.

"Grand Master: Know ye of a truth that our brother in the coffin is dead, and ripe for the long sleep of the grave?

"Sixth Novice: (Taking the hand of the dead.) The flesh cleaveth not unto the bones, nor the skin unto the flesh. He is dead.

"Grand Master: How looks his grave?

"Seventh Novice: (Looking down into the grave.) Deep—dark—narrow—cold.

"Grand Master: Knights Companions of the Order, do the last kind office to the departed, and give him a brother's blessing, for he was one of you.

"And the seven Knights Companions slowly approached the coffin, and placed their right hands upon the head, eyes, face, mouth, heart, hand, and feet of the departed brother, each accompanying this solemn rite with a fervent blessing; after which the Novices replaced the lid upon the coffin, and nailed it with seven nails. Then sang the Preceptors to a low accompaniment from the choir above, the awful words:

"'Ne recorderis, Domine! peccata illius, dum veneris judicare seculum per ignem.'

(*To be continued in our next.*)

FIGOLI; OR, THE BANDIT'S FATE.

A TRUE SKETCH.

(*Concluded.*)

THE approach of dissolution, under whatever circumstances of preparation, must always be viewed with awe. On the bed of sickness, although the mind becomes in some degree familiarised with the idea, and bodily anguish may have made life a burden, it is painful to look our last upon a world, which, with all its anxieties, holds much that is dear to us; but to receive the dread summons when health, and hope, and happiness are around us, is indeed to taste of death in all its bitterness and sorrow.

Vernon was constitutionally brave; but it is one thing to encounter death amid excitement of battle, and another to meet it in the form under which it was then approaching him.

The possessor of most earthly sources of happiness, the object of a mother's hope, a sister's pride, and the idol of one to whom a few months were to have given a name "dearer than all," it was some time before he could sufficiently abstract his mind from the world he was about to quit, in order to a preparation for that to which he was hastening.

Terence, however, though not deficient in courage, and

with fewer ties to bind him to existence, appeared much more incapable of applying himself to so serious and necessary a task, for he took his station at the grating of the prison, and watched the sentinel with great attention, until, catching his eye at last, he said:

"Is that yourself, Tim ?"

The man started at hearing himself thus called on by name, but turned away his face, and remained silent, when Terence continued :

"Tim—Tim Dolan, I say! It's the bad thing ye're doing !" and then, after a pause, during which he received no reply : "Maybe you think I don't know your mother's son behind the black crop you've sown on your lip there. I'll tell you one thing, Tim ; it's make your soul of the same colour you will."

At length, getting out of patience, Terence exclaimed :

"Is it deaf you are? or is them the manners you've come all the way from Mullinahone to learn. I might as well be talking Latin to a goose."

"Aisy now, Terry," said the sentinel at last; "what a bother you make! Don't you see I'm on duty ?".

"Is it duty ?" said Terence. "Oh! then it's a queer notion you have of that same, to be lending a hand to cut the throat of two honest men, and one your countryman and cousin-German to boot. 'Twould be more like a decent Christian, I'm thinking, to be dropping the bar outside there, and letting us out."

"I tell you I can't, Terence; it's more than my place is worth."

"And that's little enough, Tim, anyhow. It is not for myself I care so much, for, go when I will, I'll be no loss to anyone; but it's for the sake of the master, here to the fore, that I'm asking the kind thing of you. Oh, Tim! Tim! think upon his young blood, and that it will be red upon your soul, if it's shed by them ruffians, and you able to prevent it. Think, Tim, upon the old grey-headed man in Mullinahone, who'd curse the hour you were born, if he knew his son was bringing disgrace upon his name and his country in this fashion.

The last appeal appeared to touch the sentinel, for he answered in a softer tone than that which he had hitherto adopted:

"Oh! then it isn't myself would refuse to help a friend at a pinch, and that you know yourself right well; but where's the use of my opening the door when the only way out of the place is through the room which they're drinking in."

"That's our concern," said Terence ; "you might give us a squeak for our lives, at any rate."

"And get my own throat cut for my pains."

"And what's the reason you can't take your chance with us ? Wouldn't it be better to die in a good cause, than to be strung up by the neck some day between earth and heaven, as if you had no business in either? The master wouldn't be the man to forget the kind deed, I'm thinking."

At this juncture, Vernon, who had been an attentive listener to the latter part of the conference, came forward, and enforced Terence's arguments by promising to open the way for Tim's return to an honest path in life, and to reward him liberally besides, in the event of his co-operation in their escape proving successful.

Dolan, who had joined the band in a fit of disappointment, and had more than once repented of the act, was not without his feelings, and, after some further hesitation, consented to aid their escape.

Accordingly, after releasing them from prison, he restored to them their arms, to which he had access, with the means of reloading them, and furnished them each with a sword in addition.

As they approached the scene of the robbers' carousal, the boisterous sounds of conviviality which saluted their ears inspired them with a hope that the revellers were too far gone in their cups to notice their attempt, or to frustrate it if they did.

A single glance, which they were enabled, unperceived, to get at the party, was sufficient to destroy so vain an expectation.

The robbers had drank wine enough to inflame their ferocity without disarming their vigilance, and had so disposed themselves that it was next to impossible for the fugitives to gain the opposite door without coming in personal contact with one or more of the band.

A large torch was fixed on the table round which they were sitting, and, while it flung its red glare upon the forbidding countenances of the banqueters, illuminated the remotest corner of the chamber.

Dolan, as the best acquainted with the path, led the way on his hands and knees, and, crawling close under the wall, succeeded in gaining the door, unperceived by the robbers.

Terence, elated by the successful example of his countryman, followed his steps, but, either from want of sufficient care, or from the circumstance of his being a stouter man, he, on squeezing himself between the wall and the barrel on which one of the banditti was seated, overturned the latter, and thus betrayed himself and his master to the view of the robbers.

"Treason—treason !" exclaimed the band in concert, as they started to their feet, and, with their swords flashing in the torchlight, rushed upon their prey. Vernon, with a presence of mind peculiar to gallant spirits, instead of making for the door, sprang to the table, struck down the torch, and involved the whole party in darkness. He was, however, seized at the same instant by the captain, who clung to his throat like a bloodhound, and by his weight dragged his captive to the ground. A fearful struggle ensued, during which Vernon and the robber-chief were alternately uppermost, the former being deterred from discharging his pistol by the fear of discovering their relative positions by the flash, while the rest of the band refrained from using their weapons in the dark, where they were more likely to smite friends than foes.

Vernon at last succeeded in placing his knee upon the neck of his antagonist, and compelling him to relinquish his hold. After some difficulty, he was so fortunate as to gain the door, and passed through it into the court-yard, which, with the exception of an angle of it, was illuminated by the beams of the full moon. As, however, he was making his way towards the outer gate, he had the mortification of perceiving two of the robbers running for the same point, with the view of cutting off the retreat of the fugitives, while he heard the footsteps of the rest in close pursuit at his heels. Before he could decide upon the alternative of pressing forward or surrendering, two shots, fired simultaneously from the shaded angle of the court-yard, which was by the gate, stretched the robbers in advance upon the grass, and at almost the same instant, he perceived the figures of Terence and Dolan dart through the portal. Vernon followed with the speed of light, and had no sooner overtaken them, than Tim seized him and Terence by the arm, without speaking, and dragged them down an almost precipitous descent, covered with briars and underwood, by which their clothes were nearly torn from their backs, and their persons much lacerated before they reached, or rather rolled, to the bottom.

As soon as they gained their feet, Dolan whispered :

"Now run, my boys, for the bare life, and keep out of the moonshine, or it's kilt and murdered ye are, intirely."

The caution was not needless; for, as they followed in his steps, they heard the robbers, who had hit upon their track, breaking through the bushes about two hundred yards in their rear, while their random shots were whistling among the leaves about the fugitives in all directions. After running for about a quarter of a mile, they arrived at a shed, in which were tied the horses of the banditti. To select one each, and to slip the bridles over the heads of the others, and turn them loose upon the road, was the work of a moment; and the next they were galloping off, at the top of their speed, towards the river. Arrived at the brink, they pushed their horses into the stream, and were soon on the opposite bank. Thus safe from pursuit, they continued their journey at their leisure, and, after an hour's riding, arrived at the town to which Vernon had sent forward his carriage.

Dolan was rewarded for his services beyond his expectations, and is now respectably settled in his own country, an honest and useful member of society.

TALES OF BRIGANDS AND ROBBERS.

I Warn & Strike

[THE DUEL AND THE RESCUE.]

THE RED DWARF.

CHAPTER XIV.

THE MEETING OF ALLAN AND LORD KYLO.—ALLAN HEARS THE
HISTORY OF HIS FATHER'S DEATH.—ONE STORY IS VERY GOOD
UNTIL ANOTHER IS TOLD.—THE CHALLENGE.—ARRIVAL OF

TWO IMPORTANT PERSONAGES.—THE TREACHEROUS MESSAGE,
AND WHAT CAME OF IT.

MADALINE had employed messengers to search in all directions
for her father, but without success.

Foremost amongst the most anxious was Allan Buckhurst,

who, with several of his lordship's most faithful servants, used every effort to discover Sir Stuart Catemass dead or alive.

Allan begun to lose all hope, although he did not venture to tell Madaline so, but rather buoyed her up with a hope which found no echo in his own bosom.

He was proceeding with a heavy heart towards the mansion of Sir Stuart Catemass to report his fruitless search.

At the same moment Lord Kylo Smedleigh was returning from the mansion of the Duke of Buckingham, elated with the success of his cunning plan.

Like Allan, the libertine lord was so absorbed in his own reflections that he did not observe our hero's approach.

But both happening to raise their eyes at the same time, they beheld each other.

Lord Kylo's first impulse was to put spurs to his horse and fly, but upon second thoughts, he had an idea that this would look like guilt; besides, he had no doubt but Allan was as well mounted as himself, and could speedily overtake him.

He therefore reined-up his horse, and waited, as Allan, with an exclamation of rage and indignation, rode towards him.

"Be not rash, young sir," said the crafty lord, as he saw Allan place his hand upon his sword—"I am not so much your enemy as you suppose."

"False, craven knave!" exclaimed Allan. "Draw thy sword and defend thy recreant life, if thou hast the courage to do so! But what manliness can we hope for from one like thee?" added the impetuous young man, seeing that Lord Kylo refused to put himself on the defensive.

"We have been foes, I grant you; but I confess having wronged you, and trust henceforth we may be friends," said the artful libertine, in a feigned, hypocritical tone.

"Friends with such as thee!" exclaimed Allan, with disgust, about to strike him with the flat of his weapon.

"Tarry, young sir," said Lord Kylo, backing his horse beyond the reach of Allan's weapon. "The share I took in the abduction of the Lady Madaline I was forced to take."

"How forced?" asked Allan. "Were you not urged on by your own base, treacherous passions?"

"No," said Lord Kylo, boldly, his heart telling him he lied as he spoke. "I was the unwilling instrument in the hands of another—one whom I dared not refuse."

"Even if this were so, you have acted a contemptible part, in seeking to accomplish a woman's downfall!"

"I swear to you it was not myself who wished her ruin, but one of the most powerful men at Court."

"Who?"

"His Grace the Duke of Buckingham."

"The Duke of Buckingham?" cried Allan, in alarm, well knowing, if it were indeed so, the duke would never rest until he had achieved his object.

"Even so," replied the lying hypocrite, proving treacherous to the man he had promised to aid.

It is true he felt for the moment that he had done a rash action by mentioning the duke's name in the matter.

"But, then, again," thought he, "who is to prove I ever did mention it? Even if this mad-brained young spark taxes the duke with the abduction of Madaline, it is but for me to swear I never said anything of the kind. My word will go as far as his; besides, he has no witnesses."

Allan now felt that Madaline was in greater peril than ever, and longed to be by her side, to protect her from the danger which he felt assured was hanging over her.

The avowal Lord Kylo had made only served to make him appear more contemptible than ever in the young man's eyes, but he controlled the disgust he felt towards him, in the hope of gaining some information that might serve him.

Had he been more versed in the ways of the world, he would no doubt have detected the shallow trick by which Lord Kylo sought to place his own misdeeds upon the shoulders of others.

He hoped to learn something of Sir Stuart Catemass, feeling assured the libertine before him knew something of the matter.

"My Lord Smedleigh," said Allan, "were I you I should blush for myself. But if you are really sincere, and wish to make atonement for the act——"

"Which I really do," answered his lying lordship.

"Tell me, then, what you know of Madaline's father. He has been missing for some days, and if any harm befalls him, his daughter would go distracted."

Lord Kylo had not the slightest doubt but Sir Stuart Catemass had ceased to exist—he knew the difficulty of any prisoner escaping from the Black Colonel's den, and looked upon the father of Madaline as no longer living.

Remorse shook his frame as Allan's question struck upon his heart.

"You hesitate and turn pale at my question, my lord," said Allan, noticing the pallor which overspread the visage of the libertine.

"If I turned pale, it was at the thought of any harm having befallen Sir Stuart. Heaven knows I have had no hand in any plan to injure the worthy gentleman!"

Allan was credulous enough to believe this was true, and, if any harm had really befallen the father of Madaline, it was to be placed to the Duke of Buckingham's account.

"And yet, young sir, I marvel you should so interest yourself on Sir Stuart's account, for, if I have heard rightly, you find but little favour in his eyes."

"Little indeed; and yet I hope, by the humble efforts I have made in his daughter's behalf, to overcome the prejudice he bears against me."

"I doubt whether you would care about doing so if you knew all."

"Knew all?" echoed Allan. "What is it you mean?"

"Your father's sad fate is to be traced to the agency of Sir Stuart Catemass," said Lord Kylo, with a deep sigh, as if he felt it painful to speak upon the subject.

"To the agency of Sir Stuart Catemass?" cried Allan, starting with horror.

"It is as I have said," replied Lord Kylo. "That is the reason he cannot abide you—his guilty conscience tells him he has robbed you of a parent, and when he looks upon you it strikes terror to his soul."

The above words fell like a thunderbolt upon Allan's heart; if they were true, they placed an insurmountable barrier between him and Madaline, and dashed all his hopes of happiness to the earth.

"Is this really true?" he gasped, with emotion, suddenly seizing his treacherous foe by the throat, and looking into his eyes as though he would read his very soul.

"I swear to you it is!" said Lord Kylo. "Sir Stuart Catemass has been throughout his life a stanch loyalist; your father, as you are aware, espoused the Puritan cause. Upon the restoration of his present Majesty, Charles the Second, all who had been the means of bringing his father to the scaffold were singled out and hunted down, your parent, Martin Buckhurst, among the number."

"Yes, but it was by King Charles the Second's orders," replied Allan.

"True; yet many escaped to the coast, by the aid of friends, and fled to France. Such was your father's intention, but he was betrayed. I will tell you how. Although he and Sir Stuart Catemass espoused different sides, your father thought that his friend would act generously towards him, now the Republican cause was irretrievably lost, for Sir Stuart and your father had been early friends, notwithstanding the difference of their political opinions. Your father with great difficulty had baffled the soldiers of the King for several days. At last they succeeded in getting upon his track; every avenue of escape was guarded—your father was completely hemmed in. In this extremity he thought of his former acquaintance, Sir Stuart Catemass, and resolved to throw himself on his generosity for an asylum, till he could find an opportunity of leaving the country. Late one dark and stormy night, your father, weary and exhausted by the privations he had endured, sought the mansion of Sir Stuart Catemass, and asked to see him. Your father was asked in, and given food and shelter; he was then conducted to a secret chamber, to pass the night. The next morning he was awakened by violent hands being laid upon him; he started up, and found himself in the grasp of the King's soldiers. He was conducted to prison—a speedy trial and execution followed, and your father fell upon the scaffold through the treachery of the man who had sworn to befriend him."

Every word of the above went like a dagger to the heart of the bewildered and horror-stricken Allan.

"I would rather have died than listened to this!" he cried, half maddened by what he had heard. "You have done me a cruel kindness by telling me!"

"I have long hesitated whether to tell you or not," sighed Lord Kylo. "But seeing your passion for Sir Stuart's daughter was uncontrollable, I thought it best to disclose all to you. I have done it unwillingly, yet I felt it to be my duty, for had you learnt hereafter that you had wedded the daughter of him who may be justly called the murderer of your father, what would have been your future anguish?"

"True—true!" groaned the deceived young man. "Yet I was always given to understand that it was he who is known as the Black Colonel who sealed my father's fate."

"No, you have been misinformed," said the crafty reprobate. "Sir Stuart Catemass was alone the cause of your father's doom."

"Liar!" exclaimed a loud, ringing voice in Lord Kylo's ear.

He turned, and his blood curdled within him, as the form of Sir Stuart seemed to rise out of the very ground by his side.

Had his intended victim really escaped, or was this his avenging spirit risen from the grave to call him to account?

The villain reeled in his saddle, and with difficulty retained his seat, as Sir Stuart Catemass seized his horse's rein, and fixed his hollow eyes upon his terror-stricken countenance.

Sir Stuart Catemass might have been taken for a being from the other world.

Pale, haggard, and excited by the perils he had passed, he looked terrible and grim.

Allan's astonished gaze rested on the form of Sir Stuart Catemass with wonder equal to Lord Kylo's.

Did Madaline's father really live?

His doubts were speedily dispelled by what followed.

"Thou slanderous and false-speaking wretch!" cried Sir Stuart Catemass, addressing the libertine. "I now see thee in thy true colours—thou art the serpent I warmed on my hearth only that it might turn and sting me! Dismount—dismount, I say, and meet me foot to foot, and weapon to weapon, that I may call thee to account for this!"

Lord Kylo felt that his time was come.

His arm felt powerless.

To contend against an opponent like Sir Stuart Catemass would be death; and even if he escaped the sword of the indignant father, how could he avoid crossing swords with Allan, whom he felt assured would call him to account for the lying statement he had just made regarding Madaline's father.

"Young man," said Sir Stuart Catemass, seeing that Kylo was paralysed with guilty fear, "heed not one word that vile wretch has told thee. In the first place he led me to believe that my daughter had been taken from her home by thy means."

"By mine?" exclaimed the astonished Allan. "Why, it was I who defended her."

"So I have since learnt," said Sir Stuart Catemass. "And as for thy father, dear boy, I vow that, before yonder bright Heaven above us, I did not by any means compass his death! It is true we were not friends, but never was I his betrayer."

Sir Stuart Catemass spoke with all the earnestness of truth, and a heavy weight seemed lifted from Allan's heart as he listened, for hope whispered that Madaline might still be his.

Joy deprived him for the moment of the powers of speech, and Sir Stuart Catemass ascribed his silence to a different cause.

"Do you not believe me, boy?" asked Sir Stuart Catemass. "Do you really think me the wretch that this villain has painted me?"

"No, no, my lord!" exclaimed Allan, as his emotion subsided. "I believe your words to be as true as his are false!" and he pointed to the craven Kylo as he spoke.

That worthy saw himself in a dilemma from which he knew not how to escape.

A convicted liar—a discovered plotter against the very man who had saved him from a watery grave.

What refuge was there from the chastisement he saw hanging over him.

"Will you dismount and measure weapons with me, or shall I pull you from your seat?" exclaimed Sir Stuart Catemass, as he still grasped the rein of Lord Kylo's steed.

The libertine hesitated a moment as to the course he should pursue.

If he gave his steed the spur, he thought, perhaps, he might be enabled to ride down Sir Stuart Catemass and escape, to claim the protection of the Duke of Buckingham.

But then the fear of being followed and overtaken by Allan Buckhurst, who was as well mounted as himself, made him pause.

"Do you hesitate, coward?" asked Sir Stuart.

"I will meet you to-morrow," answered Kylo. "At present I feel unwell, and not equal to the task."

"To-morrow, thou vile caitiff!" replied Sir Stuart Catemass. "Why, by that time thou mayst be many miles away, scared by thy guilty conscience! Descend, I say, and meet me foot to foot where I now stand!"

At this moment the clatter of horses' hoofs rang upon the road behind them.

A couple of well-mounted cavaliers rode up, and Lord Kylo, to his great joy, saw the Duke of Buckingham and his friend Sir Pierrepoint Lucy.

"How now, my masters?" said Buckingham, addressing Sir Stuart Catemass and Allan. "What, two upon one? Surely that is not English fair play."

"Welcome—welcome, my lord," cried Kylo. "Had you not arrived so opportunely both these knaves would have set upon me at once, and a small chance I should have had for my life against such odds."

"He lies!" indignantly exclaimed Allan. "The sword of Sir Stuart Catemass alone was to be opposed against him. As an Englishman I would scorn to lend myself to any such base act as he speaks of."

The Duke of Buckingham in his heart well knew that Sir Stuart Catemass was too much a man of honour to act as Kylo had described; but his grace bore Sir Stuart Catemass little goodwill.

He remembered the scene at the banquet when he toasted the name of Madaline.

"Sir Stuart," said he, addressing the baronet, "I must trouble you to release the rein of Lord Kylo's horse. Methinks such is not the conduct of one gentleman towards another."

"When a man acts the part of a traitor and a villain to he that saved him from death and afterwards befriended him, I consider that he forfeits the name of a gentleman, and only retains that of a paltroon and a coward!"

"Those words must be accounted for!" cried Lord Kylo, assuming a bold tone, although he still trembled within himself.

"It is what I most ardently desire," said Sir Stuart Catemass, as he released the horse's rein, and drew his sword. "You little know the baseness of this villain, my lord!" continued he, addressing the duke. "He planned the abduction of my daughter in conjunction with other villains, and then tried to cast the odium of the deed upon this young man," pointing to Allan as he spoke.

The duke, thinking that Lord Kylo had done all this in order to place Madaline in his power, resolved to do his utmost to shield Lord Kylo.

He saw that fighting was the last thing in his treacherous lordship's thoughts.

"I wait for you, sir," said Sir Stuart Catemass, seeing Kylo had no idea of leaving his saddle.

Sir Pierrepoint Lucy, guessing how matters stood, came to the rescue of Lord Kylo.

"Pardon me, Sir Stuart Catemass," said he, "but it is evident my friend Lord Smedleigh is indisposed. I propose that this meeting be postponed until noon to-morrow."

"Well said, my lord," exclaimed Buckingham. "I think with you that such a course is but reasonable."

"It is but a coward's subterfuge," answered Sir Stuart Catemass. "But he must and shall meet me at noon to-morrow, if not I will post him far and wide as the most arrant knave in his Majesty's dominions, and those who shield or harbour him from my just resentment shall meet with the same exposure. Such is my resolve, gentlemen, and having explained myself, I leave you to consider the matter. You know where I am to be found. Come, Allan."

And he walked quickly from the spot, followed by the young man he addressed.

"Thank Heaven, he's gone," said Lord Kylo, breathing more freely. "Had it not been for your timely arrival, it would have fared badly with me. What is to be done in the matter to-morrow, your grace?"

This was addressed to Buckingham, who replied, after a moment's thought:

"I see no other alternative but your meeting him."

"Meeting him?" echoed Lord Kylo, in a tremulous voice. "Why, it would be rushing upon certain death."

"Not as I mean to arrange matters. Besides, if you were to refuse meeting him how could you ever show your face again at Court?"

"What the deuce care I for the Court if it imperils my life!" cried the cowardly nobleman.

"How now, my lord," exclaimed the Duke of Buckingham, in anger. "Would you bring discredit on our order? We gallants of the Court are not to be considered cowards, Master Kylo, and by my royal master, if you don't meet Sir Stuart at noon, you will have to meet me at eve!"

"But I am no match for the fellow. How is this; did I not suppose from your manner of addressing him that you wished to save me from the meeting?"

"Well, truly, I did so at first, but upon second thoughts it will be better for you to save appearances and meet him."

"Save appearances?" muttered Kylo. "I would rather save myself."

"So thou shalt, as we will arrange matters."

"What do you mean?" asked Kylo.

"Simply this," answered the duke. "You shall challenge this hot-headed spark, young Allan Buckhurst, the first thing to-morrow morning."

"Why, he may be as good a swordsman as the other," cried the abject Kylo. "I don't perceive what I have to gain by such a course."

"Then I will tell you. When this young man meets you, as he assuredly will, we'll act as your seconds, and if things are going badly with you in the encounter we'll come to the rescue, and give the young gallant a wound unobserved that shall save you and disable him."

"Good!" exclaimed Kylo, eagerly agreeing to the treacherous proposal. "Well, what then?"

"Why, then a message shall be sent to Sir Stuart Catemass, saying that Allan is in danger. His lordship will of course come rushing to the spot. In the meantime I will have some of my fellows ready to see him leave the house; the moment he does so, my emissaries shall enter the mansion, and secure his daughter, and I warrant we'll keep a tighter hold of her than you ever did, despite the mysterious Red Dwarf and his myrmidons."

"But suppose he told Sir Stuart Catemass he had received a challenge from me, would not the baronet insist upon coming with him, and meeting me first?"

"We must try to induce him to keep the challenge a secret from Sir Stuart Catemass. Come with me to my house, and I'll explain my plan."

They proceeded on their road to the duke's mansion.

Arriving there, Buckingham, followed by Kylo and Sir Pierrepoint Lucy, entered his secret cabinet, and Kylo wrote the following letter at the dictation of his grace :—

"To Master Allan Buckhurst,
        "Sir,—
        "I am challenged, as you are aware, by Sir Stuart Catemass; but, as you may imagine yourself an aggrieved party, and as you no doubt look upon me as deficient in courage, I am most anxious to remove that impression from your mind. Meet me, therefore, in the fields behind the village of Charing at the hour of ten to-morrow morning. I shall, by your agreeing to this, be enabled—if you do not disable me—to meet Sir Stuart Catemass afterwards on the same spot at twelve of the clock. Thus you see I have the courage to settle my differences with both parties, giving you the preference.

"I must ask you, as a point of honour, not to mention this to Sir Stuart Catemass; should you do so, our meeting may be frustrated, and I shall look upon you as being afraid of affording satisfaction to

                "KYLO, LORD SMEDLEIGH."

"You're sure you'll stand by me?" said Lord Kylo, when he had finished the letter.

"Thou art sure of us, I tell thee," replied the duke, as he took up the letter and glanced over it. "Nothing can be better," he said, as he gave the message to Kylo to seal.

This being done, a trusty servant was summoned, and charged to deliver it secretly to Allan Buckhurst, whom he was told was most probably to be met with at the mansion of Sir Stuart Catemass.

The messenger was immediately despatched, and the duke and his companions waited to hear the upshot.

In less than an hour the messenger returned.

He had succeeded in seeing Allan Buckhurst, and brought the following written answer :—

"To Lord Kylo Smedleigh,
    "My Lord,—
        "You have afforded me the very opportunity I most wished for.
    "I will be secret, and keep the appointment, never fear.
                "ALLAN BUCKHURST."

"He falls into the trap like the gull that he is!" said the duke.

Wine was ordered, and the two drank far into the night, Buckingham toasting the fair Madaline repeatedly in his deep potations, as if he looked upon her as being already in his arms.

In the meantime Allan Buckhurst, who was lodged that night in the mansion of Sir Stuart Catemass, lay awake thinking of some plan by which he could leave the house unobserved and meet his antagonist.

CHAPTER XV.

ALLAN GOES TO KEEP THE TREACHEROUS APPOINTMENT.—THE TWO LETTERS, AND WHAT CAME OF THEM.—LORD KYLO VISITS THE BLACK COLONEL FOR THE LAST TIME.—THE MEETING OF THE COMBATANTS.—THE TRAITOR IN AMBUSH.—GOOD NIGHT TO LORD KYLO SMEDLEIGH.

As the first ray of morning entered the chamber in which Allan reposed, he rose and dressed himself.

He looked upon his triumph over Lord Kylo as certain, and felt eager to chastise with his good sword the man who had subjected the woman he loved to such indignity.

The thought of any treachery being mixed up in the matter never once crossed his mind.

Duels were frequent in those days, and always conducted upon the nicest principles of honour.

It was the usual method of appeal, in those days, if one man felt himself aggrieved by another, and if death took place the survivor was seldom or ever punished, duelling being looked upon as the usual means of arranging a quarrel.

Allan listened at his room door, and felt convinced by

the silence that reigned in the house that no one was astir.

His idea was to return before his absence would be missed.

Then a thought struck him that he ought to be prepared for the worst.

Perhaps he might never see Madaline again—who could tell?

As he paced the room in thought, his eyes fell upon writing materials placed on a table by the window.

Thinking it the better plan to pen a few lines in case the worst might happen, he wrote the following:—

"DEAR MADALINE,—

"Honour calls me from you for a short time. By eleven o'clock I purpose returning here.

"But should Fate decree it otherwise, think sometimes of your devoted Allan, who loved you to the last."

Folding this up, and addressing it to Madaline, he was about to reopen it as a thought struck him he had not mentioned the name of her father in it, or tendered him his thanks for the night's hospitality.

A noise in the chamber overhead suddenly interrupted him.

Thinking it was one of the servants rising to resume his duties in the mansion, Allan thrust the letter he had just written into the pocket of his vest along with the challenge of Lord Kylo.

He again listened.

All was still

A few moments more passed.

All remained quiet.

Allan cautiously unlocked his door, opened it, and stealthily descended the stairs.

In so doing he had to pass the sleeping chamber of Madaline.

He had wished her good night on its threshold the night previous, and his heart beat with emotion as he thought of her he held most dear, sleeping calmly and innocently within, while he was bound upon an errand of life and death.

He placed, as he thought, the note he had written to Madaline beneath her chamber door, when it occurred to him that he might forego the meeting to which he had been summoned, and by showing the letter to Madaline's father, get his advice upon the matter.

Then again he thought Lord Kylo would ascribe his absence to cowardice, and the idea of being supposed fearful of meeting a fellow like his antagonist, made him resolve upon keeping the appointment.

Softly and stealthily he reached the hall door, withdrew the bolts with a noiseless hand, and silently left the mansion.

About the same time, Lord Kylo was on his way to the haunt of the Black Colonel to consult with that worthy as to the escape of Sir Stuart Catemass from his dungeon, and to learn how it had been effected.

"Has the ruffian leader played me false?" thought he. "If so, I must beware."

He reached the secret entrance, gave the usual signal, and was admitted to the Black Colonel's presence, who, surrounded by his band, was assisting at the interment of Geoffrey in the burial place of the gang, which we have already described.

Lord Kylo started back with horror as he found himself in the midst of the ceremony.

He always entertained a dread horror of death, and in the solemn, gloomy place he was now in, it struck upon his fears with double force.

The colonel beckoned to him to follow, and led the way into the room with the treacherous flooring through which Sir Stuart Catemass had disappeared.

"Your prisoner has escaped," said Kylo, as soon as they were alone. "How is this?"

"I would that I knew," answered the colonel.

"Do you suspect treachery amongst your fellows?" asked Kylo.

"Not that I am aware of," replied the ruffian. "And yet, who knows? It may be so. Oh, if it is, and I could learn the traitor's name, I'd grind his very life out day by day with sheer starvation in our deepest dungeon! I have looked at the matter every way," said the ruffian, after a pause, "and at times the thought strikes me that the Red Dwarf is concerned in this business."

"The Red Dwarf?"

"Ay, even he!" replied the colonel, with fear in the tones of his voice.

"But how could the Red Dwarf enter here?" asked Lord Kylo.

"Who knows? Sometimes I fancy that being must be the foul fiend himself in mortal form."

"You seem to fear him."

"Well, to tell you the truth, I do."

"What, you fear him—you, who are so feared by others? This is strange."

"Strange or not, it's true. Speak no more of it—it's a subject that troubles me. Now, what brings you here?"

Lord Kylo informed him that he had met Sir Stuart Catemass, and how my Lord of Buckingham came so opportunely to the rescue. He then imparted to the colonel the scheme he had laid for the destruction of Allan Buckhurst and the plot to regain possession of Madaline.

The colonel exulted within himself as he listened.

His wound still rankled with pain, and he burned to be revenged on those who were concerned in causing it and marring the plans which he fancied he had laid so securely.

Lord Kylo and he conversed eagerly for some time on a subject which seemed to gratify them, and then left the haunt together.

The city clocks were striking the hour of ten as Allan reached the appointed spot.

Drawing his handkerchief from his vest to wipe the perspiration from his brow, a letter fell upon the turf. He picked it up, thinking it was the challenge he had received, but, glancing at the superscription, he perceived to his surprise it was the letter he had intended for Madaline.

He then saw the mistake he had made.

It was the challenge from Lord Kylo he had placed under the door of Madaline's chamber.

She would thus learn all, and he could well imagine what her feelings would be when she did so.

He would fain have returned to quiet her fears, when he perceived his antagonist approaching, accompanied by the Duke of Buckingham and Sir Pierrepoint Lucy.

They saluted each other courteously, and Sir Pierrepoint produced a pair of rapiers from beneath his cloak.

"My lord, will you be my second?" said Lord Kylo, with a gaiety of manner which surprised Allan, who began to think the nobleman was not the coward he surmised.

But he little knew the reason of the villain's assurance.

It was not a duel he came to fight, but to assist at an assassination, if necessary.

The duke consented to act as second to the traitor Kylo, and Sir Pierrepoint proffered the same service to Allan, who respectfully declined his aid.

"I seek the aid of no one," answered Allan, "much less you. A second should be a friend—I look upon you as an enemy."

"Can I do anything for you?" said a voice behind him.

Allan turned, and the villanous form of the Black Colonel stood before him.

A thought of foul play instantly flashed across the mind of Allan.

What would he not have given for a real friend at that moment?

If they really meant him treachery, three against one were fearful odds.

He took his weapon, and stood upon the defensive, waiting for the attack.

Lord Kylo proved a better swordsman than Allan expected;

and he was thinking he should not find him the easy conquest he had bargained for, when a loud scream fell upon his ear. For a moment he glanced aside, and saw, to his surprise, Madaline advancing towards him.

With a cry of alarm, Allan warned her back, but at the same moment she was seized by Buckingham and the colonel.

To fly to her side would be to expose himself to the sword of Lord Kylo the moment he dropped his guard.

What was to be done?

He strove by a violent effort to disarm his antagonist, but in vain.

In the meantime, Madaline's piercing cries for help, as they were bearing her away, rent his very heart.

But—oh, joy!—he perceives a man leap over the bushes by his side.

It was Madaline's father, who, sword in hand, pursued Buckingham and the colonel as they bore off Madaline to the high-road.

Lord Kylo, seeing his friends had departed, sought to do the same, but Allan, guessing his motive, barred his way.

"Now, traitor and false friend, I have thee!" shouted Allan, in a terrible voice. "Thy reign of wickedness shall now cease, for, by her I love, I will kill thee!"

Lord Kylo shook with terror, for he read his fate in the young man's eyes.

He strove to keep him off; but, as Allan's attack grew fiercer, the courage of the reprobate began to grow weaker—his sword-arm shook like a reed as he strove to keep off the thrusts of his opponent.

"I—I surrender!" gasped Lord Kylo, in a faint voice. "Let us be friends. I will ask thy pardon!"

"Too late—ask pardon of Heaven!" cried the infuriated Allan; and, striking down Lord Kylo's guard, his rapier was buried up to the hilt in the wretched bosom of the libertine and deceiver.

With an agonising shriek, Lord Kylo fell backwards on the grass bathed in blood.

Allan quickly drew his sword from the body and flew in the direction taken by Sir Stuart Catemass.

(*To be continued in our next.*)

THE ROBBERS' TOWER.

A TRUE ADVENTURE.

"After the Preceptors had finished singing, they chanted the *De profundis*, while each in succession sprinkled holy water on the coffin, saying:

"'My brother! thou art dead to this world, and livest now in the Lord!'

"Then did the invisible choristers in the gallery begin to chant the *Libera*; and their voices sounded afar off, like the answerings of departed spirits. Every taper, save that of the Grand Master, was now extinguished, and all the Knights, Preceptors, and Companions, prostrating themselves in the figure of a cross, prayed silently. Meanwhile, the Novices gently and slowly lowered the coffin into the grave, and the Grand Master, again raising the iron hammer, struck the iron cross three times, and said, with a deep and solemn unction:

"'I bless thee in the name of the triune God—in the name of the ancient and venerable order of Knights Templars—in the name of the Preceptors, Companions, and Novices here assembled——'"

Here I was again interrupted by the sound of three knocks near my door, ringing like the blows of iron upon iron, and so loudly audible, that I could no longer doubt the evidence of my senses, nor reason down my apprehensions that either earthly mischief, or probably, unearthly agency, was busy near me.

The knocks were again succeeded by loud sounds of lamentation and groans, followed, as before, by a quick and sobbing respiration, which I could compare to nothing but the death-rattle.

I struggled hard with a growing suspicion that some supernatural intelligence was at work here, and yet my reason equally rejected the possible contingencies of robbers, or midnight frolics.

Thieves would not thus announce their presence, and it was utterly improbable that my afflicted relatives, or the attached sympathizing domestics would amuse themselves by trying midnight experiments upon my courage.

I had clearly distinguished that these mysterious sounds proceeded not from the sepulchre beneath me, but from the hall or corridor.

"Can it be," whispered my excited imagination, "the unquiet spirit of the murdered Bruno, or of his suicide daughter, the unhappy Leah? Or, can it be the shade of my ancestor, the long-departed Templar? Or," it suddenly occurred to me, "is it not rather some benighted traveller, attracted by the light in my window, knocking at the gate for admittance? It is, it must be, some helpless wayfarer," I exclaimed, clinging to this preferable solution of the sounds which had alarmed me.

Transferring one of my candles to a lantern which I found in the book-closet, I seized my sabre, and was hastening to the door, when suddenly the sound of solemn music floated through the apartment.

The tones were harp-like, and gradually rose with a sublime swell, which, at such an hour and place, seemed to me more than earthly.

The soaring swell was succeeded by a gradual and dying cadence, which melted away in the distant night-breeze. I paused and listened in still astonishment; but all was silent.

I endeavoured to persuade myself that it was another delusion of my fevered brain, and that the ill-cured sabre-wound on my head had contributed to the successive hallucinations of the night; but the melody had been so distinct and peculiar that I could repeat every note.

At this moment I heard the clock of the neighbouring convent of St. Clare sound the midnight hour from the vale below; it was accompanied by a long-drawn, wailing gust of wind through the corridor, and the deep-toned bell struck on my saddened ear like the knell of some one I had loved and lost.

Soon the music rose again as if from the vault beneath, and I distinctly heard the sound of harmonious voices, singing with impressive and perfect modulation, the following words from the fine opening of Mozart's Requiem:—

"Requiem æternam dona eis, Domine!
Et lux perpetua luceat eis."

A rich and powerful soprano then sang in thrilling tones the solo:—

"Te decet hymnus Deus in Sion
Et tibi reddetur votum in Jerusalem."

After which, all the voices and the harp, in fine accord, and in a louder strain, resumed:—

"Exaudi orationem meam,
Ad te omnis caro veniet."

I heard every word as distinctly as if the singers had been at my elbow; and, convinced that they were no spirits, but human choristers chanting in the sepulchre beneath me, I opened the window, and saw a blaze of light streaming through the bronze latticed gate of the vault, over a small flower garden, which embellished the approach to Cecilia's tomb.

After a brief pause, the solemn strains proceeded, when, unable to repress my curiosity, I called aloud, "Who is there?" But no answer was returned, save the echoing rocks, which responded—"Who is there—there?" with startling accuracy.

Determined to unravel this mystery, I sallied forth with sword and lantern into the corridor, descended the staircase, and cautiously approached the bronze gate, concealing the lantern under my ample dressing-gown.

Screened by a luxuriant hedge of evergreens, I reached a point commanding a view of the interior, and beheld the light of four tapers, held by as many figures muffled from head to foot in dark drapery, a spacious and lofty sepulchre, on the centre of which, on a marble basement, stood an open sarcophagus, containing a richly-decorated coffin, from which the black silk pall had been partially rolled back.

A female form, attired in white and flowing garments, was kneeling on the basement; her hands were folded as if in prayer, and her forehead was reclining on the margin of the sarcophagus.

She was a lovely blondine, her hair of silken texture, and in colour the brightest auburn, fell in graceful abundance over her shoulders; the visible portion of her face was of an ashy paleness, and on her bosom I observed a white rose.

The music had ceased before I reached my concealed station, but the dead silence which had succeeded was now interrupted by loud tokens of the approaching storm.

A gust of wind shook the mighty oaks on the adjacent slope—the kneeling figure turned her face towards the grating, and by the glare of a bright flash of lightning I saw the whole unearthly visage.

Gracious Heaven! it was the sainted Cecilia—the white rose in her bosom—in short, the perfect semblance of her portrait in the room above.

The lantern dropped from my trembling hand, and I gazed on the appalling group of figures in speechless horror, aggravated by the howling of the blast, the creaking of the branches, and the endless echoing of the thunder in the mountains.

My blood ran cold with nameless apprehensions, but soon the tide of feeling took an opposite direction.

Maddened with this inexplicable succession of alarming incidents, I determined to sever at once the Gordian knot, and rushing forward with desperate resolution, I seized and shook the bronze gates with maniacal vehemence, shouting, in the voice of one possessed, "Oh, Cecilia—Cecilia!"

"Jesu Maria!" ejaculated the pallid figure in white, turning upon me a pair of large blue eyes, which appeared glassy and lifeless.

In a moment every taper disappeared, and a horrid scream ran through the vault, succeeded by a crash which seemed to shake the massive tower above the sepulchre.

Overwhelmed with terror and surprise at the strange termination of this awful scene, I plunged through the darkness, explored with difficulty my way to the staircase, and ascended it with headlong velocity.

While feeling the way to my apartment along the wall of the corridor, my attention was roused by a noise at the other end, resembling the creak of a heavy door when moving on rusty hinges.

Turning round, I saw a faint gleam of light shoot athwart the deep gloom of this long passage, and with inexpressible astonishment I beheld the iron door of the armoury gradually open, and the lofty figure of a knight in complete armour issue from it, with a naked sword in one hand and a small lantern in the other, which he held up as if to explore the intense darkness of the corridor.

Congratulating myself that my person was concealed in the deep shadow, I gazed in utter perplexity and terror upon this spectral figure, until I saw it turn round and retreat into the armoury, the door of which, opening outwards, immediately closed, as if impelled by a spring.

Soon as I could regain the power of volition, I returned to my apartment in the tower, more perplexed than ever with the rapid succession of extraordinary and startling incidents which I had encountered in this mysterious old castle.

"Surely," I began to think, "if the dead are permitted to revisit this earth, this is the very hour and place in which to expect them."

My wonted freedom from all superstitious fancies, still, however, struggled with this thickening evidence of supernatural agency; and, opening the window, I looked out to observe if any light was again visible from the sepulchre; but the moon was obscured by heavy clouds, and all was midnight darkness.

During a short interval between the whistling blasts, I thought I could distinguish the sound of a light footstep; and, looking more intently, I saw, by a faint gleam of lightning, a figure in white drapery turn hastily round an angle of the ruins, and disappear under the trees.

I was vainly puzzling myself to account for this new incident, when the appalling knocks of iron upon iron again sounded in the corridor.

Rousing by a sudden effort my drooping courage, I hastened to the door, and opening it, listened with renewed horror to the agonizing groans of some dying sufferer.

While rooted to the spot with nameless apprehensions, a burst of loud and horrid laughter struck suddenly upon my startled ears.

It proceeded, I thought, from the armoury out of which the mailed knight had issued, and the tones had a brazen, gong-like reverberation, to which no human organs could possibly have given utterance.

This monstrous peal of merriment was succeeded by the clash of swords and armour, and I plainly heard heavy blows descending upon helmets, shields, and corselets.

No language can describe the perplexity with which I listened to this appalling uproar, which now seemed to resound from the baron's hall; and, under the insane impulse of fear, I gradually yielded to the belief that the ghosts of Bruno and Gotthard nightly visited the castle to renew their deadly conflict.

"Surely all the powers of hell are in league to-night against me!" I exclaimed, as I retreated into my apartment, barred the door in unutterable anxiety; and began to weigh whether it would not be advisable to return to the comfortable mansion of my aunt, and leave the "Robbers' Tower" to its infernal tenantry.

Suddenly, however, a suspicion flashed upon me that this old castle, having been for some months unoccupied by the family, had become the haunt of gipsies or robbers, and that the mysterious sounds and appearances which had alarmed me were the ingenious contrivances of these vagabonds to terrify the servants of the baroness, and thereby retain undisturbed possession of the ruins.

Inexpressibly relieved by this more rational view of the extraordinary adventures of the night, and fearless of human agency, I determined to solve the enigma without delay, and seized my pistols, with intent to explore immediately the hall and armoury, from one of which the clash of weapons still resounded.

My nerves, however, were still unstrung by the terrors I had experienced; and, fearing that my unsteady hand would not effectually level a pistol, I took, in preference, my keen-edged sabre, grasped it with feverish energy, and proceeded with a candle into the corridor, determined to enact myself the castle spectre, for which personification my tall figure and white drapery were well adapted.

The combat was continued with unabated energy, and the ringing sounds of swords and armour now evidently proceeded from the armoury, towards which I was cautiously advancing, when another peal of grating and satanic laughter made me pause in shivering astonishment.

At this moment, the storm-clouds, which had been, for some time concentrating, burst in fury over the ruins, the rain fell in heavy torrents, and an intensely-vivid flash of lightning was instantaneously succeeded by a monstrous burst of thunder, which shook the old castle to its foundations.

When the long-enduring reverberations of the thunder had ceased, I approached the armoury, and listened at the door, from which I now observed that the massive iron bar and padlock had been removed.

Hearing no noise within, I grasped my sabre more firmly; and, clenching my teeth in angry and bitter determination to unravel, at all risks, this tissue of mysteries, I placed my only remaining taper on the ground, to preserve it from sudden extinction; pulled the door, which opened outwards, and stepped into the armoury; when, behold! by the faint light of two small lanterns, I saw the towering figures of Bruno and Gotthard, in panoplies of steel, and beavers down, crossing their long swords to renew the combat.

Appalled to a degree far exceeding all former apprehensions, I stood in gasping and speechless terror before these colossal spectres, who paused as they beheld me, lowered the points of their tremendous weapons, and remained fixed and motionless as statues.

I fancied, as I gazed upon them in silent horror, that I could distinguish two human skulls within their barred helmets; and, ejaculating I know not what, I turned round and darted into the corridor, hurling after me the iron door with such force, as to detach the picture of the poisoned nun from the wall above, and it fell behind me with a noise which increased no little my consternation.

Overturning the candle in my rapid progress, I rushed along the corridor in utter darkness, until I found my speed arrested by some one pulling vigorously at my dressing-gown.

Desperation now supplied the place of courage, and, with a backward thrust, I plunged my sabre-point deep into the body of my pursuer.

This defensive blow did not, however, release me from his grasp; and, to aggravate my perplexity, I now heard, immediately behind me, the agonising sighs and groans which had so often alarmed me during this eventful night.

During this climax of horrors, the creaking of the armoury door diverted my attention from the awful sounds at my elbow, and my heart died within me as I beheld the two mailed spectres hastening, with long strides and uplifted swords and lanterns, towards me.

By the approaching light I now discovered, to my infinite relief, that my flight had been arrested by neither human nor superhuman interference; but simply by the iron door-latch of one of the hall stoves, which was supplied with fuel through an aperture in the corridor, as is still the custom in many modern houses throughout Germany.

My long dressing-gown had floated behind me as I rushed down the corridor; the projecting latch had caught the lining, and my sabre had pierced no hostile pursuer, but the tightly-extended skirt of my unfortunate garment.

Hastily extricating myself by severing the skirt with a sabre cut, I turned round and desperately faced my grim antagonists, who were now within a few yards of me, and held up their lanterns as if to assist their examination of my features.

Brandishing my sabre, I shouted:

"Avaunt, ye hellish forms!"

But, to my indescribable amazement, they suddenly paused, exchanged a few words, threw down their swords, and, raising their beavers, showed me the broad, bluff features of my aunt's gardeners, two old Austrian dragoons, whose tall, athletic figures I had scanned with a soldier's eye during my evening walk to the ruins.

A ludicrous explanation now ensued, and I heard that, in consequence of the appearance of some marauders in the mountains, my aunt's steward had ordered the gardeners to sleep by turns in the old armoury, as a protection to the valuable property deposited there.

The old soldiers, whose long campaigning had not much abated their dread of the supernatural, were afraid to mount guard alone in the armoury, and had agreed to watch there together; but, unable to sleep during the storm, had challenged each other to a game at broadsword, by way of killing the time, and, to heighten the joke, had donned two suits of the old armour which hung round the walls of the armoury.

The steward was not aware of my intention to occupy the apartments in the tower; and, had the men not seen me previously in the garden with the baroness, a serious, and, too probably, fatal, encounter would have been the consequence of the critical situation I have described.

On further inquiry, I found that whenever one of these lusty knights had placed an effective blow, they burst into a horse laugh, which, sounding from their capacious throats through the barred helmets, and reverberating through the lofty corridor, had produced the unnatural and gong-like peal which had so much astonished and alarmed me.

They acknowledged, too, that they had been no little terrified when they saw a tall figure in white, with a naked sabre, enter the armoury; that, however, they had gathered courage from my sudden retreat, and, beginning to suspect that I was a robber, had pursued and recognised me.

I found, also, a clue to the mysterious sobs and lamentations in the corridor, while endeavouring to separate my dressing-gown from the latch, during which operation the creaking hinges of the stove door not having been oiled for many years, emitted the wailing, groaning sounds which made my blood run cold.

While still examining the stove, another tremendous blast shook the corridor, and the storm-gust, rushing down the capacious chimney, burst open the heavy iron door, which fell back against the iron catch, and rebounding twice with the shock, explained very naturally the fancied hammer blows of the Grand Master upon the iron cross; the expiring gust then moving the door more gently on its rusty hinges, made them wail and creak as before; after which, the diminishing current rushing through the imperfectly closed door, produced the intermitting, sobbing noise, which my tortured imagination had converted into a death rattle.

Dismissing the mailed gardeners to their armoury, I retired to bed; and, deferring until morning my proposed investigation of the mysterious incidents in the sepulchre, I slept in defiance of the storm, until roused by a summons from my aunt and cousin to join them in the outer room to breakfast.

When I met my amiable relatives at the breakfast-table, I was concerned to observe the lovely Julia still more pallid than I had found her the preceding evening, and expressed my fear that she was indisposed.

"I have passed a sleepless and miserable night," she replied, "in consequence of an appalling incident which occurred last night in your immediate vicinity. Soon after you left us, four nuns from the convent of St. Clara called upon me on their way to chant a midnight requiem over the dear remains of my blessed sister, and requested me to accompany them on a harp, which is usually left for this purpose in the sepulchre. As I have found a melancholy gratification in this solemn service, which the nuns perform twice every week, when their convent duties permit, I did not allow the still distant storm, nor the cool white gown which had replaced my hot mourning dress, to deter me from an act of duty to the near departed one. I accompanied the nuns to the sepulchre, and, after they had sung the requiem, I was kneeling in silent prayer against the sarcophagus, when suddenly the brazen gates of the vault were shaken with a giant's grasp,—I beheld the figure of a colossal woman in white garments on the outside—and a voice shrieked "Cecilia! Cecilia!" in tones so wild and unearthly, that the nuns in terror dropped their tapers, and we fled into the inner vault, pulling the heavy door after us with a shock which reverberated like thunder, and greatly increased our alarm. There we remained some time in an agony of terror and in total darkness, until the hoarse voice of the approaching storm warned us to depart, and we fled through the grove to the villa, trembling at the sound of our own footsteps."

It was now my turn to explain the various wonders of the night; and, with a view to cheer my drooping and agitated relatives, I endeavoured to relieve with humorous colouring the extraordinary adventures which had crowded upon me in such rapid succession.

I enjoyed the heartfelt gratification to see my efforts crowned with success.

The pale and careworn features of my aunt and cousin relaxed into frequent smiles as I pursued my strange narrative, and the ludicrous climax of my adventure with the two gardeners created even a hearty laugh at my expense.

During a few weeks of delightful intercourse with these intelligent and amiable women, I greatly recruited my injured constitution, and at length succeeded in my earnest endeavours to prevail upon my aunt and her daughter to quit for some months an abode fraught with melancholy associations, and to pass the autumn and winter under my mother's roof in Berlin.

There, too, my daily intercourse with the unassuming and lovely Julia rapidly matured my early prepossession into a fervent and enduring attachment; and the following summer I revisited the "Robbers' Tower," no longer an emaciated and fanciful invalid, but in the full enjoyment of health and happiness, the husband of my adored Julia, and the joint consoler of her still mourning but resigned parent.

TALES OF BRIGANDS
AND ROBBERS.

[SIR RALPH GRANVILLE RECOGNISES THE RING WORN BY CLAUDE DUVAL.]

THE RED DWARF.

CHAPTER XVI.

SILVER JACK, AND HIS CHARGE TO CLAUDE DUVAL.—THE ROB-
BERY ON THE ROAD.—THE BOOTY, AND HOW IT WAS APPRO-
PRIATED.—THE JOURNEY TO THE "THREE NUNS."—SILVER
JACK'S WARNING.—CLAUDE VENTURES ON DANGEROUS GROUND.

OUR story now leads us back to young Claude Duval, whom we
left in the secret retreat of Silver Jack.

He was roused the next morning by the entrance of his
host, who inquired how he had passed the night.

"Excellently," replied Claude; "as well as if I had reposed under my late master's roof on a bed of down."

[THE RIGHT OF DRAMATISING IS RESERVED.]

"Come down, then, to breakfast," said Jack; "Amy has it waiting for us."

Claude dressed himself and descended to a lower room.

A substantial meal graced the table, at which sat one of the most beautiful girls that Claude had ever seen.

"This is my daughter Amy," said Jack, introducing Claude to her. Then, addressing his daughter, he continued: "You see him here for the first time, but not the last, I trust, as I look forward to our acquaintance being a long one,"—adding to himself, "unless anything unfortunate happens to cut it short."

"I am always happy to see any friend of my father's," said Amy, extending her hand to Claude.

He grasped it fervently and respectfully, and kissed the tips of her fair fingers, the usual mode of salutation in those days.

Claude made a hearty meal, for at the age of twenty the appetite seldom fails.

Silver Jack kept him company, eating like a man who is doubtful where his next meal may come from.

Claude had placed upon his finger the ring taken from the baronet's daughter the overnight, and it at once attracted the attention of Amy.

"My daughter is observing that ring you wear, friend Claude," said Jack. "Like myself, she has an extraordinary passion for jewellery."

"The ring seems such an antique and curious one that you must excuse my noticing it," said Amy.

"As you say, it is both curious and antique," replied Claude, drawing it from his finger and offering it to her for inspection.

"It is a family ornament—an heirloom, I may say. Were it not so, I should beg your acceptance of it."

"I thank you, young sir," blushed Amy, returning the ring, "but I have no lack of jewellery—my father is always bringing me some trinket or other. It is wonderful to me where he gets them from."

"It would not seem very wonderful to her if she knew all," thought Claude, a qualm of conscience crossing his mind as he reflected how he had obtained the ring. The fair owner of it also seemed to rise up before him, and he almost felt as if he could restore it to her, if it were possible to do so.

The meal being over, Silver Jack and Claude were left alone.

"Let me advise you, young sir," said Jack, "to follow my example, and not show yourself about town by daylight. You may be recognised; and, if so, your speedy arrest would follow—and I presume you are not ignorant as to what might be the end of it?"

"Why, I have no doubt," laughed Claude, "that the end of it would be my being found at the end of a rope."

"Not so loud—not so loud!" said Jack, looking towards the door. "I wouldn't have my daughter hear such words for the best purse that ever lined a traveller's pocket."

"But suppose you are captured some night, how could you, in that event, conceal the fact from your daughter?"

"Young man," replied the highwayman, turning pale, "don't reckon upon such a misfortune happening to me. If I am ever taken, she must never know it. She must think me dead, and never learn I had come to a shameful end."

"But even then she would want a protector," said Claude. "She does not seem sufficiently experienced in the ways of the world to be enabled to make her way through it."

"It is that which troubles me," answered Jack. "And my principal reason for asking you here was to provide against the worst. You are young, and as yet uncorrupted by the ways of the world. Will you make me a solemn promise as regards my daughter Amy?"

"What is it you wish me to promise?" asked Claude.

"This. Be a friend, a brother to her, if I am ever taken from her by the hands of the law."

"I promise," said Claude.

"Nay, but swear it."

"Then I swear it!" exclaimed Claude. "I will be what you wish—a friend, a brother to her, for her father's sake."

"Thank you—bless you, young man!" said Jack, grasping Claude's hand, while his eyes filled with tears.

"And yet I am accepting a trust I may not be able to fulfil," said Claude. "Life is uncertain, especially that of a knight of the road; and who knows but my next exploit may be my last?"

"I trust not. I think you are not doomed to be nipped in the bud so early. Something seems to tell me I am to go first; but should fortune decree that I am to escape Tyburn's triple tree, and end my days in a foreign land, so much the better."

"So say I, as regards myself," observed Claude. "And now, which road do you advise us to take to-night? If we can secure a good booty, why——"

"Hush!" exclaimed Jack, "I hear my daughter returning. Mind that you are cautious, and let no word that may cause suspicion fall from your lips while she is present."

"Trust me for that," said Claude.

The remainder of the day passed pleasantly; and when night was seen to darken the marshes around the house, Jack informed his daughter that an appointment for that evening would call him from her for a few hours, and Claude must accompany him.

"I expected you would stay at home to-night, father. You go out every evening, and leave me alone," pouted the pretty Amy.

"No, not every evening, Amy," replied her father. "For instance, I always stay at home on stormy nights to keep you company."

"That's because there are few travellers abroad in rough weather," thought Claude.

And he was right.

"Come, Claude, let us saddle our horses," said Jack, rising. "And cheer up, Amy, my wench! By the time you are asleep and wandering in the land of happy dreams, I shall have returned; but before you go to rest, fail not to place the signal-lamp in the lattice window. But I shall see you again before I go. This way, Claude," and the highwayman left the room, followed by his young companion.

When they reached the stable, Jack stooped beneath the manger in the stall where his horse was stabled, and brought out a small casket.

Unlocking it, he disclosed to the eyes of Claude a number of costly trinkets, watches set with diamonds, and gold chains of massive weight were among them.

"These are Amy's dowry," said Jack; "and, converted into money, they would fetch a pretty penny. If ever I am captured, and you retain your liberty, you will know where to find them. I shall depend upon you converting them into money and bestowing the sum they may fetch upon my daughter, so as to place her above want."

"Depend upon my doing so. Have I not sworn to do my best by her?" asked Claude.

"You have; and I believe you."

The highwayman, as he spoke, replaced the casket where he had taken it from. It was a drawer, cunningly contrived beneath the manger, so fashioned as to resemble one of the bottom planks.

Jack saddled his steed, Claude did the same, and they led them to the outside of the house.

Amy was waiting at the door, and, though she strove to appear calm, Claude perceived that her eyes were red from weeping.

Pressing his daughter to his heart, Silver Jack bade her an affectionate adieu, and, springing into his saddle, told Claude to do the same.

The young man obeyed, and, bidding Amy to be of good heart, for her father would soon return, followed Jack as he took the turning which led from the house towards the highroad.

Thoughts of the highwayman's innocent daughter were constantly crossing Claude's mind as they rode onwards. The girl's lonely situation, the ignorance she was kept in regarding her father's lawless life, and the knowledge that every day she ran in danger of becoming an orphan, troubled him exceedingly. He wished for the first time since he had left the duke's service that he had remained aloof from the path of guilt, for had he done so, he might never have seen so much innocence placed in peril, for in peril she certainly was; should her father be taken prisoner her own arrest might follow if her retreat was discovered. He longed to be honest once again, that he might offer her his hand and heart, and so place her beyond danger. But that was now impossible, for Claude well knew, should his late master the Duke of Buckingham ever cross his path, there was small hope for him.

As Silver Jack had said, the theft of the duke's favourite steed was in itself a capital offence, and he sighed to think how easy it was to drift into crime, and how different to steer out of it.

By this time they had reached the open road, and Silver Jack, looking to his pistols, told Claude to do the same.

The young man did so, for he knew the quick ear of his companion had detected the sound of a horse's feet behind them.

A solitary horseman was seen to approach as they turned their horses' heads to note the new-comer.

"As we are two against one, he will prove an easy prey," observed Jack. "Let us wait for his coming, and see if he is a bird worth plucking."

They slackened their horses' speed as the traveller neared them.

By his velvet mantle and plumed cap it was plain to be seen that he was one of the gallants of the day; behind his saddle was strapped a valise apparently well filled.

"Good evening, fair sir," said Jack, saluting the stranger as he approached. "Can you inform us whether we are on the right road for London? We are strangers to the great city, and fear we may have taken the wrong road."

"You have but to take the road which lies before you, and in an hour's time, if your horses are good ones, you may reach there."

"I thank you, Sir Stranger," said Jack, "and my young friend and I are truly glad to have met with a companion."

"I am also glad to meet you," replied the traveller; "for the roads they tell me are not over safe of late for those who travel well equipped."

"As you do, I presume?" inquired the highwayman.

"Yes, I cannot complain on that score," answered the stranger. "I have been spending a few weeks in the country at a friend's house, where my servant, unfortunately falling ill, has not been able to accompany me this evening; but I am little given to fear, and resolved, rather than lose a night's enjoyment, to travel on to London alone."

"What is this enjoyment of which you speak?" asked Jack. "A revel or masque of my Lord Rochester's or his Grace the Duke of Buckingham's, I warrant me."

"Nay, there you are wrong. This is a masked ball given by a worthy old knight in honour of his daughter coming of age, and I warrant me, when they see me in the goodly suit I have within my valise, I shall excite the envy of all beholders."

"If you ever reach there," muttered Jack, to himself.

"And the master of the house from whom you have received the invitation is an old friend of yours, I presume?" said Jack, aloud.

"There you are wrong again," laughed the cavalier. "I have never seen him in my life. He has been known to our family by name for many years, but this is the first time I have ever visited him. I bear my letter of introduction with me, and look forward to a hearty welcome. But farewell, Sir Strangers, if you do not intend putting your horses to a quicker pace. I am being looked for, no doubt. Adieu!"

As he spurred his steed and strove to ride onwards, he found his horse's rein suddenly seized by Silver Jack, who had ridden in front of him at that moment.

"How now?—what does this mean?" asked the cavalier, in a tone of surprise.

"Your money or your life!" exclaimed Claude, who was behind him, levelling, at the same time, a pistol at his head.

The cavalier rapidly stretched forth his arm towards his holsters, to seize a pistol also, but Silver Jack was too quick for him, and secured the traveller's pistols before he could reach them.

"What! have I fallen in with a couple of highwaymen?" exclaimed the cavalier, in a tone of rage and disappointment.

"We are neither more nor less, Sir Cavalier," said Jack; "so no resistance—it will be in vain, and endanger your life into the bargain. Yield up your purse and whatever valuables you may have, and no harm shall come to you."

The cavalier hesitated for a moment, and reflected.

Although a brave man, he saw it would be useless to resist these two men, especially when they held a pistol each to his head, and his own weapons were gone.

He resolved to note well the features of his assailants; but as he looked up, he perceived they had suddenly masked themselves.

Seeing it was useless so resist, the cavalier yielded with a good grace.

Silver Jack searched the traveller's pockets, while Claude unstrapped the valise from behind the saddle.

"What are you doing, fellow?" exclaimed the cavalier. "Is it not sufficient that you should take my money, but I must lose my wardrobe also?"

"I am extremely short of wearing apparel," said Claude. "You no doubt have a goodly wardrobe, which will not be much decreased by the loss of a single suit."

"But it is a suit of great price, and a new one," cried the stranger.

"So much the better for me," replied Claude. "I knew a gentleman of your position would not travel with shabby clothes."

The cavalier was about to remonstrate, when he felt his arms suddenly compressed against his sides by means of a strong leathern strap which Jack had suddenly thrown around his victim's body, who raged and stormed against this indignity, but all to no purpose. His horse was then led down a lane which intersected the high-road, and fastened securely to a tree, with the cavalier on his back; and to prevent the worthy gallant from calling for help, Jack, assisted by Claude, took the liberty of gagging him.

This being done, the highwaymen, elated with their booty, rode off towards London as fast as their horses' legs could carry them.

They halted not until they reached the neighbourhood of Whitechapel, then an obscure suburb of London, and put up at the Three Nuns Tavern, a place of entertainment which is in existence at the present day.

Being accommodated with a private room, the highwaymen began to examine their booty.

The purse was well filled, and the clothes of the most approved style and most costly material.

A letter was also found in the valise. It was the introduction and invitation to the masque of which the cavalier had spoken. By this letter it appeared that the gentleman who had been robbed was named Sir Lionel Lovel. The name was new to Claude, who knew most of the London gallants; but Sir Lionel, it appears, had been residing on the continent some time previous to Claude's accepting service with his grace of Buckingham. Had it been otherwise, Sir Lionel would have recognised Claude.

"Destroy that letter at once, Claude," said Jack, "or it may be the means of betraying us;" and he was about casting it in the fire, when Claude arrested his arm.

"Tarry, friend Jack!" said Claude. "Methinks it is a pity the opportunity of seeing this masque should be lost. I love such an entertainment above all things, having assisted at many while in his grace of Buckingham's service."

"Why, you madbrained young varlet, what are you driving at? Surely you would not have the daring to use this invite for thyself?"

"Thou art wrong, friend Jack, for I surely shall, and wear this very dress for the occasion."

"Amazement!" cried the highwayman, for, daring as he was, he could scarcely credit anyone could be so bold.

"Why, what have I to fear?" asked the audacious Claude. "Did you hear the traveller say he was a stranger to the master of the house? Truly, so am I, for by this letter I see the host's name is Sir Everard Granby, a gentleman who never visited Court while I was located there. So I pray you, friend Jack, don't attempt to dissuade me from this expedition, for I am resolved on it, heart and soul."

"But there may be many there likely to recognise you, even if you are unknown to the host," argued Jack.

"What a dull fellow thou art, my noble comrade! Do you not perceive that this is a masked entertainment, whereat every guest can conceal his face at pleasure? So, cannot I conceal mine if I see anyone there who may be likely to recognise me?"

"Well, I'll even let a wilful man have his way," sighed Jack. "But take heed you are not snared; if so, what becomes of the trust I have reposed in you?"

For a moment Claude hesitated, for he thought of Amy and what he had promised.

But his love of vanity and display got the better of his more generous feelings, and for the time he banished the young girl from his mind.

Jack again attempted to dissuade him, but all in vain, for Claude commenced arraying himself in Sir Lionel's garments, without heeding the highwayman's remonstrances.

Summoning the drawer of the tavern, Claude sent him to order a sedan chair.

In due time it arrived, and Claude was carried westward towards the mansion of Sir Everard Granby, in Temple Gardens.

Jack saw him depart; then, giving directions that the young man's horse should be cared for and put up till the morrow—a precaution which the madbrained young man had forgotten—the highwayman turned his own horse's head homewards, to rejoin his daughter Amy, well satisfied with Sir Lionel's well-filled purse, which Claude had decreed should be Silver Jack's share, providing he retained the clothes.

Vanity and love of approbation were Claude's weak points, and in the end they led to his downfall.

CHAPTER XVII.

THE MASQUE AT SIR EVERARD GRANBY'S.—CLAUDE MIXES WITH FINE COMPANY.—RECOGNITION OF THE RING BY THE OWNER THEREOF.—THE TWO MASKED LADIES.—THE SUPPER, AND WHAT FOLLOWED.—AN UNWELCOME VISITOR MAKES HIS APPEARANCE. — THE DISCOVERY. — THE IMPRISONMENT, AND CLAUDE'S MYSTERIOUS VISITOR.

CLAUDE, being set down at Sir Everard Granby's door, dismissed the sedan-bearers with an order that they should call for him at daybreak, the usual period when the revels in which he was about to join terminated.

Telling a servant in waiting to acquaint his master that Sir Lionel Lovel had arrived, Claude strolled into one of the ante-rooms, masking himself carefully before he entered.

It was lucky he did so, for many of his late master's friends were there.

The servant to whom Claude had confided his message speedily returned, requesting he would follow him to his master's apartment.

Following his guide through a lane of bowing lackeys, Claude soon found himself in the presence of the master of the mansion, who received him most cordially.

"This is the first time we have met, Sir Lionel, but I hope it will not be the last," said his host, extending the hand of friendship and welcome to Claude as he advanced.

"I trust we shall meet often, my lord," replied Claude; "and I wish your fair daughter many happy returns of the day."

Sir Everard's daughter here entered the room, blazing with diamonds.

"Oh, if they were only mine!" thought Claude. "Were I the possessor of such a treasure, I should be the happiest man alive!"

Like many young and sanguine minds, Claude thought that to be rich was to be happy.

Mistaken notion! He lived long enough to learn that the possession of money often brings increased cares, and that content was in reality the most valuable jewel that life or fortune can bestow.

"This is Sir Lionel Lovel, of whom we have so often heard," said Sir Everard, introducing Claude to his daughter.

The lady received him graciously.

Claude kissed the tips of her proffered hand after the approved fashion of the period, taking care at the same time to display the valuable ring which he had taken from Sir Ralph Granville's daughter.

At the request of Sir Everard, Claude offered his arm to Sir Everard's daughter, and led her into the ball-room, their presence being announced in a loud voice to the assembled company who began to throng the room.

"You are not obliged to wear your mask, unless it is your pleasure," observed the baronet's daughter to Claude, as she noticed he did not unmask.

"It seems ridiculous to say so, but having been so long absent from London, and meeting a brilliant assembly like this for the first time, I am somewhat bashful," answered Claude.

This seemed a reasonable excuse to the Lady Margaret, for such was the name of the baronet's daughter.

Claude monopolised his fair partner for nearly the whole of the evening, somewhat to the chagrin of Sir Everard, who feared his daughter and the new guest were becoming attached to each other.

This by no means met the baronet's notions, who had higher and more politic views for his daughter.

A cotillon was just finishing, and Claude noticed a lady opposite him in the dance gaze with evident wonder and surprise on the ring which Claude so ostentatiously displayed on his finger.

The dance being concluded, Claude led his fair partner to a seat, and moved across the room to speak to Sir Everard, who was beckoning to him.

The baronet gave him a gentle hint that it was unusual for a gentleman to lead the same lady forth to dance so often.

This was said with perfect good humour, and Claude apologised in the same strain.

Supper was shortly afterwards announced.

During this meal, some retained their masks; others dispensed with them as not wishing to remain incognito any longer.

Sitting opposite to him was the same lady who had remarked the ring he wore so conspicuously.

She was shortly afterwards joined by another lady, who was also masked.

Her attention also soon became directed to the ring.

Claude became rather uneasy, and would fain have shifted his seat, could he have perceived a vacant place.

In a short time, however, the opportunity he wished for occurred, and he rose to leave the table.

As he did so, he accidentally displaced his mask.

Striving hastily to re-adjust it, it fell to the ground.

At this moment the two ladies who had been so keenly observing him, started up with a loud cry of alarm.

"What is the matter?" exclaimed a voice behind Claude.

"The ring, father—the ring!" cried the Lady Laura Granville, for she it really was who had been sitting opposite Claude, with her sister Phillis.

Claude's quick ear in a moment detected the voice of the lady he had robbed in conjunction with Silver Jack.

He gave himself up for lost, and hastily prepared to leave the room.

But he found himself prevented by Sir Ralph Granville, who, seizing him by the wrist, demanded to know how he had become possessed of the ring upon his finger.

"I—I—purchased it," stammered Claude, for the moment taken completely off his guard.

"It is false, father!" exclaimed the Lady Laura, as she pointed towards Claude. "This is the man who robbed us as we journeyed to London. I can swear to his features, and my sister Phillis here can do the same."

"Yes—yes, I can," hurriedly exclaimed Phillis.

The next moment she felt sorry for having uttered the

words, thinking perhaps it was the young man's first offence, and not knowing what might have driven him to the act.

"He is a robber—a highwayman!" cried Laura, as a crowd began to gather round.

"Heyday! what is all this?" inquired the host, bustling among the crowd. "Are you all mad? Who is it dare accuse Sir Lionel of being a robber and a highwayman?"

"I dare accuse him!" said the resolute Laura. "And I fancy, Sir Everard, you are deceived in this gentleman, for I suspect he is not what he appears to be."

"But he must be," exclaimed Sir Everard, "or how could he become possessed of the letters he brought here?"

"He stole them from me!" cried a loud voice from the bottom of the room.

All started and looked towards the spot. A cavalier strode down the room, covered with dust, as though he had ridden long and swiftly.

Claude's heart sickened within him as he recognised Sir Lionel Lovel.

In a few words he explained all.

The ring which had betrayed Claude was taken from his finger, and he found himself in the grasp of two stout serving-men.

Several guests now stepped forward and identified Claude as the late page of his grace the Duke of Buckingham.

After a long discussion, it was resolved that Claude should be secured in one of the strong rooms of the mansion for the night, and taken before the justices in the morning.

Imagining that Sir Everard was somewhat in doubt as to the guilt of the man they had secured, Sir Ralph begged that the key of the strong room in which Claude should be placed might be confided to his care, for he was resolved to see justice done on the varlet.

"Just as you please, Sir Ralph," said the host. "Heaven knows I have no wish to let the guilty escape! All I require is that justice may be done; so bring him along and follow me!"

Sir Everard led the way, followed by Sir Ralph and the servants who held Claude in custody.

The heart of Phillis was touched with pity as she saw Claude borne away to confinement.

She heard all around say that his death was certain, and for her own part she would readily have saved him from his impending fate.

In a short time her father and Sir Everard returned, saying that their prisoner was securely lodged.

The rage of Lady Margaret knew no bounds when she learnt a highwayman had been her partner during the principal part of the evening.

"Had I my will," she cried, "the fellow should be immediately hanged out of the way without judge or jury!"

Laura Granville, who had been the first to identify Claude, began to feel some compunctions of conscience for being the cause of his arrest.

She knew not that death would follow his detection; and had she really been aware such a doom was inevitable when once the law held Claude in its grasp, no inducement would have influenced her to recognise him.

But it was now too late, and she knew his speedy death would follow.

Claude found himself in darkness, safely locked and barred in the strong room of the mansion.

The grey light of morning just struggling in at the massive barred windows revealed to him how useless would be any attempt to escape.

The room was composed of strong oak panelling, and a huge iron-sheeted door was the only entrance to the apartment.

He paced the room with impatient strides.

In two or three days he would be brought to trial, and he well knew speedy condemnation would follow.

Still, he resolved to die undaunted, and put a bold face on the matter.

Wearied with anxiety and excitement, he threw himself on a rough couch, the only piece of furniture in the room, and soon fell into a sound sleep.

He was awoke by feeling a hand laid on his shoulder.

In the uncertain light he saw a figure muffled in a cloak standing by his side.

"They are about to convey me to Newgate," thought Claude as he rose to his feet, and exclaimed: "I am ready!"

"Hush!" said his visitor, in a soft voice, which Claude fancied he had heard before—"be prudent—be silent, and I may set you at liberty!"

Claude's heart bounded within him at these words.

"May I ask who you are to render me such a service?" inquired Claude, in a low voice.

"I am the lady you robbed," answered Phillis, for she it really was.

"It seems dreadful to me," she continued, "that one so young as you are should die a shameful death. So, pitying your condition, and hoping you will see the wickedness of your ways, I have been rash enough to take the keys from my father as he slept, in order that I may set you at liberty!"

"Bless you—thank you!" said Claude, sinking on his knee.

"You are an angel on earth!" he continued; "and when I cease to think with gratitude upon your kindness, may the triple tree securely claim me for its own!"

She again enjoined him to be silent, and, showing him the open door of his prison, beckoned him to follow her.

All was quiet in the mansion.

The servants, like the guests, had caroused until the drink had steeped their senses in heavy slumber.

Claude, following his fair guide on tiptoe, soon found himself at the hall door.

It was secured with heavy bolts and bars.

Luckily, there was no lock, or Claude might have been as far from liberty as ever.

Assisted by Phillis, Claude withdrew the bolts as noiselessly as possible, and freedom opened before him.

He was about to thank his fair deliverer once more, but she motioned him to silence.

Invoking a silent blessing upon her, Claude sprang down the hall steps like a deer, and soon left the mansion of Sir Everard Granby far behind him.

He thought his flight was unnoticed, but the Red Dwarf had witnessed his escape, and quickly followed on the same road.

(*To be continued in our next.*)

THE BRIGANDS AND THE DESERTER.

A TALE OF TRUE LOVE.

——o——

Thou know'st that in my desert halls
The pride of youth and hope is o'er;
That, sunk, defaced, my crumbling walls
Repose to shelter yield no more.

Yet on this dark and dreary pile
Thy love its tender wreaths hath hung;
And all it asks is still to smile,
Bloom, fade, and die where once it clung.

C. H. Townsend.

"I WILL wait," said an old man, as he stopped under a grove of tall forest trees, "I will wait till all this splendour is past. Poor young creature! she will hear it soon enough."

He looked towards the superb palace which shone out one blaze of light amid the darkness of the night.

He saw the doors crowded with persons, and carriages rolled rapidly past him.

He recognised the imperial equipage, by the light of the flambeaux borne around it.

He drew nearer, and heard the sound of music and song.

"No, no," he exclaimed, "I cannot enter yet."

He turned back and sought the little inn where he had left his horse.

There the happy peasantry were assembled.

"DICK TURPIN'S RIDE TO YORK," and the "BURGLARY."

Unwearied with a long day of rejoicing, they were dancing, and singing, and laughing.

The whole house rang with merriment.

The old man entered one of the least crowded rooms: there he found a large party sitting round a long table covered with fruit and cakes.

They were all talking and laughing; all but one little girl, who had dropped fast asleep with joyful fatigue.

Her arms were crossed upon the table, and her bright cheek rested on them; her eyelids looked heavy with slumber, but her fresh rosy lips were partly unclosed, and her cheek was dimpled with smiles.

The old man sat down beside her, and leaned his folded arms also on the table; but he did not sleep.

The palace of the Countess Florenheim was on that evening thronged with lordly company.

Every splendid saloon had been thrown open; but among the beauteous forms assembled there, the young countess herself was the most admired.

It might be that every eye looked in almost determined admiration upon one so gentle, and so distinguished by birth and fortune.

But the young and innocent Bianca was very lovely.

The usual expression of her large hazel eyes was eloquent tenderness, her features were beautiful, and every movement of her tall and delicate form was by nature graceful: though her dress was adorned by jewels of immense value, its appearance was less magnificent than simple.

That day she had taken possession of her princely wealth; and for the first time, she appeared as the mistress of her own palace. Her manner was perfectly dignified and easy, but, during the whole evening, the rich bloom of her cheek was heightened by a continued blush.

The Empress remained some hours at the Florenheim palace, delighted with the appearance and conduct of the young and noble orphan.

The parents of the countess had deserved and enjoyed the favour of their sovereigns, and Maria Theresa loved to distinguish their child.

Every guest had departed, and the young countess stood alone in her spacious and magnificent saloons.

She pressed her hand for a moment over her eyes, for they ached with the glare of the tapers still blazing around her.

She looked at the beautiful flowers which hung in fading garlands round the room, and sighed.

With a true girlish fancy, she took down a long drooping branch of roses from the tall candelabra beside her; the blossoms were all faded: she sighed again; her heart had not been in the splendour of the evening, and now she had leisure to attend to the silent thoughts of her bosom.

She thought of her betrothed husband, and she could not help reproaching herself for having shared in any way the festivities around her, while Ernest Alberti was exposed to the dangers of war.

As the young countess was retiring to rest, the arrival of a person who earnestly requested to see her that very night was announced. She hesitated at first, but after a few moments' consideration, she consented to appear.

She returned to the deserted saloon, and there waited till the man was introduced to her presence.

She recognised at once the servant of the Count Alberti, and dismissed her attendants.

How often did she tremble, how often did she turn pale with horror, during that short interview!

Ernest had fought with his general officer, against the positive commands of the Emperor; the general had been mortally wounded, and Alberti was disgraced; a high reward was set upon his life. He had, however, escaped, but his servant knew not whither.

Many months passed away—months of doubt and sorrow to the hapless Bianca.

The young deserter was never heard of; and the festive magnificence which had flashed for a moment in the palace of the countess entirely disappeared.

All Vienna talked of her engagement with Ernest, and many pronounced the engagement to be dissolved.

It was said that the Empress had herself forbidden the young countess to think of the disgraced Alberti.

Bianca was certainly commanded to appear at Court, and she did not refuse. Many of the young courtiers determined to pay more than usual attention to the very beautiful and very wealthy heiress.

She appeared, but none presumed to insult her sorrow with their addresses: her real, artless grief invested her with a dignity which no one dared to infringe upon.

She did not attempt to conceal how severely the blow had fallen upon her; but her grief, though silent, and seeming to claim no interest, was quietly majestic.

Calm and pale, she stood among the ladies of the Court, an object of respect and admiration even to the Empress herself.

A year passed away. The general whom Alberti had wounded was not dead, but he had met with so many relapses that his recovery was still pronounced uncertain.

Bianca continued a quiet mourner, but now her alliance was sought by many of the noblest houses of Austria; gently, but firmly, every proposal was declined.

For the first time, the Empress interested herself in the suit of the prince, one of Bianca's enthusiastic admirers.

The young countess did not repel the confidence which her sovereign sought; she disclosed with affecting earnestness the feelings of her heart, and the principles on which she acted. Before she quitted the Empress, she perceived that her feelings were understood—she guessed that her principles were approved.

The mother of the Count Alberti was living, and still presided over the household of her son.

The Countess Bianca was now a constant visitor at the Alberti palace; and a few days after the above-mentioned interview with the Empress, the aged countess and Bianca were conversing almost cheerfully together: they were elated with hope, for the petitions which had been presented in behalf of Ernest seemed to be successful.

The Empress had herself written to the Countess Alberti; the letter was in Bianca's hand.

Suddenly a person entered the saloon: it was the old and faithful servant of Alberti. He told them news that almost overwhelmed them.

The young count had returned; he had been brought to Vienna with a gang of desperate banditti; he was said to be the captain of men who were outlaws, robbers, and murderers.

"Alas, alas!" exclaimed the old countess, and she gazed with a look of heart-broken sorrow on a magnificent portrait of her late husband; "this is to be the end of the house of Alberti. Your only son, my beloved Conrad, the child of our hopes, will he prove a shame to his father's name? It is well you are not here; it is enough that I survive to witness our disgrace."

"Ernest will never disgrace you," cried Bianca, eagerly. "We know him much better," she added, clasping the trembling hands of the countess, with tender affection; "there is much to be explained in this story. Dear, rash Ernest!" she faltered, leaning her head on his mother's shoulder, and burst into tears. "*We* know him better: he may be wild and faulty, but *he* will never disgrace anyone."

"He never will, you are right," replied the countess; "I spoke hastily. I ought to hope, I ought to believe, better things of my beloved son. Daughter of my love, I was very wrong to doubt him for a moment; you judge him rightly. Bless you, bless you, my sweet Bianca!"

Alberti had been indeed brought to Vienna among the banditti of Istria; every proof was strong against him.

He was condemned to be broken on the wheel, and there seemed no hope that the sentence would be mitigated.

Ernest himself told an improbable story about his not being connected with the banditti; but nobody listened to it, and he mentioned it no more. Bianca and his mother did believe him. The account was perfectly true.

Ernest had seen his antagonist fall, and he stood in stupified horror, with the bloody sword in his hand; a cold and sickening chill crept through his frame, and thought and memory seemed to forsake him.

The friend who had accompanied him to the spot where the duel was fought, roused him from his reckless stupor: he led up to him his charger, which had brought him to the spot; he conjured, he commanded him to fly.

Ernest heeded him not, but rushed to the place where the wounded general was lying: he had swooned, and the ashy paleness of death was already on his countenance.

Ernest flung himself on the ground, and groaned with anguish. The general revived, he beheld the young man, he called to him with a feeble voice, he stretched out his clammy hand to him.

Ernest half rose from the ground; he drew near the dying man, and with downcast eyes he took the extended hand.

Again the general spoke. "I was in fault," he said; "I should have known better than to be provoked by a youth like yourself. Forgive me, Alberti. If you wish that I should recover, leave me. Fly instantly—I shall be anxious, I shall have no rest, I shall die, if I think you are in danger. Leave me, I entreat you."

The young soldier obeyed; he kissed the cold hand of his general, and his friend hurried him away; he pointed towards the south, as if insinuating the direction Ernest should take. Once again, Alberti looked round: he saw the arm of the wounded man raised as if to wave him away; his hand was on the rein of the impatient charger; he leaped into the saddle and fled.

It was nearly sunset when the Count Alberti stopped at the entrance of a desolate valley.

Immense masses of rock descended to the banks of a rushing stream, on one side of which a narrow path wound apparently up the valley.

For some miles before he reached this spot, Ernest had beheld no traces of man.

He looked behind, and the broad barren moor which he had passed over marked out a uniform horizon against the clear crimson heavens.

The slanting rays of the sun spread in a threadlike blaze of golden glory over the plain.

He turned again towards the mountains and waters.

There all was dark and awful; the shadows of evening had cast even a terrific gloom over the valley; the loud and rising wind came rushing down it, and blew the foam of the torrent over his face.

Ernest threw the reins on his horse's neck, and proceeded slowly along the winding path.

The valley became narrower as he advanced, the rocks more precipitous, and the darkness increased.

At last the valley appeared to be closed in entirely by one steep precipice, over which the torrent fell with a deafening roar.

The charger stopped, and Ernest dismounted; he climbed the rocks beside him; the path which he had lost sight of again appeared; it seemed to lead into a chasm of impenetrable blackness: he sprung forward, and felt the path firm and level under his feet.

Returning to his horse, he led it after him, till they had reached what seemed to be the end of the cavern, for he saw the stars shining above him, and the ground beneath was spread with thick grass.

The horse stooped down his head to graze, and Ernest unbridled it. The fugitive threw himself down among the rocks and slept.

When he awoke, the moon was shining brightly on the plain before him, and the wind had died quite away.

Not a sound disturbed the stillness of the night, except a faint murmur of distant waters, and the ceaseless chirping of innumerable grasshoppers.

The plain seemed to be enclosed by mountains partly covered with dark pine-woods; but the black and deepened shadows which enveloped every spot not lighted by the silvery moonshine, prevented his accurate observance of the scenes he gazed upon.

He listened in vain, to hear if his horse were grazing near; he then wandered on, but forgot entirely that he was seeking his horse; he forgot everything but the thoughts most nearly connected with his own dreary sorrows.

"At this moment," thought he, "the blood that I have shed may be crying up to God for vengeance."

In the heat of passion he had found a thousand excuses for himself; he had been among gay and thoughtless young men, and they seldom troubled themselves with reasoning, where a laugh or sarcasm convinced more easily.

Alberti had often in his heart despised their silliness, but he had allowed his mind to be governed by their opinions, just because his passions and those opinions agreed; he had stooped to the palliation of crime, under the screen of worldly custom; he had become probably a murderer, and for what? because his temper had been provoked—for a trifle that was not worth remembering.

He was now alone, in calm, undisturbed solitude. He had leisure to search the very ground of his heart; and he did so. Calmly and clearly he called up the excuses which he had framed; and with firm but grieving severity he condemned them all.

He looked up into the boundless heavens above him, and the thought which he strove to fix upon his soul was, "I am alone with God, and in condemning myself, I will not, dare not, encourage a single excuse."

A rush of agonizing thoughts passed over his brain; they confused and distracted him. He leaned his burning head against the rocks near him; their dewy coldness relieved its throbbing heat; he then felt how contrasted a creature he was to all around and about him—the magnificent stillness of the scene abashed him; he felt as if his presence were a pollution to its sublime solitude: the objects that he beheld seemed to shadow forth their viewless Creator; they seemed to speak of His purity and grandeur; and he felt himself more a creature of sinful and lawless passions than he had ever done in the haunts of men.

Ernest was roused from his meditation; his charger galloped past him, he called to it, and the animal stopped; but suddenly it started again: he looked for the cause, and beheld a party of men within a few yards of the place where he stood.

The moonbeams glittered upon the weapons which they bore.

Alberti had advanced into the full moonlight, and they perceived him; he did not appear to notice them, but again called to his horse.

The animal came up to him, but at that instant one of the men approached to seize it.

Ernest lifted up his arm and struck the man down; he wreathed the mane round his hand, and demanded loudly, but calmly, the reason of their interference.

An insulting shout was the only reply he received, and they rushed towards him.

In an instant, Ernest had leaped upon his horse; the men threw themselves before him; they commanded him to dismount, they attempted to drag him down.

He swept them away with his arm, he urged on his charger, and bounded from the midst of them; but another party sprung up before him.

He had burst from them, his way seemed unimpeded, when he felt the whir and report of a bullet, as it flew past his head.

He heard again the report of a loud volley and *he* was yet unwounded.

At once his charger reared and snorted; then its legs staggered, its head plunged forward into the earth; it struggled in vain to rise, and rolled heavily over.

Ernest heard not, cared not, for the crowd that gathered round him.

He lifted up the head of his dying horse from the earth, and wiped away the foam and dust from his mouth and nostrils. The poor animal was dying: the sweat streamed out from his reeking sides, and mingled with its spouting blood.

Ernest saw an expression almost human turned for a moment on him from its staring eye.

Once again the faithful creature struggled to throw out its quivering limbs, and to strike its head into the earth: it gasped, and gasped, and its head slipped away from the arms of its master.

Alberti raised it again, but his loved charger lay motionless and dead beside him.

The tears gushed from his eyes; but he saw the men who surrounded him, who had for some minutes gazed on him in silence.

In a frenzy of rage he started up, and strove to draw his sword.

It seemed glued to the scabbard, and at first resisted his efforts.

Wild with fury, he wrenched it forth.

The blade had already struck against another sword, when it riveted his look, for it was smeared with what he knew to be the dark blood of his general.

The sight calmed him at once.

The sword dropped from his grasp; and he called out in a voice of horror:

"Enough—enough! I have had blood enough!"

His antagonist started with wonder; but suddenly a blow struck him from behind.

He turned his head, and beheld a man drawing from his shoulder a streaming dagger; he saw the face of the man; he knew him.

The man was a deserter from his own regiment.

"It is right that _I_ should fall thus," he cried out, and sunk lifeless on the body of his horse.

Ernest unclosed his eyes, and found that he was lying upon a mat, in a spacious cavern, partly roofed in from the open sky by a shelving rock at a great height above him.

By the dim light, his eye could not measure the vast extent of the cavern.

He endeavoured to rise, but the pain and weakness which he felt in his shoulder reminded him of his wound, and he sank back again.

He listened; but faint and indistinct sounds alone met his ear.

At length, amid the black shadows which hung about the vault-like roof, at the farther end of the cavern, a light appeared; it moved downwards; and he thought he heard the clanking tread of a person descending a flight of steps.

Nearer and nearer the light came, and he beheld a figure approaching.

The moon, whose light had been gradually fading, had now set; the first dun light of morning scarcely dispelled the darkness which succeeded.

The man placed the lamp on a ledge of the rock, and, drawing his cloak around him, stood leaning against the wall.

The chill morning air rushed through the cavern and almost extinguished the flame.

The man bent down over the lamp to trim it, and the light flared over the face of the deserter who had stabbed Alberti.

Ernest spoke to the man; he addressed him by his name.

The man answered churlishly.

"Do you not know me?" said Alberti.

"I know you? Not I. I only know that I wish I had killed you, or that the fellows who took the trouble of bringing you here would have stayed with you, and not sent me down to this dismal den while they are drinking above."

"Bring your lamp and look me in the face," said Ernest, in a tone of command.

The man brought the lamp, and held it carelessly before his face.

He turned pale as he gazed; and although Alberti was a helpless and imprisoned man, for awhile he thought of him only as the officer whom he had served under and obeyed.

He faltered out a few words of excuse, dictated by the feeling of the moment.

"There is no occasion for excuse, Michael," said Alberti; "I do not think you would have stabbed _me_ intentionally; but I want no excuses. I see what you now are, while I am here, a dying man perhaps, and in your power; but I ask no favours."

The man spoke not, as he stood without moving and in silence at the feet of Alberti, who turned away and closed his eyes.

Ernest looked round again, and the man was still standing before him.

"Will you answer me one question?" inquired the deserter. "Speak then! Did you come hither in search of me?"

"I in search of you?" replied Alberti, in a tone of evident surprise. "No, alas! I thought not of you till this night!"

The man did not raise his head, but said, slowly:

"I was sorry when I saw that I had stabbed my commander. I don't forget that I have met with much kindness from you, signor; but now I know that you came not here to take me, I would do anything to save you!"

Alberti was proud, but he felt ashamed in the presence of the man whose hand had been raised against his life, who was a deserter, and a common robber.

"I am justly punished," he said; "I am more guilty than yourself! _I_ have lifted my arm against my commander! I left him dying—perhaps he is now dead! _I too am_ a deserter; at this moment I am pursued; and if I should be taken, my life will be forfeited for my crime! If you are inexcusable, what am I?"

The man took up the lamp, and walked hastily from the cavern. He returned in a short time, and with him came a young woman, whose countenance displayed a strange mixture of boldness and feminine beauty.

She brought with her a basket of provisions, and, with the assistance of the deserter, they dressed the wound in Alberti's shoulder, which had been before bound only with handkerchiefs.

For days and weeks Alberti was kindly and constantly attended by the banditti. They heard his history by Michael; and his manners and martial appearance—all they observed about him commanded respect and even confidence.

His wound was healed, and his strength was gradually returning, when the cavern was entered one night by a party of the banditti, among whom was the leader of the band.

Ernest had been treated before with attention; but the request which the band then made astonished him.

They told him that they knew he could not return to his rank and to his former associates—they told him that they admired, respected, and could trust him.

They were still speaking, when Alberti raised his eyes, and fixed them on the man who had addressed him with a look of stern surprise.

The fellow looked down and hesitated; he had begun to speak in a tone which seemed to declare that he was _conferring_ a favour; as he continued, he felt that he was _asking_ a favour.

He had proposed to Alberti that he should take the command of their band.

"Never!" replied Ernest, in a tone of resolute decision.

A murmur of angry disapprobation passed through the band.

He observed it, and walked into the midst of them.

"Hear me!" he said. "I am speaking to men, and I expect to be heard as a man! You have been kind to me, and I thank you heartily! I am still weak in body, but I have not learned to fear any of you. I thank you for the admiration and respect you declare to me, but I never will be one of your band! I wish not to offend you: but I will tell you the plain truth. I will never countenance your mode of life. It is perfectly true that I am a disgraceful man and an outlaw. I feel it. But I feel that, bad as I am, I might be worse. I pretend to no superior virtue. In my opinion, I am the most sinful man among you; surely then, I have gone far enough in guilt! I will not go further! You have me in your power, kill me if you please; life cannot be very joyful to me in future! I have nothing more to say. I would not have you forget that I am grateful to you; but remember, at the same time, that I know as little of fear as any man among you."

"The men had listened to him in silence; and, after a pause, the leader asked, rather impatiently:

"What did you expect from us, Count?"

"Nothing," replied Ernest, coolly.

(_To be continued in our next._)

TALES OF BRIGANDS AND ROBBERS.

I Warn & Strike

[THE DUKE OF BUCKINGHAM'S SCHEME FAILS.]

THE RED DWARF.

CHAPTER XVIII.

BUCKINGHAM EMPLOYS THE BLACK COLONEL ON A DANGEROUS ERRAND.—THE PLAN FORMED TO CARRY MADALINE ACROSS THE SEA.—CLAUDE AGAIN VISITS THE SECRET HAUNT OF SILVER JACK.—SOME UNWELCOME STRANGERS INTRUDE.—THE ARREST.

WE must now return to Madaline, who was being swiftly hurried onward, crying for help as she struggled in the grasp of the unscrupulous Rochester and the ruffian colonel.

They heard Sir Stuart Catemass behind them in swift pursuit; but, hurrying their fair prize onwards, they came upon a carriage which was evidently awaiting them. Into this

Madaline was thrust by the colonel and Buckingham; the door was closed, the coachman told to drive for his life, and Sir Stuart, who, by this time, was within twenty yards of the vehicle, saw it rapidly driven off at a pace which defied pursuit.

Still he followed, calling in despair upon the name of his daughter, and threatening vengeance towards her enemies.

At length he sank upon the road breathless and exhausted. Allan Buckhust, who, from the moment when Lord Kyle met his well-merited fate, had been hastening to the rescue of Madaline, now came up to the baronet's side.

He saw, to his despair, that there was no likelihood of gaining upon the villians who had robbed him and Sir Stuart of one who was dearer to them than life.

Still they both resolved to follow in the direction in which she had been taken, and hastened onwards.

Buckingham's carriage, containing Madaline, the duke, and the Black Colonel, was being drawn rapidly towards the eastern quarter of London.

It was Buckingham's plan to send Madaline out of England for a short time, until imprisonment in a foreign land, under the charge of the Black Colonel, should bend her haughty spirit and make her yield to his desires.

The Duke of Buckingham at this period had numerous unscrupulous agents abroad—libertines like himself, who thought the abduction of a young and innocent girl was an achievement to boast of rather than a crime.

Onward rolled the duke's carriage until it reached the neighbourhood of Wapping, then a dissolute and dangerous locality, frequented by the lower order of seamen and captains of vessels, who were not over particular as to the business they engaged in.

The duke, masking himself to avoid being known, ordered his carriage to stop in one of the by-streets; then, descending from the carriage, he motioned the colonel to follow with the half-unconscious Madaline, who had fallen back in the carriage exhausted with her efforts to escape from the hands of her persecutors.

Buckingham gave a sign to the coachman, who withdrew to a short distance from the house where he saw it was Madaline's fate to be taken to.

The building was one of those houses of entertainment for seamen where the host was not over particular as to the means employed by him to obtain money from his customers, no matter what might be the service required of him.

When he saw Madaline brought into the house by the colonel and his companion he soon guessed how matters were.

The colonel, it appears, was well known to him, so beckoning him and his companion—for such Buckingham appeared to him—he led the way upstairs to a private room, where Madaline was forced to follow.

Disdaining to answer the libertine duke—who in vain attempted to calm her fears—Madaline resolved to resist to the last, and die rather than yield his willing victim.

Buckingham, the colonel, and the host held a whispering conference in a corner of the room, where the following arrangement was made, unheard by Madaline:

"Oh! oh! I see," said the host—"you require a vessel to convey the damsel to the shores of France. Well, it can be done at a goodly price."

He was assured that money was no object.

"Well, then, such being the case," continued the landlord, "I know the very man for your purpose, one Guy Tyrell, who has a craft at anchor. He trades to Guernsey and St. Malo, and for a consideration would, I have no doubt, sail to-night when the tide rises."

"He's our man, then," said the duke. Then, slipping a heavy purse into the colonel's hand, he added: "See it done, and when you have set sail with the haughty damsel, send word to me at Whitehall, and I will follow."

The colonel promised obedience to these orders, and Buckingham, leaving Madaline in the ruffian's charge, made his way back to the carriage, which was waiting for him, and with due speed reached London.

Locking Madaline in the room, the colonel and the host went below, and a message was sent to Guy Tyrell, saying there was business cut out for him.

Over a bowl of punch the colonel and the landlord awaited his arrival.

After a short interval the landlord was beckoned from the room by his tapster, and the colonel was left alone.

It was this worthy's intention to abandon his band from that night, and betray his comrades to the law they had so long outraged. He had long feared treachery from them, and if such were really the case it would only be turning the tables upon them. He laughed in his sleeve as he thought how he should forestall them, and drank success to himself until the punch bowl was nearly exhausted before the host returned.

"Well, what cheer?" asked the colonel, as the landlord entered the room.

"Good," replied he. "I have made matters all ship-shape for you, and," he added in an undertone, unheard by the colonel, "for myself also."

"When will the tide be up?" asked the colonel.

"In an hour's time," answered the host.

"This Guy Tyrell is a stranger to me. I should like to see him and bind the bargain," said the colonel.

"He is waiting at the bar, and shall be sent into you."

"Send in another bowl of punch at the same time."

"I will," and the landlord left the room.

The punch was brought, and the colonel began to pay his devotions to it. The landlord returned, followed by a swarthy-looking man, in a rough seafaring dress of the period.

"Is this Master Guy Tyrell, the skipper of the craft you have recommended to me?" asked the colonel.

"This is the man who will do the business for you," said the landlord, as he left them alone.

The colonel beckoned to the new-comer to sit beside him.

"In the first place, you must swear to do what is right in this business," and the colonel proceeded to unfold his plans.

When the seaman had heard all, he replied:

"I swear to do that which is right, and more, perhaps, than you require!"

"No occasion for that," said the colonel. "You know the French coast well, I suppose?"

"I do," answered the seaman.

"Ah, I heard that you are in the habit of trading to the Channel Islands; but such is not our destination at present. I will tell you where to steer for when I come on board with the lady who is to accompany us."

"Agreed!" said the seaman. "And now, what about the payment for this job?"

This was speedily settled, and the seaman said he would return on board to prepare as comfortable a berth for the lady as his vessel afforded. He also promised that the colonel should be well cared for.

"How smoothly everything goes," said the colonel, exultingly, as the seaman left the room. "By this affair I shall be enabled to make the duke my friend for life."

He again applied himself to the liquor, and by the time he had finished it the seaman returned, saying that the colonel and the lady would find everything arranged to their entire satisfaction.

Whether this really proved to be the case will be seen in the sequel.

In the meantime, let us return to the other personages who play an important part in this history.

Silver Jack rode swiftly home to his retreat, lamenting the folly of Claude in venturing on so rash an enterprise. He saw the usual signal in the chamber window assuring him that all was safe.

It was near midnight when he entered his house, and perceived, to his surprise, that his daughter Amy was sitting up for him.

"Why, how now, my wench!" said Jack. "What keeps you from your bed at this late hour?"

"I have been to bed, father," replied Amy; "but I have had such fearful dreams about you and the young stranger who left the house with you."

"Never heed them, my girl—never heed them! Here I am, you see, safe home again."

"But the young stranger?" asked the young girl, with anxiety.

"Oh, I left him safe enough," answered her father.

"But will he continue in safety, think you?"

"Why not?"

And as Silver Jack asked the question, he felt a strange misgiving which seemed to whisper danger.

"Because they say when you dream a thing twice over, it mostly comes true. Now, I dreamt the same thing *three* times over," said Amy.

"Well, well—what was it?" inquired the father, laughingly, although a strange feeling of some hidden danger seemed to strike upon his heart with an ominous presentiment.

"I will tell you, father," said Amy, in reply to his question. "Methought you and the young stranger were concerned in a service of great danger, but the nature of it was not clear to me. You seemed to enter a huge cave, in the centre of which was a deep lake, whose waters seemed to boil and heave as though shaken by some terrible tempest. The young stranger seemed anxious to leap into the lake, which now seemed to open and disclose a deep gulf or bottomless abyss. You seemed to be using every argument you could employ to dissuade him from so rash and fatal an act, and seized him to drag him from the verge of the lake towards which he had ventured. But it was in vain; for the young stranger, throwing off your grasp, suddenly leaped into the awful chasm, and I fancied I could see him being rapidly hurled down to destruction. Overpowered with horror I awoke, rose, and dressing myself, resolved to await your coming. Thank heaven you have returned safe!"

As the young girl finished her recital she threw herself on the neck of her father and sobbed as though her heart was relieving itself of a heavy load.

Silver Jack was troubled.

His daughter's dream really seemed suggestive of Claude's dangerous venture; and although he was far from being superstitious, what he heard made him fear the worst.

Suppose Claude had been discovered and arrested, might he not be induced to disclose all he knew, and be tempted, by promise of pardon, to betray what he knew of his companion?

Jack tried to conceal his anxiety from his daughter as these thoughts crossed his mind.

But with the quick instinct of womanhood she saw he was troubled.

"You have something on your mind, father—I am certain of it," said Amy, drying her tears. "If you are in any trouble or difficulty, why not confide in me? Am I not your child?—would I not do anything in the world to serve you?"

"You would—I am certain you would!" replied her father, kissing her fair brow.

"Then answer my question, father, dear, and tell me, in the first place, whether the young man who left here with you, and whom I heard you call Claude, is not in danger?"

"Not that I am aware of. And yet he may be considering his rash resolve," added Jack, half aloud.

"He may!" exclaimed Amy, starting, and showing by her sympathy for the young man's safety how much she was smitten with him.

"No more, Amy—ask me no more. There are certain matters of which you were best ignorant—this is one of them. Neither you nor I may have cause to fear for the young man's welfare. Hie thee to bed, and hope for the best."

"Yes; but, father, I——"

"Not another word on the subject, I command you! Go to your chamber!" said her father, in a voice of authority.

Amy knew when he spoke in that tone to argue further would be useless. So, asking her father's pardon if she had angered him, and being assured she had not, the highwayman's daughter once more sought her pillow.

Not so Silver Jack. He sat by the fire far into the night, anxiously wondering whether Claude had been detected and arrested.

Not being able to arrive at any satisfactory conclusion, and wishing to allay his daughter's fears—for he well knew she was listening for him to go to rest—he ascended the stairs to his sleeping-room and retired to rest.

At the same hour Claude, having been set at liberty by the fair Phillis, as we have already seen, was rapidly making his way towards London.

He longed to regain the horse of the duke, which was put up at the Three Nuns, as the reader already knows.

Fearing danger in every breeze that blew and leaf that stirred, Claude hurried on his way, pausing repeatedly to listen whether he was followed.

Glancing towards his gay attire, he suddenly became aware that it might betray him.

He, therefore, took the most unfrequented way towards Whitechapel, resolving to go back to the hostelrie where he had left his steed and suit of clothes, resolving to dispose of both, and with the proceeds escape if possible abroad.

The inn of the Three Nuns was just opening as he passed under the gateway.

The servants looked with surprise at his returning on foot, telling him that a sedan chair had been sent for him to the mansion of Sir Everard Granby as he had ordered.

"In that case they will soon learn all," thought Claude; "so the sooner I am away from here the better."

Feigning intoxication as the best means of accounting for what he termed his forgetfulness, Claude ordered forth his horse; and while it was being prepared for him, ascended to his chamber, changed his clothes for the suit he had first arrived in, packed his borrowed robes once more in the valise, paid his reckoning, and mounting on the stolen horse of the duke's, soon left the inn of the Three Nuns behind him.

He shaped his course towards Lombard Street, where the valise and its contents were pledged for a hundred crowns.

His next step must be to dispose of the horse.

"Silver Jack can best put me in the way to do that," thought he. So, giving his steed the spur, he rode with all due speed towards the highwayman's secret abode.

He congratulated himself upon not being recognised.

But he was mistaken—his proceedings were being observed by one who was as well mounted as himself.

Little did Claude Duval reckon upon a spy being in his wake.

But so it was,—and unknowingly he was the cause of Silver Jack's retreat being discovered.

Silver Jack and his daughter Amy were at breakfast as Claude rode up to the house and knocked for admission.

According to the directions Jack had always given to his daughter, Amy ascended to the upper window to learn who it was that applied for admission.

With joy she recognised Claude, and ran downstairs to acquaint her father of the fact.

"Thank Heaven, then, he is safe!" exclaimed Jack.

"Ah! then, he was in some peril," said Amy, as she noticed her father's agitation.

"Go—go and open the door, my girl," said Jack, for Claude, impatient to gain the shelter of the house, had again knocked loudly at the door.

"Patience—patience, young sir!" exclaimed Amy, as she withdrew the bolts.

Silver Jack stepped to the threshold to welcome the young highwayman.

He saw how pale and haggard Claude looked; but he ascribed that to his being up all night.

He led the way to the stable, so that the youth might put up his horse.

Claude saw how Amy's eyes beamed with pleasure as she saw him return.

He sighed to think how soon he should be obliged to leave her without any probable chance of their ever meeting again.

Having gained the stable, and finding they were alone, Jack inquired what success he had met with on the previous night at the baronet's masque.

"Not so well as I could have wished," answered Claude, resolving not to say anything about what happened to himself until he had sold the horse.

"How was that?" asked Jack.

"Well, the fact is, I was led into the play," said Claude; "and the upshot was, I not only lost more money than I took with me, but have also incurred several debts of honour, which——"

"Which of course you don't mean to pay," laughed Silver Jack.

"But I do though!" said Jack, with affected indignation in his tone at the bare supposition of such a thing. "I can assure you, my worthy friend Jack, it will be to my interest to do so."

"But how are you to do so?" asked Jack.

"I have been thinking of that as I rode here," said the artful Claude, "and have arrived at the conclusion that it must be done by my selling the horse I took from the duke's stables."

"What?—sell your steed?"

"Even so."

"But what will you do for another?"

"Fortune will soon favour me again."

"Were I you," said Jack, "I would rather sell that valuable ring you took from the finger of the nobleman's daughter."

Claude started, for the mention of the ring brought back painful thoughts.

"Let me look at that ring again," asked the highwayman. "I fancy it is of greater value than we at first anticipated."

For the moment, Claude scarcely knew what excuse to make.

At length he stammered out:

"The fact is, friend Jack, I have lost that too."

"Pardon me saying so; but you are a headstrong young fool! 'Ill-gotten, ill-spent' seems to be a proverb that may be well applied to you," exclaimed Jack.

"I shall know better for the future," said Claude. "So, to come to what I was about to ask you, how much will you give me for the horse?"

"I?" asked Jack, in surprise.

"Yes. You have only one steed in your stable; surely it will be no very great detriment to you if you were to possess two."

Silver Jack fancied the fumes of the overnight's wine had not cleared themselves away from Claude's brain, as he answered:

"No more of this, young sir! From the liking I have entertained for you, I will assist you if necessary. At present you hardly seem to be yourself. Lie down until you are calmer, and we will speak further of this."

Jack would give him no other answer, and Claude was fain to betake himself to the chamber wherein he had once before passed the night.

He found the bed a couch of thorns to him, for he felt the only safety he could reckon upon was to be gained by a successful retreat from the country.

But, then, his oath to Silver Jack as regarded Amy.

"Perhaps I had better disclose all," he thought. "My mind will be easier when Jack knows the worst; besides, he may give me better counsel in this difficulty than I can give myself."

So Claude, who had not undressed himself, rose from the bed to seek Silver Jack, in order to make a clean breast of it.

But, hark! What sounds are those below?

The rapid gallop of horses, a pistol shot, a woman's scream, and the breaking open of the door below.

Claude guessed the truth in a moment.

He had been traced, and had not only perilled his own safety, but that of his friend, Silver Jack.

He quickly opened his room door, hoping to escape by a back window which led along an unfrequented road to the marshes.

This window was nearly ten feet from the ground, but the distance seemed but a trifle to Claude, when life and liberty were at stake.

He took the leap, alighted in safety on the ground, and the next moment found himself in the grasp of two stout officers, who were guarding the house on the outside.

In vain he attempted to escape, for one of his captors, tripping up his heels, assisted his companion to handcuff him, so that Claude was rendered powerless and a prisoner.

Silver Jack was also brought struggling from the house in the grasp of several officers, Amy following, amazed and bewildered at the scene she witnessed.

"What has he done—what has he done?" cried the poor girl. "Why do you seek to take my father from me?"

"We've been on the look-out for him these five years. And now we've got you; and a pretty tight hold of you we'll keep!"

Amy could bear to hear no more—she sank lifeless to the earth.

Claude would have flown to her assistance, but he was prevented by the tight grasp the officers retained hold of him.

Silver Jack was bowed down to the earth with shame and grief.

The secret of his unlawful life was known—the fair flower that he hoped to rear and place in peace and affluence was blighted and broken down.

Silver Jack and Claude were placed in a carriage that was in readiness, and driven off to prison.

Amy was carried to her chamber insensible by the officers who were left in charge of the house, which was searched in every part for any valuables or money that might have been concealed there.

But none could be found—the secret hiding-place in the stable manger remained undiscovered.

The Duke of Buckingham's steed was seen and recognised, and forwarded the next day to his grace's stables.

Buckingham's rage against his former page, Claude, had not one whit abated for robbing him of his favourite horse, and when he learned that he had been arrested, he vowed the knave should swing for it.

His own vices he looked upon as venial ones, for in those days a gentleman and a courtier had far greater allowances made him than fair justice warranted.

The day after their arrest, Claude Duval and Jack, after a short examination before a Justice of the Peace, were consigned to Newgate to await their trial.

The fair Amy remained she knew not how long in a state of unconsciousness.

When she found her reason returning, she found herself in her chamber alone.

The past seemed to her like some hideous dream.

Her father a robber—a highwayman!

As she repeated the words to herself, she shuddered.

There must surely be some mistake?

She would seek her father, and he should explain all.

She approached the room door.

Upon her trying to open it, she found it locked.

"Father—father!" she exclaimed, "I would speak with you! Oh, come to me, your own Amy, for mercy's sake!"

She heard the door unlock, fondly hoping it was her parent.

Two of the officers left in charge of the premises entered the room, and inquired what she was making all that riot for.

"I wish to see my father!" cried the wretched girl.

"Then you'll have to wish," sneered one of the men, "for by this time the Stone Jug holds him, and is likely to do so until he dangles at the end of a rope."

Poor Amy could scarcely believe this, and, in heartbroken accents, she told the man so.

"Ask my comrade, then," said the officer.

"It's true enough, my dear," exclaimed the other man. "But, although such is the case, what have you to fear? A pretty girl like you can always find friends."

The unfeeling fellow leered at her as he spoke, and chucked her under the chin.

Amy shrunk back from him as though a serpent had touched her.

"Besides," added the fellow, glancing covetously at the few trinkets and a ring which the girl wore, "you can't be in want of money, if that's your object, for I warrant me you know where plenty of these kind of things are stowed."

"You are mistaken, sir," answered the indignant girl, "in the estimate you have formed of me. Your words are insulting and cruel, and I desire you will leave me."

"Well, so I will," said the man; "but I must have the few articles you wear as perquisites. Those ear-rings, now, will suit my wife exactly, so take them out."

"And give me also those rings," cried the other fellow, grasping her hand.

"Release the maiden, ye knaves!" exclaimed a loud voice, in tones of authority.

The officers started back, and bowed respectfully as our mysterious friend, the Red Dwarf, stood before them.

"You are exceeding orders, you rascals!" said this strange being, whom all seemed ready to obey, for the officers bowed respectfully, and appeared as though they were in the presence of their superior

The Red Dwarf motioned to them to leave the room, and they did so.

Amy looked with scarcely less alarm on her new visitor than she had upon the two fellows who had just left her.

"Don't fear, maiden," said the Red Dwarf, approaching to take her hand.

She recoiled in fear, but the few words the dwarf uttered as he went towards her seemed to breathe hope, and she listened with interest and surprise as he proceeded to tell her more.

If what he had spoken was really the truth, there was still a hope that her father might be restored to her.

"At present all is wrapped in mystery," said the dwarf. "But courage—courage! The clouds may yet pass away."

CHAPTER XIX.

THE DAY OF RECKONING.—THE KING TO THE RESCUE.—THE MEETING AT THE PALACE.—FRIENDS AND TRAITORS.—AN UNEXPECTED DELIVERANCE.—WHAT BECAME OF SILVER JACK, HIS DAUGHTER, AND CLAUDE DUVAL.—THE MYSTERY OF THE RED DWARF EXPLAINED.

ALL traces of Madaline were lost.

The hearts of her father and Allan were filled with despair.

In vain they sought an audience with the Duke of Buckingham.

His lackeys refused to let them enter the mansion, and Sir Stuart Catemass saw there was but one person to appeal to in order to see him righted—that individual was his Majesty King Charles.

To Whitehall they hastened, but were unable to obtain an interview with his Majesty, for, if the lord in waiting spoke the truth, the King had left the palace the night before, and had not returned.

"I'll not believe it!" said the disconsolate Sir Stuart Catemass, as they turned from the gate. "This mad-brained King is as unprincipled as his courtiers! Perhaps he knows of my daughter's abduction, and would shield the villain Buckingham from my just resentment. But, by Heaven, he shall not! I'll seek the libertine, and take his dastard life, even at the foot of the throne!"

Allan at last succeeded in pacifying Sir Stuart, and once more they sought in every direction for Madaline, but in vain.

The next day, to his surprise, Sir Stuart Catemass received a summons to attend his Majesty at Whitehall, by twelve of the clock. He was not to fail in his attendance, on pain of forfeiting his royal master's countenance and protection.

Allan Buckhurst was also bidden to accompany Sir Stuart.

A hope seemed to cross Allan's mind that this message might relate in some way to the recovery of Madaline.

The same hope took possession of Sir Stuart Catemass, but why or wherefore he could not tell.

They were at Whitehall by the time appointed, and, being ushered into the audience chamber, were told to await the coming of his Majesty.

The blue silken curtains which divided the apartment were shortly afterwards raised, and a page announced his Majesty.

Sir Stuart Catemass and Allan fell upon their knees, and were immediately told to rise.

The curtains in the middle of the room were again closed, and the King, bidding Sir Stuart Catemass be of good cheer, told him he knew all.

"Young man," said Charles, addressing Allan, "you have killed one of my late subjects, Lord Kylo Smedleigh; but as he was one of the very worst subjects in our dominions, I freely forgive you on that score."

These words lifted a great weight from the heart of Allan, who feared the resentment of the deceased libertine's friends.

"Tell us your grievances, and why you have sought this audience," said the King.

Sir Stuart Catemass then proceeded to speak of his daughter being so cruelly taken from him, and hoped that even the exalted rank of the Duke of Buckingham would not prevent his Majesty doing full justice to a father for the indignity, and, it might be, shame that the duke had brought upon his house.

At that moment, a page, entering the chamber, announced his Grace the Duke of Buckingham.

Sir Stuart Catemass and Allan started, and laid their hands upon their swords.

"Be calm, gentlemen, and leave all to me. I'll manage matters with his grace, and believe me there shall be a strict reckoning—ay, and a just one."

Buckingham entered the room with a gay and smiling face, to address his royal master.

But the next moment his eyes fell upon Sir Stuart Catemass and Allan, and he paused in confusion.

"Why, what ails your grace?" asked Charles. "Why do you start at the appearance of Sir Stuart and his young friend? Surely you have never done them any harm?"

"Never!" echoed the libertine courtier.

"Were we not under the King's roof, I would tell you that you lied! My daughter, thou base man—what of her?"

"I assure you, I know no more of your daughter's whereabouts than I know of the man in the moon's," said Buckingham.

"There he speaks the truth," said the King.

"The truth, my liege?" exclaimed the indignant father of Madaline.

"Have patience, and see matters out to the end," said his Majesty.

"My daughter—where is my daughter?" cried Sir Stuart Catemass, unable to contain himself, as he thought of his only child, so basely taken from him.

"You say you do not know where the lady is, my Lord of Buckingham?" asked the King.

"I repeat I do not, your Majesty," answered the duke.

"Well, then, I do," said the King, and as he spoke, the silken curtains were drawn aside, and the fair Madaline stood before her father.

With a cry she bounded towards him, and the next moment she was locked within his arms.

Had a thunderbolt fallen at the feet of Buckingham he could not have been more astonished.

Charles enjoyed his amazement heartily, and observed, as he approached Buckingham:

"When next you take a lady to Wapping, take heed the King is not there in disguise, and gains an interview with your rascally colonel, saying he is the skipper Guy Tyrell."

The truth of the matter flashed upon Buckingham in a moment.

Charles was in Wapping at the time, disguised as a sailor, on one of his mad pranks.

So thought the duke.

And he guessed rightly.

For when the landlord of the tavern left the room to seek the real Guy Tyrell, King Charles, who was in the next room, overheard all, and bribed the landlord so that he might introduce him to the Black Colonel as the captain of the vessel that was to bear off Madaline.

The King was a stranger to the villain of a colonel, and hence the successful result.

His Majesty had brought the Lady Madaline to London with him, and resolved to restore her to her father.

At this moment, the page reappearing, announced a name which caused everyone to start but King Charles.

It was the name of the "Red Dwarf."

"Ay, gentlemen, the Red Dwarf," said the King, observing their surprise. "But no longer must he be known by that title, for the game is played out, and we are the victors. Approach, my Lord Blake, sometime Captain Blake, but now one of our most faithful friends."

A tall, well-dressed man, in the uniform of the Royal Guards, now stood forward from beneath the folds of the curtain.

His former stunted and uncouth appearance was but a disguise.

He had been instrumental in discovering a conspiracy against the King's person.

The Black Colonel was concerned in the traitorous plot, and Red Dwarf, as he was called, pretended to join the conspiracy in order that he might defeat his ends.

The colonel afterwards learned who the Red Dwarf really was, hence the whispered word of the dwarf, threatening to deliver the colonel up to justice, struck such terror into the ruffian's heart.

The deeds and doings in the Red House by the river's side became known to the King.

The Black Colonel, being seized soon after he left Wapping, was executed as a traitor on Tower Hill, also a large number of his band.

Their haunt was broken up and levelled with the ground.

Hal of Hockley was pardoned.

He it was who had assisted the Red Dwarf to enter the villains' den by a secret path and save the life of Sir Stuart Catemass in the vault.

Buckingham begged permission to travel for awhile.

His Majesty gave his sanction.

The following year the duke met his death at the hands of of the assassin Felton.

Claude Duval and Silver Jack, being tried, were cast for death.

Lord Blake, *alias* the Red Dwarf, however, explained to his Majesty how they had befriended Sir Stuart Catemass and his daughter.

The King, taking into consideration that Silver Jack had formerly been a brave soldier in his Majesty's army who, by some neglect, had been discharged without a pension, ordered him to be respited, and eventually pardoned.

Claude Duval, also, on account of his youth, and the fact that neither of them had ever taken human life.

Silver Jack went, with his daughter, abroad, not forgetting to carry with him the jewel-box from its secret place in the manger. They were enabled to live comfortably on the proceeds of the jewels.

Claude was invited to go with them. He promised to follow them, but, having abused the King's mercy by again turning highwayman and proving such a bold depredator on travellers' purses, he was eventually taken and hanged at Tyburn, rejoicing to the last in the title of the "Ladies' Highwayman," a name which the fair sex had bestowed upon him from the extremely graceful manner in which he eased them of their property.

So let our youths beware of entering into any plots or conspiracies likely to lead them into the deprivation of their lives and liberties, for society still holds many who seek to attain the conviction of offenders by means as strange as those employed by the RED DWARF.

THE END.

THE BRIGANDS AND THE DESERTER.
A TALE OF TRUE LOVE.

—o—

(*Concluded.*)

"WHAT would you do were you permitted to follow your own will?" asked the leader of the men.

"Leave this place, and betray us," said one of them, instantly.

"I could have answered that question more warmly," replied Ernest, with a look of calm disdain, turning to the captain of the band. "Had no suspicion been uttered by that man, I might have told you that the same principles which forbid my becoming your companion, would prevent my becoming a pitiful informer. I ask my freedom as a man, entitled, equally with yourselves, to the common right of air and liberty. I do not insult you or myself by entreaties. You may best judge if you can believe and trust me."

It is a fact that Alberti was released a few days after the above interview; the captain of the band came to the cavern where Alberti had been kept, and told him that his freedom was granted to him.

Ernest thanked him even with tears, and, before he followed him out, he said:

"I was brought to this place senseless; I have never quitted it since that time. Bind your cloak round my head, and lead me till I am at some distance from the entrance of these caverns. I will never betray you."

Ernest from that time had no intercourse with the banditti, but he still remained among the mountains which they haunted, never molested by them.

Once he ventured from his retreat to a town at some distance from it, and he learnt there that search had been made, and was still making, for him by the imperial command.

With some difficulty he effected his return to the mountains of Istria.

In the magnificent solitudes of woods and waters, he learnt to examine his own heart, and to meditate on the follies and faults which had diverted his mind from higher and more ennobling subjects.

It was there that he was seized by the imperial troops. He declared in vain that he had no connection with the banditti, who had been taken.

He was brought with them, and as one of them, to Vienna.

The Countess Alberti, with her young and lovely friend, used every exertion to prevent the execution of Ernest; but the verdict appeared irrevocable.

The day, the dreadful day of death was fixed, and they implored an audience of the Empress; the aged mother, the betrothed wife, lay at her feet in speechless agony; they entreated, they clung to her in the delirium of their grief.

Their gentle Sovereign wept with them; she endeavoured to console them; but although her whole frame trembled, and her voice faltered with agitation, as she replied to their entreaties, her answer left them quite hopeless.

They obtained, however, permission to see the prisoner once before his execution, and even this had been hitherto denied to every one.

An unforeseen circumstance saved the life of Alberti.

The captain of the banditti, who had not been taken with his companions, heard that Ernest was condemned to die.

He had been once a man of honour himself; and he gave himself up to justice, relating clearly every particular of the count's refusal to join his band.

The sentence was changed.

Was it a merciful change?

The noble and gallant Count Ernest was condemned in the prime of youthful manhood to become a workman for life, in the quicksilver mines in Idria.

The first surprise which made known to the aged countess her son's safety was joyful; but her grief soon returned as she thought upon the dreadful termination which still awaited all her hopes for him.

But Bianca was young and ardent, and the worst that would now happen was a joy to her.

She devoted her whole heart and every energy of her mind to a plan which she instantly resolved to execute.

Since her childhood she had been a privileged favourite with Maria Theresa, but she now dreaded the opposition of her royal mistress to her intention.

After mature deliberation, she decided that the most certain method of succeeding would be to confide her plan to the

Empress herself, before it could be told to her by any other person.

The Countess Florenheim was beloved as an own child by the good and venerable confessor of Maria Theresa.

She went to him, and he listened to her kindly, and with earnest attention.

He was accustomed to examine the principles of actions rather than their effects; to consider whether they were really right, not whether they might be approved according to worldly opinions.

The father Antonio left the countess in doubt as to his opinion; but, a few hours after his departure, he again visited the Florenheim palace, and he brought with him a message from the Empress.

She commanded the immediate presence of the Countess Bianca at the imperial palace.

The confessor declined answering any of Bianca's anxious questions, and departed, declaring his intention of seeing her when she returned from the Empress.

The young countess ordered her carriage, and in a short time after she had received the imperial summons, she was admitted into the private apartments of her Sovereign.

She remained alone for a sufficient time to perplex herself with attempting to discover why she had been summoned to the presence of the Empress.

Maria Theresa appeared; she was simply dressed, and unattended; she smiled as she bowed her head to Bianca, and then sat down, fixing the full gaze of her eyes on the blushing countenance of the young countess.

She spoke at once on the subject which the latter was most interested about.

"I have been conversing with the father Antonio," she said; "you, Countess Bianca, were the subject of our conference.

"I have requested your presence; for, although I am your friend, I would now speak to you as your monarch; as such, I ask not your confidence.

"Tell me only, have your considered—do you know that, if you accompany the disgraced Count Alberti to the mines of Idria, you must literally share his fortunes?

"You will be, from the moment that you become his wife, simply the wife of an Idrian miner.

"Your title, your estates, all your rank and wealth will be forfeited.

"You will be forced to perform even the duties of a menial servant to your husband.

"Countess Bianca of Florenheim," she proceeded, "can you dare to undertake such a sacrifice?

"Are you aware that your mind may now be upheld by an uncertain enthusiasm?

"Have you thought upon the drear, dull calm of poverty and decaying health?

"Do you feel assured that when the first tumultuous feelings of self-applause have worn themselves out, when there are none around to wonder at your extraordinary devotion to Alberti, when your name will be almost forgotten in the circles where you have hitherto lived—quite forgotten indeed, by all but a few friends whom you will never behold again—do you think you will then rejoice at the decision you have made?

"When perhaps your husband may be dying, in the morning of his age, with no attendant but a weak, helpless wife, who may then be too ill even to stand beside him, then what will your feelings be?"

The Empress repeated her question; for the words which preceded it had absorbed Bianca's thoughts.

She pictured to herself the young and vigorous Ernest wasting away, dying in her presence; she forgot herself, and all but his sufferings.

Slowly she raised her head, as the Empress again addressed her.

"What will my feelings be? Ah! I can scarcely imagine what they will be. Sorrow, certainly sorrow, but only for him; that must be the pervading feeling at such a moment. Happiness," her whole face brightened with smiles as she spoke—"real joy on my own account, to know that I am with him *then, for ever !*"

Bianca continued to speak, and it was evident that her mind had anticipated and dwelt on the miseries that awaited the wife of Alberti.

Maria Theresa listened to her with profound attention; she asked, once again : "Do you determine to follow Ernest Alberti to the mines of Idria as his wife, and to resign your rank and possessions ?"

Bianca sunk on her knee, she raised her clasped hands, and exclaimed: "I am but too favoured by God and my Sovereign, if I may follow him. I resign my rank and my property with joy—with gratitude."

Again, once again, the Empress fixed on Bianca an earnest and searching look, and appeared to think deeply.

"I am satisfied—I am *quite* satisfied," she said at length, and the sternness of her look disappeared; "I cannot countenance, but I shall not oppose your marriage."

Bianca had been comparatively calm before, but now she covered her face with her hands, and sobbed almost hysterically.

Maria Theresa would have raised her, but Bianca sprung up from the ground, her face beaming with delight, though the tears hung upon her cheeks.

"Oh! forgive me," she said, eagerly ; "your highness will forgive me! Do not mistake my tears for sorrow, I am so happy that I must weep."

The Empress opened the door by which she had entered the room, and led the trembling countess into a small oratory.

"I must converse with you here, before we part," she said ; and at once, her look, her voice, her manner, became expressive of the tenderest affection.

"I have spoken as the sovereign, now listen to your friend. Here we should forget all distinctions of worldly rank. Here, my sweet Bianca, an Empress may feel herself inferior to the wife of a poor miner. Tell me really, my dear child," she said, tenderly clasping her companion's hands, as she drew her nearer, and gazed with a look of affectionate inquiry in her face ; "confide in your friend. Must you, will you pursue this rash plan? What is the chief motive that determines you?"

"I love," she replied ; and these two words, spoken as they then were, needed little comment to the heart of Maria Theresa ; "I love Ernest for himself. I did not love his rank or his riches ; he is still Ernest Alberti, he is still himself, and therefore I still love him. I can live with him in disgrace and misery—I can die with him. My words may seem like those of a romantic girl, but they are not idle sounds. I do feel that I am speaking to a friend. I open all my heart to you, when I tell you, that I see but one path before me, and that, in deciding to tread it, my principles confirm the decision of my heart."

"And I," said the Empress,—"yes, I confess that I understand and approve you. My child, you must leave me, or——"

Bianca sunk at the feet of the Empress.

She hoped—she implored for a moment.

The words died upon her lips, when she beheld the calm, but changeless refusal expressed in the look of Maria Theresa who said, instantly :

"I have now only to bid you farewell. In this oratory I shall pray for you constantly. Think of me, not as your Sovereign, but as your friend, and love me."

That very evening Bianca visited the cell of Alberti ; she had been there once before, it was to receive his last embrace.

"My love," she said, "I am very bold ; but it was not always thus. Do you look coldly on me ? Dear, dear Ernest, must I remind you of our long-plighted affection? Are you still silent ? Then I must plead the cause which has so often made you eloquent. I do not blush," she said, "to make my request ;" while a deepening blush spread over her downcast face, and completely belied her assertion. "Will you not understand me? Will you not recall the time when I should have waited like a bashful maid, to be entreated like all bashful maids? then you have often called me too reserved. But now," she exclaimed, fixing her ardent and innocent gaze upon him, "a wife offers her hand to her husband. Dear Ernest, will you not take this hand ?"

She smiled, and held out her small, white hand.

He took her hand, he pressed it to his lips, and continued to hold it trembling in his own.

"My sweet Bianca," he said, and as he looked at her the tears streamed from his eyes, "I was prepared for this. I knew that you would speak as you do now. It is heart-breaking to see you here, to hear you speak as I knew you would. I almost wish you had been less true, less like yourself. Ah! how can I refuse the slightest of your chaste favours! But I must be firm. We must part. My love, I will not speak of poverty, although the change would be too hard for you, a young and delicate lady, of high rank, accustomed to affluence and to ease. But, Bianca, you are a woman; and shall a tender, helpless woman be doomed to pine away in dark and horrid caverns, whose very air is poison?"

"Alberti," said she, with eager earnestness, "have not the miner's wives?"

"It may be so," he replied; "but those women must be poor neglected wretches, inured to the sorrows and hardships of their life; they must be almost callous of distress."

Bianca looked at him as though she had not heard him rightly.

"And do you think, Ernest, that cold and deadened feeling can produce that fortitude, that patient, heavenly fortitude, which the gospel, the spirit of God, alone inspires? Dearest, when I become your partner, the happy partner of your misery, I think not of my woman's weakness; and yet I hardly believe that I would fail. No; I look to another arm for strength, to Him who now supports the burden of all His children's sorrow. He will hear our prayers, and He will never forsake us. A miner's hut may be a very happy home; it must be so to me, for my happiness is to remain with you. Would you have me wretched with my wealth and titles? I am pleading for my happiness, not so much for yours. Must I plead in vain?"

When she finished speaking, her hand extended to Ernest, and her face, as she leaned forward, turning alternately to the aged countess and the friar, her eyes shining with the light of expression, and the pure blood flowing in tides of richer crimson to her cheek and parted lips—lips on which a silent and trembling eloquence still hung—they all sat gazing on her in speechless astonishment.

Ernest was eager to speak, but the old priest interrupted him by proposing that nothing should be finally settled till the evening of the fourth ensuing day.

Then the Lady Bianca, he observed, would have had more time to consider the plan she had formed; and till then the young count would be permitted to remain in Vienna.

"I will consent, but on this one condition," said Bianca, "that my proposal, bold as it is, shall not be then opposed, if, as you say, my resolution be not changed. You know, dear Ernest, that I cannot change."

Bianca went, and with her husband, to the mines.

The dismal hut of a workman in the mines of Idria was but a poor exchange for the magnicent palace of the Count Alberti, on the banks of the Danube, which was now confiscated to the crown; though a small estate was given to the venerable and respected countess during her life.

But Bianca smiled with a smile of satisfied happiness, as, leaning on her husband's arm, she stopped before the hut which was to be their future home.

Their conductor opened the door, but the count had forgotten to stoop, as he entered the low doorway, and he struck his lofty forehead a violent blow.

Bianca uttered a faint shriek, her first and only complaint in that dark mine.

The alarm which Bianca betrayed at his accident banished the gloom which had begun to deepen on her husband's spirits; and when he had recovered, she said:

"After all, this terrible accident and my lamentations have not had a very bad effect, as they have brought back the smiles to your dear features, my own Ernest."

The miner's hut became daily a more happy abode.

The eyes of its inhabitants were soon accustomed to the dim light, and all that had seemed so wrapt in darkness when they first entered the mines gradually dawned into distinctness and light.

Bianca began to look with real pleasure on the walls and rude furniture of her too-narrow room.

She had no time to spend in useless sorrow, for she was continually employed in the necessary duties of her situation. She performed with cheerful alacrity the most menial offices—she repaired her husband's clothes, and she was delighted if she could sometimes take down from an old shelf one of the few books she had brought with her.

The days passed on rapidly, and as the young pair knelt down at the close of every evening their praises and thanksgivings were as fervent as their prayers.

Ernest had not been surprised at the high and virtuous enthusiasm which had enabled Bianca to support at first all the severe trials they underwent without shrinking; but he *was* surprised to find that, in the calm, the dull and hopeless calm, of undiminished hardship, her spirit never sank—her sweetness of temper and unrepining gentleness rather increased.

Another trial was approaching.

Bianca, the young and tender Bianca, was about to become a mother; and one evening, on returning from his work, Ernest found his wife making clothes for the unborn infant.

He sat down beside her, and sighed; but Bianca was singing merrily, and she only left off singing to embrace her husband with smiles, he thought the sweetest smiles he had ever seen.

The wife of one of the miners, whom Bianca had visited when lying ill of a dangerous disease, kindly offered to attend her during her confinement; and from the arms of this woman, Ernest received his first-born son—the child who, born under different circumstances, would have been welcomed with all the care and splendour of noble rank. But he forgot this, in his joy that Bianca was safe, and stole on tiptoe to the room where she was lying.

She had been listening for his footstep, and, as he approached, he saw in the gloom of the chamber, her white hands stretched towards him.

"I have been thanking God in my thoughts," said Bianca, after her husband had bent down to kiss her; "but I am so very weak! Dear Ernest, kneel down beside the bed, and offer up my blessings with your own."

Surprising strength seemed to have been given to this delicate mother, by Him "who tempers the wind to the shorn lamb."

Soon after the mother was recovered, a person arrived at the mines from Vienna, anxiously inquiring if Alberti and his wife were alive. This stranger was followed by another—they were one a near relation of Bianca, the other Alberti's fellow-soldier and intimate friend. Pardon had at length been granted to the young exile.

There were many hearts that sorrowed over the departure of Alberti and his wife. The miners with whom they had lived so long had learned to love them.

Was it, then, surprising that, at their departure, their poor companions should crowd around them and weep with mournful gratitude among them his working tools and the simple furniture of his small hut?

I must not omit to mention that Ernest and his wife were publicly reinstated in all their former titles and possessions.

A short time after their return to Vienna they made their first appearance at Court for that purpose.

At the imperial command, all the princes and nobles of Austria, gorgeously dressed, and blazing with gold and jewels, were assembled.

The Empress herself hung the Order of the Golden Fleece round his neck, and gave into his hands the sword which he had before forfeited; but as she did so her tears fell upon the golden scabbard. The young soldier kissed them off with quivering lips.

The Empress then said:

"Count Alberti, every husband may envy you your residence in the mines of Idria. May God bless you both, and make you as happy with the rank and wealth to which I now fully restore you as you were in the hut of an Idrian miner."